THE BOY ACTOR;

OR.

STRUGGLES FOR BREAD.

THE BOY ACTOR;

OR,
STRUGGLES FOR BREAD.

THE FRACAS ON THE PARADE.

CHAPTER I.

THE DEATH BED—THE ARRIVAL OF A FRIEND—
MIRTH AND MISERY—THE VOW!

ALONE! Alone in the World!

What fearful meaning do not these words convey? Alone, without help, with none to love or care for you, with none to smile at your happiness, none to grieve at your distress!

Alone, with millions around us—alone, under the bright canopy of heaven—alone on this bounteous earth.

Alone, amid the giddy throng—alone, with none but God, whose ever-shielding hand sways the movements of the world.

Alone, with aching heart and tearful eye—alone with sorrow—alone with the dead!

The bright morning sun streams through the small casement, casting its warm, cheerful rays upon the low truckle bed, and lighting up the pale cold face that no more will beam with smiles.

Glistens upon the tear, as it rolls slowly down the cheek of a poor delicate boy, who, kneeling at its side, sobs convulsively.

Poor child ! He is alone—alone with the dead mother he loved—alone in sorrow and anguish!

And his young heart, swelled almost to bursting with the anguish of his feelings, sinks as he mutters—

"Alone—alone !"

And thus he remains while the bright sunlight floods the apartment, and the orb of day rises higher and higher in the horizon.

But violent grief cannot last for ever. The over-burdened heart, relieved by the gushing tears, aches less fiercely, and the low sob gives place to more violent grief.

He raises his hands from the thin coverlet of the rude couch and dries his eyes, now so red and swollen, and makes towards the door, with the intention of procuring the assistance of neighbours, who, though poor as himself, he knew would render all the aid in their power to the poor orphan boy, and see that the parish performed the last obsequies to that inanimate form of clay, which lay so pale and cold in the bright sun's ray.

He placed his hand upon the door, but ere he could lift the latch it was thrust open, and a figure dashed into the apartment with the exclamation—" Here we are—How do you do to-morrow ?" Then, starting back as the form of the dead woman met his eye, he seized the hand of the poor boy in his own, and, drawing him to his breast, said, while a tear stole to his eyes—

"My God, Harry—is she dead!"

"Yes," sobbed the boy.

And the man, who the moment before entered the room so full of life and joy, bent his head down upon the shoulder of the youth, and sobbed violently.

"I'm so glad you've come," said the boy. "I don't know what to do, you'll stop with me—you'll—but there's no food—and—and—"

"No food ?" exclaimed the man, starting to his feet—" And you're hungry. I know what it is to be hungry—yes, and know what that poor thing there has done for me, when I hadn't a bit to eat. There, don't cry, Harry—don't, it's foolish to cry—very."

And, as the last syllable left his tongue, a choking sob burst from his breast, and he wept more violently than his youthful companion.

Rough and uncouth in appearance, Charlie Evans was a man of tender heart and generous nature. His life had been one continual struggle, and the vicissitudes through which he had passed had softened his heart to the sufferings of his fellow creatures.

Ten years before, he had sat in the very spot he now occupied, without a home, and without food—he had sat there while that poor woman, who now lay dead beside him, gave him bread to allay the pangs of hunger, and proffered him a shelter from the cold night air.

To him she had been a guardian angel, and the poor strolling player, for such he was, never forgot the kindness and the hospitality extended to him.

Poor—for poor indeed are they who travel the country in this occupation—he never possessed the means to return the poor woman's kindness, as his good nature prompted him to do, but never did he pass within a few miles of Barnstable, that he did

not call and see the woman who had stood his friend. And a smile would light up the faces of mother and son, as he tumbled into their humble abode, with his ever comical greeting of—

"Here we are—how do you do to-morrow ?"

How different did he appear now to what he did a few short hours before, when, with mouth drawn from ear to ear, and a broad grin upon his face, he had tumbled head over heels on to the parade of Richardson's Show, and made the assembled multitude beneath him shout again at the same words he had uttered on entering the room of death.

But the broad grin of mirth had vanished now, and that laughter exciting leer had given place to looks of grief and sobs of agony.

The merry clown, who had often pretended to force the little boy into the capacious pockets, now folded him to his breast, and strove to comfort and assuage his grief.

It was a strange picture, that laughing, rollicking clown, playing a part so foreign to his line of business.

Foreign did we say—heaven forgive us the injustice we have done him. Charlie Evans played the part he now filled truthfully. He made others laugh to gain bread for himself and his poor motherless daughter, but his nature was sad, for he was ever cast among those who waded through the miseries of life, daily struggling like himself for a paltry pittance to keep the wolf from the door, and his heart oft ached with anguish while his face wore the grin of mirth, and his mind wandered to the poor little child at home who had scarcely sufficient to support life.

The part he now played had not been rehearsed, for it was one of those parts in which he little dreamed he should be cast. It had been thrown upon him at a moment's notice, but he fulfilled it to the letter, for his soul was in it.

With a long-drawn sigh he raised his head from the shoulder of the little boy, and met the tearful glance fixed upon his face.

"Harry—Harry—I—I am so sorry," he gasped. "So kind—so good. Would I had known it earlier. When did she die ?"

"In the night," replied the boy. "The doctor came yesterday, and said she must have some wine, but we had no money, and I couldn't get it. We hadn't money for bread, and I'm so hungry—at least I was hungry, but I ain't now."

And again the boy's tears rolled down his cheeks. The fearful affliction he had met with had drowned the pangs of hunger. Charlie dived both hands into the pockets of his trousers, and with a blank look withdrew them again, then extending one towards the youth, he said—

"It's only a button—I arn't got a halfpenny. I only joined Richardson's company yesterday, and the few pence I had I left with Mary. I wish I had got some money—I do. But there—there don't cry. I'll get some—I'll get some to buy bread, Harry. I never did beg, I was too proud, but I'll do it now, I will. Yes, you shan't be hungry long, you shan't.

"She," he continued, pointing to the bed, "was kind to me, and may God desert me if I see her boy want."

And, almost roughly, he thrust the boy from him.

"I won't be long," he continued. "Don't cry, Harry, don't cry. Oh, don't I wish the property sausages was genuine, and the penny loaves ; but here, they ain't, and it's no use regretting it—

they're only stuffed with sawdust, and you can't eat 'em, but you shan't be hungry—you shan't. I'll get some money, I'll tumble for it in the street, I'll——"

"Not for me," said the boy, "I ain't hungry now."

"That's because you're filled with grief, but you'll be hungry before I get my salary, and damme, if Charlie Evans, who found bread and shelter in this cottage when he hadn't a feather to fly with, will see the son of her who stood his friend, want. If he does may he get hissed every house. Stop here, Harry, till I come back. I'll do it even if old Richardson sees me. I don't care, I've got a heart, and damn a man if he can't feel for his friends."

And grasping his hat in his hand, the kind-hearted fellow rushed from the room.

Poor little Harry! For a moment he stood looking at the door through which Charlie had passed, then he turned to the couch on which his dear mother lay, and, sinking down beside it, buried his face in the clothes. And there he remained, his tears again finding vent, and sobs ever and anon bursting from his breast.

Meantime, Charlie Evans made his way into the High-street, and stood for a few moments looking around him as though undecided how to act.

A carriage was coming slowly along, containing an old gentleman and his two daughters, and driven by an old coachman, who seemed to think that horse flesh was not a thing on which the whip ought to be laid.

There were a great many persons passing along also, and Charlie, who never allowed anything to pass him without speculating in his mind whether it might not he turned to advantage, laid his hat on the footway, and walked quietly into the road, almost under the feet of the greys.

"Hi!—hi!" exclaimed the old coachman, "do you want to be run over?"

To this, Charlie made no reply.

The coachman drew up for a moment, and Charlie, who expected this, dashed to the side of the veichle, where, seizing the box of the hind-wheel, he lay his body along it, and, as the driver started his horses, Charlie was hurled round and round.

First his head appeared at the carriage window, then his feet, and the occupants of the carriage screamed in alarm, and the driver drew up his horses.

The instant the carriage stopped, Charlie leapt from his dangerous position, and the old gentleman stepped from the veichle very pale and frightened. But when he saw Charlie standing before him unhurt, he exclaimed in severe tones—

"What is the meaning of this? I will have you put in the stocks. I will have you to know, sir, that your buffoonery is not to frighten people out of their lives. Send for a constable. The stocks, sir, the stocks shall be the reward of your trickery."

And the old gentleman stamped on the ground with rage.

"Sir," said Charlie, "if I have frightened you, pardon me. But before you send for a constable, listen to what I have to say. I have within the last three days walked a distance of forty miles to obtain an engagement at the fair in the next town. I was successful, and wishing to see those who had been kind to me in days gone by, I visited them. But, when I arrived, I found a dead mother, and an orphan boy without food, without a friend. Sir, I am poor, so poor that I have not the means to purchase food for the day, but I care not for myself—the poor child weeping by the side of his dead parent has no food. She—his mother—gave me bread when I was starving, and I would feed him now, but I can't. I left him to beg, that I might minister to his wants—I saw your carriage, and what I have done suggested itself to me. Sir, if you have a heart, you will pity the poor orphan, and give me, the only protector he now has, the means of satisfying the cravings of hunger which must assail him when the grief of his mother's loss shall wear itself down."

"Your story," replied the old gentleman, "savours much of your actions—that of a mountebank."

The colour mounted to the face of Charlie.

"Sir!" he exclaimed, "by profession I am a mountebank, but by nature—a man. They aided me when powerless, and my feelings tell me that now I must help him."

"Humph!" said the old gentleman, "what guarantee have I that you speak the truth?"

"Come to his habitation, and judge for yourself," replied Charlie.

The tone and manner in which the words were uttered convinced the owner of the carriage, and taking his purse from his pocket, he placed in the hands of the clown a half-sovereign."

"Oh! thank you—thank you!" said Charlie, as he turned the glittering coin over in his hand.

"And now, sir," said the old gentleman, "who and what are you?"

"Clown at Mr. Richardson's show."

"Then why not solicit aid of him?"

"Sir," said Charlie, "to him I am a stranger. I joined his company but yesterday, and to be poor and seem poor is sure to bring down upon yourself contempt."

The old gentleman paused for a moment, and then said—

"You are right so far. And you are in Richardson's Show?"

"I am, sir."

"In what capacity did you say?"

"As clown."

"Very good. We may meet again ere you leave the town."

And as he spoke, the old gentleman re-entered the carriage, and pulled the check-string.

Charlie waited to hear if he had anything more to say, but the driver whipped the horses, and the next moment the carriage was gone.

Charlie stood for a moment gazing after it, then clasping his hands together, he muttered as he started swiftly along—

"Half-a-sov—real—no stage prop—genuine—poor Harry—shan't be hungry long—bread—meat—half-a-sov. I'm so glad—I'm so happy. Oh, I'll make 'em laugh when the house opens, for I shall know the poor boy wants not, but, poor little fellow, he is alone in the world—no one to care for him. None—eh? what—none? Charlie Evans, may you get hissed every house if you don't protect that boy. His mother helped you when you had'nt got a bite, and you're a damned scoundrel if you don't help him. You ain't got much to live on—sometimes nothing—but you'll stick to him, Charlie, if you don't may you get hissed—hissed—hissed! There! for if you can't feel for those who helped you, you're a disgrace to the drama—a disgrace to the profession—and a damn bad, dirty, despicable, diabolical, disreputable son of a ——. But no, Charlie Evans, you've got a heart if you are a clown, and have to play thirteen houses a day, to a set of country bumpkins as don't know a great A from a bull's foot, but you've got a heart, Charlie, and you'll do your duty to the poor orphan boy."

———

CHAPTER II.

CHARLIE PLAYS A PART—THE CHASE—DICK THE POACHER.

AWAY went Charlie, as fast as his legs would carry him, in the direction of the humble abode of death, and, knocking over in his course a small stall of greengrocery, which, in the exuberance of his spirits at the success he had just met with, rendered him forgetful of where he was and what he was doing, and, imagining that the fallen vegetables were merely the stage properties in a pantomime, commenced pelting the owner of the stall with his own property, and calling out—"Hi! hi!—here we are—here's a lark!"

"I'll lark you, you scoundrel," exclaimed the keeper of the stall, as he rushed threateningly up to Charlie.

Charlie raised his arm, and bringing it down upon the hat of the man, sent that most absurd of all articles of wearing apparel right over the eyes of the purveyor of vegetables.

"Here's a lark!" exclaimed the now happy Charlie.

"Help—officers!—thieves!" roared the man, as he almost lifted himself off the ground in his endeavours to extricate his head from the now terribly-battered hat.

But here Charley seemed to recollect where he was and what he was doing, and, observing that several persons were making towards him, he darted hurriedly from the spot.

The people who had been attracted to the scene of Charlie's gambols, now gave chase, and our poor friend saw that the exuberance of spirits at his unexpected success was likely to get him into trouble. So on he went, every moment quickening his pace, and close at his heels ran the rabble of the small country town, yelling, hooting and screaming like so many demons.

"Damn it," said Charlie, "this will never do. I must find some means to give them the slip, or I shall find myself in the stocks, and the poor boy left without food. What a fool I am!"

But still he continued to run, followed by the mob, which was headed by the proprietor of the stall, loudly calling upon anyone and everyone to stop him.

They passed through the High-street, and Charlie perceived a lane, bearing off to the right, with a field on one side.

Into the lane he turned suddenly, just as his pursurers were upon him.

So sudden and unexpected was this deviation from the straight road, that his pursuers were unable to pull up before he had got a considerable distance down the lane.

On went Charlie, and, as he turned a winding in the lane, he was grasped in the arms of a young man with a vice-like grip.

Charley struggled to free himself from this unseen enemy.

"Quiet," said the man, "this way."

"Let go," said Charley, raising his hand to strike his captor.

"Quiet," said the man hurriedly, "you are pursued—this way—I am a friend."

And the man drew Charlie towards an opening in the thick-set hedge which bounded the field.

There was something in the tones of the stranger which caused the poor pantomimist to follow him, and he had just got through the hedge when the mob turned the angle of the lane.

"Keep close," said the man, as he drew Charlie into the hedge, "and they will pass you unseen."

And such, indeed, was the case.

The mob kept straight on, and in a few minutes the sounds of their voices and their footsteps had died away.

Then the stranger drew Charlie from the hedge, where he had continued to hold him.

"You are safe now," he said, "and can pursue your way unmolested."

"Thanks—thanks," said Charlie, "for the service you have done me."

"I don't want thanks," said the man, "for they are as hollow as a rotten-turnip. I saw you pursued, that was enough for me, the law has been unjust to me, and I would save the wretch it would get into its clutches—aye, though that man had committed murder."

"Murder!" said Charlie, starting back, "surely you don't think that, I——"

"Would commit murder?" interrupted the man—No—you don't look much like a murderer—just found something, I suppose, eh?"

"What do you mean?" said Charlie, in surprise.

"Ha! ha! ha!—how very innocent—blow'd if I don't think you are a new hand at the game."

And the stranger drew back a pace or two, and gazed at Charlie from head to foot with the utmost contempt.

"If you think I have been endeavouring to escape, after committing a robbery," said Charlie, drawing himself proudly up, "you are mistaken."

"Then what was all the row about?" said the man incredulously, "here, come into this little clump of trees, and tell me all about it—you will be safe there, and it will be better, perhaps, to wait till your pursuers have again returned, disappointed at your loss to the town."

And the man led the way across the field to a clump of trees, which cast their shadows upon the green sward.

The stranger walked into the intersticies of the minature forest, until he had gained the middle, followed by Charlie.

"Here," said the stranger, "sit upon this mound. It commands a view of the lane, and we can see all that passes without being seen ourselves.

Charlie did as his new-found friend requested, and his companion, seating himself before him, the good-hearted fellow took a long survey at his features and appearance.

He was a well-formed young man, of about six-and-twenty years of age, with a fine open countenance, dark as a gipsy's, high-forehead, and a firm set chin, denoting a resolution as firm, and a will as determined, to carry out any resolve he might form.

He was dressed in velveteen smalls, and short coat of the same material, and his massive brows were surmounted by a felt hat. His hands were small, and the long tapering fingers denoted that the hard labour of a country life seldom, if ever, soiled them. There was a restless expression in the bright, piercing black eyes, which he now fixed upon the pantomimist with a questioning glance.

"Well," he exclaimed, "How was it I found you trying to escape from that rabble you deny that you are a thief ?"

"I do," said Charlie, proudly.

"Then what have you been up to ?" asked the dark man.

"Forgetting myself," returned Charlie.

"Ah! forgetting yourself," sneered his companion. "That's what we all do, when we do wrong."

"True. I have done wrong, but it was in the excitement of a moment when I felt so happy."

"Happy," said the stranger. "I have forgotten what happiness is. But, there, you promised to tell me what brought all this about ?"

"I will," said Charlie, "since you have befriended me."

"Go on then."

Charlie Evans told his deliverer how he had joined the company at Richardson's Show ; how he had paid a visit to the house of the widow who had so often befriended him, and how he discovered her dead, and her boy without bread ; his resolve to assist him, and how he had succeeded in attaining money for that purpose, and, in fact, mentioned every circumstance that had occurred till the moment when he had met him.

The stranger listened intently, and when Charlie had finished, his dark companion grasped the pantomimist's hand in his own, and shook it fervently.

"You're a good fellow," he exclaimed, "and, bad as I am, I can respect and honour the man that can feel for a fellow creature ! But the name of this woman who is dead ?"

Charlie started—so strange was the tone in which the question was asked.

"Marston," he replied.

"Marston !" exclaimed the stranger.

"Yes," said Charlie.

"Emily Marston. Is it so ?"

"It is. Do you know her ?" said Charlie.

"Know her," exclaimed the dark stranger, "know her, yes, for an angel of goodness—but—"

"But what ?" said Charlie.

"No matter," returned the stranger, hurriedly. "What is to become of the boy—the child ?"

"I shall do the best I can for him," said Charlie. "His mother helped me when I was starving, and I'll work for her boy while I can."

"You will ?" said the stranger, fixing upon him a piercing glance.

"I will," said Charlie, emphatically.

"God will bless you for it," said the stranger, grasping the hand of the surprised player. "I would take him myself, but it is better I should not. He is good and honest, and is no companion for me. Look to him, be a friend to him, and you shall find help if you ever want it. Save that boy from wrong, lead him in the paths of virtue and truth, and the good act shall find its reward at last."

"I will treat that boy as my own child," said Charlie, "for his dead mother's sake, and when I forget the duty of a man and a Christian, may heaven forget me !"

The dark stranger turned away his head to hide the tear that stole to his eye, and exclaimed—

"Your pursuers have returned while you were speaking, and the road is now clear. Go, and take with you the blessing of one who will never forget that there is one right-minded man in this cold, heartless world."

Charles rose.

So also did the stranger.

"Who are you ?" said the player. "I would know more of you 'ere I go."

"My history would but sadden you. Go to the poor boy who awaits your return in the home of the dead—go."

And the stranger turned away.

"Stay," said Charlie, catching him by the arm. "Tell me who and what you are ?"

"An outcast and a wanderer on the wide earth," replied the stranger, bitterly.

"Your name," said Charlie.

The stranger again turned away.

"Deny me not the pleasure of knowing the man who this day has saved me from the hands of my pursuers."

The man paused for a moment thoughtfully, and then fixing his eyes upon the features of the poor player, he said—

"My name is but a mockery—a lie—I am known throughout the country as—"

"What ?" said Charlie, eagerly.

"Dick the Poacher !"

Charlie dropped the hand of his new-found friend.

"There is contamination in the touch of a thief," said the man sarcastically. "An honest man dreads contact with an outcast of society."

Charlie felt that his act had wounded his friend, and again he extended his hand.

"It is stained with crime," said the stranger, as he withdrew his own.

"No matter," said Charlie, "You are not all bad—there is some good yet left, I know. Give me your hand, you are not naturally bad. Some wrong, perhaps, has made you what you are."

"Wrong !" exclaimed the stranger, as Charlie grasped his hand. "Wrong ! villany black as hell, but—there—there—farewell, we shall meet again —farewell !"

And Dick the Poacher, wringing the other's hand fervently, darted from the spot and disappeared among the trees.

Charlie stood gazing for some time upon the spot where the poacher had disappeared, and then, slapping his hand upon his thigh, he muttered—

"Strange chap, that. What a splendid heavy man he'd make—looks a gipsy to perfection. Ah, but there ain't much of the villain in him after all, his heart's in the right place. I wonder who and what he is—Dick the Poacher—that's only the character he plays now, 'tain't his natural one I'd swear, he's only made up for it. He knew Emily Marston, did he—wonder how he knew her—perhaps he was hard up like me, and she helped him—God bless her ! I should like to know more about him —he ain't what he seems. I'll ask Harry, he knows, I dare say, and I don't know a good actor from a bad one, if that fellow ain't a gentleman after all."

And, casting his eyes around him, Charlie perceived the coast clear in all directions, "I'll be off now," he soliloquised ; "the poor boy must be lonely as well as hungry. Poor boy—poor boy !"

And the good-hearted fellow drew the sleeve of

his much-worn coat across his eyes, and left the field.

Keeping a sharp look-out around him, he dashed down the lane, and gained the high road. Drawing his old hat down over his face, he keep on at a quick pace, and soon arrived at the house of mourning.

Pushing the door open, he entered the apartment with the usual exclamation—

"Here we are!"

Harry was kneeling by the couch of his dead mother, when Charlie entered, but at the sound of his voice the poor boy rose and tried to smile.

But the transient gleam of joy that lit up his pale face died away ere it was born, and a tear rolled down his cheek.

"I'm so glad you've come back," said the boy, "I am so lonely."

"Poor child—poor child," said the good-hearted man. "But I've got such glorious news for you—you shan't be hungry—you shall have food. I've got half-a-sov—only think now—two days' salary —I'll buy bread and meat—and, there, only think now, ain't I been lucky!"

"Oh, you are kind—you are good to draw your salary for my sake," began the boy.

"Hold on there Harry—I have not done that —it's the worst thing you can do, to be poor and seem poor. I wouldn't have Richardson know I was hard up on any account—once they know it, farewell to all independence. Men take advantage of poverty—I don't believe he would, but I know people do. Let a poor devil on the first day of an engagement, in any capacity, ask an employer for an advance, and the chances are the next he will want to lower your salary—and, for why. because he thinks that a hungry belly will bind you to his will, and like a true Christian and a feeling man he thinks, poor devil, he will submit to it rather than starve!"

"That is not doing to others as they would be done by," said the boy, sighing.

"Men only profess to do that, seldom practice it," replied Charlie. "They expect every man to do so to them, but they will see another damned before they will do it to him."

"Are people so bad?" said the boy, sadly.

"Not all," replied Charlie. There are some good, but very few. Men look upon these things in a business light—they buy cheap and sell dear, and he who has the most money to throw into the market, is sure to be the one to gain the most profit. But you'll find all that out in time. Now you are hungry I'll go and buy food, and then we will see what can be done about your poor mother there."

At the mention of his mother, poor little Harry Marston's tears started forth afresh.

"Don't cry my boy," said the poor clown. "If you keep on sobbing in this manner you will cry yourself away to nothing."

"I can't help it," sobbed the boy. "I can't indeed—the tears will come, and when I try to stop them they almost choke me."

"Do they my poor child," said Charlie, with a choking sensation at his throat. "But you mustn't. There, I'll come back directly with the food—don't cry now, don't!"

And the poor fellow brushed away the tear that rolled down his own weather-beaten face as he left the house, muttering to himself—

"Can't help it—can't he—no more can I—they will come to ease the bursting heart."

CHAPTER III.

THE FUNERAL—THE VISITORS—DICK TO THE RESCUE!

IT was a week after the events recorded in the last chapter, that a sad and mournful procession wended its way through the High-street of the town to the little churchyard, where lie mouldering the remains of many a brave man and tender-hearted woman, who had lived and breathed, shed light and joy, sorrow or misery, upon the little world to which they belonged. Their last resting-place marked out by the grey stone, or obliterated by the feet of heedless children, as they, all unthinking of death's dread presence, sported among the moss-covered mounds.

No sombre-toned bell tolled for the departed spirit, no gorgeous yet mournful trappings waved majestically over the coffin in which that once beautiful and tender woman now lay so cold and still, never more to rise till the last trumpet shall sound and the dead awake. No groups of sorrowing friends stood with bared heads around the church porch. for she who that day was to be consigned to the earth from which she sprang was rich only in the noble qualities of the soul, and to the worldly-minded was unworthy of a moment's sympathy—a passing prayer.

One gate of the churchyard stood open, and the bearers with their solemn burden had scarce room to pass into the precincts of the dead. This caused a half, those who bore the coffin on their shoulders expecting that the sexton, who stood some short distance up the avenue in smiling conversation with the clerk, would unbolt the other half-gate to give them free ingress.

But although this worthy saw the difficulty he stirred not, but continued his talk.

Poor Harry! Young as he was, he felt the insult offered to his mother's remains, and the tears he had long controlled now burst forth.

"Why do they not open the other gate?" muttered his companion. "Ah, Harry, my poor boy, you see what it is to be poor."

And Charlie Evans heaved a deep sigh as he spoke, and pressed his young companion's hand within his own.

And the two mourners, for they were the only two, stood awaiting with feelings of agony, the passage to the grave.

Suddenly a tall man pushed past them, and seizing the long bolts of the gate, swung it wide open. Then, stepping backwards, he raised the felt hat from his brows, and as the bearers carried the coffin past him he bowed his head till the long black curling locks fell like a veil around his face.

The sexton left the side of the clerk and approached him, and when the mournful procession had passed, he exclaimed indignantly—"Who are you that dare take upon yourself to open that gate?"

Drawing himself up with a fiery glance in his eye, the man exclaimed—

"A Christian—do you understand the word—a Christian?"

The look of ineffable contempt which the new-comer fixed upon the hard-hearted sexton, caused that worthy to recoil a few paces, and the blush of shame to mount to his face.

The man strode haughtily past him and stood at the new-dug grave.

The coffin was lowered into the grave—the minister gabbled through the solemn service for the dead—the clerk scarcely deigned to utter the responses—and the sexton looked as though he considered it unnecessary to drop the earth upon the coffin at the words—"ashes to ashes, dust to dust."

The service concluded, the minister followed by the clerk, hastily left the spot, and the two mourners and the dark-featured man who had opened the gate alone stood by the grave.

Dick the Poacher, for he it was who had given the sorrowful procession free access to the church-yard, kept the felt hat held before his face so as to shield his features from the view of little Harry and his companion as he stepped up the mound of earth at the side of the grave, to gaze upon the wooden box which contained that inanimate form. Then he too hurried away, and Harry and the clown were left alone.

Charlie assisted the poor little fellow up the little hill of soft earth, and held him by the arm as he took his last look upon the plain coffin which contained all that remained of her who in life had been to him what Heaven has destined woman should be—a mother.

Then slowly and sadly he led him from the spot, biting his under lip and setting firm his teeth to hide the emotion which shook his manly frame.

Silently and sadly they wended their way back-wards to the now lonely home of the poor orphan boy.

How cold, how cheerless did that home now appear. As he crossed the threshold, Harry felt a chill run through his veins, and a shudder per-vaded his frame—he felt he was alone.

He raised his tear-bedimmed eyes to his com-panion's face, and as if the poor player had read his thoughts, he extended his arms, and the boy, with an impulsive bound, rushed forward and was clasped to his breast.

And on the poor player's shoulder sobbed the orphan boy.

And when his grief had expended itself he once more raised his pale face, and saw the look of pity and kindness which beamed down upon him, he felt happier than he had been since his mother's death, for he saw there one word—father.

"Father," he murmured.

"Ay, boy, father," said Charlie, "to you I will be a father, while heaven grants me life. Will you trust in me ?"

"I will," replied the boy.

"Harry, I am very poor."

"I know it," said the boy.

"But I will share with you and Mary the last crust."

"And I will toil to aid you," said the boy.

"But what are we now to do?" said Charlie, after a pause. "The home where Mary is, is some miles from here—will you share it with her ?"

"Yes, oh yes !"

"The few things you have here," said Charlie. "would cost much to move."

"Oh, do not let us take them," said the boy, "they would remind me of happy days."

"What shall we do with them ?" asked Charlie.

"Sell them, and let us leave this place, all but a packet of papers which mother bade me keep —they are in the drawer there."

And the boy placed his hand upon the handles of the drawer in which the documents he now mentioned were lying.

As he did so, the door was thrust violently open and a primly-dressed, weazened-faced individual stood upon the threshold.

"Humph ! got back then," he said, striding into the room. "This way, Mr. Takeall, this way, sir," he added, addressing some one outside.

A short, stout, red-faced individual, with a pro-fusion of red hair, made his way into the room, and closed the door.

Charlie started to his feet, and confronted the new-comers, while Harry nestled close up to the side of his friend.

"What do you want?" said Charlie, gazing at the men suspiciously, for there was something in the look of both, which the player did not relish.

"My name, sir," said the man who had first entered, "is Gripe—Mr. Gripe, the steward of Squire Henley—yes, sir—and this gentleman is Mr. Take-all, the broker, you know the gentleman no doubt,"

"No I don't," said Charlie, "and what's more, I don't want to."

"Ah, no doubt, sir—no doubt—few care to made the acquaintance of Mr. Takeall—very few, but business is business, and we must do our duty."

"Well," said Charley, more and more sur-prised, "what duty brings you here ?"

"A duty which I have to perform very often. The late Mrs. Marston was indebted to the Squire —very much indebted to him—his feeling nature allowed the lady to get much more heavily in arrears than is his custom, but now that the poor woman is dead, it becomes my duty to see that my respected friend Mr. Takeall does his duty."

"And what the devil is his duty ?" said Charlie, beginning to see the motive of their visit.

"To demand those arrears, or sieze," returned the smooth-spoken Gripe.

Charlie's lip curled scornfully, and with a look of contempt, he said—

"And have you got the heart to rob that boy, but a few days made an orphan."

"We have a duty to perform," said Takeall. "It has nothing at all to do with the heart."

"Ain't it," said Charlie.

"Not a bit, my dear sir," chimed in Gripe, "not a bit, always do your duty, even the Scriptures command it."

"Look you," said Charlie, getting very red in the face, and, unconsciously closing his fists, "You're a pair of damn scoundrels, and I should like to punch both your heads !"

Gripe and Takeall started back a few paces.

"Send for a constable," said Gripe. "Here's resistance to the law."

"The law be damned," said Charlie.

"Produce your warrant, Mr. Takeall, let him see that, and then at his peril let him resist us."

Mr. Takehall produced his warrant from a large and much-worn pocket-book, and flourished it before the eyes of the disgusted Charlie.

"There, sir, there !" exclaimed Takeall, triumphantly, "do you see that, sir—do you see that now, what do you think of it ?"

"Think of it," reiterated Charlie, "why I think its a damn dirty piece of paper, and the hand that signed it ought to rot from the wrist."

"It did its duty, sir—it did its duty," chimed in Gripe.

"It's duty, when it robs the orphan," said the poor player bitterly.

"That's nothing to do with us," said Takeall. Business and duty is all we stand upon."

"What is the amount due ?" said Charlie.

"One year's rent—ten pounds—and the ex-penses of these proceedings," said Takeall.

",Then you can't have it," said Charlie.

"Can't—must—money or goods," said Gripe.

"Oh, let them have them," said the boy, " and then we will leave here for ever."

"If I do, I'm——"

"Oh, don't—don't," said Harry, seizing the arm of his friend as he advanced threatenly towards the two men, "they will put you in prison, and then I shall be alone !"

Charlie drew back.

He knew that they had law upon their side, and that the boy would be left alone.

"Let it be so, Harry," he said. " For myself, I care not but for you. They must do as they like."

"Wisely said," exclaimed Gripe, " a very wise decision."

Charlie turned from the speaker in disgust.

"Get the papers you spoke of," he said to the boy, " and let us leave them to their dirty work."

Harry opened the drawer, and drew forth the packet.

"What is that ?" said Gripe.

"Can't you see ?" replied Charlie, " papers."

"What are you going to do with them ?"

"Take them away, to be sure," replied the player.

"I cannot suffer anything to be removed," said Takeall.

And he stretched forth his hand, and tore them from the boy's grasp.

"Hand them over," said Charlie, clenching his fist, and holding it threatingly before the face of the broker, " or I'll dash you to the ground."

"Go for the constable, Mr. Gripe," exclaimed Takeall. " Go for the constable."

Gripe made his way to the door, as Charlie. now thoroughly aroused, threw himself upon the broker, who, to prevent him getting possession of the papers, held them at arm's length above his head.

At this moment the door was thrust violently open, and Gripe staggered across the room from the effects of a heavy blow on his forehead, and a hand from behind tore the packet from the broker's grasp.

Simultaneously all turned their eyes in the direction of the door, and there, with the packet in his hand, stood Dick the Poacher.

"They are safe," he exclaimed. " We shall meet again," and darted away.

———

CHAPTER IV.

THE SQUIRE AND HIS FACTOTUM—DISAPPOINTMENT AND PLOTTING.

IN a gorgeously-furnished apartment, whose long bay windows opened on to a terrace, overlooking a smooth-cut lawn, with here and there *parterres* of flowers, amid the lovely blossoms of which the bee and the butterfly sported in the sunshine or sipped the sweet fragrance from their honey bedewed petals.

A tall, severe-looking old gentleman sat in a easy chair drawn to the side at the centre window perusing a newspaper.

Suddenly his eye lighted upon a paragraph, which he perused rapidly, then laying the paper upon a side-table, he threw himself back in the chair, and became lost in thought.

Thus he continued, with his eyes fixed on vacancy, for a few moments, then he started up, and hurriedly paced the room.

"The fair," he muttered, " opens in this town to-morrow. I must see that man—that boy must be removed from my path—he now is the only obstacle to my happiness. She is dead, and I have nothing more to fear from her. But this boy he may know too much—still give me trouble, after all my plotting and scheming. Could I but blast his character as I have already done that of *his*, I could rest in peace. Peace—pshaw, there is no peace for the guilty, but I should be secure from the law's fangs. The proofs of my villany were in her hands, but she dared not use them lest I proclaimed *him* a thief, and incendiary, and brought down the over-whelming fury of outraged justice on his head. But why do I fear, Gripe is a shrewd fellow, and will have the papers I so much dread, and then I am safe—safe."

And the old man strode up and down the apartment with rapid and uneasy steps.

There was a knock at the door of the room, the old man paused in his walk, and bade the visitor enter.

The prim figure of the weazen-faced steward entered the apartment, and silently and mysterious closed the door behind him.

His thin face looked even thinner than when we last saw him, and there was an uneasy twitching about his thin lips as he strode to the side of his master.

"Good morning, Squire Henley," said the prim steward, as he bowed obsequiously.

Squire Henley returned the salutation coldly, as he exclaimed—

"Now, sir, your business."

"As was my duty," began the little man, " I, in company with the much respected Mr. Takeall, visited the dwelling of the late Mrs. Marston for the purpose of making a seizure on her goods in the event of the arrears not being paid up."

"Yes, yes," said Squire Henley, hastily, "come to the point, man—come to the point."

"As is my duty," said Gripe.

"Damn your duty," exclaimed the Squire, passionately, " those papers, where are they ?"

And the Squire leaping from the chair into which he had sunk upon his factotum's entrance, advanced hastily towards him.

Gripe retreated, so fierce was the look of his master.

"As I was saying, Squire," again began Gripe, " my duty led me to seek for the documents, but—but ——"

"But what ?" roared the Squire.

"They're gone."

"Gone—how—what means you ?"

"Lost !"

"Lost !" almost shrieked the Squire."

"Stolen ! " said Gripe, becoming more and more alarmed.

"Stolen ! By whom?"

"Dick the Poacher !"

"Liar !" exclaimed the Squire, seizing the little man by the collar of his coat.

The face of Gripe became a shade paler, but otherwise he was firm and composed.

"Squire Henley," he said, " my duty to your house has been done, and if accidents unforeseen should intervene to obstruct that duty. I have still done it, sir—still done my duty."

The cool measured tones of the little man somewhat abated the wrath of the Squire.

He released his hold of Gripe's collar, and threw himself again into his easy chair.

The steward smoothed the frill of his shirt

HARRY'S INTRODUCTION TO THE MANAGER.

front, took his pocket-comb out and adjusted his hair, and was as prim as ever.

"Gripe," said his master after a pause, "You know I cared not for the arrears—it was that packet of papers I wished to secure."

"I know it," replied Gripe.

"And I entrusted you to obtain it"

"That duty devolved upon me," said the little man.

"And have you performed it?" said the Squire.

"To the best of my ability," returned Gripe.

"By allowing another to take possession of it," said his master, bitterly.

"I could not help it."

"Why not?"

The steward pushed the hair back from his forehead, and revealed a large blue bump just above the temple.

"Look at this, Squire," he said, "and then say if I have not done my duty.

"What has that wound to do with it?" asked the Squire.

"Everything," said Gripe.

"Explain?"

"I was about to do so, but your hasty temper stayed me."

"Well, go on—I am cool now.

"As I have said, Squire, in pursuance of my duty, myself and Takeall visited the cottage under the pretence of levying a warrant upon the goods and chattels, but in reality to obtain the papers you were so anxious to get into your keeping. We found the boy and a man there, who resisted us. The boy had possession of the packet, and Takeall got it from him, the man strove to regain it, and as I was about to leave the house in search of a constable, Dick the Poacher entered, knocked me down, stole the packet from Takeall's hands, and made off."

" Did you not pursue him?" asked the Squire.

The little man looked hard at the Squire, as if he did not understand him.

The Squire repeated the question.

" Not likely," said Gripe coolly.

" Why so?"

" Dick has a hand of iron, and a will to use it," replied Gripe.

" Curse him!" muttered the Squire. " Had I gained possession of them, I could have transported that man."

" Can you not do so now?" said the steward.

" It is robbery."

" No, I cannot," said the Squire, bitterly.

" Why not?" asked Gripe.

" No matter," replied his master. " But you must yet find some means to get them from him."

" It is my duty," meekly replied Gripe.

" See that you perform it this time with better success," said the Squire.

" I shall use my best endeavours," replied the little man.

" Now, the boy—where is he?" asked the Squire.

" Gone."

" Gone?"

" Yes."

" Where?"

" I don't know."

" Why did he leave his home?" asked the Squire.

" Because he had none."

" How so?"

" Takeall seized."

" I did not require that."

" Takeall did."

" Why?"

" The things were worth more than the arrears due," said Gripe.

" The hard-hearted scoundrel," muttered the Squire.

A smile played around Gripe's mouth.

" It is his business," remarked the steward.

" Had he no feeling for the orphan?" said Henley.

Gripe raised his brows and opened his eyes in surprise.

The squire saw this, and his eyes fell before the steward's stare.

Does he suspect or know anything, he thought. Why that look of surprise.

The Squire felt uneasy.

Did his steward suspect that he was even worse than Takeall.

The broker had stripped the home of the orphan, but he had robbed him of his inheritance.

Did Gripe know this.

If so, that look was accounted for.

He would find out.

But he must work cautiously.

The smooth-spoken Gripe was a crafty man, and the Squire felt that he must be cautious.

After a pause he said,—

" Well, this is a bad job, you must do your best to remedy it. I have been a good master, and shall not forget you, Gripe. Obtain those papers and your reward shall be princely. Good morning."

Gripe took the hint, and bowed himself from the room, and, when he had closed the door behind him, he shook his fist at it and muttered—

" Squire, I'll be even with you for that shaking. You think yourself secure, but if I get possession of those documents, they go to the highest bidder. Gripe, you'll make a fortune yet."

CHAPTER V.

THE FAIR—RICHARDSON'S SHOW—THE FRACAS ON THE PARADE—THE ORPHAN MEETS WITH SYMPATHISING FRIENDS.

It is mid-day—the bright sun is shining down upon a thousand merry faces, and streaming upon rows of pedestrians, as with cheerful looks and light buoyant footsteps they wend their way from street and lane, cottage and farmhouse, village and town, to one spot—the green on which the fair that day is to be opened.

Rows of canvas stretch in long lanes over the green sward, booths and shows, swings and roundabouts, surmounted with gaudy flags and more gaudy paintings, are here scattered about in one heterogenous mass.

A babel of tongues rises in the air—shouts of laughter, cries of pain, the merry jest, the hasty word, the sudden blow, the swaying to and fro of the densely-packed mob, and a thousand upturned faces, all eager for the first flourish of trumpets that shall proclaim to the pleasure seekers that the fair is opened, and that mirth and revelry are for the time to be the order of the day.

One o'clock, and amid the beating of gongs and drums, the clashing of cymbals, the braying of trumpets, the blowing of horns, and the cheers of thousands of lungs, the fair is opened.

The musicians strike up on the parades of the different booths, each company playing their loudest as they strive to drown the others and attract the greatest numbers to their own show.

Shrieks of laughter rise from the crowd of upturned faces as the pantomimists roll on to the parade and knock each other down, only to pick them up again by the hinder part of their unmentionables, or roll over each other like a hoop, from one side of the parade to the other, shouting and screaming all the while like so many demons, whilst grotesquely-attired men shout with stentorian lungs—" Walk up—walk up! We're just a-going to begin. The best booth in the fair—don't forget Richardson's. Walk up—walk up!"

And as the smiling bumpkins and their sweethearts cross the parade and pay their money, the merry clown amuses the spectators below by kissing the girls, stealing the hats of the men, or falling about with his legs entangled in a chain of sausages, which have been appropriated to this purpose for many a long day.

Here, too, is the largest giant in the world and the smallest dwarf, the pig with three heads and the dog with no legs, the wonders of the deep, and the extinct monsters of the earth, the fire-eaters and the Circassian maiden who lives on live animals, and the proprietors of each and all are bawling themselves hoarse extolling the wonders of their caravans, and washing down their huskiness by deep potations from brown earthen jugs.

Richardson's is full, and the great sensational drama of the "Skeleton Spectre; or, the Three Bleeding Hearts of the Blighted Oak" is about to commence. The audience who had stood around the back of the parade grinning at the grotesque capers of clown and pantaloon, now leave the spot for the theatre, where they will see less than they have seen outside, and the platform is deserted of all save a few musicians and the paraders, as clown, pantaloon, harlequin, columbine, heavy ruffian, and girl in Scotch dress, are styled.

But shrinking into a corner stands a small, pale youth, gazing vacantly upon the scene around, and whose melancholy features seem sadly out of place amid that mob of pleasure seekers.

It is Harry Marston, the orphan boy.

He withdraws his gaze from the mob, and fixes it upon Charlie Evans, who, out of breath with his tumbling over the chain of sausages, is resting for a moment with his back against the side of the platform.

Slowly and timidly he left his corner and approached his friend.

"Well, Harry," said Charlie, in a kind tone. "How do you like the fair?"

A sickly smile played around the boy's mouth.

"Ah," muttered Charlie to himself, "It's not the place for him, so soon after his bereavement, but I thought it would divert his young mind from sadder recollections.

"How would you like this life?" said Charlie.

"I don't know," replied the boy, "but I should like anything I think, by which I could earn money to assist you."

"Well, I'll ask Richardson, when I get a chance, if he can give you any employment about the booth. Stand back now, Harry, I must begin again."

The boy retreated to his corner as Charlie, once more going to the front, commenced a variety of grotesque capers, whilst the harlequin and columbine, who had just concluded a dance, rested after their exertions.

The harlequin was a man of rough, uncouth bearing, with a bombastical turn, engendered no doubt by his being at the crack show. He was not much liked by the company, his disagreeable bullying manner rendering him obnoxious to his fellow workers.

He strode haughtily back from the front of the platform, swearing at the woman who had been his columbine, and who was, or ought to have been, his wife, from their relationship—a poor delicate creature, who, on more than one occasion, had to paint out a black eye ere she could appear before the public, and who now walked tremblingly by the side of her master, meekly submitting to his abuse, from fear of personal violence—not then and there, for Dancing Bill, as he was called, only practised those little feats of pugilism where the poor woman could get no help.

As he came close to where Harry stood, he turned suddenly to the boy and said—

"Here, youngster—go and fetch me a pint of ale."

The boy looked up at the black mask, and replied—

"I don't know where, sir."

Dancing Bill, his temper already ruffled, caught the poor boy by the collar, and shaking him violently, roared out—

"You won't—won't you, you lazy dog?"

"Oh, don't, sir—I don't know where, I don't" cried the boy,

"Then take that for your ignorance," said Bill, striking the youth on the side of the head with his open hand.

The first cry of the boy caused Charlie to turn, and as the youth rushed towards him, he threw down the chain of sausages, and clenched his fists.

"Oh," said the boy, clinging to his arm, "don't let that man beat me."

"What did you strike him for?" said Charlie, foaming with passion.

"What's that to you?" replied Bill. "I'll do it again if I like."

"Will you, by G—," roared Charlie.

"Yes, and you too," replied Bill, bounceably.

Charlie drew back his arm and struck the harlequin so heavy a blow between the eyes of his mask that he rolled on to the parade all in a heap.

"Come on," said Charlie—"come on, if you've got the pluck to do anything else than fight a baby or lick a woman."

This was a home thrust, and was admired much more by those present on the parade than the knock-down blow.

They all knew of the harlequin's cruelty to the poor woman, but none liked to tell him of it lest he should make their knowledge a further excuse for his brutality.

The harlequin struggled into a sitting position, and thus he remained, not daring to rise to his feet, with his hands on his knees, and glaring through the openings of his half-mask upon his assailant.

Like most women-beaters, Dancing Bill was an arrant coward. The *valour* which he displayed when thrashing a poor defenceless woman evaporated at the sight of a man's fist, and the bully and the blackguard lay like a beaten cur, grovelling at the feet of its master.

"Strike me comical," said Buskin Bob, the pantaloon, "if you ain't done a blessed service to humanity in knocking him over, but I expects that ere poor devil will get it when he gets her home."

"There, come here," said Charlie, drawing the boy back again from the front of the platform. "He won't touch you no more, or if he does, it won't be well for him. Look here, Bob," he added, turning to the pantaloon, "Did you ever see such a damn dirty piece of work as to hit a poor orphan as ain't got no mother, only me, and all because he didn't know where to get the ale."

"Strike me comical, it is a shame. Who is he?" asked the pantaloon.

"Why the little chap as I was telling you of—don't you know," said Charlie.

"In course I do. Here, never mind, youngster. Strike me comical, I've got an apple here for you, a nice one too."

And Buskin Bob dived his hand and arm into the capacious pocket of his pantaloon dress, and drew forth the fruit he had stolen from a young country lass as she crossed the parade.

"There it is—a beauty. Munch that, and don't mind Spangles. I'll get you another next house, or else something else. I will, strike me comical if I don't."

The boy took the apple and smiled his thanks, and through the flake-white and red ochre on that man's face he could see a countenance beaming with pity, and he felt that there was one more to befriend him.

"Strike me comical, the drama's over," said Bob. "You stand there, and don't move for Spangles or anyone else. Now then, Charlie."

Charlie gave the boy a pressure of the hand to reassure him, and then rushed forward to the front, followed by pantaloon, whom he knocked over on to the platform. but not with such force and determination as he had done the harlequin, and in this respect he extended his hand to the fallen man and assisted him up, as he cut a few capers and screamed out—

"Hallo—here we are—here we are!"

The fracas between the clown and harlequin was taken by the mob below as all fun, and therefore the affair passed off less seriously than it otherwise might have done.

The drama being finished, the satisfied spectators took their leave, and the company on the parade was strengthened by those who had been engaged in the representation of the drama.

The fresh arrivals were soon made acquainted with the quarrel between Charlie and Dancing Bill, and our poor friend the clown was commended by them all for the part he had played, and many who before feared the bully now jeered at him openly.

And a good feeling, too, was also raised for the poor orphan, and, in a very short time, he found his pockets full of fruit, ginger-bread nuts, and various knick-nacks, which had by some means or another found their way into the hands of the donors.

Poor boy, he began to feel more happy every moment, and almost wished that he too was an actor—they were so kind to him, so good, spoke such cheering words, and felt so much pity for him.

"Surely," he thought "these men have feelings in spite of the ruffians some of them look."

And he was right. There are no class of men in the world who sympathise more with the poor, the friendless, and the oppressed.

CHAPTER VI.

THE CLOWN AND THE PROPRIETOR—THE VISIT TO THE DRESSING-ROOM—HARRY OBTAINS EMPLOYMENT—THE OLD STAGER AND THE YOUNG ASPIRANT.

In all vast assemblies whether for pleasure or otherwise, there is sure to be one portion of the time in which the space so thickly covered, will, as if by magic, become thinned, as if the greater portion, as though actuated by a sudden impulse, shifted their position or sought relief from the crowd by becoming scattered.

This would seem to be one of the characteristics of a congregation of people. In the midst of a sermon, when the silence is only broken by the words uttered by the minister, if one shift his position or cough, the spell is broken, and a hundred shift in their seats or a chorus of a'hems are sure to echo throughout the building. So it is with a mob, it seldom thins gradually, but all at once. One minute where there is not room for a human being to squeeze itself into, the next a thousand could stand with ease and comfort.

It was during one of these sudden lulls in the pressure of the fair that Mr. Richardson sat in the money-box, smiling blandly and doubtless reckoning up in his mind the prospect of the fair being successful or a failure, when Charlie Evans approached the old show proprietor and requested the favour of a few moments conversation.

"Deary me," said Richardson, "what is it—what is it?"

"A favour sir," replied Charlie.

"A favour, every one wants favours, and business is bad, very bad."

Charlie smiled.

Business on the contrary had been very good.

But when Richardson was asked for money before it was due he invariably replied that business was very bad.

He thought the favour which Charlie now required was an advance.

He objected to this upon the plan that it was bad, and that the men invariably spent in drink that which they borrowed.

Strictly upright in all his dealings, he liked to see his people the same.

One of his characteristics was whenever he left a town to send and make inquiries if any of his company had become indebted during their stay, and if so, he always paid the bill, hence it was that any poor player had only to say that he belonged to Richardson's company, and that he was welcome.

What a fool, doubtless some will say, but we think differently.

Richardson seldom or ever lost by this. He was respected wherever he went, and the members of his company for shame's sake seldom overstepped the boundaries of their means.

"Here, you, Jones, just come and take the money," said Richardson, addressing one of the company, "and just keep your eyes open, do you hear?"

"Yes," replied the individual addressed, as he stepped into the box as Richardson retreated from it.

"Now then," said the old show-keeper," as he smoothed the frill of his shirt. "What is it you want?"

"Employment for a poor youth," replied Charlie—"a poor boy left without friends or home."

"Deary me. Where is he?"

"Here," replied the clown.

"Call him then."

Charlie stepped back, and caught Harry by the hand, and drew him forward.

"This is him," said Charlie.

"Deary me. Ain't he got no friends?" asked Richardson.

"None, sir," replied Charlie.

"None at all, boy, eh?" said the proprietor addressing the child.

Harry turned his gaze first to Richardson, then to the clown, and answered—

"Yes, sir—one!"

"And who is that?"

"Him," he replied, pointing to the clown.

"No father?"

"No, sir."

"No mother?"

"No, sir."

"Nobody at all?"

"Only Charlie."

"Why don't you seek elsewhere for employment, does the paint and tinsel of the stage charm you?"

Harry cast his eyes upon the ground, he knew not what to reply.

Charlie came to the rescue, and told Richardson all that we have recorded, and wound up by expressing a wish that he would find the poor boy employment, so that he could be near him to protect and guide him.

Richardson dived his hands into the pockets of his small clothes, and paced up and down the platform for a few moments thoughtfully.

Then he stopped suddenly before the clown and the youth.

"What can you do?" he said to Harry.

"Anything, sir."

"You think you can, but I'm many years older than you, and I can't do anything now."

"Anything in an ordinary way," chimed in Charlie.

"Dance?" said Richardson.

"No," replied Charlie, with a smile.

"Sing?"

"No."

"Tumble?"

"No, sir."

"Then you can't do nothing," said Richardson, sharply.

The boy turned his head to hide the tear, the sharp remark called forth.

"I can do anything, sir—clean or polish."

"Bah," replied the proprietor.

Then seeing the sad look on the boy's face—he said kindly—

"My poor boy, I do not know what I can do to assist you."

Charlie sighed.

His hope had vanished.

"Is there no employment, sir, about the booth which he could do, nothing," said the kind-hearted clown.

"Nothing," replied Richardson, as he re-entered the money box.

Charlie turned away disppointed.

"Here," called the good old man, "I tell you what you can do."

Charlie listened intently.

And the face of the boy brightened.

"You can take him to the manager, and say I sent you—he knows best."

"Thank you, sir," said Charlie.

"Thank you," sir, iterated Harry.

Charlie felt that it was all right now, and he drew his young companion away from the platform, and took him down underneath to the space appropriated to the dressing-rooms.

Entering the one appropriated to the male portion of the company, Harry cast his eyes around in surprise.

Dresses of all times, shapes, and materials lie scattered about on benches, the wooden partition was hung with hats, helmets, and head-dresses of various sorts and periods, sabres, daggers, and pistols, forming a strange and fantastic background to the picture this room presented.

In the centre stood a heavy, bearded ruffian, with slouched hat and long scarlet cloak, a massive head of ringlets, one of which he had trained to fall over the left eye, and which gave to his countenance a villainous expression.

This ringlet served the double purpose of making him look the part he played, and hiding from the public gaze, the sightless orb which lie beneath it.

Poor fellow! He was blind in one eye.

In the belt around his waist two enormous pistols were stuck, and a large sword lie against his left leg.

He was a strange looking character in his present costume, and the heart of poor Harry sank within him as he gazed upon him. Sitting or standing around were several others all attired, or partially so, for the various characters of the 'Skeleton Spectre!"

One sat before a small broken glass applying to his upper lip a little black, and giving the youth an idea of how to "make up."

All this the poor boy took in at a glance, and truly his impressions now of a theatrical life, were anything but flattering.

It was the dark side of the picture—the bright one is to be seen in the glare of the footlights.

There the faded plush and the begrimed tinsel become velvet and gold and silver—it glitters then, but it is not gold.

How cold, cheerless, miserable, and wretched in daylight, does it appear behind the scenes.

The wretched daubs, the leaden gilt, that at night sparkles forth in lustrous beauty, charming the eye of the beholder, now looks dead and miserable.

Charlie introduced his protogée to the assembled company.

"Poor little fellow!" said the heavy man.

"Hard lines," said the man, turning from the glass and surveying the boy curiously.

"What's his line?" asked the heavy man, after a long look at the youth.

"Oh, utility," said Charlie.

"That be blowed," said he who was making up. "Where's he been operating?"

"At home with his mother," said Charlie.

"What is his line?" asked the heavy man—"Anything or nothing?"

"Nothing," said Charlie, "never was in the profession."

"Then, how can I help him?"

"By finding him something to do."

"Yes, but what?"

"Anything."

"That's nothing," replied the heavy man.

"Can't he help the store-keeper?" suggested Charlie.

"He might."

"Then, give him that."

"He would get scarcely anything for it."

"It may lead to something better," said the clown, unwilling to let any chance slip.

"But I don't think he wants help."

"Yes he does. He has more than he can do to keep everything in order."

"Well let it be so, then," said the heavy man, "but he'll starve upon the salary."

"No he won't," said Charlie.

"Could you live on five shillings per week?" asked the heavy man.

"No."

"Then how can he?"

"He won't have to do it."

"But he must if he can't get more."

"I will see to him," said the clown.

"You?"

"Yes, me."

"It ain't one of your own, is it Charlie?" said he who was making up.

"Yes."

"The devil it is. I thought you had only got one—a girl.

"No more, I ain't, but I've adopted this one you see."

"Adopted him?"

"Yes."

"Why, you can hardly keep yourself, or at least you couldn't, but I suppose now you've got into the crack show, you mean to do the grand."

"I mean to do my duty," said Charlie.

"It ain't a man's duty to keep all the orphans in the world, is it?"

"Perhaps not," replied the clown. "But I consider it my duty to adopt this one."

"Why?"

"Because when I was starving, his mother fed and sheltered me."

"Did she?"

"She did."

"Then she was a true woman?" said the man,

"She was an angel," replied Charlie, emphatically, "and I would not see her boy want while I could get a crust."

"Bravo," said the heavy man, "Charlie you're a brick, and I'll do all I can to help the boy for your sake. Let him help the property man for a time, and something will turn up better."

"Thank you," said Charlie. "He's a good boy, and so you'll find him."

"I hope so. And now youngster just listen to an old stager's advice. Do your best, and do it willingly, and if what you see and learn here leads you to fancy the profession, take to it, but do not let the tinsel and feathers lead you to adopt a life which may be hateful to you hereafter. The life of a player is no easy, gentlemanly calling—it is one continual struggle for bread. I adopted it because I thought that Drury Lane would command my presence. I believe that I had but to appear once upon the stage to take the world by storm, and carve out for myself a name and fame as great as any who have stood before the footlights; and to attain this end I sacrificed position, friends, all—but it was a vain delusion. I found the gold but dross, and the applause I sighed for came but in fitful gusts, and died away ere it was almost given. I never could reach the position for which I aimed, and now, after twenty years, I am still a poor player in Richardson's Show. Boy, you had better seek any other calling than go through life a poor and strolling player."

Harry listened to all that was said to him, and the words of the man sank deep in his heart. And he resolved then never to become an actor.

But resolves are like promises, often broken—and so was Harry's.

But when he commenced to set the dressing-room in order, and fold and dust the dresses, which he did at once, he determined to take advantage of anything that might offer the means of obtaining bread. But the momentary dislike he had taken to the life when he first entered that dressing-room soon wore off, and the continual change of scenes and characters before him made anxious to become an actor.

And ere the fair closed for the night, he determined to persuade his friend to obtain for him an engagement as a BOY ACTOR.

CHAPTER VII.

THE LAST HOUSE—THE TEMPTER—THE SQUIRE AND THE POACHER.

IT was the last house as it was called—that is to say, it was the last performance which was to take place that day, or rather night.

The fair was half empty, the grease-pots in front of the platforms of the various shows were going out, the swings and roundabouts were still, and only the dancing and drinking booths could boast of much company.

The scratching of "the fun of the fair" was less frequent, the strains of the brass bands less lively, the paraders less active, and the half-extinguished lights lent an unearthly appearance to their spangled dresses.

The players, tired and worn out with the arduous toil of the day, scarcely sauntered along the platform, and the request to walk up was more husky and less frequent—all now looked tired, jaded, and worn.

Charlie had given Buskin Bob the last touch that night with the red-hot poker, and fallen over the chain of sausages, which he had now gathered up round his arms to be placed with the other properties till to-morrow's opening, and now leant against the side of the platform in conversation with his friend the pantaloon, while the young lady in Scotch dress danced the Highland fling for the thirteenth and last time that day.

The few persons who had passed up the steps to the parade, and paid their money to see the spectral drama, now passed through the canvas partition to the theatre, and the paraders were about to leave the platform for the dressing-rooms to doff their ordinary clothes, when a gentlemanly-looking old man made his way up the steps to the parade, and, paying his money, walked over to Charlie, and said—

"I would speak with you, when you are at leisure."

Charlie turned, and beheld the man who had given him the half-sovereign on the day of the death of Mrs. Marston.

"I am at leisure now, sir," said Charlie, leaving the side of his friend, and walking to a part of the parade where no one could hear their conversation.

"You remember me, I presume?" said the gentleman.

"Yes sir, and shall ever remember your kindness."

"This is a hard life, is it not?" asked the gentleman.

Charlie sighed.

"Indeed it is, sir."

"And but poorly remunerated."

"You are right, sir."

"Should you like to leave it?" asked the man.

"In truth, I should," replied Charlie, "but I have no other means of gaining bread."

"You spoke of an orphan boy, did you not, when last we met?"

"I did, sir."

"What has become of him?"

"He is here with me."

"You cannot afford to keep him, can you?" said the gentleman.

"I can but ill afford," replied Charlie, "but I have resolved to try and do so."

"Humph!—a relation, perhaps," remarked the gentleman.

"No, sir."

"You take a strange interest in him then."

"A Christian's interest, sir," was the reply.

The gentleman shrugged his shoulders, as if he could not understand that a poor player could be a Christian.

"Perhaps he may at some future period be enabled to repay your kindness?"

Charlie shook his head.

"I fear, sir, that that will never lay in his power."

"What then can induce you to take so much interest in him?"

"I do so, for his mother's sake."

"His mother's?"

"Yes. She was kind to me, and my heart tells me I should protect her orphan child."

"I feel interested in this boy," said the gentleman, after a pause, "and should like to be of service to him,"

"I am happy to hear it, sir."

"I would send him to London, and place him in a position where he could carve out a means of living respectably."

"In a few years he will doubtless be glad to accept your offer."

A look of disappointment crossed the face of the visitor.

"It must be at once," he said.

"He is too young," replied Charlie.

"Pshaw!" said the other. "Many younger than him would be glad to avail themselves of such an opportunity."

Charlie paused for a few moments thoughtfully.

"May I ask why you take so great an interest in him?" he inquired.

"I knew his mother."

"Indeed."

"And I thought of interesting myself in her son's behalf, when she lay ill."

"You knew she was ill, then, sir?" said Charlie.

"Yes."

"And yet you permitted her to die of want?" said Charlie, bitterly.

The man coloured to his temples, and his eyes dropped under the piercing glance of the clown.

Charlie felt that there was something behind this apparent kindness, and he resolved to be cautious.

"Sir," he remarked, after a pause. "May I ask the name of the gentleman I am addressing? Mine is Charlie Evans."

"Henley," replied the stranger, but he tried to draw back the word, and it came only in a whisper."

"Henley," Charlie muttered, "Squire Henley?"

"The same."

"Was it not your steward, sir, who wished to deprive that poor boy of some papers entrusted to him by his mother?"

"Ah," said the other, hurriedly. "How do you know that?"

"I was present."

"Then you are the man who resisted——"

"I was," interrupted Charlie, coolly.

"You have laid yourself open, sir, to prosecution —you have interfered with justice."

"Justice!" said Charley. "Was it justice to rob the orphan?"

Henley quailed under the eye of the poor clown.

He paused to consider.

He wished to get that boy out of his path, and he saw that Charlie was an obstacle in his way.

Threats he felt would avail him nothing. He must resort to coercive measures.

"You are poor?" he said,

"Very," said Charlie, "but honest," he added emphatically.

"Look you," and he sank his voice to a whispers. "I wish that boy no harm, but he stands in my way. Give him over to me. I will provide well for him and for you?"

Charlie had knocked about the world too long not to have some knowledge of human nature, and he read in a moment that his visitor would make his poverty the means of gaining him over to some act of villainy.

He drew himself proudly up, and in a tone of sarcasm, he replied—

"Squire Henley, the man who could send his myrmidoms to rob the orphan ere his mother's corse was scarcely cold, will stop at no villany. You have some reason for wishing to remove this boy, but that reason is not a honourable one. I know and feel that his mother was not what she seemed, she never was born and bread a poor labourer's child. I know not what, but I suspect that all is not right, and if you stand between that boy and his just inheritance, you are a scoundrel, and, poor as I am, I despise you."

"You refuse then to let me have the boy or assist me?"

"I do."

"You are poor?"

"I am."

"I will give you the means of living in affluence."

"I refuse them."

"Fool!"

"Rogue! for now I know you to be one," said Charlie, turning from him in disgust.

"You will repent it," said Henley, losing his temper.

"I should scorn myself did I fall in with your plans."

"Think of my offer."

"My answer would still be the same," said Charlie, and he walked across the platform to the canvas, and disappeared behind it.

Henley stood for a few moments irressolute, whether or not to follow him, then he turned and dashed down the steps, and made his way out of the fair.

On he went till he had passed the people who had formed little knots here and there, till he arrived at a part of the road which was comparatively deserted, then he stopped and looked around him.

"A fine evening, Squire," said a voice close at his elbow.

Henley started.

"You here," he gasped.

"Yes, I am here," was the reply.

"How came you here?"

"I followed you from the fair," was the reply.

"What do you want?"

"Money."

"Ah!"

"Don't be frightened," said the man who had wished him good evening. "I am not a robber."

"But a poacher," said Henley. "Let me pass."

"Stop, Squire."

"What do you want with me?"

"Only some of that of which you have robbed me and mine."

A cold perspiration broke over the face of the Squire, and again he moved to pursue his way, but Dick the Poacher, for he it was, placed himself before him, and barred his passage.

"Let me pass," again said the Squire.

"Look you, Squire," said Dick, "I want money. You want certain papers that were lately in the possession of Mrs. Marston —they are now in mine."

"Will you part with them?" asked the Squire, eagerly.

"If you will make it worth my while," replied Dick."

"They are not worth much," said Henley.

"Yes, they are," replied Dick, "the possession of them will render the boy's removal unnecessary."

"What will you take for them ?"

"A hundred pounds."

"Come to the hall in the morning, and bring them with you," said Henley—"the money shall be yours."

"That won't do, Squire Henley, "I know you to well. Here are the papers—give me the hundred pounds, and they are yours."

"I have not got the money," said Henley.

"That's a lie," said Dick.

"How ?" said the Squire, indignantly.

"I say it's a lie—you have got the money, you placed that amount in your pocket-book to buy over the clown at Richardson's."

"How do you know this ?"

"No matter how I know it—I know more, that you could not buy him, and that you have that money with you now. Will you take them or not—to-morrow I shall ask two hundred for them."

"Yes, yes," said Henley, fearful that delay might prevent his getting them.

And he drew forth his pocket-book and extracted the notes therefrom.

"Give me the packet," he said.

"No, no, money first," replied Dick.

"How do I know that you will give me them, when you have got the money ?"

"How do I know I shall get the money when they are in your possession. Look you, Squire, had I wished to rob you, I could have done so. You know me to be a poacher, and you fear me. I know you to be a thief, and I will not trust you."

Squire Henley winced, but replied not.

"How's it to be ?" said Dick. "Are we to trade or not ?"

"Show me the packet," said Henley, suspiciously.

Dick drew a packet from his pocket and held it up before the Squire.

Henley gazed upon it, and read the writing on the cover by the moon's light.

"That is them," he said, hurriedly, "take the notes and give them to me."

Dick extended his hand and grasped the notes.

Then he handed the packet to the Squire, who hurriedly placed it in his breast.

"Now," said Henley, "take my advice and leave this part of the country."

"Why, Squire ?"

"To save yourself from a prison,"

"He, he," laughed the poacher. "Squire Henley, I have less fear of a prison than you have. I only take that which heaven has sent for the common food of man, but you rob the orphan, and the widow, I would not change places with you, Squire, if I had to change conscience as well."

The Squire turned away biting his lip and continued his journey to the hall.

Dick stood watching his retreating figure for some time, then a smile broke over his countenance as he muttered :—

"Fool and villian, does he think I have robbed my own flesh and blood. No, no, Squire, you have made me a hundred pounds richer, but I have made you that amount poorer."

———

CHAPTER VIII.

THE PANTOMIMISTS AT THE "RED COW"—HARRY'S RESOLVE TO ADOPT THE PROFESSION.

THE little parlour of the "Red Cow" was gradually emptying itself of the numerous company which had assembled within its walls, and the haze of tobacco smoke, which had hung like a black cloud over the rough deal tables, covered with rings of a sticky substance caused by the overflowing of the twopenny over the sides of the brown earthenware jugs, had cleared away, and the noise and bustle of the day had subsided.

Old Joseph Grimhall sat in the little bar parlour—a little square compartment parted off from the public gaze by a screen some six feet high, into which a square of glass had been let, in order that the worthy host might have an uninterrupted view of the rows of barrels and bottles which were arranged around.

A broad grin was on his face, and a look of satisfaction beamed in his eye.

Business had been brisk that day, and old Joseph was congratulating himself upon the run of custom he had received from the attendants at the fair.

He was thinking of closing and seeking rest from his arduous duties, when casting his eyes in the direction of the little square of glass, he perceived the figures of two men and a boy enter the bar.

Joseph rose from his seat with alacrity to attend to the wants of his new arrivals.

"Just give us a quart of twopenny," said Buskin Bob, for the new arrivals were our old friends, the clown, pantaloon, and Harry.

The beverage was drawn and passed swiftly from hand to hand.

"That's the stuff to wash the dust out of your throat, gentlemen," said the landlord. "Been to the fair ?"

"Well, I rather thing we have," replied Charlie.

"And, as we happen to live at some distance from this town, we wish to be accommodated with a lodging."

Grimhall shook his head.

"Very sorry, gentlemen. Can't oblige you, all full," said the host.

A shade of disappointment passed over the features of Charles Evans.

"Strike me comical," said Bob, "you don't mean to say you can't find accommodation for three of Richardson's company."

At the mention of Richardson's name, Joseph Grimhall pricked up his ears.

"Richardson's, did you say ?" asked the landlord.

"That's it." replied Charlie, "the crack show."

"And do you belong to his company ?" asked the worthy landlord, a look of admiration beaming from his eyes.

"Strike me comical, if I don't," said Bob.

"Well, gentlemen, I'll do my best to accomodate you. I shall be only to happy to do anything for Mr. Richardson—he's safe—he is very safe."

Then turning from the new-comers, he leant over the bar, and called out loudly—

"Tom ! Tom !"

"Hallo !" came a voice from the back of the house, and in another moment, a strapping lad made his appearance.

THE FIRST REHEARSAL.

"Get the bed ready in the next room to mine. These gentlemen will sleep here to-night."

Tom opened his eyes as wide as possible, and fixed an somewhat inquiring stare upon his master.

"Now, make haste, we must not keep any one from Richardson's waiting."

Tom, like his master, fixed a glance of admiration upon our friends, and darted off to perform the duty assigned him.

"Won't you walk into the parlour while the room is being got ready for you?" said the landlord, now only too happy to minister to the wants of his customers.

Well he knew that he would be well paid; for, should the men fail in settling their account, he was sure that, on the last day of the fair, the usual notice would be issued by the show proprietor, that all demands upon his company would be met by the manager ere they departed from the town; and, furthermore, Grimhall knew that the strolling player was no mean customer when in an engagement.

"To be sure we will, and smoke a pipe in the bargain," said Charlie. "Come along, Harry. Here we are, right and tight!"

"Strike me comical, Charlie," said Buskin Bob; "we must have another quart of twopenny, and a snack of bread and cheese. You're hungry, ain't you, youngster?"

"No," said Harry, "I've had such a lot of apples and ginger-bread."

"That's all a owing to Charlie exciting the sympathy of the company by flooring Dancing Bill. I reckon his old woman will get it when he has a chance. She'll have to lay the colour on thick to hide a black 'un, I expect. If anything puts him out, he always slogs the missus."

"He is a great coward, then," said Harry, his eye flashing indignantly.

"Yes, you may well say that, Harry," replied the clown; "but there are a good many like him in our profession, I am sorry to say, and I often think the applause bestowed upon one or two in our line, when they are cast in characters which excite the sympathies and admiration of the audience in their heroic struggles to protect a defenceless woman, would turn to hisses and groans, did they but know the insults, miseries, and often blows, heaped upon their partners in life."

"But they are very few," said Harry.

"God forbid all should be alike," said Charlie. "They are few and far between, yet they are characters that do exist, and those it is who cast a slur upon an honourable profession, and give to the enemies of the drama a triumph they but ill deserve. A scabby sheep infects the flock, my boy, and the disgraceful act of one man often casts a stigma upon the whole body."

"Strike me comical if that ain't true," remarked Buskin Bob, taking a long and deep draught of the twopenny to wash down his indignation.

"True; I should say it was! Why, I once operated in a company where the leading juvenile, after rescuing the heroine from a band of villains, and making a long palaver about dying in the defence of a woman, and bringing down the house till it shook again, rushed off at the wings, and knocked down his own wife, with a child in her arms, because she asked him for money to buy bread."

"Strike me comical," said Buskin Bob, "if I wouldn't have let him have one."

"We did better than that," replied Charlie. "We paid a man to tell him of it from the middle of the theatre, whilst going through his part the next night; and the groans and hisses with which he was assailed made him bolt as if he had been shot, and he never again made his bow before the footlights."

"Wasn't you all glad?" asked Harry.

"Rather," replied Charlie; "and that I believe would be the best way to get rid of the scabby sheep, and then the profession would be honoured by those who now despise it."

Harry became thoughtful.

He was fascinated with the profession, but he feared to enter it, lest he should encounter such as those whom Charlie had been speaking of.

"You are tired, ain't you, my boy?" said the good-natured clown, observing the abstracted look of his young protegé.

"No," said Harry; "I was only thinking."

"What about?" said Charlie.

"That I should like to be an actor; but what you have just told me has made me feel sad."

"Ah, my boy! seek what profession you will, you will be sure to find good and bad connected with it. The only difference is that, our profession being a public one, our private characters are often pried into, and it would appear to be in the nature of mankind always to confound the good with the bad, and tar one and all with the same brush."

"That's it," said Buskin Bob. "In the eyes of some people a man can't enter a tavern but what he's a drunkard."

"It's only one part of the community, though, who so judge their fellows," remarked Charlie; "fanatical fools who can appreciate nothing but their own ideas, and who believe they are only doing right in holding up everything and everybody not connected with them to shame and contempt. Look at some of their doings," he added. "To enforce their own principles they would ruin another, as a proof of which did they not endeavour to set fire to the booth? And that's what they call Christianity. Damn such Christianity, say I."

"Strike me comical," said Bob, "if they didn't nearly do it too!"

"Yes," said Charlie; "but the mauling they got for their pains will prevent them trying on that game again."

"And so you want to come out, do you, youngster?" asked Bob, turning to the poor orphan.

"I should like to," replied Harry.

"You're too little yet," remarked Charlie.

"All the better for that," said Bob.

"How so?"

"Sure not to get hissed if he made a mess of it. People don't like to hiss a young 'un."

"More they don't," said Charlie. "But what line is he fit for?"

"Oh!" said Harry, "I should like to save the young woman, when the robbers carry her away."

"Ah! like all new hands, wants the best part," remarked Charlie, with a smile.

"Don't blame him either," said Buskin Bob. "Many a good actor's been damned by being cast for a bad part."

"And many a bad actor has damned a good part, too," said Charlie with a grin.

"So they have, but a part that excites the sympathy of the audience is half the battle, and if he comes out at all, I say, give him a good one, let it be ever so small."

"That, of course, would remain with the manager," said Charlie.

"True; but if they don't give him a decent one, don't let him try a duffer. Remember, the first appearance either makes or mars him. If he is damned the first time, it's a chance if he ain't damned for ever."

"Well, I'll see, to-morrow, Harry, and if we can get him on, why we'll do all we can to assist him."

"Aye, that we will. I've took a fancy to him, and I'll help him all I can, though he will find me but a poor prompter."

"And me too," remarked Charlie.

"Still we can parrot him—show him how to go on and off—tell him where to cross—how to stand—how to walk, and, in fact, teach him all we can; and then, if he don't succeed, it will be no fault of ours."

"Your room is ready, gentlemen, when you are," said Grimhall, entering the little parlour.

"That's right," said Charlie, "for I am tired out."

"It's no child's play, thirteen houses a day," remarked Buskin Bob.

"No," said Charlie; especially tumbling."

"Acrobats?" suggested Grimhall.

"Not exactly," said Charlie; "clown and pantaloon."

"Indeed! This gentleman, then, is clown?" said Grimhall, pointing to Buskin Bob.

"Do you think so?" said Bob.

"I do," replied the landlord.

"And what makes you think that?" asked Charlie, grinning.

"He's got such a happy look," remarked the landlord.

"Ah!" said Charlie; "that's his contented mind."

"So I should say. It must take a happy man to make a clown."

"Wrong there, my friend," said Buskin Bob. "Strike me comical if you ain't."

"You are already comical enough, I'll wager, or Mr. Richardson's show would not be your field of operations."

"You are mistaken, landlord. My friend is clown: I am pantaloon," said Bob.

"I should not have thought it," said Grimhall. "You look most like—"

"A fool, eh?" interrupted Bob. "Thank you for the compliment."

"I did not mean to infer that," stammered the host.

"I know that," replied Bob, laughing. "But you see how easily men can be deceived by people's looks."

"Indeed! Then I was deceived."

"And you are not the only one," said Charlie. "The most comical fellow I ever met with off the boards could bring the water into the eyes of the most callous by his pathetic acting; and the most miserable one would send a house into fits of laughter before he opened his mouth."

"And the heavy villain is generally a good hearted fellow," remarked Bob.

Harry felt pleased at that; for was it not the heavy villain to whom he had to trust to gain a position in the profession he longed to adopt, thought the boy.

"Let's get to bed now, Harry," said the clown, rising from his seat. "I wish we were at home with Mary, poor little thing; but we ain't, and so we must content ourselves as we are. The next fair will place us nearer to her, and then we'll go home, after the booth is closed."

"I shall be so glad," said the boy; "for I am sure I shall love her."

"I know you will," remarked Charlie. "Everybody loves her. God bless her!"

And a look of sadness overspread the countenance of the good-hearted fellow, as he thought of the poor little girl left at home by herself.

"Strike me comical," said Bob, "if that girl was mine I'd have her with me."

Charlie shook his head.

"Don't you mean to bring her up to the profession?"

"Not if I can help it," said Charlie.

"Why not?"

"Too many temptations," said the clown. "I want to keep her away from the boards if I can."

"Well, can't say I blame you," said Bob; "it ain't a life every girl would like."

"Nor yet one that every man would like to see his daughter take to for a living," remarked Charlie. "But there, none of us know what we may come to in our struggles for bread."

And taking Harry by the hand, he led him from the parlour, followed by Buskin Bob. As they passed through the little bar, Charlie cast his eyes towards the door, and observed the face of a man peering at them.

The landlord had extinguished all the lights but the one candle he was lighting his guests to their room with, and consequently the features of the watcher could not be traced by the clown.

He passed on, never giving one thought to the circumstance, and in another minute was in the room prepared for them.

But had he have recognised the features of the man at the door, he might have felt less comfortable than he did when he threw himself upon the side of the bed, and bade his young companion seek his rest.

It was the eagle eye of the weazen-faced Mr. Gripe, which had watched them from the fair, and his ear had been glued, as it were, for some time past to the window of the little parlour in which they had been sitting.

CHAPTER IX.

DANCING BILL SHOWS HIS SPIRIT—APPEARANCE OF DICK THE POACHER—COWARDICE AND CONTEMPT.

DANCING BILL left the show in company with his ill-used partner, in no very favourable mood, and was making his way along to a little alehouse where he had engaged a bed for himself and wife, muttering maledictions against the boy, the clown, and everybody else.

His poor trembling wife walked silently on by his side, fearful to utter a word either of condolence or censure.

Poor broken-spirited thing! The life she had led with the brute at her side during the last ten years had indeed been a bitter one. She had meekly and uncomplainingly submitted to every insult, for she loved the wretch who, lost to all feelings of self-respect, could raise the hand of violence towards her whom he had sworn to cherish and protect.

Strange it is that woman—gentle, kind, loving woman—can pass through life with such fiends uncomplainingly. Yet Margaret Simmons never spoke of her husband's violence; never held him up to the scorn of his fellows; never sought protection from his blows; but, on the contrary, was ever the first to interpose between him and his enemies—would throw around him the shield of her own gentle body, and blame herself as the cause of the misery she endured.

And the unmanly wretch, feeling himself screened from punishment by the gentle nature of his abused wife, gave to his vile passions their full scope, and heaped insult upon injury.

Out upon such worthless scum of society—out upon such defaced and degraded images of a beneficent Creator — out upon the loathsome thing who degrades his manhood below the level of the brute creation; for the beast shields its mate, and battles to the death for its protection.

Let man shun the wretch who can thus degrade his manhood: shun him as he would a pestilence—loathe and spit upon the cur who can thus abuse the strength the Almighty has endowed him with, and place in woman's hands a whip to lash the brute, and cut from his venomed carcase the poisoned sting.

Away with love for such as these! It is a base slander upon a pure and holy passion—an impediment to justice and mercy. Away with all feeling, all pity; expose him to his fellow men; point at him the finger of scorn; hold him up to the derision of the good and true. Away with all maudlin sentimentality! Woman was sent upon the earth to cheer man's path through life, not to be a thing on which to vent his passion and his blows.

"You'll get it for this, Meg, I tell you," said Bill, placing his hand on his swollen cheek.

"It was no fault of mine," remarked the poor trembling creature, meekly.

"We'll see if it ain't. I'll have my revenge," muttered the harlequin.

"Have it on those, then, that would harm you," said the wife, with a sigh; "I cannot help it."

"Then you ought to," growled the man.

Margaret spoke not: she saw that her husband only wished for some excuse to inflict punishment upon her.

Like all cowards, he felt it would be a relief to his feelings to thrash those who could not retaliate.

"It was your fault," he growled.

"How my fault, Bill?"

"Didn't you want a drink?" he asked.

"Yes, and so did you," she replied, meekly.

"I know I did; but I shouldn't have tried to get it if you hadn't wanted it."

"You had been drinking before," she replied.

"Had I?"

"Yes."

"What if I had?"

"You could not be surprised that I should be thirsty, with the dust flying in clouds about us, and the heat of the fat pots almost scorching us up."

"You had no right to want it," growled Bill. The woman only sighed.

"Curse you, you are always getting me into a row."

"No, Bill, I am always studying how to save you from one."

"It's a lie!" roared the bully.

"You know that it is true," she meekly answered.

"Now, don't you get my monkey up," said Bill, "or it'll be the worse for you."

Margaret looked around her. The road was deserted, and she began to tremble.

She walked on quietly beside her husband, dreading his every movement.

"A pretty look I shall have to-morrow," he said, after a pause.

"You have never thought of how I should look," replied the poor woman, "when you have beaten me."

"Now, shut up. You want a row, don't you?"

"No, Bill; we have too many, I am sorry to say."

"And yet you are always trying to provoke me," he said.

"No, I do not."

"Yes, you do."

"I strive all I can to prevent it."

"That's a lie."

"It is not, Bill."

"Now, don't contradict me, or it'll be the worse for you."

"I am not contradicting you," said the woman, almost bursting into tears.

"Tell me I'm a liar!" yelled the ruffian, raising his arm.

The woman shrunk back.

"Oh, Bill, why do you seek to make me so unhappy?" pleaded the woman.

"I will make you unhappy if you contradict me—make me out a liar!"

Again the poor woman retreated from the side of her brutal husband, who, doubling his fist, advanced threateningly after her.

At this moment a man broke through the hedge that ran along the side of the footway, and stood before him.

Dancing Bill dropped his uplifted arms, and retreated back a few paces.

"Well," said the new-comer, "if you ain't the damndest disgrace I ever come across. Make you out a liar! I tell you what I make you out to be—a damned dirty, mean, disreputable cur. I've been following you on the other side of the hedge, and learnt your game. You call yourself a man, don't you?"

"You mind your own business," said Bill, all his valour running down to the tips of his toes, and prompting him to seek safety in flight. "Who are you?"

"Who am I?—not a thing like you. Why, damned if I'd use a bird I had snared like you use that woman."

"It's no business of yours," remarked Bill.

"That woman's my wife."

"Your what?"

"My wife," iterated Bill.

"Then the greater reason that you should use her kindly," exclaimed the man, indignantly, and doubling his fists.

Poor Margaret: grateful as she was for the timely arrival of the stranger, she feared for the safety of the brute who a moment before would have struck her, and she interposed her thin form between them.

"Well," said the man; "if you ain't the most despicable hound in creation, to plead as an excuse for your cruelty that it is your wife. Stand back, missus, and let's plant these two bunches of fives under his ogles, and see if he's got the pluck to stand up before a man."

"Oh, don't! don't!" pleaded Margaret, whilst Bill sidled close behind his wife, so that if the stranger struck out she might receive the blow intended for him. "Oh, don't, sir! It was all my fault."

"Look here, missus. Dick the Poacher ain't the man to call a woman a liar, but I tell you I have heard all you have both been saying, and I know what's what."

"Well, it ain't no business of yours," said Bill, gradually becoming bolder now that his body was shielded by that of his wife.

"Ain't no business of mine, ain't it?" said Dick.

"No, it ain't," replied Bill.

"It's the business of every man," said Dick. "Why don't you come from behind the woman, and show yourself like a man?"

But Bill did not seem much inclined to avail

himself of Dick's invitation. On the contrary, he only kept the closer to his wife.

"You snivelling cur!" exclaimed Dick, contemptuously curling his lip; "you ought to be kicked to death by butterflies, you ought. Look at her, opposing her weak, ill-used frame, to protect such a worthless dog. Shame on you, you brute, to vent your wrath on a poor weak woman, and that woman, too, your wife."

"Just you go about your own business," said Bill, "and leave me and my wife to settle our own affairs."

"Settle them, then, like a man, not like a cur!" exclaimed Dick.

"We can do without your interference. She don't want none of your help," said Dancing Bill, recovering from the fright into which the threatening attitude of Dick the Poacher had thrown him.

"I can tell you what," said Dick: "whether she wants it or not, it won't be well for you to hit her, for if you do, you'll find my mauleys playing a tune on your nasal organ, and painting your face so as you won't want a mark to-morrow, Mr. Harlequin. Didn't think I knew who you was, did you?"

Dancing Bill did not; and what was more, he was much annoyed that the poacher had recognised him, for he might impart the knowledge he possessed to others, and thus he might find himself held up to contempt throughout the town.

Blackguard as he was, he felt ashamed at his actions being known.

All this time poor Margaret stood before her brutal husband, to shield him from the wrath of Dick.

Dick the Poacher, whose passionate indignation had somewhat cooled down, stood gazing with the most supreme contempt upon Dancing Bill.

"Now, look you," said the poacher, after a pause, "I'm a man of my word, and you may take your 'davy I shall keep it in this instance. If you beat this woman I'll maul you. I'll keep my eye on you, my fine fellow, so just you mind what you're up to. And now for something else I have got to say to you. Don't you be too fast with that boy. The clown gave you a towelling for hitting him this afternoon; I have got an interest in that youngster, and it won't be well for you or any one else to harm him. I know Charlie Evans will protect him, but so will I; and if you attempt to do him an injury I'll stop your dancing for one while, I promise you."

"What's the boy to me?" growled Bill. "I don't want nothing to do with him."

"Perhaps not, now," said Dick; "but you owe Charlie a grudge for the one from the shoulder he let you have, and you might find it to your interest to do him a bad turn, but I warn you not to try it on."

"I don't know what you mean," growled the harlequin.

"Perhaps not, but you may soon; and when you do, just watch it, that's all," said Dick, in a meaning tone. "Now, make yourself scarce, and if you can't be a man, try and be a little better than a cur."

So saying, Dick the Poacher turned upon his heel, and walked rapidly away.

A sigh of relief broke from the lips of Dancing Bill.

A sigh of fear escaped his wife.

She dreaded that the little incident just enacted would only the further excite the wrath of her husband, and enhance his cruelty towards her.

But in this she was mistaken.

The bully and the coward had found his master.

There was something about the Poacher that had cowed the evil passions of the panto-mimist.

He could not tell why, yet he felt that it would not be safe for him to assail the trembling woman at his side.

And then, again, what could he mean about that boy whom the good-natured clown had introduced to the booth?

True, his evil nature would have prompted him to injure both the clown and his *protegé* at any opportunity which presented itself, out of revenge for the blow he had received from the former, but why should the poacher suspect him of any intention to do so?

Then, again, what interest had Dick in the boy?

There must be some mystery about the youth, he thought, but what that mystery was he was at a loss to define.

He walked slowly on, without speaking a word to the poor trembling wife at his side, till he arrived at the little alehouse where he had procured lodgings.

The house was fast closed, but a glimmer of a candle showed that some one was yet stirring, and, in answer to his summons, the door was opened, and he was about to follow his wife into the house, when a hand was laid upon his shoulder.

He turned somewhat nervously round, and encountered a short, spruce-looking little man, with a patronising smile upon his thin, weazened face.

As their eyes met, the little man placed his finger on his lip, to enjoin the harlequin to silence.

"Hush," said the little man. "Can I speak to you in private?"

"What do you want with me?" growled Bill.

The little man bent his head forward, and whispered,—

"To make your fortune, and give you your revenge on your enemies. Send your wife to bed, and then come here to me. You will not repent it."

"Shan't I?" said Bill, puzzled at this new circumstance.

"No, my dear sir, you will not," replied the little man. "But will you come?"

"For what purpose?"

"I will explain all then," replied the man.

Bill took a long look at the little figure before him.

He saw that he was an elderly man, and appeared anything but a strong one.

Dancing Bill thought he need have no fear of him.

"All right," he said, after he had taken a good survey of the old gentleman, "I will join you here in a few minutes."

"That is well," said the little man, smoothing his shirt frill.

Dancing Bill walked into the little tavern, and the little old man strode along the road with a satisfied smile.

He had no wish to be observed loitering about the alehouse.

The moment he had moved away from the house, the face of a man peered through the little palings which parted off the garden of the tavern from the high road, and watched the form of the old gentleman as he paced to and fro.

"Humph!" said the man, "I thought so, old Gripe. I'll know your little game, or I am not Dick the Poacher."

CHAPTER X.

SQUIRE HENLEY DESTROYS THE SUPPOSED EVIDENCES OF HIS GUILT.

LIGHT and buoyant was the step of Squire Henley, as he sped along the road after he had gained possession of the much coveted packet from Dick the Poacher.

A satisfied smile played around his mouth, and a feeling of gratification had taken possession of his breast.

A few hours before, his whole thoughts were centred upon getting the poor orphan boy out of the way, but now he cared not what became of him.

He had no fear now, either of the boy or his friends, for he held that in his hand which rendered them harmless.

He had plucked the sting, and they could no longer harm him.

And Dick the Poacher, too, the man he had hitherto feared, he was now powerless to defy him.

And Squire Henley chuckled as he thought how easily he could now dispose of him.

"The fool!" he muttered; "the fool! He has sold his liberty—placed himself in my power. I gave him credit for more sense than that. Ha, ha! Dick, you can defy me no longer."

And the Squire rubbed his hands in glee, and clutched at the packet which he believed had secured to him the orphan's just inheritance.

On he went, heeding not the cold night air—his heart was warmed by the possession of that little square packet.

He reached his noble house, and to his loud and hasty summons the ponderous door swung open.

With a light step he mounted the broad staircase, and, entering his sitting room, threw himself into a chair.

"At length," he muttered, "that weight of fear is removed from my breast, and the only evidence of my guilt is in my own possession, and I breathe freely once more. Now can I defy them all. Dick knows too much, but who would believe him? None; for is he not an outcast? This," he added, raising the packet from the table on which he had laid it on his entrance, "this only can wrest from me the proud position I now occupy, and steep me in poverty, but that long-dreaded incubus is now removed from my breast, and I have done with fear of exposure for ever."

And he placed his hand upon the seal to break it.

Then he paused.

"I will not read them," he said at length. "Enough that they are in my hands."

And he laid them again upon the table, and, throwing himself back in his chair, gazed intently upon the packet.

After a time he rose, and paced the room thoughtfully for some moments, then, pausing before the packet, took it up, and held one corner of it over the lamp.

In another moment the papers were in a blaze.

He held it between his fingers till the flames almost burnt his hand; then threw it from him into the fire-place.

He watched it till it was entirely consumed, a smile playing all the while around his mouth.

When the last spark had died out, he raised the blackened tinder from the grate, and powdered it between his hands till not a vestige of it remained.

"Now," he muttered, "who shall dispute my right to this proud manor? Ha, ha!"

Had not Squire Henley stood with his back to the large ornamental lamp, and thus cast the shadow of his body upon the tinder of the packet, he might have seen that on the charred paper which would have raised a doubt in his mind whether Dick the Poacher had really placed in his hands the documents he so much feared.

But his shadow fell upon the consumed embers, and he saw it not.

He saw not printed letters thereon.

The papers were written that he required.

Those he had burned, save and except the wrapper, were printed.

Still, he knew it not, and he chuckled in glee when no trace of them existed save the black marks they had left upon his hands.

As he held them up to the light, he smiled at their blackened appearance.

But they were not so black as his heart.

"Thus perish the proofs of my villany," he muttered. "Now I can defy them all."

And he laughed aloud.

But his laughter would have turned to groans did he know all.

But he knew it not, and was happy.

That is, if man can be happy with the hand of crime upon his soul.

He raised the lamp from the table and left the room, mounted the staircase, and entered his chamber, and washed his blackened hands.

But he could not wash the black stain from his conscience.

No; that could not be obliterated.

But Squire Henley cared nothing for the crimes he had committed—he only feared discovery.

Once he could prevent that, he heeded not the deed he had done.

Unrobing himself, he retired to his couch, but he could not sleep. He felt so secure now that even the favours of the drowsy god could not be courted to his eyelids. He lay thinking how effectually he had destroyed all proofs of villany, and gloating over the wealth he had secured to himself.

But not one thought of the misery he had entailed upon others.

His selfish mind could feel no pity for the poor orphan he had robbed—for the poor woman he had murdered.

And thus he lay till the first grey streaks of early dawn lit up the eastern horizon.

And then his eyelids closed, and he slept.

But not the peaceful sleep of innocence.

His mind still wandered, and carried him back to former years.

Carried him back to the time when his hands were hardened by honest toil, and his soul was free from crime.

But ambition had soured the fruits of his labours, and he sighed for riches.

By plodding industry he could not accumulate wealth, and he resolved to sacrifice honour at the shrine of Moloch.

He steeled his soul to the voice of the conscience, and he sinned.

From that hour he had known no peace.

He had gained riches, but at what a cost?

The ruin of the widow and the father!

But still the proofs of his crime existed, and he feared their production.

He felt it necessary to avoid this.

And he plotted and planned to ward off the day of retribution.

And how he had done so will be seen anon.

Days of anxious thought—nights of sleepless misery—had been his reward.

The proofs of his guilt existed, and he could not rest.

But now they were destroyed, and he was safe.

At least, so thought Squire Henley.

But Dick the Poacher knew better, and intended to make a good market yet of the squire's fears.

Dick had resolved that the orphan should not want, whilst he who had robbed him of his just rights enjoyed his ill-gotten wealth; and he had hit upon the idea of taking off the cover from the documents, and enclosing an old newspaper in it, and selling it to the squire for the genuine packet.

He had gone to the house of the squire for that purpose, and, whilst endeavouring to seek an interview with him, unknown to any of the domestics, had seen him place the money in his pocket-book, and leave the house.

Dick had followed him to the fair, and up on to the parade of the booth, and, unobserved, overheard the conversation between him and the clown.

And if Dick had entertained any respect for the pantomimist before, it was doubly enhanced now.

When the squire left the fair, Dick had followed him, and accosted him in the dark part of the road, as we have seen, and with what effect is already known.

Chuckling at the success of his little plot, the poacher had made his way through the hedge into the field, where he sat down to think how he could best devote the use of the money to the poor little orphan, when the sound of angry words met his ears.

He rose and listened, and was not long in tracing their cause.

He had heard of the *fracas* on the parade, and the words which now came to his ears satisfied him that the speaker was none other than the harlequin.

Dick kept pace with them along the road, listening to all that was said, and broke through the hedge on to the footpath just in time to prevent the poor columbine from receiving violence from the hands of her husband.

Scarce had he left the pantomimists to pursue heir way to the alehouse than he perceived the spruce little figure of the steward of Squire Henley, and, feeling assured that something unusual had brought the little man on that road at that hour, he resolved to learn his intentions.

Consequently, Dick kept the field, and walked on beside the unsuspecting Gripe till he arrived at the door of the alehouse, and accosted the harlequin.

Dick listened intently to catch the words, but he could not hear them distinctly, as the steward spoke in so low a tone.

But he heard the promise of Dancing Bill to meet him again in a few minutes, and he resolved to know what was on the *tapis*.

Dick felt sure, whatever it was, it was no good, and his mind naturally conjured up some harm intended to the orphan, and he resolved to hear all he could, and, if he found his surmises were right, to adopt measures to thwart them.

CHAPTER XI.

THE INTERVIEW BETWEEN GRIPE AND DANCING BILL—AN UNEXPECTED STROKE OF LUCK, AND A MYSTERIOUS LOSS.

IN about ten minutes Dancing Bill left the alehouse, and, drawing the door gently to after him, looked right and left for the old steward.

Gripe was by his side in a moment.

And Dick the Poacher, with his face close to the rails by the little garden, placed himself in an attitude of listening.

"Now, then," said Dancing Bill, when the form of the little weazen-faced steward stood before him, "what is it that you want with me?"

"Your aid, my friend," said the little man.

"In what?" said Bill.

"A little business which I have on hand," replied Gripe.

"What is it?"

"Have all retired in the house?" said Gripe, nodding his head towards the alehouse.

"Yes."

"No fear of being overheard, eh?"

"Not that I know of," said Bill, looking up at the windows. "I think they're all snoozing."

"Well, then; I want the aid of a man I can depend on, and I believe I can trust you in this."

"What is it?" asked Bill.

"You have an enemy in the show—a man you would revenge yourself on if you could get a chance?"

"Perhaps," said Bill.

"The clown, I mean. You owe him no good will," remarked Gripe.

"Damn him! no," growled Bill.

"He struck you to-night," said Gripe.

Dancing Bill made no reply.

"And you would be revenged on him for that blow, would you not?" said Gripe.

"I would," said Bill.

"You can do so, my friend," said Gripe, insinuatingly, "and at the same time make something handsome for yourself."

"How?" said Bill.

"By following my instructions," said Gripe.

"What about?" asked Bill, becoming interested.

"The clown has a boy with him?"

"Yes."

"And seems very fond of him, don't he?" said Gripe.

"Yes."

"And he takes the boy with him, wherever he goes?"

"Yes, I believe he does," said Bill.

"Well; I have reason to believe that a gipsy-looking man, called Dick the Poacher, will take some opportunity of placing in the hands of either the boy or his friend the clown a packet of papers."

"Well?"

"I wish to get possession of them," said Gripe.

"I don't see how I can help you," said Bill, with rather a dissatisfied growl.

"But I think you can," said the little man.

"How?"

"Your business throws you much into each other's company?" said Gripe.

"On the parade it does, but not else," said Dancing Bill.

"Your wife, now, could be induced to show some sympathy for the boy, and thus worm herself into his confidence," said the steward.

"And if she did?"

"She might find some means to extract the documents, and place them in my hands," insinuated Gripe.

Dancing Bill thought a moment.

"What are they about?" he said at length.

"Oh, they have reference to a few private affairs, and are useless to the boy. If I could get possession of them, I might turn them to good account; and for your assistance, or that of your wife, I will pay liberally. Besides, the obtaining them will give you your revenge on the man who struck you, and who brought upon you the jeers of his insulting companions."

Gripe knew that the best way to win Dancing Bill over to his assistance was to play upon his passions, and excite his hopes of vengeance.

"But the boy ain't got them yet, you say?" remarked Bill.

"No, I think not; but I believe he will have them. This is what I want to find out—whether he gets them or not."

"And if he does?" said Bill.

"I want to get them into my possession," answered Gripe. "Now, I believe you can assist me; and if you do, I'll come down handsome."

Bill shook his head.

"You see, me and Charlie Evans ain't pals, and I don't suppose we shall be again."

"He is not a man to bear animosity, I should say," remarked Gripe.

"But I am," said Dancing Bill.

"Yes, so I should say. All men are not alike. I never forgive the man that injures me; still, if I could turn anything to my interest by disguising the true nature of my feelings, I should feel myself in duty bound to do so. Now, what I have seen of this clown, leads me to believe that he is a good-hearted, easy-going fellow, that would rather shake a foe by the hand than bear him any ill-will, and he'd sooner smoke a pipe with you over a glass of ale than remain bad friends. Take advantage of this: seek a reconciliation to all outward appearances, and then you may worm out of him whether he or the boy have got the documents, or if he is likely to get them, and then you or

your wife may find some means of placing them in my hands."

Dancing Bill nodded his head. He thought that what Gripe had said was perhaps right, and he might be able to have his revenge upon the clown, and put something into his own pocket in the bargain. But then he recollected that his tempter had mentioned the name of Dick the Poacher, and he thought surely that was what the man who had accosted him in the road had called himself.

"Didn't you say something about a Dick the Poacher?" he asked, suddenly.

"Yes," replied Gripe. "Confound him! he is the fellow that stole them from Takeall."

"Who's that?"

"Takeall?"

"Yes."

"Oh, a very respectable gentleman, and much esteemed friend of mine—a person with whom I often have dealings."

"Then this chap that's got them now stole them?"

"Yes. You see, my duty led me and my friend Takeall to the house occupied by this boy's mother, and there it was that the poacher wrested them from Takeall's hands."

"Why didn't he give him into custody?" said Bill. "It was robbery!"

"Why, you see, that would have rendered necessary the production of the documents before the magistrate."

"Suppose it did. You would have got them then?"

"Perhaps not," said Gripe.

"Perhaps you have no right to them," insinuated Bill.

Mr. Gripe coughed.

"That's it, ain't it?" said Bill.

"Well, I can hardly say," returned Gripe.

"I think I can see how the cat jumps," said Bill, after a pause. "You have no more right to them than I have, but you think if you can get hold of them that you can turn them to your own advantage."

"Just so."

"And as you don't want to be seen in the affair, you want to put me on the scent."

"That's it," said Gripe.

"But why did you choose me for the work?" asked Bill, still rather puzzled.

"Because I believe you would do anything to be revenged on the clown and the boy."

"And so I would," replied Bill. "Curse him, I would!"

"Then set to work. Before you leave the town, I believe that Dick will place them in either the boy's or the clown's hands, and if so you may be enabled to obtain possession of them at some time or other; and if you can hand them over to me, I'll reward you handsomely."

"I'll try," said Bill. "We shall travel for another month before the booth closes for the winter. But what guarantee have I that you mean to act square by me?"

Gripe drew a purse from his pocket, and took from it a couple of sovereigns.

"There," he said, placing the gold in the hands of Dancing Bill. "Is that sufficient proof?"

"Whew!" whistled the pantomimist.

"And look you," continued Gripe, "if you succeed in placing them in my hands with the seal unbroken, you shall have twenty more."

THE FIRST APPEARANCE.

"Then I reckon they are worth something to you," said Bill.

"To me; but to you or anybody else they are useless," said Gripe, hastily.

The little man had no wish that the pantomimist should imagine them of any value to himself, or that his curiosity should be excited for him to peruse them did he succeed in getting them into his hands.

"Do you know what they are about?" asked Bill.

"I think I do," answered Gripe.

"What?"

"That is my business," answered the little man, haughtily.

"Oh, well, I didn't mean to offend you," said Bill, surlily.

"No offence," said the little man. "Only your business is to obtain them—mine to learn their nature. You perform your part of the contract, and be secret, and the reward I have promised you shall be yours."

"Very well," said Bill; "that's a bargain. Now how am I to find you if I succeed?"

Gripe hesitated whether to divulge his name and residence to the pantomimist.

He was too shrewd to lay himself open to the player, so he considered how best to act.

"You are likely to remain with the same company?" he said.

"Yes, for the season," answered Bill.

"And when does that end?"

"In about a month."

"Then I can see you at the booth?" said Gripe.

"But we leave the town in two days," said Bill.

"No matter," replied Gripe.

"But I may not be able to obtain them in that time."

"True. But I can seek you in whatever town you may be stopping," said Gripe.

"You can do that, certainly," remarked Bill; "but you may have your trouble for nothing."

"I don't mind that."

"But I could let you know, if I knew where to send to, when I had got them, or whether I had any chance of obtaining them or no."

But the old man resolved not to place himself in the other's power.

"Never mind," he said. "It will be no trouble for me to walk into the show on the last day of the fair, whatever town you may be in. I have no need to speak to you or you to me. A look will let me know how you have succeeded."

"As you like," said Bill.

"Then let it be so," said Gripe. "Set your wits to work, and remember there's twenty pounds for you when you get them. Good night."

And without waiting for any reply to his salutation, the prim little old man turned upon his heel, and walked swiftly down the road.

Dancing Bill stood watching his retreating figure for some moments; then, taking the two coins from his pocket, in which he had placed them, commenced trying them with his teeth, to make sure they were good.

"This is a rum go," he muttered. "I can't understand it. There's something queer about it all. But there, that's no business of mine. If I can earn the twenty pounds I'll do it, if only to be revenged on Charlie—damn him, I will! I won't forgive him that blow, nor the youngster either, that was the cause of it. I'll worm round him, and let him fancy I've forgot all about it; but he'll find I ain't, though, if I get a chance. Up in the stirrups now, I reckon. Two pounds for nothing! Well, I can't tumble to it. There's something wrong—can't make it out. Still, if it will harm Charlie or that boy I'll do it if I can. Two pounds, and twenty more to come! Blowed if I ain't in luck, and I'll follow it up to the end."

And giving the coins another grip between his teeth, Dancing Bill was in the act of transferring them to his pocket, when he felt his wrist grasped, and his arm drawn through the opening between the rails of the garden, and, ere he could turn or utter a cry, he felt the coins taken from his hand!

Surprise and fear now took possession of him, and he gave vent to a half-shriek, half-cry, and bounded almost into the middle of the road.

And there he stood, glaring at the spot where he had been the moment before.

He could see no one there, and his heart commenced to throb violently.

Summoning up courage at length, he went up to the paling, and looked over.

There was no one there.

He opened his hand, and looked at it, to make sure he was not deceived.

The coins were gone!

Again he peered over the fence. Nothing was to be seen but the vegetables which grow within the enclosure.

A cold sweat broke over his face, and his limbs trembled. A strange feeling possessed him that some supernatural being had assailed him, and he rushed into the house in an agony of fear.

CHAPTER XII.

AN OPPORTUNITY PRESENTS ITSELF OF WHICH HARRY TAKES ADVANTAGE—THE FIRST REHEARSAL.

WORN out with the exertions of the previous day and night, and the late hour at which they had retired to rest, Charlie Evans, Buskin Bob, and little Harry Marston slept soundly till the bright morning sun had risen high in the pale blue firmament.

Buskin Bob was the first to open his eyes, but he quickly closed them again to shut out the glare of the sun's rays, which streamed full upon his generous-looking countenance.

However, he soon became accustomed to the strong light, and, sitting up in the bed, he placed his hand upon the shoulder of his friend and fellow-labourer, and shook him heartily.

"Strike me comical," he exclaimed, as Charlie opened his eyes, "if anyone wouldn't think all the grunters in the town had been turned out among the acorns. Just wake up, will you? You have been snoring at such a rate that you almost shook me out of bed."

"Stow it," said Charlie, stretching himself. "I know better than that, for I tallowed my proboscis before I went to bed."

"That was with the property candle, then," said Buskin Bob, "for I never heard a fellow play so many tunes on his nasal organ in all my life. I only wonder that poor little chap could sleep at all."

"Don't wake him," said Charlie, "poor little fellow! Let him sleep if he can—it ain't much rest he'll get now."

"No," said Buskin Bob, with a sigh, and lowering his voice almost to a whisper, so that he should not disturb the boy's slumbers. "His troubles have just begun, and so young, too! Well, it is hard to begin so young in life the struggle for bread."

Charlie gave vent to a sigh.

Too well *he* knew the struggles of the poor strolling player.

"Well," he said, leaping from the bed, "let us hope that he may have a better time of it than we've had."

"I hope so," said the pantaloon. "Buskin' ain't what it used to was. I've known the time when it paid well—licked all the engagements. People gets more stingy, or else poorer than they used to be, I don't know which."

"'Tain't that," said Charlie, "it's competition. Don't matter what line you start—what game you're a-fly to—up springs a lot of rivals, and a dozen now has to share what one used to collar. Why, Bob, when you first went buskin' about the country, there wasn't another chap like you on the road, but now there's fifty."

"There's not one of them, though," said Bob, indignantly, "as can come the hanky-panky like me. Show me the chap as can do the 'tater trick like me. Is there a cove as can keep thirty balls going for half an hour, and never make a miss? I tell you what it is, Charlie; the British public — the enlightened British public, I suppose I ought to say—don't care a damn for real talent. It's the gab that pleases them, and that's what done for me. I hadn't the gift of the gab. I done the tricks clean, but I wasn't a good hand at palavering. Why, look at 'em! they're all bounce and jaw, and when they've soft-soaped the audience till they are slippery enough to swallow anything, and chucks out the halfpence, they covers up their tights and bolts, and don't do not nothing at all, because they can't. When I went buskin', I did give the people something more for their money than jaw, I did."

Charlie smiled.

"You should have done the same, Bob," he said.

"Should I!" said Bob, drawing on a stocking with such vengeance, that he sent his great toe right through it.

"Yes, you should," replied Charlie.

"It ain't in me, I tell you," said Bob; "I can't patter."

"Then you should have joined company with one who could," said Charlie. "You don't mean to say you have chucked it up altogether?"

"Yes, I have," said Bob.

"What will you do in the winter, then, when there's no fairs?" asked Charlie. "Try the theatres?"

"No; go to the workhouse," said Bob, sadly.

"What?"

"Go to the workhouse."

"That be —— there, I won't swear," said Charlie.

"I mean it," said Bob.

"Then I don't," said Charlie. "If I can't get an engagement anywhere, I'll start on my own hook."

"What line?" asked Bob, looking up incredulously into the face of the clown.

"Tumbling—anything," replied Charlie.

"You will?" asked Bob.

"Yes, I will."

"Well, I'm blowed!"

"Are you?"

"Yes."

"Why?"

"'Cos I am," said Bob.

"'Cos you are — that's no answer," said Charlie.

"Ain't it?"

"No."

"Well, then," said Bob, "I thought you was too proud."

"Too proud?"

"Yes—above it."

"Above what?"

"Buskin'," said Bob; "or begging, if you like it better."

"I was," replied Charlie.

"And ain't you now?" asked the pantaloon.

"No."

"Why's that?"

"Because I can't afford to be proud any longer," replied the clown.

"How so?"

Charlie pointed to the still sleeping boy.

"There's another to get food for," said Charlie.

Bob turned his eyes full upon the face of his companion with a fixed stare.

"Do you tumble now?" asked Charlie, after a pause.

"Strike me comical!" exclaimed Bob, and the pantaloon gave his old brace such a tug that he broke it.

"You'll destroy all your 'props,'" said Charlie, "if you go on in that way."

"Damn the 'props,'" said Bob, throwing the broken brace across the room. "Charlie, you're a brick."

"Am I?"

"Yes," said Bob. "Strike me comical if you oughtn't to have been a gentleman."

"Ought I?" said Charlie, with a smile.

"You ought," said Bob. "For there's many a cove as calls himself one ain't got a heart like yours."

"Nor yet a purse," said Charlie, pulling one of his pockets inside out.

"It ain't the money as makes the man, strike me comical if it is," said Bob.

"What then?" said Charlie.

"The heart," said Bob, thumping his breast, but on the right side instead of the left; "and there's some mistake, Charlie. You was cut out for a gentleman—not what the world calls one, but what nature intended one should be."

"And what's that?" said Charlie, smiling.

"A thing with a heart in its bosom," said Bob; "not a lump of stone, but a heart as can feel for another."

"I can feel for anyone," said Charlie, "who deserves sympathy."

"That carries out my argument," said Bob, warmly. "You was meant for a gentleman. If you wasn't, why—why, strike me comical! that's all."

"Then I suppose I was," said Charlie.

"I know you was," said Bob; "and there's some mistake."

"Well, perhaps there is," said Charlie, with a grin. "I was made by contract."

"Then, strike me comical, if the man didn't die before he'd finished you, and that explains it all!"

"Stow it," said Charlie.

"It must be that," said Bob.

"Well, then, let it be so," said the clown.

"But I say, Bob."

"What?"

"None of the workhouse—it must not come to that."

"Why?"

"What am I to do for a poll all the winter?" said Charlie.

Buskin Bob scratched his head, and stood thinking for a few moments.

"I tell you, Charlie," he said at length, "I'm no use. I can't patter, and the profession ain't worth a curse without it now."

"Nonsense!"

"It ain't nonsense, I tell you," said Bob. "Time was when the drum and the mouth organ was all that was wanted; but now, it's all jaw and no do—strike me comical if it ain't!"

"Well, look here, Bob. You can do what I can't: I can patter—you can't. Suppose we join and go shares? It's better than the workhouse, Bob, and a good deal more independent."

Buskin Bob stood for a moment, as if he did not believe he had heard aright.

He knew Charlie's aversion to begging.

He thought that his companion could not possibly mean what he had said.

Bob hardly knew what to think of the proposition.

Certainly it was better than the workhouse, and he said,—

"Charlie, do you mean it?"

"I do."

"Then, strike me comical! give us your fist. It's a bargain."

"You agree?"

"I do. And I'll chuck in something extra for the kid, because I know it's for him you do it."

"And for myself," said the clown.

"No it ain't," said Bob; "you'd never have taken to buskin' for yourself. But there, it is just what I said; you was meant for a gentleman; if you wasn't, strike me comical!"

"Then that's settled," said Charlie.

"It is."

"When the fairs are done we start on a provincial tour?"

"Yes."

"And share the proceeds?"

"No, strike me comical if we do!" said Bob, "the boy shall have his share."

"Well, well, settle all about that another time. Just give him a shake now, and then we'll have a bit of breakfast and go to the booth, for it's near eleven o'clock."

Bob shook the still slumbering Harry by the shoulder.

The orphan opened his eyes, and gazed bewilderedly around him.

"Hi, hi, hi! here we are!" said Charlie.

Little Harry rose up in bed, with a smile upon his pale face.

"Get up, my boy," said the good-natured clown. "It's late."

"Is it?" said Harry.

"Yes; just upon eleven."

"Eleven?" said Harry, as if he had not heard aright.

"Yes, eleven."

"Then I have slept late. I used to always rise at six."

"But you didn't go to bed at two, did you?" said Buskin Bob.

"No. About seven."

"Well, you ain't had no more sleep than you used to get," said Charlie. "But it's the worst of our profession—we turn night into day, we do."

"And sow the seeds of disease in our frames at the same time," said Bob. "Strike me comical if I ain't an old man at forty!"

"Ah, sunk into the 'lean and slippered pantaloon.'"

"Yes, and before my time," said Bob, "and all owing to late hours."

"And the rest," said Charlie.

"Perhaps you are right," sighed Bob. "But there—young chaps will be careless, and I suppose Buskin Bob ain't any exception to the rule."

"No," replied the clown; "we all learn experience as we get older, and then regret the past. But it's no use—the thoughts of to-day won't obliterate the acts of yesterday; so let's have some breakfast, and then to business."

In a short time Harry, Charlie, and Buskin Bob sat down to a plain but substantial meal, to which each did ample justice; and at about half-past eleven they left the "Red Cow" for the fair.

"Well, Harry," said the clown, as they walked along, "what do you think of an actor's life now?"

"I have been dreaming about it all night," said Harry.

"And got disgusted with it, haven't you?" asked Charlie.

"No; I feel the more inclined to adopt it, if I can get a chance."

"You do?"

"Yes."

"Then, strike me comical," said Bob, "if we don't try and push you on."

"Thank you," said Harry.

Here the conversation dropped, and thoughtfully and silently the trio wended their way to the village green, on which the fair was held.

Arriving at the booth, they perceived the old proprietor pacing up and down, with nervous yet hurried steps.

Richardson had thrust his hands deep into the pockets of his velveteen smalls; and, with his eyes fixed intently upon the large steel buckles of his shoes, seemed lost in thought.

As our friends passed him, Charlie wished the old gentleman good morning.

"But it ain't a good morning, Muster Evans —it ain't a good morning, sir."

"I trust nothing has occurred unpleasant," said the clown.

"This is an unlucky fair, sir," said Richardson; "a very unlucky fair."

"May I ask," said Charlie, "what has occurred to make you think so?"

"Everything goes wrong, Muster Evans."

"I trust that nothing has occurred of an unpleasant nature?" said Charlie.

"But there has, Muster Evans—but there has. Deary me! only to think now! to be disappointed, when I had the promise of a visit from a very influential company."

"But what disappointment do you complain of, sir?"

"The absence of one of the ladies," said Richardson.

"It is not yet time, sir," said Charlie, "for the booth to open, and she may yet be here."

"No, she won't—she sent me word she won't. Deary me—the piece can't be played without her! Deary me!"

And the good old man drove his hands still further into his pockets, and recommenced his walk.

Charlie and his friends made their way to the dressing room, where they learned that, at the express desire of some of the aristocratic inhabitants of the town, the proprietor had undertaken to play a certain drama that day, which rendered it necessary that he should obtain the services of a very young lady actress to personate a page, the ladies of his company all being cast either in other parts, or too old to make up to advantage for the character.

"Why not let one of the males play the part?" asked Charlie.

"There's not one in the company young enough," said the manager. "A girl of eighteen can dress for a boy of twelve, but a man of twenty can't do it, and the governor must have the right thing or none."

Charlie was thoughtful.

Would not this be a good opening for the orphan?

He turned to the manager:

"Is the part heavy?" he asked.

"No—light."

"Many lines?"

"Not more than six," said the manager; "but there's a combat."

"What do you think of my boy?" asked Charlie.

The manager shrugged his shoulders.

"No go," he replied.

"Why not?"

"Because, small as the part is, it must be done to rights, or it'll damn the piece entirely."

"You say there are few lines to speak?" said Charlie.

"Not more than six."

"I'll teach them to him," said Charlie.

"But there's the combat, and that must be done."

"I will learn him that too," said Charlie.

"It's no go," said the other, after a pause, "it's a double fight."

"Will you give him the chance?" said Charlie; "me and Buskin Bob will put him through it."

"I am afraid it's no good: he'll get frightened, and ruin all."

"No he won't," said Charlie; "let him try?"

The man paused for a few moments, and then he said,—

"I'll ask Richardson."

"Do so," said the clown, "but before you go give me the part."

The part was found, and handed to the clown, and the manager left the room to confer with the proprietor.

"Strike me comical," said Bob, as soon as the manager had disappeared, "if this ain't a chance!"

"If Harry can do it," said Charlie, "it may prove a lucky circumstance for him."

"He'll do it," said Bob, "never fear."

"But I do fear."

"What?"

"His confidence," said Charlie. "He is so young."

"So he is; but that's all the better," remarked Bob.

"I'll try him, anyhow," said Charlie. "Here, Harry."

The boy was by his side in a moment.

"Do you think you could speak that much?" said Charlie, pointing to the part.

"When I had learned them I could," said Harry.

"Do you think you could learn them?"

"Yes."

"In how long?"

"Oh, a very little while," said Harry, running his eye over the manuscript.

"And do you think you could recollect them when you got on?"

"On what?" said Harry.

"On the stage, to be sure."

"Yes; there's not much."

"No; I know that. It's very little; but bold, daring men have become spellbound, and forgotten every word when they have stood in the glare of the footlights."

"I shan't," said the boy confidently.

"Now, ain't he got confidence," asked Buskin Bob, gazing at the boy in admiration. "Strike me comical if he'll make a mess of it!"

Still Charlie feared that when the boy found himself on the stage he would break down.

He knew too well the strange oppressive feeling which the young aspirant to dramatic honours experiences when he makes his first bow before the public—a feeling which none but those who have experienced it can divine.

"We all have got confidence behind the scenes," said Charlie, after a pause; "but when the curtain's up it's all gone, and a fellow stands at the wings with his heart thumping against his side, and his tongue sticking to the roof of his mouth. And what's the consequence?—a hiss, and it's all over with him, for the enlightened British public have no sympathy for the new actor. They paid their money, and they will have its worth, and damn a fellow's feelings! What's that to them?"

Buskin Bob knew the truth of this, and he merely shrugged his shoulders, and entered his own dressing-room.

Here, in a few moments, he was joined by Charlie and his young protegè.

The proprietor, who had no wish to disappoint those whose patronage he had sought, had consented that Harry should play the part, but had enjoined his manager to see that the boy was letter-perfect ere he allowed him to go on.

"Now, Harry," said the clown, placing the part in the boy's hand, "Look at that while I make up, and let's see how soon you can learn it."

"You must be perfect," said the manager, "You're not up to gag: it wants an old stager to do that."

Harry sat down, and commenced learning the few lines, while Charlie and Buskin Bob made up for their respective characters.

Dancing Bill, who dressed in the same compartment, here entered.

Charlie looked up at the harlequin, and, forgetting, or being too good-natured to remember, the fracas of the day before, wished him good morning.

Dancing Bill returned the salutation with apparent cordiality, but turned away to hide the revengeful look which overspread his face.

Neither Charlie nor Buskin Bob took long over their toilet, and when the clown had given the last touch to his face, he turned to the orphan.

"How do you get on, Harry?" he asked.

"I know it," replied the boy, with a smile.

"Let me hear you," said Charlie.

The boy handed the part to the clown, and commenced speaking the lines.

When he had finished, Buskin Bob slapped him on the shoulder, exclaiming—

"Strike me comical, he's letter-perfect!"

"Yes, now," said Charlie.

"And so he will be when he's on, see if he don't," said Bob, looking admiringly at the boy, whose face was now radiant with smiles.

"I hope so," said Charlie, "but still I fear he will break down."

"Strike me comical if he won't," said Bob, "if you keep on like that—you will frighten him into it. Look here, Harry, don't you be frightened: go on plucky, and don't look at the audience, and I'll wager you'll pull through all right."

"I'll try," said the boy, resolutely.

"Then you'll succeed," said Bob. "Make up your mind to do it, and you'll never say die till you're dead."

Here the property man entered the room with a page's suit, which had been obtained expressly for the young lady who, from some cause or other, had failed to fulfil her engagement.

"There's the 'props,'" he said. "They are a little too large, I expect, but you must make them do."

"I'll dress him," said Charlie.

"All right," said the man, laying down the things and quitting the room.

"You will look spanking!" said Bob, "strike me comical if you won't!"

The boy examined the dress he was to wear with a smiling countenance.

The gilt slashings on the doublet—the tall feather in the hat—held there by the sparkling tinsel, fascinated the youth, and he was impatient to have them on.

Charlie and his friend soon robed the young lad; and when the last string was tied, and they led him before the broken glass, Harry clapped his hands together in glee.

He looked so much taller and stouter: the colour, too, had made his pale cheek glow with roseate freshness; and the tall plume waving above his head gave a noble bearing to his little figure, and he almost danced for joy.

"Strike me comical," said Bob, "there's a make-up! Looks an angel, don't he, Charlie?"

"Fine," replied the clown. "But I expect you have forgotten your part."

"Oh, no," replied the boy, turning from the glass where he was admiring himself.

"Go over it again. Let's see what's the cue. Oh, here it is."

And having given the boy the cue, Harry once more spoke the lines correctly.

"All right," said Charlie. "Now for the combat."

"It's a double one," said Bob.

"The devil it is!" said Charlie.

"Yes it is."

"Then he can't do it," said Charlie, in a disappointed tone.

"Yes, he can," said Bob.

"I tell you he never tried it before," said Charlie.

"No matter," said Bob. "He'll do it. See if he don't."

But Charlie shook his head.

Buskin Bob procured four swords.

"Now, Charlie," he said, "the boy shan't fail for the want of teaching. There, my boy, lay hold of two, and we'll show you how to do it."

Harry did as he was desired, and, Charlie taking one of the weapons in his hand, himself and Bob threw themselves into position, and instructed the youth in the various strokes.

"I wish it had been a single combat," said Charlie. "He would do the round eights to perfection in a quarter of an hour."

"And so he will this," said Bob. "If he don't, strike me comical!"

And after a few moments' pause the rehearsal was continued, and by the time the gong was sounded to summon the company on the parade, Harry had become so proficient that Charlie confessed (to use his own expression) that he was perfectly licked, whilst Buskin Bob wished

he might be struck comical if the boy wasn't a perfect genius.

"Now read your part again," said Charlie, "and keep up your spirits. I can't stop with you, but the manager will tell you all you'll have to do. Don't fail, Harry, if you can help it. Speak out plainly and distinctly, and keep a bold and unflinching eye. Remember, my boy, that the first appearance either makes or damns you."

"It will make him," said Bob. "See if it don't."

"I hope it will. Keep up your spirits, Harry. Keep up your spirits. I must go now—indeed I must."

And pressing the hand of the youth, the noble-hearted fellow left the room for the parade.

Buskin Bob remained behind for a moment, to give the lad some further counsel, and then Harry was left alone in the little room.

He read and re-read his part, folded it up, and strutted before the broken piece of glass, speaking the words and striking the attitudes which the part suggested, then paused and smiled at himself.

How fine he looked! How noble his bearing! Surely he had but to walk on to the stage to meet the applause of the assembled pleasure-seekers. He knew every word of his part. He had not missed a stroke in the last rehearsed combat.

He felt he must succeed.

True, he had done well—far exceeded the expectations of his friends.

But then, Charlie and Buskin Bob had formed both the audience and the tutors.

They were generous in their criticism, and forgiving in their natures.

The glare of the footlights had not dazzled his sight, nor were a thousand eyes focussed upon his little form.

Save the clashing of the swords and the kind words of his friends, all was silent in that little room; but now he had to meet the stare of a multitude, and receive at the hands of a not over-generous public condemnation or approval.

* * *

CHAPTER XIII.

THE POACHER'S HIDING-PLACE—DICK SECRETES THE GENUINE DOCUMENTS—HIS RESOLVE TO DEFEAT THE STEWARD, AND HIS VISIT TO THE FAIR.

THE first grey streaks of early dawn which had brought sleep to the eyelids of Squire Henley threw also a faint light upon the form of Dick the Poacher.

That worthy, after nearly frightening to death the harlequin, and extracting from his hands the two sovereigns which the little steward had given him, crept away noiselessly under the shadow of the hedge, until he came to a gap, through which he once more gained the high road.

Casting his eyes about him, and perceiving the coast clear in all directions, he walked sharply on till he gained the spot where we first made his acquaintance.

The damp night air fanned the dark ringlet

locks on his brow, and struck a chill to his frame, but Dick heeded it not. The night air was no stranger to him, and he had little fear of any evils arising from it.

He gained the little clump of trees where he had sat with Charlie Evans on their first meeting, and, throwing himself upon the mound in their centre, gave himself up to thought.

And in this position the first streak of day found him.

As the light clouds spread further over the horizon, Dick arose, and, parting the branches of some bushes which grew in luxurious abundance around the spot, he passed through the opening he had made, and stood, as it were, in a little enclosure.

Arranging the branches so that they should bear no evidence of having been tampered with by mortal hands, Dick knelt down upon the earth, and grasped the turf in his hands.

The grass yielded easily to the force Dick applied to it, and left the earth as clean as though it had been cut out with a knife.

Then scraping the mould away for the depth of a few inches, Dick inserted his hand in the little hole he had made, and pulling his arm back, he seemed to lift up the grass, earth and all, for the space of about two feet square.

Holding it in a perpendicular position he rose to his feet.

There, where a few minutes before seemed to be nothing but a smooth, shady, grass-grown spot, was an opening into the earth.

A rudely-constructed ladder rested against the side of the cavity, and assisted to form a support to the trap-door, so ingeniously covered on the outer side with vegetation as to hide its existence.

Placing his hand upon the root of turf first removed, he forced it into the place from whence he had torn it to get at a ring let in the outside of the trap, and passing his hand over it two or three times, so as to give it the appearance of not having been removed, he descended the ladder, holding the trap up at arm's length above his head, and gradually lowering it as he disappeared into the cavity.

Before he had arrived at the bottom of the ladder the trap had been properly adjusted in its position, and its appearance on the outside was exactly the same as it had presented before the poacher had entered the enclosure. Having satisfied himself of this, Dick stepped down the few remaining rounds of the rude ladder, and stood on the damp ground which formed the floor of the cave or underground passage.

Here he paused.

All was as still as the grave.

The air was noisome and damp.

Still the place was ventilated by a few small natural fissures in the ground about the roots of the trees above, and little specks of light, like stars through a dark cloud, beamed down upon the poacher's cavern.

Dick took from his pocket a flint and steel, and in a few moments procured a light, and ignited a small wax taper. The flicker of the little candle only served to light up the space around Dick for about a yard, and had the effect of plunging the more distant parts of this subterranean passage into Stygian darkness.

But Dick moved silently and firmly on.

It was not the first time he had trod the damp floor of that dark place.

Many a time had he disappointed the gamekeepers and others, by suddenly disappearing at the moment they made sure of his capture.

Where he went no one could form any conjecture.

Once Dick entered that field, they believed all pursuit useless.

Many had tried to discover the means of escape, but all had failed.

Yet they had searched every inch of ground in and around that miniature forest.

But all to no avail.

The existence of the passage had never occurred to them.

The inability to account for his mysterious disappearance engendered a superstitious dread in the minds of the ignorant country people.

Dick kept on, holding the light above his head till he had accomplished some twenty paces.

Every now and then he had to stoop, to avoid striking his head against a huge root of one of the trees which had penetrated into the passage.

Having arrived at the end of the cavern he paused, and, placing the taper on one of the projections of the uneven sides, he cast his eyes upon the ground.

"All right," he muttered, " yet why I should ever think otherwise I don't know. Yet the same circumstances that led me to discover this place may lead others to do the same. But I have obliterated the traces that led me hither, and the probabilities are more against than for discovery."

And stooping down he raised a rough trap at his feet.

This trap, unlike the surface one, was in no way concealed.

As Dick raised it and threw it back against the side of the passage, the faint ray of light from the small taper revealed a small square hole about two feet deep, and of the same length and breadth.

This was used by Dick to store his powder, or any article which he might desire to conceal.

It was perfectly dry, the sides and bottom having been cemented.

"So, so, squire," he muttered to himself, " I think I have done you this time. You believed I was fool enough to place myself in your power, and rogue enough to rob the orphan, did you? Ha, ha! how I should like to see the look on your face when you discover the trick. "There," he added, taking the packet of papers —minus their wrapper—which he had torn from the grasp of the worthy Takeall, at the cottage of the deceased woman, " are the genuine documents, and not all the gold you could place before the poacher would induce him to place them in your hands."

And as he spoke he stooped down, and laid them in the cemented hole.

"You won't find them very easily, Squire," he continued, as he closed the trap over them; "and if you did I would tear them from your possession, if I had to cut your heart out first. They belong to that boy, and he shall have them, but not yet. And Gripe, too," he muttered, "the man is like his master—a worthy pair—a well matched brace of scoundrels. He would get them, would he? What service can they be to him, unless to extort money from the squire. Gripe is no fool; he knows what he is about. Should he obtain them, I don't believe he would let Henley have them: no! he would play upon his fears—make the fear of producing them the means of his own aggrandisement. But, Mr. Gripe, I will be even with you for the dirty piece of business I overheard last night; and the harlequin, too. I have given him one fright, he shall have another yet. That woman beater is superstitious, and I'll play upon his fears, I warrant me. And Gripe, I will play upon your purse as I have done your master's. You have both conspired to ruin me—to blast my character, and I will blast yours. The man who can fawn and cringe and bow to the dictates of a villain and a usurper, and strive to bring a fellow-creature to infamy and shame for gold, will need but little working on to become himself a thief. Gripe, you would have these documents, and would stop at nothing to obtain them—not even the appropriation of your master's property. Beware, old man! I will track you like a shadow; play upon your ambitious soul; and when I have made you the thing you would make me, I will laugh in your face, taunt you with your dishonour, and hold you up to the scorn and loathing of your fellow-men!"

And Dick sat himself down upon a ledge of earth which projected from the wall of the cave, and buried his face thoughtfully in his hands for some time.

Then he rose and paced the passage several times with hasty and uneven steps.

"Squire," he muttered, through his clenched teeth, "you have much to answer for, and the day of retribution will come. That poor boy—would that I could protect him! But no, no! he is better with the good-hearted clown; for though he be poor, he bears an honest name. The black stain of infamy sits not on his brow, for poverty has saved him from the designs of villainous men. Envy has not blighted his hopes; nor unrequited love driven him to desperate acts. Oh, would that I had been born to honest toil! then—then—but no matter! the guilty cannot ever triumph. Justice will tear the bandage from her eyes in her own good time, and weigh the wrongs and sufferings in the balance, and the bared sword with sharpened edge will fall upon the guilty! Vice triumphs for a time, but in the end virtue rises on its fall. Justice may be delayed, but it will come—it will come!"

And again the poacher paced the damp flooring of the cavern with hurried steps; proudly, defiantly his foot pressed the soft earth.

There was a bright glare in his dark eye, a glow upon his bronzed cheek, as he drew from his pocket the notes the squire had given him as the price of his supposed villany."

"All for him," he muttered, holding them out at arm's length, and shaking them in the air. "All for the poor orphan, for they are his by all laws of right and justice. Not one will I appropriate to myself—not one. Dick the Poacher robs not the orphan of his due; it is only the proud, rich, ambitious squire who can rob the widow and the fatherless!"

Dick turned them over in his hand, and let the light of the little taper play upon the notes.

"A hundred pounds," he muttered. "Harry, you will not starve. These will last some time, and when they are gone I'll find the means to get more. Squire Henley, you little suspected into whose hands these notes were destined to

fall, and the worthless rubbish you received in exchange for them. Ha, ha, Squire; you have only one more to get over if you outwit Dick the Poacher!"

Folding them up carefully, Dick returned the notes to his pocket, while a smile of triumph lit up his dark eye and played over his handsome bronzed features.

Casting another look at the trap-door over his hiding-place, and assuring himself that it was properly fixed, he took the little taper from the wall, and made his way along the passage till he stood at the foot of the rude ladder.

Then he blew out the light, and placed the taper on the ground at one side of the passage, where he could again obtain it at his next visit.

Ascending the ladder, he gently and cautiously raised the trap a few inches and looked around to see that no one was near.

Nothing met his gaze but the vegetation growing around.

He raised the trap till it allowed his body to pass through. Then he closed it, and stamped down the grass around its sides, so as to effectually hide any traces of its existence.

This done, he parted the bushes as he had done before, and passed through them, again arranging the bent branches. He drew his felt hat over his eyes, and made his way rapidly from the field into the lane, thence to the high road, along which he walked hurriedly in the direction of the fair.

It was not long before he reached a small inn which stood by the roadside.

The sun had now risen, and the people of the house were stirring.

Dick entered the bar, and asked if he could be accomodated with breakfast.

He was answered in the affirmative, and ushered into a small room at the back of the building.

A fresh, rosy faced, buxom country lass was about closing the door of the little apartment, after receiving the poacher's orders, when Dick called her back.

"Have you pen, ink, and paper?" he asked.

"Yes," replied the girl.

"Then let me have them," said Dick, "I'll write a note while breakfast is being prepared."

The girl departed, and in a few minutes returned with the desired materials.

"Now," muttered Dick, after she had closed the door and left him to himself, "visitors will not arrive yet awhile, and I'll amuse myself with writing to Old Gripe, to inform him that the documents are in my possession, and if he should have heard that the squire had got them, I will tell him the trick, and offer to sell them to him. He will jump at the chance of getting the squire in his power, and I will obtain more money for the boy.—Oh, I'll make you all pay for it, you thieving scoundrels! but not one of you shall get them after all.

And taking the pen in his fingers, Dick the poacher wrote hurriedly on the paper before him, consuming sheet after sheet.

Then folding them up he wrote the same words on the outside that had appeared on the outside of the packet he had sold to the squire and formed the letters as near as he could like those which had caused Henley to part with his hundred pounds.

A BRUTAL BLOW.

"There!" said the poacher, throwing down his pen and leaning back in his chair, "Now, Mr. Gripe, I am quite ready to ease you of any cash you may possess, or any you may be enabled to obtain. You are a shrewd man, but Dick the Poacher is no fool! Adversity is a first-rate school, if it is a new one—it puts a man up to a dodge or two, and this is one of them. You haven't done with me yet, nor I with you; you are too valuable a bird to let off without plucking, and I am just the boy to do it."

The door opened, and the young girl entered with the breakfast.

Dick hurriedly placed the writing in his pocket, and fell to at the viands, on which he did ample justice, not having broken his fast for some hours.

The meal ended, Dick allowed his head to drop on the table before him, and gave himself up to sleep.

Tired and wearied, he slept long and soundly; nor was it till the folks on their way to the fair began to drop in that he awoke.

Rousing himself, he arose and left the house.

He paused a moment before the inn; then, drawing his hat over his eyes, he walked hurriedly away, in the same direction as the stream of pleasure-seekers, who now thronged the road.

The road was somewhat more noisy than it had been on the day before, and Dick the Poacher was roused from the reverie into which he had fallen several times, by the "fun of the fair" being drawn down his back by some smiling country damsel, who gave vent to an immoderate fit of laughter as the thoughtful man started at this sudden interruption to his ideas.

But on he went, looking neither right nor left, and all heedless of the smiling, happy groups which he passed.

Dick felt in no mood to join in their merriment, although the pleasure-seekers seemed to have thrown off all restraint, and courted the company of all or any with whom they came in contact.

It's all fair in fair time, they thought, and so gave full licence to the exuberance of their spirits; and not a few of the rollicking country lasses set the poacher down for a surly, disagreeable fellow, as he passed on his way, all unheeding the words or deeds of his merryhearted fellow pedestrians.

Soon a turn in the road brought the flags and streamers which surmounted the booths, swings, and roundabouts into full view, and then, for the first time, Dick the Poacher raised his thoughtful eyes from the ground, and gazed about him with some degree of interest.

Laughing in wild glee—running and tearing after each other—the young holiday folks sped by, whilst the elder people stood looking on with smiling faces at the mad pranks of their more youthful companions.

Happiness and content, peace and joy, sat upon every face; and Dick sighed as he thought that he only wore a look of sorrow amid the cheerful throng. The fair was no place for him, he thought.

Those whose hands were hardened by honest toil, and whose minds were contented with the means of procuring their daily food, surely were more happy than he.

They at least had not suffered from oppression and villany; no revengeful feeling assailed their breasts—no recollections of bitter wrong usurped their minds.

They were happy: and Dick wished that a beneficent Providence had made him one of them.

Had his first cry been heard in the labourer's cottage, instead of the gentleman's mansion, he might have stood there that day a happy and contented man.

But now—like a dark cloud in the bright sky —he felt that he cast a shadow upon the joyous scene.

It was not pleasure that turned his steps in the direction of the fair.

He cared nothing for the various amusements scattered so plentifully over the green.

The frolicsome capers of clown and pantaloon had no charm for him, nor did the tinsel-bespangled parades charm his eye.

His senses were not to be flattered by the gaudy trappings of the motley groups outside the shows, nor his mirth excited by the many incidents which provoked the laughter of the crowd.

But he had come there to do what he considered an act of justice.

He had come to see the orphan, and relieve his wants.

What cared he for the invitations to "walk up"—the sights offered to his view for a few half-pence?

Dick considered it but a waste of time to devote an hour to laughter or tears conjured up by the player, yet he was about to visit one of the shows!

He walked on and pushed his way through the crowd, till he stood opposite the far-famed Richardson's booth.

His eye wandered over the parade in search of the boy.

But no Harry was there!

Dick ran up the steps, crossed to the money-box, paid his money, and, drawing himself up into a corner, watched and waited.

The business had not yet commenced, but while Dick stood impatiently looking round, a man of rather short stature, attired in a long-tailed black coat, velveteen smalls, grey worsted stockings, shoes and large buckles, with a white neckcloth and low, broad-brimmed hat, bustled on to the platform.

"Strike up the gong!" he exclaimed. "Deary me! ain't the gentlemen ready yet? The fear is getting full, and it's time to commence. Where's Muster Evans and Muster Bob?—call them up. Now, Mr. Lunn, just tell the gentlemen to begin."

The last-named person—a black drummer— in answer to the request of the proprietor, for such was the little man we have described, whirled his drumsticks round his head, and the next moment the double band struck up, and as its first sound floated away over the upturned faces, Charlie Evans and Buskin Bob rolled on to the parade, amid the joyous screams of hundreds of delighted pleasure-seekers.

"Here we are! How do you do to-morrow?" yelled the clown, turning round to knock down the pantaloon.

At that moment the eye of Charlie caught that of Dick, who placed his finger on his lip, as an intimation not to recognise him there.

CHAPTER XIV.

THE FIRST APPEARANCE—THE QUEEN AND THE PAGE—THE COMBAT—THE PART PLAYED TO NATURE.

THE overture was finished, and the green baize curtain rose slowly upwards, revealing to the anxious gaze of a thousand eyes the pretty little set scene, lighted by the numerous little variegated lamps, hung in various devices at the sides by the proscenium and in the wings of the world-famed Richardson's Theatre.

The rows of seats, draped with red cloth, were filled with the motley throng which composed the audience, and the thousand pair of eyes were focussed upon the little scene, which lay like a little picture embedded in a sparkling frame.

The drama which the aristocratic portion of the inhabitants of the little town had promised to patronise was about to begin, and little Harry Marston, the orphan boy, was to make his first appearance.

But under what difficulties had he, with a boyish impulse, undertaken the part at a few minutes' notice.

No word of apology or explanation to the audience was to be made. The lady engaged for the character was little known to those assembled, and the management resolved not to undeceive them unless the boy should break down, when a few words would abate the wrath of the audience, and exonerate the manager from blame.

The piece began, and the old stagers, who had walked through their respective parts many a time and oft, made "their entrances and their exits" amid the clapping of hands, and other tokens of approbation of the satisfied sight-seers.

It would soon be Harry's turn to leave the wings, and make his bow in the centre of the stage.

Confident as he had been of carrying out the little part, as the piece progressed he became more and more nervous; his lips became dry and parched, and his limbs trembled.

He strove to murmur the words he would have to utter, but—horror!—he had forgotten them! He tried to recall them to his memory, but, alas! he could not! Not one line could he recollect; and yet a few minutes before he was letter-perfect.

What could he do?—he would ruin all!

He looked behind, towards the entrance to the parade, in the hope of seeing his friend Charlie, but the clown was on the outside.

Then he thought he would run to the dressing-room for his part, which he had left there, and read it over again.

He turned away from the wings to do so, but the voice of the manager bade him stay, as in another moment he would have to face the audience.

Every moment his lips became more dry—he trembled more violently— became more and more confused, till at length the agony of his feelings almost caused him to burst into tears!

Oh, what would he not then have given to be released from his undertaking!

He would speak to the manager—tell him his fears. Better do that than stand appalled before the eyes of the audience.

With drooping head he advanced towards him, but as he was about to speak his name was called.

The manager imperiously motioned him back to the spot where he had stood, and the next moment a voice whispered hurriedly in his ear,—

"Go on—there's your cue."

Poor boy! he could not move—he seemed rivetted to the spot; but the next instant he felt himself pushed forward, and, ere he knew where he was, a loud clapping sound rang in his ears, and a closely packed mass of heads rising one row above another, with eyes which seemed to dance up and down in mad glee, came athwart his vision, and he stood with bowed head and trembling limbs before the thousand spectators of the drama, in which he was that night to perform a part for the first time, confused, bewildered, and affrighted! He staggered backwards, when a voice whispered,—

"Kneel—the letter—kneel!"

The spell was broken, and he looked up.

Before him stood a tall, commanding female figure, in long, flowing velvet robes, with a diadem encircling her brow.

It was the lady who played the queen, and whose page the boy was to personate.

He placed his hand within his vest, drew forth a sheet of paper folded as a letter, dropped on one knee, and handed it to the stately woman who stood so imperiously before him.

She stretched forth her hand and took it, and as she did so she felt the hand of the boy tremble within her own.

He had nearly spoiled her part by his nervousness, but her true woman's nature rose above her chagrin, and she whispered,—

"Fear not, my boy; I will help you through. It's only the stage fright, it will soon pass away."

The tones of kindness in which these words were whispered by the stately, awe-inspiring figure before him struck a warm glow to his heart, and as he rose to his feet and retired to the wing, he turned his eyes boldly upon the mass of faces before him, and unflinchingly encountered their gaze.

But his part—the part he learned so correctly —the part he had now forgotten—preyed upon his mind.

What could he say?

Alas! he knew not!

The queen had read the letter, and now turned and addressed him—then paused for his reply.

But he knew not the words he was to answer.

A frown gathered upon the brow of the austere woman, and she stamped her foot impatiently.

Harry almost burst into tears.

He raised his eyes to the rouged face which glared down upon him; raised them with a look so full of agony—so beseechingly—that the frown gave place to a look of pity, and she whispered a few words of the part he had learned, and now forgotten.

He almost bounded with joy!

The words came back to his mind, and he spoke them to the end in a clear and distinct tone.

Scarce had the last syllable died away on his lips, than the loud and prolonged plaudits of the audience rang in his ears.

He turned his eyes to the wings, and there stood Charlie Evans and Buskin Bob, their painted faces radiant with joy at the success of their young friend.

But in a moment they were gone.

They had stolen away from the parade in their anxiety to know how the boy got on, while Dancing Bill and his poor wife went through their performance.

In a short time, the lady who played the queen, having finished the scene, bade him follow her, and with head bowed, and his plumed hat in his hand, he strode across the stage after the haughty-looking woman, and made his exit at the wings amid another shower of applause.

Oh, what a sigh of relief escaped from his breast as the audience was shut out from his sight!

Like some poor wretch who, by an unexpected interference of Providence, had escaped the fangs of a wild beast at the moment of its spring, the boy seemed to give vent to the long pent up breath in one deep, bursting sigh.

But he had not done yet: once more must he confront that mass of faces—stand before those numberless rows of eyes—ere the green baize should descend, and he could seek his friends.

He had spoken all he had to say but one

word; but he had yet to fight the double combat, and his hands still trembled and his brain was giddy.

But there was no help for it! he had promised to do it, and it must be done; but if he failed in this, he felt he could never more attempt to face an audience again.

The lady who played the queen, and so kindly strove to carry him through the scene, came to his side, and in pitying tones—so different from those she had used when on the stage—said, as she took his hand within her own,—

"My poor child, what could induce your friends to send you here?"

"To assist them," said Harry.

"Are they then so poor?" asked the woman.

"I have only got one friend—yes, I have two," said Harry, suddenly recollecting Buskin Bob.

"Father and mother, I suppose?" said the woman.

Harry sighed, and his eye became moist.

"No," he replied, "I have no father, and no mother now."

And the hand she still held trembled within her own.

"No father—no mother!" she said, with a sigh; "poor child! Who then are your friends, that they can suffer you to take a life like this?"

"Charlie Evans and Buskin Bob," replied the boy.

"Charlie Evans, the clown?" said the woman, in some surprise, "are you related to him?"

"No, but when mother died he took me, and is kind to me; but he is too poor to keep me, I know, and I don't like to take the bread his kind heart would give me without doing something towards earning it."

"And you have done this to-night because you would help to do something for your support. Is it so?" asked the woman, bending down her head till the diadem almost touched the head of the boy.

"Yes, mum."

"Alas, my poor child! your nature has prompted you to choose a life which has many bitters, but few sweets—a life made up of lies and tinsel and deceit! Look at me," she added, drawing her tall form proudly up, till she looked every inch the character she played, "what do I look like? To your young eye, what do I appear to be?"

Harry gazed with admiration upon the stately figure before him, as he answered,—

"A lovely queen."

The woman laughed hoarsely.

"Boy," she said, again stooping over him, "the ignorant, admiring, and gaping crowds before whose eyes I stalk, in tinselled diadem and flowing plush, think not of the struggles with poverty the stately queen has to endure—know not that the imaginary draught quaffed from the painted goblet, and the rich fruit and mock viands which grace the stage banquet, but too acutely remind the poor player of the scanty fare with which she keeps life within her frame! Oh! what a mockery is the stage!—the parts we play so foreign to our nature! We live for a time in an ideal world, till the fall of the curtain breaks the spell which binds us, and plunges us back again into the real miseries we endure in our struggles for bread."

"But I hope to get on," said Harry; "to get on to one of the larger theatres, and earn plenty of money."

The woman shook her head.

She, too, had hoped so, years before. But she felt she would not say anything that would damp the ardour of the boy; she would rather help him, though she grieved to see him adopt the profession.

"I hope you will," she said, after a pause. "But, come, we must go on again directly, so no more trembling, but hold your head up bravely, and walk the stage firmly. Have confidence in yourself, and the audience will have confidence in you."

And she hurried from his side and walked on to the stage.

"Now then, youngster," said a voice at his side, "got the toasting-forks ready?"

Harry turned as the gruff voice fell on his ears, and encountered two bearded and ruffianly-looking men, each armed with a short fencing-sword.

These were the individuals with whom Harry was to fight the double combat, and who personated first and second hired ruffians to slay the queen.

The boy started as his eyes first encountered them.

The parts they played were very low in the profession, but their make-up was perhaps equal to any of the company.

Rough and uncouth in their appearance, yet they were two good-hearted, rollicking fellows, and the half look of fear which the boy fixed upon them, caused them to burst into a roar of laughter.

"Why, you ain't frightened, are you?" said the one who had spoken before.

"No—yes—no," said Harry.

"That's right, my lad," said the other. "If we look robbers, we ain't, that's all! I dare say you're nervous—I was, first time—but we'll carry you through somehow. Just chuck the swords about well—we'll hit them; that's all you've got to do."

"And look here," said the other, "don't you be afraid of your fingers—the basket will save them; but amateurs will flinch—they are such flats."

"I won't be frightened," said Harry, reassured by the kindly tones of the men.

"All right! Get the 'props,' or there'll be a stage wait."

Harry procured the swords, and returned to the side of the two fierce-looking men at the wings.

Meantime the queen was playing the part assigned her, and the two robbers were awaiting the cue to go on.

In a few moments it came, and then he who had first spoken turned to the boy, and said,—

"Now then, youngster, look out and rush on when I stab the queen."

The next moment they were on the stage, and with palpitating heart the young boy watched the movements of the man who had addressed him.

He saw the ruffian steal stealthily along behind the queen, and then, drawing a dagger from his belt, raise it above his head, and plunge it, handle downwards, into the back of the female, who, with a loud shriek, sank down at his feet.

It was now time for the boy to appear once more before the audience, and summoning up all his courage, he rushed on, and, amid loud applause from the audience, confronted the two robbers, who, appearing surprised, fell back, and drew the swords which they had placed in their belts.

"Keep your back to the audience," whispered the one who had stabbed the queen, "and don't be frightened—we'll carry you through it. Hold up your swords."

The boy did as he was ordered, and the next moment the clash of the steel resounded through the house.

The audience were in raptures, and their plaudits almost drowned the noise of the clashing swords.

In the excitement, Harry forgot the injunction he had received to keep his back to the audience, and gradually walked round till he faced them.

Now that he saw the faces of those assembled to view the drama, he began once more to grow nervous, spite of the applause, which one of his opponents perceiving, and wishing to save the lad from any chance of failure, dropped his sword as if it had been struck from his hand, and fell upon the stage, leaving only one for the boy to contend with.

For a few moments more, Harry and the remaining ruffian struck at each other's weapons, when down went the man by the side of his companion.

Having thus overpowered his adversaries, it became necessary, for the completion of the part, that he should endeavour to raise the queen, who was supposed to be dying.

He knelt down beside the prostrate woman, and, placing one arm beneath her head, raised it on to his knee.

Now came the pathetic part of the drama. The queen dies; but ere she breathes her last, she reveals to the page that he is her own child.

The woman played the part well: and as she proceeded with it, the eyes of the poor orphan boy filled with tears, for it brought so vividly to his young mind the death-bed at which, so short a time since, he had stood and received his mother's last blessing.

As the woman proceeded, his feelings became worked up till he could scarcely refrain from giving them vent, and when at last she had finished, and her head dropped back, in one agonised cry the words of his part burst forth,—

"Mother, mother!"

———

CHAPTER XV.

THE HARLEQUIN AND COLUMBINE—DANCING BILL AND HIS PUGILISTIC PROPENSITIES—THE TWO BLOWS.

THE green baize curtain rolled slowly down, amid the clapping of hands and voices of approbation, to shut out from the gaze of the audience the Boy Actor, at the termination of his first appearance on the stage.

The last scene was a great success, so well and so naturally had he played the part.

And played it he had, as truthfully as ever part was played.

But it was not a part studied to please an audience: it was a part true to life—it was the bursting of an overcharged heart—which felt and acted true to nature.

For nature had planted in the breast of the youth love for the mother who bore him, and grief for her death and respect for her memory.

But the audience knew not how the heart of the poor boy ached during the last scene, and they left the theatre without one pang at his sufferings.

The manager, too, was in raptures. So was Charlie, and so was Buskin Bob; but they felt at the same time what moments of agony it must have caused him.

Perhaps there was only one behind the scenes who felt pleased at his suffering, and angered at his success.

This one was Dancing Bill, the harlequin.

He hated the boy for the blow he had received from the clown, and his triumph was to him a thorn in his side—a canker in his heart.

His own brutality had brought the punishment upon him, but his mean spirit would not acknowledge the fact.

The coward generally hates those whom he has injured.

No sooner did he hear of the triumph of the Boy Actor than his ill-temper rose, and the poor columbine received at every step a volley of abuse.

Poor thing; she bore it meekly!

She feared to answer him, lest her words might be heard by any of the company, and her lord and master called to account for his unmanly conduct.

For since Charlie Evans had sent him sprawling upon the parade, there was not one in the whole company but would have interfered to protect his wife from his ill-humour.

The bully had been curbed, and the most timid feared him no longer.

Like the braggart and bounceable boy at school—once he is thrashed, not one but despises him.

And Dancing Bill knew and felt this. Hence the abuse he lavished on his wife was muttered only in hissing whispers, that could travel no further than the ears of the person it was intended for.

If he hated Charlie and the boy before, that hatred now grew the more intense, and he ground his teeth together as he strove to think of some means by which he could injure them.

Then he thought of his interview with Gripe, and the promise he had made to that worthy to endeavour to worm himself into the good graces of the clown and his *protegé*, in order to learn whether the documents so much coveted by the steward were in their possession, and, if so, strive to obtain them.

He felt that, by so doing, he could satisfy his own greed for money, and at the same time be revenged on them both.

Yet he felt nervous; for, like most ignorant men, he was superstitious.

He could not account for the loss of the two sovereigns which had been so mysteriously abstracted from his hand on the night before.

He felt assured in his own mind that it was not the act of a living being, or he must have heard or seen it; and he could only come to the conclusion, after mature consideration, that some evil spirit, incensed at his villany, had deprived him of its first fruits.

Had not his coward soul been galled by the blow received from the clown, he would have resolved to have no more to do with the plot of the steward; but then that blow cankered in his heart, and revenge was strong as fear.

Having concluded a dance, much to the delight of the gaping crowd assembled in front of parade, and now having ten minutes to rest, Dancing Bill commanded his wife to attend him in a sort of green-room down under the stage.

The poor woman followed him, half fearful of personal violence.

Having arrived at the room, and finding none of the company present, Dancing Bill entered, followed by his wife, and shut the door.

"Now, Margaret," he said, surlily, "you're always pretending you'd do anything for me. Now, I'll try you."

"I would do anything," said the woman, "that would render you more kind to me."

"There, shut up, you're always on to that game. I want to tell you what I learned and did last night, and then hear what you think of it; and see if you are willing to carry out your promise to help me in anything for our good."

The woman sat down upon a box, and turned an inquiring eye upon her husband.

Dancing Bill related all that had passed between him and the steward, and likewise the loss of the fee he had received.

The columbine listened without interruption to the end.

"What do you think of it?" asked Bill, when he had concluded.

The woman shook her head.

The question was repeated.

"I hardly know," she said.

"You see, there's a chance of making money out of this ruffian," said Bill.

"Yes; but it would be a wicked work," replied Margaret.

"How so?"

"To rob the orphan," replied his wife.

"What's that to us?"

"It should be everything," she replied. "Had we a child, Bill—which, thank Heaven, we have not—what should we feel did we know that others plotted its ruin?"

"Well, we ain't got one, and we ain't a-going to have any feelings for him. I tell you I hate that boy—hate him worse since I've heard him praised so to-day!"

"Why should you hate him? I am sure I feel glad at his success."

"Do you?" yelled Bill.

"I am glad at anyone's success," murmured the woman, meekly.

"Of course you are, if it annoys me," said the brutal fellow. "You would do anything to annoy me, you would!"

"No, Bill, no! I would do anything to please you—I would indeed," said the poor woman, her face becoming pale, spite of the rouge laid so thickly on her cheeks.

"Then why do you object to what I want you to do now?" growled the harlequin.

"Because—because—"

"What?" interrupted her husband.

"It is wrong—unfeeling—unnatural," said Margaret. "Oh, Bill! why wish to wrong this poor boy? Money gained by villany never does any good. You say yourself that even the first payment was mysteriously taken from you; it was the devil's money, Bill! and you would lose it all the same way—I'm sure you would. Don't have anything to do with it. Let the man who would tempt you to this sin do his own hellish work, and warn the poor boy to save him from the loss."

"Curse me if I warn him!" said Bill, spitefully. "I tell you you must work the oracle. He thinks you are friendly to him, but he feels I ain't. You must worm yourself into his confidence—promise to be a mother to him—and learn all you can; then tell me, and I'll do the rest."

The poor woman shook her head.

"Do you mean to say you won't?" said Bill, savagely.

"I can't, Bill!"

"Can't! why not?"

"I haven't the heart."

"Then you'll have to get it, I tell you," said the harlequin.

"Bill, it is not in my nature, I cannot lend myself to wrong that poor child."

"I tell you you shall!" roared the savage brute, his passions now fully aroused, and all his evil nature bursting forth at the knowledge that no one was present. "I tell you you shall," he iterated, "or I'll ——"

"Oh, Bill! don't! don't!" shrieked the woman, as the ruffian raised his arm.

"Will you do it, then?" he almost yelled.

"I can't, Bill, I can't!" she gasped, retreating towards the door.

"Fury seize you, take that, then!" he exclaimed.

And ere the words had left his mouth, the ruffian struck her a blow on the cheek.

But ere the sound of the blow died away, another echoed through the room, and Bill fell like a log at her feet.

She looked up, and stood face to face with Dick the Poacher!

CHAPTER XVI.

THE INTERVIEW IN THE DRESSING-ROOM—AN UNLOOKED FOR STROKE OF FORTUNE—THE HARLEQUIN PLAYS A NEW PART.

WITH flashing eyes and threatening mien, Dick the Poacher gazed scornfully down upon the prostrate harlequin.

With all her woman's forgiving nature, the poor ill-used columbine flung herself before the indignant man.

Interposed her bruised body to save the wretch—who but a moment before had struck her—from the vengeance of a noble-hearted man!

"Coward and villain!" said Dick, "is there not one spark of manliness in your nature, that you can thus degrade yourself by such conduct? Shame on you! shame!"

Dancing Bill struggled to his feet, but still kept behind his wife.

"Oh, sir," cried Margaret, "do not touch him! He did not hurt me—indeed he did not."

And as she spoke she held her handkerchief to her cheek, now red and swollen.

A look of pity stole over the face of Dick, as the poor columbine thus gave the lie to her words.

At this moment, Charlie Evans, Buskin Bob, and young Harry entered the room.

"It's your turn on," said Bob, addressing the harlequin. "The governor is in a rare state at your not being on the parade."

This was a good reason for the harlequin to escape from the room, which he did without a single word, and slunk out like a beaten cur, his poor ill-used partner meekly following him.

The new comers had not observed how affairs stood at their entrance, but they saw now that something was wrong, and turned to Dick for an explanation.

"What's been the row?" asked Charlie.

"Why, that scoundrel who has just slunk out has been beating his wife," said Dick. "I came down here as you wished me to do, to await your arrival, and just as I entered, the fellow struck the poor woman a blow in the face."

"He's a cowardly hound!" said Buskin Bob.

"Can only fight a baby, or lick a woman!" said Charlie.

"But he won't fight no more babies here in a hurry," said Bob. "I rather think he had enough of that yesterday, when you put him on his back—eh, Charlie?"

Charlie smiled, but said nothing.

"And I knocked him down for his brutal action just now," said Dick, "and would have thrashed him well, but his wife stood between us, poor thing."

"More fool she!" said Bob. "But, there, she's like all the rest of the women—the more they are beat, the more they try to shield the brute, instead of smashing him down with the first thing they could lay hold of."

"He knows she's a poor frightened thing," observed Charlie; "he'd run away from a woman as had got any pluck in her. But Mr. Dick—for that is the only name I know you by—I have but a few minutes to spare before I go on the parade again."

"One minute will transact the business I have with you," said Dick; "but —" and he looked towards Bob.

Charlie saw that Dick wished to speak to him in private, and he gave Bob a hint to that effect, and the good-hearted fellow left the room.

"Now," said Dick, "the last time we met was at the cottage."

"It was," said Charlie.

"You remember what took place there?"

"I do."

"I decamped with a packet belonging to this boy."

"You did."

"Do you know anything of the contents?" asked Dick.

"Not the least idea," said Charlie.

"Do you, Harry?" said Dick, turning to the boy.

"No," replied Harry, "but mother told me before she died to keep them secure till I became a man."

"I know the contents," said Dick.

"You!" said Charlie.

"Yes: but do not think me guilty of perusing them since they have been in my possession. I say I know the contents, and their value to this boy, when he is old enough to act for himself. I have them safe, and will keep them for him. I intended placing them in your hands, but I have learnt sufficient since to satisfy me that they will be safer in mine."

A pained look passed over the face of the clown.

Did the poacher think he could not trust him?

Dick observed his look, and hastened to explain the meaning of his words, and his reasons for wishing to detain them.

"There are three persons bent upon getting possession of that packet," said Dick.

"Who are they?" asked the clown.

"Squire Henley."

"Ah," exclaimed Charlie, "the man who was here last night?"

"The same; but for the present he is satisfied that he has got them. Let that pass—still beware of that man. The next is his steward, Gripe; and the third the villain who I knocked over a few minutes since."

"What! Dancing Bill?" said Charlie, in a tone of surprise.

"Yes."

"What does he know about them?" asked Charlie.

"Nothing," replied Dick.

"Then why should he wish to get them?" asked Charlie, still more surprised.

"He is bribed by Gripe," replied Dick, "so beware of him. You see you have three persons to watch, and under these circumstances I think it would be better that I should retain them."

Charlie became thoughtful.

He felt satisfied that there was something connected with them which would benefit the boy, and he would like to have them, for the boy's sake.

Still he could not doubt that Dick meant well by the boy.

"I have hidden them," said Dick, "where none can find them. If I gave them up to the boy or yourself, the probability is that one or another of those I have mentioned would find some means to deprive you of them. I will keep them securely, for I have almost as great a stake in them as has this youth. You may trust me," he added, "for, though I am a poacher, I rob not the widow or the fatherless."

"I will trust you," said Harry, "for I like you."

"And you shall never regret doing so," said Dick. "It is not every one, however, would trust me, though, God knows, I have been more sinned against than sinning!"

"But," said Charlie, "should anything happen to you, they would be lost to the boy."

"True, as it stands at present; but I will reveal to you their hiding-place, so that, in the event of my being put out of the way, you can get them. You know the little mound of earth where we sat on the first day we met?"

"Yes," replied Charlie.

"You observed the bushes on one side of it?"

"I did."

"If you forced your way through those bushes, you would find yourself in a little open space."

"Well?"

"In the centre of this clearing is a trap-door, covered with grass, so as to appear like all around it."

"Well?" said Charlie, becoming interested.

"Beneath that trap is a small ladder, leading to a passage beneath the trees, and at the end of this passage is another trap, covering a small hole, and in that are the papers."

"It is a strange place," said Charlie.

"It is. I discovered it by accident, many

years since, and it has often served as a place of concealment for me."

"But may not some one else discover this place, as you have done?" said Charlie.

"No, for I have rendered it so secure from observation, that any one might walk over it a thousand times and never suspect its existence."

"The trap, you say, can be raised from the outside?" said Charlie.

"Yes; and its position is exactly in the centre of the little clear space between the bushes."

While Dick the Poacher was speaking, the door of the little room was opened about an inch, and the ear of Dancing Bill was placed against the opening.

So intently were the minds of all engaged in the apartment, that they neither of them observed this circumstance.

"And now," said Dick, after he had made the clown fully understand the position of the little hollow in the earth, "to prove that I am interested in the welfare of this boy, and that I place implicit faith in your honour, I will place in your hands the sum of one hundred and two pounds for his support."

"What!" said Charlie, fairly leaping back.

"One hundred and two pounds," repeated Dick. "Rather a strange sum, is it not? but it belongs to the boy. I knew the anxiety which Squire Henley felt to get possession of that packet, so I took off the cover, wrapped it round an old newspaper, and sold it to him for the sum of one hundred pounds. He would rob this child as he has robbed others; therefore I felt no compunction in robbing him. The two pounds were paid to the harlequin to rob the boy by old Gripe, but I eased him of them, and here they are."

And Dick drew forth the notes and the gold, and offered them to the clown.

But Charlie drew back.

"I cannot take them," he said.

"Why not?"

"They are the proceeds of robbery," he replied.

Dick opened his eyes to their utmost width and gazed with surprise upon the man before him.

Then his features relaxed, and a look of pride beamed from his eyes.

"You are a noble-minded man!" he said, "and I am thankful that this poor boy has such a one for a protector. But I offer you not that which belongs to another; every penny of the hundred pounds is that boy's money—money withheld from him; he has more right to it than he who formerly possessed it. Take it—use it for the boy; and believe me you will lend yourself to no dishonest act."

"Then does this squire——"

"You will know all in time—the boy is too young to act now. Bring him up honestly, and when years have passed he can claim his own. But take the money," he said, "for, by all that is true and just, it is his own."

Charley took the roll of notes.

"But the gold?" he said, pointing to the two sovereigns, which Dick laid down upon a small table. "He has no right to them."

"Well, as you like," said Dick, placing them in his pocket. "Now I have performed the duty which brought me here to-day. Leave the papers where they are for safety, and remember that Dick the Poacher will not forget that he,

too, has a duty to perform, in watching over this poor orphan boy."

He extended his hand to the youth as he spoke, and Harry grasped it as he turned his tearful eyes upon the face of the gipsy-looking man, who had shown so much sympathy for him.

Then grasping the hand of the now-delighted clown, Dick said,—

"Beware of that harlequin; and if you should not see me for some time, think nothing of that, for I will be by your side when I know that I am wanted. Now farewell."

And with a final shake of the hand, Dick left the room.

Charlie stood gazing at the open door for a few seconds, and then gave vent to the expression,—

"Well, I'm blowed!"

"Charlie, Charlie!" exclaimed Buskin Bob, rushing into the room, "make haste! make haste!—the governor's in a rare way at your not being on the parade!"

"All right, I'll come. Such luck! tell you all about it presently."

And snatching up his coat, which lay on a bench, he thrust the roll of notes into the pocket of it, and, hurriedly folding it up and replacing it, darted from the room, followed by the pantaloon, up the rude steps to the parade, on to which he rolled, with the usual "Hi, hi! here we are!"

"Now then, youngster! you'll keep the stage waiting if you don't mind," said one of the company, looking in at the door upon the boy, as he stood in the centre of the room, wondering at the events of the last few minutes.

The words of the man aroused him, and he stammered out,—

"Oh, I forgot—I forgot!"

"Come on!" said the man.

Harry followed the man, and was just in time to prevent a stage wait, for he gained the wings at the very moment that his cue was spoken.

Whilst Harry was on the stage, and Charlie was creating roars of laughter among the mob outside by some of his grotesque capers, Dancing Bill entered the little room in which Dick and Charlie had been conversing.

He glided stealthily in, and silently closed the door.

Then he raised his black half-mask.

His face was flushed, and a demoniac look gleamed in his eyes.

He listened intently for a moment, then crossed the room to the bench on which Charlie's coat lay folded.

He raised it, then listened again.

Apparently satisfied, he cautiously unfolded the garment, and inserted his hand in the pocket.

The gleam in his eye brightened as he drew forth the notes.

Hastily he secreted them in his breast.

But his hand trembled nervously as he did so.

He refolded the coat, and placed it in the position it had occupied before his entrance.

Then he recrossed the room, and threw open the door.

He looked cautiously out.

No one was near.

The deed had not been seen, and he breathed freely.

"Now, Charlie Evans," he muttered, between

CHARLIE EVANS SEES AND HEARS MORE THAN HE EXPECTED.

his clenched teeth, and shaking his clenched hand above his head, "I am revenged for that blow. Ha, ha! You triumphed yesterday—it is my turn to-day! You little thought I overheard every word. I swore to be even with you and the boy, and I will, too! This is the first blow in return, but I'll strike another: I know where the papers are concealed, and it shall go hard with me but I'll have them. You will pay dearly for that blow, Charlie Evans. Ha, ha, ha!"

And darting from the room, he once more gained the parade, unsuspected and unseen.

CHAPTER XVII.

THE STEWARD AND THE POACHER—THE BARGAIN STRUCK.

MR. GRIPE, the weazen-faced Steward, was standing sunning himself in front of the office of Mr. Takeall, auctioneer, valuer, and sworn broker.

There was a smile on his little weazened face as, with his hands underneath his black sparrow-tail coat, and head bent forward until his nose almost touched the spotless large shirt frill, he was doubtless reckoning the per centage on the goods which had been seized that day from a poor labourer's cottage, and which was always punctually paid over to him by the short broker.

They were a worthy pair of unfeeling scoundrels, and were never so happy as when engaged in making other people miserable.

Squire Henley was a bad man, but he was made even worse by his steward. But for Gripe, his tenants would meet with more grace when sickness or want of work rendered them unable to pay their rent.

But Gripe had it all his own way, as the Squire seldom or ever interfered; and as the more seizures Takeall had, the more money it put into Gripe's pocket, why, the old man preferred tenants who could not pay to tenants who could, always providing said tenants' goods and chattels were worth considerably more than the year's rent.

But suddenly the little smile that played round the little mouth of the little steward evaporated, and a look of surprise stole over his weazened features, and he opened his little eyes till the lids would go no further.

Then giving vent to a little cough, he swung his little body round, and commenced walking away.

"Hold on there!" said a voice.

Gripe suddenly pulled up, for the tone was so imperious.

"Well, old shrivelled jib," said Dick the Poacher, for he it was who had brought the steward to a standstill, "in a hurry, ain't you? generally are when you see me."

And Dick brought his hand down on to the shoulder of the little man with a hearty whack.

"Oh!" said Gripe, cringing under the pressure of the poacher's hand, and recollecting the blow he had received from the same weapon a week before.

"That don't hurt you, does it?" said Dick, a mischievous light gleaming from his bright dark eye, and a roguish smile lighting up his bronzed handsome features.

"Why do you molest me?" said Gripe, indignantly.

"Because I have got a word or two to say to you," replied the poacher.

"I wish to have nothing to say to you," returned Gripe, "unless it is to tell you that you have again laid yourself open to the law."

"Indeed," said Dick.

"Yes sir, 'indeed!'" iterated the steward. "Give me that packet of papers you wrested from that worthy gentleman, Mr. Takeall, at the cottage of the Widow Marston. It was felony, sir—felony!"

"They did not belong to you, did they?" said Dick.

"It was my duty, sir—my duty to take possession of them, under power of the warrant I held," replied Gripe.

"And it was my duty to see that you didn't have them," said Dick.

"No, sir, it was not. It is your duty to respect the law, and you have outraged it," said Gripe; "and I feel that I am not doing my duty in not handing you over to the constable, and placing you in the stocks."

"Then why don't you do it?" said Dick.

"Because I am a humane and merciful man, that's why," replied Gripe.

"A what?" said Dick, opening his eyes to their utmost width, "a what? Well, that beats me, and no mistake! Shall I tell you why you

don't? It's because you know that I would twist that head of yours off your contemptible little carcase, or crush you beneath my heel!"

The little steward drew his small form up to its utmost stretch, and, shaking his head defiantly, exclaimed,—

"You dare not do it!"

"Well, that's plucky!" said Dick, a look of admiration beaming on his smiling face. "But I could, and would, did I not feel it would be a desecration to that piece of leather!"

And he held up his foot as he spoke.

The little eyes of the little man fell before the determined look of Dick the Poacher.

He felt that Dick had the strength to carry out his threat, and the will to do so, did he give him cause.

He therefore remained silent.

Gripe was a very prudent man, and always weighed the results of any action before he put it into execution.

He did nothing without there was a prospect of gain to himself.

He never entered upon any speculation whereby he might encounter loss.

Therefore he deemed it better not to vex the gipsy-looking being at his side.

"Now look here," said Dick, after a pause, during which time he had been watching the movements of the little man's countenance, "that packet didn't belong to you, and you know it."

"But it became the property of the squire," replied Gripe. "As the widow was in arrears, and as became the duty of myself and the worthy Mr. Takeall, we must seize it with the rest of the property."

"Because the other lot didn't pay the arrears—is that it?" said Dick.

"Exactly."

"Now, Mr. Gripe," said Dick, with a scornful curl of the lip, "I have known you for a long time to be a thorough heartless villain, but I did not know that you added to those base qualities the title of liar!"

"Sir, do you dare to defame my character! Do you impute——"

"Hold on there, you dried up mummy!" exclaimed Dick. "I say you are a liar as well as a knave!"

"Those words are actionable!" said the little man, his face becoming flushed with wounded pride.

"Actionable be ——there, I won't swear," exclaimed Dick, "but I know you to be a mean-spirited, contemptible, designing little cur, who, if justice were meted out fairly, would be dragged by the heels through a horsepond every twenty-four hours, and pelted with the refuse of the town by every boy who resides within it."

Gripe really foamed at the mouth.

He clenched his little fists, and drew his little body menacingly up.

But he did no more.

The gleam in the dark eye of the poacher held him fascinated, as it were, by its influence.

What would he not have given to be revenged on Dick for the insults offered him.

But he feared to bite.

Physically the little steward was no match for the poacher.

Dick could have crushed him with a blow.

But Dick had laid himself open to the law,

and it was in the power of the little steward to hand him over to its mercies.

But he hesitated even to do this.

He felt that, at the first attempt to be revenged in this manner, the hand of the poacher would be at his throat.

And as Gripe was a prudent man, he resolved to pocket the affront, and bide his time.

But Gripe likewise determined not to forget it.

Like all mean natures, the steward neither forgot nor forgave.

He hoped now that Dick would leave him; and by way of giving that personage a hint that his room would be preferable to his company, he commenced moving away.

"Don't be in a hurry," said Dick.

"But I am in a hurry. I've no time to waste with you," said the little man.

"Then you must wait till your hurry's over," said the poacher.

"What do you mean?"

"What I say," coolly replied Dick.

"Do you dare to stop me on the king's highway?" said Gripe, his face becoming red and pale by turns.

"It will be to your interest to stop," said Dick.

"My interest?" said Gripe.

"Yes."

"How so?"

"You know I have got the papers," said Dick.

"Ah, yes," said the little man, quickly becoming interested.

"And you want them, don't you?" asked Dick.

"Yes," hurriedly replied the steward.

"What for?"

"To place them in the hands of their owner."

"And who is that?" asked Dick.

"Squire Henley," replied Gripe.

"Mr. Gripe," said Dick, "if all the lies you told in a day were piled one on the top of the other, they would reach higher than your head."

The steward turned pettishly away.

"Hold on," said Dick, "or you won't get them."

Gripe turned hastily.

"You will give them to me then?" he said.

"Well, perhaps I shouldn't mind, if you wanted them; but as you would place them in the hands of Squire Henley, I think I had better keep them myself."

Gripe's countenance fell.

"Well, I—I—that is," stammered Gripe, "I want them."

"For the squire?"

"No, not exactly."

"Now, look here, Gripe," said Dick, laying his hand upon his arm, "you either know or suspect that the squire has no more right to them than yourself. Your object in wishing to get them is to play upon the squire's purse, through his fears; is it not so?"

Gripe was silent.

"You know," continued Dick, "that I hate the squire, and despise you. I would make Henley suffer for the wrongs he has done to me and mine, and would make you the instrument by which those sufferings might be enhanced. Those papers would make your fortune, but in so doing they must also make mine. I will

strike a bargain with you: what will you give for them?"

"Five pounds," said Gripe, hastily.

"Five devils!" roared Dick. "Not for five hundred will I part with them!"

"Then keep them," said Gripe, endeavouring to look unconcerned.

"No, I shall not do that. I shall go to London, and place them in the hands of a solicitor."

"No, no, don't do that," said Gripe hastily, as Dick turned away. "I'll give a hundred pounds for them, and that is twice as much as they are worth."

"Squire Henley would give a thousand," said Dick.

"Oh no," said Gripe; "don't think it."

"But I know it," replied Dick; "and those who have the greatest right to them would give ten. Now, do we trade or not?"

"I have not got so much money," said Gripe.

"Borrow it of Takeall."

Gripe shook his head.

"He would require too much interest," he replied.

"Then you can't have them," said Dick coolly. "I shall start for London directly—do an honest action, and receive a good reward into the bargain."

And he commenced moving away.

Gripe followed him, and placed his hand on the poacher's arm.

"Stay till to-morrow," he said, "and I will try and borrow the money."

Dick pretended to think for some moments.

"No, no," he said at last, "I think I'll take them to London."

"Stay till to-morrow," pleaded Gripe, now really afraid that he should lose them.

Again Dick pretended to think.

"Well," he said, after a pause, "I will wait till this time to-morrow, not a minute later, and if you have not got the money then, I'm off to London directly."

"Then meet me here at this hour," said Gripe.

"No, not here," said Dick. "In the lane that runs beside the church — there we can arrange all without interruption."

"Let it be so then," said Gripe. "You will not fail?"

"I will not—but I wait no longer," said Dick, resolutely.

And turning round, he walked hurriedly away, leaving the weazen-faced steward rubbing his hands in glee at the prospect of obtaining the packet.

CHAPTER XVIII.

DANCING BILL PLAYS A NEW PART—THE ROBBERY DISCOVERED—DOUBTS AND FEARS—THE MIDNIGHT JOURNEY.

It was near the termination of the "sixth house."

The fair presented a most animated appearance; and the fat-pots which had been lighted threw a lurid glare over the mass of upturned faces.

The roars of laughter caused by Charlie Evans and Buskin Bob had died away, and

Dancing Bill and his ill-used wife were amusing the assembled crowd by the quick movements of their legs and feet. All eyes were centred now upon these worthies, while Charlie and Bob rested for a time from their labours.

Bill ever and anon leapt over his wand, but his mind seemed to be intent upon other than his business; his eye ever and anon wandered to Charlie, as though it wished to read there the discovery of his loss.

But the good-hearted fellow's countenance was as cheerful as ever, and Bill seemed to heave a sigh of relief after each look.

To Dancing Bill the day seemed as if it would never come to an end, and his anxiety to leave the booth preyed upon his mind.

He feared discovery, and he was conjuring up in his mind some excuse to enable him to get away.

But nothing suggested itself to his mind for some time.

At length he hit upon an idea, and resolved to act by it.

He threw a summersault at the very moment when the eyes of the worthy proprietor were fixed upon him, and purposely slipped on to the parade.

There he lay, as though unable to move.

Charlie and Buskin Bob rushed forward to assist him up; while his wife—who knew nothing of what had happened, or his intention—bent over him.

"Have you hurt yourself?" asked Charlie, raising him from the boards, assisted by Bob.

Dancing Bill only groaned in reply.

"Deary me! deary me!" exclaimed the old proprietor, coming to the spot; "what is the matter, Muster Evans?"

"He has hurt himself, I fear," said Charlie.

"Slipped," said Bob.

"Oh!" groaned Bill, "I can hardly stand!"

"Where are you hurt?" said Richardson, a look of commiseration stealing over his face. "Deary me, where are you hurt?"

"I've sprained my ankle," said Bill.

"Deary me, what a sad thing! How unfortunate! and the fear not half over."

Dancing Bill screwed up his mouth, and appeared to be in great pain.

Margaret stood by in an agony of grief.

She was a woman, though an ill-used one, and felt sympathy for the wretch who styled himself her master.

"Deary me!" said Richardson, "just lead him back, and sit him down for a little while. He'll be better perhaps directly; and, Muster Evans, you and Bob just commence again, for the people are shifting away to other parts of the fear. Deary me, how sad!"

Dancing Bill was led back, and seated by the money-box, where his wife leaned tenderly over him; while Charlie and Bob rushed to the front, and strove their hardest to stay the sight-seers, whom this event had commenced to disperse.

It became hard work now for our two friends, but they went at it willingly: though neither of them could feel the least respect for the harlequin, they both pitied him, and felt grieved at the accident.

Dancing Bill sat holding his foot in his hand, and rocking his body to and fro, as if suffering the most acute agony.

And so well did he play the part, that the old proprietor suggested that it would be better he should go to his lodgings, and call in a doctor to look to his hurt.

This was what Dancing Bill wanted, and being assisted to the dressing-room, he changed his clothes, and, bidding his wife remain till the close, limped out of the booth, apparently in great pain.

It was an unfortunate circumstance for the proprietor, but could not be helped; and each and all endeavoured to do their best to keep the game alive without him.

His wife danced, scarcely resting for a minute, although her mind was in a state of suspense respecting her husband; and Charlie and Bob strove their hardest to make up for his loss, scarcely allowing themselves breathing time.

In fact, one and all did their best, not out of any good feeling to Dancing Bill, but from respect to Richardson.

Perhaps no man ever gained the love and esteem of his employées as did the old show-proprietor.

His character was summed up in one word, and that word—man!

Enterprising, self-made man he was. From an orphan in a poorhouse, he rose to be the greatest show-proprietor of the day.

Beloved while living, his memory is respected in death, for there are not a few who have tasted of his bounties, and shared in his benevolence.

As the king of showmen he stood pre-eminent; and his good name will live as long as a fair is held in England.

It was with wearied frames, and aching limbs, that the pantomimists entered the dressing-room after the last house, to throw aside their professional dresses.

The promise of Charlie, to explain to Buskin Bob the slice of luck, as he termed it, had not been fulfilled, in consequence of the supposed accident which had befallen Dancing Bill, and the extra labour which devolved upon themselves; but now, as Charlie commenced unrobing, he related the gift he had received on behalf of the boy.

"Strike me comical!" said Buskin Bob, when he had heard all that Charlie felt himself justified in telling his friend, "but the chap, whoever he is, is a brick! What does the young one think of it?"

"I scarcely know," replied Charlie, "for I have had no opportunity of speaking to him since. We shall soon hear, though, for he's doing the combat, I hear, bless his little heart! Ah, you don't know how I love that boy," continued the good-hearted clown, "love him for his mother's sake, poor woman! She oughtn't to have been what she was, I know; so good—so kind—so feeling. I shall never forget her kindness to me; and if the spirits of the departed can look down upon those they leave behind, she shall have no cause to regret all her goodness to me."

Charlie had taken off his clown's dress, and was putting on his walking attire, when Harry, flushed with the excitement of the combat, and the applause he had received, entered the room.

"Hallo, here we are!" exclaimed Charlie. "How have you got on?"

"First-rate!" said Harry, with a smile. "I shan't be frightened any more now."

"Strike me comical," said Buskin Bob, "if it ain't just what I said. He's gone right slap bang through thirteen houses without once getting hissed! I knew he would, strike me comical if I didn't!"

Meantime Charlie Evans was thrusting his hand into the pocket of his coat, as he threw it across his arm: a deathly pallor was on his face, and a nervous twitching around his mouth.

"Strike me comical! how white you look. What's the matter?" said Bob, looking at his companion in surprise.

"Why—why—" gasped Charlie—"the notes —the notes. Harry, have you had the notes?"

"What notes?" asked the boy, looking up in surprise.

"The notes—your notes—those Dick the Poacher gave to me: where are they?"

"I don't know," said the boy, still more surprised; "you put them in your pocket."

"I know I did. But—but—"

"What?" gasped Harry.

"What?" iterated Bob.

"They are gone—gone!"

And Charlie Evans dropped the coat from his arm, and sank down upon the bench, covering his face with his hands.

"Gone?" said Buskin Bob, drawing out the word as if it stuck in his throat.

"Gone?" repeated Harry.

"Yes, gone—gone! lost! stole!" gasped Charlie.

Buskin Bob looked at the seated man for a few moments, and then exclaimed,—

"Strike me comical!"

Then he dropped as it were all of a heap by the side of his friend.

Little Harry stood looking from one to the other, in consternation.

"A hundred pounds," he thought, "which would have saved us from want, lost as soon almost as received!"

And then he too sat down, heaving a heavy sigh.

Buskin Bob was the first one to recover himself.

"Are you sure you put them in your pocket, Charlie?" he asked.

"Sure as I am sitting here," replied the clown. "Harry saw me do so."

"I did," said the boy.

"Then they must have dropped out. Let us search for them," said Bob.

All three rose, and commenced searching the room.

Dresses were shaken—benches moved—every corner looked into—not an inch of the place but was thoroughly searched, but all of no avail, they could not be found.

"See if they have slipped into the lining," said Bob, taking up his friend's coat, and feeling it all over.

But there was no indication of such being the case.

"They are gone," said Charlie, "but how? where?"

"They must have been stolen," said Bob.

"But who could steal them? No one knew that I had them, and none have been here but ourselves."

"And Dancing Bill," said Buskin Bob.

"But he knew nothing of them," replied Charlie. "Harry, have you mentioned it to any one?"

"Not a soul," replied the boy.

"Do you know the numbers of them?" asked Bob.

"No," replied Charlie.

"Then you can't stop them," said Bob.

"No," sighed Charlie.

Bob thought for a few moments, and then, turning his eyes full upon Charlie's face, he exclaimed, emphatically,—

"Charlie, if them notes is stolen, Dancing Bill is the thief; if he ain't, may I be struck comical!"

But Charlie was unwilling to judge him so hastily.

"He is, I tell you," said Buskin Bob, striking his fist upon the little table. "I feel he is. I can't help it, but I do feel he is; if I don't— there, strike me comical!"

"Did he know of their existence I might think so," said Charlie, becoming more cool; "but he did not know."

"Perhaps," said Bob.

"I am sure he did not."

"Who, then, could have took them?" asked Bob.

"Alas, I know not! I only know I placed them there, and they are gone!"

"Do you think this poacher chap was only having a lark with you, and has nailed them himself? If he's a poacher he ain't far off a thief, you know."

These remarks set Charlie thinking.

It might be so: yet why should the man wish to sport with his feelings?

He had warned him to beware of Dancing Bill; but might he not, after all, be in league with the harlequin?

He resolved to attest the sincerity of Dick.

He would visit the spot where he had stated the papers to be hidden, and learn whether he had spoken the truth respecting them.

If he had, then he could have no suspicion of his good will towards the boy; but if he had not, he must believe him to be the one who had extracted the notes from his pocket, and consider him the enemy instead of the friend of the poor boy.

Knowing, as he did, that he could trust Buskin Bob, he revealed to him all that Dick had said respecting the packet and the hidden packages; and his determination to lose no time in learning the truth or falsehood of the story.

Buskin Bob agreed to accompany him, and after another fruitless search they left the booth, resolved not to mention the loss to anyone for the present.

With a heavy heart little Harry followed his two friends out of the now-deserted fair.

All the bright hopes he had cherished during the past few hours were dispelled; the success of his first appearance, which had caused his young heart to bound with joy, was now forgotten, and silently and sadly he walked along, beside the thoughtful pantomimists.

"Harry," said the clown, after they had walked some distance in silence, "myself and Bob are going to learn the truth of what Dick, as he calls himself, has told me. You go to bed, my boy, and leave us to do the work."

"I will go with you," said the boy.

"You can if you like, but you can do no good if you do. Better go to bed, for you are tired, and it is late for you to be up. You can depend upon us."

"Oh yes," replied the boy.

"Then go to bed, Harry," said Buskin Bob,

"and, strike me comical, we'll find out whether it's all right or all wrong."

The boy would fain have accompanied them, but he wished to please his friend, who, he felt sure, advised him for his good, and when they arrived at the little alehouse, Harry went up to the room where he had slept the night before, whilst Charlie and Bob framed some excuse to Grimhall for not being prepared to retire yet, and, having procured the means of obtaining a light, they again started on their journey to the hidden passage.

Half an hour's walk brought them to the little clump of trees where Dick the Poacher and Charlie Evans had sat, on the day of the death of the poor widow.

Making sure that no one was about, they forced aside the bushes and passed through them.

Here they found—as Dick had stated—the little smooth square completely surrounded by the trees and bushes, and resembling a small lawn.

They groped about for some time, till at length Charlie, seizing a turf of grass in his hand, it left its fellows without any force being applied to uproot it.

He thrust his hand into the cavity thus formed, and an iron ring came in contact with his fingers.

This he felt sure was the trap covering the entrance to the passage Dick had spoken of.

CHAPTER XIX.

THE STEWARD RESOLVES TO ROB HIS MASTER, IN ORDER TO PLACE HIM IN HIS POWER.

GRIPE, the steward, remained watching the form of Dick the Poacher till a turn in the road hid him from the old man's sight, and then he turned his little form round, and started off towards the mansion as fast as his legs would carry him.

Rubbing his hands together gleefully, and chuckling to himself as he went along, the little steward soon reached the place of his destination.

Having entered unseen, he made his way stealthily to his own room.

Throwing himself into a seat, he gave vent to a low laugh.

He felt that the possession of the coveted papers would make him the master of his employer, and he resolved, come what would, to possess them.

But then there was an obstacle in his way—Gripe only possessed in ready money some fifty or sixty pounds.

But he could obtain the sum he required in the course of a month.

Now, the great difficulty was how to get sufficient to satisfy the demand of Dick the Poacher.

He felt certain that that personage would keep his word, and carry the documents to London, if he was not prepared on the morrow to hand over the sum demanded for them.

This he must prevent, for two reasons.

One was to get the squire in his power, and by playing on his fears, play at the same time on his purse.

The other was the fear that, if Dick took them to London, Squire Henley himself might lose his property, and so the steward would lose his place.

In either case Gripe felt he would be the loser.

Now how was he to prevent this?

If he borrowed of Takeall, the broker would require enormous interest, and, besides, exhibit some curiosity to know what the steward required with so large a sum.

Though professing the utmost friendship for each other, yet neither would trust the other.

Both being rogues, both were suspicious of any private transactions connected with the other.

Taking all things into consideration, Gripe thought that borrowing the money of the broker would not be wise.

Therefore he dismissed that idea from his mind, and tried to find another.

He sat buried in thought for some time, then, rubbing his hands together, he muttered,—

"That's it—that's it! I have over that sum in my desk, belonging to the squire. I will make free to use it for my own purpose, and refund it when I can draw my own out."

Mr. Gripe was a thinking man, and a shrewd man to boot. He never did anything without weighing the consequences of the act.

He had weighed this well. He knew that, although he had no intention to keep that money—he knew that he could well refund it at a certain time—yet he knew that legally it was a dishonest act, and one that left him open to prosecution as a felon.

But then, again, he knew—or, rather, he thought he knew—that the possession of the papers which that money would give him, would place the squire in his power; and in the event of that personage discovering the guilty act of his steward, he would not dare to prosecute, lest Gripe should produce them, and thus beggar or disgrace him.

Gripe did *not* positively know the tenour of the documents, but he guessed it, and he was seldom wrong in his surmises.

He put this to that, as he said; and then, by addition and subtraction, he always worked the thing into its real worth.

He knew a little, and he guessed a little; and when he put the two littles together, he made a great deal, and out of that he could extract enough to prove to him that his master was a villain.

And having come to this conclusion, Mr. Gripe had no fear of him, nor any compunction in appropriating the squire's property to his own uses.

For—he thought—if it is not mine it is not his, and I have as much right to it as he has, if the question of right is taken into consideration.

And so Gripe resolved to become a thief.

Morally he did so, but whether legally or not we must leave others to determine.

However, the little man deemed it necessary to wait till the last moment ere he took the money.

There was yet some twenty hours before the time arrived to meet Dick again.

In twenty hours kingdoms have been overthrown ere now, and Gripe resolved to wait till the last moment.

"Who knows," he thought. "Did I take it

now, the squire might discover his loss; but if I wait till the appointed time I shall run less risk of discovery."

So Gripe passed the remainder of the day speculating upon the prospects of a good fortune to be made out of the squire.

So certain did he feel of this, that his little weazened face was covered with smiles, and—as Gripe always did when in a good humour—he resolved to give Takeall another job in the morning, to make a levy upon a poor sick cottager's furniture.

For, as we have said, Gripe was always happy at the prospect of making others miserable.

During the night he obtained little sleep, his mind was so much disturbed by the prospect of getting Squire Henley beneath his thumb.

Although the squire had been a good and liberal master to his steward, and would have trusted him with anything, Gripe did not consider that he was bound in any way to return good for good.

His motto was *self;* and self was his god.

Could he place his foot on the neck of his dearest friend and raise himself thereby, he would do it, and feel not the least compunction in the act.

Upwards and onwards was his motto—no matter at what price.

Good or bad the action, it mattered not to him, so that he was the gainer.

He rose with the sun, and attired himself with his usual neatness, and went about his ordinary duties with his usual bustling, fussy manner.

The squire had gone out upon a hunting excursion, and this circumstance favoured the intentions of the steward.

He opened his desk, took the money he required, and, smoothing his shirt-frill, left the manor, and made his way towards the old church.

Punctual as he always was, no matter on what business he was bent, the little steward cast his eyes around him, in the hope of seeing Dick.

He had not long to wait, for the poacher met him almost immediately upon his arrival.

"Humph!" exclaimed Dick, "so you are here?"

"Business is business," returned the little man, "and I always make it a point never to keep any one waiting."

"Do you now," said Dick. "Well, it strikes me that you do."

"Not so; I am always punctual. I don't like to wait, and I never let others."

"Yes, you do," said Dick; "Jack Ketch has been waiting for you a long while."

Gripe started, and unconsciously placed his hand upon his neck.

"Now," said the little man, "have you brought them with you?"

"Yes," replied Dick. "Have you brought the money?"

"I have," replied Gripe.

"I thought you hadn't got it," said Dick.

"Oh, yes," said Gripe, averting his glance from the piercing eyes of the poacher.

Dick saw in a moment the change in the steward's countenance, and a smile broke over his handsome bronzed features.

"Ha, ha," he muttered to himself, "Mr. Gripe, I have you on the hip now, and I'll pay off old scores, I warrant me."

Then taking the papers from his pocket which he had written at the roadside inn, before his visit to the fair the previous day, he held them towards the steward.

Gripe's eyes sparkled as he did so.

He stretched forth his hands to grasp them, but Dick drew them back.

"Money first," he said.

"It is not usual to pay for any article till you possess it," said Gripe, looking suspiciously at his companion.

"Ain't it? then I must make an exception to the rule, Mr. Gripe. I won't trust you."

"Why not?"

"Because I know you to be a rogue," replied Dick.

A spiteful glance was in the old man's eye, but he said nothing.

"Now then—money," said Dick.

Gripe drew forth the cash.

"There it is," he said.

"And there's the packet," replied Dick, handing to the steward what that worthy believed to be the documents stolen from the cottage of the Widow Marston, on the day of her funeral.

"Now, Mr. Gripe," said the poacher, "you are satisfied, I hope?"

"Yes," replied the steward.

"And so am I, but not with this transaction."

"With what, then?"

"That you are as base a rascal as ever I encountered."

"What do you mean, sir?"

"Simply that you are a thief."

The face of Gripe turned pale with rage and terror.

"Me, a thief!" he gasped.

"Even so, Mr. Gripe."

"What—what mean you?"

"Simply what I have said," returned Dick coolly. "Yesterday you denied that you had the money to pay my demands, but to-day you have it. Where did you get it from, eh, Mr. Gripe?"

And Dick fixed upon the face of the now trembling steward so searching a look, that Gripe almost wished he had had nothing to do with him.

Dick enjoyed his confusion, and in revenge for the many insults he had received at the hands of the steward, resolved to make him as contemptible as possible in his own eyes.

"Mr. Gripe," he said, after a pause, "you are as consummate a rascal as your master, and, bad as I am, I cannot descend so low as to remain one moment longer in your company than the transaction of our present business necessitates, so I now leave you, sir, to your own bad work—for bad I feel are the intentions of yourself with respect to these papers. But be careful you do not overbalance yourself—the child plays with the fire till it is burnt: it must be experienced hands that use edge tools with safety, so be careful, Mr. Gripe, or you may burn or cut yourself when you least expect it!" and Dick turned upon his heel and walked rapidly away.

Not so Gripe. He held the packet tightly in his hand, and, as he heard the papers crumple beneath the pressure, his heart beat with joy, for now he felt himself his master's master.

What cared he now if his peculations were discovered—would Squire Henley dare impeach his character? If he did, woe be to him! he would show that packet to the man he had robbed, and then—what then?

And Gripe chuckled in glee as he strode home.

CHAPTER XX.

THE PANTOMIMISTS DISCOVER THE HIDING-PLACE IN THE PASSAGE—DISAPPOINTMENT AND SUSPICION.

THE bright moon shed her mellow light upon the spot where the trap-door leading to the hidden passage was situated, and revealed to each other the looks of gratification which lit up the faces of Buskin Bob and his friend Charlie Evans.

To a certain extent the doubt of Dick's veracity was eradicated.

At least, they had discovered that one portion of his story was true, namely, that which related to the trap embedded in the earth.

And this removed a weight from the mind of Charlie; yet still he resolved to be satisfied as to the whole.

They raised the trap, and looked down the dark opening.

"Strike a light, Bob," said the clown; "this looks like the entrance to a well, more than anything else."

In a few moments a light was procured, and then they commenced to descend the small ladder.

Arriving at the bottom they paused.

"This here's a rum place," said Bob.

"Well, rather," replied Charlie. "But, hi, hi, here we are! Come along."

Strike me comical," exclaimed Bob, "if I ain't half frightened."

And as he spoke, he raised a small piece of candle above his head, so as to throw its rays further into the passage.

But as he did so he received a blow on the head, which made him turn so sharply that he received another ere he could determine its course.

Not knowing anything of the nature of the place, and being a tall man, he had received the blows by striking his head against the projecting roots of the trees overhead.

But at the moment Bob knew not what it was that had assailed him, and instinctively he clenched his fist, and turned sharply round to defend himself from the attacks of some unseen enemy.

But casting his eyes upwards, he soon perceived what it was, and, muttering an imprecation on the objects which caused his fright, he led the way, followed by Charlie, down the passage.

When they had reached its end they gazed upon the ground, in expectation of discovering the second trap.

So nicely and compactly was it fitted into the earth, that for some moments they could not perceive it.

"Strike me comical," exclaimed Bob, "if you ain't been sold!"

"Why do you think so?" asked his companion.

"Because we can't see no trap here," replied Bob. "I made sure we should, after the one up above was all right, but the one here is all humbug."

"No it ain't," replied Charlie, "for here it is."

And as he spoke the clown raised the trap, and revealed to his companion the little square opening.

A cry of surprise escaped them both.

The secret place was empty!

The papers placed there by Dick the Poacher were gone!

The two friends stood looking at each other for some time in silence; then each spoke at once the one word,—

"Sold!"

And they believed now that Dick had deceived them—believed that he it was who had abstracted the notes from the pocket of the clown, after having placed them in his hands.

But why should he thus sport with the feelings of the clown and his *protégé?*

Alas, they could not understand it.

"Strike me comical," said Bob, after a pause, if I can tumble to it now—no, I can't; there's something behind all this. If that chap you call Dick don't mean right, why did he tell you of this place?"

"Ah, that's what beats me," said Charlie; "it's a strange piece of business. But the notes are gone, that's certain: and there's no papers here, that's certain, too. I can't make it out. I wish I had not seen him, for it did but awaken hopes in the poor boy's breast to dash them from him directly. Poor little fellow, I do pity him, I do."

"And so do I, strike me comical if I don't. But there, pity's not much use—not half so good as bread. That's what the poor want. Many a starving wretch had been saved from crime, had bread taken the place of pity. It's all very well, but it don't feed the hungry nor clothe the naked, strike me comical if it does."

Charlie sighed.

He had found more than pity from the mother of the poor boy in whose welfare he now took so great an interest; and that which she meted out to him would he mete out to her offspring.

He had fondly hoped that the offering of the poacher would have prevented him seeking a living in the streets during the winter; but now that hope had passed away, and he saw nothing to save himself and the poor boy from earning a livelihood in that manner.

It was with a sorrowful heart that Charlie Evans and his poor friend Buskin Bob left the underground passage.

"Strike me comical," said Buskin Bob, when himself and companion once more gained the top of the ladder, "if I ain't half inclined to leave this here blessed trap open, so as others can find out the place. It would just serve that poacher right, it would, if he wants to keep it dark, strike me comical if it wouldn't."

"No, no," said Charlie; "although I believe he has played us a trick, I am not quite certain of it, and it is wrong to condemn before we have proof. He, as well as us, may be the victim of others' perfidy. Secure the trap, and let us wait—time will bring the truth to light."

"I hope it may. But if it's square, depend upon it that Dancing Bill is the thief!" said Bob, emphatically.

Charlie shrugged his shoulders.

"How could he know of it?" he asked.

"STRIKE ME COMICAL! YOU DON'T SAY SO."

"Can't say," replied Bob, "but can't help thinking it, strike me comical if I can."

"Well, time will show," replied Charlie, "so let us go home, and trust to Providence to unravel the mystery in favour of poor little Harry."

They left the spot, and in silence made their way to the little alehouse, where they found the Boy Actor fast asleep.

Without any further conversation on the matter, Charlie and Bob retired to rest, and soon forgot, in the slumber which sealed their eyelids, the strange adventures of the past few hours.

Hours in which hopes and fears had struggled within their breasts; in which bright sunshine and dark clouds had been thrown across the soul.

It was a cruel blow to all the fond hopes of the poor pantomimist—a blow the more crushing because so unlooked for.

Poor Harry perhaps felt least acutely the loss.

His young mind could not realize the fearful struggles for bread which beset the poor.

Hitherto his wants had been supplied, although in a humble manner; and it was not till her mother's illness rendered it impossible for her to procure food for her child, that he knew what hunger was.

And even then his want was not of long duration, for Charlie had come to the rescue.

Come, with his smiling face and cheerful words, to gladden the heart and minister to the frame of the poor bereaved boy.

True, he thought of the better prospects in store for him, when Dick the Poacher placed a hundred pounds in the hands of his friend, to be applied to his necessities; and he felt a keen disappointment when Charlie discovered his loss, but still not so acute as his friend.

Charlie knew what it was to fight his way

half starved through the world; knew that when poverty cried for bread it often received but stone; knew what it was to meet only the frowns of those who, in prosperity, would grasp the hand with warm and fervent pressure; knew what it was to meet the cold reply, the insulting taunt, so often offered to the poor by those whom a gracious Providence had taken under its care, and provided with the daily wants of men.

All this he knew—all this he felt—would be experienced by his young *protégé*, in his path through this cold, unfeeling world.

A gleam of sunshine had been thrown across it, but the black cloud of adversity had cast its shadow upon it, and left the first dark spot on the young player's career—a career which opened so well, but which was blighted and soured by one who should have aided him in his " Struggles for Bread."

CHAPTER XXI.

DANCING BILL VISITS THE PASSAGE AND SECURES THE PAPERS—THE EXPLOSION—THE WOUNDED MAN—THE STRUGGLES TO ESCAPE.

LIMPING as though in great pain, Dancing Bill slowly made his way from the booth through the fair, out into the high road.

Here the look of anguish which he had worn on his features gave place to a triumphal smile, and, striking off into a back lane, it was truly wonderful how soon he recovered the use of the sprained foot.

In fact, the cure was instantaneous.

No one could have limped more painfully in the high road—no one could have walked with greater ease than did Dancing Bill, after a turn in the lane hid him effectually from the view of anyone who might pass along the high road.

The smile of triumph deepened into a loud, demoniac laugh now, a laugh at the success of the ruse, and the prospect of being revenged on the clown, Harry, and Dick the Poacher.

He hated all three.

Hated them because they had each been instrumental in chastising him for his ruffianly conduct; hated them only as the coward can hate.

He had sworn to be revenged on them, and fate had placed him in a position to find out the means.

And he had done so.

He had overheard all the conversation which had taken place between Dick and the clown, respecting the hiding-place where the documents lie concealed.

He had heard, also, that which had relieved his superstitious mind, namely, that it was the act of the poacher, and not some supernatural being, who had deprived him of the two pounds which was to secure his services in depriving the orphan of that which was justly his own property.

He almost danced with joy now, so light and springy was his step.

On he went down the lane, chuckling in high glee at the prospect of his voyage, and the profits which his intentions would doubtless realize.

He made his way through the gap in the hedge which bordered the field, crossed it, and in a few moments stood within the little enclosure where the trap hid the entrance to the underground passage.

The spot was soon found; for so attentively had he listened to its position, that he could not fail to discover it.

He raised it, and descended the ladder.

The darkness of the place for a time terrified him, and he hesitated to proceed.

He strained his eyes greatly, but could distinguish nothing but a deep, dark space before him.

He feared to enter.

Yet he was loth to leave the place without possessing that for which he had deceived the company at Richardson's, and for which he had come thither.

Still, he could not summon up courage sufficient to penetrate that darkness.

He turned to ascend the ladder, when his foot struck something on the ground.

He stooped to ascertain what it was, and found it to be a tinder-box.

A cry of joy escaped his lips.

He sat down upon the last round of the ladder, and, holding the box between his knees, struck the flint against the steel.

A shower of sparks was the result, and as they fell upon the tinder, he blew them with his breath, and the glow emitted therefrom revealed to his eyes a few matches and a wax taper, lying in the spot where Dick had placed them for future use.

It was not long now ere he procured a light, and, holding the taper above his head, he moved slowly and cautiously along the passage.

Arriving at the end, he searched for and found the trap.

This he lifted, and there, upon the cemented bottom of the square hole, lay the coveted papers.

With a cry of joy he seized them in his grasp, and thrust them into his breast.

" Mine! mine! " he exclaimed. " Now, Charlie Evans, I am avenged for the blow you struck me. Who triumphs now? Ha, ha, ha! who triumphs now? "

And again stooping over the opening, the harlequin examined the other objects in the hiding-place.

Those, he felt sure, belonged to Dick the Poacher; and his revengeful spirit prompted him to take them, in retaliation for the treatment he had received at his hands.

" He had my money, and I'll have his goods," he muttered, between his clenched teeth. " Ah," he added, as the thought struck him, " when he finds these things gone, he will believe Charlie has taken them; that will dissolve their friendship, and make it still worse for the man I hate."

And taking the articles out of the hole one by one—which consisted of traps, snares, knives, and two or three small tin boxes—he secreted them about his person.

As each article was disposed of, the smile on his face grew broader, and his heart beat fiercer at the thought of how he was being revenged upon his enemies, as he termed those whose manly spirit had prompted them to defend a helpless and insulted woman.

But one article now remained—a small, curiously formed tin case.

The curiosity of the harlequin prompted him to make himself acquainted with its contents, ere he consigned it to his pocket.

He knelt down, and, placing the taper upon the floor of the passage, forced off the lid.

The better to examine his prize, he held it close to the light, and, drawing out a piece of paper which had been placed in the top, it touched the flame of the taper.

There was a bright flash—a loud report; a shriek broke from his lips.

A sickening and painful sensation—as though his arm had been torn from its socket—came over him.

The passage was wrapped in darkness, and he fell forward on his face, insensible!

The shock for a few minutes entirely deprived him of his senses, and when he did recover, his mind was a prey to the most agonizing misery.

He was in utter darkness; his face and arms lacerated by the powder which had flown into them.

A horrible feeling came over him—he feared that the powder had blinded him.

So dark was all around.

Not a single ray of light could his gaze encounter, and he trembled lest his villany had been punished by the fearful doom of blindness.

Oh, that he were once more in the open air! Oh for the knowledge that his eyesight was uninjured!

He feared the worst, yet hoped for the best.

He knew that the light had been extinguished by the powder; he knew that the passage in which he was was pitchy dark, and that no ray of light had penetrated it from the outside when he made his way into it; but he thought that, dark as it had been, he could yet distinguish its outlines, but now, not even that could he do.

He groped his way along the passage by placing his hands upon the damp, moist walls, and his superstitious nature caused him to tremble with fear, despite the pain he was suffering.

In the darkness by which he was beset, he fancied himself surrounded by supernatural beings eager to seize him.

So strongly did this fear gain upon him, that he quickened his pace to get out of the place, and in so doing he caught his head in the roots of the trees, which held him prisoner.

With a shriek, he tore himself away, leaving a quantity of hair hanging thereto.

In his anxiety to escape from the place, he gave no thought as to the true cause of the circumstance—he believed it to be the work of some supernatural agency, and his terrors increased.

He dashed quickly forward, and his foot striking a projection in the uneven ground, he fell.

His hands came in contact with the damp slimy greenness of the walls towards the floor of the passage, and a shiver of horror pervaded his frame.

With a cry of terror he rose to his feet, and made his way along.

He reached the laddder, and crawled up it.

The trap he raised with his head, but the light—which came from the moon—was faint, and he could scarcely see.

The powder had injured his sight!

He struggled through the trap, closed it, and groped his way out of the little enclosure into the field.

Burnt and bleeding, he hurried into the lane, and thence into the high road, as well as he could, and took his way towards the little alehouse, where he had lodged during the time he had been in the town. Arriving there, he sought his bed, on which he threw himself, and waited the return of his wife.

Bitterly, indeed, did he now curse his wickedness; he felt that it was a judgment on him for injuring the fatherless.

CHAPTER XXII.

THE DISCOVERY THROUGH THE WINDOW. — THE RESTITUTION OF THE STOLEN NOTES.

It was the latter end of October—the leaves were falling from the trees, dried and withered, and the air was chilly.

Richardson's show had closed for the winter, and its company had to seek occupation elsewhere.

Some had been engaged at the various theatres, others had started entertainments on their own account, and some were starving, being unable to obtain employment of any shape.

Dancing Bill was laid up in the hospital, and the doctors were trying every means to cure the wounds and restore the injured sight of the man, and his wife was struggling on heaven only knows how.

Charlie Evans had entered into partnership with Buskin Bob, and little Harry had undergone a series of lessons in tumbling, walking on stilts, and juggling; whilst little Mary, the daughter of the clown, had taken lessons in dancing, and had become so proficient that she could step through the highland fling and the sailor's hornpipe.

Buskin Bob played the drum and mouth organ, whilst Charlie tumbled on stilts, assisted by his *protégé*, and for some few days they had succeeded in picking up money sufficient for their wants.

It was a life which Charlie objected to, but he felt that it was necessary to throw aside all delicacy of feeling to get bread, and in a few days it wore off, and they now worked the streets of the different towns with more or less success.

What had become of Dick the Poacher they none of them knew.

He had not been seen by them since the night when he placed the notes in the hand of the clown, to be applied in keeping the orphan; and Charlie had made up his mind that Dick had taken them again himself, and that he had sent them to the underground passage for no other object than making them believe the packet had been stolen, whilst he kept it for his own purposes.

It was towards evening one day when Charlie and Harry and Buskin Bob were going through their performances, to the delight of a gaping crowd, that Charlie, whose head reached to the windows of the first floors as he capered about on the stilts, caught sight of a face in one of the rooms which brought him to a perfect standstill.

It was the face of Dancing Bill, who had that day come out of the hospital and taken a furnished lodging for himself and wife.

After a moment's pause Charlie looked again into the room, to make sure that he was not mistaken.

"It's him, sure enough," he muttered, "but what can he have that shade over his eyes for?"

Drawing himself between the windows so as not to obstruct the light with his body, he peeped through one of the panes of glass.

Dancing Bill had not observed him, and was in the act of gazing at a bank note which he held in his hand when the clown first looked in.

Charlie saw that it was a note in his hand, and the words of Buskin Bob flashed like lightning across his mind that Dancing Bill was the thief.

Charlie well knew that Bill had no money when at the fair, and he naturally imagined that the note now held in the hand of the harlequin was one of those which Dick had given him.

As he stood there surprised, and scarcely knowing whether to make the harlequin acquainted with his presence, the door of the room opened and Margaret entered the apartment.

Charlie drew further back against the wall.

"Well," said Bill, looking up as his wife entered, "did you get it changed?"

Charlie listened intently.

"No," replied Margaret.

"How's that?" asked Bill.

"Because we are not known here," replied Margaret.

"You ain't put yourself out of the way to try, I suppose," exclaimed Bill, "you didn't seem much inclined to go."

"I can't help it, Bill," said the woman, "I know the money is not ours, and we have no right to it."

"We've as much right to it as anybody," said Bill. "That poacher stole it, I reckon, or he wouldn't have been so generous."

"That is nothing to me," said his wife.

"Ain't it? Well, it just is to me. I can't follow the profession for some time; and it will help us till I can."

"It will never do you any good," said Margaret, seating herself.

"We'll see," said her husband. "But even if it don't, it shan't do those who it was meant for any."

"Strike me comical!" exclaimed Buskin Bob, shifting his chin over the pipes of the mouth-organ; "if I don't think you're gone to sleep! Don't stay there any longer, licking the steam off them windows!"

The voice of his friend called Charlie to himself; and he darted from the pathway into the road, beside his friend.

"Hullo, here we are!" he exclaimed. "Well I'm blowed!"

"What's up?" said Bob.

"I've seen something."

"Sign you ain't blind, then," replied his friend, flourishing the drum-stick over his head, and bringing it down upon the drum head with force enough to burst the blackened parchment.

"But he is nearly," said Charlie, stooping down.

"Who?"

"Bill."

"Bill who?" asked Bob.

"Dancing Bill."

"What do you mean?" said Bob, looking up into the face of his friend. "Going off your chump, ain't you—getting light headed on the top of those stilts?"

"I tell you I've seen Dancing Bill; and what's more, I've seen one of the notes the poacher gave me."

"Where?" asked Harry.

"In his house."

"The devil!" said Bob.

"Shut up shop," said Charlie, "and let us go home."

"I ain't been round for the half-pence yet," replied Bob, ducking his head from under the straps, and setting the drum on to the ground.

He knew that Charlie would not have expressed a wish to close the entertainment, had he not good reasons for so doing; consequently he went round the assembled company, hat in hand, whilst Charlie unstrapped the stilts from his legs and those of the boy.

The company gradually dispersed, and the players were left to themselves.

"Now just explain what's up," said Bob; "for strike me comical if I can tumble."

"Dancing Bill and his wife are in that room," said Charlie, pointing up to the window through which he had been gazing. "He has a shade over his eyes, as though something was the matter with him; and he has got a bank-note in his hand."

"I said he was the thief—strike me comical if I didn't."

"I know he is now," said Charlie; "but we have no proof."

"Do you know the numbers of the notes?" asked Bob eagerly.

"No; like a fool, I never thought to look at them."

"Then you can't swear to them?" said Bob.

"But I can!" said Charlie. "From what his wife said to him, I know them to be the same as taken from my coat pocket, in the dressing-room."

"But how can you get them?" said Bob, after a pause.

"I'll take them away from him, the mean-spirited rascal. Harry shall have the money the poacher left him, or I'll hand him over to justice."

Buskin Bob shook his head.

"You can't swear to them," he said, "and if he denies that they are the same, you have no proof to the contrary."

"I have," said Charlie.

"What?"

"The words of his wife, which I overheard just now."

"Won't do," said Bob, shaking his head dubiously.

"Why not?"

"'Cos it ain't evidence. She's his wife, you know, and a wife can't appear against her husband."

"No more she can't," said Charlie, with a sigh.

"But don't you think Dick the poacher knows the numbers?" remarked Harry.

"Oh," said Bob; "if he does, that would do."

"But we don't know where to find him," said Charlie.

"No more we don't," remarked Bob. "Well, it is vexing."

"But I am resolved that Bill shall not retain them. They are Harry's, and he shall have them, if I tear them from him."

"Don't be rash," said Bob. "Let us go home and think what's best to be done. When Bill finds that we know he has got them, he will no doubt be glad to give them up, for fear of a prison."

"Not knowing where to find the poacher, is worse than all; as, if we give Bill in custody, his evidence would be wanted."

"Harry," said Bob, "do you know where Dick is likely to be found?"

The boy shook his head.

"I don't know," he replied.

"Even if he did," remarked Charlie, "he might not feel disposed to come forward. We must do without. I will force my way into Dancing Bill's presence, and tear them from him."

"Not now," said Bob. "He can't get rid of them all at once. If you go in now, he will get rid of them. Wait till dark; then, watch the house, and perhaps we may pounce upon them unawares."

"Well, come Harry," said the clown; "let us go home now, and change the props; and by and bye me and Bob will return and get your money. It will not do to make a disturbance about it, as even Dick the Poacher did not come by it all fair and square."

The two wended their way homewards, changed their dresses, and Bob and the clown went out on their mission, leaving Harry and little Mary, an engaging little girl of ten years, to themselves.

It was quite dark by the time that Charlie Evans and his friend stood before the house where Dancing Bill had taken up his abode, and they looked up at the window of the room where the clown had seen him a few hours before.

"If we could only get into the room without anyone in the house knowing it, I should be glad," remarked Charlie.

"So should I," said Bob.

At this moment the door was opened by Margaret.

Bob drew Charlie aside, so that the columbine could not distinguish their features.

Pulling the door to behind her, Margaret ran hurriedly down the street.

"Now's your time," said Bob. "She's just gone for some errand, and left the door open. In you go. Strike me comical! won't he stare when you tell him what you've come for!"

And pushing the door open, the two friends silently entered the passage.

A stream of light from the open door of the room where the harlequin sat, enabled our friends to make their way up the stairs without difficulty.

Dancing Bill sat before a table, with his back to the door, his head leaning thoughtfully upon his hands, and the green shade protecting his eyes from the light of the candle.

Charlie walked noiselessly into the room, and laid his hand upon the shoulder of the harlequin.

With a cry, Dancing Bill sprung to his feet, and faced the clown and pantaloon.

"Charlie Evans!" he gasped.

"Here we are," said Charlie. "Happy to see you."

Dancing Bill felt anything but happy to see his visitors, though.

His guilty conscience smote him, and he turned pale as death.

"You don't look well," remarked Bob; "strike me comical, if you ain't like a ghost."

"What do you want?" gasped Bill. "How did you know I was here? Did Margaret tell you?"

"No," replied Charlie. "I found you out by accident, and I have likewise found out that you are a thief."

"Ah!" gasped the man.

"Aye, Mr. Dancing Bill. "I am here to demand from you bank notes to the value of one hundred pounds, which you stole from my coat pocket on the night you pretended to sprain your ankle."

"I stole!" said Bill, endeavouring to look surprised.

"You stole!" replied Charlie.

"I don't know what you mean," said Bill, putting on a swagger. "Do you come here to insult me, or is this only one of your clown's tricks?"

"I come here to demand the restitution of stolen property," said Charlie.

"I don't know what you mean. Where was you to get a hundred pounds to lose, I should like to know?"

"That is my business. That I did have it you know. That you stole them from my coat pocket you also know, and that you have the notes in your possession now I am sure you cannot deny."

"I can," said Bill. "I never had such a thing—no more did you, I believe."

"You lie!" exclaimed Charlie. "Through that window I saw one of them in your hand, and through that window I also heard the conversation between yourself and wife, a few hours since."

"Ah!" gasped Bill.

"Now, look you, Bill," said Charlie; "hand them over, and I'll let you off; but if you refuse, I call in a constable, and place you in a prison."

"I tell you I know nothing about them."

"Will you hand them over?" asked Charlie, advancing to the stairs, "or shall I brand you as a thief, and give you over to the mercies of the law?"

The guilty man hesitated.

"Strike me comical, if you hadn't better fork out," said Buskin Bob, "and save your character; that is, if you've got one—which you ain't."

"I'll give you one minute," said the clown; "and if you don't hand over the notes by that time I will arouse the people in the house, and expose you to them—then place you in the hands of justice."

"How do I know they belong to you?" said Bill, the fear of a prison causing him to give way.

"Because you took them from my pocket," replied the clown.

"Well, then, you confess you have got them," said Buskin Bob.

"No, I don't," said Bill.

"Yes, you do," said Bob; "though you didn't mean to, perhaps."

"I found them," said Bill, after a moment's pause; "and I don't believe they belong to you."

"Yes; but you found them in my pocket," said Charlie.

"No, I didn't," said Bill.

"Where then?"

"On the floor of the dressing-room."

"That's a lie," said Bob. "And even if you had, you knew they didn't belong to you; and you ought to have found out whose they was."

"Ought I?"

"Yes, if you was a honest man you would."

"But he is not," said Charlie. "Come, I don't mean to stay here all night. Give me the notes at once, or I place you in the hands of an officer."

The determined manner of the clown satisfied Bill that he would keep his word, and, drawing the notes from his breeches-pocket, he slowly said,—

"There—take them—and much good may they do you."

At this moment Margaret entered the room.

In a moment she saw what had occurred, and with a heavy sigh she sat down without speaking a word.

She did not regret that the clown had got back the property; but she feared the brutal passions of her husband, which he would no doubt vent on her.

Charlie concealed the notes in his pocket, and turned to leave.

But the look on the face of the poor columbine stayed him, and he turned and addressed her.

"You know that these notes are the property of the poor child," he said; "and you know that Bill robbed me of them. I have got them back, and if he spits his spite on you he is a cur!"

"If he does," said Buskin Bob, "why, strike me comical if I don't blue about the robbery."

With a look of contempt at Bill, and a glance of pity at Margaret, the two friends left the room and descended the stairs.

CHAPTER · XXIII.

THE RESOLVE TO TAKE A PROVINCIAL THEATRE.

On through the bright moonlight went the two friends, in the direction of the little house which served now for the home of both.

Buskin Bob, since his partnership with Charlie, had a room in the clown's habitation, and wonderful indeed was the change which it had made for him.

Though not a man given to over indulgence, Bob had lodged for the most part of his life at the alehouses.

Having no friends or relatives, he had found that at least the most handy, if not preferable manner of living; but now little Mary, the clown's daughter, acted as housekeeper, and provided for their every want, as far as their precarious means would allow. Bob regretted that he had not thought of Charlie before, and spent his time otherwise than he had done.

Besides the extra comfort, this experienced little Mary was an intelligent and affectionate child, and her smiling face, and generous and willing disposition, spread a charm around the little household.

Bob thought of her as they wended their way along.

He knew that she would be so glad at their success, and he knew also that the money would assist her to many little things she really wanted, and which the earnings of herself and her father could not procure.

In the happiness of others Bob always felt happy himself, and consequently he strode on by the side of his friend with a smile on his face and joy in his heart.

They reached the little cottage, and were welcomed by the little folks with a kindly greeting.

"Well, Harry, my boy," said the clown; "we have succeeded."

"Oh, I am so glad!" exclaimed the youth; "for now Mary can have a new dress."

"That's it," said Bob. "I like to see you think of others, I do. Strike me comical! but I do like you for that—a kind thought for another. You are a brick—you are."

"But the money is yours, Harry; not mine," said Charlie.

"Yes it is," replied the boy. "Dick gave it to you."

"But for your use," said Charlie.

"For all our uses," remarked the lad. "I couldn't be so mean as to wish it all laid out on me. No, no, father—for that is what you are to me—it is yours, to do as you like with."

"And what shall I do with it?" asked the clown.

"Why, buy Mary a new dress with some of it, first. We have been talking about one while you were out."

"Well, I suppose Mary don't object to that?" said Charlie, laying his hand upon the girl's head, and stroking her hair. "Eh, do you?"

"I should like one, father; but Harry wants a pair of boots more than I want a dress."

"Well, Harry, I am glad to say, will be able to have them now, and you can get the dress as well."

"Oh, how nice!" exclaimed the little maid, a beam of pleasure sparkling in her eye.

"Do tell us how you got it away from him?" said the boy, referring to the notes which the clown had so strangely discovered.

The man related the circumstance.

"He was rather surprised to see you, then?" asked Harry.

"Well, rather—eh, Bob?"

"Strike me comical if he wasn't!" said Bob. "What a first-rate ghost he looked, without any make-up, too."

"Yes; but I wonder what he has been doing to his eyes."

"Can't think, and didn't care to ask him, neither," replied Bob.

"Seems as if he'd been burnt," remarked Charlie.

"Looks as if he had fallen with his face in a fat-pot," remarked Bob.

"So it does, but that cannot be, for I don't believe he's been doing anything since he sprained his ankle, or pretended to do so."

"Ah, depend upon it that was only a dodge to get away with the money," said Bob.

"Very likely," said Harry. "But he walked lame after the fall."

"So he did; and he may have hurt himself. Be that as it may, I have no wish to speak further ill of him than he deserves," remarked Charlie.

"Strike me comical if it wasn't a good job for all that you had the stilts on, and happened to twist your ogles into the window."

"And at the very moment, too, when he held one of the notes in his hand," replied Charlie; "I could not have suspected him had I not seen it. But things are to be, I suppose, and it was the hand of Fate which guided me thither at that very moment."

"Strike me comical, you ain't a fatalist, are you?" said Bob, looking hard at his friend.

"I scarcely know," replied Charlie; "I sometimes think there is more than accident, when people are thrown into the presence of that which they would seek; but there, be that as it may, I have got poor Harry's money, and there'll be no need for him, this winter, to go out into the cold streets for a living."

"Oh, I am so glad!" chimed in Mary.

"Are you, my little maid?" said Bob, lifting up his pipe from the hob, where Mary had placed it for him.

"Yes, that I am," she replied.

"And why should you be glad?" continued Bob.

"Because he is so kind to me; and I love him because father loves him, and you love him; and he has got no friends but you and me and father."

"You may well call father my friend!" said Harry, a tear moistening his eye.

"I don't know what I should have done, and where I should have gone, after poor mother died, had he not come to me!"

"Surely it must have been the hand of Fate that led me there at such a moment!" remarked the clown.

Harry sighed; and a tear sparkled for a moment on his eyelid, ere it rolled silently down his cheek.

"Cut it!" said Bob. "Change the subject. The scene is still fresh, and the boy's heart still tender; so bring down the curtain on the pathetic."

Charlie laid his hand on the boy's shoulder caressingly, and looked kindly into his mournful face.

"Harry," he said; "the money I have got back to-night cannot last for ever; and though Dick the Poacher promised to see that you did not want, he may never interest himself again on your behalf, or a thousand things may intervene to prevent him. If we use the money, it will gradually dwindle down, and at last all will have gone; but if it could be invested in any way, by which you might be enabled to get a sufficient profit from its outlay as to find you in food and clothes, that would be the best thing."

"Strike me comical, if you ain't right!" exclaimed Bob. "Keep the capital, and live on the profits."

"He can't do better," said Charlie.

"Yes, he can," said Bob.

"How?"

"If he gets the value of his money, it is as good as the money, ain't it? and can be sold again, if necessary. What a pity it is only winter that's coming on: if it were spring, now, you might do some good, you might."

"How so?" asked Harry.

"Get a show, and work the fairs," said Bob. "Strike me comical! who knows but you might get on as well as Richardson in time. He was once as poor as you, Harry, if not poorer."

"A hundred won't go very far in the purchase of a portable theatre," remarked the clown; "and the money might be better laid out, perhaps, although there's one thing to say, we might all assist in that line, where we could give him no aid in another."

"I should like to be a show proprietor," said Harry, his mind wandering to the genial countenance of Richardson.

"It is very precarious," remarked Charlie; "and no hundred pounds would purchase the booth and provide for the company in dresses. No, no; better rent and not purchase anything of the kind, till luck sets in; and remember that you must lay up six months in the year, and you can't do without food during that time.

"Or we shouldn't have been doing the hanky-panky in the streets, I know," said Bob.

"Nor would Charlie have discovered Dancing Bill," remarked Harry.

"Nor you have been a hundred pounds richer than you were this morning," chimed in Mary. "Oh, Harry, I'm so happy! What a lot of money!"

"Not so much," said Charlie, "but that, without careful management, it will soon dwindle away. To live on it during the winter would never do; when spring came, it would have lost much in bulk. Something that would yield immediate profit is what is necessary."

"You see, the theatres have got all the pull this time of year, and keep it till spring sets fairly in. Strike me comical if I don't think that would be as good investment as any," said Bob, "and the easiest thrown up if it don't pay."

"What?" asked Charlie.

"A small theatre," replied Bob. "Here's four of us, and each of us on the pinch can do a little. Christmas is coming on. There's the pantomimes, and you and I know our business well enough to please an audience in a working town. Besides, you will only rent a theatre, but the chances are you must purchase a booth."

"Humph," exclaimed Charlie, "I don't know but what you are right, after all. If they are managed anything like they will pay during the season, and we have enough experience to judge of how to look after a small concern. But then, if Harry likes it, I expect all that are any good have been let."

"I don't think so. There's the Royal Star, at Chatham, what do you say to that?" asked Bob.

"That might do," said Charlie, "but that all remains with the boy himself."

"Not so," replied Harry. "What you deem best I will agree to, for I know that you will advise for the best."

"You're right, youngster," said Bob, taking his pipe from his mouth, and re-placing it upon the hob. "Charlie is not the man to do wrong wilfully, and whatever he decides on he'll have done for the best—and I say agree to it."

"I shall certainly do so," replied Harry.

"Not if you don't think it will do," said Charlie.

"But I feel convinced that you would propose nothing but what you think would do; and, as you have had much experience, you must know what is best," remarked the boy.

"Perhaps so," replied Charlie. "Yet I might propose that which might be distasteful to you."

"Not so," said Harry; nothing you can say or do will be distasteful to me. I know your generous soul, and I shall ever revere and love you."

"Strike me comical," began Bob, "if you ain't just what a chap ought to be—got a little gratitude in you. Well, there's nothing like it."

"I shall always be grateful for the many kindnesses I have received at his hands," remarked the boy.

Charlie held forth his hand, and the youth grasped it with a fervent pressure. A thrill of gratitude ran through the heart of the poor orphan.

A thrill of pity through the heart of the kind-hearted clown.

A smile lighted up the jolly features of Buskin Bob, and he refilled his pipe.

A gleam of pleasure was in Mary's eye, as her glance rested alternately upon her father and her young friend.

Partaking largely of that generous disposition inherent in her father, like him she felt happy at others' happiness; and the prospect of Harry becoming a proprietor instead of a servant, had in it such a charm that her heart bounded with joy.

Poor child, she knew nothing of the struggles of the poor proprietor to obtain a livelihood. To Mary's ears the word sounded better than servant, yet often—very often—is the servant better off than the master.

He may receive but a paltry pittance for his labours—toil hard and incessantly to gain even this; but how often has the lessee or proprietor, or employer, to sacrifice more than this to obtain the means of paying the little salary.

Often indeed!

The fluctuations in public places of amusement are so great, that even when entered upon at a time when yielding a good surplus, in one week the gains turn to losses, and crowded houses to empty benches.

Still the expenses are as great as hitherto, and even a short continuation of this bad business will break the most enterprising manager.

In many of the provincial towns the theatres are only open a few months in the year, hence some managers possess three or four of these places of entertainment.

There is a good reason for this.

A liberal support may be bestowed upon him at one, and, with a desire to cater well for the amusement of his supporters, he will invest the greater portion of his profits at the next house, in the hopes of drawing a larger audience, and finding supporters when the success of the former house here gives place to empty benches; and, spite of all his expense, all his trouble, all his determination to succeed, his efforts are not appreciated, and the piece—which he has almost ruined himself to produce—has to be withdrawn from the bills, and he finds himself, after days and nights of anxious toil—almost ruined—still fighting bravely on to win the smiles of the fickle goddess Fortune.

What a life of toil, anxiety, hopes and fears!

Bright sunshine to-day, to-morrow Stygian blackness.

And ere the friends retired to their beds that night, they had resolved to "Struggle for Bread" as managers of a provincial theatre.

May success attend them!

But we shall see anon.

CHAPTER XXIV.

THE FRIENDS START IN A NEW LINE OF BUSINESS —AN UNEXPECTED VISITOR.

THERE was a large concourse of people around the doors of the Royal Star, which that evening was to be opened under a new management; and, as the bills set forth, an entertainment second to none ever produced before an enlightend British public.

There was the usual squeezing and thumping at the doors long before the gas was alight; the catcalls and whistling of the frequenters of the gallery; the more demure, solid-looking people who now and then pay a visit to the pit, accompanied by market baskets, enormous reticules and bags filled with viands, and the little bottle and glass without a foot, from which their owners regaled themselves between the acts.

A genuine good humour, however, pervaded the motley assembly, despite the efforts of several of the younger persons to make their way close up to the doors, and get positions which the earlier arrivals occupied.

Various were the comments and speculations made by the crowd upon the somewhat gaudy decorations of the exterior, and the prospects of success of the new management.

The Royal Star had never really answered the expectations of the various managers who had taken it.

It was but a poor paying property at best; but those who loved to pass an evening within its walls were anxious that it should succeed, in order that they might have the place open more than it had hitherto been.

The promises, too, held out by the management were enough to ensure its success, even in that small town; but the people knew very well that their support was necessary, and upon this evening a very liberal one was promised.

Charlie Evans was pacing up and down the little stage, assisting to fit the scenery, and attending to every little want that was necessary, and which, at the last moment, is sure to be discovered; while Buskin Bob was counting out checks in the little money box, listening, with a look of pleasure on his generous countenance, to the noise outside.

Harry, too, was there, and so was little Mary, her fingers aching from the days of stitching which she had had, in mending up the old "props," tacking ribbons here and laces there, fixing feathers, mending pants, sewing up a rent in a doublet, and fastening strings and buttons on the frocks and fleshings.

And she had worked with a will, scarcely giving herself time to rest, so anxious was she that the piece should not fail for the want of proper dressing.

Harry, too, was to play that night. The lady who had sustained the part of the queen in the spectral drama had been engaged expressly for

RERTEAT OF DICK THE POACHER.

the part, and Harry was once more to make his bow as the young page.

He was nervous and fidgetty, and his handsome face wore a look of sadness.

He knew not why, but he felt ill at ease.

A foreboding of something usurped his young mind.

It was not the fear that he would fail in his part.

What, then, could it be?

Alas, he knew not.

Charlie attributed it to anxiety of mind, and Buskin Bob said he'd be all right after a little while.

But as the time wore on he became more and more depressed, and sank into a thoughtful reverie, which was broken only by the noise of the feet of the audience, as they ran over the seats of the pit and gallery in their search for places.

The house was open.

The gas was alight, the orchestra ready to begin; yet there was much to do behind the curtain.

A new scene, painted expressly for the piece, would stick in the groove now, although it had slid easily enough in the morning.

This must be remedied.

Too well Charlie knew the thunder of indignation it would bring down, and he felt they could ill afford, on the first night of their management, to allow even a scene to stick.

Consequently it had to be planed, to allow it to run easy.

Then a feather for a hat could not be found—a sword hilt was loose—and one of the heavy men could not squeeze into a doublet.

The audience were impatient; Charlie and his friends anxious.

But they must begin to time, and so the bell rang for the lights to be highered, and the musicians to begin the overture.

No. 8.

As the gas became brighter, the first round of applause from the audience came to the ears of those behind.

Harry just drew aside the curtain, to take a survey of the house.

It was full; and for the first time a beam of pleasure sparkled in his eye.

If such houses would only continue, he felt sure that success would attend them, and then Charlie, Mary, and Buskin Bob would have no more to depend upon the generosity of a street mob for bread.

As he turned away from the curtain, a figure in one of the boxes at the side raised his head, and glanced spitefully towards the spot.

It was Dancing Bill.

But so changed was he since last we have seen him.

The green shade no longer rested over his eyes.

The smooth-shaven face was covered by a luxuriant crop of hair.

He kept his face buried as much as possible in his breast, as though he wished not to be seen or recognized.

But though so altered in appearance, the same demoniac gleam of his dark eye showed the vengeful spirit beneath.

What had brought him there?

It was not anxiety for the success of the Boy Actor and his friends.

No, for he bit his lip with chagrin as he looked around the well-filled house.

Empty seats would have been more congenial to his mind.

But they were full, and his spirit grew more revengeful each moment.

He drew himself back to the side of the box, and kept his head bowed on his breast, peering out of his upturned eyes.

Though he appeared to see nothing, he saw all that passed.

Once more the prompter's bell rang, and the green baize curtain rose slowly up, revealing to the vision of the audience the pretty little scene with which the piece opened.

Buskin Bob left the money box for one moment, to bestow applause upon our little hero, as he strode on; then darted back, with a smile on his face, to await Charlie Evans, who was to look after the money when the first piece was over.

For Buskin Bob was to appear that night in his juggling entertainment.

The worthy old fellow had been practising for the last fortnight all his old tricks, and the gilded balls and long-bladed knives had been thrown around his head till his arms had ached.

But he cared not for that.

It would save expense, and increase the entertainment; and though he had often vowed never again to have anything to do with his old line of business in his buskin' days, he resolved to render all the aid he could in furnishing a good evening's amusement to the supporters of the Royal Star.

Meantime the spectral drama progressed favourably, round after round of applause being bestowed upon the actors; but—as at Richardson's—it was not till the double combat that the audience became enraptured, and the plaudits mingled with the loud clash of the actors' weapons.

Absurd though it is, these feats are sure to tell, and the more especially when it is "two big un's agin' a little un';" the more juvenile portion of the audience feel more delight in a back fall than in the elocutionary part of the drama.

"Can't he fight!"—"Don't he die fine!"—"Can't he fall straight!"—"Ain't he a stunning crawler!" and a host of similar exclamations may be heard by the young frequenters of the gallery of the minor theatres every evening, thus showing with what they are best pleased.

A skilful manager panders to this taste, without destroying the other portions of the piece, or giving offence to the more intellectual portion of his audience.

He has two classes to please—the intellectual and the ignorant.

Should he study the former, he will raise the curtain to an empty gallery; if the latter, his boxes will present rows of unfilled seats.

Consequently the skilful manager blends the two, giving satisfaction to the public, profit to himself, and often disgust and annoyance to the author, who, in many instances, can only recognize his production by its title.

But it is hard to please all.

Some one must suffer, and, as a rule, the weakest go to the wall.

However, the piece drew to a close, as must all things in the course of time, and the green baize rolled down amid the applause of a very indulgent audience, and had to be drawn up again to enable the company—who all assembled on the stage—to receive that reward for their labours which all, from the highest to the lowest, value so much—the approbation of those in the house.

There are some who assert that they value not applause.

Our friends were none of them.

Had the curtain dropped in silence, the spirits of our friends would have sunk very considerably; but their fears were lightened with smiles, and a feeling of joy was in their hearts, for it outbid their hopes.

The public had appreciated their endeavours to please them, and had acknowledged those endeavours by the shower of warm plaudits which echoed around.

It proved the success of the piece, and the feelings with which the audience viewed them.

And success to them was all in all.

Charlie relieved Buskin Bob of his post in the money box, and the worthy fellow hurried behind to prepare for the entertainment.

A lady had promised to dance, in order to prevent too long a stage wait whilst Bob dressed, but at the last moment sent an apology for not complying with her promise, but informed Charlie that she had prevailed upon another to take her place.

And during the time when Charlie and Bob were in the money box, that person entered the house, and, without seeking an audience of the managers, hurried to the ladies' dressing-room, and speedily announced herself as ready to go on.

Bob heard the music, and the plaudits with which she was greeted, during the time he was dressing; and just as he had tied his slipper, and was about to go on, the figure of a female stood before him.

"You did not expect to see me here, did you, Bob?"

The worthy fellow looked up, and, striking a most ludicrous posture, held up his hands in surprise.

"Strike me comical! you don't say so! What, Margaret? Well I'm blowed!"

"It's me. I little thought who I should find here, when Mrs. Lorners asked me to come in her place."

"And it's much obliged to you I am," said Buskin Bob, rising to his feet. "But how, in the name of fortune, is it that Dancing Bill let you come?"

"He don't know anything about it," replied Margaret.

"But he'll hear of it, safe enough," said Bob, "and then —"

"Then what?" said the woman.

"He'll — you know. He hates us all, he does."

"You think he will beat me?"

"Yes."

"But he won't," said the woman.

"I hope he won't," said Bob.

But the worthy fellow thought he would, and felt sorry that the poor woman should have laid herself open to his brutality.

"I tell you he'll never strike me again," said Margaret, "he has had enough of that."

"Oh?" exclaimed Bob, looking questioningly up at the woman before him.

"When you had left that night, after making him give up the notes, he vented his ill-humour upon me, and, goaded to madness, I returned the blow."

"You did?"

"I did."

"Strike me comical, you are a brick!" exclaimed Bob, fixing upon the poor columbine a look of admiration.

"Yes, I struck him again."

"What then?" asked Bob eagerly.

"He was frightened."

"I knew him to be a cur," began Bob, but recollecting that the woman before him was his wife, he hesitated.

"And I know him to be one, too," said Margaret. "I could bear with him no longer, and I left him."

"And you don't live with him now, eh?" exclaimed Bob.

"No," said the woman, "and never will again. Thank heaven, I can earn my own living."

"So you can."

"And so I will, Bob. I have born every species of insult and injury at his hands, but I can bear it no longer."

"Well done, Margaret. He is a bad fellow, and ill deserves so good a wife. But I must go on now—you won't go yet. Charlie's round in front, go and see him. There may perhaps be an opening here for you, if we can only make one, and the house will pay."

And the good fellow left the room in high glee at what Margaret had told him.

"Ah," he thought, "he trod on the worm till it turned and stung him. I know who'll be the gainer by the separation, and it won't be Dancing Bill. No, no, he won't have her money to play with, nor her body to practise his pugilistic propensities upon. I'm glad of it, strike me comical if I ain't!"

And as the curtain once more rose, Buskin Bob stepped on to the stage, and made his bow.

The eyes of Dancing Bill followed every move and trick of the pantaloon, as he went through his business, and malignant was the scowl that gathered on his brow.

Great, indeed, had been his surprise when he saw his wife.

Like all evil-minded men, he was a jealous one, and the sight of his wife among those whom he styled his enemies, was galling in the extreme.

He had resolved to be revenged on our hero and his friends for the loss of the notes, which his guilty mind had prompted him to steal from the dressing-room, and his feelings were now, if possible, more bitter towards his old mates than ever.

He resolved never to lose sight of them till he had done them every injury his ignoble nature could invent.

But he always had the fear of Dick the Poacher before his eyes.

He had recovered the injuries inflicted upon him by the fire in the hidden passage, and was only awaiting some favourable opportunity to be revenged on the pantomimists.

He had feared that Charlie might suspect him of having in his possession the packet spoken of by Dick, as well as the notes, and great indeed was the surprise he felt, when the friends left him without one word respecting them.

They had no suspicion that he had a knowledge of the passage.

This fact was gratifying to him.

He might do them an injury yet.

So he watched and waited.

But while so doing he heard of their being about to open the Royal Star.

He felt that he might have done the same had he been allowed to retain the notes.

They might have laid the foundation of a fortune for him, and perhaps would do so for their owners.

But he resolved to plot their ruin.

And, disguised, he visited the theatre that night for that purpose.

Each burst of applause bestowed upon them acted only as so many incentives to his evil passions.

But how could he accomplish his wishes?

That was the question he kept asking himself.

He saw but one means, and that was— Fire!

Could he succeed in firing the house, his revenge would indeed be great, and the ruin of those he was striving to effect sure.

But how?

He would wait till the house was over, and then, as the audience left the theatre, he might find means of carrying out his hellish designs.

The light, flimsy curtains of the box in which he sat should be the torch to fire the pile on which the hopes of the friends rested.

And he drew back behind them and waited.

He had not to wait long.

———

CHAPTER XXV.

THE INCENDIARY FIRE—DICK THE POACHER APPEARS AT AN OPPORTUNE MOMENT.

THE green baize curtain descended slowly on the last act of the *petite* drama which closed the first night of the new management.

The audience rose from their seats, and commenced to leave the theatre; the musicians packed up their instruments, and departed from the orchestra by the little door under the stage; the gas was lowered, and the benches were fast showing their white deal tops, as they were vacated by their yawning and stiffened occupants.

But there is a quick movement among the crowd—cries and shrieks rise from the throats of those who have not yet left the theatre, and then, in one wild, awe-striking tone, rings the loud shout—

"Fire! Fire!"

A broad glare of light illumines the darkened theatre, and spreads confusion and horror around.

The thin curtains of the box in which the bearded man had sat are in a blaze, and the flames are rising to the roof!

Panic-stricken, those who have not yet escaped rush towards the door, and block it in a solid mass; while shrieks and cries fill the air, mingled with the groans of those who, having fallen, are being trampled to death.

But Dancing Bill—where is he?

The box he occupied is empty.

Amid the confusion rings clear and loud the voice of a man, exhorting the people to be calm.

Calm! with that sheet of flame rising into the air! Calm! with death in all its terrors staring them in the face!

Strong men are blanched with fear, and weak women fall fainting to the floor, to be trampled on by those behind them.

Only that flimsy curtain is on fire, but men stand appalled as the sheet of flame illumines the place.

Charlie Evans and Buskin Bob are struggling to reach the box from the pit, heedless of the danger to which they expose themselves.

The curtains of the next box have caught, and the fire is spreading and threatening destruction to the whole house.

The friends are in an agony of fear. They feel that they are powerless to avert the threatened destruction of the house, when the figure of a man bounds hastily over the seats in the pit.

He has lost his hat in his struggles to force his way to the fire, and his long black curling locks fall in disorder over his forehead.

He clears the seats with the rapidity of lightning, and takes one terrific leap among the burning muslin.

He tears the lighted fabric down, and hurls it into the pit, calling upon Charlie and Bob to trample out the fire.

His voice rings loud and clear around the almost empty theatre, and as the light of the burning mass glows upon his face, it reveals to the pantomimists the features of Dick the Poacher.

He it was who fought his way through the panic-stricken mass at the door, and struggled to save the house from the doom intended for it.

But having accomplished his object, and seen the last spark extinguished, he sinks exhausted in the box at which the fire originated.

Those who had been unsuccessful in their endeavours to escape, now fell back into the theatre, with blanched cheeks and palpitating hearts.

They see that the danger is past, and they call loudly for vengeance on he who had fired the curtain.

For that it was the work of an incendiary all believe.

Not a jet of gas could get near it—it had clearly been set on fire.

By whom?

One man only had occupied that box, but he was gone!

He had been seen by many, but recognized only by one.

And that one was Margaret, the wife of Dancing Bill.

She had recognized him as she stood at the wings, watching the labours of Buskin Bob.

Knowing the vindictive feelings her husband entertained towards those who had opened the house that night, she felt sure that Dancing Bill had done this wicked deed.

But should she betray him?

He was her husband, though a brutal one to her; but she had sworn to love and cherish him, in weal and woe, could she, then, be the one to denounce him?

Spite of all his ill-treatment to her, she still would shield him.

She would not harm him—him who had so often harmed her.

She was a woman; and with a woman's love possessed a woman's feelings.

And those were—spite of all she had had to bear—mercy.

This deed of Dancing Bill's would have rid her for ever of the worthless wretch, yet she hesitated to denounce him.

She had sworn to stand by him, and she would not violate her vow.

But still she despised him, for he had proved himself unworthy her—unworthy the title of man.

And with a heavy sigh, she turned away and left the theatre.

In a few moments Dick recovered from the exertions he had made, and, swinging himself over the front of the box, dropped into the pit of the theatre, by the side of Charlie and Bob, who were gazing upon the remains of the curtains at their feet.

The good-hearted clown extended his hand to Dick, and muttered his thanks for the service he had done them.

Then silently they made their way over the stage, to where Harry and little Mary stood clasped in each other's arms, and mingling their tears together.

Harry had recognized the features of the gipsy-looking Dick, and he rushed forward to meet him.

"Oh, thank you! thank you!" he gasped, looking up into the bronzed face of the poacher. "If it hadn't been for you the house would have been burnt down. I am so glad you were here—so very glad."

"And so am I," replied Dick. "I promised you I would be by your side in the hour of danger, and while heaven spares me, I will keep my word."

"You have done so nobly," remarked Charlie, "though not having seen you since the night when you gave me the notes, I feared something had happened, and we should meet no more."

"It seems that Providence has destined me to be near this child when ill assails him, for had this occurred a day earlier, I had not been here."

"Thank heaven it did not!" said Bob, "for had it not been for you, the house would have gone."

"But explain," said Dick, after a pause, "how is it that I find you here?"

"The money you gave me to support this boy has been devoted to opening this house, where I hope to be enabled to gain a livelihood for us all."

"We had a good house, and every prospect of a successful season," said Buskin Bob, "but I fear this accident to-night will do us much injury."

"Accident!" exclaimed Dick. "No, no; that was no accident, it was the work of an incendiary."

"I fear so too," said Charlie; "but who would do so base a thing?"

"Many," replied Dick. "Worse deeds have been done ere this."

"But why should anyone wish to do us an injury, who never harmed them?"

"I cannot say," replied the poacher; "but remember, there are those who wish that boy no good, and would gladly see him out of the way. But I say not those have done it, still, I know what men will do; they will stop at nothing to rid themselves of those who they believe stand in their light, even when their hopes, by injuring another, lead them to the contemplation of deeds which, if discovered, would place a halter round their necks."

"It is an unfortunate circumstance for us," remarked Charlie, "as it may make people fearful, and thus give us half-empty benches to play to."

"Let us hope not," replied the poacher. "I should be sorry to see you fail, for you are a good-hearted, feeling man, and deserve the sympathy of all right-minded people."

"I strive to do so," replied Charlie.

"And you do," said Dick. "I am not a man to think too well of others, for I have felt the stings of some—stings that have sunk deeply in my heart, and cankered in the wound; but you have shown yourself a man in the interest you have taken in that poor child."

"I have done but my duty," said Charlie.

"But you have done it nobly, my friend. No thought of gain or self-interest actuated your motives."

"None," said Charlie.

"It was but the nobleness of your nature," continued Dick. "Poor yourself, yet you could offer to keep him, knowing full well that every crust bestowed was taken from yourself. This is more than what most men call duty—it is an act that ennobles a man, and proves that there is some of that feeling left which the Almighty implanted in our breasts, but which our selfish passions eradicate."

The confusion having now entirely subsided, and the theatre emptied of all save those on the stage, Charlie, Buskin Bob, and Dick the Poacher inspected every part of the edifice, to see that all lights were out, and everything completely safe.

Finding all was right, they returned to Harry and his little companion.

"Will you come home with us," asked the clown of Dick, "and have a little bit of supper?"

"Oh, do come?" added the boy.

"My boy," said the poacher, "if I refuse, it is not from any wish to refuse you, but I will say this, that Dick the Poacher has no right in the houses of honest men."

"And why not?" asked Charlie.

"Am I not an outcast?" said Dick.

"Are you not a man?" asked Charlie.

"I was once, ere wrong and oppression drove me without the pale of society," said Dick, bitterly.

"And are now," said Charlie.

"I forfeited the title," replied Dick.

"And redeemed it by your actions to-night," said the good-hearted clown.

"It can never be redeemed," said the poacher, "till —"

Dick hesitated.

"Till what?" asked the clown.

"No matter," exclaimed Dick, "time will explain all."

And he turned away.

"Stay," said Charlie, placing his hand on the arm of the poacher. "We must not part thus. I have much to tell you—much to ask. Come with us. Our home is humble, and its fare rough, but a kindly welcome shall greet you there."

"Not now," said Dick.

"Why not?" asked Charlie.

"It must not be," replied the other.

"Oh, it must—you must come!" said Harry, in pleading tones. "Do persuade him, Mary—do. He is so kind—so good; and see what he has done to-night—saved the theatre from fire, and us all from ruin. Do ask him, Mary—do ask him?"

Little Mary approached the gipsy-looking being, and placed her small hand in his, and, looking pleadingly in his face, she murmured—

"Oh, do come, sir—oh, don't refuse?"

Dick looked down upon the pretty upturned face, so pleadingly fixed on his, and a tear, like a glistening dew-drop, sparkled in his eye.

He clasped the little girl in his strong arms, and lifted her up.

But quickly—almost roughly—he set her down again, saying,—

"No, no! it would be contamination! The lips of a branded felon must not desecrate the cheek of loveliness and innocence."

"But you will come—you will, won't you?" still pleaded the child.

There was a struggle going on in the breast of the strong man.

But he turned away.

"Not now," he murmured, "not now. When Justice tears the bandage from her eyes, and judges me truly, then—then you shall not ask in vain. We shall meet again, but the stain of a prison is now upon my hand, and the black spot shall not cast a shadow in an honest man's home."

And ere the friends could prevent him he was gone.

CHAPTER XXVI.

DANCING BILL AND HIS WIFE—THE REQUEST—THE REFUSAL AND THE THREAT—THE BULLY COWED.

WITH aching heart, and tearful eye, poor Margaret left the theatre, which the intrepidity of Dick the Poacher had saved from ruin, and strode along the dark street in the direction of her lodgings.

Acutely, indeed, did she feel the wrong her base and revengeful husband had endeavoured to inflict on the Boy Actor and his guardian, and her woman's heart rose in love for those as her husband's revenge increased.

But the marriage tie held her soul in bondage, and the yearnings of her heart to do justice to those so deeply wronged were fettered by it.

Though Dancing Bill had broken every vow—cancelled every sacred obligation, still the victim of his cruelty clung to the vows she had made before the altar.

She felt, as his wife, she must shield him from even those whose ruin he sought.

The fetters of Hymen bound her, tongue, heart, and soul—she was a wife.

A wife!

And to whom?

A villain, whose every word—whose every act degraded the name of husband and of man!

Human statutes are founded upon divine laws, and such, doubtless, they should be; for what higher authority and guide can we have than the laws of God?

Yet our law-makers have found that divine doctrines must be set aside, in mercy to those who suffer under their binding influence; and a wise parliament!—heaven be thanked!—have found it necessary to make a decree, whereby a poor, suffering, ill-used woman may snap the fetters which bind her, heart and soul, to a thing who sinks so low in the scale of humanity, as to degrade his manhood below the level of the brute creation, and contaminate by his evil influences the righteous and the just.

But at the time of which we write there was no such law—at least, not for the poor, and Margaret had not the means to break her bonds.

Her cup of bitterness had been filled to overflowing.

It is the last straw which breaks the camel's back; it was the last blow which caused the poor columbine to turn upon her master.

She had flown from his presence, resolved never more to return.

At first, Dancing Bill cared little for the circumstance, his selfish mind leading him to believe that it would better his circumstances, as he would only have himself now to support.

But a few days told a different tale.

He had now but what little money he himself could earn, and not the handling of the proceeds of his wife's toil.

And he also discovered that he was unable to make a shilling go as far as Margaret could do.

Then he turned his attention to Gripe.

But not knowing where to seek that worthy, he could not dispose of the packet he had suffered so much to obtain, and he had to struggle harder to get the means of a livelihood.

Then for the first time he regretted the loss of his wife.

But not one pang of compunction for the acts which had driven her from him.

These things, combined with the knowledge that the Boy Actor and his friends were now in a position to better their circumstances, galled his selfish mind almost to madness, and he sought relief to his bitter feeling in endeavouring to encompass their ruin.

And he visited the Royal Star on the first night of the new management for that purpose alone.

How he succeeded we already know.

He had escaped from the house ere the first alarm was raised, and was hurrying away from the scene of his villany ere the curtain had burst fairly into a flame.

Margaret walked slowly on, her head bent, and pressing the little bundle in her arms which contained the dress she had worn on the boards that night, when her progress was suddenly stopped by a man standing before her.

Starting, she looked up.

Dancing Bill stood before her.

But so different to what he had appeared while sitting in the box at the Royal Star.

The massive growth of whiskers had disappeared, and he was as smooth-faced as ever.

Margaret strove to pass him, but he placed himself before her.

"Let me pass," she said.

"I have something to say to you," he replied, still standing before her.

"I wish to have nothing further to do with you," replied his wife.

"Perhaps not," exclaimed Bill; "but recollect I am your husband, and I command you to listen to me."

"Husband!" exclaimed the woman, bitterly and sarcastically.

"Yes—husband," replied the man.

"Say rather master!" said Margaret.

"Well, then, master, if you like it better," replied Dancing Bill, half savagely. "Come home!"

"I shall not," said the woman, in a determined tone.

"You won't?"

"No."

"We'll see," exclaimed the brutal fellow.

Margaret again endeavoured to move on, but Bill grasped her by the hand, and held her stationary.

"Let me go," she exclaimed, "or it'll be the worse for you."

"Do you threaten?" hissed the harlequin.

"I will perform," she said, "if you do not take your hand from off me."

"I say you shall come!" he said.

"And I say I will not," said the woman, firmly. "Had you wanted me to live with you, you should have acted like a man. Let go of me, or I will tear your face for you! You have struck me a hundred times, and I meekly submitted to your brutality, but I do so no longer; raise your hand to me, and I will leave the marks of my nails upon your face, and call upon the first man that passes to chastise the thing that can beat a woman!"

So determined were the tones of the woman, that Bill instantly released her arm, but still kept his position before her.

"Will you come home?" he asked.

"No, Bill," she replied, "I will not."

"You are my wife, and the law will compel you to return."

"Will it?"

"Yes."

"And you would seek its aid to compel me?" asked the woman, sarcastically.

"I will," replied the man.

"You dare not!" said his wife.

"Dare not!"

"Yes, dare not!" she replied.

"I am your husband," said Bill.

"But I am your master," said the woman, pointedly.

"You?"

"Yes—me!"

"We shall see," said Bill.

"We shall see," exclaimed the woman, "if you have the courage to try the point, but you have not."

"But I have, and will," exclaimed Bill.

"Try it, and take the consequences."

"What consequences?" said Bill.

"The consequences of your villany to-night," exclaimed Margaret. "Wretch! do you think I did not recognize you in the box, in spite of the manner in which you strove to hide your identity."

"What box?" stammered Bill, turning pale.

"What box?" exclaimed the woman, contemptuously, "the box you fired. Mean-spirited villain! I recognized you, and, by heaven, if you dare attempt to molest me I will denounce you, and hand you over to the mercies of that law you have dared to threaten me with!"

"Ah!" exclaimed Bill, threateningly. But he stopped suddenly, and added,—

"Margaret, you are mad—you know not what you say!"

"Liar and villain! Stand aside, and let me pass."

"Margaret—"

"Let me pass, I say, if you would not have me denounce you as the villain whose revengeful hand has been raised to hurl ruin and desolation upon those who never harmed you. What have you to answer for! the lives and limbs of the poor beings crushed and trampled to death, through your hellish work. Fiend! stand from my path, or my voice shall bring the officers of justice upon you!"

"Hush!" exclaimed the now thoroughly affrighted man.

"Stand aside then," said the woman.

"Margaret, hear me!" pleaded the trembling man.

"I will have no more to do with you," said Margaret. "The climax of your villany has come—henceforth we are strangers."

"Will you leave me thus?" he exclaimed, as Margaret passed him.

"I leave you," she replied, "to your own conscience. But beware no harm comes to that boy, or those who would befriend him, or this night's work shall be hurled upon you, and a felon's doom shall rid society for ever of so base and unfeeling a villain!"

And with a haughty stride she passed on, leaving her crest-fallen and guilty husband fearful to further molest her.

He would have struck her, but he dared not—the master had now become the slave!

But bitter thoughts rankled in his heart, and wicked ideas usurped his soul.

His evil passions had led him on till the crime of murder stained his soul!

The brand of Cain was on his brow, and the victims of that night's work called aloud for vengeance.

And one there was who could bring down upon his head its overwhelming fury.

That one was his wife.

The woman he had sworn to love and cherish, but whom he had insulted and outraged.

She scorned and defied him, would she denounce him?

His cheek paled at the thought, and his heart trembled.

Already, in imagination, he felt the rope of the hangman around his neck, and he could scarcely breathe.

How could he save himself from the doom he feared.

There was but one way.

Death!

But to whom?

The only evidence of his crime—Margaret, his wife!

And by what means could her death be encompassed?

The demon in his soul whispered:—

"Murder!"

He shuddered at the thought. Could he perpetrate so fearful a crime?

The demon answered—

"Already is your soul stained with blood—already art thou damned!"

Could such a deed be blacker than those he had already perpetrated?

No!

Then Margaret must die!

The crime of that night would then be buried in mystery, for there would be none to accuse him.

The only witness would be removed, and he would be saved!

How many have thought so before and since —but how few have escaped.

"Murder will out," for the all-powerful finger of a wonderful Providence points out the perpetrator of the deed, and weaves around him a web from whose meshes he cannot escape, and justice slumbers not till the crime is expiated upon the gallows.

But, like others, Dancing Bill felt sure of escape, and he resolved that Margaret should die.

And by his hand—the hand that should have shielded her from every harm, protected her from every pang.

He walked moodily on towards his lodgings, the determination he had made every moment taking firmer hold upon him.

He resolved not to lose sight of her till he had accomplished his hellish purpose, and her life's blood flowed at his feet.

But when should the deed be done?

He would watch and wait.

The late hours which her profession led her to keep, would be favourable to his purpose, and he resolved to track her footsteps till an opportune moment.

CHAPTER XXVII.

DANCING BILL DISGUISES HIMSELF FOR A PURPOSE
—THE STORM—THE MURDER—THE RECOGNITION.

WITH the resolve he had formed embedded in his heart, Dancing Bill entered his lodgings, and threw himself upon the bed.

But he slept not! His evil passions kept him awake throughout the greater portion of the night, and when, at last, the drowsy god visited his eyelids, his mind still reverted to the scene enacted that night, and the wicked resolve he had formed of taking the life of his poor, heart-broken wife.

Morning came, and he awoke from a slumber that refreshed not, and found himself as determined as ever.

Throughout the day he was wretched and miserable. The least noise sounded in his ears like claps of thunder, and he started ever and anon without any apparent cause.

His nerves were shaken, and his guilty conscience smote him till he bordered upon distraction.

Evening came, and he attired himself as usual—save that he drew over the legs of his stockings a pair of gaiters, which he had often worn in the pantomimes in which he had played.

Dancing Bill, besides being a dancer and pantomimist, had sustained many characters in dramas, farces, and interludes.

He had never been very great in this line of business, yet had been sufficiently handy to get many a night's salary, when he could procure nothing in his ordinary line, consequently Bill had a small wardrobe; and as he was one who would never lend a "prop" to a fellow "pro," and took great care of them himself, he had many which were of great service to him.

And one of these were the gaiters we mentioned.

He then took from the box in which he kept his "props" a smock frock, and a red wig and whiskers, which he tied up in his handkerchief into a small bundle, and left the house.

But he had not gone far when he paused for a moment, then turned back.

Gaining his room, he once more opened the box, and took therefrom a long, thin stage dagger.

Drawing it from the sheath, he felt its point, and a growl of dissatisfaction escaped him.

The edge was not of sufficient keenness.

He threw up the window and sharpened it upon the sill.

At length, being satisfied that he had rendered it fit for his purpose, he closed the window, repossessed himself of the little bundle, and, secreting the dagger in his breast, once more left the house.

It was fast growing dark, and the day—which had been sultry and oppressive—was closing in with every indication of a storm.

Dark clouds were rising, and a sulphurous odour pervaded the air.

But Dancing Bill heeded it not.

The clouds were not so dark as his soul, for it was bent on murder.

He had learned on the previous day the movements of his wife, and he now bent his steps in the direction of the place where that night she was engaged to dance.

It was at an entertainment in an Assembly Room near Edmonton, and in that direction he now bent his steps.

His way lay through narrow lanes and over broad fields—at least, such was the course he chose, to avoid observation, which he might have met with in the high road.

About the centre of one of these lanes he paused, and, taking the smock frock from his bundle, attired himself therein.

Then he put on the carrotty wig and whiskers, and drawing his hat down upon his head, looked the countryman to perfection.

Dancing Bill could have taken to the high road now in safety, so completely was he metamorphosed, that his most intimate friend would have failed to discover the lineaments of Dancing Bill, the harlequin, in the country-looking man he appeared to be.

But Dancing Bill kept on his way through lane and field for some time longer, then he made his way into the high road, and entered a small roadside inn, about a mile from the place where his wife that night was engaged to dance.

Calling for some refreshment, he sat down in a little room at the side of the bar, and became buried in thought.

But those thoughts were not of mercy.

They were what would be the best means to avoid detection of the crime he intended perpetrating.

The hours flew by, and Dancing Bill drank till he was half intoxicated.

His eyes ever and anon wandered to the old eight-day clock in a corner of the room, and when the hands pointed out the hour of ten, he shifted his position to a seat by the window.

Raising one corner of the dirty red curtain, he peered into the road.

There were few passers-by, but Bill's eyes followed them eagerly.

In this manner he continued to look from the window of the little room, of which he had been the sole occupant since his entrance, till the figure of a female passed the window in the direction of Tottenham.

For a moment his eyes followed the figure along the dark road, and when it could be no longer seen, Dancing Bill rose from his seat.

His face was pale, and his limbs trembled.

Drawing his hat low down over his forehead, he strode from the room, through the little bar, into the road.

Casting an anxious glance behind him, he darted swiftly on, till the female figure whom he had watched from the window once more came in sight.

Then he slackened his speed, so as to keep about the same distance between them.

He felt assured that the woman in advance of him was Margaret.

The being whom that night he had resolved to murder!

She carried, as on the night before, the little bundle under her arm, and this tended the more to convince him that it was her he sought.

Had it not been for this circumstance, he would have gone up to her for the purpose of seeing her features, as in the dim light he could not be certain of her lineaments.

But the dress, carriage, and bundle were sufficient, and he followed on, with his hand grasping the handle of the small dagger.

THE VICTIM OF THE HARLEQUIN SEEKS SHELTER FROM THE STORM.

Along the high road, never for one moment losing sight of his intended victim—casting anxious glances around him, and impatiently awaiting the first favourable opportunity of putting his diabolical intention into practice—Dancing Bill followed his unsuspecting victim, till she had arrived at the legendary trees, planted on Page Green, and better known by the name of the Seven Sisters.

It was at this moment that the first flash of lightning illuminated the dark clouds, and lit up the country in all directions.

Simultaneously with the flash, a loud clap of thunder reverberated through the air, and, as though all the portals of the skies had been opened at the same moment, the long pent-up rain descended in torrents.

The woman rushed from the high road, and took up a position beneath the trees, to shelter herself from the fearful storm.

Dancing Bill followed in the long grass.

The fury of the elements drowned his footsteps, and keeping behind, he was himself unobserved.

Stealthily, yet tremblingly, he stole behind the large tree against which the woman leaned, and the lightning—which now followed in quick successive flashes—lit up the spot in gorgeous magnificence, as it played among the fast-falling foliage of those giant trees.

An exclamation of fear escaped the woman's lips as each successive flash darted across her vision.

With fear and trembling she clung closer to the massive trunk of the tree, and with stealthy strides the assassin drew each moment nearer to his intended victim.

The warring of the elements awed, but at the same time strengthened the project of the harlequin.

In the noise caused by the thunder and the rain, the cries of the victim would be drowned; and on such a fearful night it was not likely that anyone would be about.

We have said that Dancing Bill was a superstitious man, and this circumstance he looked upon not as an omen of evil to him, but of good.

And as this conviction grew upon his mind, his nerves became strengthened and his resolves more firm.

Gradually he worked his way round the tree, till his arm could reach the unsuspecting woman, who, all unconscious of the fate awaiting her, stood tremblingly wishing for the abatement of the storm.

Closer—closer—crept the assassin.

No. 9.

He drew the small sharpened dagger from its sheath.

Then he paused.

The words of Shakespeare forced themselves upon his mind:—

> "If I put out thy light,
> Where is that Promethean heat
> That shall again rekindle," etc.

But then the thought of the secret known only to her came across him, and he hesitated no longer.

He crept nearer.

He raised the glittering steel.

But again he paused.

"Thou shalt do no murder" rang in his ears, but his imagination conjured up the phantom gallows to which she could consign him.

He hesitated no longer.

He still crept nearer the shivering woman.

His breath almost fanned her cheek.

She, all unheedless, watched the rain as it descended in sheets, and listened with terror to the awful roll of the thunder as it died away in the distance.

He was close to her now—so close that the shining steel glittered above her head.

There was no one near to see the deed.

His grasp tightened on the handle of the weapon.

One step nearer he crept.

He held his breath.

Then—down—down descended his arm, and the glittering steel was buried in the bosom of his victim!

A lurid flash of lightning lit up the heavens, and the tree belched forth a sudden flame.

And the shriek of the murdered woman was hushed in the loud report of heaven's artillery!

As she fell, Dancing Bill fell with her.

The lightning had struck him down!

Down by the side of her he had stabbed!

And his face was covered with the hot blood which oozed from the wound in her breast.

With a cry of horror he sprang to his feet: with a cry of agony the woman also arose, and leaned against the now blighted trunk, bereft of its foliage and branches.

Another flash, and the white face of his victim met his gaze!

He stood appalled, and trembled in every limb.

Another flash! and the lineaments of the murdered woman were distinctly visible.

With a yell of horror he sprang back.

He grasped a tree for support.

The dagger, which he still retained, fell from his grasp, and he hid his face in his hands.

Hid it, to shut out the glare of those eyes, now fixed so reproachfully upon him.

Hid it, that he might not see the victim of his work—his passions.

Hid it, that he might not gaze upon the innocent being whom his ruffian hand had struck, and whom he had mistaken for his wife!

It was not Margaret!

It was the woman for whom she had danced the night before at the Royal Star, and who in return had danced for her that night!

Dancing Bill saw it all in a moment, and strove to fly, but his limbs refused their office, and he was unable to leave the spot.

The dying woman approached him.

He could not fly!

A shudder ran through his frame, but he was powerless to move.

She seized him by the arm and looked into his face, but he could not stir.

The agonies of death were upon her, and she clutched at his face.

The wig and whiskers were torn away, yet he could not move.

The lightning flashed again, and lit up the glassy eyes of the woman with an unearthly glare.

"Ah, murderer!" she gasped, "I know you you—you are Bill Simmons! Wretch! a curse rest on you for this deed! Oh! heaven save me. —I—I—Oh!"

The thunder drowned the remainder of her words, and as its echoes died away over the fields, she fell back upon the wet grass—dead!

The light of life's beacon had gone out: the last ray had shone upon the face of the murderer, and lit up to his conscience the deed his blackened soul had led him to perpetrate, then had vanished, leaving his mind in blackness and despair.

Each successive flash revealed to his fascinated gaze the bloodstained and murdered woman at his feet, and the thunder, in loud and angry tones, seemed to upbraid him for his villany.

With a cry of horror, he seized the dagger he had dropped, and fled from the spot into the high road.

Fled from the sight of that pale face and bleeding form!

But could he flee from his conscience?

No!

Sleeping and waking that deed would haunt him, till he expiated it upon the scaffold.

Yet no one had seen the deed.

But the evidences of his guilt were clasped in that dead woman's hands, to rise in judgment against him.

CHAPTER XXVIII.

DICK RESOLVES TO TRACE THE PAPERS—HIS VISIT THE MANOR.

DICK THE POACHER made his way from the little theatre with a sad and heavy heart, for the endeavour which had been made to injure the boy Harry and his friends, had somewhat damped his ordinary devil-me-care spirit.

From the time that we saw him at Richardson's show, till that which brought him to the aid of the managers while the burning curtains were causing destruction to the house, Dick had suffered incarceration in gaol for the crime of poaching.

Crime! said we?

Is it a crime for man to take of that which Providence sent for his food?

Shall one man hoard up, for his own pleasure, that which a beneficent Creator sent for the benefit of all?

It would seem that the law denies the right of the poor to obtain the food with which this bountiful earth teems, and which heaven sent for the use of man; so Dick had to suffer imprisonment for taking that which was sent to feed man.

Not that he took it from those who required it, but because the law says that one man shall hold all that is on his lands, spite of the hunger without.

So Dick went to prison for snaring a rabbit, and Gripe prosecuted, in the name of his master.

It was his duty—at least, so the little man said, and as such he was bound to do it.

Bound by duty to prosecute the man whom the day before he bargained with for the mysterious papers.

But Gripe always did his duty, spite of fear or consequences; but in this instance he felt not only his duty, but his interest, demanded that he should prosecute the poacher.

Dick had threatened him, but the smooth talking Mr. Gripe had laughed him to scorn.

He had sold his power to the steward, and Gripe could now pay him back the grudge he owed him.

So he persevered, and Dick was sent for a few months to prison.

Confinement, to the wild, free nature of Dick was torture unbearable, and his health gave way under it.

His cheeks, blooming with the tint of health, became pale, and his eyes sank deeply in his head.

But he bore up, and vowed that he would make the steward suffer for the pain he had inflicted upon him.

And Dick was not the man to forego his intentions, or break his word.

On the day of his liberation he had sought the passage, and to his horror discovered that it had been entered in his absence, and the papers abstracted.

At first he thought the clown had been there, but that thought was quickly obliterated.

Other things besides the packet were gone.

He knew nothing of Charlie Evans, save what he had learned in the two interviews he had with the pantomimist, but he had then learned enough to satisfy him that if Charlie had really been in the passage, he would have scorned to take anything but the packet.

So firm was he in this conviction, that he knew some one else had been there.

But who?

He fancied that, by some means, either Gripe or his master had learned the secret.

He trembled as this thought crossed his mind, for then he would be powerless to cope with them, or aid the Boy Actor.

He resolved to find out, if possible, into whose hands they had fallen.

Gripe or Henley, he felt certain; yet how should they suspect or discover the hiding place?

Doubtless, he thought, they had discovered the fraud he had practised upon them both, and knew that he still possessed the documents; but how they had made the discovery of their whereabouts puzzled him not a little.

They must have watched him, and thus discovered the secret of the underground passage.

He feared for the injury the possession of these papers would do to the poor nephew; for too well he knew the unscrupulous character of the master and his steward.

Besides, once in their possession, he had much to fear for himself, as he would then no longer possess any hold upon them.

The inveterate hatred which they both bore him, and the desire which they both cherished

of getting him completely out of the way, they would be enabled to carry out, unless he again wrested them from their hands.

But how was he to discover which of them had them?

This somewhat puzzled him, but he determined to find out by some means or another.

He resolved to intimidate Gripe into a confession, should other means fail.

He doubted not that he would be able to do this, as he felt certain that, to possess the packet which Dick had sold to him for the genuine one, the steward had made use of his master's money.

Under threats of exposing him to Henley, Dick believed he could work on his fears.

And with this resolve in his mind, he made his way to Barnstable, a few nights after that on which he had done such signal service to the managers of the Royal Star.

It was about ten o'clock at night when he arrived at the large swing gate which gave entrance to the grounds.

Warmed by his long walk, and somewhat fatigued withal, he paused, and leant against the low rails which surrounded the beautiful grounds in which the house stood.

For some time he looked upon the different windows, so that he might judge by the lights what persons were in the house.

The squire's room was in darkness, and Dick felt sure that that personage was not within the mansion.

But the room assigned to Gripe was lighted, and Dick resolved to seek that gentleman, without, if possible, making his presence known to anyone else.

With this intention, he walked some distance past the gate, and climbed over the wall into the grounds.

Instead of crossing the lawn, he kept within the shadow of the trees which bordered it, and took a circuitous path to the house.

It was not long ere he arrived beneath the window of the room occupied by the worthy steward.

Dick cautiously crept up to the glass, and looked in.

Mr. Gripe was seated at his desk, which stood upon a large table in the centre of the room, dotting down various figures in a large vellum-bound book.

His back was to the window, and his attention seemed wholly wrapped in the work before him.

"If I could only get in without disturbing him, or arousing anyone else," muttered the poacher to himself, "I might so take him by surprise that before he could collect himself, I might learn all I wish to know. I'll try, anyhow. If the worst comes to the worst, I can but run for it."

So Dick placed his hand upon the sash, and tried to raise it.

It gave no resistance to the little force he used, and Dick felt satisfied that it was not fastened.

Looking around him, to make sure that no one was about the grounds, he raised the sash gently, but at the same time quickly, and it slid up noiselessly.

Gripe had not heard it, but the cold air entering the warm room caused him to shiver and turn.

A cry rose to his lips, but Dick leaped through the window, and grasped the little steward by the throat.

"Hush!" he exclaimed.

"What—wha—wha—a—t" gasped the little man, "means this?"

"Silence, and you shall hear!" hissed Dick. "But if you raise a cry above a whisper, I'll break every bone in your little body across my knee!"

Then releasing the steward, he thrust him back into his chair, and pulling down the sash of the window, he drew the curtain across it.

Gripe turned red, then white, as this little operation was going on, and his little eyes almost started out of his little head as they followed the poacher's movements.

When he had done all that suggested itself to prevent observation, Dick drew a chair up to the table, and seated himself opposite the now trembling steward.

"Well, old fellow," he said, "I'm out again, you see. Prison fare don't agree very well with my constitution, but still I am strong enough to make mincemeat of you in five minutes, if you are not very careful how you treat me."

"What do you want?" said Gripe, shifting his chair a little farther from his visitor.

"Just a little conversation," said Dick, giving his chair a hitch to the side of the steward. "There, don't move again, I want you within reach of that hand."

And the poacher held his hand before the steward's eyes.

The little man drew back his head, but spoke not a word.

"Don't you think," began Dick, leaning his head forward, and looking into the eyes of the little man, "that you're a despicable scoundrel?"

"Why should I?" said Gripe.

"For doing your best to put me in prison," exclaimed Dick. "For depriving me of the fresh air and the green fields—for taking from me my liberty, only for taking that which God has sent for the benefit of all."

"It was my duty," stammered Gripe.

"Your duty!" exclaimed Dick.

"Yes," said Gripe.

"To whom?"

"To my employer," said Gripe.

"And was it only duty which caused you to add to the evidence against me all the crimes of which I have been guilty," said Dick, bitterly.

"I had a duty to perform, and that duty I owed to my employer. As his servant I only did my duty. Yes, sir, my duty," said the little man, haughtily.

"Oh! you do your duty then, I suppose, as you call it, to your master?" questioned the poacher.

"I do."

"And pray, may I ask, Mr. Gripe, what are your duties towards him?"

"Obedience to his orders, attention to his interests—"

"And pilfering his money," exclaimed Dick; "ah, Mr. Gripe?"

The little steward started, and the colour, which had slowly returned to his cheek, now again left it, and he was pale as death.

"Is it not so?" asked Dick, enjoying the little man's agony.

"No—no!" gasped the steward.

"Then, since you are such a stickler for duty, why the devil did you rob your master to pay me?" exclaimed Dick, fixing his hand upon the steward's shoulder, and fixing a piercing glance upon his eyes.

Had a can of gunpowder been exploded beneath his chair, Mr. Gripe could not have been hurled from his seat with greater alacrity than he himself bounded from it.

"Sit down, sir—sit down," said Dick, sarcastically. "I have no desire to humble any man by allowing him to stand in my presence, although morally he is not my equal."

Gripe winced—he not the equal of a poacher!

But the retort died upon his lips, and his eye fell before the eagle glance of the dark orbs which glared upon him.

"You appear surprised, Mr. Gripe, at my knowledge of your transactions," said Dick, after a pause. "But sit down, sir, I exact no ceremony, though you are a thief."

"Me a thief!" gasped the little man: "me a thief! Do you know what you say, sir—do you know that those words are actionable? Do you know sir, what you say? Me—me a thief!"

And the little man endeavoured to summon a look of virtuous indignation to his features.

But Dick broke out into a violent fit of laughter.

"Look here, Gripe," he exclaimed, "if you try to swell yourself out like that, you'll certainly be like the frog in the fable—you'll burst yourself."

"How dare you! A poacher—a man who has been in prison—talk to me! me, the steward of the squire, call me a thief!"

"Yes," replied Dick, "and a damned infernal rascally old thief into the bargain! The laws make me one, and the tyranny of others brought me to do that which rendered it the only course by which I could obtain food. I steal only that which is sent for all; but you, who had plenty, robbed the man who fed you, that you might turn your hand against him—bite him who gave you food, turn upon him as the adder nourished in his bosom, and sting him who befriended you!"

The steward fairly foamed at the mouth, and clenched his teeth with rage.

But the eye of his tormentor held him fascinated and powerless.

"You come here," he said, after a pause, "to annoy and insult me for doing my duty. You should not lay yourself open to the law, if you would not suffer its penalties."

"Nor should you," said Dick calmly.

"I do not."

"You lie!" exclaimed Dick.

"Leave this place," said Gripe, "or I will summon those who will hurl you from it!"

And he placed his hand on a bell-rope.

"Drop your mawley," said Dick, "or I'll drop it for you! Remember I hit hard."

"Begone!" said Gripe.

"Drop it, I say."

"You have no right here. Begone, or I will hand you over to the constable."

Dick rose from his seat.

"Look here, Mr. Gripe, if you don't want to feel that bunch of fives, drop your hand from that cord."

And Dick advanced threateningly towards him.

Gripe hesitated, but the flash of the poacher's

dark eye told him that Dick meant mischief, and he let go his hold on the bell-pull.

"A sensible man," said Dick, seating himself again in his chair, "come, I see you are to be reasoned with. Sit down, Mr. Gripe, sit down, and let us understand each other better."

"Why are you here," asked Gripe; "what is it that you require?"

"Information," said Dick.

"What if I refuse to give you any?" asked Gripe.

"Why, then it will be the worse for you," replied the poacher.

"How so?"

"Because I shall acquaint the squire of certain things about which he is at present in the dark."

"What's that to me?" said the little man.

"Everything."

"That's nothing."

"Yes it is—much."

"What?"

"Character—reputation," said Dick.

"I don't understand you."

"I will be more plain then," said Dick, "I will inform him that his steward robbed him to purchase certain papers from me to be used against him."

"You will state that which is untrue, then," said Gripe.

"Not so."

"But I say you would."

"Where did you get the money, then?" said Dick.

"What's that to you?" said Gripe.

"Much."

"Much?" iterated the steward.

"Yes, for by the information you may save yourself much unpleasantness."

"Well, then, it was my own—my savings," said the steward.

"Mr. Gripe," said Dick slowly, "you are either a most confounded liar, or a most consummate rogue. Either you lied or you robbed, for you told me you had not got the money, but when you found I would not part with those papers till you had obtained it, you procured it—but how? By robbing your employer—by appropriating his money to your own use! This is a crime which the law holds heinous, and punishes with severity. Were I to inform the squire of your pilfering, he would assuredly hand you over to its mercies. How would the poor wretches whom you have deprived of their homes, and sent forth into the cold world to beg or starve, gloat in your misery! it would be a glorious revenge for them, and the squire would give them that gratification, did he know it."

"He dare not," said the little man, trembling. "He dare not, he is in my power—mine. If he but uttered one word to harm me, I would hurl him from his position, blast his fame, and drive him out into the world a despised and degraded beggar!"

"Ha, ha!" chuckled Dick to himself, "I shall learn the truth yet."

And fixing his dark piercing eye upon the steward, he said,—

"You could not do it."

"But I could and would," replied Gripe, "he is in my power, not me in his. I have the papers in my possession which will enable me to ruin him."

"Where did you get them?" asked Dick, innocently.

"Where?" iterated the little steward, in a surprised tone.

"Yes, where?" replied Dick.

The little man looked at the poacher, as if he thought he was going out of his mind.

"Well," said Dick, after a moment's pause. "You don't answer?"

"From you, didn't I?" asked Gripe.

"From me?"

"Yes, you. Did I not give you five hundred pounds for them?" exclaimed Gripe.

"Oh! those you mean," drawled Dick, as though he had forgotten all about them.

"Certainly I did," exclaimed Gripe.

"I thought you meant the others," said Dick, slowly.

Mr. Gripe, who had hitherto kept out of reach of the poacher's arm, bounded up to his side, and fixed an infuriated glance on him.

"What others?" he exclaimed, hastily.

"Why, the other ones," said Dick.

"Are there any others?" asked Gripe, anxiously.

"Well, there was," drawled Dick.

"Where are they—what are they?" asked Gripe, eagerly.

"Well, I did have them, but—"

"But what?"

"I haven't got them now," said Dick.

"What were they about?" asked Gripe, tremulously.

"Oh, nothing," said Dick carelessly.

"Are they about this estate? Do they contain anything respecting this manor?" asked the little man tremulously, and almost pleadingly.

So anxious was the manner of the little steward, that Dick saw at once, as far as Gripe was concerned, he knew nothing about the documents stolen from the subterranean passage, but he resolved to learn, if possible, whether Henley had been there and taken possession of them.

"Oh, nothing particular," he said, in answer to the steward's question.

"What are they about?" asked the steward.

"You seem anxious to know," said Dick.

"I am."

"Then, first, tell me where the Squire has been while I have been in prison?"

"He went to Paris, on the evening of the day when you were convicted."

"Did he go anywhere else?" asked Dick.

"Nowhere."

"Made no calls in the neighbourhood, before he went?"

"None. I went with him to London, and did not leave him till he was on board the ship."

"Mr. Gripe, you sometimes lie; is this one?" asked Dick, watching eagerly the countenance of the steward.

"It is true."

"Well, I believe you."

"Now, about these other papers?" said Gripe, eagerly.

"Well, I'll be candid with you. They are useless to you; you will lose nothing by their loss, gain nothing by their possession. To me they are of value, hence I wished to know whether they had fallen into your hands or those of your master. My presence here has not been known to anyone, nor shall my departure. Good night."

And without another word, he threw up the window and leaped out.

———

CHAPTER XXIX.

THE HOUSE OF DICK THE POACHER—THE IDIOT WIFE —THE RETURN OF DICK.

LYING about two miles off the high road to Barnstable, and on the banks of a pretty mill-stream, an old-fashioned farm house reared its head over the luxuriant vegetation with which that part of the country abounded.

Standing in the midst of a small patch of land, which on one side sloped down to the water's edge, the white gable roof shone in the sunlight, and presented a fairy-like aspect of comfort and peace.

A few fowls strolled about before the house, and ducks paddled on the banks of the little stream.

Here and there, a small patch of vegetables broke the smooth covered earth, but save and except these, no further evidence existed of the ground being turned to advantage.

A thin wreath of white smoke curled up to kiss the sunbeams, as they played upon the white-tipped roof, and a young woman sat in the open door-way, gazing vacantly out upon the grass-grown earth before her.

Her cheek was pale, and the marble whiteness of her brow—partially shaded by the glossy black tresses of her raven hair—gave her features the hue of death.

There was a strange, vacant, glassy stare in the dark eyes of the woman, which lent to her face an unearthly aspect.

Poor thing! reason had partially fled that brain.

Weird Minnie, the once prosperous farmer's daughter, the pride of the country around, the joy of her parents, the wife of Dick the Poacher, was an idiot!

In the full blush of her virgin pride and strength, Dick had wooed and won her youthful love.

The cheerful, happy nature of the poacher had engrafted in her heart a passion pure and holy as ever woman formed, and happy was the moment when, hand in hand, they stood and plighted their vows before the altar.

No dark cloud then had crossed their path, no evil destiny threw its shadows upon their love, and days, weeks, months wore on in one uninterrupted stream of peace and joy.

But the clouds rose, and the storm burst in overwhelming fury.

The beauty of Minnie had caught the gaze of a distant member of the family, a well-to-do farmer.

This man, Henley by name, was fascinated by the beauty of Minnie.

A stern, overbearing man, devoid of all those impulses with which a generous heart is filled, his bosom was fired with the beauty of the young wife, and he resolved to devote himself to her ruin.

But the virtue and retiring modesty of the fair girl was an obstacle difficult to surmount, and Henley was too shrewd to commit himself in any way by which he might lay himself open to the law.

Could he but bring them to poverty, he thought he might succeed.

He was rich: the broad acres which he rented stretched far on every side, whilst Dick was but a small hard-working farmer, but with expectations of considerable wealth at the death of an uncle.

Henley planned and plotted, and ere the second year of their union had passed, he had bought almost all the land around the homestead of Dick.

This was a sad blow to the young farmer and his wife, as it effectually prevented them from bettering their circumstances.

Indeed, little remained to them now but the homestead and the small plot of ground on which it was built, and this being a freehold, Henley was unable to obtain it.

He caused many flattering offers to be made for it, but all in vain; Minnie, who had been born there, begged of Dick never to part with it, and he, too fond of his wife to ever deny her slightest wish, promised to keep the old homestead spite of any offer—no matter how great it might be.

But the loss of the land soon entailed poverty upon them, and Dick was driven to seek food for himself and his wife in other channels.

He became a poacher, and many, indeed, were the heads of game he trapped on the estate which Henley had wrested from him.

Time went on, and the uncle of Dick died, but the expectations of the poacher were not realised; himself and sister, who had always been led to anticipate a good inheritance from their relative, did not receive a single shilling.

This was a sad blow to their hopes—rendered more galling by the knowledge that their enemy Henley had inherited all.

Henley had been with the old man for some time previous to his death, and it was believed that he had induced him to make a will in his favour.

But, be this as it may, a will was found which bequeathed all his property to the prosperous farmer.

Then, again, was Dick solicited to sell the homestead, but in vain.

Galled by the refusal, Henley, who had heard from a lawyer's clerk in the neighbourhood that Dick had several times poached on his land, resolved to trap the young farmer and send him to gaol.

He had not long to wait ere an opportunity offered itself.

One night, as Dick went to his traps to search for game, he was pounced upon by several men, headed by Mr. Gripe, whom Henley had taken into his employ as steward.

The moment that his capture was made known to Henley, that worthy sought the homestead, where Minnie awaited the return of her husband.

Sought it with the intention of offering to save her husband from a prison, on the condition of her consenting to purchase his freedom at the sacrifice of her honour.

But the woman repelled his advances, and defied his power; upbraided his villany, scoffed at his insults, and, maddened to fury by the bitter sarcasm of her manner, he returned to his home resolved to blast the character of the poor farmer, and embitter the peace of his wife.

Hence Dick was sent to prison, and a more vindictive prosecutor never stood in a court of justice than Henley.

But, spite of the manner in which Henley pressed for punishment, Dick's term of incarceration was not long, and in a few weeks he was once more free.

But his reputation was gone; the stain of a prison was on him!

He hurried home, to that wife whom he fondly believed awaited to welcome him—to that smile which would repay him for all the misery he had suffered.

The sight of Minnie as she sat at the door of the homestead lent wings to his feet, and he flew to meet her.

But she came not forth to meet him, as was her wont.

He stood before her, but her eyes were bent upon the ground; he placed his arm around her neck, and raised her face, it was pale and cold; the smile had faded, the lustre of her dark eye was dim, and a vacant stare only met his anxious gaze.

He spoke to her, but she answered incoherently; he drew her towards him, he strained her to his breast, he spoke words of kindness and love, but a low, unnatural laugh was the only response; and with a cry of agony he sank at her feet, as he saw that reason had tottered from its throne, and his once happy wife had been bereft of her senses.

What were the sufferings he endured between the four stone walls from which he had just been liberated, compared to the agony of mind he now experienced?

He bore her into the house; he sought medical aid; he strove by every means in his power to shake the lethargy which bowed her senses in thraldom, but all in vain! the eye had lost its lustre for ever, the brain its reason.

Bitter, indeed, were the curses which Dick now heaped upon the man who had plotted his ruin, and loud the threats he held out towards him.

Gripe, who overheard these threats, considered it his duty to make his employer acquainted with them, and Squire Henley—as he was now called—resolved to do all that lay in his power to remove the man from his path.

It was not long after Dick had been freed from prison, that a large haystack on the squire's property was discovered to be on fire, and Dick was found trespassing on the grounds.

Here was a chance for Henley to rid himself of the man whom he both feared and hated.

The only evidence which could implicate Dick was the fact of his being on the premises at the time of the fire, the threats he had been heard to use, and his having been convicted of poaching, but these Henley well knew were sufficient to deprive him of liberty for a long time.

That Squire Henley believed him to be the party who had fired the stack, was not the case.

He knew too well the character of the poacher, to believe that he would stoop to vengeance by such means.

Dick, he knew, would not hesitate to strike in the face, but would scorn to stab in the dark.

Still, the squire found it necessary to remove the young man from his path, lest any unforeseen event might make him acquainted with circumstances he fondly hoped were known only to himself.

Therefore Dick was arrested on suspicion, and remanded.

During this remand, the squire received a visit from the Widow Marston.

What transpired at the interview was known only to themselves, but at its conclusion, the squire, pale and trembling, sought his steward, whom he sent with a message to the magistrate, who, having perused it, made out the order of release for Dick the Poacher.

From this time, Squire Henley was nervous and fidgetty, whenever he received any intimation that Dick was seen poaching on his grounds; and to the solicitations of his steward to prosecute the poacher, his answers were short and evasive.

It was evident that Squire Henley could not carry it with so high a hand with Dick as he had before done, and he also gave up all hope of winning over to his arms the wife of the poacher.

Thus things had been for some years when our story opened, and Dick was first presented to the reader.

But, of late, Minnie had some moments when a gleam of reason broke forth, and the dull face was lit up with a glow of reason.

Such was the case on the morning on which we first make her acquaintance.

She had not seen her husband for some weeks, but she took little heed of his absence, as he was often away for days together.

Poor Minnie had no conception of time; she knew not how long he had been away, she only knew that it was some time.

But she sat waiting for him at the door of the homestead, as usual, with her gaze fixed vacantly upon the ground before her.

Suddenly she raises her eyes.

A voice falls upon her ear, in tones so well known.

It is the voice of Dick the Poacher, as he has been called ever since the fatal time which robbed poor Minnie of her reason.

"Minnie."

The word falls like music on her soul—the dull eye brightens.

"Minnie, my poor Minnie!"

She rises from her seat, and moves forward.

She is clasped in the arms of him for whom she alone lives—him for whom one gleam of reason only glows upon her cold, expressionless face.

"Minnie, dear, I have been long absent," said Dick, caressing the dark hair of his wife, and imprinting a kiss upon her pale cheek.

"Is it winter time, then?" she asked, looking up into the dark eye, bedimmed with a tear.

"Winter time, Minnie?" said Dick. "Oh, no—it is Autumn. Don't you see the leaves are turning brown upon the trees. But it will soon be winter."

"Yes, and the snow will cover the green grass, and then—then—"

"Then what, Minnie?"

"I can see your footprints in the deep white snow. I look for them on the grass, but it grows up and hides them from my sight. I have looked for them, but they were not there—they were not there."

Dick encircled her waist with his arm, and led her towards the house.

"You have looked for them in vain, my poor Minnie," he said, "I have been absent a long time, but I am with you now, Minnie."

"Yes, and you will stay with me?" she asked, looking vacantly into the bronzed face.

"I will, Minnie, dear one, I will! The squire—"

"Ah!" interrupted Minnie, for the first time an expression of curiosity, not unmingled with fear, spreading over her features; "they call him squire, but he is not, no, no."

"The squire, Minnie," continued Dick, "has been at his work again, but he shall not part us more. He believed that he had me entirely in his power, but I will disabuse his mind of the thought. So fear not, Minnie, I will remain with you now, spite of him."

"Bad man," said Minnie, "bad man!"

"Indeed he is," replied Dick.

"The grass withers where his feet fall," said Minnie, "and the flowers die. The birds will not sing when he is near, and the birds sing to me, Dick, darling—sing to cheer me when I am sad."

"They must love you, Minnie, for who would not?"

"Love!" exclaimed the woman, "who loves —the squire? Ha, ha!"

"The squire, Minnie?"

"Aye, said he not he loved? Loved me—the idiot, me — weird Minnie, me — the poacher's bride. But the birds did not sing, Dick, and I knew he lied!"

"Has he been here?" asked Dick, in an anxious tone.

"The birds have," she answered.

"The squire?" exclaimed Dick.

"Is the grass withered?" she asked, looking down.

"No, dear one."

"Then he has not been here. No, no; he leaves his footprints—it dies, and where he steps the earth is barren. Ah, no!"

Dick looked anxiously and inquiringly into the face of his fair companion.

But after a moment he seemed satisfied that her words had reference to the visit of Henley ere reason had left her.

"Come, Minnie," he said, "let us go in."

"Yes," she replied, "for now you have come, the old house will not be so dull."

"You are happy to see me again then, Minnie?" said Dick, looking tenderly at her.

"Hark!" she said, pausing, and pointing upwards.

"What, Minnie?"

"The birds!"

"What of them?"

"They welcome you home."

"And so do you, do you not, Minnie?" he asked, tenderly.

"Yes, for the birds tell me I must love you," she replied.

"Then come, dear one, come and tell me how you have been while I was away."

And he led her into the house, and seated her on a chair in the kitchen, where a bright fire glowed in the grate, and the utmost order and cleanliness prevailed.

Dick cast his eyes around the apartment, and thought that were it not for her household duties, not one spark of reason would remain, for attention to those distracted the melancholy into which she fell when she could find nothing to do.

Seating himself beside her, he placed one arm around her neck, and imprinted a kiss upon her lips.

"Oh, God!" he muttered to himself, "will this fearful ban be never taken off? Shall she go on through life without any return of that reason which my own acts have deprived her of? Forbid it, heaven! If I have sinned, punish not her, but let thy vengeance fall upon my guilty head!"

CHAPTER XXX.

THE ANONYMOUS LETTER—THE DEFALCATIONS DISCOVERED—THE SQUIRE THREATENS—THE TABLES TURNED.

SQUIRE HENLEY sat in his little breakfast parlour the morning after his arrival at his mansion from Paris; sat looking out upon the leaves, as, withered by the autumn blast, they fell from the branches, spinning through the air to the ground.

A self-satisfied smile was on his face, and a feeling of satisfaction was in his heart, as he looked forth upon the stately trees and smooth mown lawn; viewed what he believed it was now in the power of none to wrest from him.

The last fear had been removed from his heart by the possession of the dreaded packet; removed, too, by the very man he most feared and hated.

The deep reverie into which he had fallen was broken by a knock at the door of his apartment, and a servant placed in his hands a letter marked private.

He broke the seal, and perused its contents.

As he did so, a dark frown gathered upon his brow, and he rose to his feet.

"What can this mean?" he muttered; "deceived where I most trusted! But there is no signature; the letter is an anonymous one, and may be all a lie, yet I will see to it. Some poor tenant, whom Gripe has pressed hard, has doubtless sent it, to be revenged upon him. Yet there may be truth in it. I will act upon its suggestions, and if I find he has robbed me, I will have no mercy upon him—none—none!"

And he strode from the room with the letter in his hand.

He took his way to the little room used by his steward as an office, and entered without, as usual, announcing himself.

Gripe was seated before a ledger, making out his accounts.

The little man looked up with a smile on his weazened face, then rose from his seat and handed a chair to his master.

Henley took it, and sat down.

The little man remained standing, rubbing his hands together, and waiting to hear the reason of the squire's visit.

"Sit down, Gripe," said the squire.

The little man obeyed.

"I have been thinking," said Henley, fixing his eyes full upon the face of the steward, "that I have been somewhat neglectful of late."

"In what, sir, may I ask?" said Gripe.

"In not making myself acquainted with the nature of my estate, and paying more attention to its profits and expenses."

Gripe bowed.

GRIPE TRACKS THE FOOTSTEPS OF MINNIE.

"I have, therefore, come to look over the accounts," said Henley, watching intently the face of the steward.

"Certainly, sir," said the little man, in a calm tone. "The books shall be made up and submitted to your inspection in the course of the day."

The squire moved impatiently on his chair.

"Why are they not ready now?" he asked.

"Because I have several entries to make, which other business has denied me the opportunity of doing before."

"How long will they take to do?" asked Henley.

"About an hour," replied Gripe.

"Then I will assist you," said the squire.

"As you please," returned the steward.

And drawing one of the books to him along the table he placed it before Henley, in a cool and collected manner.

The squire looked hard at his steward, and hesitated.

"Surely," he thought, "he would not be so calm and collected were anything wrong in his accounts."

Yet, as he had entered the room with the avowed intention of examining the books, he scarcely knew how to leave without giving some explanation to his steward.

And that explanation would imply a doubt of his steward's honesty.

He resolved therefore to go on with the business he had come upon.

Together they went through the accounts,

and in the course of an hour every item of receipt and expenditure had been dotted down and reckoned up.

Now came the moment for the accounts to tally.

Gripe was calm as ever, as he watched the squire, as he placed the finals of each column before him.

A frown gathered on the squire's brow.

"How is this, Gripe?" he exclaimed.

"What, sir, may I ask?" said the steward, calmly.

"What, sir, may you ask?" iterated Henley.

"Yes, sir," said Gripe.

"How do you make these accounts balance, sir—how do you reconcile this?"

"What?" asked Gripe.

"A difference of five hundred pounds!" said Henley.

"In your favour, sir?" inquired Gripe.

"In my devils!" exclaimed Henley. "How do you account, sir, for five hundred pounds, which you acknowledge you have received, but which is not here accounted for?"

Gripe rose from his chair.

So did the squire.

The face of the little man was as placid as a statue's.

The smirking smile still remained—not a nerve moved.

On the contrary the squire. His face flushed with passion, and he clenched his fist, whilst his whole frame trembled with excitement.

"How do you account for it—how do you account for it?" almost yelled the squire.

"My dear sir," said Gripe, in cold, cutting tones, "do not excite yourself."

"Answer my question!"

"Such is my duty."

"Damn your duty, sir! Have you done your duty?" exclaimed Henley.

"I always make a point of doing so," replied Gripe, smoothing his shirt frill.

The calm demeanour of the little man was more than Henley could bear.

Satisfied now that the letter contained some truth, he flung it upon the table before his steward, exclaiming,—

"Read that—read that!"

Gripe took up the epistle, turned it over in his hand, examined the post-mark, and deliberately unfolded it, then slowly and calmly he perused its contents.

Having read every line carefully, he slowly refolded the letter, and presented it to the squire, who stood watching the calm, unruffled features of the little steward as he read the words therein written.

"You commanded me to read it, sir," he said, "and, as was my duty, I have read every line attentively; but, by the way, I perceive the writer has forgotten to sign his name."

The calm, measured tones of the steward, as he gave utterance to these words, goaded the squire almost to madness, and he yelled out,—

"What do you think of that, sir—what do you think of that?"

"The gentleman writes a good hand," replied Gripe, "and the wording is far superior to many I have seen."

Henley fairly staggered back at the cool effrontery of the steward.

That Gripe could not honestly account for the money he felt assured, but the cool manner in which he took the discovery of his shortcomings quite staggered him.

For a moment he looked at the little man in surprise.

Then the passionate glow mounted once more to his face, and he said,—

"Mr. Gripe, I require an explanation of this deficiency."

"It is doubtless my duty to comply with your request, sir, but circumstances may prevent me doing so," replied Gripe.

"Sir, I demand an explanation!" exclaimed the squire, taking a step nearer to the little man.

"Sir," exclaimed the steward, coldly but respectfully, "what if I decline to give any?"

"Then, by hell——"

"Hush, sir," interrupted Gripe, "you forget yourself."

"Forget be——"

"Again, sir, I must remind you that you set a bad example to your servants, by allowing your temper to get the better of your reason."

For a moment, Henley stood looking upon the little man as if he believed he had lost his senses; then stretching forth his hand, he grasped the steward by the collar.

"Either give me some account of these deficiences, or I will this instant hand you over to the mercies of the law," he exclaimed.

Still Gripe was calm.

"Speak!" exclaimed the squire, "If you would save yourself from a prison!"

"A prison," said Gripe.

"Yes, unless you can render an account of this sum," replied Henley, "I will prosecute you with the utmost rigour of the law."

Gripe fixed his eye full upon those of his master, as, in calm and measured tones, he said,—

"Squire Henley, you dare not!"

So firm and convincing were the tones of the little man, that Henley released his hold of Gripe's collar, and stood looking at him in wonderment for some moments.

Gripe pulled up the collar of his coat, smoothed down his shirt frill, and stood calmly awaiting any further remark the squire might have to make.

"Dare not!" he exclaimed, in slow, measured tones.

"Aye, dare not!" replied Gripe. "Such was the remark, squire, I made use of."

Henley became more and more puzzled; the manner of the obsequious little steward quite confounded him.

Detected, yet so cool, calm, and defiant, he knew not what to think.

Gripe watched the workings of his countenance, with the same cool, collected look.

"Mr. Gripe," continued Henley, after a pause, "I have hitherto placed the most implicit confidence in your honesty."

Gripe bowed.

"But now, sir, I find that I have been deceived. Your boast that you ever perform your duty is false, and, spite of the generous manner in which I have always treated you, you have descended to rob me. The confidence I reposed in you has been abused, and I have but one duty to perform, and that is, to hand you over to the officers of justice, to be dealt with as the ministers of the laws you have outraged shall think fit."

Gripe bowed again, this time very low.

"I believed you trustworthy, and should not have hesitated to believe your bare word, had not this letter have come to hand. But I find I have been deceived, and you must now take the consequences of your guilt."

And the squire crossed the room, and placed his hand upon the bell-rope.

Gripe followed him with his eyes, and as the squire took the silken cord in his hand, said,—

"Squire, what are you about to do?"

"Hand you over to justice," replied Henley.

"I would advise you to take your hand from that cord," said Gripe.

"How, sir!" indignantly exclaimed Henley.

"It may not be pleasant for your servants to hear me denounce you as the robber of an inheritance—the wretch who can rob the widow and the orphan—the thing whose baseness drove a gentle being to madness, and seeks the destruction of a man whom your villany has reduced to a life of shame!"

With a start, Henley let the rope fall from his grasp.

The crimson hue on his face gave place to a deathly pallor.

His limbs trembled, and he staggered forward to a chair, into which he sank.

Gripe watched him with the same cold look upon his little weazened face.

Not a smile betokened his triumph—not a gleam brightened his small grey eye.

Overpowered, Henley buried his face for a moment in his hands.

Gripe closed the books upon the table, and piled them one upon the other, as if nothing had happened; then seated himself at the table, and commenced cutting a quill with a penknife, which lay beside the inkstand.

Nor was it till Henley, ashamed of the weakness he had exhibited, started to his feet, that Gripe looked up from the work on which he was engaged.

Various were the emotions which rapidly coursed through the mind of the squire. Did Gripe know all—did he know anything? or was it but a trick—a suspicion?

But even if he suspected, or knew, of what avail would it be; had he not destroyed the evidence of his guilt—was not the only thing that could be brought against him, consumed and powdered till not one grain remained?

Bitterly did he curse his weakness.

But he would now be firm.

No word of Gripe's should turn him from his purpose.

Once more he seized the cord.

Gripe fixed his little grey eye upon him, and his hand remained motionless on the cord.

"Squire," he said, "you were once a shrewd man, or you would never have been able to have done as you have; surely, now that you have succeeded thus far, you will not place yourself in a position to lose what you have toiled and sinned so much to gain."

"What mean you?" said Henley.

"The Widow Marston's inheritance."

"I do not understand you," said Henley, turning even a shade paler.

"Don't you?"

"No."

"Shall I refresh your memory?" asked Gripe, paring away at the quill.

"How?" asked the squire.

"By producing the packet which Dick the Poacher wrested from the hands of Takeall at the cottage of the widow, on the day of her funeral."

"Ah!" exclaimed Henley, thrown completely off his guard, and advancing to where the steward sat.

For the first time, Gripe's features relaxed.

"Oh," he said "you are becoming interested."

"What know you of those papers?" asked Henley eagerly.

"Not much."

"Anything?" asked Henley.

"Well, yes."

"What?"

"Simply that I have got them."

"You?"

"Yes, me."

"Liar!"

"Rogue!" answered Gripe.

"Ah!" yelled the squire.

And Henley again stretched forth his hand menacingly, but Gripe fixed that peculiar glance upon the squire that he hesitated to strike.

"Facts are stubborn things, squire—tough, too, for you don't like to swallow or digest them," said Gripe, slicing off the nib he had made to the quill, and commencing to cut another.

The coolness of the steward was fast telling upon the nerves of Henley; he became agitated and nervous.

Gripe looked out of the corner of his eye, and saw the pallor deepening upon the cheeks of his master, and the nervous twitching around his mouth, and knew that soon he would be able to do as he pleased with him.

"Sit down, squire," he said, after a pause.

Henley hesitated.

Gripe repeated his request, this time rising and placing a chair for his master.

Henley looked hard at him for a moment, then dropped into the seat.

"That's it," said Gripe, following the squire's example. "Business can always be transacted better sitting than standing."

Still the squire made no reply.

Gripe, finding that Henley waited for him to commence, said,—

"Now, squire, you perceive I am not a man to be frightened by any ridiculous outburst of passion. You have demanded to see the accounts, and you have examined them; you have found a deficiency, and threatened me. I despise those threats, because I know you are powerless; had I not have had you sufficiently in my power, I should not have laid myself open to your wrath, or to the law. The money I have appropriated to the purchase of the evidence of your guilt—guilt black as hell! I bought the packet of Dick the Poacher—the proofs of your villany. Now summon your servants if you will, and bid them carry me to a prison, but remember, at the least attempt to denounce me as one who has made a breach of trust—at the the first attempt to bring disgrace upon me—I will hurl you from the proud position you occupy, wrest from you your ill-gotten wealth, and cover you with shame and infamy. Now, squire, we will change places—I will become the master, you the slave. Aye, you may wince and grind your teeth, but I heed you not; your sting is drawn, and you are powerless to wound, for I have you on the hip, Squire Henley, and I can loathe and despise you!"

CHAPTER XXXI.

GRIPE IN DANGER—THE SQUIRE OUTWITTED—
TRIUMPH OF THE STEWARD.

HAD a thunderbolt fallen at the feet of the guilty squire, he could not have been more appalled than he now was.

With cheeks of deathly whiteness, and limbs that trembled till they shook the chair upon which he sat, he glared in horror-struck amazement upon the smiling face of the little steward before him.

Gripe—cool and calm as ever—smoothed his shirt frill, and fixed his cold grey eye upon his master; held him fascinated, as it were, by the calm, cold glance.

Now was the moment of Gripe's triumph, yet not one movement of his weazened face divulged the feelings in his breast.

Henley remained in the half stupefied position into which the words of Gripe had plunged him for some few minutes, then he sprang to his feet, gasping forth—

"Fiend—devil—liar!"

But Gripe took little or no heed of the words.

He only finished making the fresh nib to the quill, dipped it in the ink, and scrawled his name upon a sheet of blotting paper, which lay on the table before him.

"Where—where," gasped Henley, after a pause, "are these papers?"

"Safe," replied Gripe.

"Where, I say?"

"In my possession."

Henley thought for a moment.

"Gripe," he said at length, "You have outwitted yourself."

"Indeed?"

"Yes."

"How, pray?"

"They are forgeries."

"Oh," replied Gripe, calmly.

"Yes, forgeries," replied Henley.

"How do you know that?"

"Because those papers fell into my hands before I went to Paris," replied the squire.

"Did they now?"

"Yes."

"How did you get them?"

"From Dick the Poacher."

"What?"

"From Dick the Poacher."

"When?"

"On the first night of the fair," replied the squire.

"That's strange," said Gripe, "for I got them since then, so you must have lost them, squire."

"No," replied Henley, "I destroyed them instantly."

"How?"

"Burnt them."

"You did?" said Gripe, becoming somewhat uneasy at the convincing tones of the squire.

"I did, and if you have really obtained any papers from Dick, he has palmed off spurious documents upon you."

"Or upon you," said Gripe, "which is most likely."

"Why?"

"Because you have striven to injure him," said Gripe.

"If I have, it was at your suggestion," replied Henley.

"Suggestions which you acted upon."

"That may be."

"Then you were his greatest enemy, not me, so the greater reason that he should deceive you," said Gripe, gaining the courage he had lost at the mention of the second packet, and the knowledge that it was destroyed.

Squire Henley cursed himself bitterly for not having examined the packet ere he destroyed it, for now he felt it impossible to say that it was the genuine one taken from the cottage of the widow.

Yet he felt the probabilities were as great one way as the other, and perhaps, after all, the one Gripe possessed was the true packet.

What had he better do?

He could not determine upon the best course to pursue.

Oh that he were certain!

But he was not, and he must be wary.

He might compromise with Gripe.

He would try.

"Gripe," he said, laying his hand upon the shoulder of that worthy gentleman, "give me the packet you possess, and whether it be genuine or a forgery, I will forgive your delinquencies."

"Will you," said Gripe.

"I will."

"You are very kind."

"To you I have always been so."

"True, I cannot complain of any want of kindness on your part towards me," replied the steward.

"Then let us be friends."

"That is my wish."

"Give me, then, the packet, and accept in return the five hundred pounds you have robbed me of."

"Won't do, squire."

"Why?"

"The offer is not fair."

"How so?"

"I should gain nothing thereby."

"You would lose nothing."

"I fear I should."

"What?"

"By placing that packet in your hands," said Gripe, "I place myself in your power."

"But I give you my word never to harm you," said Henley.

"I cannot take it."

"Why?"

"The word of the man who can rob the widow and the fatherless is worthless," said Gripe, sarcastically.

Henley winced.

"I will add to it another five hundred," said Henley.

"It won't do, squire," said the steward, "I know the worth of them, and the power they give me."

"What if I dispute their genuineness?" said Henley, after a pause.

"It would be of no avail," observed the steward.

"Why not?"

"Dick the Poacher can swear to them."

"He is a convicted felon."

"What of that?"

"His word would not be believed," answered Henley.

"There is Takeall."

"He can know nothing of them."

"There is the boy, then—the boy to whom they belong."

"Curse him," muttered Henley.

"You see, squire, that course would avail you nothing."

"What will induce you to surrender them into my hands?"

"Nothing."

"Name your price."

"I will not part with them."

"Will you destroy them?"

"No."

"What, then, do you purpose doing?"

"Keeping them as a passport to your fears—to your fortune."

"Gripe," said Henley, worked to desperation by the cool, taunting tones of the little steward, "I must have them."

"Mr. Henley," replied Gripe, equally coolly, "you shall not."

"No."

"Positively no," replied Gripe.

"By hell, then, I will tear them from you!" exclaimed the now exasperated man.

Gripe leaped from his chair, and retreated from the squire as he advanced threateningly towards him, the veins in his forehead swollen almost to bursting, and his teeth locked firmly together.

"Stand back, squire!" exclaimed Gripe, now fearful of the wrathful man.

"Devil!" shrieked Henley, "where are they? Speak, or I will tear the secret from your heart!"

And with a bound he sprang upon the little man, and grasped him by the throat.

"I would not have your blood upon my soul," exclaimed Henley, "but if you place them not in my hands, I will lay you dead at my feet!"

"For mercy's sake!" gasped Gripe.

"I will show none!" yelled the squire. "Taunting devil! you have stung me to madness, goaded me on till I care not what I do. If you would save your life, yield up the papers!"

"Let me go, then," said Gripe.

"Give them to me!"

"I cannot, while you hold me thus," gasped the steward.

Henley released his hold, and Gripe staggered back against the wall of the apartment, his face swollen and blackened by the pressure of the squire's fingers on his throat.

"Would you murder me?" he gasped.

"The papers!" said the squire.

"Would you add another crime to the black list of your sins?" asked Gripe, evidently wishing to gain time for thought.

"Peace!" exclaimed the squire. "I am a desperate man, so beware what you do, or how you try me further. Get them—place them in my hands at once—or I will crush you beneath this foot!"

And the squire stamped upon the floor of the apartment.

Gripe saw that he must make some semblance of compliance, and he moved towards the door.

The squire followed.

Gripe was annoyed at this circumstance, but he feared to make any remark.

He had hoped to have been enabled to escape from the reach of Henley while the fit of passion into which he had worked himself lasted.

But the squire kept close upon his heels, his hand ready to again grasp his throat, at the least appearance of treachery.

Gripe made his way up the staircase, still followed by the squire, and entered his own sleeping apartment.

Still Henley followed.

The steward advanced to a chest of drawers, and opened one just sufficiently to get his hand in.

Then he turned and looked at the squire, still keeping his hand in the partially opened drawer.

"Quick, sir!" exclaimed Henley, impatiently, "your obstinacy is all you have to thank for losing them, without any gain to yourself. I made you offers which would have satisfied the most exacting; you have refused them, and now you must lose your cherished prize altogether."

"I must succumb to brute force," said Gripe.

"You should have listened to reason," replied Henley. "You believed me in your power, but see you are in mine. Fool! did you think I was to be cowed by a thing like you!"

Gripe made no reply, but continued fumbling in the drawer.

"Haste," cried Henley, "and end the farce, lest you again excite my passion. The packet, quick, or my fingers shall again be at your throat!"

And he extended his hand towards Gripe's neck.

"They are not here," said Gripe.

"Liar!"

"They are not, I say."

"Then where are they?"

"I know not," said Gripe.

Henley seized the steward again by the throat, but in an instant he released his grasp, and recoiled back several paces.

Gripe had taken a pistol from the drawer, and presented it at the head of the unsuspecting squire.

The packet was not there—it was the weapon which Gripe sought to defend himself with.

Again the tables were turned, and Gripe held the squire at bay.

Foaming with passion, Henley stood gazing upon his steward.

"Foiled!" he hissed. "Fool, why did I not throttle him!"

"So, squire," said Gripe, after enjoying for a few moments the confusion of his victim, "it is not only brute strength that wins the day."

"Curse you!" exclaimed Henley, again advancing.

But Gripe kept the muzzle of the pistol turned to the head of Henley, and again he fell back.

"Squire," said Gripe, in his usual calm tone, "you have taught me a lesson, and that is not to trust you, and you may rest assured that I shall always be prepared to defend myself from your attacks.

"The papers!" fairly roared the squire.

"Are safe," replied Gripe.

"They must and shall be mine!"

"No, squire, at least, not at present. They must not yet leave my possession. You see, it would be madness for you to endeavour to take them from me. Go to your own room, and when this passion has worn itself out, we can better understand each other. Better that we be friends than enemies. We hold each other in power, and our interests are mutual. When rogues fall out, honest men get their due."

Squire Henley hesitated a moment, then turned and left the room.

"Ha, ha!" exclaimed Gripe, "to-morrow we shall be friends."

CHAPTER XXXII.

THE FLIGHT OF THE MURDERER—CONSCIENCE AT WORK.

AWAY, with the hand of Cain upon his brow—away, with the guilt of murder on his soul—away through lane and field, street and high road—away over hedges and ditches—away from the scene of his crime—the bleeding victim of his murderous hand, the festering corpse.

Away, away, from all but his conscience—that ever upbraiding voice, that will penetrate the soul, and awake the mind to the guilty deed.

From this Dancing Bill could not fly.

From the last look at that pale upbraiding face—from the last glare of those glassy eyes—from the last words of his innocent victim.

He could not shut them out. In every passing object he saw the last fearful look—heard the last words.

On, on, he flew, amid the raging of the storm.

The lightning flashed, and the thunder rolled, the wind howled, and the rain poured down in torrents; but still, above the voice of the elements, he could hear the dying words of her whom he had mistaken for his wife—of her who that night had died for Margaret, died by the hand of him who should have loved and cherished the wife of his bosom—his partner in life.

In vain he strove to shut out the glare of those eyes—that last fearful look—that glassy stare.

Turn which way he could, there he saw them —saw them fixed upon his guilty face, penetrating his very soul.

He placed his fingers in his ears, that he might shut out the sound of her voice; but above the howling of the storm it came on his senses, and drove him almost to madness.

He hurried on in despair.

Never again, he thought, should he free himself from the glance of those eyes—the sound of that voice.

Bitterly, too, did he curse the evil fortune which had led him to track an innocent and unsuspecting woman—one who, by word or deed, had never done him wrong.

Had it have been Margaret, he believed he should have felt none of those qualms of conscience with which his breast was now so violently assailed.

Her he believed he could have murdered without one thought of the guilty deed.

But his victim had never wronged him—could have no reason to do him harm—had no power to assail him; and he cursed his want of forethought, in not making sure the figure he was following was his wife—she who held the secret of his villany in her breast—she who could have consigned him to a prison.

He had thought to crush the only evidence of his guilty work—to remove the only evidence of his crime.

But how had he succeeded?

As most guilty men do.

He had placed his foot upon the first round of the ladder which leads to destruction.

He had descended to the second to retrieve the first, but he had slipped lower, and the break became wider.

Now, two crimes had been committed, and the evidence of the first remained, instead of being blotted out.

He was worse off than before—further from the goal to which he had aspired.

Thus it ever is with the guilty man; he struggles to regain his position, but in vain; he slips down, down, till a fearful gulf yawns at his feet, and he is carried away into the vortex of destruction.

Dancing Bill was not the only man whose evil passions had led him to plunge his soul into crime and misery, nor was he the only one who hoped to retrieve the first false step by the descent of the second.

The gambler throws the dice to retrieve his shattered fortunes—the drunkard takes the second glass to kill the effects of the first.

Vain delusion!

They but add to the already vile defects—add to the poison which is working in their mind.

As well might a man grasp at a sunbeam to save himself from falling, as descend the second round of the ladder of crime to retrieve the first step.

To hide one lie a second is uttered; to hide one crime a second is committed; and the double crime must be answered for, for the guilty cannot escape, and the recording angel registers them both, dots them down in characters of fire, to burn the evil-doer.

"Thou shalt do no murder! saith the Lord."

Shall man expect to escape the penalty of a crime which the Supreme bade his viceroy on earth to write with his finger upon the solid rock?

Yet man deems it necessary to commit such deeds that he may escape the penalty of his former crimes.

Fool! knows he not that there is one who knows and sees all? one whose hand shall hurl him to destruction?

But Dancing Bill thought not of all this.

He only knew that Margaret had the power to consign him to a felon's doom.

And that power must be annihilated.

Too late he had found how uncertain are the hopes of man.

On he strode, trembling at every step.

Once or twice he paused to wipe the bloody weapon upon the wet grass, and obliterate the traces of blood from his hands.

Whenever he saw a human form approaching towards him he crossed to the opposite side, so that he might run no risk of being recognized.

In this way he reached his lodging.

Nervously he turned the key in the lock of the outer door, and silently he made his way up the stairs to his own room.

He feared to strike a light, lest the noise of the flint upon the steel should betray the hour at which he arrived home.

This was a circumstance he feared to be known, and he fondly hoped that no one had any knowledge of the time when he entered the house.

Accustomed to keeping late hours, which his avocations necessitated, no one would have considered it strange that Dancing Bill should return at such an hour; but the nerves of the harlequin were shaken, and he feared even this being known.

So he threw off his clothes, and concealed them between the bed and the mattrass, lest any one should enter the apartment, though why he should expect such a circumstance it is impossible to divine.

It must have been the whispering of a guilty conscience.

That still, small voice, which wakes the giant to the consciousness that there is a law higher than the dictates of man, a power greater than earthly justice.

After secreting his dress beneath the bed, Dancing Bill crept in between the sheets, and laid his head upon the pillow.

If he expected the drowsy god to drown his senses in forgetfulness, he was greatly mistaken.

He tossed about uneasily, still sleep would not press his eyelids.

The features of his murdered victim were still present in his mind's eye; the curse of the bloodstained woman still rang in his ears.

He closed his eyes to shut out the pale and fearful vision, but in vain—it still stood before him—still upbraided his murderous soul.

So strong did the feeling of fear which pursued him take hold of his imagination, that at length he fairly believed the corpse of his murdered victim stood beside him.

So plainly did he trace every feature—so clearly did he hear every word she uttered.

It seemed to bend over him, and the pale, cold face almost touched his own.

He would have shrieked, but he feared the sound of his own voice.

He put forth his hand to push it from him, but his arm passed through the fearful shadow, as though it were composed of air.

He trembled in every limb, and a cold, clammy perspiration broke out upon his brow.

A sensation which he had never before experienced crept over him, and the bed beneath him shook with the tremulous agitation of its occupant.

Still the figure stood by his bedside—still those glassy eyes were fixed upon his face.

Oh! that it would leave that spot.

He drew his head beneath the counterpane to shut it out, but still it was there.

Still the pale face and glassy eye was before him.

With a cry of horror he started up in the bed, and struck forth with all his force.

But this had no effect upon what he believed to be the spectre of his murdered victim.

His blows fell harmlessly upon the shadow, and he sunk back again upon the pillow.

Oh! if he had but a light.

Yet he could not—dared not—leave his couch to procure one.

That fearful shade stood in his path.

What could he do to rid himself of its dreaded presence?

He tried to think, but nothing definite could he summon to his aid.

Would it leave him if he slept?

Fondly he hoped it would.

He closed his eyes again, and pretended to sleep.

But still the pale form was there, and the glowing eye gleamed upon him.

Despair sat upon his soul.

What would he not now have given to recall that fearful deed.

He felt that that shade would haunt him through life.

Should he pray that it might be removed?

Pray!

Him—a murderer—pray!

He strove to utter a prayer, but his tongue clove to the roof of his mouth, and he could not articulate a single word.

And the voice of the murdered victim fell upon his ears in taunting tones.

Down—down—down into the bed he crept, to shut out sight and sound, but in vain; turn which way he would, still could he trace the lineaments and hear the tones of his innocent victim.

He could bear it no longer.

He strove to leap from the bed.

His limbs were cramped and powerless.

In trembling suspense he lie, panting and trembling.

At length he drew up one foot, with the intention of leaving his couch and obtaining a light.

But he started with fear, and his pores opened, and a cold sweat breaks out upon him.

Something cold, clammy, and death-like moves down the limb he has drawn up.

What can it be?

He feared to think.

Was it the hand of his dead victim? He shudders, and his breath comes short and quick.

Still there it lies—cold, damp, and clammy. His flesh creeps and his hair stands on an end.

He strove to speak, but he could not utter a sound.

The tones he would utter died away in an inarticulate whisper, and still the cold substance presses against his limb.

He lay and shuddered, and his brain whirled in the agony of fear which beset his mind.

Wretched, miserable, powerless he lie, unable now to close his eyes, and shut out the horrible vision before him.

He feared he should go mad, so fearfully did his imagination play upon his brain.

And thus he lay for some time longer.

He makes one more struggle to rise; the fearful incubus is taken from his heart, and he starts up in the bed.

As he does so, the cold pressure on his leg is removed.

A feeling of joy takes possession of his breast, but ere it is kindled it dies away, for again the clammy substance presses upon his leg.

With a cry of horror he thrust his hand down the bed-clothes, and grasps the object.

A cry of joy broke from his lips—the fearful substance was but his own dead foot.

The blood had stagnated in the member, and his fears had conjured up the rest.

But that fear was still upon him, spite of the discovery he had made.

His guilty conscience would not permit him to sleep.

He bounded from the bed, and struck a light, and as the gleam of the candle shed a lustre through the darkness of the room, Bill breathed more freely.

CHAPTER XXXIII.

THE MANAGERS AT THE ROYAL STAR—MARY IS RESORTED TO, TO SAVE THE FORTUNES OF THE HOUSE.

WITH a long, lingering look of admiration, the eyes of Charlie and his companions followed the stout form of Dick the Poacher, as he hastily quitted the theatre, after his refusal to partake of the hospitality extended by the pantomimists.

Little Mary was so disappointed, that she fairly burst into tears, and Harry, in his endeavours to soothe her, kissed away the pearly drops as they rolled down her pretty cheeks.

"Strange chap, that," said Buskin Bob.

"Very," replied the clown. "There is something about him I can't make out. He ain't what he seems to be."

"Strike me comical if he is!" exclaimed Bob. "I tell you what, somebody's been and gone and done him some sort of injury, that's my belief.

"What injury?" said Charlie.

"Well, in course I don't know, but there's been some hankey-pankey dodge or other played on that chap. Just you take a look at his physog, there's no make up there, it's true to nature. Strike me comical, if I'd have had a face like that chap, I'd have made a fortune out of it, that I would, strike me comical if I would'nt!"

And Buskin Bob emphatically drove his fist into the crown of his hat, causing a sound to emanate therefrom, something like that which his drum gave forth at the blow of the stick.

"I tell you what, Charlie," he added, placing his hand inside his hat to force out the dent which his fist had made in the crown. "I tell you what it is, I've been a buskin' about the country too long not to know a thing or two, I'm fly to every fakement on the boards, and I know a real gentleman, and I says this here individual—this here gentleman, because, if he is a poacher, he is a gentleman—I say this cove—this Dick—this whatever you like to call him—is a man, a true man, a good man, and strike me comical, if he ain't a real right down gentleman, I'm — no, not that, but I don't know nothing of the hanky-panky line, if I do, strike me comical, there!"

"He is not what he seems, I believe," said Charlie.

"Well then, I believe he is," said Bob.

"What, a poor —"

"But ain't he got the looks of a gentleman?" asked Bob.

"True."

"Then he is one. But, Harry," added Bob, "surely you must know something of him."

The Boy Actor shook his head.

"Then how does he know you, and why should he be so eager to befriend you?"

"Strike me comical if there ain't some mystery here."

"Did you never meet before, Harry?" asked Charlie Evans.

"Not till the time when he stole the papers from Takeall, the broker," replied the boy.

"Never before?" asked Bob.

"No," said the boy; "And yet I sometimes think that when I was a little child—so small that I can't recollect—I have seen those dark eyes and black ringlets; but I am not sure, it may be only fancy."

Charlie Evans shook his head.

"Well," he said, after a pause, "time works out the greatest puzzle, and it will doubtless unravel this mystery."

"I hope it may," said Bob; "and if it does, just you see if I ain't right. Look here, Charlie, I'll bet you a pot of fourpenny I'm right, I will, strike me comical!"

But Charlie only smiled at his good-hearted friend, and intimated that it would be as well to get home, as the young ones were getting tired.

Taking the hand of his little daughter in his own, the clown led the way out of the theatre, followed by Buskin Bob and Harry.

The excitement caused by the fire, and the interview with Dick, had for a time chased away all feelings of exhaustion from the hearts of the players.

Now, as they left the theatre, that feeling returned; for their duties during the last few days had indeed been arduous, and they were tired and worn out.

Arriving home, they sat down to their humble meal, and counted out the proceeds of the first night's performance.

It exceeded their expectations.

Harry's face became radiant with smiles, as the amount of money taken that night was mentioned to him.

"Oh," he exclaimed, "we shall be poor no more. I am so glad you opened the house."

But Charlie felt otherwise.

The affair of the fire, he feared, would do more to injure them than anything else.

He regretted that the boy should be so sanguine, and he said,—

"Harry, I truly hope such may be the case, but do not make up your mind that it must be so. That fire to-night has done us more injury than you think for. The public will be frightened, and stay away, and the curtain will be drawn up to empty houses—at least, I fear so, but I hope—sincerely hope—that such will not be the case."

"And so do I, strike me comical if I don't," exclaimed Bob.

Harry only sighed.

The words of Charlie had thrown a chill upon his sanguine mind.

He could not but acknowledge that the opinion of the clown was worth taking.

Young and sanguine, he looked upon success as certain.

He retired to bed that night with a gloomy feeling at his heart.

So also did little Mary.

Poor child! as she flung her arms round the neck of her young companion, she murmured,—

"Oh, Harry, that fire. I do hope it will not injure us."

"And so do I," said the Boy.

DICK AND SQUIRE HENLEY IN THE CHURCHYARD.

"I will ask in my prayers to-night that it may not," said Mary.

"And so will I," said Harry; "and pray, too, that he who could do so wicked a deed may be pardoned, and led to feel the horror and wickedness of the crime he has committed."

And, with a parting kiss, these two children—these young ones, who were doomed to be cast upon the cold world to struggle for bread—retired to rest.

And laid their heads upon their pillows with the vision of the fire before their mind's eye, but hopeful that they still might succeed in the career which had been marked out for them; and prayed that, though it is noble to toil, the fruits of their labours might be good, and that their struggle for bread might not be rewarded with stone.

Up betimes on the following morning, and away to the theatre.

There is little rest for the managers of a provincial play-house. Pieces have to be altered almost every night, and there are scenes to paint and alter, dresses to turn and mend, checks to make, parts to write, and a thousand other things, known only to those engaged in the profession.

Little time, indeed, had the new management at the Royal Star to be idle, unless they engaged others to do the work.

But this would not pay, and Charlie Evans, Buskin Bob, and the two children had all to turn to and do something.

No. 11.

This they did with a will, and left nothing undone which they could possibly do.

Under such circumstances, the new proprietors of the Royal Star bid fair to raise the old property out of the slough into which previous managements had plunged it.

But, alas! a dark cloud had passed across the bright horizon of success.

The fire had done more to close the theatre than all the neglect of the new managers could do.

It was with a sad heart that the Boy Actor and his friends heard the comments on the accident of the night before, and the surmises as to how many people would be in the house when the curtain rose that night.

Old "pros" shook their heads ominously, and related the effects experienced at other places of amusement, under circumstances of a similar nature.

Ere midday, the friends had decided that it would be necessary to put forth some new attraction, to induce the people to pay a visit to the house.

"It won't do," said Charley, in a desponding tone, "to trust to the same entertainment as last night. We must promise more, and perform it, too, to get them in."

"Strike me comical if we mustn't," said Bob. "But what can we do extra to-night?"

Charlie shrugged his shoulders.

"I don't know," he said.

"Nor I either," said Bob. "I only wish we could burn the fellow that set fire to the crib last night, strike me comical if I don't, and the public would like it, too, I know."

"Vengeance is not for us," said Charlie, solemnly.

"Aint it?" replied Bob. Strike me comical if I wouldn't have vengeance on him, if I only knew who he was. I'd play such a tune on his skull with my drum sticks, as would make him recollect the part he played last night, I would, strike me comical if I wouldn't—there!"

And Buskin Bob clenched his right hand, and struck the palm of his left, as indicative of the nature of his feelings towards the ruffian whose nature had prompted so diabolical a deed.

"We don't know who he is," said Charlie, "so must leave him to be dealt with by heaven."

"Then I hope it will send him to hell, that's all I hope," exclaimed Buskin Bob, turning quite red in the face. "He deserves to have it as hot as he tried to make it for us, strike me comical if he don't."

"Well, let us leave him to his own conscience, be he whomsoever he may," said Charlie. "All I know is, I would not have his feelings."

"He can't have any," said Bob, "or he'd never have done it."

"He could not have thought of the consequences of his deed," said Charlie.

"But something must be done to save the house—to counteract the feeling which has taken possession of the public."

"What can be done? Nothing for to-night," said Bob.

"Suppose we send for Margaret," said Charlie.

"She was here last night, so that could make no difference."

"But she is not announced for to-night," remarked Charlie.

"Might do that, then," said Bob.

"Let Mary dance," said Harry, who had heard a portion of the conversation.

"Ah! that would do," exclaimed Bob. "Get a few bills stuck about the doors, that a young lady will dance to-night, and it might draw in a few."

Charlie paused a few minutes.

At length he said,—

"I fear she is not well enough up in her steps."

"Why, you know she can do the hornpipe to perfection."

"Yes, on a cellar-flap, or to a street band; but not on the stage," answered the clown.

"I think she can do it well enough," remarked Harry. "It would be a novelty if she danced the hornpipe in costume, and she would make a pretty little sailor boy."

"So she would," said Bob; "and I tell you what, Charlie, suppose she does it in fetters?"

"Good," said Charlie, "the fetters will hide a few false steps. So she shall do the hornpipe in fetters, and we'll have a few bills on the doors, that a young lady from London has been procured to dance, at an enormous outlay to the management, who have been induced to place this novelty before them on account of the generous support received from the people of this town on the first night of the new company."

"Strike me comical, Charlie," said Bob "you've just hit the right nail on the head. Nothing could be better, and I will tell you what I'll do. I'll paint a young girl dressed as a sailor, dancing in fetters, on a piece of canvass, and we'll put it over the entrance with a light behind it, and see if it won't draw the people in."

Away flew Harry from the little room in which this decision had been come to, to the apartment in which Mary sat mending a doublet for one of the characters that evening.

The young girl looked up as he entered, and a smile stole over her sweet face.

"Have you come to help me, Harry?" she asked.

"I wish I could," replied the boy, "but I don't know how to sew."

"I am glad that I do," she answered, "for there is so much wants doing, that the dresses would all be spoilt if I couldn't, and father says a stitch in time saves nine."

"So it does, Mary."

"Yes, for look here, that little hole would have gone much larger if I hadn't drawn it together."

"Do you know what I have come to tell you?" asked the boy, bending down over the head of the smiling girl.

"No, what?"

"Guess?"

"I can't."

"Do try?" asked Harry, his youthful face lighting up with a smile.

"I don't know what to guess, upon my word I don't," replied Mary.

"Well, then, you are going to play to-night."

"Me?"

"Yes, you."

"But I can't play."

"Oh, yes, you can."

"Why, what can I do?" asked Mary, turning her smiling face in surprise to her youthful companion.

"Why, dance to be sure," replied Harry.

" Dance ! "

" Yes."

" Me dance ! here ? "

" Yes, Mary, you dance, here."

" Why, what can I dance ? "

" The hornpipe."

" He, he," laughed the little maiden. " I could do so in the streets perhaps, if father wished me to do so, but not on the stage."

" And why not ? "

" I cannot do it well enough," replied Mary."

" Oh, yes you can."

But Mary shook her head.

" I wish I could," she said. " If I could only dance like Mrs. Simmons, I should be so glad."

" Father says that you can do it nicely in a boy's dress."

Little Mary blushed up to her eyes.

" And in fetters," said Harry.

" Oh! I can't, I'm sure I can't," said the girl.

" And I am sure you can," said Harry. You will try now, won't you ? " he added, as she turned her gaze from him.

" I am sure I should be hissed. I am sure I should."

" No you wouldn't," pleaded Harry. " Now do try. I know you will succeed. Now do promise me you will. You won't refuse me Mary, will you ? " and the boy placed his arm, round the neck of the little maiden, and looked plead ingly into her soft blue eyes.

" I can't," she answered.

But at the same moment she threw her arm over the neck of the youth, as she saw the look of disappointment which overspread his features, and imprinted a kiss upon his cheek.

" You will promise me, Mary," he said, " now won't you ? "

Mary was silent.

" I would do anything for you, indeed I would."

" I know you would, Harry," she exclaimed fervently.

" And will you refuse me this ? " he asked

" I—I——"

" Well, try, Mary," he interrupted.

Mary could not bear again to refuse his request, so she placed her little hand in his, and said,—

" I won't promise——"

" Oh, yes, you must ! " pleaded the youth. " It is the only hope we have of counteracting the depressing effect caused by the incident of last night. People will stop away unless we can do something to bring them in ; and I'm sure we could do nothing better than get you to dance a hornpipe in fetters. So you see, Mary, our hopes are in you. You can save the house, and be the means of saving us from ruin. You will do it, Mary—won't you ? "

The young girl drew his head down to her lips ; and, imprinting another kiss on his cheek, she murmured,—

" Do it, Harry ?—yes. If they hiss me all the while, I will do it."

" Oh! I'm so glad ! " exclaimed the boy; " so very glad! You won't be hissed, Mary ; no one could be so cruel as to hiss you, for you are so good—so kind, and I love you so much! Oh! I'm so glad ! "

And clasping the little maiden in his arms,

and kissing her affectionately, Harry darted from the room.

With light and childish steps, he made his way to the spot where Charlie and Buskin Bob were conversing.

" It's all right," he exclaimed, in pleased tones.

" What's all right ? " asked Charlie.

" Mary."

" What of Mary ? "

" She'll do it."

" What ? "

" The hornpipe in fetters."

" Oh ! " said Charlie, who had almost forgotten all about it in pursuit of other matters.

" Yes ; she'll do it—she promised me she would."

" In course she would," remarked Bob. " Strike me comical if I thought anything else. Well, I'll just go and get the transparency ready ; and, Charlie, send Harry to the printer's for a few bills. They'll do them while he waits ; and have them put up at once."

And away darted Bob, to daub over a piece of canvas with the figure of a youth dancing in fetters.

The bills were procured, the transparency painted and fixed over the principal entrance to the Royal Star, and a light placed behind it as soon as dusk.

As far as possible, every preparation had been made for the evening, both before and behind the curtain, and Charlie and his friends only awaited anxiously the hour of opening.

Not that they were in any hurry to commence business, but they were anxious to see what effect the fire of the previous night would have upon the public.

They feared empty benches.

They hoped a full house.

In fact, so anxious were both Charlie and Bob, that neither cared for any tea, although they had been toiling hard for several hours.

The time at which the people commenced assembling around the door was drawing near ; the lamps had been lighted, the transparency illuminated, and Mary had been escorted to the opposite side of the road by Harry, to see the portrait of herself in boy's attire, with chains fastened to her wrists and ankles, and hanging down her form like the string of sausages stuffed with sawdust which her father had so often fallen over on the parade of Richardson's show.

Mary's lip curled scornfully as she looked upon this little piece of clap-trap.

" Don't you like it ? " asked Harry, in a disappointed tone of voice.

" It will do," she replied, " for what it is intended, but Bob has not done it nice."

" I think he has," said the boy.

" Do you ? " said Mary.

" It's just like you."

" Like me ? "

" Yes."

" With that large mouth ? " exclaimed the little maiden, half playfully, half hurt.

Young as she was, Mary knew that she was pretty.

" Oh ! " exclaimed Harry, " I did not notice the mouth. Yes, that is a little too large."

A *little* too large! Mary thought it was a very great deal.

" And look at the nose," she said.

The boy did as she requested.

The nose was worse still.

"And the eyes and the hair. Oh, it is a daub!" she said; "I wouldn't let Bob paint my portrait."

And the little maiden walked indignantly back to the theatre.

But Mary was too kind-hearted to remain angry long, and when Bob ran against her on the stage, and asked her if she hadn't seen the beautiful picture he had painted for her, she only smiled and replied,—

"Bob, you are a bad judge of beauty."

And with a merry laugh she bounded past him, leaving the good-hearted pantaloon gazing after her slight form with a look of admiration on his rough yet honest countenance.

"Strike me comical if I ain't though. My name's not Buskin Bob if Charlie Evans ain't the father of as pretty a girl as ever ran across the boards. If he ain't strike me comical—there! Ah," he added, thrusting his hands into the pockets of his small-clothes, and letting his head sink meditatingly on his broad chest, "she oughtn't to be brought up in the profession, she oughtn't. It's all very well while she's a child, but she ought to cut it bye and bye. She's too pretty, much too pretty for the boards, and the temptations are great. But there, they ain't all bad, and very few are as bad as they are made out to be; still, there would be no thieves if there was nothing to steal, and poor girls would do no wrong if there was no temptations. Well, well, she is a good girl, she is, and I hope no harm will come to her, I do, strike me comical if I don't."

And Bob walked thoughtfully off the stage to see how the house looked in front, and whether the doors were thronged as on the previous night.

Harry had gone to the dressing-room to make up—a difficulty which he had learned to surmount by this time, and Charlie was engaged in the prompter's box, in seeing that everything was ready for the rise of the curtain.

Little Mary had sat down to fix the last sword-knot, and the man engaged for that duty was lighting the gas in the flies, by the means of a long pole.

The bedaubed scenery was becoming brighter and more dazzling, and the cold, cheerless, miserable theatre—as it ever appears by daylight—was fast assuming a far more cheerful aspect.

Buskin Bob had walked round to the front of the house, and surveyed the crowd in front of the entrances.

A sigh broke from his lips.

The number assembled did not reach one quarter of the previous evening, and even among those pushing towards the doors, remarks were being freely made about the fire, and the casualties attendant on it, the previous night.

Some of the more timid females seemed more inclined to seek an evening's amusement elsewhere; the fear of a repetition of the last night's sad drama taking possession of their minds.

"This won't do," muttered Bob, to himself, as he observed the uneasy feeling among those present. "The doors must be opened at once, or half of them will go away frightened by the remarks of the others. Strike me comical, if whoever he was that set fire to the box wished to do any of us a bad turn, he could not have thought of anything more likely to injure us. He has carried out his work better than he expected—curse him!—strike me comical if he ain't."

And Bob hurried back to the stage.

"Charlie," he said, when he found that personage, "you must open the doors at once."

"It ain't time yet," replied the clown; "it wants twenty minutes."

"Never mind if it wants forty," said Bob. "I tell you it must be done, or half those who are waiting will go away."

"Why?" asked the clown.

"Because that infernal fire is all they can find to talk about, and those as ain't frightened themselves are frightening others, so as they can get close up to the doors and have the best seats."

Charlie sighed.

"Well, open the house then, Bob; it will be better for them to wait after they have paid their money than go away again."

"And better for us too," said Bob.

"Light up as quick as you can," said the clown, addressing the man with the long stick with a light stuck in a cleft of one end. "Light up the front; you can do this while the people are coming in."

The man passed round to the front, and in a few minutes the theatre was ready for the reception of the audience.

Bob took up his post at the money box, and the doors were opened.

There was a rush as the bolts of the doors were drawn, for it would appear that the frequenters of theatres must rush, even if there were but two persons present, but the pressure was not near so great as it was on the previous evening.

Nor was Bob's duty so hard to perform, for in the space of a minute and a half the rush had gone by, and Bob was leisurely counting the money he had received.

He shook his head ominously.

True, it was still early, much earlier than the time of opening, but Bob knew too well that there was no chance whatever of a good house that night.

The patrons of the place had to wait considerably longer before the gas was turned up and the band entered the orchestra than their patience could submit to, and the clapping and whistling gave place to groans and hisses.

To avoid one evil, Charlie had been compelled to court another.

It was with a feeling of relief, then, that the band entered the theatre, for the moment that the bald head of the leader appeared in the orchestra, the demeanour of the audience changed, and bursts of applause echoed through the half-empty house.

It was not long ere the first chord sounded, and the lights were turned up; and, as the strains of the little band floated around, the audience forgot their ill-temper, and became silent and decorous.

Charlie looked long and anxiously through the slit in the side of the curtain, and turned away with a sigh from the view of the half-empty benches.

"The fire has done its work," he murmured. "The house is half empty."

Harry, who had finished dressing, at this moment approached his friend, and, over-hearing the remark, exclaimed,—

"Half-empty?"

"Yes," replied Charlie. "The fire has kept the people away."

"But the recollection of it will soon die out, perhaps," said the boy; "and, a few nights passed, we may find the theatre as full as yesternight."

Charlie shook his head.

"I trust it may be so, Harry, for all our sakes, but——"

"But what?" interrupted the boy.

Charlie hesitated.

He feared to say anything which might have a depressing effect upon the mind of the boy, and perhaps cause him to fail in his part.

"But what?" repeated Harry.

"I hope it will, my boy—sincerely hope it will."

And, not wishing to deceive the boy, he turned away, and busied himself in seeing that all the properties required in the piece were at hand.

All was ready, and the bell rang for the curtain to rise.

And, as it rolled up into the flies, Charlie turned away from the wings with a look of pain upon his face.

"The second night, and an almost empty house," he muttered. "It's hard lines, after so bright a promise. Poor boy, I had hoped better for him; but luck seems against us, and, strive as we will, we still are doomed to "Struggle for Bread."

CHAPTER XXXIV.

MR. GRIPE MAKES HIMSELF AT HOME—DOUBTS AND THREATS—A RANDOM SHOT, AND ITS CONSEQUENCES.

MR. GRIPE sat in the large easy chair in the squire's sitting room, his feet encased in a pair of prettily worked slippers, the gift of his much esteemed friend Takeall, the broker and appraiser, and which had fallen into that gentleman's hands in the course of one of his seizures, and having forgotten to put them down in the inventory, had presented them to his esteemed friend the steward.

With one foot resting on the fender, and the other placed upon the bright hob of the grate, in which a large coal fire was burning, he lolled back in the soft cushion, and, with a smile upon his little weazened face, amused himself by perusing the newspaper, which had been left in the room for the squire, as soon as he should rise from his breakfast.

He had sat thus for some time in an attitude of the greatest ease, when the door of the apartment opened, and Squire Henley stood upon the threshold.

As the eyes of the squire lighted upon the form of his steward they gradually opened till they could go no further, and a look of the greatest surprise overspread his features.

Gripe raised his little eyes from the paper, and fixed them full upon the squire, the smile still remaining upon his thin lips, but he never shifted his position in the least.

For some few moments Henley stood gazing at the figure of the little steward, as though he could not believe the evidence of his senses; then,

thinking that perhaps the little man had not observed him, he coughed to attract his attention.

"Come in," said Gripe, "and close the door, squire, there's such a confounded draught."

And the little man gave a little shiver, and again turned his eyes upon the paper.

If it had been possible for the squire to open his eyes any wider than they already were, he would have done so.

The cool, calm tones of the steward, combined with the attitude which he had taken up in his chair, and in his private room, completely confounded him, and he hardly knew whether to leap upon the little man and kick him out of the apartment, or obey the command which the steward had uttered.

While debating in his mind which course to pursue, Gripe again looked up from the paper.

"Whew! what a draught," he exclaimed. "Pray come in, squire, and close the door after you."

Henley slowly entered the apartment, and closed the door, but remained standing by it.

"Sit down," said the little man, "I won't keep you long waiting for the paper, I have only got a column and a half to read before I have finished this leader."

And again Gripe lowered his eyes to the paper, and read, or pretended to read.

Squire Henley placed his hand upon the back of a chair, and stood looking at the little man, as if he could not believe the evidence of his senses.

Then he raised the chair about a foot from the ground, and bringing it down with all his force upon the slippered foot, which Gripe at that moment drew from the hob, sat himself down upon it with all his might.

"Oh! Oh!" shrieked Gripe, endeavouring to extricate the imprisoned foot.

Henley ground his whole weight down upon the seat of the chair for a moment, then rising, Gripe released his foot, at the same time overturning the chair.

Grasping the maimed member in his hand, he dropped the newspaper on the floor, and hopped about the room with his foot in his hand, and with such a comical expression upon his weazened face that even Charlie Evans, had he seen the little steward at that moment, would have confessed that it was done better than he himself could have done it, after the pantaloon had dropped the red pointed property poker on his toes.

So irresistibly comic was the appearance of Gripe, that the squire, annoyed as he was at the cool impudence of his steward, allowed a grin of satisfaction to creep over his features.

It was not by accident that Gripe had received such a blow.

Annoyed beyond measure at finding Gripe in his own private room, and the cool impudence of the little man, Squire Henley was goaded to fury; and it is somewhat doubtful whether the squire, if the foot of the steward had not attracted his attention, would not have raised the chair considerably higher from the floor than he had done, and brought it down with still greater violence upon the little head of the imperturbable Mr. Gripe.

Throwing himself into his own easy chair, the squire lifted the paper from the floor, where Gripe had dropped it, and holding it before him, fixed his eyes upon its columns, and took no further notice of his steward, or the antics which the little man was pursuing.

"Oh! my foot! Oh! my foot!" yelled Gripe, sinking into a chair at the other side of the room from the fireplace, and, still holding that member in his hand, rocked himself to and fro.

"Oh! squire, I do believe you have broken it. I do indeed!" he exclaimed, seeing that Henley took no notice of him, and appeared busily occupied in perusing the news.

"Damn your foot!" growled the squire, "and you too. Your foot had no business there, this is my room. What brought you here?"

"Duty," exclaimed Gripe.

"What duty?" said Henley.

"Duty I owe to myself," returned Gripe.

Henley merely shrugged his shoulders, and again pretended to read.

Gripe continued rocking himself to and fro for some time; then the pain having somewhat abated he limped across the room, and taking the chair which the squire had inflicted the injury with, he sat himself down at the opposite side of the fireplace, and fixed his little eyes full upon the face of his master.

For some time Henley pretended to read, but not one line did he peruse.

Annoyed, yet scarcely knowing how to act, he gazed over the top of the paper at the face of the little man, on which the faint smile was fast returning.

"Curse him!" thought the squire, "the cool, impudent rascal, and yet I fear to kick him out, for he holds me in his power."

Thus they sat for some time, till Henley could bear the cool gaze of the steward no longer, and shifted uneasily in his seat.

"I say, squire," said Gripe, at length, throwing himself back in his chair, and placing one leg over the other.

Henley returned no answer, but still pretended to read.

"I say, squire," again exclaimed the little steward, "you won't be long before you have finished that article, will you?"

"Curse you, what's that to you!" growled Henley, mortified beyond measure at the coolness of his companion.

"Oh, nothing," drawled Gripe, "I can wait till you have done."

And turning his face towards the glowing fire, he placed his feet on the fender, and fixed his eyes upon the ornaments of the chimney piece.

A sigh of relief escaped the breast of Henley, as he felt that the glance of the steward was taken from his face.

The eye of the little man had such an influence over him, that while it rested on him, it seemed to hold him spell bound.

It was the voice of conscience, whispering to his soul, "the guilty shall have no rest."

For some time Gripe continued in the same position.

At length he turned his gaze upon the face of his companion, and said,—

"Have you done, squire?"

"Go to——," roared Henley, flinging down the paper.

"I have no wish to do so," said Gripe, in the cool, measured tones so common to him, "as I should be sure to meet you there, some time or other."

The squire bit his lips, to suppress the wrath which rose in his breast.

"Insolent," he muttered.

Gripe shrugged his shoulders, and smoothed his hair with the palm of his hand.

"What the devil is the meaning of this conduct," exclaimed the squire, beginning to lose all control over his temper. "Why do I find you here in this apartment, when you should be attending to your duties?"

"That's just what I am doing now, squire," replied Gripe calmly, "I never neglect my duty, no matter how difficult or unpleasant it may be to perform. Duty is duty, squire, and duty brings me here this morning."

"What duty?" said Henley.

"A duty which I owe to myself and to you," replied Gripe.

"Explain."

"A perfect understanding respecting the business which engaged our attentions last evening."

"Then let us have it, and begone," exclaimed Henley.

"Well then, squire, to the point. I hold you in my power, and you know it," said Gripe.

"Indeed!"

"Yes, squire, such is the fact," exclaimed Gripe.

"So you believe."

"I am sure."

"I am not."

"Shall I convince you?" asked Gripe.

"By what means?"

"The production of the packet," said the steward.

"Produce it, let me see it," said Henley, as a feeling took possession of his breast, that if he could but lay his hand upon it, he might hold Gripe by the throat, while he consigned it to the fire which burned so brightly in the grate.

"I will do so," said Gripe, "should your obstinacy render it necessary."

Henley looked questioningly at his companion.

"How?" he said, "I don't understand."

"In a court of justice, I mean," replied the steward, the smile deepening around his little mouth.

"I have but your bare word that you are in possession of these supposed documents. I would be convinced."

"No doubt you would, squire," said Gripe, "but you may take my word for it, that I have got them, and mean to keep them into the bargain."

"What purpose do you intend putting them to?" asked Henley.

"That will entirely depend upon circumstances," replied the steward.

"Look you, Gripe," said Henley, after a long pause, "you have been made the tool of a clever rascal, who bears me some ill-will. Dick the Poacher, knowing your grasping, avaricious nature, has played upon your cupidity, and palmed off upon you the concoction of his own imagination. There are no papers in existence which can injure me—no documents which can wrest from me one foot of these broad lands."

"But I say there is, squire," returned the steward.

"You have been deceived."

"No, I have not."

"Think you that that poacher, had he possessed such documents, would have sold it to you for five hundred pounds, when this estate is worth as many thousands. He has played upon your credulity, to avenge himself for the prosecutions he has suffered at our hands. The packet he sold you—if he really did sell you one —is worthless."

"Won't do, squire, won't do," said Gripe. "Remember that you commissioned me to get it at the cottage of the late Widow Marston, that I saw it there, that Dick the Poacher wrested it from the hands of Takeall the broker."

"Well?"

"Well, squire, if those papers were worthless, why were you so anxious to get them?" asked the steward.

Henley was silent.

"Your anxiety proved to me their value," said Gripe, "and my own suspicions made me resolve to obtain them."

"For what purpose?" asked Henley.

"That of placing you in my power," said Gripe.

"And you believe you have succeeded?" said Henley.

"I know I have."

"Then," said Henley, "you are mistaken. The papers I was so anxious to obtain were but memoranda of past transactions, and worthless to any one save myself. Dick discovered this fact, and sold them to me, those he has placed in your hands are forgeries, and now Mr. Gripe, instead of me placing myself in your power, it is your own grasping, avaricious nature has placed you in mine. To obtain what your sordid mind desired, you sacrificed the reputation of an honest man, and laid yourself open to the law. I have borne your insults and your threats too long, but will bear them no longer, Mr. Gripe, your cleverness has quite outwitted you."

And rising from his seat, Squire Henley. placed his hand upon the bell-pull, and rang it violently.

For a few moments the steward sat gazing at the squire in perfect amazement.

Could it be possible that, after all, he had been deceived in his surmises, that the squire was really and truly an honest man, and that Dick had only been making a market of his cupidity.

The calm, measured tones of the squire, too, and the firm and unflinching demeanour he had assumed, caused the little steward, for the first time, to doubt whether he really had not outdone himself.

But he resolved that the squire, at least, should not think he had given up all hope, so he exclaimed,—

"Why have you rung that bell?"

"To summon the servants," replied Henley, "and denounce you, Mr. Gripe, as a thief, the robber of an indulgent employer—the false steward, and hand you over to the tender mercies of that law which you have outraged, and which your base nature so fondly hoped I dreaded."

Gripe rose from his seat.

"Squire," he said, resolved to stand firm to the last, "dare but speak one word against my reputation, and I denounce you."

"Fool, as well as knave!"

"Assassin, as well as robber!" roared Gripe, scarcely knowing what he said.

For a moment Henley stood gazing at the little man before him, then an ashy paleness overspread his face, and staggering to a chair, he grasped the back of it in his hand, and fell forward on his face in a fainting fit.

———

CHAPTER XXXV.

DISCOVERY OF THE BODY—THE ACCUSATION.

THE storm died away. Heaven's artillery had expended all its fury—the flood-gates of the skies had closed, and the morning broke beautiful and fair.

One by one the feathered songsters brought their heads from beneath their wings, and carolled forth their melodious notes in hymns of praise to the coming day.

The sun rose fiery red, throwing golden-burnished beams athwart the clear grey clouds, deepening in colour, contracting in space, and lighting up the already golden hues of the fast-falling leaves of the magnificent elms, beneath whose shades lie, with her face pale in death, the unsuspecting victim of the hellish deed of Bill the Harlequin.

The glassy eye, which never would beam with joy or weep with sorrow, was fixed immovable upon heaven's vault; the lips that no more should curl in anger or part with smiles, had parted, till the lower jaw had dropped upon the bosom, no more to rise and fall with each inspiration; the limbs which the night before had moved so quickly to the lively music, were stiff and rigid. She had danced her last dance, breathed her last breath, and now lay with the bright sunbeams' slanting rays playing through the branches of the trees upon her form—cold and dead!

A worthy son of toil, one of nature's true nobles, with his basket of tools upon his back, and the food for the day swinging in a cotton handkerchief from his hand, passed beneath the trees on the way to his daily labour.

Refreshed with his night's rest, at peace with himself and all the world, he was singing forth the lines of some favourite ditty, when his eye, resting upon the earth, the song died from his lips, and, with a shudder of horror, he became pale as death.

He had come close upon the murdered woman ere he had discovered the body, and the shock his system had received at the suddeness of the discovery completely, for a few moments, prostrated his energies.

But he was a feeling-hearted man, and as soon as he could collect himself, he threw down his basket of tools from his shoulder and the food from his hand: he stooped down and raised the head of the poor murdered woman on to his knee, and gazed pityingly, yet half-frightened, upon that cold pale face.

He cast his eyes around him, in the hopes of seeing some other wayfarer, of whom he could ask advice or assistance; but not a soul was in sight.

What, he thought, had he better do?

He entertained no doubt but that the woman was dead; yet he could not bear to leave the cold remains where he had found them.

He taxed his brains for a few moments, in the hope of hitting upon some course of action.

At last he thought it would be better to warn the people at the nearest inn, and, with this resolve, he gently laid the body down upon the long wet grass, and hastily snatching up his basket of tools and bundle of food, he darted out of the green into the high road, and strode on in the direction of Edmonton.

He would be late at his work, he thought; but never mind, he must not let the body lie where it was, although he had never seen the woman in life.

Walking and running, he made his way along till he came to a small ale-house, which the worthy landlord was at that moment opening for the day, and, as the man came hurriedly up to him, the landlord, opening his eyes very wide and fixing them upon his visitor, exclaimed,—

"Why, Slater, not at work to-day? Hallo!" he added, with a start, "what's the matter with you, ain't you well?"

"Yes—no!" replied Slater, out of breath with his exertions, and confused and bewildered by the fearful sight of the murdered woman.

"Why, what be the matter with you, man?" exclaimed the landlord. "Why you shake as if you had been and done a murder."

"Ah!" gasped the man, "me do it."

"Do what?" said the landlord.

"The murder—the murder!"

The landlord was puzzled at the manner of Slater, and eyed the man from head to foot in the greatest surprise.

"Oh! such a fearful sight," gasped the man. "A woman has been murdered under the seven trees."

"No!" exclaimed the landlord. "A woman murdered!"

"Yes—yes! Come and see. She must not lay there. Come and see."

"Who is she?"

"I don't know."

"Who murdered her?"

"Heaven only knows."

"Wait a minute: I'll get my hat and go with you," said the landlord, rushing into the house, and calling his wife to look after the bar, seized his hat, and once more joined Slater.

"How has she been murdered?" asked the landlord, as they hurried along.

"Been stabbed."

"Are you sure she is dead?"

"I think so; she's so white and cold," replied the man.

"We'd better call on Wilks, the constable," said the landlord, "and let him know."

"I never thought of that," replied Slater.

"That's what you ought to have done first," said Collier.

"Well, we can do that now," replied Slater. "Yes."

And turning off from the high road, the two men summoned the constable, and made him acquainted with the circumstance.

"I'll be there in a minute," said Wilks, retiring into the house as the landlord and the man who had discovered the body hurried on towards the fatal spot.

It was not long ere they came in sight of the body.

The constable had followed almost immediately, and arrived there as soon as they; but in hurrying along he had been asked by one or two persons if anything was the matter, and on his answering that a woman was murdered, they had joined him, and there was now assembled some six or seven persons around the corpse.

Now Mr. Wilks, the parish constable, was a good-hearted man in his way, but he had his failings, like other people; besides, he thought himself a very clever man, having been commended upon one or two occasions by the justices, who, by the way, in most country places, know as much about law as a new-born child.

But in the eyes of Mr. Wilks they were great men, and commendation from great men was enough to convince the constable that he was possessed of great tact.

So no sooner did he come upon the body, than he ordered everyone else to stand back.

The woman had been murdered, that was certain, and if anyone could find any clue by which to have the assassin, Mr. Wilks was the man.

At least, so thought the parish constable.

So Mr. Wilks bent over the body, placed his hand on the heart, shook his head mysteriously, as though he had discovered something very wonderful, then exclaimed,—

"Quite dead."

"In course she is," said the man, who had first come upon her. "I knew that long ago."

Mr. Wilks rose from his knees, and twisting his face into an expression he meant to be severe, and which he believed to be a true copy of the physiognomy of the local magistrate, at the time he was committing some poor child, of seven years of age, to prison for six weeks, for stealing a turnip, that grew temptingly near the roadway, exclaimed in a very low tone,—

"How did you know?"

"Because she looked just as she does now," replied Slater.

"Humph!" coughed Mr. Wilks. "Looks is nothing to go by."

"I did not go by looks," said Slater.

"What then?" asked Wilks, fixing his eye full upon the poor workman, as if he would count the joints in his backbone.

"Why, the feel," replied the man.

"The feel?"

"Yes."

"Have you disturbed the body?" asked Wilks, severely.

"No," said the man, becoming half frightened at the peremptory tones of the would-be great man.

"Then, how did you feel it?"

"I lifted her up."

"Then you have disturbed the body. You have taken upon yourself, sir, a duty which does not belong to you. You had no right to touch. You should have waited upon the officers of the law, instead of which, you take upon yourself the duties of others; and make private individuals acquainted with the deed, before the officers of the public."

"Well, I didn't know," stammered the man.

"Everyone is supposed to know the law, sir— you, sir—me, sir—everyone, sir. It places suspicion upon yourself; such conduct does, sir."

"Do you think I murdered her?" said the man, half frightened—half indignant.

"I don't know," replied Wilks, severely. "You were the first that saw the body."

"Well, I was the first as see it," said Slater.

"And you should have come and informed me," replied Wilks, "instead of running half a mile further up the road. "The circumstance is very suspicious, to say the least of it."

"I tell you what it is," said the workman, losing his temper at the bombastical tones, and

MARY AT THE FAIR.

insinuation of the officer, "you're not fit to be an officer. You're too fast, you are, and a fool into the bargain."

"Don't insult me in the execution of my duty," exclaimed Wilks, "or I'll take you into custody."

Slater slunk back, and Mr. Wilks, looking severely and triumphantly around him, upon the few assembled, turned again to the body.

He examined the clothing of the woman to see if he could discover anything that might lead to her identity, untied the little bundle which lay by her side, and held up the short Spanish dress in which she had figured the night before in the glare of the footlights.

Here Mr. Wilks smiled. This surely was something by which to find out who and what she was.

A theatrical costume—then she must be known in some of the places of amusement.

"Clue number one," exclaimed Mr. Wilks. "This will lead to her identity."

Then he fumbled in the dress pocket of the poor murdered woman, and then drew forth a card.

He held it up and read the few printed lines upon it.

It was a ticket of the entertainment, the attendance at which had proved so fatal to her.

"Clue number two," said Mr. Wilks, and the heart of the officer fairly thumped against his breast at the prospect of promotion for the clever manner in which he would, he felt sure, bring the perpetrator of the horrible deed to justice.

"Now," thought Mr. Wilks, "this wound could not have been inflicted without the aid of some instrument; dilligent search must be made for that."

So he austerely waved the assembled persons back, lest they should discover the object for which he intended to seek.

Slowly the persons fell back before the wave of the constable's hand.

Sticking his hands beneath his coat tails, and bending his eyes upon the ground, Mr. Wilks slowly walked around the tree, beneath which the woman lay.

But his search was fruitless.

No weapon could he discover.

No. 12.

A look of disappointment overspread his features, and he again approached the corpse.

"She must be removed," he said, "to await an inquest. Mr. Collier, yours is the nearest house?"

"Yes, I believe it is," said the landlord, not much relishing the body being conveyed there.

"Believe, sir! you know it is," exclaimed Wilks. "The body must be removed there."

"Can't you take it somewhere else?" said Collier; "the missus ain't very well, and it might upset her."

"The law, sir," exclaimed Wilks indignantly, "must be studied before the missus."

And Wilks fixed his eye upon the landlord, as much as to say,—

"I would advise you not to trifle with it."

With a shrug of the shoulders Collier remained silent.

Wilks beckoned to the bystanders to step forward and raise the body from the grass, for the purpose of having it conveyed to the alehouse.

This two of them did, and one taking the poor woman under the arm-pits, and the other under the knees, raised the inanimate mass of clay from the ground.

A loud exclamation escaped the lips of the officer.

The eyes of all assembled were turned upon him.

"Clue number three," he exclaimed.

And stooping down, he raised from the earth a small carpenter's chisel, which the dress of the woman had hitherto concealed from his sight, and which was stained with her blood.

Holding it aloft, he exclaimed,—

"This is the weapon with which the murderous deed has been committed."

Collier, Slater, and the others advanced towards him to get a glimpse of the weapon.

"Why," exclaimed the man who had first discovered the body, swinging his basket off his shoulders, and looking into the inside of it, "that's my chisel!"

"Yours?" exclaimed Wilks.

"Yours?" exclaimed the others.

"Yes, mine."

"Ah, ha!" almost yelled Wilks, leaping upon the man, and grasping him by the collar: "the evidence is clear—the guilty discovered; you are the murderer!"

A deathly pallor overspread the man's face; his eyes almost started from his head; his jaw dropped and his limbs trembled, and his basket of tools fell from his hand on to the grass at his feet.

"Me!" he gasped. Me—the—murderer!—Oh, God!"

"You!" hissed Wilks. "This weapon stained with blood is yours—you first gave information to shield yourself: the evidence is strong, the guilt is clear, and I arrest you as the murderer of this poor woman!"

"No, no! as Heaven is my judge, I am innocent!" gasped the man, now powerless as an infant.

"Convey the body to Collier's house," said Wilks, "whilst I convey this miscreant to gaol."

Slater looked appealingly around, but all shrank from him, and half fainting he suffered himself to be led away by the officer, a victim of circumstantial evidence.

CHAPTER XXXVI.

GRIPE VISITS THE IDIOT—THE BITER BIT.

THE loud summons which Squire Henley rang upon the bell was not long ere it was answered, for as the Squire fell fainting into the chair, the door of the apartment was opened and a servant stood upon the threshold.

The eyes of the man rested in surprise for a moment upon the pale face of his master, then turned with an inquiring look to the face of the little steward.

"Your master is not well," said Gripe; "I rang for some cold water."

The man instantly disappeared, but soon returned with the water, which he placed upon the table.

"You can retire," said Gripe, "I will attend to him."

The man lingered for a moment, then left the room, closing the door after him.

To say that Gripe was not surprised at the effect of the random shot he had fired at the squire would be untrue.

The little man was surprised, and very much surprised too.

The word assassin had escaped him without thought or meaning, but the effect it had had upon Henley proved to the quick-sighted steward that it must have contained some particle of truth.

Yet he could not divine who, or for what purpose, the Squire could murder, and become an assassin.

But still he felt sure that Henley had been guilty of some deed which placed him within the pale of the law, and he resolved to leave no stone unturned to make himself acquainted with the previous acts of his master.

Gripe had often gazed with pride and admiration upon the broad lands known as Henley Manor, and wished that he were their owner.

By worming out a few secrets of the squire's life, he soon found that Henley's right to them was somewhat doubtful; and when the squire had shown so much anxiety to obtain the packet from the cottage of the widow he imagined a great deal more than he had ever done.

Well knowing that the guilty ever live in fear, he resolved to work cautiously, and if he found the squire give way ever so little from his usually austere and exacting manner, he was certain that Henley was not an innocent man.

Thus it was that he had entered the private apartment of the squire that morning, a room in which he had no business to be, and set the squire at defiance.

But the end of it had nearly been fatal to his hopes, and it was but the last words of the steward that had saved Gripe from being placed in the hands of the officers of justice.

And if Gripe had so found himself placed, he would have felt convinced that his power over the master of Henley Manor existed only in his imagination; but the climax had put a different colour on his mind, for it convinced him that although he himself might be unable to prove it, Henley was a guilty man.

The momentary fear which had seized him when Henley rang the bell, and gave utterance to his determination to unmask him, now gave place to one of triumph, and he awaited the recovery of the squire with the greatest anxiety.

For some few moments Henley remained in the same state of unconsciousness, but at length a shudder ran through his frame, and he heaved a heavy sigh.

"All right," muttered Gripe, as these indications of returning consciousness were exhibited by the squire, " he'll come to in a minute. Now, Mr. Gripe, what had you best be about ? Stop or go for a time ? Let me see; it is evident I have nothing to fear from him, and it is likewise evident that I have yet got much to learn; but where am I to get the information ? There's Dick the Poacher—if anyone knows anything it's him, but there's not much chance of drawing him out. Catch a weasel asleep. You might just as well try as pump Dick; the sucker's dry in that quarter; and yet he is the only one who could put me in possession of all I want to know. I have it;—his wife, the idiot. Now if I could but get her to listen to me for a few minutes I might succeed. Egad! I'll try, and at once too; but I must look out for that poacher. He's a dangerous chap, and may not like my pumping his wife. Still, delays are dangerous; 'strike the iron while it's hot' is the motto for me, and as I am in duty bound to do the best I can for myself, why I'll be off at once, and leave the squire to recover from his fit at his own convenience."

So soliloquising, Gripe rose from his chair and, after looking carefully around him, prepared to leave the room.

"Whew !" he exclaimed, "how my foot pains me. Curse him, I believe he did it for the purpose; but I'll be even with him yet—I'll be even with him."

And Gripe hobbled rather than walked out of the apartment into his own room.

Attiring himself for his journey, he stole quietly out of the house, and took the road leading to the little farm house, where he felt sure of seeing Minnie.

Gripe approached the place as cautiously as possible, lest Dick should be present and perceive him.

He had no wish that the poacher should know of his presence, for Gripe felt assured should he be detected by him, Dick would suspect he was after no good.

At the same time the steward felt sure that if Dick was absent he should discover Minnie sitting in the porch, a position she most always occupied when her husband was absent.

Keeping within the shadow of the trees and fences, and ever and anon casting furtive and anxious glances around him, Gripe approached until he could gain a good view of the farm house porch.

There sat Minnie, her hands in her lap, and her eyes bent upon the ground at her feet.

A smile of satisfaction beamed from the eyes of the steward.

He felt sure, from the position and the pensive attitude of the poor imbecile, that she was alone.

So he boldly struck into the path which led to the house.

He had made his way up to within a few paces of the porch ere Minnie discovered his presence.

But as she rose her expressionless eyes from the ground and fixed them on the figure of Gripe, a frightened expression stole over her features, and she rose to her feet.

Gripe saw that she intended to avoid him, and he hurried forward.

Stepping within the porch, he laid his hand upon her arm.

A slight scream escaped her lips and a shudder pervaded her frame.

Gripe saw that it would be necessary to soothe her fears and endeavour to banish from her mind the aversion she felt for him.

Idiot though she was she could distinguish a friend from an enemy.

"Minnie," said Gripe, softly, "Minnie, why do you fear me ? Do you not know me ?"

A low, hollow laugh escaped the lips of the woman as she muttered—

"Know you ? See, the grass withers and the birds sing not; the air is sultry, and your breath kills all that feels it. I know you—I know you."

"Then, Minnie, do you fear me ?" asked the steward, smiling.

"Demons laugh only when they destroy," said Minnie. "Judas betrayed with a kiss."

"Come, Minnie, I will not harm you," said Gripe, softly. "Where is Dick ?"

The woman started round and fixed her expressionless orbs upon his face.

"Where is Dick ?" asked Gripe again.

"Gone, gone," sighed the woman.

"He leaves you much alone," said Gripe.

"But the birds sing when he comes back, and the flowers bloom, and the grass grows green," she said.

"And so they do, Minnie, when he is not about," said Gripe.

"No, no. Look, it withers, for you are here. See there is the print of the burning foot upon the ground; the foot that fired the hay stacks and blamed it to Dick—but Dick's feet dry not the grass—ah, no! ah, no!"

And her head drooped on her breast, and she seemed to become entirely lost to the presence of the steward.

Gripe began to consider how best to worm out of her whether Dick had any papers in his possession or not.

"Minnie," he said, "Dick is a good man, a noble fellow."

A smile for the first time lightened up the expressionless features of the poor idiot.

"Ah! " she exclaimed, " so the birds tell me."

"And they tell you true, Minnie."

"And the flowers," she added.

"They tell you true."

"Aye, for they never lie; they are true as ye are false," she exclaimed.

"Nay, Minnie, I am not false."

"Not to Dick ?"

"No."

"Ah! the birds said you were, and they never lie."

"How can the birds tell you, Minnie ?" said Gripe; "birds cannot speak."

The woman looked at him almost fiercely.

"They sing, they sing: now their voice is still, for you are near. Poor Minnie knows when the wicked come this way, for the birds are silent, and the grass is withered and shorn."

"Nonsense, Minnie, I am your friend, and would do much for you."

"Oh, no! oh, no ! " sighed the woman, "you

would take Dick away—you would leave me here
alone."

"No, Minnie, I would keep him here with
you," said Gripe.

"No, no; you and the squire would take him
away, but he will not let you—he will not let
you—oh, no."

"Why not, Minnie?"

"He is strong; he fears not the wicked
squire, he could tear him to pieces—he could
make him poor again—ah, ha!"

"Ah," muttered Gripe to himself, "then
Dick does know—does possess some secret. If
I can but prevail upon this fool to divulge it to
me I can defy them all."

Then he added aloud,—

"Oh, yes, Minnie, Dick told me."

"Told you—what did he tell you?" she
asked.

"That he held the wicked squire in his power,
and that, if I would help him, he would crush
him."

"Dick told you," murmured the woman.

"Yes."

"Ah, poor Dick," sighed the woman.

"Indeed you may sigh for him, poor fellow,"
said Gripe. "He has suffered much at the
squire's hands."

"Bad man—bad man," said Minnie.

"He is a bad man," said Gripe, "but he will
never be able to have Dick more if he does as he
said he would."

"What did he say?" asked the woman, looking in his face.

"That he would place the evidence of the
squire's guilt in my hands, and that I should
crush the squire for him."

"Then the grass would not wither nor the
flowers die," sighed the woman.

"No, Minnie, they would always be fresh and
beautiful."

"Oh! I should be so happy—so happy then."

"You would indeed."

"Yes, so happy," said Minnie.

"Can you go and tell Dick that I have come
for them!" asked Gripe, fearful of her relapsing
into one of her totally unconscious moods.

"Dick has gone—gone."

"Where?"

"Where the grass is green and the birds
sing?"

"But he will soon return," said Gripe, inquiringly.

Minnie shook her head.

A smile of satisfaction at this circumstance
played around the mouth of the steward.

The longer Dick remained absent the better
chance for him to succeed.

"The squire wants to hurt Dick," again he said,
after a pause.

The woman started.

"But I will not let him, Minnie," continued
Gripe, if I can help it.

"And you will not let him," said the idiot.

"Not if I could see Dick."

"He has gone—gone."

"Well, the squire can't hurt him, if you
could give me the papers."

Gripe felt convinced now, that there were
other documents in existence. Had not Dick
said so the night he entered the manor house
by the window—and that they were of the
greatest importance he felt assured, although Dick
had said they were in no way connected with
the estate or those which the steward had purchased of him.

"Papers," said Minnie.

"Yes, the papers, you know—the papers, that
would ruin the squire and save Dick from
further harm at his hands."

"Oh, yes—oh, yes, I know—I know," said the
woman.

A cry of joy almost escaped the lips of the
little steward.

"Get them, Minnie," he said. "Give them to
me, and I will save him."

"Save him?" she exclaimed.

"Yes, Dick, your husband."

"Poor Dick—poor Dick," she sighed again.

"Get them, Minnie. "Do not delay a moment
or it may be too late," said Gripe, his anxiety to
obtain them becoming so great that he could
scarcely contain himself.

"Where are they?" she asked, in a quiet
tone.

"Oh, you know—you know, Minnie," exclaimed
Gripe.

But a black look sat on the woman's face.

Gripe was in an agony of suspense.

Did she not know where they were, or had she
forgotten. He feared that the opportunity of
becoming their possessor would be lost.

"Oh, you know, Minnie," he exclaimed, "they
are where he keeps all his private things."

"Oh, yes," said Minnie, "I know."

"Get them, Minnie dear—get them," urged
Gripe.

The woman entered the kitchen, and taking a
plaid shawl from off a hook, threw it over her
head and pinned it beneath her chin.

"Where are you going, Minnie?" asked Gripe,
anxiously.

"To get them—to get them," she answered,
walking out of the porch round to the back of
the house, then taking a key from her pocket
she applied it to the door of an outhouse, which
flew open.

"Are they there, Minnie?" asked Gripe.

The woman nodded her head, and Gripe
bounded into the place.

With a loud clang, Minnie pulled the door to
and locked it—then slowly returned to the front
of the house, with the expressionless look still
upon her face.

CHAPTER XXXVII.

MARGARET RECEIVES A VISITOR AND PAINFUL IN-
TELLIGENCE—IDENTIFICATION OF THE BODY—THE
FALSE HAIR—A WIFE'S DESPAIR.

MARGARET SIMMONS, the columbine, and wife of
the guilty harlequin, sat in a little humble room,
where she had taken up her abode since the night
on which she had summoned up courage to strike
her brutal husband, in retaliation for the blows
he inflicted on her, and left him.

The apartment in which she sat was shared
by a friend and fellow pantomimist—a lady of
no mean talent; but one who had been unfortunate in her engagements.

She was a widow, and thus Margaret, besides
finding it considerably cheaper to share a lodging with another, found a companion and a
friend.

The breakfast which Margaret had prepared

remained untasted on the table, and she sat with a pensive look upon her face, and a feeling of depression at her heart.

Mrs. Luton, her fellow lodger, had not been seen or heard of by Margaret since the night on which she had undertaken the latter's engagement to dance at the Assembly Rooms, near Edmonton.

There was something so strange in the continued absence of the lady from home, she being a woman who had always found comfort at her own fireside, and one who never remained from home longer than the time necessary to fulfil her professional duties, that Margaret had become alarmed, and, a fear taking possession of her mind that some accident had befallen her friend, she resolved to go that evening to Edmonton, and make inquiries respecting her.

The gloom which the absence of Mrs. Luton cast over the spirits of her friend deepened, and Margaret felt so sad and miserable, that she could scarcely save herself from weeping.

When the mind is ill at ease the thoughts generally turn to the more gloomy moments of our existence, and so it was with Margaret.

Her mind reverted to the miseries of her past life—the brutal treatment of her husband, and her own undeserved sufferings.

The thought of her husband, and his now lonely condition, and the blows and unkind words which had led to their separation.

She wondered, too, what would become of him. His evil nature, she feared, would lead on to some fearful deed, which he would be called upon to expiate upon the gallows.

Indeed the fearful act he had committed at the Royal Star had been sufficient to place him under restraint for the rest of his existence, if not to deprive him of life. But the author of that crime was known only to himself and her, and he would not be called upon for judgment for the wicked deed.

Margaret wished that she had not recognised him—wished that she had not known it was his hand that fired the curtains. The knowledge sat like an incubus upon her heart, and made her wretched.

Her past sufferings—her parting from her husband, the knowledge of his villany, and the unaccountable absence of her friend, all combined to render Margaret Simmons one of the most wretched beings in existence.

It was about midday that she was aroused from the painful train of thought into which she had fallen by a knock at the door of the apartment in which she sat.

Hastily brushing away a tear, which, spite all her efforts to keep off, had forced itself to her eyelid and hung like a diamond on the long drooping lashes, she arose, and bade the visitor enter.

She hoped it was some one who came with news of her friend, and her heart beat with expectation.

The door opened, and Mr. Wilks, the parish constable, entered the room.

Margaret started; there was something in the appearance of the man she did not like, though why or wherefore she would have been puzzled to tell.

They had never met before, yet a feeling of dislike rose to her heart towards the new comer.

"Humph!" exclaimed Mr. Wilks, endeavouring to cough a very pompous cough, similar to that which the justice he so much admired was addicted to, and at the same time to make Margaret believe he was a very shrewd and clever man.

Then casting his eyes scrutinisingly around the apartment, he brought them to focus full upon the pale and melancholy face of the poor columbine.

"This," he said, "is the apartment occupied by a lady named Luton, if I mistake not."

At the mention of the name of her friend, Margaret started, and laying her hand upon the arm of the officer, and looking up in his face, she exclaimed, eagerly.

"Oh, sir—where is she—has anything happened to her?"

Mr. Wilks paused, ere he answered.

He had learned at the Assembly Rooms the name of the murdered woman, and the place of her residence, also the fact that she had not been the person engaged; but had undertaken to fufil the engagement for a friend, with whom she resided.

So to this friend Mr. Wilks had come to seek further evidence.

But why? he asked himself should Margaret show so much anxiety—why did she expect that anything had happened.

Did she get the woman to fulfil her engagement so that she might be murdered on her return home? was she an accessory to the deed?

Mr. Wilks hoped she was.

Yes, hoped!

For would he not be commended from the bench? would not the public, whose servant he was, say he was a clever officer, if he could only bring another person to justice?

Stooping his head, he whispered mysteriously into the ear of Margaret,—

"Slater's taken!"

The look of surprise which rose to the face of the columbine appeared to the mind of the over zealous officer to be one of blank despair.

"Yes," he said, in a very low whisper, as though he feared he might be overheard,—"Taken!"

Still Margaret only looked in the face of the officer in mute surprise.

"The crime was discovered before he could escape," whispered Wilks, "and when he found that it was all up with him, he bade me, one of his dearest friends, to let you know."

Margaret, more and more confused and confounded, exclaimed,—

"Who's Slater? I really don't know such a name."

"Not know him. Come, I am his friend; you have nothing to fear from me."

"I do not understand you," said Margaret, "there must be some mistake; it cannot be me you seek, although you mentioned the name of a friend for whose long absence I entertain great fears."

"Don't you know Slater, the carpenter," said Wilks.

"Never heard of him," said Margaret.

"But you knew what was to befall Mrs. Luton," said Wilks, insinuatingly.

"Has anything happened to her?" asked Margaret, eagerly.

"You know there has," said Wilks. "What need is there to beat about the bush?"

"Oh, heavens! what has happened. Tell

me, sir, I beg of you? I have been wretched at her absence. She was kind enough to fulfil an engagement for me, as I had danced for her the night before; but from that time I have not seen or heard from her. Oh, sir, if you know anything of her tell me, I beg of you?"

"Then you don't know," exclaimed Wilks, the words and manner of Margaret being too convincing even for that officer that she was *not* an accessory to the deed.

"No, indeed! I am only too anxious to learn," exclaimed Margaret.

Annoyed beyond measure that he could find no excuse to make another charge, Mr. Wilks exclaimed, half savagely,—

"She's murdered!"

"Oh, God!" shrieked Margaret.

And, tottering to a chair, she sank into it, and buried her face in her hands.

The grief of the poor woman, caused by the shock these words had produced, almost made that clever officer ashamed at the brutal manner in which he had broken the sad intelligence.

"Murdered!" she gasped. "Murdered! oh, that I had not let her gone!"

And Margaret sobbed violently for some moments.

When at length her grief had somewhat abated, Mr. Wilks, who had meantime taken an inventory of everathing in the apartment, in the vain hope of finding something which would justify him in arresting Margaret, exclaimed,—

"It will be necessary, for the sake of identifying the murdered woman, that you should accompany me to the place where she lies, and attend before the coroner, and state what you know about her."

With a deep sigh Margaret arose.

The shock which she had experienced had been so great that it had left her face bloodless as marble.

Her limbs trembled violently, and she felt so weak that she could scarcely stand.

But Mr. Wilks had a duty to perform, and he must perform it.

He could not allow himself to feel any sympathy for the poor woman. The coroner's jury were to assemble that evening, and he must produce all the evidence he could rake up, so, ill or well, Margaret must go with him to Tottenham.

Urging her to be quick, he sat down, and impatiently awaited while the columbine attired herself for the journey.

Margaret was usually an energetic woman; but the sad news of the fate of her friend had driven all energy out of her, and it was some time before she was ready to accompany the officer.

"You have been a long while getting ready," said Wilks, in a dissatisfied tone; "but, there, you wouldn't be a woman if you wasn't."

"I should not be a woman if I did not feel for a friend who had met so sad a fate," replied Margaret, with a look of pain upon her features; "and I should have expected that a man, though an officer, could have some feeling for the woman who can feel distress at the loss of a friend."

Mr. Wilks winced.

The words of Margaret made him feel rather contemptible in his own eyes.

It was evident that she did not think him so great a man after all.

So Mr. Wilks said no more, but led the way out of the house.

Poor Margaret, she felt that she was always to be unhappy. So, with a heavy heart and tearful eyes, she followed the parish constable to the little ale-house, where the murdered body of her friend lie in its blood-stained clothing, and the twelve intellectual tradesmen who were empannelled as a jury were to sit and condemn a fellow creature for her death.

The self-considered great officer led her into a room, in which the body lay covered with a sheet.

Margaret tottered rather than walked towards it.

Wilks drew the covering down from the face and breast, and revealed the features of the corpse.

A shudder passed through the frame of the poor columbine, as she gazed upon the cold dead face of her who had shared their humble home but two nights before, so full of life and health, and as she bent over the rigid form her tears fell fast upon those features which never more would wear the impress of joy or sorrow.

"Do you know this woman?" asked Wilks.

"I do," replied Margaret.

"Is she the person with whom you lived?"

"She is," said the columbine.

"Then you recognize the body," said Wilks.

"I do," replied Margaret.

"That will do for the present," said the parish officer, in a patronising tone, at the same time proceeding to cover up the face of the corpse.

Margaret placed her hand upon his breast, to stay the operation for a moment: then bending her head down till her lips touched the cold clammy cheek of her dead friend, she imprinted a kiss upon it, and a tear dropping upon the forehead of the murdered woman was a greater tribute to her memory than all the epitaphs recorded in stone,—the chisselled lies that so oft profane the tomb.

In another moment the corpse was hidden from her gaze, and she was ordered to wait in an adjoining apartment till she should be called before the coroner.

The jury assembled, and poor Slater, with handcuffs upon his wrists, was brought before them to hear the evidence of the different witnesses.

One by one were they called up, and ordered to stand down.

At length Margaret was summoned.

The poor columbine was the last witness.

With haggard face and throbbing heart she stood before the assembled gentlemen. The oath was administered to her, and the coroner, fixing a penetrating glance upon her face, asked her if she knew the prisoner.

Steadfastly the poor woman looked at the accused man, and equally as steadily Mr. Wilks watched her countenance as she did so.

But no glance of recognition could that clever officer detect between the pale haggard prisoner and the equally pale witness.

Margaret shook her head, and answered,—

"I never saw him before."

A sigh of relief broke from the lips of the accused.

"Look at this," said the coroner, handing to

Margaret a wig and false whiskers, made all in one. "You may not recognise the prisoner as he at present appears, but you might do so were he disguised in that wig. It was found clasped in the dead woman's hand."

Margaret took the wig in her hand and examined it intently.

A deathly pallor overspread her face—her limbs trembled—her eyes started almost from their sockets. She tottered forward and grasped the back of a chair for support, or she must have fallen to the floor.

Margaret had recognised the wig—recognised her own work. She herself had sewn the whiskers to the wig, and placed the elastic which secured it to the face—that wig she had made for her husband.

"Does that wig belong to the prisoner?" asked the coroner.

"No," said Margaret.

The face of the accused man lighted up with a look of joy.

"To whom then does it belong?" asked the coroner: "for that you know the owner is certain, and the wearer of that wig must have been the woman's murderer!"

"That man is innocent!" gasped Margaret. "Innocent of the fearful crime! Oh, God! I see it all! I see it all!" and relaxing her grasp of the chair, Margaret fell to the floor insensible.

CHAPTER XXXVIII.

HOPES AND FEARS—CHARLIE SEEKS A FAVOUR, AND FINDS A PARTNER MUCH AGAINST HIS WILL.

THE second night of the new management had drawn to a close. Little Mary had danced the hornpipe in fetters much to the gratification of the gods, who bestowed upon the clown's daughter a very fair amount of applause, and summoned her re-appearance with loud, shrill whistles, and various other noises, so peculiar to the frequenters of the gallery of a minor theatre.

But the curtain fell as it had risen, on empty benches.

Dancing Bill had partially gratified his revenge.

It was with a sad heart that Charlie Evans wended his way home on that night—the money taken at the doors was not sufficient to cover rent and lighting.

Buskin Bob, too, was miserable, and so were the young folks.

Their hopes had been blighted, nipped in the bud by the work of Dancing Bill.

The supper of boiled pork and pease pudding which Charlie took home in a borrowed basin from a cook-shop, was eaten in silence, Buskin Bob never once wishing himself struck comical during the time of the humble meal.

With wearied frames and depressed spirits the "good night" was uttered, and sorrowfully and sadly each sought their couch.

Tired as he was by his arduous duties, Charlie Evans could not sleep. He tossed about uneasily, bemoaning their ill-fortune, and endeavouring to think of some means by which he could make the house pay till Christmas.

For at Christmas he felt sure of a week's good houses.

If they could but struggle on till then, he thought all would go well.

But before that time he could see nothing but failure.

With a continuance of such business as they had experienced that night they would be unable to pay the company; but if the company would stand by him till Boxing night, he might be enabled to pay all demands, and return during the week all their losses.

Charlie knew full well that, as far as the feelings of the poor actors which composed the staff of the Royal Star were concerned, they would not object to do so, and likewise knew that the fabulous salaries actors are often asserted to receive was all moonshine, and that scarcely one knew where to get bread when out of an engagement.

That the will was good to assist him—for take the players as a body, a better hearted set of men never existed, men who will sacrifice time, labour, and even money to assist a fellow creature when misfortune has overtaken him—Charlie well knew; but that their means would not allow he also felt assured.

Charlie could see but one hope of keeping the house open till Boxing night, and that was by throwing himself upon the generosity of the lessee, and endeavouring to obtain the consent of that personage to accept a portion instead of the whole of the rent, and thus enable him to pay something to his company.

It was but the shadow of a hope after all, for lessees are not as a rule inclined to be indulgent.

Not that they are naturally exacting, but it unfortunately occurs that there are many in the profession who enter upon the management of a theatre without a farthing to work with, or any reasonable prospect of success.

Hence the lessees cannot be over indulgent, or advantage would be taken of it.

Besides, lessees are but men, and they wish their property to bring them in as much as possible.

If a theatre will pay at all it will do so at Christmas, during the time of the pantomime, and at such a season a lessee may make a good deal out of his house; therefore the inducement to take it out of the hands of an unsuccessful manager is greater than the wish to assist him till he can turn himself round again, and retrieve his fortunes.

However, it was Charlie's only hope, and he resolved to try it.

With this determination he arose the next morning, and when they were all assembled at the breakfast table he mentioned the subject to Buskin Bob.

"Well," said Bob, "I hope he'll do it; but don't build on it, Charlie."

"I shall not do that; but it is the only means I can see of saving ourselves from ruin."

"Oh, father," exclaimed little Mary, "I am sure the lessee would not wish to ruin us."

"Perhaps not," remarked Charlie; "but he is but a man, trusting to the rent of the house for his own living."

"But he will surely wait till Christmas," said Harry. "It's not long now."

"It is not long," said Charlie; "but short as it is he may be unable to grant our request."

"Or unwilling," said Bob. "Strike me comical if I don't think that's most unlikely."

"However," said Charlie, "I'll try him after breakfast."

"Tell him that its ill-success is only owing to the accident," said Bob.

"That may embitter him against us," said the clown.

"I don't think so," replied Bob; "because you see if the fire has injured us, it will do no good for any one else."

"But Christmas is so near. He may feel inclined, now that the house has been done up, to take it from us, and provide a company, and turn manager himself."

Charlie looked blank.

Nothing was more likely than that the lessee should do so, and at the expiration of the good season let it off his hands again.

"Well, we can't tell till we try," said Charlie, "and it shall be no fault of mine that we do not keep it on for the poor boy."

"I am sure it will not," remarked Harry, "and I shall never be able to repay the interest you take in my welfare."

"I am only doing my duty," said Charlie. "I have not and never shall forget your mother's kindness to me."

At the mention of his mother, Harry's eyes filled with tears.

Charlie felt sorry that he should have uttered anything which would bring a pang to the heart of his young *protégée*.

Little Mary threw her arms around the neck of her youthful companion, and imprinted a kiss on his cheek.

Harry felt that if he had lost a kind mother he had found kind friends, and the tears soon dried up, and, like the showers in summer, the bright sunshine of happiness broke over his face and cheered away the gloom.

The meal ended, Charlie prepared for his visit to the lessee, whilst the others got ready to leave for the theatre, and do all they could themselves about the building to curtail the expenses.

The lessee received the clown in the most courteous manner; but his brow darkened when Charlie told his business.

"People who are not prepared," he said, "for such cases, ought not to enter upon speculations."

"Sir," replied Charlie, "we entered upon the speculation with one hundred pounds, every farthing of which has been laid out in renovating your property. The unfortunate accident to which our ill-success is attributed was no fault of ours; indeed, we risked our lives to save the property from ruin. The favour I ask is small; the time short, and I trust that the endeavours we have shown to turn the house into a good paying property may induce you to look favourably upon my suit."

"I admit that you have done much as far as decorations and such like; but I have experienced so many losses from previous managers that I have resolved that I will suffer no more."

"But, sir, the Christmas season will enable us to meet our deficiencies," anxiously pleaded Charlie.

"The Christmas season will be still heavier in expenses," replied the lessee.

"Not much, sir."

"Indeed it will, if you want to draw an audience. You will require pantomimists."

"I myself play clown," said Charlie.

"Then there is the rest."

"My friend and fellow-manager is pantaloon —so, you perceive, sir, we shall keep the expenses down as much as possible."

The lessee paused.

Charlie watched the workings of the man's countenance eagerly, for any expression that might bid him hope.

"Mr. Evans," he said at length, "I am not disposed to entertain your application — not from any wish to injure you, but should you be unsuccessful, and even at the best seasons success is not always certain, I should be a loser. This I can ill-afford. But as I have no wish to compel you to give up the theatre altogether, as I should be unable to meet my demands, I will enter into an agreement by which I take a certain share, leaving you to settle with your company as you please."

Charlie paused before he replied to this proposition.

There was much to consider.

Would the remainder, after the lessee had taken his share, which he would do every night, by putting a man on the check, be sufficient to pay his company.

That the lessee would be no loser he was certain; but would he?

He feared he would—yet it appeared that his acceptance of the proposition were the only means by which they could retain the management.

It would be unpleasant, too, for the lessee to have anything to do with the theatre, inasmuch as he would bind their hands.

But still Charlie had no hope but to agree with him.

The lessee waited patiently for his answer— for he well knew that he would lose little by the acceptance of his proposition; and if Charlie decided upon refusing it he might have some difficulty in obtaining a tenant till Christmas.

At length Charlie spoke.

"Is there no other arrangement we can make?" he asked.

"None," replied the other.

"Then I suppose I must agree?" replied Charlie.

"Very good," said the other, "I will draw up an agreement in the course of the day, and bring it down to the theatre to-night for your signature."

Charlie bowed, and having no further business he left the house.

A smile of gratification broke over the face of the lessee as he bowed the clown out of his dwelling.

He was pleased at the arrangement.

It would insure his rent.

But it might ruin the management.

He was a man of business, and that was no business of his.

He looked to himself, made himself secure, and that was all he cared about.

Charlie made his way to the theatre, where he found Buskin Bob daubing a scene; his daughter, as usual, mending the "props," and Harry sweeping out the pit.

"Well, what luck?" asked Bob.

"Not much," replied the clown.

THE RECOGNITION.

"Strike me comical, if I didn't think so," said Bob.

"Why."

"The look of your phiz," replied the pantaloon.

"He would not consent to wait," said Charlie.

"Would not consent to wait?" iterated Harry, who had made his way on to the stage the moment he caught sight of the good-hearted clown.

"No, Harry."

"Then, unless we are more fortunate than last night, we are ruined," exclaimed the boy, a look of pain crossing his features.

"He would not consent to my prayer," said Charlie, "but he made a proposition, which I

eventually accepted, as I could see no other means of remaining where we are if the house still keeps bad."

"What was it?" asked Bob.

Charlie explained.

"Well, strike me comical," exclaimed Bob, "he is a hard-hearted fellow. Look what we have done for the house; when we took it it wasn't fit for a dust-hole, and we've made it a pretty decent place. Strike me comical, if we ain't."

"So we have," said Charlie; "but I could get no better terms, and I thought it better to accept and try them than give up the theatre."

"I don't know but what you have done the best as could be done," said Bob, "but, strike me comical, if we shan't find things very unpleasant with him about the place. However, we must do our best, and if fortune only smiles on us, we shall be able to shake him off, and start on our own hook again."

"So I thought," said Charlie.

"And so we'll try. It's a long lane that has no turning, and it's always the darkest the hour before day. We are down on our luck now; but we've got the will to strive to rise; and, strike me comical, Charlie, we won't despair, no matter how hard are our struggles for bread."

CHAPTER XXXIX.

MR. GRIPE, FINDING HIMSELF IN AN AWKWARD POSITION, FORMS A PLAN TO ESCAPE—THE PLAN UPSET, AND MR. GRIPE IN THE BARGAIN.

"THERE is a method in madness," has been somewhere written, and it would appear to bear undoubted truth.

The poor idiot, whom the villanous little steward had striven to make his dupe, had outwitted him.

At the very moment when Gripe had felt sure of possessing the secret he so much coveted, he had been overcome by the stratagem of an idiot.

After the first feeling of surprise had passed away, the little steward strove to force the door open, and finding himself unable to accomplish this feat, he sat down upon a rude bench, and endeavoured to think.

The place in which he found himself was a kind of outhouse, filled with implements of farming, tubs, troughs, and an heterogenous mass of lumber, and as it was often used for storing vegetables, it had no window, save a kind of trap, high up in the wall, but which, at this time, was firmly closed and secured.

A dim light, though, pervaded the place, and forced its way into the small building from the chinks of the rough door and trap, so that Gripe was enabled, though indistinctly, to trace out the objects which this place contained.

"Surely," he thought, rising from his seat, "this is not the kind of place a man would keep any secret or valuable documents he might possess. An idiot might, it is true, but then Dick is not an idiot, if his wife is. Idiot do I call her? I believe she knows well what she is about. I have been deceived. I thought her a fool, on whose stupidity I could play, but she has proved herself the shrewdest of us both, and cooped me up here in this confounded place, from which it seems I have little chance of escape. Confound her, I almost wish I had twisted her neck, and then searched the place; but I'll be even with her for this. She shall find that it is dangerous work to play with me. Curse her, the demented fool."

And Mr. Gripe again tried the door, through which he believed he had entered to gain something more congenial to his wishes than imprisonment.

Still he was unable to force it, and thinking that perhaps Minnie might still be within hearing, and only fastened him in without knowing what she really did, he called out loudly—

"Minnie! Minnie!"

Then he listened intently.

Not a sound came back to his ears in return.

"Minnie!" he again called, after a pause.

Still no answer.

Gripe became agitated.

"Why had she fastened him in that place? Was it that she possessed sufficient sense to feel that Gripe really wanted to take advantage of her impaired intellect to induce her to betray the secrets of her husband, and that, by leading him to believe she would do so, had made him a prisoner, and intended keeping him so till her husband's return."

He began to fear such to be the case.

Gripe had led her to believe that he was anxious to see Dick, and he feared that he would now be compelled to meet him. He cursed his folly for being so eager to enter the place, when one moment's reflection would have convinced him that documents, if Dick really had any, would not be consigned by any sensible man to such a locality for security. But in his anxiety to possess what he believed Dick to have in his keeping, he never gave a single thought to this.

Now, to meet the poacher was what the little steward had no wish to do, for he felt assured that Dick was not the man to forgive anyone who would take advantage of his wife's imbecility to do him wrong.

Finding that Minnie did not return to open the door and let him forth, he began to feel more and more uncomfortable, till at length he almost fancied he could feel the chastisement he knew Dick would mete out to him for his villany.

"She certainly means keeping me here till her husband returns," he soliliquised, "and then, instead of leaving the place with a greater knowledge of the squire's villany, I shall perhaps leave it with sore limbs. This comes of a man doing his duty."

And Gripe looked around the place to see what article he could make use of to raise his little body up to the shutters which covered the opening used as a window.

An old tub, which had been used in the more flourishing days of the farm, stood in one corner, and on this Gripe fixed his eyes, which were becoming every moment more accustomed to the gloom.

"Now, if I can get that tub out of the heap of rubbish which surrounds it," muttered the little man, "and roll it up to the window, I might stand upon it, and see if I could force open the shutter. Anyhow, I'll try. Never give up is my motto; do your duty—always do your duty, Gripe; and it now becomes your duty to escape from this place one way or another, and save your bones from feeling the weight of an enraged man's arm."

With this resolve the steward commenced clearing away the heap of lumber which surrounded the tub.

It was no easy matter, for many of the articles were of considerable weight, and as Gripe had seldom lifted anything heavier than a ledger, he soon became tired.

But the fear of Dick returning lent him fresh strength, and by dint of great exertion he succeeded in clearing a passage to the article which was to raise his small form to the level of the shutters.

Grasping the damp and dirty barrel in his

hands, he rolled it along on its end till he had placed it beneath the opening.

Then he paused to take breath for a few moments.

"Now for it," he muttered. "I ain't very heavy, and it will bear my weight easily enough."

Placing his hands on the top of the stones, he drew himself up, and stood upon the end.

But although he was now raised some four feet above the ground, he found he could not draw the bolt at the top, it being fastened top and bottom.

"Confound it," he muttered, "I am not high enough yet. I must place something on the top of this, to raise me up a little."

So down he got again, and once more looked about the place.

A rude shaped half-tub, half-trough, he selected from among the lumber, and after two or three attempts, placed it on the top of the barrel.

"That will do," he said, as he adjusted it in the position he required.

Climbing up the barrel once more, he stepped on to the trough, and stretched forth his arm and grasped the bolt.

It required more than ordinary force to draw it from the socket. Not having been used for some time, it had corroded with rust.

Working it backwards and forwards, he pulled down at the same time with all his might.

It commenced to yield to the pressure.

"That's it," muttered Gripe, "it's coming. Ah! ah! Minnie, I shall be one too many for you yet. Here it goes."

One more pull he gave, and down came the bolt from the socket.

But the grin of exultation died away on the face of Gripe, and a cry of terror escaped him.

The trough, rotten with damp and age, gave way beneath him, and the suddenness of the fall, combined with the weight of the little steward, stove in the top of the barrel, and Gripe, releasing his hold of the handle of the bolt, he fell into the barrel, and ere he could put forth an arm to save himself the broken trough fell upon him, inflicting several blows upon his face and shoulders, and greatly assisted in preventing his escape from the wooden walls in which he so unexpectedly found himself a prisoner.

Surprise or fear for the moment quite rendered the little man powerless; but when, after a few minutes, he could collect his confused thoughts, he looked up. There, above him, was the opening—the shutter having swung back as he fell—and the bright daylight poured in upon him as he stood, with bleeding face and scratched hands, in his unpleasant and unlooked-for position.

For a few moments Gripe stood like one in a dream.

His usual coolness deserted him, and he could not determine the best course to pursue.

His eyes wandered away from the opening to the lumber strewed about the floor, then to the opening again—then to his dusty and dirty clothes.

But he soon found that it was necessary for him to extricate himself from his unpleasant situation.

Throwing off the pieces of timber which had formed the trough, he endeavoured to climb out of the barrel.

To get on to it he found pretty easy—to climb out of it was quite another thing. When he had ascended it to get at the bolt of the shutter he had the wall to prevent the barrel from tippling over; but to get out from the inside was far more difficult, as there was nothing to counteract the pressure which he must use in so doing.

Still, it would never do to remain where he was. So, placing his hands on the top of the staves, he drew his knees up till they rested beside his hands.

But, alas, for the immutability of human affairs, the whole weight of his little body resting on the side of the barrel turned it over, and Gripe was precipitated on to his head, the barrel falling on the top of him.

The force with which he fell partially stunned him, and his legs were very much bruised by the barrel, as it rocked up and down on its belly, the end each time striking him in its descent.

Covered with dirt, his limbs aching from the blows he had received, and looking as unlike himself as possible, Gripe, after a time, raised himself into a sitting position, and looked bewilderedly around him.

For some few moments he was unable to perfectly realise his position, but at length, when he had made himself thoroughly acquainted with the extent of his injuries, and the true nature of his situation, a deep groan broke from his breast, and he bowed his head in shame and despair.

The errand on which he had come was dishonourable, and the punishment he had received was, to say the least of it, well merited; and still he was as far off the consummation of his wishes as ever.

And as he sat in the middle of that place, amid the heap of rubbish with which it was filled, Gripe bitterly cursed himself for the part his selfish nature had prompted him to play.

He had thought, by taking advantage of the impaired intellect of an unfortunate woman, to succeed in inducing her to betray the secrets of her husband; but he had met with one, if not so gifted with reason, at least as cunning as himself.

That instinct which the idiot possesses was inherent in Minnie. She felt that the prosecutor of her husband could mean nothing but injury to him she loved, and she had hit upon the means by which to render Gripe powerless to harm him.

Many a woman possessing all her faculties would not have thought of confining the steward as Minnie had done.

Gripe thought her a fool; she had proved herself wiser than he had been.

And as he sat there he acknowledged that she had done so.

His prospects of escape were now less than they had hitherto been.

True, the shutter was open, but how was he to reach the window?

Again he look around the place in the hope of finding something to assist him to reach the opening.

But nothing which would answer that purpose met his gaze.

The barrel was no longer of use, both ends having disappeared.

The staves still held together, but the slightest pressure would send them into a heap.

Gripe fairly broke out into a perspiration, as he could discover nothing which would aid him to leave the place.

The prospect of meeting Dick appeared certain, and his fears became stronger and stronger.

"Confound my folly," he muttered, "for proceeding on the business as I have done. I should have forseen some such danger as this. Now I shall have ruined all chance of learning that I so much covet. I should have gone to work differently. Had I have schemed to place Dick in my power—and with his impulsive nature I might easily have done so—I could then have served my purpose better. But now I have ruined all my hopes. He will find me here—that idiot will make him understand the business on which I came, and if I escape without further injury, I shall have placed the poacher on his guard. What a fool I have been. Oh, Gripe, Gripe, you should have known better—you who so well know how to plot and plan to be outwitted by an idiot! Confound her."

And, vexed with himself, Gripe rose from the floor.

As he did so the sound of voices saluted his ears.

He listened intently.

The voices sounded louder and nearer. The steward turned pale, for in another moment he heard a key placed in the lock of the door.

CHAPTER XL.

HENLEY RESOLVES TO KNOW HOW FAR GRIPE HOLDS HIM IN HIS POWER—THE INTERVIEW IN THE CHURCHYARD.

WHEN Squire Henley recovered from the swoon into which he had been thrown by the words of his steward, he opened his eyes and gazed about the apartment for some time like one in a dream.

His eyes wandered, however, to the chair which Gripe had occupied, as the truth of what had happened dawned upon his senses, and a sigh of relief broke from his lips when he found that the steward was gone.

Rising from his chair, he tottered rather than walked across the room to the bell-pull, and seized it in his grasp.

In a very moments the summons was answered.

"Where is Gripe?" he asked.

"I thought he was here, sir," replied the man. "Shall I seek him?"

"No matter," replied his master.

The man bowed and withdrew.

"Oh, the curse of avarice," exclaimed the squire, throwing himself into a chair· "Why —why was I not satisfied to remain a well-to-do and honest man. But no, my grasping nature rebelled against honour, and I could not rest satisfied with sufficient to render me happy. I would be wealthy and powerful, and I found the means to become so, but at what a price—what a price!"

And Henley buried his face in his hands, and racked his body to and fro, whilst his heart heaved with the violence of the emotions which raged within.

"I had enough—enough for my wants," he murmured, after a pause; "but the demon of avarice would not let me rest. It engendered in my breast a desire for more, and I covetted that which should have been anothers. I resolved to possess it, and I planned and plotted and sinned to get it within my grasp. Lied and perjured myself that I might rob another of its inheritance, and I succeeded; but what has it been to me, an incubus more fearful than the mind can conjure up. I had expected wealth to bring happiness in its train; but it brought misery—brought its punishment with it."

"Oh, that I had never possessed it—I might then have been happy. Now what have I become, the slave of my own servant, the despised of my own menial."

Squire Henley rose and paced the room, as though by so doing he hoped to still the feelings which raged within his heart.

"Conscience," he continued, "has never slumbered—night and day has its upbraidings made my life a torment of misery, but I felt secure. Alas the guilty will never know rest. The secret I believed buried in the tomb rises against me, and I am defied by one whom I have befriended. Was not the knowledge of my own guilty deeds sufficient, but that I must be tormented by this villain who purchased his power over me with my own gold. My own. No, no,—not mine—not mine. Yet I believed that none knew that but *her*. I must know the truth of what Gripe has ascertained. I must hear whether or no he holds me in his power. If he does, then farewell to peace of mind for ever. But if he has lied—if I have still the power to defy him, I will trample the serpent beneath my heel—pluck the taunting sting from the adder I have nourished, and hurl destruction upon his head. I must know the truth—though I learn it by kneeling to him I have so deeply wronged."

Henley left the apartment and retired to his dressing-room.

Here he donned a low broad brimmed hat and great coat; then listening for any sound that might indicate that the servants were about that part of the house, he opened a drawer and took from it a beautifully mounted pocket pistol.

He held the weapon in his hand for a few moments, and looking at it intently he murmured,—

"You may yet do me service. Your friendly aid I may require. To live in fear of one whom I have fed and sheltered cannot be."

And the squire placed the weapon in his pocket with a heavy sigh.

"Rest there," he said, "till I know the worst, and if I need thy aid be speedy and sure in thy friendship."

Again he listened.

No one was about.

With slow steps he descended the stairs, and made his way into the grounds by a side door,

"I will see him," he muttered as he strode along. "I will see the man I have wronged—the husband of her whose reason I have blighted. He can save or destroy me. Will he show me more mercy than I have meted out to him. Dare I hope it—yes, for he is true and noble;

the soul of honour beats within his heart and he will scorn to lie even to the man who lied to injure him. Oh, did he know the agony of mind I have so long endured—did he but dream of the miserable existence which has been my portion these many years he would pity me—he would know that he had been avenged. But he knows it not, for to the world I have ever been the same. He has known and seen but the mask worn in society—to him the hours of remorse have been unknown. Dick—Dick," he added, " much as I have wronged you, you have been amply and terribly avenged."

Forcing his hat low upon his brow, so as to hide his features as much as possible from the gaze of any person whom he might meet, and drawing the huge collar of his great coat up high over his face, he strode onward towards the spot where the little farm of Dick the poacher was situated.

Like Gripe, he well knew by what means he should find out whether Dick was absent or not.

Were he absent he felt assured he should find Minnie sitting in the porch awaiting his return.

As he neared the place, he looked anxiously towards the door of the little farm house.

Minnie was there, her hands resting on her lap, and her eyes fixed upon the ground as usual.

A sigh of disappointment escaped the breast of Henley.

"Not there," he murmured. "And I must bear this fearful suspense some time longer; but doubtless he will soon return. I will wait and watch. I will not return without knowing the truth, though it may plunge me into deeper despair."

And casting his gaze around him, Squire Henley walked away in the direction of a little church, the steeple of which rose above the trees, at some little distance from the old farm house.

With his head buried in the ample collar of his great coat, the squire still kept on, ever and anon raising his eyes and looking about him, in the hope of seeing Dick.

But hours passed away.

No Dick made his appearance.

Still Henley resolved not to return to the manor till he had seen him.

Striding along, almost heedless which direction he took, he found himself near an old ruined church, which had formerly been built for a monastery, but which was now fast falling into decay.

He strolled within the precincts of its crumbling walls, and walked half fearfully amid the tombs which lie scattered here and there, moss grown and neglected.

Suddenly he paused.

His eye had rested upon a carved stone tomb, which time was fast crumbling to decay.

As he gazed upon it a shudder ran through his frame.

"Why have I wandered here?" he muttered. "To the last place that I should love to look upon."

And he turned to leave the spot.

He had gone about three paces, when a voice fell upon his ears.

He paused.

A cold perspiration broke upon his brow.

There was something in that voice which caused his heart to beat violently within his breast.

He feared to turn—yet dared not move away.

"Can the dead arise to upbraid me," he gasped.

Fearfully he looked around.

A man was seated upon the tomb.

Henley gave an involuntary start as his eyes encountered the form of Dick the Poacher.

"It was his voice, then," muttered the squire—"how like—how like!"

"So, squire, there is some fascination for you still in this mouldering block of stone," said Dick.

"You here," said Henley.

"Yes."

"I did not think to meet you here," said the squire.

"Perhaps not; nor did I expect to meet you," said Dick. "Can you not do without desecrating the grave of one you have so basely wronged."

"Hush!" said the squire.

"Ha!" exclaimed Dick. "Conscience, then, is not quite dead within you."

A deep sigh broke from the heart of Henley.

"Squire, you know this tomb," said Dick, bringing down his clenched hand upon the damp stone.

A shudder was the only reply.

"Know who slumbers beneath this carved cerement?" he continued.

"Alas! too well," replied Henley.

"And yet," said Dick, "you can dare to pollute the spot with your presence! Oh, man, man! are you so callous, so lost, so fallen, as to desecrate the last resting place of one whose dying moments you embittered, whose relatives you robbed and slandered?"

"Peace!" gasped Henley.

"Peace!" iterated Dick, with a scornful curl of the lip. "That word has no right upon your lips. Peace you have refused others, and can never know it yourself. Oh, man! what have you to answer for?"

Henley lowered his head before the penetrating look of the poacher.

"Shall I tell you, Squire Henley?" exclaimed Dick, after a pause.

"No, no!" gasped the squire.

"You fear to hear," said Dick.

"I—I—"

"Do fear," exclaimed Dick. "You fear not to bring your hated presence within the precincts of the remains of those whose friendship you won, whose confidence you abused, whose lives——"

"Hold!" gasped Henley. "I am here by accident."

"Accident," said Dick.

"Yes."

"What accident, squire?"

"I was seeking you."

"Was?"

"Yes; and heedless of the direction I was taking, I wandered unintentionally hither," answered Henley.

"Indeed."

"Yes, indeed."

"You were seeking me?"

"I was."

"For what purpose?" asked Dick. "What hellish villany have you now in your soul?"

"I wished to see you," said Henley.

"For what purpose?" asked Dick.

"To gain rest for my troubled soul," said the squire.

"Squire, you will never know rest," said Dick.

"Why not?"

"Because your crimes will ever rise in judgment against you. Sleeping or waking, that still small voice called conscience whispers to your soul that thou art accursed."

Henley was silent.

Dick watched him intently.

A gleam of pleasure shot from the dark eye of the poacher, as he saw the deadly pallor which overspread the features of his companion.

Dick was not the man to feel joy at the agony of others.

In that white face he read that at least the squire felt some horror now for his previous acts.

He was not all stone. There was one soft spot in his heart which conscience could assail.

"Squire," said Dick, after a pause, "you have sought me for that which it is not in my power to give. Look, squire, can you ever hope to know rest again whilst memory will cling to the knowledge that beneath this tomb lies mouldering the remains of one for whom you professed a brotherly love, yet whose property you covetted, and whose very life you dared—"

"Hold! for the love of heaven!" gasped Henley, trembling violently.

"You fear to hear of your guilty work," said Dick.

"No—no. You labour under some strange delusion. I never wronged him."

"Never!"

"Never!"

"Oh, man—man—are you not fearful that his fleshless bones should rise from the tomb to upraid you."

And rising from his seat Dick clasped the wrist of the squire, as he turned to hide the flush on his cheek, which the words of the poacher called up.

With a cry of horror Henley shook off the grasp of Dick.

As the cold fingers of the poacher grasped his arm he almost feared that a spectre from the tomb had issued forth, to check the lie upon his lips.

"Shame, squire, shame," said Dick; "add not liar to your already overcharged soul."

Henley cast his eyes upon the ground.

"Can you ever hope to know peace again," exclaimed Dick, his voice trembling with emotion as he spoke, "after the injury you have inflicted upon me."

"What wrong have I ever done you?" asked the squire.

"What wrong?" exclaimed Dick. "Have you not branded me as a felon? Have you not been the means of driving reason from the brain of her I so fondly love? Wretch!" added Dick, advancing towards him with clenched hands—"What wrong have you ever done me—wrong that goads this brain almost to madness, and prompts me to rid the gallows of its due, and crush beneath my heel the serpent whose venomed sting has sank so deeply in my soul, and poisoned my happiness for ever!"

"Man!—would you murder me?" gasped Henley.

"I would avenge my poor wife!" exclaimed Dick.

"Would you hurl your soul to perdition!" exclaimed Henley.

"I would do an act of justice, and avenge the injuries of those you have so basely injured!"

And Dick stretched forth his hand to grasp the tall form of the squire.

Henley darted back.

He drew the pistol from his breast, which he had secreted there when he left the manor.

"Stand back, Dick," he said, pointing the weapon at the poacher's head.

Dick smiled scornfully.

"Fire," he said, "if you have the courage."

"I would not have your blood upon my soul," said Henley; "but I will defend my life."

"Squire Henley," exclaimed Dick, "you dare not pull the trigger of that weapon, for with my death grasp would I clutch your throat, and tear your treacherous heart from out your guilty breast."

"I seek not your life," said the squire; "but will defend my own until it is no longer worth the keeping—then will I turn this barrel against my heart, and bid farewell to life and misery."

There was something so convincing in the tones of the squire, that Dick dropped his threatening arm, and drew back a pace.

As he did so, the squire returned the weapon to his breast.

When he had done this, he fixed his eyes upon the poacher, and said,—

"Dick, let us be friends."

"What!" exclaimed the poacher, with a start.

"Friends," said Henley.

Dick drew himself proudly up, and fixed upon Henley a glance of withering scorn.

"Squire," he exclaimed, "the world calls me a poacher; the stain of a prison is upon me; those who know my poor demented wife believe that my villany has deprived her of reason; they look upon me as without the pale of society, but they know not what has driven me to pursue the course of life I have done. You, in the eyes of most men, are wealthy, honourable, and just; but I, the despised poacher, the gaol bird, scorns the proffered friendship. I would not take your hand, for there is pollution in the touch. Squire, bad as I am, I cannot descend to acknowledge for my friend the man who can rob the widow and the orphan, and place beneath the cold, grey stone the body of the man for whom he professed respect and honour by unnatural means. Ah! start, squire, for well you may. Were that body exhumed, what might not be found? what hellish work might it not bring to light? Squire Henley, we can never be friends till justice is done to the oppressed, poor Minnie's reason restored, and the heap of bones which lie beneath this cold slab are restored to life."

"That can never be," gasped Henley.

"No more can our friendship," said Dick.

"Dick," said Henley, after a pause, "you are poor."

"In wealth, I admit; but, squire, I am richer than you in honour," exclaimed the poacher.

"The farm will not yield you sufficient to support yourself and your wife."

"Thanks to you, it will not," answered Dick.

"It shall be restored to you as of former years."

"Indeed."

"It shall."

"On what terms?"

And Dick fixed his dark eye penetratingly on the face of Henley.

"The answer of a few questions," replied Henley.

"It may serve my purpose not to answer them truthfully."

"No, it would not."

"Why not?"

"Because, Dick, you are too honourable to lie," said Henley.

"I wish I could return the compliment," said the poacher, sarcastically.

Henley winced.

"Will you accept the terms?"

"Squire, I will accept nothing from you."

"Why not?"

"Because the day will yet come when I shall *demand* all."

Henley started.

Then Dick did possess proofs of his villany.

But he must be satisfied that Gripe held no power over him.

"Dick," he said, "answer me one question. Has Gripe the power to do me harm?"

"Why do you ask?" inquired Dick.

"He has threatened me."

"And you fear him?"

"I—I do."

"Then you acknowledge you are guilty?" said Dick, fixing his eye upon his face.

"No, no; but—"

"But, Squire Henley," said Dick, "if you are an honourable man, it can be in the power of none to injure you. Knowing that you are guilty, you tremble lest he holds the proofs that can consign you to a felon's doom."

"I know not what to think—how to act. Speak, Dick, you can bid me live or die."

"How so?"

"Tell me, has Gripe any power over me? If he has not, then I can defy him; but if he really does possess anything by which he makes me his slave, I will place a pistol to my head, and bid farewell to the world for ever!"

Dick paused for a moment, so determined were the tones of the squire, that he really believed he would carry out his threats.

He had no wish that the squire should die yet—his time had not come.

"Squire," he said, "Gripe is powerless to harm you, but there is one who can."

"Who?" asked the squire.

"Me—Dick, the Poacher."

Henley was about to speak again, but Dick warned him off, and strode from the church-yard.

CHAPTER XLI.

THE WINTER LESSON—THE PANTOMIMISTS AT HOME — UNWELCOME NEWS — A RESOLVE — GOOD TIDINGS.

THE air was bitter cold, and laden with particles of ice, which, drifted by the keen piercing wind, cut painfully as they were hurled against the face.

The snow lie frozen and crisp upon the ground, and the tall leafless trees appeared like gigantic pieces of beautiful needlework.

The houses looked as though they had been covered with white sheets, and the hedge-rows presented the appearance of a fairy scene, and the spiders' webs hanging in festoons from bough to bough, thickly coated with the frozen rain, gave to them an appearance at once beautiful and charming.

The pedestrians hurried along with their heads buried in the collars of their coats, and their hands thrust into their pockets, to shield them from the biting wind and the sharp pricking sleet.

Winter had set in, cold, bleak and cheerless, bringing to those whom a bountiful providence had vouchsafed every requirement, "tidings of comfort and joy," but to those whose portion it is to struggle for bread—struggle with aching hearts, and weary limbs for a bare subsistence, to those to whom luxury is but a name, and want a constant companion, to the poverty-stricken portion of the vast community, it brought with it all the horrors of want, misery, and cheerlessness.

Thousands, indeed, welcome the snow-crowned king with joy, for it betokened the approach of reunions, festivities, and happy hours by the fireside.

But thousands there were, who shrank with fear at the snow white locks of hoary winter— abject poor, the houseless wanderer, to them the festive season was the most to be dreaded in the whole year—without food, without covering, with the bleak snow falling around them, with the biting winds penetrating to their very vitals, with little or no prospects of work during the inclement season, to these indeed the approach of winter is to be dreaded.

What is it to these that it tells of the birth of our Saviour—tells us of Him who came to redeem the world. In the warmly clad circle— before the cheerful grate, around the well filled board, it may bring "tidings of comfort and joy," but not to the ill-fed, ill-cared for masses can it bring such cheering thoughts.

It's approach is looked for with horror, welcomed with wailings, borne with lamentations, and supported with despair.

To the Boy Actor and his friends Christmas was both longed for and dreaded.

Wished for that it might redeem their shattered fortunes, dreaded lest it should not answer the expectations fondly indulged in.

Ever since the arrangement by which the lessee took a part in the management was made, the Royal Star had failed, the bright "spec" on which the hundred pounds had been devoted had gradually faded, till Charlie Evans, after settling with the lessee, had not sufficient to pay for the lighting, and hand over to the company half salaries.

Still he fondly hoped that Christmas would redeem the fortunes of the house—that good audiences would take the place of empty benches, and that boxing night would yield sufficient to pay up the salaries of those who had so kindly supported them in their Struggles for Bread.

It was the day before Christmas.

Charlie Evans, Buskin Bob, little Harry, and the pretty Mary were seated before a small fire—so small, indeed, that its warmth scarcely reached them.

Their faces were sad, and wore a look of anxiety and care.

"To-morrow's Christmas-day," said Charlie, "but it ain't much of a Christmas for us. You and I, Bob, are used to being hard-up on Christmas-day; but little Harry, there, will feel it. I don't care for myself, but I can't help feeling for him."

"Oh, I don't mind," said Harry. "I know you have done the best you could, and I am satisfied."

"Yes, I have, my poor boy. Perhaps I have done wrong to struggle on night after night, paying half salaries and half light, and leaving ourselves without a penny; but I have done it in hopes of pulling in during the Christmas week."

"The company has stuck to us better than I thought they would, strike me comical if they ain't," said Bob.

"Yes, poor creatures, they have; and, like us, they will have a sorry Christmas, I fear. Their money is not much when they get it all, but when they can only get half for two months, and sometimes nothing, it must go hard with them. I only hope that Boxing-night will enable us to pay them."

"I hope so too," said Bob.

"We have done all that we can with the little means at command, to draw a good house, and heaven knows we have saved all the expenses by doing the work ourselves," said Charlie. "But still there is much to be done, and we shall have to be at the theatre all day to-morrow to get ready."

"So there will be no plum-pudding to-morrow," said Bob, looking hard at Mary and the Boy Actor. "Strike me comical, if there will. There, never mind; what's the use of having any; we shouldn't have time to eat it."

A faint smile rose to the face of Charlie Evans.

"It would only be a property one that we could get," said Charlie; "and they are somewhat hard of digestion."

"Yes, as hard as poverty. Strike me comical if it ain't. But, never mind, if our luck only turns, we'll have a plum-pudding yet."

"And it will turn, I believe," said Harry.

"Why?"

"Because father plays clown, and he will be sure to draw good houses," replied the boy.

"And Bob plays pantaloon," chimed in Mary.

"Yes; and you are fairy queen," said Harry. "There's a company without any one else."

"Ah, my boy," said Charlie, "the public would be but ill-satisfied with such a bill."

"But see how you can make the people laugh," said Harry; "you are so jolly."

Charlie sighed.

He had often laughed, and brought forth roars of laughter, when his heart was sad.

He had many a time tumbled on to the parade and the stage, and stolen the slice of bread and butter from a child, and would fain have eaten it, so hungry had he been, but that false feeling which assails the heart has prompted him to throw it off at the wings, because he would not let his fellow players see that he was starving.

He thought, too, that this Christmas would be the same, for they had no money, and but little food.

So little, indeed, that Charlie Evans could not find it in his heart to share it with Harry and his daughter.

The Royal Star was closed, so it was announced in the bills, whilst the pantomime was in preparation; but in truth because it would have been quite useless to open it till boxing night.

At that time pantomimes were not produced, as is now the case, on Christmas Eve, and so there was no prospect of obtaining anything in the shape of good fare on the Christmas Day for the poor pantomimists.

But though each felt acutely their hard lot, neither complained.

It would seem that each one rather endeavoured to cheer the other.

Buskin Bob, who was perishing with cold, moved back from the little fire, in order that Mary might get the nearer to it, and hoped that he might be struck comical if he wasn't so hot he couldn't bear it.

Charlie Evans felt as if he could have hugged his friend to his heart, for he saw that the action was prompted by his generous heart to make the poor girl more comfortable.

It was the same feeling which had prompted Charlie at the humble morning meal to pretend that he could eat no more when he cast his eye upon the last loaf.

"Me and Bob," said the clown, "must go down to the theatre and put things in order."

"I will go with you," said Harry.

"And I, too," said Mary; "there is sure to be something wanted."

"No, no," said Bob; "strike me comical if you shall, it's too cold. You both stop at home, and if you must have something to do, just darn that hole in my pants."

"You both stay at home," said Charlie, "there's not much to do now—me and Bob can see to all that's wanted."

"But had I not better come and help you?" asked Harry.

"No, my boy," said Charlie; "stay with Mary—stay and cheer her."

The boy returned to his seat by her side, and Charlie and Bob, wrapping themselves up as well as they were able, were about to leave the house for the theatre, when a loud knock at the door arrested them.

Harry leapt up to answer the summons, and returned in a moment with a note, which he placed in the hands of the clown.

Charlie opened it, saying, as he did so, "Don't I hope it is some one wants the boxes for a large party on Boxing night."

"Strike me comical, so do I," exclaimed Bob.

But, as the good-hearted clown cast his eyes

HARRY AND MARY.

over the letter, his face paled, and the paper fell to the floor.

"What's the matter?" asked Harry, looking anxiously into the clown's face.

Charlie only pointed to the paper.

"What's up?" asked Bob. "Strike me comical, if you ain't as white as a ghost."

With a sigh, Charlie sank into a chair.

"We can't open on Boxing night," he gasped.

"Can't open!" exclaimed Harry and Mary in a breath.

"Can't open!" exclaimed Bob.

"No."

"Why?"

"They are going to cut the gas off," said Charlie.

"Who is?"

"The company."

"What for?"

"Because it has not been paid for," replied the clown.

"Then damn them. I hope their Christmas dinner may choke them. Strike me comical, if I don't," exclaimed Bob. "Cut the gas off, when we've struggled so hard to keep the house open, and paid them, and gone without ourselves. Cut it off, and know that they will get the money the next morning."

"They care not for that," said Charlie.

"But they know it would ruin us," said Bob.

"What do they care."

"Cut it off—and at a time, too, when men

No. 14.

profess to be delighted at doing acts of charity, and showing good-will to all men. Cut it off—ah, they can't—will not do it."

Charlie shook his head in despair, and Harry and Mary fairly burst into tears.

"And these men," continued Buskin Bob, "profess to be Christians. Surrounded by every comfort, yet they cannot feel for the poor player, who struggles on without food, without warmth, till better times can enable him to turn round and say—'Here is the money I owe you, and I am grateful for your indulgence.' They know how we have struggled; they know, too, that we have paid them and gone without ourselves, and they know that we would pay them on the following day. Yet they take advantage of the time to make the demand, or execute the threat. They may be but men, but they can afford to wait one day. It would not ruin them, but it would be sure to ruin us. Well, I would rather now be the poor, half-starved pantomimist than the man who penned these lines; for, thank God, I can lay my hand upon my heart, and say I would not thus take advantage of ruining my greatest enemy. No, strike me comical, if I would."

And, indignantly, the pantaloon hurled the letter into the small grate.

"What's to be done?" asked Harry.

"Oh, father, it will never do to let them close the house on such a night," said Mary, looking up in the pale face of the clown.

"Alas, Mary, I know not," exclaimed Charlie, in tones of utter despair.

"How much is it?" asked Harry.

"Three pounds ten," replied the clown.

"And we can't get even that little sum," said Mary.

"No, child," said Charlie, "we have struggled on till sixpence only remains."

"And I should like to force that sixpence down the throat of the fellow that wrote the letter," said Bob, "I should, strike me comical."

"He is but a servant," said Charlie, "who has obeyed the orders of his masters."

"Then if he'd been a man," said Bob, fairly roused into a passion, "he'd have flung the paper in their face, and said—'If you would do this now you will utterly ruin them, and lose the money in the bargain, but if you give them grace you may save them and yourselves from loss, so if you can be so hard on them, and such fools to yourselves, do your own dirty work.'"

"Bob," said Charlie, rising from his seat and taking his friend's hand in his own, "all men have not got hearts like yours."

"No, or they wouldn't have done that, strike me comical if they would," exclaimed the pantaloon. "But when did they say it must be paid."

"On the morning of the boxing day or they will cut it off before the curtain rises."

Bob thought for a few moments.

Then turning quickly round, and striking his hand upon his thigh, he exclaimed,—

"Charlie! Harry! I have it."

"What?" asked all in a breath.

"How to save the house."

"How, how," asked all eagerly.

"The money is to be paid before night," said Bob.

"Yes! yes!"

"We'll give a morning performance, and get the money for them, strike me comical if we won't."

"Hurrah!" exclaimed Charlie, fairly jumping back in glee. "Here we are, that will do it! that will do it! Lor I never thought of that. But," he added, with a blank look on his face, "how can we announce it."

"Have some bills printed," said Bob.

"But we still owe money for the last," said Charlie.

"No matter, we shall be able to get them," said Bob; "I'll just run down and see about them at once."

"Do so," said Charlie, "and I'll run over to the theatre, and at rehearsal mention the morning performance."

And hastily snatching up their hats, the clown and pantaloon started off on their different errands, with lighter hearts than beat within their breasts a few short minutes before.

It was late in the evening before Charlie and Bob returned to their humble home.

But there was a look of pleasure upon the features of both as they entered the room, where the Boy Actor and little Mary sat over the small fire in the little bath stove.

As the young folks rose to greet them, and take their snow covered hats, Charlie caught Mary in his arms and imprinted a kiss on her lips.

"Mary," he said, "we will be able to keep Christmas to-morrow."

"Oh, I'm so glad," she said, clapping her hands together.

"Yes," replied Charlie. "When I arrived at the theatre, I found another letter waiting for me. At first I feared to open it, lest it should be some fresh demand with which we could not comply; but when I did open it, I found—"

"What! what!" interposed Mary and Harry in a breath.

"What do you think?"

"I don't know," said Harry.

"Oh, do tell!" exclaimed Mary.

"A ten pound note!" said Charlie.

"A ten pound note!" exclaimed both the young folks in a breath.

"Yes, a ten pound note," said Charlie.

"Oh, my!" exclaimed the girl.

"Strike me comical if he didn't," chimed in Bob.

"Yes," said Charlie, "and what do you think I have done with it."

"I don't know," said Mary.

"Not lost it?" asked Harry.

"Oh, no; I paid the printer and the gas," said the clown; "and discovered that the lessee had been the cause of that letter."

"Why?" asked Harry.

"Because, knowing that we had not got a feather to fly with, he had induced them, under false pretences, to send them down upon us."

"But what interest could he have in doing so," asked Harry.

"He would have paid the money himself and taken the house upon his own hands while the good season lasted."

"And you have foiled him," exclaimed Harry.

"I have," said Charlie,

"And I'll kick him the moment he appears behind," said Bob, "if I don't, strike me comical."

"The traitor!" said Harry, his youthful face lighting up with indignation.

"But we know him now, and can be upon our guard," said Charlie.

"And will show him up before the audience," said Buskin Bob. "I will—if I don't, strike me comical."

"But I have not told you all," said Charlie, "after paying gas and printing, I shared equally with the company. So there is not much left, yet there is sufficient to provide for to-morrow."

"Who sent it?" asked Harry.

"There's no name to the letter, but I know of one only who could so befriend us," said the clown.

"And who is that?"

"Who?" said Buskin Bob. "Why, Dick the Poacher. Didn't I say he was a gentleman, spite of his dress; didn't I say he wasn't what he is—couldn't I see as he was a right down, slap up, good-hearted, first-rate chap. I did, and here's proof of my words, if there ain't, why strike me comical.

CHAPTER XLII.

THE PANTOMIMISTS—CHRISTMAS DAY—BUSKIN BOB AND THE LESSEE.

CHRISTMAS day.

Perhaps of all the days in the year there is none looked forward to with more joy or more sorrow.

The boy at school dwells upon it for months ere it arrives, for to him it is a holiday, a round of pleasure.

The father will once more see the pride of his life, the mother the hope of her joyous days, the festive board will groan beneath the cheer provided for loved ones who have deserted the parental roofs, and built homes for themselves in the wide, wide world.

The wine cup will flow, and generous hospitality expand wide its wings.

Lovers meet and kiss beneath the miseltoe, and old friends long parted will once more clasp the hand of friendship, or imprint the kiss of affection.

The poor boy who has left home and kindred to seek a fortune far away, will return to the old house at home, and sit once more in the seat of his childhood; listen to the voice which has sung the sweet lullaby in the days of infancy; grasp the hand which has chastised his childish faults, led his thoughts to virtue and happiness.

The wife will return to the home of her childhood; to that home where a mother's watchful care has guided the slippery path, and led her steps to virtue, honour, and peace.

Once more the broken links are joined, once more glad hearts assemble beneath the roofs of their childhood, and the memories of days gone by enter their souls.

The wayward child is welcomed home; the fallen daughter forgiven—family quarrels made up, envious feelings drowned in the social cup, animosities forgotten, and true and brotherly love reign supreme.

It is a day of rest, a day of joy, a day of happiness to most all.

But there are one class at least to whom Christmas is a day of toil.

That class are the pantomimists.

There are rehearsals, parts to learn, and a host of other things connected with their profession.

And it often happens that Christmas is to them a day of misery.

Perhaps it may have been their fate to have had no engagement for some time; they may be "hard up," and have eked out an existence till the season, but when it arrives it often finds them poor in the extreme, and they may be seen around the stage doors of the various theatres ill-clad, ill-fed, and wretched.

Christmas is to many of them but the prospect of employment—the hope of better times, and Christmas day but a day of toil to prepare them for the morrow.

So it was with our friends.

True, they had now the means of procuring a few comforts for the Christmas day, but there was work to be done at the Royal Star, and hard work too.

Charlie and Buskin Bob, Harry and Mary, had plenty to keep them employed.

There was the transformation scene to be gilded, the masks to be painted, scenery to plain up, dresses to be mended, feathers to be wired, wigs to be sewn, benches to be swept, curtains to shake, wings to be cleaned, gas lights to alter, and the thousand other things which turn the theatre in the day time into a huge workshop.

All this had to be done, and more, on Christmas day, the determination to open the house on the Boxing morning giving less time than had been expected.

With cheerful hearts and willing hands these duties were performed, and about nine o'clock at night the friends went home to their humble lodgings to spend the Christmas.

It was but poor fare they sat down to, for Charlie had so laid out the gift of the poacher that little was left for themselves.

But still, poor as it was, it was eaten with thankfulness and joy.

Thankfulness to the generous donor—joy at the knowledge that the rest of the company had at least the chance of faring as well as themselves.

So it was, with cheering hopes and contented minds, the pantomimists and their young friends sought their couch on the Christmas night.

Boxing day opened cold and frosty; yet the sun shone forth, and, as far as the weather was concerned, everything bid fair for the success of the pantomime at the Royal Star.

All were up betimes.

The morning meal was hurriedly partaken, and Charlie and his companions started for the theatre.

The house was announced to open at two o'clock, and hurried preparations were made to have everything in readiness.

The company were all at their posts at the time the call was made for, each one willing to do his best.

The God-send in the shape of the few shillings which Charlie had given them the day before had caused their hearts to beat in friendliness towards him, and each one strove to do all they could to assist the managers.

Buskin Bob, whose indignation never for a moment cooled at the base conduct of the man who would have taken advantage of their poverty to get the house into his own hands at such a time, made the whole of the company acquainted with the facts, and a murmur of indignation was heard from all.

At mid-day the doors of the house were surrounded, and, an hour before the time announced for opening, a huge mass blocked up either entrance.

Buskin Bob was in raptures, Charlie delighted, and the young folks happy.

Still Mr. Grabham, the lessee, did not make his appearance.

This circumstance was thought strange by the pantomimists, inasmuch as he had never been absent from the theatre since the agreement made between him and Charlie Evans.

"It's rather strange that Grabham has not dropped in," said the clown to his friend, who was putting a finishing touch upon one of the scenes. "Perhaps he don't know we are going to open."

"Perhaps he hopes we ain't," said Bob. "I reckon he'll be a little flabergasted when he finds how we have licked him about the gas."

"Yes, no doubt he will," said Charlie, with a smile. "But he'll drop down to take his share directly he finds it out."

"Will he?" said Bob.

"Yes, you may depend he will," replied his friend.

"Then strike me comical if I don't hope he'll come before I'm made up," said Bob.

"Why?"

"Because then I should have my slippers on."

"What of that?" asked Charlie.

"What of that?" iterated Bob.

"Yes."

"Why, I can't kick him so hard as I can with these boots," replied Buskin Bob, holding up his leg, and showing his friend the toe of his boot, thickly studded with nob nails.

"Treat him with contempt," said Charlie.

"Yes, I'll treat him with contempt," said the indignant pantaloon. "But I'll treat him with leather too, or my name's not Buskin Bob; strike me comical if I won't!"

"Be careful, Bob," said Charlie; "we are poor, he is rich."

"We are men and he's a humbug," said Bob, getting quite red in the face.

"He has not treated us as generously as he should have done," said the clown.

"And I shan't treat him as tenderly as a baby neither, I can tell you," exclaimed Buskin Bob.

"Be careful, Bob; he has the means, and doubtless the will to do us much injury," said the clown.

"I have the means and the will to do him one," said Bob, again lifting up his foot; "if I haven't, strike me comical!"

"Yet I fear ——"

"Fear what?" interrupted Bob.

"That he will find some other means to get the house out of our hands," replied his friend.

"Very likely he may," replied Bob.

"For myself I should not care, but for the boy's sake I should be sorry," said Charlie.

"Not a bit of it," said Bob; "he can't get us out while we pay the rent."

"Yes, he can give us notice."

"To be sure; but at that time expires, the house won't be worth anything," said Bob, with a knowing wink; "and strike me comical, Charlie, if I think you are such a fool as to chance it again after the pantomime."

"No. It would not be worth the risk again," said the clown.

"In course it would not," said Bob, "and besides, you know in that agreement he got you to sign, it stipulated that you could go back to the old terms whenever you liked."

"That's true," said Charlie.

"Then chance it; go back to them at once," said Bob. "and as soon as the house begins to fall off, throw it up, and we'll try our fortunes elsewhere."

"I scarcely like to drive out of it at the very best time," said Charlie.

"You don't?"

"No."

"Why?"

"It would be mean and ungenerous," replied the clown.

Buskin Bob drew back a few paces, and looked his friend in the face with an expression of surprise.

"Be what?" he said.

"Mean and ungenerous."

"Strike me comical, there" exclaimed the pantaloon.

"Would it not," said Charlie.

"No."

"But it would, Bob."

"But I say it wouldn't. He has forfeited all right to respect, or sympathy."

"Still I would do to others as I should wish them to do to me," said Charlie.

"So would I."

"I know you would, Bob."

"But, strike me comical, if I would to him. Charlie, I am not the man to council any unfair dealings, but I say this much; the man who would act as he has done towards us, should not be allowed longer to desecrate this place with his hated presence. If he can stoop so low as to endeavour to injure us behind our backs, your duty to that boy, as his guardian, is to kick the viper out; if it aint, why, there, strike me comical."

"Certainly I can do so."

"And justice demands it!" exclaimed Bob.

"Well, we'll think it over; an hour or two perhaps may alter our feelings," said the clown.

"They may yours, but strike me comical if they will mine," said Bob, as Charlie turned away to attend to his duties. "I only hope if he comes at all to this house he'll come before I make up. It would be vexing only to have my slippers on, that it would, strike me comical if it wouldn't."

And thus easing his mind a little of his indignation at the conduct of the lessee, Bob stooped down and tightened his boot-lace. Rising from his recumbant position Bob turned to cross the stage, when his eyes fell upon the very individual who had so excited his indignation.

Mr. Grabham had just arrived.

Having been from home on the Christmas day he was unaware of the intention to open the theatre for a morning performance, till a bill had caught his eye an hour before.

He swaggered up to the wings, and almost insolently staring at Bob, said,—

"When was it arranged to give a morning performance?"

"Day before yesterday," said Bob looking down at the toe of his boot.

"Indeed."

"Yes, indeed," said Bob.

"Why was I not acquainted with the intention?" asked Grabham.

"Why wasn't you?"

"Yes, why was I not?"

"Because we didn't choose to tell you, that's why," said Bob.

"Are you aware, sir, that you will not be allowed to light up?" asked Grabham.

"No, I ain't."

"Ain't you?"

"No."

"Then I can inform you," said Grabham, with a malignant look, "that you will not be able to do so."

"And why, pray," asked Bob.

"Because you are in arrears with the gas," replied the other.

"Oh, indeed."

"Yes."

"Well, what does that matter?" asked the pantaloon.

"I have received a notice that the gas is not to be used."

"When?" asked Bob.

"This morning."

"What reason did they give?" asked Bob, innocently.

"That, being in arrears, you would not be permitted to use it," said Grabham.

"And they sent you a notice this morning to that effect, did they?" said the pantaloon, again looking very hard at the toe of his boot.

"Yes, sir, and it must be abided by," said Mr. Grabham, pompously.

"Ladies and gentlemen of the company," exclaimed Bob, calling out loudly, "will you please to step towards the prompter's box?"

A smile lit up the face of Grabham.

He believed that Bob was about to inform the company that he would be unable to bring up the curtain.

In a few moments nearly all the company had obeyed the summons, and stood awaiting the object thereof.

Casting his eyes around, Bob said,—

"Ladies and gentlemen, Mr. Grabham informs me that we shall be unable to light up, as he has received a notice this morning that the gas must not be used, as we are in arrears. That is what you state, I believe?"

"Such is the case," replied Grabham.

"Mr. Grabham," roared Bob, "you are a liar!"

Grabham fairly leapt back three feet towards the wall.

"Ladies and gentlemen," continued Buskin Bob, turning to the company, and drawing a paper from his pocket; "here is a receipt for the gas, which my friend Mr. Evans paid the day before yesterday, which you will see by the date."

Grabham opened his eyes, and his mouth too, in the greatest astonishment.

"Now," said Buskin Bob, "is not this man a liar?"

"To be sure he is," said Tom Slater, who was engaged as harlequin, "or it would be dated the 24th."

"No," replied Bob; "nor is this all I wish to bring to your notice. We have had to struggle hard, as you all know, to keep the house open. We laid out a hundred pounds upon it, and it would have been too bad not to give us a chance of at least getting some of it back. Business has been bad, very bad, and we have left the theatre night after night without a penny for ourselves; but we struggled on because we hoped the pantomime would pull us out of our difficulties. All the while that things looked gloomy, this person permitted us to keep on the house in consideration that he should receive the lion's share. We have done so, but directly he finds everything prepared, and the house ready to open, he goes to the gas company, represents us as a set of swindlers, and prevails upon them to send us a notice that if all arrears are not paid up by this morning, it would be cut off before the time of opening the house. Under these circumstances we resolved to give a morning performance, but when we arrived here to make the arrangements necessary, Mr. Evans received a letter from a friend, enclosing a ten pound note; out of this he paid the gas and the printer, and shared the remainder among these ladies and gentlemen of the company, who have so kindly supported us, and extended to us such kind indulgence. Now, ladies and gentlemen, what can you think of the man who can be guilty of so mean an action?"

And Bob, pointing at Grabham, who stood abashed before him, turned questioningly to the company assembled.

"What did he do it for?" asked Slater; "he must have had some motive."

"To get the house entirely into his own hands. He knew that we were unable to comply with the demand. He would have paid it and taken the property off our hands."

"But what would he have done for a company?" asked Slater.

"He would have engaged you all," replied Bob.

"Then I'm damned if he would have got my services!" exclaimed Slater.

"Nor mine! nor mine!" exclaimed several others.

"Nor mine, nor Charlie's," said Bob. "So, even if we had not had the good luck to satisfy the demand for the light, Mr. Grabham would have been none the better off for his dirty work."

Mr. Grabham, thoroughly ashamed of his conduct, slunk towards the stairs, as Charlie and young Harry came up them.

"Stop a minute, Mr. Grabham," exclaimed Bob, "I have not done with you yet. I have proved you to be a mean-spirited cur and a disgraceful liar, but I have not yet shown the ladies and gentlemen of this company the treatment which your dirty conduct will justify."

And, making two or three steps rapidly forward, Buskin Bob caught the lessee by the collar of his coat, and, holding him firmly, inflicted half a dozen hard kicks in the vicinity of his coat tails, then thrust him violently down the stairs leading from the stage.

CHAPTER XLIII.

BOXING-DAY AT THE ROYAL STAR—A GOOD HOUSE—
THE LETTER.

AMID shouts of laughter, and the ironical jeers of the company, the lessee shrank like a beaten cur out of the theatre.

His dirty work had brought upon himself just punishment.

"There," said Bob to Charlie, "I said I'd do it, and, strike me comical, I've kept my word."

"Serve him right," said several.

"Now, Bob," said Charlie, "we must make up, the house is full."

"Glad to hear it," said Bob. "I should have been wild, and no mistake, if I had been dressed when he showed his ugly face in between the wings. I should, strike me comical if I shouldn't!"

Charlie only smiled, and inwardly hoped that the indignity offered to the lessee might not bring down upon them the wrath of that unprincipled personage.

The pantomimists flew to their dressing-rooms to make up for their respeceive parts.

Harry and Mary were both cast in the opening, and the kind-hearted little maiden issued from her dressing-room attired as a fairy, with a long wand in her hand, and a tiara of roses upon her brow.

The colour had been laid on her pretty cheeks with taste and moderation, and she looked really beautiful amid the cloud of gauze, which extended like a balloon around her pretty little figure.

Harry, who had made up for a demon, made towards her as she glided on to the stage, and lifting his ugly gilt mask from his head, he threw his arms around her, and imprinted a kiss upon her lips.

"Oh, Mary," he exclaimed, "how beautiful you do look!"

"Am I not always pretty?" said the little lady, with a toss of her flower-covered head.

"Oh, yes," said the boy, "but not so beautiful as now."

"Then, it's the dress you love most, Harry, after all," smiled Mary.

"Oh, no, no!" exclaimed Harry; "I always love you, but I feel as if I could love you more, now that you look so very beautiful, so much more beautiful than when at home in your old cotton frock.

Mary sighed.

Why did she so?

Young as she was, she felt that budding affection, which with her would ripen into love for the poor orphan, and the words he had uttered caused her little mind to wonder whether he could love her in poverty and rags as truly as he could in affluence.

A shade passed over her young heart, and she almost became sad.

Harry saw the alteration in her features, and knew that he had unintentionally wounded her feelings.

He flung his arms around her again, and pressed her to his heart.

"I am sure I shall always love you," he exclaimed, "no matter how you look or what you wear, for you are so kind, so good, and so pretty."

Mary looked into his face, and her eyes filled with tears.

But like the summer shower, however, it dried away, and a smile, like a bright sunbeam, overspread her features.

She pouted her pretty lip, and Harry once more clasped her in his arms and kissed her.

"Strike me comical!" exclaimed Bob, at this moment coming on to the stage, followed by Charlie Evans; "look here, Charlie, if the young rascal and your daughter aint a billing and a cooing just like two turtle doves!"

Charlie laughed, and Mary and Harry blushed, whilst the little maiden ran off the stage, as if ashamed at being caught.

The pantomimists were made up, and everything being in readiness, the bell rung for the curtain to ascend.

Up it went, and revealed to the gaze of those who stood at the wings a house crowded to suffocation.

"Thank God!" exclaimed Charlie.

"Strike me comical!" muttered Bob.

How happy they both felt at that moment, as they gazed upon the sea of heads which rose from pit to ceiling.

"Ain't you glad we opened, Charlie?" asked the pantaloon.

"I am."

"So am I—strike me comical if I aint!" replied Bob.

Charlie, smiling, pressed his friend's hand in silence.

"It's a spanking house," said Bob.

"A week like this will bring us our money back," said Charlie.

"More than that, strike me comical if it won't. Because you ain't going to be such a fool as go whacks with that mean-spirited cur as I made acquainted with my shoe, are you?"

"I should not like to cheat him," replied the clown.

"Cheat, be ——. Strike me comical, I won't swear, but he has broken the contract with you."

"Still, I would be more generous and honourable to him than he has been to us," replied Charlie, who, though he could but despise the man who would have so injured them, could not bring himself to act unfairly towards him.

"Well, Charlie, of course you will do as you like, but he don't deserve it; strike me comical if he does—there."

And Bob brought his fist emphatically down upon one of the wings.

The pantomime went on, till at length the transformation was at hand.

Charlie and Bob had taken up their positions, and listened eagerly for the cue at which they were to tumble on to the stage.

At length it came; and, amid roars of laughter, and shouts of applause, our good-hearted friend rolled towards the footlights with the ever welcome exclamation—

"Here we are! Hallo! How do you do, to-morrow? Happy to see you. Oh! ain't we jolly!"

But Charlie thought as he knocked Bob down with a property carrot, which he pulled out of his capacious pocket, that had it not been for the ten-pound note so generously sent them, that their jollity would have been less than it really was; for had they have appeared at all before the large audience in that theatre, it would have been not as managers, but servants, toiling for the man who had done his best to ruin them.

But their hearts were light now, and they played with a spirit.

Never before had Charlie and Bob gained so much applause—never before had they sustained their parts with greater credit.

The audience were in raptures, and so was the company.

That house contained sufficient to pay off all demands; and all knew that Charlie Evans would not fail to settle with his friends before he took a sixpence for himself.

At length the bell rang, and the curtain rolled silently down upon the last tableau.

The pantomime was over.

The audience commenced to leave the theatre, highly delighted with the entertainment provided for them; and not a few resolved to return again at night to see it over again.

After a few minutes rest, Charlie returned to his room, accompanied by Buskin Bob.

Both were in a perspiration, and throwing each a property cloak around them to keep them from catching cold, they seated themselves before a small table, on which were placed two boxes.

Charlie lifted one of these in his hands.

A smile broke over his painted face.

"Feel the weight of it, Bob," he exclaimed, turning to his companion.

Bob took the box, and weighed it on his hand.

"Strike me comical!" he exclaimed. "It's the heaviest we ever had."

"It is," said Charlie; "and it will remove a heavier weight from my heart."

"How?"

"It will pay those who have so long trusted us—so long toiled with us uncomplainingly in our struggles for bread."

"So it will," said Bob. "And, strike me comical, if they ain't acted like bricks."

Charlie unlocked the box, and turned the money out upon the table.

"Tell them to come in, Bob," he said; "I wouldn't let them wait another minute longer than I could help."

Bob rose from his seat and left the room.

The good fellow smiled as he took his way across the stage and entered the different dressing rooms, telling each one of the company to go to Charlie and get his money.

If Bob felt happy at being the bearer of the request, the poor players felt happy also at the prospect of receiving their wages, for not a few of them had been sadly put to it during the past few weeks, and their pleasure was doubly enhanced, as they had expected to wait till after the night's performance.

But Charlie Evans was not the man to forget that the money was due to them, and that their wants should be studied.

He had been too hard up himself not to feel for others.

One by one they entered his little room, and received the balance due to them for their services.

Nor was this all they received.

Charlie tendered thanks as well as money—thanks for the kind manner in which they had stood by him in the hour of adversity.

Scarcely one of them but offered to take a part only, lest he should have none left for himself; but this Charlie firmly but feelingly refused.

There was enough for all.

Had it been otherwise, the good-hearted fellow and his friends would have waited for the proceeds of the next house.

It was five o'clock, and the performances were to commence again at seven.

Those who could, hurried home to get refreshments. But Charlie and Bob, who took some time to make up, decided upon remaining at the theatre.

Tea was procured from a neighbouring coffee-house, and set out in the little room; and with grateful hearts the pantomimists, and Mary and Harry, sat down to partake of it.

"Fortune once more seems to smile upon us, Harry," remarked the clown; "but we must not hope for its continuance. During this week we shall, doubtless, have good houses, and perhaps for a month afterwards, paying ones. But we have seen sufficient to convince us that the property is not up to much, in the long run. I think it will be better for us to give a month's warning, and leave the theatre at the expiration of that time. Should business continue good, we may get back your hundred pounds; but if we remain longer, I feel assured we shall again lose it."

"You know best, father," said the boy. "I will willingly agree to anything you may think for the best, for I am sure you have my interest so much at heart that you would do nothing but what you thought for the best."

"Strike me comical if he would," said Bob; "and what Charlie says is about the best thing he could do. Besides, the spring won't be long coming, then; and a booth to travel the country will pay better than a theatre."

"I only wish, if we can get a booth, that we could take the company with us," said Harry.

"So should I; for they work well, and have got hearts, Harry, and bless them for it. They have clung to us whilst hunger gnawed their vitals without a murmur; they have left the theatre with empty pockets, and I shall never forget their kindness—never!"

"Nor I," said Bob. "Strike me comical if I shall. But still, there are some of them who would not accept an engagement in a booth, and others whom it would be ruin to employ."

"So it would," said Charlie. "Still, we could not expect to get a company together like Richardson's."

"Nor a booth, neither," laughed Bob.

"No," said the clown, "at least, not unless luck should run high for some time. I should have been glad to have had some of our old pals here."

"I'm rather surprised," said Bob, "that we haven't seen one, at least."

"Who?"

"Why, Margaret—Dancing Bill's wife."

"So am I; it's strange where she disappeared to all of a sudden," remarked Charlie.

"Can't make it out," said Bob. "I made sure she'd be columbine for us."

"There's a mystery about her sudden disappearance," said Charlie, "and I believe she's gone away out of fear of Bill."

"Maybe so," said Bob; "but, strike me comical if I don't sometimes think she ain't gone in a natural manner. I don't like to say things as ain't exactly right, but I fancy Bill knows where she is, and is keeping her out of the way for some reason or another."

"Well, I hope she is all right," said Charlie, "and perhaps she may turn up in a day or two. Hallo! it's just six—we must get to work again; and the people outside are getting impatient for the doors to open."

As they crossed the stage, the noise of the people crowding around the doors fell upon their ears.

"Another good house," said Buskin Bob. "Strike me comical if they won't have the doors down, if they go on hammering at them in that manner."

Charlie was about to reply to his friend's observation, when a youth crossed the stage with a letter in his hand, and laying his finger upon the clown's arm said,—

"Are you Mr. Evans, sir?"

"Yes, my boy," replied the clown.

"Here's a letter for you," said the youth, placing a note in the clown's hand.

Charlie turned it over in his fingers, then broke the seal and perused its contents.

"Poor thing," he muttered.

"What's the matter?" asked Bob.

Charlie placed the note in his friend's hand, and Bob, after reading it, said,—

"Strike me comical, and we were only just talking about her."

It was from the poor columbine, Margaret, who had but just recovered her consciousness, having been attacked with brain fever, caused by the fearful discovery she had made in the inquest room.

She was now a patient in the hospital, to which she had been conveyed by Mr. Wilks, at the coroner's request.

"Tell her," said Charlie, turning to the boy, "that I will see her in the morning. Poor thing," he added, "we will do all we can for her, for we have got hearts in our breasts, Bob, and can feel for others, though we are but pantomimists."

CHAPTER XLIV.

THE ACQUITTAL OF SLATER—THE POOR COLUMBINE IN THE HOSPITAL.

THERE is something awfully solemn in twelve men seated around a table, and weighing in their mind evidence given for or against a wretch accused of murder!

There is a something fearful in the knowledge that to these assembled gentlemen is entrusted the fate of a fellow creature!

To them is left the decision whether or not the accused shall take his trial for life or death.

Awful is the silence which reigns around when the foreman has announced that they have decided upon their verdict.

A silence so deep, so profound, so painful, that it is only broken by the loud beating of the prisoner's heart.

Who could pourtray the feelings of that pale, haggard man, at the moment of the intimation that the jury had agreed.

The pallor on his face deepened, and his manacled hands were clasped firmly together,

as though he hoped thus to still the violent beating of his heart.

With strained eyeballs, as though he would penetrate into the innermost recesses of the foreman's heart, and with body bent forward he awaits, with agonising suspense, the fiat of the jury.

"Do you find the prisoner Guilty or not Guilty?" asked the coroner.

"Not Guilty!" replied the foreman.

A sigh of relief, so long, so deep-drawn, burst from the heart of Slater, and his manacled hands, which he had extended as though appealing for mercy, fell with a heavy sound upon his thighs.

The words of Margaret, together with the evidence of the doctor respecting the weapon used to inflict the fearful wounds, had had such weight upon the minds of the gentlemen who composed the jury, that they could find no other verdict.

Slater was acquitted.

Mr. Wilks was now as eager to take the manacles from his wrists as he had been to place them there.

The poor carpenter's character was cleared of the foul stain which had accidentally been cast upon it.

He was again free.

But what had he suffered?

Could the verdict of those men reinstate him in all his previous happiness and health.

They had decided that he was innocent; that he had been wrongly accused; that he was deserving of the sympathy of all men, instead of censure.

He would leave that court without a blemish upon his character; he could hold up his head again before his fellow men; he could look proudly and defiantly around and say, "I have stood the ordeal, and am proclaimed pure by a jury of my own countrymen!"

But could he feel as he had hitherto done; look as he ever had; be merry, joyous, and happy,—

"No!"

The agony of mind he had endured; the fearful stigma under which he had lain; the agonising suspense he had been subjected to had done its work.

Slater had become prematurely old.

His hair had turned prematurely grey; the upright form of the healthy man was bent; and the ruddy glow had faded for ever on his cheek.

The elastic step had given place to a tottering gait, and the laughing eye had become dim.

In health and spirits alike was he broken; and though time might allay, it never could wholly eradicate the fearful change he had undergone in so short a time.

Collier was profuse in his congratulations, for he was really glad at the escape of the young carpenter.

Mr. Wilks, too, was equally so.

But the accused man turned away from the pompous officer with a look of intense disgust.

This hurt the feelings of the worthy policeman, and he remarked,—

"Won't you take my hand?"

"No," said Slater.

"Why not?"

BUSKIN BOB IN A NEW CHARACTER.

"How can you ask, when you have caused me so much anxiety," said the other.

"If I have," said Wilks, "you are clear now, and all the better for what you have undergone."

"Am I?"

"Yes."

"Your innocence is thoroughly established," replied the officer.

"You were not justified in accusing me," said the young man.

"It looked black against you, and I only did my duty."

"Perhaps so; but I think different," said Slater.

"Had you been in my place you would have acted as I have done," said the officer.

"No I should not."

"Indeed!"

"Indeed I should not."

"Then you would not have done your duty."

"I would do my duty in any channel," replied the carpenter; but I would not have accused a man of the crime of murder with no evidence to back it."

"But there was evidence."

"What?"

"The chisel stained with blood," replied the officer.

"It had fallen from my basket when I raised the murdered woman from the ground."

"It looked black against you, but I am only glad you are innocent," said the officer.

"I never believed you guilty," said Collier; "for guilty men don't often run about to make people acquainted with their work."

No. 15.

"Sometimes they do," said Mr. Wilks, who, although he had professed to be pleased at the established innocence of the accused man, was terribly annoyed at the circumstance; inasmuch as it had shown him to be at fault, and on the wrong scent.

However, Mr. Wilks fancied he should yet be able to find out the perpetrator of the fearful deed.

He felt convinced that Margaret knew the assassin.

The words she had uttered had proclaimed as much, and he resolved to keep a sharp eye upon her.

He thought himself clever enough to worm out of her who was the possessor of the wig which was found in the dead woman's hand, and which the clever Mr. Wilks had himself overlooked.

He had removed her from the room in which the inquest was held, into an adjoining apartment, and laid her upon a bed, sent for a medical man, as the one engaged to examine the body had left the house, and then locked the door to prevent her escape.

But Mr. Wilks, at any rate, would have to wait some time for the knowledge which he sought.

The shock Margaret had received, caused her reason to totter, and she was in a raving fever.

The coroner ordered her removal to the hospital, and gave directions that she should be questioned as to her knowledge of the owner of the wig, as soon as she recovered, should she be fortunate enough to do so.

So Mr. Wilks, having procured a vehicle to carry the poor columbine to the hospital, left the house with his charge.

"That's as great a fool for an officer as ever I knew," said Collier, turning to the carpenter, who still remained in the house, surrounded by several of his friends.

"In his zeal to bring some one to justice, he overlooks things which would establish the entire innocence of the man he accuses," said Slater.

"Never mind," said the landlord; "your innocence is thoroughly established, and you have nothing to care for now."

Slater sighed, and shook his head. He could not but observe that several persons had already avoided speaking to him.

"They still," he thought, "believe me guilty."

However, he knew himself innocent, and he strove to shake off the feeling of oppression which still hung on him, in vain.

He could not conjure up his usually buoyant spirits; and he left the house in which the pale cold corpse of the murdered woman still lay—the house in which he had undergone hours of suspense and agony—and proceeded to his own home—that home which he had feared he might never see again.

But it is seldom that the innocent suffer for the guilty.

That Providence which sways the destinies of the world, watched over the poor carpenter, and shielded an innocent man from the gallows.

Worn out with the excessive fatigue of the previous day, with aching limbs, yet thankful heart at the success which had crowned their efforts at the theatre, Charlie Evans rose at an unusually early hour from his couch, and having lighted the fire and procured breakfast, he awoke his friends.

"Bob," he said, "breakfast is ready; get up and go down to the theatre earlier than usual, as you will have to do my work as well as your own to-day."

"Strike me comical!" exclaimed Buskin Bob, sitting up in the bed, "ain't I tired!"

"So am I," replied Charlie.

"What in the name of fortune did you turn out so early for?" asked Bob, giving himself a stretch.

"I am going to see Margaret," replied the clown.

"Oh, yes, I had forgotten her, poor thing! strike me comical if I hadn't," said Bob, springing out of bed with the agility of a cat.

"Tired as I was, I have thought of her all night," said the clown; "I've done nothing but dream about her and Dancing Bill."

"The varmint," muttered Bob; "I can't help hating that fellow, I can't; strike me comical if I can—there."

And Bob drew the stocking up his leg with such a vengeance, that he nearly drove his toes through it in his indignation.

The meal was soon ended, at least so far as Charlie Evans and his friend Buskin Bob were concerned; both Mary and Harry were allowed to continue their slumbers, and Charlie rose and attired himself for his visit to the hospital.

"I don't know when I shall get back," said the good-hearted clown, "but I will do so as soon as I can."

"All right," said Bob, "don't hurry yourself, I'll look to the theatre and see all right for business."

Charlie opened a little drawer, and took therefrom a sovereign.

"We can ill afford to be generous," he said; "but, poor thing, she must be hard up after laying there so long. I'll give her this, for I think we ought to do something for a fellow creature in the hours of adversity. She'd have done it for us, and, as we've got it, we'll do it for her."

"In course we will!" exclaimed Bob. "Strike me comical, if I don't think we should have an empty house to-night if we allowed her to lay there in want and got the means to prevent it."

"Well, I am not superstitious enough to think anything of that kind would happen because we forgot to act like Christians. No, no! it ain't from any fear of that, it's because we have got hearts as can feel for the sufferings of others; because we are human, spite of being poor, despised, strolling players."

"Those who affect to despise us," exclaimed Buskin Bob, "might often learn a lesson from both the actions and the teachings of such as us, strike me comical if they mightn't! They call us rogues and vagabonds, but we preach morality, and the triumph of virtue over vice. They preach justice and truth, but often lie and wrong. They would condemn us for pourtraying the miseries of crime, and wrong us by driving the poor player from the stage to seek food by dishonest means, and struggle for bread in the paths of dishonour."

"Not all, Bob," remarked his friend.

"No, or none would patronise us. But the miserable, fanatical humbugs, who make a trade of religion, and insult the Maker they profess to serve."

"And there are many of them," remarked Charlie.

"Strike me comical if you ain't right, there," exclaimed Bob. "But, never mind, the poor player may be driven about by them like a dried leaf in the autumn winds—they may stop the fairs, refuse to allow us to occupy the barns, but the more they strive to put us down the faster and stronger will be the rise of the drama; men will see through the hypocrisy, and aid the strolling player; will assist him in his labours, and when fairs shall no longer be an institution of free and enlightened England, the poor player will still stand forward for public approbation, in the gilded house, built for the representation of the drama."

"But we shall not live to see it," said Charlie.

"Shan't we; perhaps not, for we are daily growing older," said Bob; "yet, depend upon it, the time is not far distant when the fair will be a thing of the past, and the barn no longer fitted up as a playhouse. The canting mawworms are up and doing, and the strolling players are fast fading away. We may yet live to see it, Charlie, and if we do, mark my words, the poor player will be respected where he is now condemned, and the end for which these fanatics labour will be frustrated; they would crush us, but we shall rise in proportion as they would keep us down; the fair and the barn will fade away, but the splendid homes of the drama shall rise and flourish, and the poor player find a spot on which to exhibit his talents, and learn the masses a lesson, and hurl back scorn and derision upon the heads of those who would so ignobly encompass our overthrow. The players will yet see better days, strike me comical if we won't, there!"

"There," said Charlie, offering his hand to his friend, "perhaps you are right, perhaps you are wrong, but meantime we must not forget we are Christians, willing to aid a distressed fellow creature, so I am off to see poor Margaret; good bye."

"Good bye," said Buskin Bob, shaking the extended hand of the good-hearted Charlie, "give my love to her."

"I will," said Charlie.

"Strike me comical, what would Bill think of it, though, if he heard you," said Bob.

"Think," said Charlie, "why, that there were those in the world who had more feeling for his poor wife than he had."

So saying, Charlie Evans started on his journey; and Buskin Bob, lighting his pipe, set down to meditate upon the fate of the poor players, and puff away his indignation at the acts of the fanatics and shortsighted idiots who at that time were striving their hardest to do away with the time-honoured amusements of the people.

After having smoked all the tobacco out of his pipe, and knocked out the ashes upon the hob of the grate, Buskin Bob rose from his seat and called upon Harry and little Mary to awake.

In a short time the young folks appeared.

Leaving them to get their breakfast, Buskin Bob started for the theatre.

Meanwhile, Charlie Evans made his way to the hospital, and arrived at its gates just as the clock struck nine—the hour at which persons were admitted to visit the sick inmates.

He was not long in finding the ward in which poor Margaret was.

Standing at the door, he cast his eye down the long row of beds in search of her well-known face.

But he saw it not.

Waiting for a few moments to inquire where he could find her, Charlie saw a hand beckoning him at the far end of the room.

Mechanically he walked towards it.

Surely it was not the hand of the poor columbine!

The head and face which protruded above the bed clothes were not her's.

Margaret was a fine, pretty, dark-haired woman; but the occupant of that bed was a pale-faced, bald-headed, old woman.

He drew near.

Then the sufferer spoke.

"Charlie," she exclaimed, "how can I thank you?"

The poor clown drew back.

The tones of that voice were familiar to his ears, but the face he had never seen before.

"It is me, Charlie! it is me!" said the woman, endeavouring to raise herself upon her elbow.

"Margaret!" he exclaimed. "Oh, God, what a change!"

And striding to the bedside, he raised the poor sufferer in his arms, and gazed with anguish into her face.

"A change indeed," she murmured.

"Yes, a change indeed," said the noble-hearted Charlie; "a change so great that, used as I am to make-ups, I did not recognise you."

"I have suffered much," she murmured, with a sigh.

"You must have done," said Charlie.

"More, more than ever I thought I should have suffered," sighed the poor woman.

"Doubtless," said the clown.

"You have heard—of course you have heard," said Margaret.

"What?" asked Charlie.

"Of the murder—the murder at Tottenham."

"At Tottenham?"

"Yes."

"No."

"Not the murder under the Seven Sisters?" exclaimed Margaret.

"No," said Charlie, in some surprise.

"You have not?"

"No."

"Strange," said Margaret.

"Poor thing!" muttered Charlie, "she still raves.

And he cast his eyes around in search of the nurse.

"No, no," said Margaret, who heard the words, "I'm not raving now. Recollection has returned to me; I have awoke to the terrible truth. Oh! Mr. Evans, what I have suffered!"

"You have suffered much, I can well see that; and you have not yet recovered. Be silent, do not speak, you will soon be well again."

"Never, never!" sighed the poor woman.

"Why not?"

"There is a weight here," she said, "which can never be removed."

And she laid her hand upon her heart.

"A weight," she continued, "that can never be removed; a weight that will bear me down to the grave in sorrow and dismay."

"Why?"

"Oh! can you ask?"

"I do not understand."

"Bill!"

"What of him?"

The poor woman cast her eyes fearfully around the room.

"He—is—"

"What?"

"Ah! God—I fear to tell," she exclaimed.

"You can trust me," said Charlie Evans.

"Dare I?"

"Yes."

"Then—Bill—is—"

"What?"

"A—Oh, heaven! I dare not confide the fearful secret to you."

"You may, Margaret," said Charlie; "indeed you may."

"And you will never divulge it?" she asked.

"Never, on my honour," replied the clown.

"Can I trust you?"

"Margaret."

"Oh, yes, I know I can," said the woman; "but still I fear."

"Who?"

"You—all—everyone."

"Why?"

"I know not."

"Margaret, have you ever found me false?" asked Charlie, in a tone which denoted that his feelings were pained.

"No, never."

"Then why fear to trust me now?" he asked.

"Alas! I know not."

"You have no cause."

"Charlie."

"Then why hesitate?"

"I cannot tell."

"Speak freely and fear not," said the clown, bending over her.

"I would fain do so, yet I fear," said the poor invalid.

"You can trust me," said Charlie; "you know you can."

"But the secret is a fearful one," said Margaret, her white face becoming even more deathly in hue.

"Yet it shall be sacred within this breast," replied the clown, laying his hand upon his heart.

"I know it—yet I dread."

"What?"

"To divulge it."

"To me?"

"Even to you."

"You need not fear."

"I cannot prevent it."

"Speak, and if I can aid or advise you I will do it," said Charlie.

"I know that."

"Then why hesitate?"

"Because—because—"

"What?"

"The secret is a fearful one!" exclaimed the woman.

"Still you need not fear."

"But I cannot prevent it—indeed I cannot!" she exclaimed.

"Speak freely, Margaret," said Charlie; "whatever you may confide to me shall be held sacred—I swear it. No word or deed of mine shall ever betray that which you may confide to me."

"Then—Bill—is—is—"

"What?"

"A—a—oh, God!"

Charlie bent forward.

"What! what?" he gasped.

"A—ah—my poor brain! I—I—cannot betray him."

And with a deep sigh Margaret sank back upon her straw pallet.

Her eyes closed, she had again become lost to all around.

CHAPTER LXV.

THE POACHER AND THE STEWARD—GRIPE PLEADS FOR MERCY—AN OLD DEBT PAID.

PALE and trembling, Mr. Gripe listened to the sounds which smote upon his ears.

That they were the tones of Dick the Poacher he had no doubt.

What should he do?

Where should he hide himself from the vengeance of the man whose secrets he had been endeavouring to worm from his idiot wife?

He cast his eyes around the place which formed his prison.

But there was nowhere in which he could secrete himself.

Cold drops of perspiration broke out upon his face.

His limbs trembled.

Still the sounds came nearer and nearer.

There was a hand upon the fastening of the door.

He heard the key turn in the lock, and he sank down upon the floor of the outhouse in the most abject fear.

The door opened!

Dick the Poacher stood upon the threshold!

Behind was his idiot wife.

A smile was on her face—her eye was brighter than usual.

Dick entered the place, and looked around him.

His eye lighted upon the form of the little steward, as he sat, all of a heap, upon the cold, damp ground, with the ruin of the barrel and trough around him.

Their eyes met.

Gripe trembled.

Dick could scarcely repress a smile which rose to his lips.

For a few moments they stood glaring at each other.

Gripe never before in his life felt so small.

Dick never before felt so indignant.

Still, neither spoke for some moments.

At length Dick advanced to the spot where the little steward sat.

He fixed his dark eye upon him, and exclaimed—

"So, Mr. Gripe, you have again been up to your dirty work?"

"Me—me!" stammered the steward, scarcely knowing what to say.

"Yes, sir, you."

"I—I—"

"Came here in my absence," exclaimed Dick, "and endeavoured to seek information from my poor idiot wife,"

"I—"

"Silence, you contemptible cur!" roared the poacher. "I have always known you to be a thing unworthy the name of a man, but never till now did I believe you could stoop to wrong me by making the shattered reason of my poor wife the instrument to minister to your ends."

Gripe quailed beneath the searching glance of the poacher.

"I—I—" he stammered, "came hither to seek you."

"Liar!"

"Upon my soul, I did," exclaimed Gripe, thoroughly aroused by the fierce glance of the other.

"Liar! I repeat," exclaimed Dick. "You came here in the hopes to work upon the imbecility of this poor creature."

"No, no."

"Yes," I say.

"Indeed I came to speak to you," said Gripe, becoming more and more alarmed.

"For what purpose?" asked the poacher, fixing his penetrating glance upon him.

"For—for——"

"For what?"

"To seek information respecting the papers I purchased of you," stammered Gripe.

"And for which you paid with stolen money," said the poacher.

"Me!"

"Yes, you, Mr. Gripe; allow me to give you a bit of information."

Gripe crept up from amid the lumber by which he was surrounded.

"The papers I sold you are worthless," said Dick.

"Worthless," gasped Gripe.

"Yes."

"Are they not genuine?"

"No."

"Then you deceived me?"

"I did!"

"And robbed me of five hundred pounds!" exclaimed Gripe.

"No," said Dick, "you wished to get the squire into your power. To gain this end you offered a large price for the supposed means. It matters little to me how you gained the money. I sold you the documents, that I might be revenged upon you and Henley; they are useless, and Squire Henley has now the power to brand you as a felon."

"Brand me as a felon," gasped Gripe.

"Even so, for have you not robbed him," said Dick.

"I could not rob a thief," exclaimed the steward.

"Indeed."

"No."

"You have placed yourself in a very awkward position, Mr. Gripe," said Dick, "and doubtless the squire will reward you according to your merits."

"He dare not."

"Ah!"

"I say he dare not," exclaimed Gripe.

"And why, pray?"

"I have the proofs of his villany," said Gripe.

"They are fictitious," said the poacher, with a most galling tone of voice.

"Then I can prosecute you for defrauding me of my money," said Gripe.

"Your money," said Dick, sarcastically.

"Yes, my money."

"Come—come," said Dick, "that won't do. I knew that you had not the sum you offered for the papers, and likewise knew the source from whence you derived it. It was me who sent the anonymous letter to the squire, and caused him to become acquainted with the doings of his steward."

"You?"

"Yes, me."

"After persuading me to become their purchaser?" said Gripe.

"I did not persuade you," said Dick. "I wanted money, and I hated both you and the squire, for both had wronged me; I found you willing to purchase supposed evidence of Squire Henley's guilt, and took advantage of your greedy disposition to sell you spurious proofs."

"Robber!"

"Villain!" replied Dick.

"You shall suffer for this," exclaimed Gripe.

"Indeed."

"Yes."

"How?"

"I will prosecute you," replied the steward.

"For what?"

"For obtaining money under false pretences," said Gripe.

Dick burst into a loud laugh.

"Mr. Gripe," he said, after a pause, "I always thought you a shrewd man, now I find you are only a fool."

"You shall see what I am," said Gripe.

"Where?"

"In a court of justice," replied the steward.

"Ha, ha!" laughed Dick; "why there you dare not show your head."

"Why not?"

"Because you are a thief," replied Dick.

Gripe winced.

"Because the money you paid me was not your own," continued the poacher.

"How do you know?" asked the steward.

"Henley told me so."

"Ah! Have you seen him?" asked Gripe, eagerly.

"Oh yes."

"When?"

"Just now."

"Where?"

"In the old churchyard," replied the poacher.

"He there?"

"Yes, and I told him how you had obtained the papers."

"What did he say," asked Gripe, eagerly.

"That justice should have its due," replied the poacher; "that you should answer for your crime."

"He dare not."

"But he dare," said Dick, interrupting the steward, "his books prove your defalcations; and a felon's doom awaits you. Now, Mr. Gripe, you will feel the horrors you have inflicted on me."

"He cannot, will not do it," said Gripe.

"But he will," said Dick, who seemed to take a pleasure in the fears of the steward.

"No, no."

"Yes, yes. He has said so, and I have persuaded him to keep his word."

"You?"

"Yes, me."

"You, who have yourself suffered," said Gripe.

"Yes, I, who have suffered through your accursed means. Gripe, I have long owed you ill-will; I now take the opportunity of repaying you. The papers you hold are worthless; the money devoted to their purchase was stolen; you thought to get a prize; you have found a blank; you have laid yourself open to the law, and you must abide the consequences of your crimes. Mr. Gripe, you have made me suffer, it is my turn now; I am only a poacher, you are a thief."

Gripe covered his face with his hands and trembled violently.

Dick stood calmly watching him for some time; at length the steward looked up.

"Dick," he said, "you owe the squire no good will."

"On the contrary," replied the poacher.

"You hold the evidence of his guilt," said Gripe.

"Well?"

"Share it with me, and let us both rid society of a villain."

"Hark you, Gripe," said Dick, "I owe you both anything but good will; together you have worked to encompass my ruin; to a certain extent you have succeeded, but spite of all your machinations, I can still defy you both; I loathe and contemn you, and sooner than enter into a partnership with the scoundrels who can rob the widow and the orphan, I will endure anything. No, no, I have fallen; but not so low that I cannot redeem the past. That I have deceived you both, I will not deny; but the motive I had in so doing was an honourable one. You thought to get the squire in your power, you have placed yourself in his. A few years imprisonment will have a salutary effect upon you; you will then learn that mercy should be extended to the erring and oppressed, and, I sincerely hope, that when you find yourself cooped up within four prison walls, you will acknowledge the truth that, justice and mercy should be extended to the poor suffering wretch whom cruel fate has left to the mercy of the oppressor—the robber of the widow and fatherless."

"Dick, Dick," gasped Gripe, now fully convinced that he had laid himself open to the power of the man he had affected to despise, "you—you can save me; remember it was you who led me to this crime, it was you who persuaded me to wrong."

"I can save you," said Dick, "but I will not."

"I implore you!"

"You implore in vain," said the poacher.

"Dick, you have suffered," exclaimed Gripe.

"I have."

"Have pity, then, on me," gasped the steward.

Dick turned away.

"Dick—Dick!" exclaimed Gripe, in agony, "have mercy."

"No!" replied the poacher, "for you refused it to me. Look!" he added, pointing to his poor idiot wife, "can you ask for mercy and look upon her? Had mercy been shown me, I had been an honest, toiling man, instead of a poacher. Had mercy been extended to me, my poor, poor wife had not now been bereft of reason—the light of my home, the joy of my life had still been fresh and green. But it was re-fused, and I suffered. But what were my sufferings compared to her's? Oh, God! can you ask me for mercy, and gaze upon your work? Can you sue to me to save you and look upon the poor wretch whom your villany has thus wrecked? No, no! Were all the powers of Heaven and earth arranged against me, I would not stretch forth a hand to save you from the fate which awaits you. I am not one who can feel pleasure in the sufferings of another; but, I am a man—possessing a man's heart—a man's feelings—a man's love. Go to the gaol, whose portals are open to receive you, and there think on the wreck your hard heart has made, and the vengeance of Dick the Poacher!"

CHAPTER LXVI.

THE LAST OF THE PANTOMIME AT THE ROYAL STAR—AN AMATEUR'S ASPIRATION AND FAILURE—CHARLIE TO THE RESCUE.

THE pantomime was a great success.

During the Christmas week the house was crowded nightly to suffocation; and happy, indeed, were the Boy Actor and his friends.

It was not till about the middle of the second week that the audience began to show a decrease; but, as soon as it did, Charlie Evans gave the requisite notice to the lessee, that he should resign the house at the expiration of a month.

He had not forgotten the dirty trick the lessee had played them.

Yet, towards that gentleman the clown acted with the strictest honour.

Night by night, now, the company grew less, till, a few nights before the final one, the pantomimists again played to half-empty benches.

It was intended that Charlie should take his benefit on the last night of their management: but a circumstance occurred which altered their resolution.

A young, effeminate-looking man, who was ever hanging around the back of the theatre, treating the players, and endeavouring to make their acquaintance, was ambitious to "fret his hour upon the stage;" and finding, spite of all endeavours to place his foot upon the boards, he could get no one to aid him in his ambitious hopes, he had hit upon the idea of taking a benefit himself to aid him in his wishes.

So Mr. Foggleton Phipps, by which name this individual was known, sought audience of Charlie; and, the terms being agreed to, the clown set forth the last night of their management for the benefit of the young aspirant, and announced his own for the night previous.

Charlie, with an old stager's eyes, saw in a moment that Mr. Foggleton Phipps would, vulgarly speaking, make a mess of it; so he had no wish to announce his own benefit after a failure.

Besides, Mr. Phipps taking his benefit first might possibly prevent Charlie disposing of many of his tickets.

The night of Charlie's benefit came round, and, though he was not honoured with a crowded, yet he had a good house; and when the curtain fell upon the bowing clown, it likewise closed his management of the Royal Star, and for one night only Mr. Foggleton Phipps had the theatre under his own control.

Never did Mr. Foggleton Phipps appear so tall in his own eyes—never did he look so patronisingly upon the poor players.

He wanted to play "'Amlet," as he himself pronounced it, for his benefit, but from this the good-hearted clown persuaded him.

"It would never do here," said Charlie. "Shakespeare is no draw at the Royal Star."

"That's because there is no one in the company could play the part," said Mr. Foggleton, "for everyone admires Shakespeare."

"It would never be appreciated at this theatre, sir," said Charlie; "and besides, the part is a heavy one, much too heavy for an amateur; I would advise you, sir, not to attempt such a part."

"Why not?" asked Mr. Foggleton.

"Because, as one who has trod the boards for many years, I feel assured you would fail in the first act."

"Indeed, sir; I am well up in Shakespeare," said Mr. Foggleton, looking daggers at his adviser, "especially 'Amlet."

"Do as you please," said Charlie, "but if you would take the advice of an old stager, who wishes you well, you would play something else."

"What else can I play?" asked Mr. Foggleton, annoyed that he could not sustain the character on which he had set his hopes, yet certain in his own mind that the clown was advising him for his good.

"Well, there's the 'Bleeding Heart or the Enchanted Moon,'" replied the clown; "that, I should say, would draw as well as anything."

"But that's not Shakespeare."

"True, sir," said Charlie; "but it will pay better at this house."

"I don't care about its paying, I only want to play it."

"To an empty house?" asked Charlie.

"Well—no," drawled out Foggleton.

"Then, depend upon it, you will get no one in if you play any of Shakespeare's; you must have a blood and thunder piece, or you may as well not draw up the curtain."

"But I'm not fit to play in any such piece," said Mr. Foggleton Phipps.

"Nor any other," thought Charlie, but he kept it to himself, and said, "You can find several parts in the drama I have mentioned more suited to your abilities than "Hamlet."

"Of course I shall play the principal character," said Mr. Phipps.

"If you insist upon it, I have no power to prevent you," said Charlie; "but if you will act wise, you will not attempt above a dozen or twenty lines on your first appearance."

"What!" exclaimed Mr. Foggleton Phipps, "a dozen or twenty lines?"

"Yes, sir."

"Why, I shouldn't think of playing a part under at least two or three hundred lines!" said Mr. Phipps.

"Wouldn't you?"

"No."

"You would not be able to get perfect in time," said Charlie; "and depend upon it, you would forget your cue when on the stage."

Mr. Foggleton Phipps turned away, chagrined and disappointed.

He believed that he possessed the ability to play the part he had selected.

But still he could not shake off the feelings that, since the remarks of the clown, had entered his heart that things would go wrong, so he resolved to adopt some other piece.

Finally he made up his mind to play in the "Bleeding Heart."

Of course he selected for himself the most difficult part.

He had not been an amateur if he had not.

Setting himself diligently to work, he endeavoured to learn the words, ever and anon starting up and flinging his arms about, then closing the book, and looking up at the ceiling, repeat the lines in a melodramatic tone, or at least one which he believed such.

The rehearsal in the morning was attended by all cast for the piece, and amongst them were Harry and Mary.

Mary herself had not been cast for it, but the lady who sustained the lead at the Royal Star feeling satisfied that Mr. Foggleton Phipps would not only ruin his own part but hers as well, she had prevailed upon the juvenile lady to undertake her business, thus leaving them to fall back for a juvenile upon little Mary.

Mr. Foggleton Phipps was somewhat annoyed at this, as he wished to be able to say that he had played the lead with Mrs. Bilton at the Royal Star.

But there was no help for it now, so the rehearsal commenced.

"Strike me comical," said Buskin Bob, in a low whisper to his friend the clown, as they stood at the wings watching the progress of the rehearsal, "if he ain't acting now!"

This remark was called forth by the antics of Mr. Phipps, for whom, by-the-by, the stage of the Royal Star did not seem half large enough.

"He'll make a mess of it to-night, I expect," said Charlie, in a whisper.

"Sure to, strike me comical if he ain't," said Bob.

"Never knew a fellow act at rehearsal as could act at all," said Charlie.

"Nor I."

"The greatest duffer in the morning is generally the best at night," said Charlie.

"And vice versa, as they says in the prayer-book," said Bob. "Why, strike me comical if he ain't a-going to do a back fall!"

"More fool he," said Charlie, as the young aspirant for dramatic honours rolled all in a heap on the stage.

This was too much for the assembled company, and a loud shout of laughter greeted his rising.

The stage had not yet been swept, and consequently, when Mr. Phipps again stood upright he cut a peculiar figure.

His black coat was now covered with dust, as also were his trowsers.

This created a fresh burst of laughter, and the Boy Actor, unable to control himself, fairly roared out.

A spiteful gleam shot from the eye of Mr. Phipps, and he bit his lips, so indignant was he, that his talent was so little appreciated.

However, he took no further notice, and the rehearsal proceeded.

By the time, however, that it was over, Mr Phipps discovered that he was anything but perfect in his part; still he resolved to be so by night, and urged upon the rest of the company the necessity of the same.

Of course all promised, but one or two of the old players merely folded up the parts, which they had only looked at for a moment, and thrusting them in their pockets, intended to let them lie there, till called upon to hand them over to the prompter.

They had played the parts so often, and if they were not acquainted with the words, they were with the business and situations, "gag" must do the rest.

It is very seldom that actors are perfect on benefit nights, and on this occasion there was little exception to the rule.

Night came, and Mr. Foggleton Phipps, in a state of nevous anxiety, was first on the stage.

As the time for commencing drew nigh, Mr. Foggleton Phipps grew momentarily more nervous.

He could not recollect so much of his part now as he did at rehearsal.

Yet he hoped to be all right by the time he was made up.

Hurrying to the dressing-room, he selected his costume, and having attired himself for the character, and rather extravagantly painted his face, he seized his part in his hand, and stalked up on to the stage with all the dignity of a prince.

Across and across the boards he paced, alternately reading his part and stopping to admire himself.

It was not long ere all was ready.

The gas was turned up, and the overture began.

It was a very indifferent house.

Long rows of benches only here and there dotted by a human form, whilst scarcely one was in the boxes.

As the overture proceeded, and the few persons in the house commenced to show their impatience for the curtain to rise, the impression that he should cause quite a sensation began to desert the mind of Mr. Foggleton Phipps.

Instead of being quite perfect in his part, he could scarcely recollect a dozen lines of the first scene.

His nervousness increased, and as he had rung for the green baize to ascend, he wished he had taken the clown's advice, and endeavoured to play a smaller and more insignificant part.

However, it was too late now to withdraw from what his vanity had prompted him to undertake.

The curtain was up, and the audience must be met.

He must face his friends, too, to whom he had boasted of his talents.

His nervousness was so great that he absolutely trembled, and his features were pallid, despite the paint upon his face.

Frantically he ran his eye over the first lines of his part.

The cue came at which he was to enter, and, thrusting his part into his breast, he tottered rather than walked on.

If he was nervous before, he was doubly so now, now that he saw so many eyes fixed upon him.

A few hours before he had felt assured that a burst of applause would have greeted his appearance.

But an ominous silence only greeted him.

His fellow actor gave him his cue, but he had forgotten it.

It was repeated, and Mr. Foggleton Phipps burst through the lethargy which bound him, and succeeded in getting on with a few lines.

Then his hopes revived.

But some ill-natured "god" called out to him to speak up.

Phipps was in agony.

He strove all he could to satisfy the wishes of that personage; but, somehow or other his tongue seemed to cleave to the roof of his mouth, and he could but utter the words of his part in a low voice.

"Speak out—don't go to sleep!" and several other exclamations of a similar character saluted his ears.

This added to his nervousness; and, after struggling hard for several minutes to sustain the character with credit, he almost burst into tears, and hurried off at the wrong side.

This brought down a shower of indignation from all parts of the house, and poor Mr. Foggleton Phipps would have given his ears off his head to have been able to slink away and hide his ambitious head.

"Strike me comical, if it ain't just as I said," muttered Bob, who was acting as prompter. "Tell Charlie," he added, in a loud tone, to Harry, who stood beside him, "to hurry up, or we shall have a stage wait."

The boy turned to do his bidding, but, at that moment the clown, attired in a dress similar to that worn by Mr. Phipps, made his way into the prompter's box.

"Strike me comical, you are just in time," exclaimed Bob. "He can't go on again."

"No;" replied Charlie. "It's a strange thing, but amateurs always will select parts they are unfit for."

"You are not going to play the part, are you?" said Harry.

"Yes."

"But you haven't learnt it," said the boy with a smile.

"That's true, but I know pretty well all about it. What I can't recollect I must gag."

"And its only an old stager as can do that, strike me comical, if it ain't!" exclaimed Bob. "It's not a bit of use an amateur trying it. If he can't recollect every word of his part, he'll never go through it, strike me comical, if he will!"

With what a feeling of relief did Mr. Foggleton Phipps receive the information that Charlie Evans had made up for the part, expecting that he would break down, and was now come to his rescue.

With a deep sigh he leaned back against the wings, and fixed his eyes upon the flooring of the stage.

He never felt so small in his life.

He believed that he had but to make his appearance on the stage to ensure success.

But he had been undeceived, and he cursed the fascination which had led him on till he had made a fool of himself.

Mr. Foggleton Phipps was not the only man who had tried and failed.

Many have attempted, and discovered to their horror that they were unfit to cope with the work they had cut out for themselves.

"Never mind," said the good-hearted clown, making his way to the side of the abashed amateur, and laying his hand confidingly upon the young man's shoulder, "better luck next time."

TRAGEDY.

"I shall **never try** again," said Mr. Phipps, dejectedly.

"Why not?" asked the clown.

"Because I've had enough of it now," said Phipps. "I did think that I could make an actor."

"And so you may stand a chance of doing yet," said the good-hearted fellow, who was really sorry for the other's failure, "if you will only take the advice of one who has seen more ups and downs in life than ever I hope you will see. If ever you attempt to play a part again, take a small one and you may succeed; the stage, like everything else, cannot be tempted at once; to play a heavy part requires long practice, to face an audience as you must face them in the part you wished to play, and the one you have selected requires an old acquaintanceship with the boards. The boy must serve an apprenticeship to become a good workman, and it is only by degrees that you can master all the requirements necessary for an actor. I am sorry, for your own sake, that you have attempted so difficult a part; but because you have failed now, do not let that deter you from trying again, only, if you would succeed, bear this in mind, take an insignificant part, and rise by degrees. A man cannot leap over a mountain, but he can walk up the one side and down the other. Do not aim so high till you have become proficient; and if after long practice you have gained sufficient confidence, try it, and I sincerely hope success may attend you. There's the cue, I will go and finish the part for you."

And grasping the hand of Mr. Foggleton Phipps, Charlie shook it warmly, and dashed on to the stage.

The piece went on till the end, and what seemed a failure turned out a success.

CHAPTER LXVII.

THE PANTOMIMISTS IN A FRESH LINE OF BUSINESS —THE FIRST HOUSE OF THE FIRST DAY.

THE curtain was rung down, and Charlie, the Boy Actor, and his friends stood for the last time on the little stage of the Royal Star.

That night ended their management.

After thanking the company for the aid they had rendered them in their Struggles for Bread, Charlie dismissed them with a sorrowful heart.

"We must part now, kind friends," he said, "but I trust it will not be for long. Could I have entertained the least hope of getting a livelihood here I would not have given up the house, but I have seen sufficient to convince me that it will not pay, and I should not be doing my duty to this poor orphan boy did I recklessly use his money, for, friends, the money with which we opened this long-closed establishment was his, not mine. I grieve to part with you, for you have clung to us when I dared not hope to receive such kindness at your hands. You have struggled with us, shoulder to shoulder, uncomplainingly, without a murmur of dissatisfaction. We shall soon meet again, I hope, and labour on together, but for the present we are undecided how we shall act, but I do not think it at all likely we shall risk taking another theatre for the present. But whether we become the proprietors of a booth, and travel the country, or whether we accept engagements, we shall always feel it our bounden duty to think of those who so generously assisted us here, and if it ever lies in our power we will return that kindness, won't we, Bob?"

"Strike me comical, yes!" exclaimed Bob; "to be sure we will. We shall never forget they stuck to us when we were hard up; strike me comical if we do—there!"

With mutual good wishes, for each others welfare, the company departed, and the Royal Star was closed.

As they walked home to their humble lodging, Charlie laid his hand caressingly on the shoulder of his young *protége*.

"Harry," he said.

"Yes, father."

"I am happy to tell you that I have got your hundred pounds back, with thirty more added to it."

"Have you," said the boy in a pleased tone, looking up in the smiling face of the good hearted clown.

"Yes, my boy," said Charlie, "I have saved that, and I am happy to leave the house under such circumstances."

"Had we kept it an—"

"We should have lost it all again," interrupted Charlie.

"To be sure we should," chimed in Bob. "And, besides, strike me comical, if I would have run any chance of that with such a humbug as Grabham."

"He will be the loser now," said Harry.

"And serve him right too," said Mary.

"Strike me comical if it don't," said Bob.

"We will go to-morrow or next day," said the clown, "and see if we can't manage to purchse a booth."

"That's the best game," said Bob, "strike me comical if it ain't, pays well in the summer, if it is only managed properly, and strike me comical, if I don't think both me and Charlie knows a little how to do that, eh, Charlie?"

"Rather," replied the clown.

The subject dropped for the time, and after partaking of their humble supper, they retired to rest; the Boy Actor, to dream of the booth, and the struggles for bread in store for them all.

The next day, Charlie and Bob started out to look at a booth which was for sale; the proprietor of it having amassed sufficient to keep him from work, for the rest of his days.

After some haggling as to the price to be paid for it, Charlie eventually became its possessor for seventy pounds, the former proprietor to keep charge of it till the pantomimists were prepared, and the weather sufficiently cheering to start with it round the country.

They now had sixty pounds in hand, amply sufficient to re-decorate, and provide the required properties.

But, then, two months must elapse, ere it could be brought into use, and during that two months, they must live.

Bob proposed their not touching any of the sixty pounds, but offered to go into the streets alone, and endeavour to pick up sufficient to keep them, by his feats of legerdemain.

But to this the others would not agree, so at length it was resolved to use the money as sparingly as possible, and to remain at home during the remainder of the winter months, and that time to be devoted to the teaching of dancing and tumbling to the Boy Actor and little Mary.

Time flies swiftly when the heart is light and the mind contented.

And the two months passed happily away in the little circle of pantomimists.

The bright sunshine had taken the place of cold winds and frosty skies, and the booth, newly painted and gilded, was ready for the fairs.

The young folks who had now, under the tuition of Charlie Evans and Buskin Bob, become proficient in the business for which they were destined, were anxious to start on their travels, and again struggle for bread.

A horse was purchased to draw the booth from town to town, not a particularly handsome one to be sure, but at least a serviceable animal; and on a bright sunshining morning in the month of April, the Boy Actor and his little companion Mary sat nestled in a truss of clean straw at the bottom of the caravan, whilst Charlie and Buskin Bob walked merrily alongside the shaggy horse, as he dragged the caravan over the stones of the little town, towards the spot where a fair was to be held on the morrow, and where for three days the pantomimists intended to pitch their booth, and court the patronage of the "enlightened British public."

And no less light were the hearts of the young people, as they sat in the lumbering vehicle, breathing fond hopes for successful and brighter days.

They reached the ground about nightfall, and having partaken of refreshments, and provided the horse with a good meal, they lay down in the caravan, and sought rest to refresh them for the morrow's toil.

Charlie, Buskin Bob, and little Harry rose betimes the next morning, and commenced to get things in readiness for the building of the booth.

About seven o'clock they were joined by two others, the Brothers Tumblini they styled themselves, but in fact, were no relations to each other.

They were named John Cross and Thomas Stubs, and had been pupils of a celebrated tumbler.

They had since worked together at the fairs and gafs, and had adopted the title of the Brothers Tumblini.

They had been engaged by Charlie, to perform their daring feats in his booth, and these, to·

gether with his own party, for the present, formed the entire strength of the company.

With willing hands and cheerful hearts, they all set to work, and by ten o'clock the booth was erected.

The sides of the caravan worked on hinges, and being let down, formed a small parade outside the booth.

On this parade Buskin Bob was to give an entertainment in juggling, and little Mary, the Infant Venus, by which name she was announced on a not very neatly executed painting, was to dance the flag dance.

Having got all in readiness for the time the fair opened, the little company sat down to a meal of bread and cheese.

"Eat hearty, my boy," said Charlie, pushing a huge hunch of bread and cheese before Harry, "we shan't have much chance I hope of stopping for any more till the fair closes to-night."

However, the Boy Actor wanted little pressing, and having made a good substantial meal, they commenced their toilet.

By the time that each was made up for their character, the hour of opening had arrived.

Standing beside a gong, Charlie lustily announced to the gaping crowd that they were just a going to begin, and invited them to walk up and see the wonderful feats to be performed therein, at the low charge of twopence.

Striking the gong two or three times, he moved aside, and Buskin Bob appeared on the parade, attired, not as we have seen him in Richardson's show, but in tight fleshings and doublet.

He carried with him an immense number of gilded balls, and these he threw about with wonderful rapidity, forming in the air circles, squares, diamonds, triangles, and an infinite variety of different shapes, to the great delight of both young and old, who surrounded the little booth and gazed in wonder and admiration upon the fantastic tricks he performed.

This little feat had the desired effect, and one by one the pleasure-seekers complied with the continued request of Charlie, to walk up.

Bob now disappeared behind the canvas, and Charlie once more made the welkin ring, with heavy strokes upon the gong.

"Walk up, ladies and gentlemen," he bawled out at the top of his voice, "the best booth in the fair, the wonderful brothers, and a host of talent. Walk up—walk up, the Infant Venus, acknowledged by all the world, to be the most graceful dancer of the age, is to be seen within; walk up, only twopence. To satisfy you, ladies and gentlemen, of the talent contained in this booth, the young lady shall step forth and give you a specimen of her abilities."

The canvas again opened, and little Mary, radiant with smiles, her pretty form enshrouded in drapery, and bearing in either hand a small union jack, stepped on to the parade, and bending her graceful figure before the gazing crowd, waved her hand to the musicians, who struck up a tune they had been in the habit of playing about the streets for some years past, and then away went her little feet, as fast as they could go, through the many steps of a fantastic dance.

Her appearance seemed to have a happy effect upon many of those assembled beneath her, and they flocked up the steps to pay their twopence, and view the wonders to be seen within.

The booth was soon full, and the Brothers commenced their feats

Although they could hear little or no comparison to feats of the kind exhibited in our day at the various music halls and theatres, still they were very clever, and neatly executed.

The Brothers had little to complain of in the applause which greeted every fresh surprise.

They worked with a will, and the audience were pleased and gratified.

This over, Buskin Bob and little Harry came forward, and tumbling of a somewhat different description to that performed by the Brothers, was executed between them.

Harry was somewhat nervous, but Bob wished he might be struck comical, if he didn't take the greatest precautions to prevent his being hurt; so, after the first few tumbles, he became reconciled, and went to work with all the coolness of an old and practised hand.

This was followed by a variety of tricks with knives by Buskin Bob, and the entertainment wound up with a dance by the Infant Venus inside the booth.

It occupied about half-an-hour in all, and the audience appeared thoroughly satisfied with the amusement they had received for the low price of twopence.

The first house had been a good one, and all connected with it were well pleased at the patronage they had received.

"Strike me comical," said Bob, addressing his friend Charlie, "that boy and girl stick to it well."

"Yes," said Charlie, "but I fear they will be sadly tired ere night."

"No doubt of it, we must have fourteen houses to day, strike me comical if we mustn't."

"We ought to," said Charlie, "but I am half afraid the young ones will break down before that."

"Not a bit of it," replied his friend.

"I hope they wont."

"I don't expect they will, strike me comical if I do," exclaimed Bob, getting his tools in order for work on the parade.

The gong was again sounded, and again the invitation given to walk up.

Once more, Buskin Bob commenced his hankypanky, as he termed it, and little Mary sat down to rest, till the time came for her to again appear on the parade.

Harry drew near her.

"Are you not tired," he asked.

"No," she replied.

"But you soon will be," he exclaimed, "two dances each house is a good deal for you Mary."

"Oh, I don't mind that," she replied, with a smile.

"Don't you."

"No, not if it will assist us to live," she replied.

"But if you make yourself ill," remarked the youth.

"I don't think I shall," she answered.

Harry threw his arms round her neck, and kissed her pretty cheek.

"I know you would do anything to insure success," said the boy, "but, Mary dear, if it is purchased at the sacrifice of your health, I should be so unhappy."

"Should you?"

"Yes."

"Why, Harry."

"Why," said the boy, looking into her smiling eyes, "because, Mary, I love you so much, that I should die if you were ill, I do really think I should."

And again he pressed his lips to her cheek.

The little maiden's eyes filled with tears as she returned his caress.

"I will be careful," she said, "for your's and my dear father's sake; but I will not be lazy; we have struggled with poverty so long, that I must do all I can to assist in earning for us bread, and happier days. Besides, suppose I do dance twice every house, don't I dance all day at home."

"Yes, but—"

"That's more than I shall have to do here," she interposed. "So don't be frightened, Harry, I shan't make myself ill, I shall only be a little tired, and if we are as successful as we all hope to be, why I shan't care for that a bit, I shan't."

And, rising from her seat with a smile, she kissed her young companion, and hurried away to perform her duties on the parade.

The Boy Actor stood gazing after her pretty figure till it was lost to sight, then a sigh broke from his breast, and he murmured,

"Heaven has been kind to me, if it has robbed me of my poor mother, it has thrown me among those whom I can love, and who can love me in return, given me friends to guide my path, and lead my footsteps through the world. Oh, I am thankful that I am in such hands; I will always strive to be good and kind, for had not my mother been so, I might now be a poor despised orphan, without food, without home, without friends; but I have found them all, and I fancy I hear the last words of my mother saying, 'Be good to your fellows, and you shall ever find friends in this cold wide world.'"

CHAPTER LXVIII.

GRIPE IN DIFFICULTIES—THE STEWARD DETERMINES ON A JOURNEY TO LONDON—AN UNEXPECTED AND UNLOOKED-FOR RESULT.

LIKE a beaten cur, Mr. Gripe, the little steward, slunk tremblingly out of the shed in which he had expected to find "something to his advantage."

With a contemptuous curl of the lip, and an indignant gleam in his eye, Dick watched the base-hearted little man till his form was hidden behind the trees in the distance.

Then, throwing his arm round the waist of his demented wife, he led her gently into the house.

Gripe wandered on for some time, his mind a prey to no very pleasant thoughts.

He felt that he really was what Dick had termed a contemptible cur, and he looked ever and anon behind him as though he expected to be followed by the poacher, and chastised by his strong arm for the dirty business in which he had been engaged.

It was with a sigh of relief, then, that he found himself some distance from the old farmhouse, and the road clear both before and behind.

His rage and disappointment at finding he had been duped by Dick and placed himself in the power of the law, had rendered him for a time forgetful of the injuries he had received in his endeavours to escape from the outhouse and anything but prim and respectable appearance he bore.

But now, the first burst of fear and passion having subsided, he recollected the strange and not very pleasant aspect he bore.

So Gripe paused before a large pond, and stooping down, bathed his scratched face and hands.

Having dried them upon his handkerchief, and combed his hair, brushed his hat round, and otherwise adjusted his toilet, he sat himself down upon a low fence and began to review his present position.

It was no enviable one, to be sure.

Full of hope and joy he had left the manor-house in the morning, certain of his power over a most illiberal master.

Now he dared not return to it lest the officers of justice awaited him on its threshold.

Here seemed to be the end of all his ambitious hopes.

Not satisfied with holding a position which in itself was good, he had aspired to become the master where he was the servant.

And for a time it seemed he was so.

The little man, who had bowed, and cringed, and fawned, no sooner believed himself in power than he became arrogant and insolent to such a degree that, driven to distraction, he had caused Henley to throw himself in the way of Dick the Poacher, and upset all the fond hopes of the little steward.

Gripe was now worse off than ever.

With but a few pounds in his pocket, he knew not what to do or whither to go.

He felt that it would be unsafe to go to the manor, since the insulting manner in which he had treated Henley he was sure would induce that gentleman to put his threats into execution.

And again, he knew that he was so thoroughly disliked by all there that he would be unable to induce any of the servants to obtain for him the property he had left there.

Bad and designing men may gain the semblance of friendship from those beneath them whilst in power, but if they fall they are sure to find them enemies.

A tyrant may exact homage, but he never gains respect.

The worm will fly from man, for it knows he hath the power to crush it; but when the power is gone and it can no longer harm, it will feast upon his body.

Too well Gripe knew that each one of the servants at the manor-house would more willingly consign him to the hands of justice than aid him in any way.

So back to the manor-house he resolved not to go—at least for the present.

He would watch and wait.

He did not entirely despair of getting the squire into his power yet.

But for the present he was in the squire's.

And as he himself had shown no mercy he could not expect any himself.

Still he knew not where to go or how to act.

First he thought of applying to his worthy friend Takeall for assistance, but then he recollected that the broker was only generous when there was something to be made.

True, he could, in the event of that gentleman refusing him assistance, have threatened to make public some of the not very creditable transactions of which he had been guilty in his business.

But then the public would scarcely believe that Takeall was in the habit of swearing that property seized for rent was only worth a quarter its value, and share with the steward the proceeds of his villany, when such an assertion came from a thief.

So, for the present, Gripe resolved to seek no assistance from the auctioneer and sworn broker.

Suddenly a thought struck him.

He recollected the conversation he had had with Dancing Bill, the harlequin.

He recollected, too, that Dick the Poacher had appeared anxious to know whether the squire had gained possession of other papers, which he avowed to be useless.

That there were other documents he now felt satisfied.

But had Dick got them? or had he, as he asserted, lost them whilst in prison?

If so, might not the harlequin have possessed himself of them?

Here was food for his mind!

Here was hope to his soul!

If Dancing Bill had really obtained them, he might still have them in his possession.

He himself had refused to tell the harlequin where he could be found, and believing that the poacher had sold him the genuine packet, he had forgotten all about what had passed between him and the murderer.

He resolved to find him out.

But how?

Gripe thought long and seriously.

The colour returned to his cheek, the gleam to his eye, and he held his head more erect than he had done since he left the house of Dick the Poacher.

"I've got it!" he exclaimed. "I'll go to London, and make inquiries of the theatrical agents; some of them are sure to know his whereabouts."

And the little weazened face of the plotting steward beamed up, till the smile on his face became a grin.

"Ah, ah, squire," he muttered, "you may yet find yourself in my power as much as I am now in your's. And you, Master Dick, may find yourself outwitted, with all your cunning. I am no match for you physically, but I flatter myself that intellectually you are no match for me."

And Mr. Gripe rubbed his little hands together in high glee.

"I'll start at once," he muttered. "I won't delay. Delays are dangerous; and it is a duty which I owe to myself to wriggle out of the clutches of the squire—and I always do my duty! I'll walk all night. I'll be in London to-morrow. And who knows but the power now possessed by the squire may be mine in a few days—aye, mine!"

Gripe was himself again.

His was a spirit not easily broken.

It might be bent by the force of circumstances; but once the pressure was removed, up it sprung again, and was erect as ever.

Gripe was one of those men whose motto is,— "Strike the iron while it is hot."

No sooner did he form a resolve than he commenced to put it into execution.

Buttoning up his coat, and forcing his hat firmly on his head, the steward prepared for his journey to London.

The shades of evening had fallen, but there was every prospect of the night being a fine one, as the first rays of a young moon tinted the blue vault of heaven.

Taking one long look in the direction of the habitation of Dick, the little steward shook his fist at it, and turning away, strode lightly on.

Buried in thought, and counting up the prospects of success to his journey, he started suddenly, as the voice of a man saluted his ears.

He raised his eyes, which had been turned on the ground, and encountered the tall figure of a man, wretchedly clad.

The face of the stranger was pale and haggard, and the beard, which was of some days' growth, gave to his features a wild and dirty appearance.

Gripe would have strode on his way, but the man again spoke.

"I am starving," he said; "give me money for bread."

There was something in the tones of the man's voice which checked the churlish reply that rose to the lips of the steward.

Gripe gazed intently at the haggard features for a few moments.

A cry of surprise and pleasure almost burst from his lips.

But he looked again to make assurance doubly sure.

"For God's sake pity my distress, and give me the means to purchase food," said the man, almost fiercely.

"Ah!" exclaimed Gripe, leaping towards him, "you are the man I seek! Oh, how fortunate!"

But the man sprang back, and threw himself into an attitude of defence.

"Stand back!" he said; "I will never be taken! Stand back, or it will be the worse for you. I am a desperate man—so stand back, I say!"

If Gripe was surprised before, he was doubly so now.

He looked at the man in doubt.

"Surely," he thought, "I am not mistaken? I do not so very easily forget faces—it must be him."

And again he advanced towards the stranger.

"Don't lay your hands on me, or it will be the worse for you!" again exclaimed the man, retreating backwards as he spoke.

"My dear fellow," said Gripe, in that soft tone of voice he could so well assume, "don't you know me?"

"No!" exclaimed the man, still standing in attitude, as though he feared an onslaught from his questioner.

"Come, come," said Gripe; "I know you; we have met before. You were the harlequin at Richardson's Show."

"It's a lie!" exclaimed the man, hastily, and his pale, haggard face became still more ghastly.

"Nonsense!" said Gripe; "I never forget a face I have once seen. You are the man I commissioned to procure some documents for me late one night after the fair had closed.

The man started.

He moved round, so that Gripe might bring his face in the faint moonlight.

"What do you want with me?" he asked, after a long and piercing look at the little steward.

"I was now on my way to London to seek you," answered Gripe.

"For what?" asked the man, eagerly.

"To find out if you had been successful," answered the little steward.

"Is that all?" asked the other, anxiously.

"No," said Gripe.

"What then?" exclaimed the man, again retreating a few paces.

"To reward you if you had," answered Gripe.

"Ah!" said the other, apparently satisfied that Gripe spoke the truth; "well, I recollect you now."

"Then why did you deny that you were the man?" asked Gripe, suspiciously.

The man hesitated for a moment.

"Why, because—because," stammered Dancing Bill, for he indeed it was, "I—I have run in debt, and they meant to arrest me—that's why."

And Dancing Bill drew a heavy breath of relief.

He had not recognised Gripe at first, and the words the little steward had spoken caused him to imagine that he knew of the guilty deed his hand had perpetrated, and that he was about to arrest him for the crime.

Truly, a guilty conscience needs no accusing.

His crimes had brought him to misery and starvation, yet he clung to that life which was now a burthen to him.

He now suffered Gripe to approach him.

"Did you succeed?" asked the steward.

"I did," replied Bill.

A cry of joy broke from the lips of Gripe.

"Where — where are they?" he asked, eagerly.

"I have them here," said Bill, laying his hand upon the breast of his ragged coat. "I have long wished to meet with you, so that I could get the money you promised me for them, for I am starving."

"Give them to me!" said Gripe, anxiously.

"Where is the money?" asked Bill.

And he extended his hands.

Gripe paused.

He remembered too well the trick of Dick the poacher.

"I dare say," he said, "you are a fair-dealing, honest fellow enough, but I am a man of business; I must first examine them to see that they are correct."

"They are all right," said Bill; "I have never interfered with them."

"How did you get them?" asked the steward.

"I overheard where they were secreted in the dressing-room."

"Overheard?"

"Yes."

"Who?"

"A man they called Dick the Poacher," said Bill.

"How came he there?"

"He came to see the clown and that boy he has with him," returned Bill.

"Harry Marston?" asked Gripe.

"The same."

"Yes! yes!"

"I overheard him tell them where those papers were to be found by the clown if anything happened to him."

"You did?"

"I did."

"And where were they?" asked the steward, eagerly.

"In a passage under a field."

"Where?"

"In a lane in Barnstable," replied Dancing Bill.

"Yes! yes!"

"I pretended to sprain my ancle, and got away from the booth to go there," continued Bill.

"Well?"

"I found the place and the packet," replied Bill.

"But is it the packet?" asked Gripe, half doubtfully.

"It is."

"How do you know?"

"Because I heard the man tell the clown that he had only sold the wrapper, wound round an old newspaper, to the man who wanted to get them?"

"You did?" exclaimed Gripe, in a tone of joy.

"Yes, I did."

"Show them to me, and if they are the documents I seek, I will keep faith with you," said Gripe.

"They are the right ones, I am sure," said Bill.

"Why should you think so," asked the steward.

"Because of the manner in which they were hid away. I should never have found them, if I had not heard the place described so minutely by the poacher."

Gripe was in ecstacies.

"Let me see them," he said, "and I will deal fairly by you."

Bill drew the papers from his bosom, and held them in the moon's rays.

Gripe stretched forth his hand to grasp them.

"Stop," said Bill, "I have told you I am starving. I want the money."

"And you shall have it, when I am satisfied you are not playing me false," said the steward, resolutely.

"You will not deceive me," queried the harlequin.

"I will not, on my honour," was the reply.

Bill placed the packet in the steward's hand. Nervously, yet hastily, Gripe unfolded them, and holding them so as the faint moonbeams played full upon them, he took his glass from his breast, and scanned them eagerly.

A low chuckle emanated from his throat.

He folded them up, and placing his eye-glass in his breast, he turned to Dancing Bill.

"Let me see, I promised you a pound, did I not," he said.

Dancing Bill made a grasp at them.

"Stop, stop!" said Gripe, fearful that the other might refuse to part with them.

"A pound!" exclaimed Dancing Bill, indignantly.

"Wasn't it?" said Gripe, slowly, as if he had forgotten the price agreed upon.

"No."

"How much then," innocently inquired Gripe.

He saw the man before him was in the last stage of poverty.

He had heard him say that he was starving, and his mean spirit prompted him to take advantage of his condition.

It was his duty, he thought, to buy cheap, and sell dear.

It was his duty, to take any advantage he could, even of the starving wretch, who gave him the power to defy the squire, and save himself from a gaol.

"You know how much it was," said Bill.

"I have quite forgotten," said the steward.

"That's strange."

"Why so?"

"Because you have a good memory."

"Do you think so?"

"Yes, or you wouldn't have reccollected me."

"Oh, that's nothing."

"Ain't it?"

"No."

"I think it is, seeing as how I have altered, since last we met," returned Bill.

Gripe winced.

"Well, I have quite forgotten," said Gripe, "it must have been five, then."

"No, it wasn't," grumbled Bill, "and you know it, too."

"Oh, two was it," said the steward, misconstruing the word.

"No, twenty."

"Twenty," echoed Gripe, "that's a large sum."

"Is it?" said Bill.

"Yes, too much, too much," said the steward.

"That was what you promised," said Bill.

"Oh, I must have been mad," said Gripe, still wishing to get it reduced.

"I don't know anything of that," said Bill, "it's not too much for the risk I ran, and the sufferings I had to endure."

"Sufferings," iterated Gripe.

"Yes, I was laid up in the hospital through it," said Bill.

"How was that?"

"Because there was a cannister of powder placed alongside of them, and it blew up in my face and nearly blinded me."

"Ah!" said Gripe, "then Dick set a guard over them."

"He did," answered Bill, unwilling to tell Gripe how the accident really occurred, "and if that ain't worth twenty, I don't know what is."

"Come," said Gripe, "you must take less than that, I am poor now, if I was rich then—"

"I shan't take any less," said Bill, moodily.

"Say ten."

"No, for Dick would give more for them," said the harlequin.

This settled the question.

Gripe thought it would not be policy to strive longer to beat down the price, lest the harlequin should resolve to let the poacher have them.

"Well," he said, "I was a fool to offer so much, but if I did, I suppose I must keep my word. I consider it the duty of all men to keep their word, and certainly I must do my duty."

Gripe drew his purse from his pocket and counted out twenty soverings into the extended hand of Bill the harlequin.

The eyes of Bill glistened fiercely.

He could now allay the pangs of hunger.

Oh, if he could but allay those of conscience, famished as he was, how willingly would he have given the gold he held in his hand for such a boon.

But that he could never do. It haunted him night and day, for it was stained with blood.

If the famished man gloated with pleasure upon the gold, Gripe yielded it up with anything but a good grace.

He could not bear to part with it.

True, it would leave him with but a few pounds in his possession; but then, the packet in his hand could be made to bring him thousands.

"There," he said, as he grudgingly placed the last coin in the blood-stained hand of the famished and guilty wretch. "You ought to be very happy now."

"Happy," said Bill—"

But he paused, lest an unguarded word should betray him.

"Yes, very happy. Now go and get yourself some food, for you seem as if a good meal would do you some service."

Bill closed his hand tightly over the sparkling coins, and turned to go.

"Good night," said Gripe, now that he had served his purpose, only too anxious to be rid of the company of one whom he feared might be prompted to rob him of his purchase.

"Good night," replied Bill, in a low tone; what would not he have given for a good night's rest?

He knew not now what it was to rest in peace.

His slumbers were broken and unrefreshing, for the pale face of his murdered victim haunted his pillow and drove sleep from his eyelids.

And in the silence and darkness he could hear that voice which he had stilled for ever beneath the giant trees.

"Good night!"

What a mockery were the words, what a taunt did they not imply.

Silently and sadly he strode along the road in the opposite direction to that which Gripe had taken.

Casting his ever restless glance around him, starting at every shadow, and every gust of wind as it shook the foliage of the trees.

Peace he would never more know, happiness had flown for ever.

The blood of his victim called aloud for vengeance, and that call would one day be answered.

Justice was only deferred for a time, but in the end murder will out.

* * *

CHAPTER LXIX.

GRIPE RETURNS TO THE MANOR—A SCENE IN THE HALL — THE ACCUSATION — THE THREAT — THE DESIGN FRUSTRATED.

"It is always the darkest the hour before day."

There is truth in this, for how often do we see men brought down to the very lowest depths of despair, when prosperity dawns upon them, the dark cloud which overhangs their destinies, till, like a funeral pall, it enshrouds their existence, suddenly pierced by a bright ray of good fortune which hourly becomes brighter till the mists are chased away, and a glorious halo of peace and happiness encircle them.

It was black enough a few short hours since with the little steward.

The dark cloud of destiny had encompassed him till it almost threatened to destroy him.

But prosperity dawned, and despair gave place to satisfaction.

A few hours since, and he dared not show his face at the manor-house, now, with light and buoyant steps, he wended his way thither.

The fear he entertained of the squire putting his threats into execution troubled him no longer, for he carried that in his breast which would crush him.

It was now late, and the inmates of the manor-house had doubtless retired to rest.

Still Gripe feared not to disturb them.

With a smile on his weazened face he strode on.

As he saw the gable roof of the farm house of Dick the Poacher, he again shook his clutched fist towards it.

"Ah! ah! master Dick," he muttered, "I am one too many for you yet."

On he went, with head erect and step as firm as ever, till he gained the gates of the mansion.

Not a light was to be seen at any of the windows.

As he had expected, all within had retired to rest.

He rang a heavy peal upon the bell, and, smiling, awaited the answer to his summons.

In about five minutes the form of a footman was seen wending his way along the gravel walk which led from the gate to the house.

The man exhibited some surprise when he perceived that it was Gripe who had summoned him from his bed.

As he threw the gate open the little steward politely thanked him, and apologised for having called him out of his warm bed at such an hour.

The man made no reply; but, as he followed Gripe towards the house, the look on his face plainly showed that he was not the best pleased at having to answer his summons.

Gripe entered the house, and proceeded at once to his own room.

The footman, however, instead of seeking his chamber, made his way to his master's sleeping apartment, where, having solicited admittance, he stood at the bedside of the squire.

"What is it, Thomas?" asked Henley, in some surprise.

"Mr. Gripe, sir, has returned," replied the man.

"The devil!"

"No, sir, Gripe."

"Where is he?"

"In his own room."

"Have all the servants retired to rest?" asked the squire.

"Yes, sir."

"Summon all to appear in the hall," he said.

"When, sir?"

"In ten minutes."

The man bowed.

"Thomas."

"Sir?"

"You know the residence of the constable?"

"Yes, sir."

"You will at once summon him hither."

"To-night, sir?" asked the man, in surprise.

"Immediately."

The man again bowed, and left the apartment.

As soon as he had done so, Henley leapt from his bed, and hastily attired himself.

"The viper!" he muttered; "the insolent wretch! Shall I submit to his cool insults? Shall I suffer myself to be robbed, and then defied in my own house? No; I will remove him from my path, crush his overbearing spirit, and give justice her due. Mr. Gripe, you have played a desperate game; you bit the hand that fed you, but you will find that I am not the man to tamely submit to your insults and indignities!"

And Squire Henley strode haughtily from his room, down the grand staircase into the hall, where several of the servants had already assembled, and were discussing among themselves what could possibly be the cause of the strange summons from their beds.

Meantime, Gripe had thrown himself into a chair, and sunk into a deep train of thought.

Suddenly he was aroused from his reverie by hearing footsteps on the stairs.

He arose from his chair, and cautiously opening his door, looked forth.

The hall, which, when he entered, was in utter darkness, was now lighted.

What could it mean?

Whilst considering, he saw that the servants were assembling, and conversing in eager whispers.

In a moment the truth flashed upon his mind.

The squire believed his power gone since his interview with Dick the Poacher, and was about to carry out his threat of exposing him to the servants and handing him over to justice.

A smile broke over the face of Gripe.

How he would undeceive Henley and defy him!

He chuckled in high glee at the prospect of humbling the man before his own servants, who would hold him up to scorn.

"Ha! ha!" he muttered. "Play your game, squire, but you will be the loser. You little know what has fallen into my hands to-night—little know that I still have the power to work your ruin. Fool, as well as knave; I can defy you and degrade you!"

And Gripe placed his hand in his breast, and clasped the packet he had received from Bill the harlequin but a short time before.

"Ha! ha! Let those laugh that win, squire," he muttered, as he saw the tall form of Henley cross the hall, followed by the glances of the wondering servants.

Still standing within the doorway of his own room, Gripe watched all that was going on, for some time.

There was a loud ring at the gate bell.

"Now for it," muttered Gripe. "I am much mistaken if that is not the officer sent to bear me to gaol. Capital, Squire Henley; but I will humble you yet; you think to hold me up to scorn and derision, but you shall sue to me for mercy, ha, ha!"

At this moment, the man who had been sent for the constable, ran up the stairs.

Gripe drew back into the shadow of his room.

The footman entered.

DANCING BILL'S APPEAL TO MARGARET.

"Mr. Gripe," he called out.

"Now sir, what do you want?" asked the steward.

"The squire commands your attendance in the hall immediately," answered the man.

"The squire?"

"Yes, sir."

"At this hour," said Gripe, appearing to be surprised.

"Yes, sir."

"Strange, but I will attend him in a minute."

The man left the room, and descended the staircase.

Gripe placed his hand to his breast to assure himself that the packet was all safe there, then with the usual smile on his weazened face he left the room and advanced to the stairs, arriving in the hall, he looked round upon the assembled servants as though greatly surprised at the unusual scene.

Stepping out into the centre of the hall, Squire Henley fixed his eye upon the still smiling face of the little steward, and said,—

"Mr. Gripe, you are perhaps surprised that I should command your attendance here at this late hour, but, sir, there is a villain in this house."

"Doubtless, squire," said Gripe, fixing his cold grey eye upon Henley.

"A villain, sir, who has repaid the trust I reposed in him, by robbing, and then presuming to insult me. One whom I trusted and should have continued to trust, had not I been warned of his guilty doings. In justice to myself and every person under this roof, I call upon the constable to take into custody one who can repay my kindness with such base ingratitude.

The constable, who till now had stood in the back ground, advanced and placed his hand upon the shoulder of the steward.

"Squire Henley," said Gripe, "at your peril."

No. 17.

But Henley turned away contemptuously.

"Fool!" hissed the steward, "I would save you, but the fault lay upon your own head. Behold!" he added, drawing the packet from his breast, "I hold that which shall crush your haughty spirit, hold you up to infamy and disgrace, wrest from you these broad lands, and consign you to an ignominious doom."

And Gripe waved the packet triumphantly above his head.

"Liar!" exclaimed a loud voice, and Dick the Poacher, darting through the hall door, which had been opened for the passage of Gripe and the constable, seized the packet from the steward's grasp. "Gripe, you are not yet master of Henley Manor!"

And ere a hand could be stretched forth to stay him, Dick was gone.

***

CHAPTER LXX.

THE INVALID AND THE OFFICER—A DISGRACE TO THE LAW AND A CREDIT TO THE STAGE.

THERE are persons in this world whose touch it would appear, like that of Midas, turns everything to gold. There are others who, strive as they will, can never thrive; the apple for which they toil and labour turns to dust within their grasp, and emits a bitter taste; so it is with some whose destinies are cast beneath a fatal planet, strive as they may, do what they will, disappointment and misery dogs their footsteps through life, ill-fortune haunts them like a shadow, and they pass through the hours of existence meeting at every turn misfortune or woe.

Such would appear to be the case with Margaret Simmons, the columbine.

Poor thing, her's indeed had been a life of misery; scarce one happy hour had she experienced since she were old enough to judge the difference between happiness and misery. Born of poor yet respectable parents, the days of her infancy were passed in peace and contentment, though the means were small and the fare hard; but ere six summers had passed over her head, she was left an orphan, and fell into the hands of some distant relatives, who, under the pretence of caring and providing for her, took her under their protection.

But the kindness which these people professed to feel for the poor orphan girl, was actuated by self interest, as they resolved to bring her up to a line of life which they believed would speedily reimburse them for any outlay they might incur on her behalf, and yield a good profit into the bargain.

Young as Margaret then was, she showed great disposition to become a dancer, and she was placed under the tuition of a woman who had possessed great talent in her day, but could hold no engagement for any length of time, owing to her propensity for drink.

Hence it was that, driven from the boards, she sought the means of pandering to her disgusting passion by taking pupils.

Whilst under this woman's tutorage, Margaret was submitted to every species of unkindness and cruelty, and to save herself from further indignities, finally ran away from her apprenticeship and went to London, where she succeeded in obtaining an engagement at a salary of one shilling per night.

This was little enough to keep a poor girl, without friends or home; but she strove hard to live upon it, till a better chance should offer.

This came at last. She was to form one of the front row of the corps-de-ballet, and her salary was doubled; but on the very first night of her new position, poor Margaret had the misfortune to fall through a trap which had been carelessly left unbolted, and though the injuries she received were not fatal, yet they were of a serious nature to her, as they precluded her from fulfilling her engagement, and threw her out of employment without the means of obtaining the common necessaries of life.

Without friends, without money, without one to guide or advise her, poor Margaret lived for a few weeks upon the sale of every article of clothing which she could part with, and nothing but an asylum in the poor house seemed left to her.

It was when the last coin had been spent for bread, and she could no longer occupy her lodgings, being in arrears, and unable to comply with the demands of her landlord, and she had resolved to seek shelter in the workhouse, that a troupe of strolling players became acquainted with her position, and requiring a female dancer to accompany them on their summer tour, entered into an arrangement with Margaret, and in the towns and villages she danced in the open air, on a board some four feet square, attired in an Highland costume.

This life was anything but congenial to her feelings, but necessity compelled her to put up with it till prosperity should shine upon her.

Many a night was she compelled to sleep in some outhouse or barn, the proceeds of the day's toil not yielding a sufficiency to procure them a lodging.

Among the troupe was a young man, a dancer, who professed to feel for her a more than ordinary interest, and endeavoured to persuade her to unite their destinies, and seek their fortunes as dancers on the parades at the fairs.

In an evil moment, believing in the truth and honour of her lover, she consented, and having at length saved sufficient money, they were united.

But ere a week had passed away, Dancing Bill, as he was called by the rest of the troupe, showed himself in his true colours, and the poor girl, when too late, discovered that she had allied herself to a brutal and unprincipled villain.

Daily did she receive some fresh insult or indignity at his hands, and broken in spirit and in health, she left the troupe with him, and obtained an engagement as columbine in a show which worked the fairs.

Striving her utmost to obey his every wish and please his every whim, receiving in reward blows for all her love and kindness, years passed, till at length they procured an engagement at Richardson's show.

Of her various sufferings since that time we are well acquainted, sufferings which for a time had deprived her of reason, and laid her a broken-hearted woman upon an hospital bed, where the fatal secret she was about to divulge to Charlie Evans was prevented by a relapse into insensibility.

When she recovered from the unconsciousness into which she had fallen it was late in the day, and as the hospital regulations allowed no visitors on the premises at that hour, Charlie had departed; but ere he left he had placed in the hands of the nurse a sovereign, to procure anything which the suffering woman might require.

Alas, no gold could purchase what Margaret sighed for, peace of mind.

But she was none the less grateful for the generous gift, and a sigh escaped her as she thought how happy she might have been did Dancing Bill but possess a heart like that of the good-natured clown's.

On the day after the visit of Charlie Evans, Mr. Wilks, the constable, who had been daily informed of the state of the poor columbine, called at the hospital and presented himself at the bedside of the sufferer.

Even in that abode of pain and sickness, the great man, as he considered himself to be, put on his severest look, and gave his most pompous cough.

Margaret shuddered as she observed him walk up between the long rows of beds, and a deep sigh escaped her bosom.

"Humph," said Mr. Wilks; "better, eh?"

"Yes," replied Margaret, in a low voice.

"Strange circumstance this," said Mr. Wilks, fixing his little grey eye upon her pale and attenuated features, "very strange."

Margaret made no reply.

"But it will all be cleared up now," said the officer.

Still Margaret made no answer, she knew too well the business which brought that man to her bedside, and though she had nearly betrayed the secret to the clown, she would not to the officer.

"Shall I," she thought, "be the instrument to consign my husband to the gallows. Bad as he has been to me, I am still his wife, and is it not my duty to shield him from every harm, oh, would that I had never known it."

The look of the officer became more severe and the cough more pompous.

"Now you know all about it," he said, "so take my advice and make a clean breast of it."

"I don't know what you mean," stammered Margaret.

"Don't you, now."

"No."

"Then I must refresh your memory," said Mr. Wilks.

"Well."

"The murder at the Seven Sisters."

"What of it?" asked Margaret, with a heavy sigh.

"That's what I want to know," replied Mr. Wilks. "I beg you to understand that I am here in my official capacity as constable of the locality, in which the deed was prepetrated."

"Well," said Margaret.

"I advise you to inform me where the murderer is, and who he is," said Wilks.

"Don't you know," said Margaret.

"No, otherwise I should not be here," said Wilks.

"You told me that you had him in custody when you compelled me to accompany you from my home, to the place where the inquest was held."

"Did I?"

"Yes."

"Then it wasn't him; you know that," said Wilks.

"Then why was he arrested?" asked Margaret, feeling disgusted at the haughty and bombastical manner of the constable.

"Because suspicion pointed to him," replied Wilks.

"And do you deprive a fellow creature of liberty because circumstances look suspicious?" asked Margaret. "Do you fix upon an innocent man the stain of murder without any evidence to show that he was the guilty party? Do you consign a man to a prison because he happened to be near the spot where a cruel and merciless deed is committed? Can the law allow its officers to deprive a subject of liberty without some proof of their guilt?"

"That matters little to you," answered Mr. Wilks. "Your actions at the inquest prove you to know to whom that wig belonged, and that it is some one in the theatrical profession there cannot be the shadow of a doubt."

"Then why did you arrest a man of another calling?" asked Margaret.

"Because—because—" stammered Wilks, somewhat disconcerted by the question.

"I will tell you," interrupted Margaret, "because in your zeal to bring a wretch to the gallows, you forgot your duty as an officer; because in your anxiety to arrest an innocent man, you overlooked that which might have prevented the guilty from escaping the just punishment of his crime. Had you done your duty as becomes an officer of the law, one poor innocent man might have suffered less, and the guilty one have been consigned to the doom he merited."

Mr. Wilks began to feel very small; but like most arrogant natures, he began to show his petty spirit when he found the rebuke was merited.

"That is no business of yours," he said. "I want to know to whom that wig belonged, and if you would save yourself from standing a very good chance of being placed in prison you will tell me."

"Is it any part of your duty to come here and threaten a woman, who has scarcely recovered from a long and dangerous illness," asked Margaret, in a contemptuous tone. "Begone, sir, you neither possess the spirit of a man nor the qualities of an English officer."

And, laying back upon her pillow, Margaret drew the bedclothes up around her throat.

Had Wilks dared, he would have dragged the poor suffering columbine from the bed and conveyed her to gaol; but as it was, he bit his lips with vexation, and vowed inwardly that if ever he got an opportunity he would have no mercy on her.

"Look you," he said, "I am here by the orders of the coroner."

"Did he command you to insult an invalid," asked Margaret. "If not, you have exceeded your orders."

"Will you inform me to whom that wig belongs?" asked Wilks, now pale with passion.

"What wig?" asked Margaret.

"The wig taken foom the hands of the murdered woman," exclaimed the constable.

"I will."

"Who, who?" asked Wilks, eagerly.

"To me," replied Margaret.

"To you?" said Wilks.

"Yes, to me."

"Then you are—"

"What?"

"The murderess!" said Wilks.

Margaret rose in the bed.

A flush of pleasure overspread the face of the constable.

"Me?" she said, in surprise.

"Yes, you."

"Why should you think so?" asked the columbine.

"Because you admit the wig to be yours."

"So I do," replied Margaret; "but remember that myself and the murdered woman resided together, that she had access to my boxes; that she met her death at Tottenham whilst I was at home, miles away, from which home I had not stirred from the previous night, till the time you sought me to identify the body, and which every person in that house, and there are several, can truly testify to; it seems to me, Mr. Wilks, that it matters little to you who you accuse of this fearful crime, so that you can swell your vanity by making it appear to your superiors that you are a clever officer, whilst, in fact, you are but an ignorant and insulting man, who abuses the power entrusted to him."

Wilks ground his teeth with rage. He believed that he had found out the guilty wretch at last, but the reply of Margaret had satisfied him to the contrary.

Willingly would he have placed her in a goal upon the charge, if only to be revenged upon her for the biting sarcasm of her words; but already had he arrested one innocent person, and that circumstance had redounded little to his favour with his superiors.

He hesitated, then, between his duty and his inclination.

Fondly he hoped that he might yet be enabled to be avenged upon the poor woman for the rebuke she had given him.

Like most bully's, he was a paltry coward, and determined to watch and wait for any opportunity that might present itself, to inflict some kind of punishment on the woman that had outwitted him.

He could see that she was still suffering, yet he hesitated not to threaten her. So, bending over the bed he exclaimed,—

"Think not to escape easily; suspicion is strong against you; you shall yet give an account of your acts on the night of the murder; you shall yet find the majesty of the law too strong to allow either the guilty party or an accomplice to treat an officer with contempt; I will keep my eye upon you, so look to it, for my name is not Wilks if I don't place you in a gaol yet."

"Strike me comical if you ain't the damnedest mean-spirited cur of a whelp as ever disgraced the uniform of the law, to threaten a woman as has got one foot in the grave. And if the authorities of this place allow it, there is one here as wont't stand by and see a poor invalid annoyed and insulted by a wretch who disgraces the clothes he wears, and the name of justice!"

And Buskin Bob, foaming with indignation and disgust, seized the forlorn Mr. Wilks by the collar, and thrust him violently from the side of the bed, into the middle of the ward.

The pantaloon had called to see poor Margaret, and had arrived at the bedside of the columbine as the officer uttered his threat.

"Do you dare to molest me in the execution of my duty?" exclaimed the officer, after a moment's pause, which had given him time to recover himself.

"Strike me comical," exclaimed Bob, turning upon him, "I dare do all that becomes a man. I dare knock down the scoundrel who can insult and threaten a woman upon a bed of sickness. I dare tear the coat from the back of a vagabond who can disgrace alike the cause he is deputed to serve and the name of man, if I can't, why, strike me comical, there!"

"You mind your own buisness," exclaimed Wilks, scarcely knowing what to say, and feeling that he had exceeded his duty.

"It is the business of every man to defend a weak and defenceless woman from the insults of a blackguard, strike me comical if it ain't," exclaimed Bob. "Now go. The law must have officers to execute its mandates. But justice demands that *men* fulfil the office. If you had a duty to perform it was not to threaten a dying woman. You have exceeded that duty, and ruined the cause you have been called upon to serve. 'Tis such as you that bring the law into contempt, and do more to divert justice than obtain its ends. If justice be done, you will not escape the penalties of your villany, nor shall you, while Buskin Bob can raise his voice in condemnation of the wretch who, to serve his own vile purposes, can threaten a dying woman, strike me comical if you shall, there!"

CHAPTER LXXI.

MARGARET SEEKS AN ENGAGEMENT AND MEETS WITH FRIENDS—BUSKIN BOB RELIEVES HIS HEART AND PAINS HIS FOOT.

THE rebuke he had met with, and the look of contempt on the pallid faces of the occupants of the long rows of beds in the hospital ward, caused that would-be great man, Mr. Wilks, the parish constable, to feel anything but a pleasurable sensation; and muttering something about seeing whether the law would allow him to be interfered with whilst in the execution of his duty, he made his way out of the hospital, with anything but the pompous step with which he entered it.

Unconsciousness had deterred Margaret from revealing the fearful secret to Charlie Evans, and now she had thought over the matter, she resolved not to make a single soul acquainted with it, so her interview with Bob, was none other than could be expected from acquaintances, and Bob himself had too much sense to wish to know the object of Mr. Wilks's visit to the hospital.

Wishing to prevent suspicion gaining ground, Margaret enjoined Buskin Bob not to mention to Charlie the fact of Wilks having been to the hospital. Which he promised not to do. And deeming themselves bound in honour not to reveal what either had heard or said, neither Buskin Bob nor Charlie Evans mentioned what had occurred at the hospital.

That night, Margaret having obtained an order, left the asylum, and went for a time none knew whither.

Charlie and Bob called the next day, and were

surprised to find her gone, and all inquiries as to her whereabouts proved fruitless.

So the friends started on their tour of the fairs, each thinking of the poor columbine, but neither mentioning her to the other.

Finding her home had been sold off to pay the rent, which her three months illness had permitted to accumulate, Margaret, with no other wardrobe than that which she carried on her back, and the sovereign given to her by Charlie Evans, started for Brent, in Devonshire, at which place a fair was to be held, two miles from the spot on which we first made the acquaintance of the Boy Actor.

Wishing to husband her money, Margaret determined to walk the whole distance, for in those days the iron rails had not formed a girder round the earth, and the expenses of travelling were considerably more than they are at the present day.

It was a long and tedious journey; and, heartsick and footsore, the poor columbine arrived at the little town on the night before the fair was to take place.

Here she went from booth to booth, as they drew up in the fair field, and sought employment.

But the pale face and attenuated form of the poor woman was to her a great denial. No one would engage her, as she seemed too weak and ill to undertake the arduous work of columbine for twelve or fourteen hours a day.

Dispirited with her ill-success, Margaret was about to leave the fair-field, when a small caravan drew near the spot.

"There is one chance more," thought Margaret, "and only one."

Sadly she approached the lumbering vehicle as it took up its position, and a cry of surprise escaped her lips, as she perceived the driver to be none other than our old friend, Buskin Bob.

"What, Margaret! strike me comical!" exclaimed Bob, dropping his whip in surprise, as his eyes rested upon the pale face of the columbine.

"Oh, Bob, I hardly expected to see you here," said Margaret, grasping the extended hand of the pantaloon.

"Strike me comical, if I expected to see you, either," exclaimed Bob. "Hi, Charlie," he added, raising his voice. "Here's Dancing Bill's wife, strike me comical if there ain't."

Margaret shuddered as the name of her guilty husband fell upon her ears.

The head and shoulders of Charlie Evans protruded out of the little window of the caravan, and the exclamation escaped his lips,—

"Hillo! Here we are!"

Then the face of the good hearted fellow disappeared as quickly as it had been seen.

But it was for a moment only, for the next, the door of the caravan was opened, and the clown leapt to the ground.

"What, Margaret," he exclaimed, as he took her hand in his own, "I am glad to see you. Here, Harry, drop the steps out, my boy."

Harry was not slow to obey the wishes of Charlie Evans, and, lowering the steps from the caravan to the ground, he ran quickly down them, and gazed with a look of pain upon the features of the poor columbine.

"Strike me comical, Charlie, don't she look queer," said Bob, in a commiserating tone of voice; "looks as though she was made up for a spectre."

"Walk up," said Charlie, "we don't charge you anything, because you are a "pro," and on the free list. Here, let me go first and give you a hand. Who'd have thought of seeing you here. Well, I am glad."

"So am I!" exclaimed Bob. "Strike me comical if I ain't, there!"

And Bob smacked the whip he held in his hand, or rather the apology for one, to give more emphasis to his words.

Charlie led Margaret up into the caravan, where she was greeted by Harry and Mary, and Buskin Bob having unharnessed the horse, and tied on the nosebag, ascended the steps and joined his friends.

"Well, Margaret," said the pantaloon, laying his hat and whip aside. "How are you?"

Margaret merely shook her head in answer.

"You don't look well, strike me comical if you do," said Bob. "But what on earth brought you here?"

"To seek for employment," answered Margaret. "I have tried every booth, but could not succeed."

Charlie sighed.

"It's very hard times," he said, "to Struggle for Bread."

"If you are surprised to see me," said the columbine, "I am equally surprised to see you."

"We sought you at the hospital with the intention of asking you to join us," said Charlie, "but you had left, and none knew whither you had gone."

"Yes, I could not stay longer," replied Margaret, her features assuming a still paler hue.

"How was that?" asked Bob. "Didn't they treat you kindly?"

"Yes," replied Margaret, "but—"

And here she paused.

"They are not places people want to pass the whole of their existence in, strike me comical if they are," said Bob, observing that he had asked a question to which it would have been painful to reply.

"No," said Margaret, with a sigh, "though, thank heaven, that the benevolence of the rich, have founded such places for the poor."

"It would be hard lines indeed if there were not such places for some of us," said Charlie.

"Strike me comical, if it wouldn't," said Bob, "many a poor player has found the benefit of them ere now, and many will again, no doubt, so all honour, say I, to those who have the means and the will to subscribe to them."

"So, Charlie," said Margaret, "you have started for yourselves."

"Yes," replied the clown, "the theatre wouldn't answer, so we bought a booth and hope to make it pay."

"Is this your first fair," she asked.

"No," replied Charlie, "this is our second."

"And if it turns out as good as the first, strike me comical if we can grumble," said Buskin Bob.

"I am glad to hear it," replied Margaret.

Then she lapsed into silence.

She wished to ask if they could make room for her, but feeling assured that they had to struggle hard for bread themselves, she feared to put the question.

"And so you have met with no success?" said Charlie, after a pause.

"None at all," replied the poor columbine.

"Bob," said Charlie Evans, turning to his friend, "we've been hard up, and know what it is?"

"Strike me comical if we ain't!" said Bob. "Many a time."

"Known what it is," continued Charlie, "to walk a hundred miles to seek an engagement, and find every post filled."

"Aye," said Bob, "and had to do the hankey-pankey on the road for a meal. Strike me comical if I ain't, many a time."

"Margaret can't do the hankey-pankey on the road," said Charlie; "and she has not succeeded in her errand here."

"Who says so?" asked Bob.

"Herself."

"Then, strike me comical if she ain't out of her reckoning. Charlie Evans is not the man to refuse a fellow 'pro' a part, if he can only make room for her."

"Right," said Charlie. "We could struggle on by ourselves, but Margaret seeks aid. She shall not ask for it here in vain. We did well at the last fair, and hope to do so here. It is but bread that can be gained by the poor player, but we will share the crust with one who needs our help."

"We will," said Bob, catching Charlie's hand in his own, "we will, Charlie; strike me comical if we won't. Margaret shall work with us while we can draw a single house, and sooner than see her want, we'll play twenty houses a day."

"Oh, Margaret must stop with us," said Harry; "and it will help to ease the labour of Mary."

"So it will," said Charlie.

"Yes," said Mary, "we can share the toil: Mrs. Simmons does not seem well, and if we take the work in turns, it will do us both good."

"To be sure, it will. Strike me comical if it wont," said Bob.

The eyes of the poor columbine filled with tears as she looked first at one and then at the other.

"Charlie—Bob," she said, "I know that you find it as much as you can do in this small booth to keep yourselves. You require no aid, but your generous hearts prompts you to share with me that which you require for yourselves. I am grateful, but I ought not to deprive you. I will walk back to London and seek employment there."

"If you do, I'm damned!" exclaimed Charlie.

"I hope I may be struck comical, till I can't leave off laughing for a week, if you do!" exclaimed Bob, placing his back against the door of the caravan. "I tell you what, Margaret, you don't go down those steps till you promise to stop and help Mary, who, poor girl, has too much to do for one so young."

A smile of gratitude broke over the poor woman's face, and she sat down and burst into tears.

They were tears of joy.

The smile of thankfulness mingled with them.

"There, that's settled," said Charlie; "I don't believe we should get a house at all if you wasn't here."

"Strike me comical if I don't think the grub would choke us if we didn't give her some!—there. So just you make yourself happy; I am going to see and give the horse some water now."

And Bob opened the door of the caravan a very little way, and squeezed himself out, closing it rapidly after him, as if he feared Margaret would endeavour to escape.

"Well," muttered Bob, as he took the nose-bag off the head of the shaggy brute, and balanced a pail of water on his knee for it to drink, "I am glad as Charlie is willing to help her. Poor thing, she's had a hard time of it! She deserves a better fate. She's a nice-looking woman, and a good-hearted woman, and a damn'd sight too good for the wretch she married! I don't wish anybody ill, but strike me comical if anything would please me better than to hear some fine morning as how she was a widow. I'd marry her if she'd have me; I would, even if her husband was hung, strike me comical if I wouldn't—there!"

And Buskin Bob dropped the now empty pail with such force upon his toes, that he danced about the shaggy horse, and cut more capers than ever he did whilst playing the part of pantaloon on the parade of Richardson's Show.

Whilst Buskin Bob was performing his part outside the caravan, little Mary and Harry were preparing supper within.

The fare was humble, but to poor Margaret it was a luxury, and with a thankful heart she seated herself at the little table to partake of the hospitality of her friends.

Never once did Charlie refer to the words she had uttered when he visited her in the hospital.

That they had made an impression on his mind could not be denied, but he could only come to the conclusion that they were the ravings of one suffering from brain fever, and had literally no meaning.

The meal over, a portion of the caravan was parted off to serve as sleeping apartments, and Margaret was invited to share the bed of Mary.

With a grateful heart she retired to the rude couch prepared for her, but, worn out with fatigue as she was, for some time sleep was denied her.

Her mind was a prey to the most agonising thoughts.

She reflected upon the events of the past few months, and the fearful deed which had been committed by her husband, and her eyes were filled with tears, when at length sleep stole over her senses.

CHAPTER LXXII.

THE VISIT TO THE OLD HOUSE AT HOME—AN UN-EXPECTED MEETING—THE PROMISE AND THE COMMISSION.

ON the following morning the players were up betimes, and the morning meal ended, they set about building the booth.

The Brothers Tumblini were also at the booth, and Charlie, anxious that Harry and his daughter should have as much rest and recreation as possible, begged they would not assist in the erection of the booth, as it could be easily done in time without their aid.

The young folks, eager to lighten the labours of their friends, were for a time unwilling to comply with their wishes, but eventually gave way to the desires of Charlie.

"We have nothing to do," said Harry, "and it is dull sitting looking at you at work."

"Why not take a walk till it's time to dress?" asked the clown.

"Oh, yes! in the fields," said Mary.

"No," said Harry, suddenly, "if you will come with me, Mary, I will go and look once more upon the house where my mother died, and from which your father so kindly took me."

"Do so, boy," said Charlie. "It is not more than two miles from here, and you can get back plenty time enough for the opening. Besides, there is a charm in gazing upon spots so dear to us. Go!"

And a sad look overspread the clown's face as he spoke, for he remembered the kindness he had received from the mother of the boy by his side.

It was not long ere Mary was attired for the journey, and together they started forth to view the home of the Boy Actor.

In less than an hour Harry Marsden stood before the little cottage in which his first hours of grief had been passed, and in which the father of his companion had sworn to protect him.

Various were the thoughts which passed through the mind of the Boy Actor as he gazed upon the walls of that house where he had passed his childhood's days, and the tear of sympathy and love rose to his eye and rolled down his cheek as he turned his head away from that spot so dear to his memory.

Little Mary could not but sympathise with him.

She, too, had lost a kind and gentle mother; and she flung her arms around the neck of her companion, and mingled her tears with his.

"Do not cry, Harry," she said. "'Tis hard to lose those we love, but regret will not bring them back again."

"I can't help crying," said Harry; "the tears will come. I try to keep them back, but it is no use. The sight of that house makes me unhappy. I know I ought not to be wretched, for you love me, your father loves me, and Buskin Bob loves me, and all try to make me happy; but I can't forget my mother—I can't forget her."

"No," said Mary, "nor can I. So we must cry, Harry—we must cry!"

And with their arms encircling each other's forms, the youthful players wept in unison.

"I will go and see my mother's grave," said Harry, when his grief had somewhat subsided. "I will go and see if there are any flowers growing upon the mound of earth which covers her remains. It may be some time ere we are in this part of the country again; perhaps we never shall be; so come, Mary, let me show you the spot where she lies."

Mary took his hand, and together they wended their way towards the little churchyard, at the gate of which Dick the Poacher had upbraided the unfeeling sexton.

The bright sunbeams were playing upon the little grass-covered mounds which marked the last resting-places of the dead, as the two youthful players arrived at the gates of the little churchyard.

Silently and sadly they wended their way among the grave-stones, till they came to the spot where the late Mrs. Marsden lay mouldering in her shroud.

The little mound of earth which covered her remains was black and cheerless.

No flowers decked her last resting-place; no stone marked the spot where she lay; no lying epitaph was written o'er her grave; no marble slab covered the body from which the soul had fled.

Blank, cheerless, and miserable was the last resting-place of the widow.

No hand had planted blossoms on her grave; no tears had watered the dry, black earth, for it was the last home of poverty.

Harry bent over it and wept.

His tears were a greater tribute to her memory than sculptured stone or polished marble.

The grief of the poor boy became so visible, that Mary drew him from the spot.

"Come," she said, "this place makes me feel wretched."

Harry turned instantly.

He felt a melancholy pleasure in gazing upon the grave of his mother, but he would not cause a moment's unhappiness to his young companion.

No; he loved her too much for that.

Boy as he was, his heart yearned towards his lovely companion with more than a brotherly love.

Out of sight of the old churchyard, the grief of the Boy Actor became somewhat moderated, and he pointed out to his fair companion spots dear to his memory, and where he had often wiled away the hours between sunrise and sunset.

Thus occupied, Harry and his companion strolled into the field where Charlie Evans and Dick the Poacher had had their first interview.

They strolled away together towards the little wood, and sat down upon the grass to rest themselves ere they returned towards the fair.

Charmed by the wild-flowers that grew around them, caused Mary to pluck several from their stems.

As she did so, the thought entered her mind how beautiful they would look growing upon the grave of her companion's mother.

But not wishing to cause Harry any more melancholy reflections, she kept her thoughts to herself.

Selecting some of the finest, she drew them from the ground, then turning to her companion, she remarked,—

"Harry, we have got two hours yet before it is time to dress, you stay here and rest yourself, while I take a walk and see about the place."

"I will go with you," said Harry, leaping to his feet.

"No, no," said Mary, "I want to go alone. Now you have said you love me, and if you do you will let me have my own way this once."

"But you will lose yourself in this strange place," said the boy.

"Oh no," said Mary; "I shall not go far, and will soon return. Now, do stay here, I won't be long."

Harry saw that she was bent upon going

alone, so, he sank down again upon the grass, exclaiming,—

"Now don't go out of the high road, or you may find it difficult to regain it."

Promising to comply with his wish, Mary rose to her feet, and grasping the flowers she had drawn from the earth, smilingly waved an adieu to her companion, and took her way across the field towards the road which led to the little churchyard.

Harry watched her retreating form, as she skipped lightly over the grass, till it was lost to view in the bend of the lane.

Wondering what could be her motive, he laid his head back against the trunk of a huge tree, and gazed vacantly upon the blue sky above him.

Suddenly he was aroused from the reverie into which he had fallen by a rustling among the branches which hid the spot where the secret hiding-place of Dick the Poacher was situated.

Turning hastily round and raising himself upon his hands and knees, he gazed in the direction of the spot from whence the sound came, and a cry of surprise escaped his lips, as he saw the figure of a man, making his way through the branches in front of him.

Wondering who it could be, the boy retained his position, and in a few moments a tall man, with heavily bearded face, and attired in well-worn garments, stood before him.

Over his shoulder and across his breast, was a broad belt, attached to which was a large hunting knife, and in his hand he carried a gun, with a strap attached to it, for the purpose of slinging it over the shoulder.

Dropping the stock of the gun to the earth, he grasped the barrel by both hands, and leaning upon it he gazed intently at the recumbent youth.

He was a strange figure; his wild appearance, his heavy beard, moustache, and whiskers, torn habiliments gave to him the semblance of an escaped madman, than aught else.

It was Dancing Bill the harlequin.

He had been paying a visit to the underground passage, for the purpose of procuring the weapon which he had seen there on the night, he stole the packet, he had since sold to Gripe.

It was his intention to leave the country with the money the papers had fetched him, and proceed to the backwoods of America, where he believed he should be free from the fangs of justice and escape the penalty of his crime.

Hence it was that he had paid a visit to the cave to obtain the weapons he believed would be of so much service to him there.

For some time they stood gazing at each other in surprise.

There was something in the features of the man before him that caused a shudder to run through the frame of the youth.

He felt that the strange being who now gazed so intensely upon him was his enemy.

Suddenly the Boy Actor leapt to his feet.

He had recognised in that pale, wan face the features of the man who had struck him on the parade of Richardson's Show, and whom Charlie Evans had chastised for the cowardly deed.

Retreating a few paces, Harry exclaimed,—

"Dancing Bill, the harlequin!"

The man drew back with a start, and his hands tightened around the barrel of the gun.

"Oh!" he exclaimed, "now I know your face. You are the boy whom Charlie Evans brought to Richardson's?"

Harry answered not, but still retreated.

"Stay," said Dancing Bill, "I will not harm you. I was angry when I struck you. You have nothing now to fear."

Harry paused, but still looked suspiciously upon the man.

"Why are you here?" asked Bill. "I thought you were far away. Are you playing here, or are you at the fair?"

"At the fair," replied Harry.

"Is Charlie Evans there?" asked the harlequin.

"Yes."

"And Buskin Bob?"

"Yes."

"And my wife?" asked Bill, eagerly.

"Yes," replied the boy.

"Aha!" exclaimed Bill. "Here, boy," he added, advancing towards Harry, "what do you fear? I will not harm you."

But Harry retreated as Bill moved forward.

"Do you think I mean to blow your brains out?" asked Bill.

"I—I—don't know," answered Harry, tremulously.

"I tell you I will not harm you," said the harlequin, in a softer tone of voice.

And as he spoke he threw the gun to the earth.

"Come here," he said. "You say Margaret, my wife, is at the fair?"

"Yes," replied the boy.

"In whose booth," asked the harlequin.

"In mine."

"In your's?" said Bill.

"Yes—Charlie Evans's," said the Boy Actor.

"Ah! has Charlie got a booth?" said Bill.

"Yes."

"What is she doing?" asked the harlequin.

"She ain't done nothing yet," replied the youth.

"When did she join?"

"Last night."

"What will she do to-day?" said the harlequin.

"Dance."

"Have you been to any other fairs?" asked Bill.

"Yes—one."

"Was she there, too."

"No."

"Where was she?"

"In the hospital."

"What was the matter with her," inquired Bill.

"She was ill."

"I don't suppose she was well, or she wouldn't have been there," replied the man.

"No; she was very ill," said the Boy Actor.

"She is better now, I suppose?" said the harlequin.

"Yes, but far from well," replied the youth.

"Look here; I wish to see her," said Bill.

The boy made no answer.

He only hoped that Bill would not come to the booth.

He had no need to fear that he would.

He had not forgotten the reward of his cruelty, and had no wish to encounter Charlie Evans.

"I wish to see her," he continued. "Will you carry a message to her for me?"

THE PROCESSION AT COVENTRY.

"Yes."

"And not mention to any one else that you have seen me?" said Bill.

"Not to Charlie?"

"No."

"Nor Buskin Bob?"

"No."

"Nor little Mary?"

"No."

"Why not?" asked the boy.

"Because—"

"Because what?"

"Because I do not want anyone to know that I am in this part of the world."

"Why not?"

"No matter," replied Bill, "I have good reasons."

"You have not done anything wrong, have you?" asked Harry.

"Wrong! what wrong?" exclaimed Bill, turning a shade paler.

"Well, I don't know," said Harry, innocently. "Only it seems strange not to wish anybody to know where you are."

No. 18.

Dancing Bill fixed his eye upon the boy's face, as if he would read his thoughts.

Did that boy suspect him!

Did the stain of blood rest upon his hands.

Could he detect the hand of Cain upon his brow.

But the unmoved countenance of the youth assured him that he knew nothing, and he said,—

"I have reasons for not wishing anyone but my wife knowing where I am at present. Will you take a message to her for me?"

"Yes."

"And to her only."

"Yes; if there is no harm in it," said Harry."

"None."

"Then I will do it."

"You are not deceiving me?" said the harlequin.

"No."

Bill looked fixedly at him.

The boy's face was immoveable.

There was nothing there to lead the harlequin to believe that he would do other than he promised.

"Listen," he said.

The boy drew nearer.

"Tell Margaret you have seen me," said Bill.

"I will."

"And tell her that I would see her."

"Yes."

"To-night."

"Where."

"Here."

"Here!" said the boy.

"Yes, here. Tell her that I am going away, and that I would see her ere I go. She must come alone. I will not harm her, but I must see her. At one o'clock I will be here, and if she comes not, she will never see me again; tell her that."

"I will."

"You will not fail?"

"No."

"Now, boy, that blow I struck you was done in anger. Forget it, and do as you have promised me; but not to another soul whisper that you have seen me. Good-bye!"

And as the harlequin gave utterance to the last words, he raised the gun from the ground and disappeared in the little wood.

Harry stood gazing in the direction of where Bill had vanished from his sight, till he felt the pressure of a hand upon his shoulder, and turning, saw Mary at his side.

"Come," she said, "we must make haste back, or we shall have no time to dress."

Without a word, Harry took her hand in his, and slowly walked across the field towards the highroad which led to the green on which the fair was held.

CHAPTER LXXIII

THE BOY ACTOR DELIVERS HIS MESSAGE TO MARGARET—THE SUFFERINGS OF THE POOR COLUMBINE.

BACK to the booth, hand in hand, went Harry and his young companion.

Wondering in his mind whether or not to mention to Charlie and Buskin Bob his meeting with the harlequin, he fell into a train of thought from which the remarks of his young companion almost failed to arouse him.

The pantomimists had retired to make up when the young players arrived at the caravan, so Harry and Mary went immediately to their respective dressing apartments, and in his anxiety to prevent his friends having to wait for him, he forgot to mention the affair to Margaret, till the circumstance again occurred to his mind, when he met her on the little stage after the first house had commenced.

But immediately the curtain fell, and little Mary had gone on to the parade, Harry followed the poor columbine to the dressing-room.

"Mrs. Simmons," he said, "I have got something to tell you."

The poor woman turned to him with a smile, expecting only some childish remark.

"Well, what is it Harry?" she inquired.

"Now guess," said the boy.

"I cannot."

"You will be so surprised," continued the youth.

"Shall I?"

"Yes."

"Well, tell me then what it is," said Margaret.

"I've seen him."

"Who?"

"Can't you guess."

"No, indeed I cannot."

"Why, Dancing Bill," exclaimed the boy.

"My husband," she gasped, turning deadly pale, and grasping the panneling of the wall for support.

"Yes," replied the youth, "but why are you so pale, are you ill again. I'll go and tell father or Buskin Bob to come to you, you are ill; you tremble so and are so very white."

And the boy stepped towards the door with the intention of summoning some one to her assistance.

"No, no," exclaimed Margaret, hurriedly, starting forward and laying her hand upon the arm of the Boy Actor, "do not go. I—I am better, better now."

"Do let me go and tell father," he said. "He will be sure to come, and perhaps he can send for something to do you good."

"I am better now," she repeated. "I am not very strong yet, Harry, that's all—that's all."

And the poor woman cast her eyes to the floor to hide the look of anguish which passed across her face, at being compelled to lie to a child.

Harry stood irresolute whether to go or stay.

"Where, where did you see him?" she said, eagerly.

"In the little wood in the field past the church at Barnstable," replied the boy.

"Did he see you?" she asked, quickly, and looking intently in the boy's eyes.

"Yes," replied Harry.

"Did he recognise you?" she inquired, in the same eager tone of voice.

"Yes."

"And Mary?"

"Oh, no. Mary had run away from me for something, and left me awaiting her return beside the little wood, when all of a sudden I heard somebody getting through the branches, and I turned round and saw Dancing Bill right before me. At first I did not know him, he had got such a long beard and was so ragged, but he knew me in a minute, and spoke to me."

"What did he say?" asked the woman, bending over the youth, and speaking only in a whisper.

"He asked where you was," replied the youth.

"Yes, yes."

"And I told him."

"Told him!" gasped Margaret.

"Yes. Told him that you was with us," replied the youth.

"Well."

"He said he must see you," remarked the boy.

"He did?"

"Yes, Margaret, he made me promise him that I would tell you and you only, that I had seen him, and that he must see you, as he was going a very long way off."

"Where?"

"He did not say where. He only said he was going away and must see you before he went. He told me to say he would meet you to-night after the fair was closed."

"Meet me!" exclaimed Margaret.

"Yes."

"Where?"

"At the wood in the field," replied the boy.

Margaret sank upon a seat with a deep sigh.

"He said you need not fear for he would not harm you, only he must see you, if only for a minute, before he went away."

"Have you said anything to Charlie or Bob about this?" asked Margaret, after a long pause.

"Not a word," replied the youth.

"Do not—do not," she exclaimed.

"Why not," asked the youth, innocently.

"I—I cannot tell you now. Some day you will know why, but do not ask me, Harry; do not ask me now. Say not a word to anyone that you have seen him, if you would not make me wretched."

"I won't make you wretched, Margaret," replied the youth. "I won't tell any one, upon my word, I won't."

Margaret threw her arms round the neck of the youth, and imprinted a kiss upon his cheek.

"Thank you," she said, "thank you."

Harry could not but feel the arms of the woman tremble, and observe the cheek, as it pressed his own, cold and clammy.

Then, as the boy left the apartment to attend to his duties, poor Margaret sank down again upon her seat, and buried her face in her hands.

Hot scalding tears forced their way through her thin white fingers, and her whole frame shook with violent emotion.

"Would to God that one of us were dead," she muttered to herself; "would to heaven it were so! What should I do? As his wife, I should obey his desires; as a woman who would be true and just, I should spurn him. Shall I see him, and beg of him to fly the country, and in another land endeavour, by rectitude and prayer, to atone for the deeds he has committed in this? Shall I pity him, and grant his request? Or shall I stifle every feeling of love in my breast, tell him that I know he is a murderer, as well as incendiary, upbraid him with his villany and the disgrace he has heaped upon me, and denounce him as the assassin of my friend, the spoiler of all my hopes, the robber of my peace of mind for ever? Shall I hurl down upon him the overwhelming fury of the outraged laws, and give to justice her due? Alas! alas! I know not what to do. Conscience tells me that I should denounce him, but my heart prompts me to save the husband, the man who has so basely and deeply wronged and insulted me."

And the poor columbine rocked herself to and fro upon her seat in an agony of mind, to which the copious flood of tears could even give no relief.

Oh! for a friend to guide or advise her how to act.

Friends she knew she had, and good and noble ones, too, in Charlie and Buskin Bob, but she could not betray the life of her husband, even into their hands.

True, she had nearly done so to Charlie Evans, but now she feared to do that which she had previously resolved upon to ease her overburdened heart.

In this matter she felt she was alone in the world.

Surely fate had been unkind to her in revealing the guilty acts of her husband.

Deeds at which humanity must shudder, and the heart stand appalled.

Poor Margaret!

Her's had indeed been a hard fate.

Her existence had been one round of misery.

And black despair seemed hurrying her to an untimely death.

From her fearful sufferings she was aroused at last.

The bell rang for the curtain to ascend.

The second house was full.

Hurriedly bathing her tear-bedewed face, she tottered rather than walked from the room.

Struggling to repress the sobs which almost choked her, she hurried to the wings.

She must meet the upraised faces of smiling rows of happy persons.

She must summon to her own features a look of pleasure, whilst her heart was lacerated with pain.

She must wear a smile on the face, while her soul ached with misery.

Who can pourtray the sufferings of poor Margaret as she bounded on to the stage, amid the plaudits of the happy sight-seers?

Who can describe the depth of agony raging in her heart as she bowed to the audience?

No one.

Instead of smiles, would not tears have greeted her had that happy mass known what she felt?

And instead of calling her back to repeat the dance, would they not have rose in pity and left the booth in sorrow?

CHAPTER LXXIV.

CHARLIE EVANS RECEIVES A VISIT, AND THE BOY ACTOR AN OFFER—BUSKIN BOB AND THE CLOWN —AN INCITEMENT TO WALK UP.

IT was towards evening.

The "houses" began to fill up, and Charlie

Evans was using all his endeavours to prevail upon the mob assembled in front of the booth to "walk up," that a middle-aged, gentlemanly-looking man mounted the steps, and, standing at the back of the parade, seemed rather anxious to catch the eye of our old friend the clown.

But he had to wait some time ere he could effect this, Charlie being too much engaged in beating the gong, and extolling the wonders of his caravan.

But at length, finding all attempts fruitless to prevail upon more to walk up, he turned to give the order to begin inside.

As he did so, the gentleman placed his hand upon his arm.

"Are you the proprietor of this booth?" he asked.

Charlie was about to reply in the affirmative, but hesitated a moment, then answered,—

"I am the manager, sir."

"That will do as well, I have no doubt; when you are at liberty for a moment, I should be glad to speak with you."

"You shall not have to wait long for an opportunity," replied Charlie. "In a minute I will wait upon you."

And pulling aside the canvas, he gave the necessary order for the entertainment to commence, and returned to the stranger's side.

"Now, sir, I am at liberty for ten minutes," he said, as he stepped back into a corner of the booth, alike free from observation and hearing.

"Well, sir, you will no doubt think my application strange, but the fact is, I am passionately fond of the drama, and all my family seem to be equally so. My son and daughter, together with several young friends, have been laying their heads together to get up a theatrical entertainment at home, and as I do not like to thwart young folks in their amusements, so long as they do not tend to corrupt the morals, I have given them my full consent; but a difficulty has arisen at almost the last moment. A young lady and gentleman, children of a neighbour of mine, have unfortunately met with a domestic bereavement, and are unable to sustain the parts they selected for themselves. This has caused no little pain and annoyance to the others; and as I should be sorry that their hopes should be disappointed, I resolved to pay a visit to the fair to-day, and endeavour to find two young people who would undertake to fill the gap, and prevent a disappointment to the young minds. Two such children I have seen upon your show, and if you are willing, and can induce them to sustain the characters, for I am well aware that travelling players often combine Thespian with other pursuits, I shall be glad to reward them generously for their labours, and consider a favour conferred upon me in the bargain."

Charlie listened patiently, and a gratified smile broke over his face.

He was happy to think that Harry and Mary had attracted the notice of one who, if an enthusiast, appeared likewise a gentleman, and one disposed to act liberally.

Still, Charlie Evans was not the man to take advantage of a generous offer, without first candidly stating the merits or demerits of the article for which the offer was made.

"I feel flattered, sir," he said, "that you should have selected the two young persons in my booth, the more so as I am the guardian of the boy, and the father of the girl; but I feel it a duty I owe alike to myself as well as to you, to state that you can form no opinion of their abilities to play a part by what you have seen them do on this parade, and I should be sorry to jump at your kind offer without saying that they may fail, and you would only be disappointed, and regret you had ever sought their assistance."

"That's candid," replied the gentleman, "and I respect you for it, as it convinces me I am speaking to an honourable man."

Charlie bowed.

"Though, understand me, I am not one of those who profess to believe the strolling player nothing better than a rogue and a vagabond, and only seek his aid to further my own schemes. Nothing of the kind. I admire the strolling player, sir, the man who can teach a lesson from a barn, and read a moral in a booth. I am satisfied that the young people I saw here are not likely to break down for want of confidence, and no one with any grain of sense can expect a child to play a part equal to a long practised man."

"What is the piece that has been selected by your young friends, sir?" asked Charlie.

"Well, they have decided upon playing a farce, for which the characters are all filled; but the last two acts of Othello has also been studied; but unfortunately Othello and Desdemona cannot play their parts, and the others are hurt to tears at not being able to go through theirs, after having learnt and practised them for some days past. Poor little things, it is hard they should be disappointed; we should minister to their joys when young, they will find sorrow enough to contend with in riper years; unless they escape the fate designed for us all."

"There spoke a man and a christian," thought Charlie.

For it brought to his mind his own happy childhood, and the after-life Struggles for Bread.

"My motto," continued the gentleman "is, 'chase the tear with a smile from the face of a child,' and, sir, I trust that you will be willing to assist me in doing so, by permitting, if the young people have no objection, your ward and daughter to fill the parts I have mentioned."

"May I ask, sir, when you would require their services?" asked Charlie.

"Their favours, sir," interrupted the gentleman.

"As you please," said Charlie, with a smile.

"The evening after to-morrow," replied the applicant.

Charlie paused thoughtfully.

"So soon," he said.

"That is the night on which the young people have fixed," replied the gentleman.

"You see, sir," said Charlie, anxious that Harry and Mary should fill the parts, yet fearful of overtaxing their strength, which already with their arduous duties was sorely tried, "there is still another day's fair, and the young folks are so fully occupied that I cannot see how they can possibly learn their parts in time."

A shade of disappointment passed over the face of the gentleman.

"It would be hard," he said, "to tax them too much; already their duties are too arduous for so young people."

"True, sir," said Charlie, "but in our Struggle for Bread, we are often compelled to sacrifice rest or comfort to obtain it."

"I am sorry, very sorry," said the gentleman, "I wish it was a day or two later, but the young folks are all invited, and looking forward eagerly, no doubt, to the treat. But still, it cannot be helped, and better perhaps that they be disappointed, than these poor children sacrifice the few hours of rest to their amusement."

"I am sorry, sir," said Charlie, "that it is to take place so soon. I am sure they would be as happy to oblige you as I should."

"I am sure you would," said the gentleman, "but you have a duty to perform, and I am convinced that you are one who will perform it, spite of any tempting offer. But," added the gentleman, suddenly, "suppose they read their parts, instead of learning them, could they do that?"

"Yes," said Charlie, "if you would be satisfied with that, for that would entail no extra labour on them."

"Then let it be so," said the other. "It may not look so well, but it will save the others from losing that on which they have set their minds."

"I am sure they will be willing to do that," said Charlie.

"Then I may depend upon them, you think."

"No, sir, I am sure," replied the clown.

"And the young folks will have no objection?"

"None, sir; they are only too happy to do anything which they believe will please me," replied the clown.

"I am glad to hear it," said the gentleman, "for it proves that you study them all in your power, that you win their love and respect by kindness and affection."

"There is one thing," said Charlie, "which had not entered my mind till now."

"What is that?"

"In our wardrobe, we do not possess a dress fit for the parts," replied the clown.

"No matter, it will not be required," said the other. "Since dresses are provided for all."

Thrusting his hand into his breast-coat pocket, the gentleman drew forth his card-case, and extracting a card therefrom, he placed it in the hands of the clown.

"Send them there, sir, in their walking apparel," he said, "and they will find everything they may require for the character. Now, I have detained you too long, so will take my leave, and bear home to those who are anxiously waiting my return, the cheering news that I have succeeded in finding some one to fill the parts, and that their pleasure will not be foiled by the absence of their sorrowing friends."

And extending his hand to Charlie, the gentleman ran down the steps, with a smile on his face and joy at his heart.

For some time Charlie Evans stood on the edge of the parade, gazing after the retreating form of his visitor, as he made his way through the mob which stood gazing up at Buskin Bob, as he went through his hankey-pankey performances, as he himself styled them, on the parade.

"A good man that," muttered Charlie to himself, "and a christian to boot; it ain't everyone as would take so much trouble to minister to the gratification of children; but, there, he has got a heart, he has, and that's more than a good many have in this world."

Buskin Bob had caught the last ball in his hand, made his bow to the gaping rustics, and now made his way to the side of his friend, Charlie Evans.

"Are you counting how many people there are in the fair and wishing they'd all walk up," said Bob.

"No," said Charlie, starting from the reverie into which he had fallen and stepping backwards from the front of the parade, "I was watching that gentleman."

"Strike me comical if you ain't been having a long chow with him," said Bob; "who is he."

"A man," replied the clown.

"Well, I didn't think he was a woman," said Bob.

"Yes, Bob," said Charlie, "a man and a Christian."

"Strike me comical, then," exclaimed Bob, "if I shouldn't have liked to take his portrait. It ain't often you get a glimpse of those kind of things now-a-days."

"No, indeed," replied the clown with a sigh. "There are little Christianity in men of the present time. Every one seems as if he would place his foot upon the neck of his fellow, and raise himself up by trampling on the prostrate body of his brother."

"Strike me comical, Charlie, cut it," said Bob; "you are getting into your sentimental fit again. It was a great mistake you didn't study for a preacher, instead of a clown. But, there, strike me comical if I don't think you'd have spoiled their trade."

"Why?" said Charlie, with a smile.

"Because, Charlie my boy," answered Buskin Bob, "I believe you would have practised what you professed, not professed what you did not practise."

"What's that?" asked Charlie.

"Chrstian charity and goodwill to all men," replied Bob, "that's what your mealy-mouthed, white chokered fellows don't feel for us. Strike me comical if they wouldn't trample us under their feet, if they dared!"

"Ay, indeed," said Charlie, with a sigh; "they who boast the most of their good qualities, seldom possess any; the true Christian is he who strives to make others happy, and feels a pleasure in doing so, and such a man, Bob, was he with whom I have just been speaking."

"Was he, now?"

"Yes he was."

"Then strike me comical," said Bob, "tell us all about it."

"To be sure I will," said Charlie, "you and I, Bob, have no secrets."

"Strike me comical, no," said Bob. "Do you know why that is?"

"Because we can trust each other," replied the clown.

"Yes," said Bob; "because we know what it is to Struggle for Bread, and find even in our darkest moments, a friend at our side."

"No, no, Charlie, you and I have no secrets. We have toiled together, and starved together, and the crust that could be obtained by the one has always been shared with the other. Strike me comical, if I don't think it would have choked us if we had swallowed it all and not given the others a bit!''

"It would, Bob—it would," exclaimed Charlie, shaking his friend warmly by the hand. "But brighter days seem dawning upon us; but whether we rise or fall we will stand side by side in our Struggles for Bread."

"We will, Charlie, we will; if we don't, strike me comical, there!" said Bob, emphatically, as he hurled a gilt ball high up into the air, and caught it in a leathern cup fastened to his forehead.

"Wait till I strike up the gong, Bob," said the clown, and do a little patter, and then I'll tell you what it was that gentleman wanted with me."

"All right," said Bob, getting up his tools, as he called his juggling properties, and going to the back of the parade so as to give a clear space for little Mary, whose turn it next was to come on and go through her performance on the parade.

Charlie sounded the gong loudly, and advancing to the edge of the parade, commenced bawling out at the top of his voice,—

"Walk up, ladies and gentlemen, the best booth in the fair, the only show where can be seen the wonder of day, the Infant Venus, acknowledged by all who have seen her to be the greatest prodigy of the times, including the Lord Chancellor, the Lord Mayor, and all the crowned heads of Europe; also the wonderful and truly astonishing India-rubber backed Brothers Tumblini, whose feats have astonished all beholders. Walk up, ladies and gentlemen, and see these wonderful and surprising boneless brothers, who puzzled the whole medical fraternity, and have sold their bodies to a celebrated anatomist for a thousand pounds, in order that he may confer upon that professionable and much respected body a great boon, and reveal to the public in general the secret of their formation. Also the talented Simonsi, from the Opera House in Paris, where she was offered a considerable sum to prolong her engagement, but declined, on the advice of the Emperor's physician, to proceed to England for the benefit of her health, which has now been thoroughly established by our glorious climate. Walk up, walk up, we are just a-going to begin. If you go away from the fair without paying us a visit, you will never forgive yourselves, when you hear from your friends the character of the entertainment we offer you for the low charge of twopence! I will not allow you to be disappointed in only seeing a portion of the performance, so, while you are getting your money ready, I will summon the Infant Venus to go through a few steps on the parade. Walk up, ladies and gentlemen, the price is only twopence."

And inflicting two or three blows upon the gong, Charlie Evans retired to where Buskin Bob stood grinning at the further end of the parade, as Mary, full of smiles, dashed through the canvas, and pirouetted around before the assembled people.

CHAPTER LXXV.

WAVERING AND INDECISION—MARGARET RESOLVES TO MEET HER HUSBAND—DOUBTS OF BUSKIN BOB.

THE last house was over, and Charlie Evans, as was his wont, had returned thanks for the patronage he had received, and solicited the favours of the generous British public for the morrow.

The curtain was rung down, and the players, wearied with the arduous toil of the day, retired to their rooms to rid themselves of their "props," and don their ordinary attire, previous to sitting down to their frugal supper.

Margaret was sad and wretched.

Wavering and undecided how to act, she paced the little dressing-room to and fro for long after Mary had left it to join her father and his friend.

"What shall I do? what shall I do?" she kept muttering to herself.

Then she placed her bonnet on, with the intention of granting her husband's request.

"But then," she thought, "perhaps he meant some act of violence towards her."

And she took off her bonnet and laid it aside, determined to pay no heed to the request of her guilty husband.

Might he not only seek her destruction?

Was it not her life he had sought upon the night of the storm, when he dogged the footsteps of the woman he believed to be herself along the high-road from Tottenham?

It must have been, or why was he there?

He knew not that the poor murdered woman had undertaken the duties of his wife on that fatal night; and besides, there was an absence of motive towards her.

But to his wife he bore ill-will.

She held him in her power.

A word from her could have consigned him to a felon's doom, and he sought to destroy her hold upon him.

Might he not still fear that she would betray him to Charlie, and wish to prevent her doing so by encompassing her destruction?

She did not think he was aware that she had the least suspicion or knowledge that it was him who had assassinated her friend, still he was aware that she knew it was his hand that fired the Royal Star, and would he not expect the woman he had so basely treated, to denounce him to those he sought to ruin, especially when they extended to her the hand of friendship and protection.

She dreaded to go, lest she encountered his violence; she wished to meet him, and beg of him to fly the country, ere the strong arm of the law was laid upon his shoulders.

Thus, a prey to conflicting thoughts, she sat down, and rocked herself to and fro.

"He knows where to find me," she murmured, "and if I go not to him, may he not come to me."

This, above all things, she would wish to avoid.

She would not have the poor but honest shelter of the kind-hearted pantomimist's, degraded and polluted by the presence of a murderer.

To avoid such a circumstance, she must go to

the little wood, where Dancing Bill had been seen by young Harry in the morning.

Go to meet the destroyer of her happiness, the murderer of her friend.

Again she placed on her bonnet, and threw her thin shawl across her shoulders, and prepared to start on her wretched journey.

But again she paused.

Would not her kind friends think it strange that she should wish to leave the caravan in which they had made everything as comfortable as possible for her to remain.

What excuse could she make to them for going away at that hour.

Whilst she thus stood perplexing her brain for some excuse for her conduct, Buskin Bob arrived at the half open door of the dressing room.

"Margaret," he exclaimed, "supper is waiting. Why, strike me comical if you ain't as pale as if you had made up for a ghost. What's the matter? And what have you got your bonnet and shawl on for? Surely you don't think of leaving the booth to-night? You are not well enough yet, to do so much work as you have done to-day. It's enough to kill you, your strength ain't equal to it. Perhaps a breath of air might do you good in the day time, but it will do you harm at night. The dews are falling heavily. Take my advice, don't go out to-night, but come and have a nice little bit of supper and perhaps you'll be better after it; you have worked too hard you have, much too hard, and you shan't do it to-morrow. I'll do a few extra tricks to lighten your labours, strike me comical I will, there!"

Poor Margaret! a look of gratitude spread over her sorrowful countenance, and a faint smile lit up her pale cheek at the good-natured resolve of Buskin Bob.

But it died away instantly, as she felt the necessity of complying with the desire of her husband.

"Thank you, Bob," she said, extending her hand to the pantaloon. "I am sure I can never be grateful enough to you and Charlie, for the kindness you have already shown me. I am not well. I could not eat any supper, and I think a walk would do me good."

"Not to-night, Margaret, not to-night," said Bob.

"Yes, Bob, to-night. I should like to go to-night," she said, sorrowfully.

"Why, Margaret?" he asked.

"I—I don't know," she stammered confusedly.

"Well," said Bob after a pause, "as you like. But let me go with you. There are many drunken fellows about now, and you may be molested."

Margaret shook her head.

"They will not harm me, Bob," she said. "I have been out by myself at later hours than this too often, not to be easy by myself."

"Yes, yes," said Bob, "but if Bill left you to go by yourself, that's no reason that I should."

"No, Bob, you get your supper, and rest yourself, you are too tired," said Margaret.

"Tired," said Bob. "Why, strike me comical, if I was thrice as tired as I am, I should be only too happy to be by your side, wherever you wished to go."

"Bob!" said Margaret,

Buskin Bob, dropped his eyes to the ground.

He had unintentionally revealed to Margaret an affection for her, stronger than ordinary friendship. But the look of surprise in the eyes of the columbine, led him to think that he had overstepped the bonds of propriety, in thus addressing the wife of another.

Margaret, with a woman's, tact, saw in a moment the confusion under which the pantaloon laboured, and she hastened to remove it.

"Bob," she said, "I feel your kind heart would prompt you to do anything for me, whom you believe weak and ill. But I will go alone. Excuse my absence to Charlie, and tell him I will be back if possible, in an hour."

"As you please, Margaret," said Bob; "but take care of yourself, don't go too far. If anything was to happen to you, I—I, oh, strike me comical."

And Bob turned away to hide the confusion he felt, at almost again giving vent to words that might have pained the poor heart-broken columbine.

With a tottering step, Margaret left the dressing-room, and made her way out of the booth into the now deserted fair field.

Buskin Bob stood thoughtfully for some moments gazing after her, then turned to join his friend.

"Strike me comical," he muttered, "if I don't think it is something more than a walk that takes her out at this hour. I don't like that pale face and trembling limbs. There's something more in it than I can tumble to. She ain't all right yet; that fever has left something behind, or I am much mistaken. How wild and abstracted she appeared during the day. Ah," he added, suddenly, "strike me comical, she can't be tired of her life, and intend to commit suicide; poor thing, she has suffered enough to make her do it, but she has too much sense to contemplate such a deed, and yet she has been out of her mind, and may be even now. I don't like the thought of this walk, strike me comical if I do. I must see to it. I will follow her unseen, and if she attempt such a deed, the hand of Buskin Bob shall save her from it; strike me comical if it shan't—there!"

And darting hurriedly from the booth, by the same way as Margaret had taken her departure, the good-hearted fellow hurried across the fair-field in the direction taken by the columbine.

During the meantime, Charlie Evans, the Boy Actor, and little Mary, had assembled in the apartment of the caravan devoted to a sort of sitting and dining-room, and were anxiously awaiting the arrival of Bob and Margaret, to share the humble meal, which was spread out on a little table before them.

"Harry," said the clown, "a gentleman has been here to-day to ask me to allow you and Mary to play the parts of Othello and Desdemona, in a private performance at his house. The piece will be represented entirely by young people, and as it is to take place the day after to-morrow, I consented to allow you both to go."

"The day after to-morrow," said Harry; "I don't think I could learn it by then."

"It is only the last two acts, and if you like you can both read your parts, instead of learning them."

"I should like to learn mine," said Mary, "it spoils the piece to read it."

"And I should like to learn mine, too," said

the boy. "I have read the play and seen it acted, and I think we could learn the lines of the last two acts in time."

"Well, that you will please yourselves about," said the clown. "You have no need to do so if you have not time."

"Oh, we will learn it, won't we Mary?" said Harry.

"Yes," replied Mary. "But where is it to be?"

"A short distance from here, at a gentleman's house," replied the clown. "I should have hesitated to accept the engagement for you, but that I believe the person who sought your services to be a thorough gentleman, and one who will reward you liberally."

"That don't matter to us, father," said the Boy Actor. "If you wish us to go, we shall only be too happy to comply."

"I know that, Harry; hence, the reason I did not speak to you or Mary about it at the time."

"There was no need, father," said Mary, "for you would not, I am sure, desire us to do anything which you was not well assured would please us both."

"No, Mary, I would not," said the clown, firmly. "But at the same time I could not help feeling that you would be too much overtaxed if you were to learn the part, so the gentleman was quite willing that you should read them instead, rather than that the children invited should be disappointed."

"But how about a dress, father," asked Harry.

"They are provided. So you have nothing to do but to carry your parts with you, and endeavour to do your best to amuse and give satisfaction. You know what Shakespeare says, Harry,—

' There is a tide in the affairs of man,
  Which—taken at the flood, leads on to fortune.'

and who knows, Harry, but that this gentleman may stand your friend at some future time."

"I shall do my best, father," said the Boy Actor, "and so will Mary, I know, to merit the good opinion of anyone whom you believe worthy of respect."

"Nobly spoken, my boy,," said Charlie. "Always make it your aim to merit the good opinion of mankind, and depend upon it, that whether good or bad fortune attend your footsteps through life, you will ever be respected, honoured, and esteemed."

"I will," said Harry, "if only for your sake."

"Do so likewise for your own," said Charlie; "for a man can have no better inheritance than a clear conscience and a good name. Now let us to supper. Wherever can Margaret and Bob be? Just run and ask them if they are going to stop away all night?"

Harry leapt up from his seat to obey the wishes of the clown, and in another minute returned, saying,—

"I can't find them anywhere, father."

"Strange," said Charlie. "But we will get our supper, and no doubt they will soon return."

CHAPTER LXXVI.

THE MEETING OF THE HARLEQUIN AND COLUMBINE—THE ATTEMPTED MURDER—A TIMELY RESCUE.

IT was not long ere Buskin Bob came in sight of the columbine, as she wended her way along, on her sad and painful errand.

Keeping within shadow of the high hedge, which divided the high road from the fields on either side, Bob stepped cautiously along in the wake of Margaret.

The columbine, all unsuspecting of the vicinity of a watcher, kept on her way.

Her eyes were bent upon the ground, and her sight ever and anon dimmed by tears, whilst sighs broke from her breast as she thought of the crimes of him she now hurried on to meet.

A shudder ran through her frame as she passed the spot where Dick the Poacher had interfered to save her from her husband's violence, and basely as he had used her, she wished that she stood there by his side now, and the stain of blood not been on his soul.

She felt that she could, and would again submit to his brutality, if by so doing, she could remove that fearful crime from his shoulders.

But, alas, that could never be; and she pursued her way in an agony of mind better to be imagined than described.

On, on she went, past the little ale-house where she and her husband had lodged, past the church in whose enclosure lie mouldering the remains of her who gave birth to the Boy Actor, and following at a short distance behind her, went Buskin Bob.

She gained the lane and entered the field, and stealthily the pantaloon hung upon her footsteps.

Across the field with tottering steps, Margaret made her way to the clump of trees which hid the secret entrance to the underground passage.

And cautiously Bob glided on behind her.

She reached the little wood and paused.

Bob waited his opportunity, and as she turned for a moment and gazed towards the high road, the pantaloon darted forward, and concealed himself in the bushes.

But if he had hidden himself from Margaret, she was fully exposed to his gaze.

For some minutes Margaret looked anxiously around her, as if in search of some one, and Bob never for a moment allowed his eye to wander from her form.

Suddenly he heard a rustling amid the trees in whose shadow he stood, and saw the form of a man break through the enclosure and stand before Margaret.

"You have come," said the man.

"I have," replied Margaret. "Why have you sent for me, Bill?"

Buskin Bob started at the sound of the name Margaret uttered.

He ground his teeth, and clenched his hands.

He feared, he knew not what, and stood ready for the spring.

"It is well that you have done so," said the man.

"Why?" asked Margaret.

"Because I had resolved to see you, Margaret, ere I left England for ever," he replied.

A SCENE FROM A NAUTICAL PLAY.

"What do you want of me?" asked the columbine.

"To tell you you are my wife, my true and lawful wife," said the harlequin.

"Alas! too well I know it," replied the columbine, sadly.

"To remind you of a wife's duty," said the harlequin.

"That I have ever done," she replied.

"You have left me," he said. "Did you not mean to cling to me till death?" he asked.

"Bill, Bill," exclaimed Margaret, "to you I have been a true and loving wife. At your hands I have suffered indignities which would have broken the heart of the most callous. I suffered till I could suffer no longer, and I left you."

"Yes; but not of your own free will," he said.

"It was," she replied.

"I say it was not!" he exclaimed almost brutally.

"Of whose, then?" she asked.

"Of whose?" he iterated.

"Aye, of whose?"

"Of those accursed people with whom you now are," he replied. "Of Charlie Evans and Buskin Bob."

"'Tis false," she exclaimed.

"'Tis true," he replied.

"It is as vile a lie as ever was uttered," said Margaret.

"Why, then, did you go?" said the harlequin.

"Your cruelty drove me from you," she replied.

"Enough, I have thought better of that now

You need not feel afraid that I will harm you any more," he said.

Margaret sighed.

"Margaret," he said, "I have resolved to leave this country and seek a home in America. I swear to be a better man. Leave those people and join me."

Margaret recoiled before him.

"Never!" she exclaimed.

"Never?" he repeated, surlily.

"Never!" she continued. "The last tie between us is broken. Go, in heaven's name, go! Fly from the scenes of your wickedness, and in another land make atonement for the fearful crimes you have committed in this."

"I cannot go alone, Margaret; you must accompany me."

"No," she replied firmly. "I cannot, will not accompany one whose soul is stained as your's is with crime."

"What mean you?"

"Too well you know," she replied, meaningly.

"The fire?" he said.

"Yes," she replied.

"They were my enemies, and I but had revenge upon them," he exclaimed.

"Enough," said Margaret, "I heard that you intended to leave England, and I obeyed your wish to see you ere you went, so that I might implore you to pray for your sins; to seek salvation by acts of religion; and endeavour by leading a better life, to atone for the crimes your guilty hand has perpetrated."

"All this will I do, Margaret," he replied, "if you will come with me."

"No, I cannot."

"Why not?"

"Have you not disgraced me," she asked; "have you not blighted my happiness for ever; have you not made life a burden to me."

"Pshaw!" he exclaimed, testily. "You are like some romantic school girl. I admit that revenge prompted me to fire the house, but it was saved, and there is little harm done."

"That is not all," said Margaret. "Black as was that deed, there is yet one more fearful."

Dancing Bill started and trembled.

"What?" he gasped.

"Ask your own heart," she said.

"I—I know not what you mean. I can recollect nothing else," he gasped.

"Liar!" hissed Margaret. "Oh, man, man, how have you fallen; into what sin has not your evil passions led you. Never can you forget your crimes, never! never! Sleeping and waking, it is ever present to your mind. The blood of your victim calls aloud for vengeance upon her murderer. See, the stain of blood is on your hand; the brand of Cain upon your brow. Oh, Bill, Bill, my heart bleeds with agony as I think of the fearful deed you have committed, of a deed that will sooner or later consign you to the gallows—me to a life of misery and despair."

"Margaret," he hissed. "It's a lie! it's a lie! I did not slay her."

"It is true. Your coward hand was raised not against her life, but mine; would that your guilty steel had found the sheath intended for it; but in the darkness of the night and amid the warring of the elements you mistook your mark and slew my friend."

"'Tis false," he gasped; "believe it not, Margaret! believe it not!"

"It is true, true as heaven!" she exclaimed. "You have escaped; but the bloodhounds of the law are now on your track."

"They, they have no proof that I did the deed."

"They have," said Margaret. "In the hands of your murdered victim was grasped the proof of your guilt—the evidence of her murderer!"

"What? what?" he gasped.

"The wig, torn from your head in the struggle for life—worn by you on the night of the murder."

"Ah!" gasped the harlequin, starting back in terror. "But—but no one knows it belonged to me."

"Yes—one."

"Who?"

"The woman you have consigned to a life of misery," said Margaret. "Your broken-hearted wife."

Bill sprang forward and caught her by the arm.

"Margaret?" he hissed, "would you betray me."

"Bill," she said, "did you ever spare me."

"Speak! speak!" he exclaimed, in an excited tone.

"Touch me not," she said; "take your hand from me, for it is stained with blood."

"Answer me!" he exclaimed. "Swear you will not betray me."

"I will not swear," she answered firmly.

"Margaret, you hold my life in your hands. I would not have your blood upon my soul, but I will protect my liberty even at the sacrifice of your life. Down on your knees and swear never to betray me."

"I will not swear," she said. "Heaven will work out its own ends, and justice, if she now slumbers, will yet awake. Go, leave me, repent if you can!"

"Margaret, I am a desperate man. Swear never to divulge to whom that wig belonged. Swear, never by act, or deed, or word to intimate that you know who was the murderer of that woman."

"Ah!" said Margaret, "then your own tongue confesses your guilt."

"No matter!" he exclaimed. "Will you swear never to betray me?"

"No!" she exclaimed, "I will not."

"Then, by hell, your tongue shall be silenced for ever. I can but die once; if there be blood upon my hands I cannot stain them more. I cannot suffer more for two murders than I have done for one. I would spare you but you refuse to live—Die! then! . Thus do I destroy the fatal evidence."

"Help—help! Oh, God!" shrieked Margaret, as Bill drew the hunting knife from his side, and raised it above his head.

"Strike me comical, if you ain't the damndest villain I ever saw on or off the boards!" exclaimed Buskin Bob, darting from his concealment.

And with a heavy blow he struck the villain to the earth, as the knife fell harmless by the side of Margaret.

CHAPTER LVII.

THE PRIVATE PERFORMANCE—SUCCESS OF THE BOY ACTOR AND HIS COMPANION—AN UNEXPECTED REWARD.

DESPITE the arduous duties of the youthful players, the Boy Actor and little Mary set to work with a will to learn the parts assigned them for the private performance at the house of Mr. Hardy, the gentleman whom we have seen conversing with Charlie Evans on the parade of the show.

"Where there's a will there's a way," and as the will was good, the young people soon found the way to render themselves perfect in their parts, despite the little time which they could devote to the learning of them.

They knew that Charlie would be happy in their success, and they resolved to do all in their power to give satisfaction to those who had sought their aid, and bring credit upon themselves.

Together they studied, and together they rehearsed; and when the time came for them to start for the place where the performance was to be held, they were "letter perfect."

Charlie accompanied them as far as the house, and giving them a few words of encouragement and advice, left them to introduce themselves.

They were received by Mr. Hardy, and by that gentleman, introduced to his children and their friends, by whom they were ushered into their respective dressing-rooms, where they found everything ready for them.

Their arrival having been announced to the several guests, and the children anxious to begin their evenings entertainment, they all retired to the drawing-room to witness the farce which was to be performed, whilst Harry and Mary "made up" for the tragedy.

The drawing-room had been filled up as well as possible to represent the front and back of a theatre; the back portion of the house forming the stage, and the front, the place for the audience.

By means of coloured paper, the sides of the folding-doors were made to represent the proscenium, and so well had it been done, that but for the fact that audience and actors were on a level, it might have been taken for a veritable stage.

A piano and harp formed the band, and which were played by two of the elder ladies of the family.

When all was ready to commence, and the guests had taken their seats, instead of the curtain rising, the folding-doors opened, and this caused no little merriment, as it was somewhat a novelty in the stage.

However, the farce commenced, and the little actors made their entrances and their exits, perhaps not always at the right side, or the right time, but that mattered little; the generous British public, who, by the way, are often anything but generous to the poor players, in this case demanded not its shillings worth, and mistakes or failures passed current, and those who made the greatest blunders, received the most applause.

It seemed but to enhance the amusement of those present, to see a pretty, timid girl, suffused with blushes, walk on, laugh, place her hands over her face, and rush off again, without saying a word, and then at the urgent request of her fellow actors make another trial, which ended in a loud burst of laughter, and "I can't, really I can't," and once more dart away.

Again, the most unpardonable of all, the "stage waits," were forgiven, and instead of hisses and groans, only loud shouts of laughter reverberated among the guests, as some before anxious but now frightened amateur kept the stage waiting, whilst his fellow players endeavoured to force him on from behind the folding doors.

However, the farce went on, and at length came to a close, and if justice was not done to the author, he had no cause to be angry; on the contrary, he could feel gratified by the knowledge that he had ministered to the happiness of several young people and the amusement of old ones.

The little players had "fretted their hour upon the stage," and now hurried away, some to change their dress and take up their position with the audience; others to go and see how the professionals were getting on, whilst the two old ladies enchanted the senses of the assembled guests with the strains of music, till the folding-doors should once more open upon the scene, being prepared by the servants for the last two acts of "Othello."

Meantime, Harry and Mary had "made up" for their parts.

The dress which had been procured for the Boy Actor was indeed a gorgeous one. A frock of blue velvet, figured with silver lace, white pants, red velvet shoes, and red velvet cloak, which hung in graceful folds from his shoulders, whilst a band of velvet, studded with imitation jewels, encircled his brow.

In truth the youth looked noble in his attire; his tall, graceful figure was set off to the best advantage, and a smile of gratified pleasure overspread his handsome countenance as he viewed himself in the long glass between the windows of his dressing-room.

Never before had he worn such a dress; nothing so elegant in make or material had he yet met with; never before had he looked so well.

But suddenly he gave vent to a sigh.

He must colour his face for the part, might not that destroy to a certain extent his handsome appearance.

Fain would he have foregone this last touch in the "make up."

But he knew his character would not be perfect without it, so he turned to the toilet table for the colour.

But in vain he searched—no colour could he find.

Whilst standing and wondering what he had best do, he heard the door open behind him, and as he turned, a young gentleman entered the apartment to know if he was ready.

"All but the colour," replied the boy.

"What colour?" asked the youth.

"For my face."

"Why, you have a good colour enough," replied the youth. "Your cheeks are as rosy as the morn."

"Yes," said Harry; "but Othello is a Moor."

"True; but you never think of blacking your face?"

"It should be," replied the boy.

"On the stage it might, but not here. Why you would frighten us if you blacked your face."

"Oh, I don't mind playing the part as I am," said Harry.

"That's right—don't think of colouring. Shall I say you are ready?"

"Yes, replied Harry, not a little pleased at foregoing the colour.

As he stepped out upon the landing, he met little Mary.

A smile of pleasure broke over his face, so beautiful did she look, attired in a blue satin robe, with white satin petticoat and shoes.

But there was no time now to speak to each other on their appearance, and they followed the youth down to the room set apart for the stage, where, taking up their positions, they awaited the opening of the folding-doors.

With the impetuosity of youth, his fellow players instantly gave the order for this to be done.

This was done, and a solemn silence reigned among the guests, as each sat anxiously awaiting the appearance of the young professionals.

When Harry stepped on from the side to the centre of the room, and bowed his head gracefully to the assembled guests, it was evident that the ease and grace of his appearance was appreciated.

Weighing carefully every word, studying his points, acting without extravagance, he played his part.

So did little Mary, and it was evident that they had imprinted a favourable impression upon those assembled.

Violent outbursts of applause at such a place could scarcely be expected, yet if not loud it was fervent and generous.

But it deepened into murmurs of approbation when, in the last act, the boy stood before the bed.

"I would not send thy soul unshriven before its maker!"

So deep and solemn were the tones in which these words were uttered, that they caused a thrill to run through the veins of those who heard them, and a rapturous burst of applause greeted the last lines of the part, and continued some moments, after the graceful fall beside the bed on which Desdemona lay.

The piece was ended, and the folding-doors closed slowly upon the youthful actors, who had so well sustained their characters, and given the liveliest satisfaction to themselves and their patrons.

The Boy Actor and Mary retired to the rooms assigned them, and changed their dress, and when they again met on the landing, Mr. Hardy made his appearance, and invited them in the room which Harry had just left. He said,—

"Now, my young friends, first of all, let me tell you that you have afforded myself and guests much pleasure in the able way in which you have sustained your respective parts, and I thank you for your presence here this evening. As an earnest of my satisfaction and goodwill towards you, I beg you will accept this."

And the gentleman placed a sovereign in the hands of both Harry and Mary.

As Harry was about to thank him, he stopped him by saying,—

"You looked remarkably well in that dress, and I hope it pleased you."

"Indeed it did, sir," said Harry. "They were magnificent dresses."

"And did yours please you, miss?" he asked, turning to Mary.

"Yes," she replied. "It is the prettiest dress I have ever seen."

"Will you fetch it and let me look at it," he said.

"Yes, sir," answered Mary, leaving the room for that purpose, and returning in a moment with the articles.

Mr. Hardy took them in his hands and pretended to examine them minutely; then holding them towards her, he said,—

"I beg you will accept it, as a mark of my esteem for you."

"Accept it, sir," she said, in surprise.

"Yes, my dear. It may serve you to play the part in again."

And he forced the articles into her hands.

"Oh, sir, how can I thank you!" she exclaimed, her eyes lighting up with joy at the magnificent gift.

"Say no more about that," he said. "And now, sir, the dress you wore to-night is yours."

"Mine?" said Harry.

"Yes, yours; and I feel assured you will never dishonour it. Now let me once more thank you for the gratification you have caused us, and bid you good-bye. Though I doubt not, if heaven spare us all, it will not be the last time I shall see you, for I feel assured that you will yet carve for yourselves a name and fame in the dramatic world."

And shaking them both by the hand, he walked with them to the door. And with grateful hearts they both left the scene of their first public performance.

CHAPTER LXXVIII.

BUSKIN BOB AND THE COLUMBINE—THE REQUEST AT THE HEDGE—MARGARET RETURNS TO THE BOOTH.

HAD a thunderbolt fallen at the feet of Dancing Bill, the harlequin, he could not have felt more surprised and discomfitted than when he lay upon the earth, stretched there by a blow from the fist of Buskin Bob, and perceived the arm of that worthy encircling the trembling form of his wife.

So great was his confusion that for a moment he scarcely knew how to act.

But he soon recovered himself, and awaited the opportunity to rise and fly from the spot.

Nor was the surprise of Margaret less than that of her guilty husband.

"Bob!" she exclaimed, "you here?"

"Yes, Margaret," replied the pantaloon, "and strike me comical if I don't think it is a lucky job I am, or that varmint there had cut your throat. But don't be frightened, Margaret, he shan't hurt you, the spider-legged villain. Strike me comical if I ain't half a mind to throttle him, I am."

"No, no!" exclaimed Margaret, "leave him to himself and his conscience."

"To his what?" said Bob, turning in surprise

and looking in the pale face of the columbine, —a time of which Bill took advantage, and leaping hastily to his feet, made off as fast as his legs would carry him— "A what? Why, strike me comical, Margaret, you don't think he's got a conscience, do you? Leave him to the hangman you mean."

Margaret started.

Had Bob, then, heard the conversation between herself and her husband, or had the remark only been called forth by the act of attempting her life.

"Let us leave this spot," she said, "let us go, Bob."

"The damned villain," muttered Bob, in tones of deep indignation, "the consummate scoundrel. And so he has cut pantomime for tragedy, has he. Strike me comical, if you ain't got a vagabond for a husband. Look here, Margaret, say the word, and I'll drag him to a gaol, or my name's not Buskin Bob, strike me comical if it is, there!"

"No, no." she answered hurriedly. "I—I cannot destroy my husband."

"He would destroy you," said Bob.

Margaret sighed.

"Murder you, as he murdered—"

"Ah!" exclaimed Margaret. "Bob, Bob, what have you heard?"

"All, Margaret—all. Enough to make my blood curdle within my veins with horror."

"Then you know—"

"The reason of that officer's visit to you at the hospital—the cause of your illness. Strike me comical, I feel for you, I do. You have suffered fearfully."

"Aye, Bob, I have. But come let us leave this spot; let us return to the show. But stay, I have no right there," said the columbine, pausing.

"No right there!"

"No."

"Why not?"

"Am I not the wife of a murderer?" asked Margaret.

"Well."

"And shall I contaminate the abode of those whose lives, though poor, are at least above reproach."

"Come on," said Bob.

And he took her arm and gently forced her along before him.

"No, no. I cannot."

"I tell you you must."

"I am the wife of that villain!" she exclaimed.

"You are a woman," said Bob.

"And a wretched one."

"Then the greater reasons why you should find sympathy."

"While the fearful secret was locked in my own breast, I could encounter the glance of those who were kind to me; but now—now, I feel I cannot sit again with those who can say, behold the wife of a murderer."

"Strike me comical if it would be good kokum for any one to say so in my hearing," exclaimed Bob. "I'd — I'd — damned if I wouldn't—there!"

And Buskin Bob buried the knuckles of one hand in the palm of the other with a loud clap.

"Look here, Margaret," he said. "If you deserved sympathy before you doubly deserve it now, and strike me comical if you shan't have it

from Buskin Bob. Poor thing, I pity you; yours has indeed been a life of misery since that wretch led you to the altar, but it has been no fault of yours."

"None, none."

"I know. It is his own bad passions—passions which prompt him to injure all whom his evil nature leads him to believe his foes. Little did I think, bad as I knew him to be, that he would strive to ruin Charlie and the boy by firing the Royal Star."

"And that is not his worst crime," sighed Margaret.

"No; murder!" exclaimed Buskin Bob. "Hidden behind the trees I heard all, saw all that took place. Thank God I was there, or another crime would have been upon his soul, another victim fallen beneath his brutal passions."

"Bob," said Margaret seriously, "I scarce know whether to thank you for saving me. Perhaps it had been better that his knife had done its work, for then I had ended a life so full of anguish and misery; better perhaps that I had died by his hand, than live a wretched, despised, and broken-hearted woman."

And covering her face with her hands she burst into tears.

"Come, come, Margaret," said the good-hearted fellow with some emotion. "Don't weep for such a wretch. He is not worthy a tear. No one can despise you because he is a villain; no one can censure you for his acts. All must pity you; I pity you; Charlie will pity you and—and—there, strike me comical we will. Now don't cry—don't. Strike me comical if I can bear to see a woman cry; it seems as if the tears she shed got in my throat and stuck there till they nearly choked me, they do, strike me comical if they don't—there!"

And the voice of Buskin Bob, as he gave utterance to these words, was choked with emotion.

His tender heart could not bear to witness the sufferings of his companion, and his eyes moistened as he led her from the field towards the high road.

Poor Margaret, absorbed in her grief, scarcely noticed the gentle pressure used by Bob to urge her forward towards the fair field.

With his right hand he grasped the trembling fingers of the columbine, and his left arm imperceptibly even to himself, stole around her waist, as each, engaged with their own thoughts, pursued the road to the fair.

They had gone some distance down the road, when both were startled from the reverie into which they had fallen, by hearing a voice exclaim,—

"Seek the haunted oak the night after to-morrow. In the hollow you will find my last request. Farewell for ever!"

It was the voice of Dancing Bill on the other side of the hedge.

Buskin Bob leaped towards the spot from whence it came, and in the dim light he perceived the figure of a man stealing swiftly over the field.

"You heard?" said Bob.

"I did. Thank God he has gone for ever."

"Do you think he will fly the country?" asked Bob.

"Yes."

"I doubt it."

"I do not."

"Why?"

"Because others know his secret beside myself now," said Margaret. "He felt that I might not betray him, but you he must fear."

"Why should he do so?"

"You would betray him."

"Humph."

"From you he could expect no mercy," she said.

"Why not?"

"Because of the work at the Royal Star," she replied.

"For that I could forgive him." replied Bob.

"And the rest?"

"I know not what to think. My conscience tells me I should do my duty, and hand him over to justice; but my heart prompts me to spare the husband for the wife's sake."

"And which will conquer?" asked Margaret.

"Strike me comical if I know," said Bob. "Could I give him up to the outraged laws without inflicting pain upon you, I would do it. I know that it is the duty of every man to surrender up a murderer; but I likewise know that I should never be happy again if I caused your sufferings an extra pang."

"Bob, Bob; would to heaven his heart had been like yours!" exclaimed Margaret.

"It wouldn't have been much to boast of if it had," said Bob. "But strike me comical if it would have ever harmed a woman. No, no, Margaret, I am a rough fellow. I have been dragged up in a rough way, and taught in a rough school. I've seen a few ups and downs in life; I've had to struggle hard for bread, and have often only found a stone; but that has not hardened my heart—that at least is soft and feeling. I can pity you, Margaret; feel for the woman who suffers at the hands of a brute. If I could not give to a wife all the happiness she deserves, I would never stoop so low as to degrade the name of man by ill-using or insulting her I had sworn to love and cherish, strike me comical if I would, there!"

"No, Bob, no. You at least have the heart of a man beating in your breast. You would have done all that lay in your power to render a woman happy."

"I would have striven so to do," said Bob. "Anyhow, I don't think I should ever have raised my hand in anger towards her, strike me comical if I do. But there, Margaret, perhaps better days are in store for you now. If Bill leaves the country you will be no more annoyed by him, and though you can never hope to forget his crimes, time will assuage your grief."

"Never, never," she sighed. "Oh, Bob, dare I ask you to keep from Charlie and everyone else the fearful secret you have learned. I cannot say one word in favour of him the law calls my husband. I cannot put forward one extenuating act from the deeds of which he has been guilty. Well, I am aware he deserves to meet an ignominious doom; but I am his wife, Bob, and as such what pain must it inflict upon me were he to be hung—what continual misery would it cause me, to feel that every gaze I encountered I could read the knowledge of his guilt. Oh, Bob, if you would be my friend—if you would spare me further anguish, lock up in your own bosom the fatal secret you have learned this night."

"For your sake, Margaret," said Bob, "I will do so. To me a wish from you becomes a command. I would not add to your sufferings for the world, for—for—strike me comical, there!"

Bob had again nearly found himself going too far.

But he recollected himself in time, and stopped the words he would have uttered with his usual exclamation.

"I know I can trust you," said the poor woman.

"You can," said Bob.

"I will."

"You may indeed, strike me comical if you may not."

"Then I will return to the booth. I well know I am unworthy to partake of the hospitality of such kind friends."

"That is all nonsense," said Bob. "Why, strike me comical if I would give a fig for the man who could only extend hospitality to those who needed it not. No, Margaret, Charlie Evans is not the man to blame an innocent wife for the deeds of a guilty husband. You are alone in the world, without friends save us. And never shall you look in vain for a cheering word or a kind smile to dispel the anguish of your mind while Buskin Bob or Charlie Evans in this cold, unfeeling world Struggle for Bread."

CHAPTER LXXIX.

BUSKIN BOB PERSUADES THE CLOWN TO VISIT THE NEXT TOWN, AND SUCCEEDS

BUSKIN BOB was not the man to act in any underhand manner towards his friend Charlie Evans, but he felt that for the sake of both parties, it were better that he complied with the wishes of Margaret Simmons, and made no allusion whatever to the adventure of the evening, or what he had learnt whilst concealed behind the clump of trees which hid the entrance to the underground passage.

When they arrived at the fair field, therefore, Buskin Bob prevailed upon the columbine to go on to the booth without him, telling her that he would follow in the course of a few minutes, as by so doing, Charlie would not know they had been in company, and it would prevent the clown from asking questions which he had no wish to answer or to evade.

This plan was adopted, and Margaret entered the booth alone.

"Why, Margaret," said Charlie, kindly, "I began to fear you had run away from us. Been for a walk?"

"Yes," she replied, "I did not feel well."

"You are not strong yet," said the clown. "Perhaps it was the best thing you could do. I sent Buskin Bob to look for you, but I think he has lost himself; he has not been back."

"Has he not?" said Margaret, in a low tone of voice.

"No," replied the clown; "but never mind, perhaps he has gone to see to the horse; he is very fond of the animal, and the beast seems fond of him. Sit down and have your supper. I'm sure you must want it."

"No, indeed," said Margaret. "I do not feel as if I could eat. I am tired Charlie, so, if you don't mind, I will retire to bed."

"Oh, have a bit of supper," said Charlie, pushing a plate towards her. "It ain't much, certainly, but it will do you good to eat a bit."

"Do excuse me, Charlie," she said, "I am not at all hungry, and I believe a little sleep will do me more good than anything else."

"Do as you like, Margaret," said Charlie, "I don't wish to press you against your will, but don't refuse it because you think we have none for ourselves, for we have supped already."

"No, it is not for that," said Margaret, "but I am not well, and should prefer to go to bed."

"Go then, Margaret."

The columbine rose and bade him good night,

"Good night," replied the clown, "I hope you will be better to-morrow."

Margaret answered only with a sigh.

"Better," she thought, "I shall never be better more. The sufferings of the body may be eased by medicaments or time, but the sufferings of the heart, never. Who—

'Can minister to a mind diseased ;
Pluck from the memory a rooted sorrow,
Raze out the written troubles of the brain,
And with some sweet, oblivious antidote,
Cleanse the stuffed bosom of the perilous stuff
Which weighs upon the heart.'

None but God."

It is not in the power of man to root out the fearful canker-worm that lies festering in the mind. Science is great and noble, and powerful. It can lift mountains from their base and hurl them into the sea. It can shiver huge rocks to atoms, as easily as a strong man snaps a rotten reed. It can encircle the earth in an iron girder, and connect the eastern and western hemispheres by a single wire, along which, with the speed of the lightnings flash, the denizens of the one may hold communion with the other. It can dive into the bowels of the earth, and soar up into the boundless expanse above it. But it cannot minister to a soul diseased.

Too well did Margaret know this.

She retired to the place parted off for her and little Mary to sleep, and flinging herself upon the bed, she felt that she could there give way to her sorrow; there hide her grief from the gaze of her kind friends.

And on that rude pallet she sobbed herself to sleep, but the mind rested not, and throughout the night, visions of her guilty husband and his victim floated through her brain; and she rose the next morning, pale and unrefreshed.

But she resolved to do all in her power to go cheerfully through her duties, and so well did she succeed in hiding her sufferings from her friends, that Charlie congratulated her upon her health, which he believed to be rapidly returning.

Buskin Bob had not forgotten the words uttered at the hedge by Dancing Bill. He had turned them over and over in his mind, and could come to no other conclusion, than that the harlequin had used them to induce his wife to go to the spot, in order that he might carry out the hellish deed which Bob had frustrated.

But where was this haunted oak ?

Bob had no idea, never having before heard of it ; but still he believed it must be somewhere in the neighbourhood.

Perhaps Charlie knew, but then it would not do to ask him, lest the clown should wish to know why the question was asked, and he had no wish to pain Margaret by asking her.

Besides, she would then feel that Bob intended going there himself.

At length he resolved to ask Harry, so strolling up to where the boy stood, he carelessly remarked,—

"Harry, what place do you call that, where the haunted oak is ?"

"Hender Wood," replied the boy.

"Oh, Hender Wood is it," said Bob. "Let's see, what part of the wood is it, Harry, I almost forget."

"Why just at the entrance of the wood, about a dozen yards from the road," said the boy.

"To be sure it is," remarked Bob. "It's a very—"

"Large tree," said Harry ; "with withered branches, and hollow at the bottom of the trunk. I've often played about there."

"Oh, yes, I recollect," said Bob. "Strike me comical if I mustn't be getting old to forget so soon. The entrance up this end you mean."

"Yes," replied the boy, as he hurried away in answer to a call from Charlie.

"All right," muttered Bob. "It's too bad, though, to pump a youngster ; but still, the cause is a good one, and therefore I don't commit any very great wrong, strike me comical if I do. So having learned where this tree is, I will be there at the time, and just see what Master Bill's game is. I must consider of some means to prevent Margaret going. Poor thing, the wretch has done her enough injury already, without her running the risk of meeting with more."

The day passed over, and though the number of visitors to the booth was not so great as on the previous one, it was by no means a failure ; and at supper, the question was discussed as to what they should do till the time of the next fair, which would not take place for seven days.

The Brothers Tumblini had accepted an engagement for a few nights at a place of entertainment some few miles distant, consequently they could not offer to the public a display of talent equal to that which had been seen at the fair.

So Bob proposed that they should stop where they were for a few days and rest.

To this Charlie agreed, believing that relaxation from labour, would be alike beneficial to Margaret and to Mary.

It was towards the close of the day, on which Dick had requested his wife to be at the haunted oak, that Buskin Bob strolled up to Charlie Evans, and looked him in the face and remarked,—

"Charlie, my boy, why, strike me comical, how queer you do look."

"Do I ?" said Charlie.

"Do you ? don't you feel so ?" asked Bob.

"No," replied the clown ; "thank God I am well enough."

"I don't think you are."

"Why ?"

"You look pale."

"I have not noticed it," said the clown.

"Well, no ; perhaps not, people can't generally see their own phisog," said Bob. "Strike me comical if I don't think the best thing you could do, would be to go to the next town, and see the sprites that are playing there. It will do you good; a little change you know is good for us all at times; and I really believe it would be for you.

"Well Bob, I don't think there is anything the matter with me," said Charlie, "to render a change necessary; but I have thought of going to see them, so that I could form an idea as to whether it would be worth our while to engage them."

"Then why don't you go?" said Buskin Bob.

"Suppose we go then," said Charlie after a pause.

"I don't care about going," said Bob, "besides, we can't both go."

"Why not?"

"Who's to look after the booth?" asked Bob.

"Oh, Margaret," replied Charlie.

"She ain't well, poor thing," said Bob, "I wouldn't bother her."

"Well, you go," said Charlie.

"No, I'll stop and look after the booth," said Buskin Bob, "and you trot over and see what they are like."

"Well, just as you like, Bob," said the clown. "I'll go to-night."

Buskin Bob turned away with a grin on his face.

"I don't like double dealing," he muttered; "but if I can get Charlie out of the way, I can come out in a new character without having any questions asked. I have got a little idea in my head, which I think will prevent Margaret from ever being troubled again by that Dancing Bill, strike me comical if I ain't."

No more was said about the visit to the next town till after tea, when Charlie rose and remarked,—

"Well, if I go, I may as well go at once, and see what sort of an entertainment it is."

"What entertainment?" asked Margaret.

"Oh, a varied one in the next town," said Charlie. "I hear they have got two clever sprites there, and I want to see if they would be of service to us, and their terms moderate."

"Are you going to-night father?" asked Mary.

"Yes," replied the clown. "I am going at once; Harry would you like to go with me!"

"Oh, yes," replied the boy, leaping up quickly.

"Take him, with you Charlie, he'll be company for you, and it will amuse him," said Bob.

"Oh, yes, take me," said Harry, "I shall be delighted."

Does it not appear strange that persons connected with the theatrical profession are always eager at every available time to visit a theatre; to sit in front of the stage, and see that which they themselves are so intimately acquainted with. Yet so it is. The professional on an off night invariably finds his way into a theatre, and is perhaps one of the most interested and best pleased of the audience.

Buskin Bob watched them eagerly as they prepared to start.

He was not a little pleased that Harry was going with his friend as he had a little business on hand, which he desired to keep as secret as possible.

Business which he believed would prove advantageous to Margaret, and for ever rid her of the worthless wretch who had caused her so much misery.

Bidding little Mary good-bye, the clown and the Boy Actor took their departure from the booth.

Buskin Bob stood by the little window in the caravan watching them as they wended their way in the direction of the next town, then with a smile he turned and entered his sleeping apartment.

CHAPTER LXXX.

BUSKIN BOB IN A NEW CHARACTER—THE MEETING AT THE HAUNTED OAK—TERROR OF DANCING BILL —THE PROMISE.

FOR some time Buskin Bob remained in the apartment, during which he was engaged in turning over the contents of a box in which he kept his "props."

From among them he selected a short, dark frock, devoid of lace or ornament, a long black velvet cloak, black pants and high boots, to which he added a small round cap with eagle's feathers, and a long thin sword, in a black scabbard.

These he laid upon the bed, and returned the other articles to the box.

Then taking down a small bag which hung on a nail, he extracted therefrom a bundle of tow, and a piece of phosphorous wrapped in paper; these he thrust into the pocket of the doublet or frock, together with a flint and steel and a piece of German tinder, which he took from the pocket of the coat he wore.

Having laid the things smoothly across the bed, he rubbed his hands together and muttered to himself—

"The fellow is a superstitious cur, and if I don't do a little hanky panky that will frighten him a bit, my name's not Buskin Bob, strike me comical if it is."

Then strolling into the compartment where Margaret and little Mary sat, he took up his pipe, filled and lit it, and seating himself at the table commenced reading.

Margaret, meantime, sat conning over in her mind the words she heard her husband give utterance to, respecting the haunted oak, and his last request.

But she had resolved not to visit the place at the time he said; she intended to go to the haunted oak, but her visit she was determined should be in the day-time.

Not that she feared to visit the spot at night from any superstitious feeling, but she dreaded lest she should meet with Bill, and pay for her temerity with her life.

Had Buskin Bob have been assured that she would not attempt to go that night, he would have been less secret in his actions.

His object in inducing Charlie to go to the next town, was so that he might be enabled to carry out a little plan of his own without being asked for explanations.

The hours wore away, and ten o'clock came.

Buskin Bob, laid down the book, threw himself back in his chair, and yawned.

As is usual, one in company has only to yawn or cough, to set the others off on the same course, and consequently, no sooner did Bob

MARGARET SIMMONS.

begin to yawn, than little Mary did the same, and when she left off, Margaret commenced.

"Strike me comical," said Bob, "if I don't feel sleepy."

"Yawning is catching," said Mary.

"So is coughing," remarked Bob, "especially in church. Let a chap cough and every one in the building is safe to do the same, from the beadle to the minister."

"Then, Bob, I wish you would neither cough

No. 20.

nor yawn till I have finished my work. I declare you have made me feel quite sleepy, and I have got all this side to hem."

And the girl held up some work on which she was engaged.

"Then I shouldn't do it to-night," said Bob. "Strike me comical if I should."

"Why not?"

"Because it ain't good for you, is it, Margaret, boring your eyes out by candle light," said Bob. "You're tired enough as it is, and a good night's rest will do you more good than that will."

"I would not do any more to-night, dear," said Margaret.

"I don't think I will," replied Mary, laying down her work. "I think I'll go to bed."

"That's right," said Bob. "And if I was you, Margaret, I would do the same."

"I think I may as well," she replied, rising. "Good night, Bob."

Bob looked up in her face as if he would read there whether she had only said she would go to bed in order to induce him to retire to rest, so that she might slip away, and visit the haunted oak.

But there was nothing in the woman's countenance to lead him to believe that she had any such intention, so bidding both her and Mary good night, and seeing them enter the part appropriated for their bed-room, he slipped quietly into his own apartment.

"Strike me comical if this ain't better than I expected," he muttered. "Now for a bit of hanky panky."

Throwing off his clothes, he commenced to robe himself in the dress he had taken from his box a short time before, and when he had put on the cloak, he stood before a looking glass and gazed intently upon it.

"Not perfect yet," he muttered.

So opening the box, he drew forth a pair of whiskers and a moustache, and drew them on to his face, then blacking his eyebrows, he exclaimed,—

"There never was a better make up for Mephistopheles than this, Bob. Strike me comical if you don't look the devil to perfection!"

Giving his long sword a hitch up, and drawing the feather from his cap and placing it in his belt, he drew the long black cloak closely around him, so as to hide the dress beneath, and strode towards the door of the caravan, opening it softly, he called out,—

"Margaret."

"Yes," she answered.

"I'm just going to run out, I shan't be long."

"Very well," replied the woman.

"Good night."

"Good night."

And Buskin Bob closed the door hurriedly, and leapt to the ground.

Casting his eyes around him, he strode away muttering,—

"Now for Henden Wood and the haunted oak."

In the course of half-an-hour, and without meeting a soul on the road, Buskin Bob arrived at the entrance to the wood, into which he penetrated.

He was not long in finding the tree, which bore the repute of being haunted

It was a huge oak, withered and blighted; not one green leaf fluttered on its branches, and it stood amid its fellows like a corpse among the living.

Bob stood gazing up at its leafless branches for several minutes. Then he took the long feather from his belt and placed it in his cap, unhooked his long sword, and threw back the large cloak. Then he stooped down, and thrust his hand into the hollow cavity of the trunk, and drew forth a packet.

"Strike me comical," he muttered, "if Bill ain't put his last request there, as he said he would, and perhaps after all he has left the country. However I will wait and see."

And Buskin Bob walked round the huge trunk of the tree to the opposite side.

"Hullo!" he said, "are they beginning to cut down this wood. It seems like it, for here is one giant of the forest laid low. It's a pity to destroy the woods as they do. Well, it will answer some purpose I suppose, if it's only for me to sit on."

And he sat down upon the trunk of a large tree, which the woodman's axe had recently laid low.

As he did so, the sound of the parish church clock, as it struck the hour of midnight, was borne on the wind to his ears.

"Twelve o'clock," muttered Bob. "If Bill means harm to his wife it won't be long before he is here, so I'll just get ready to welcome him."

Bob took from his pocket the flint and steel, the tow and phosphorous, and laid them beside him on the tree.

Placing a small piece of German tinder upon his knee, he struck the steel with the flint, and a spark falling upon the tinder, it instantly ignited.

Thrusting the packet he had taken from the hollow of the oak into his pocket, he forced the piece of tinder into the centre of the tow, then opening the paper he wet the phosphorous with his saliva. Scarcely had he accomplished this, than he fancied he heard the sound of a footstep.

Thrusting the flint and steel back into his pocket, he rose to his feet and listened.

The footstep sounded nearer, but upon the other side of the tree.

Bob kept close to the withered trunk, so as to conceal himself, and waited.

"Margaret," said the voice of Dancing Bill, "are you here?"

Bob thrust the tow in which he had placed the burning tinder into his mouth, and taking the phorphorous in his hands, he rubbed it over them, and over his face and body.

"Margaret," again said the voice of Bill, close to the tree.

"Who calls upon Margaret?" exclaimed Bob, in a voice rendered husky and unnatural by the tow in his mouth.

And as he spoke he sprang round the trunk of the oak, blowing from his mouth sparks of fire and smoke almost into the face of Dancing Bill, who, uttering a cry of terror at the fearful sight before him, stood powerless to move from the spot.

And no wonder that the superstitious harlequin was appalled at the sight of the figure before him, as blue flames played from its hands and breast, and sparks of fire emanated from its mouth.

Such a sight, at such a time, and in such a

place, would have appalled stouter hearts than Dancing Bill's; it would have struck terror to the souls of the innocent and pure, how much more, then, must it have done to the guilty breast of the murderer.

In vain he strove to fly, his limbs refused their office, and down upon his knees he sank, and buried his face in his hands, to shut out the horrible sight.

"Why have you called upon Margaret?" asked Buskin Bob.

There was no answer.

"Bill Simmons," said Bob, in the same unnatural tone. "Know you in whose presence you are?"

"Mercy! mercy!" cried Bill.

"Who am I? speak!" exclaimed Bob.

"The—the—de—de—devil!" gasped Bill.

"Right," said Bob, "and you are mine."

"Spare me—spare me!"

"But for a time," said Bob. "I will spare you so long as you obey my will. You are mine, for murder as made you such. You are here to-night bent on more crime. Is it not so? It is useless to lie to me, for I can read your soul."

"Yes," gasped Bill.

"You came to murder your wife?"

"I—I—did."

"There has been blood enough already shed by you, to make you mine," said Bob, blowing forth another volley of sparks from his mouth. "Now mark me well. Never more seek your wife to slay her. Never more harm her by word or deed; for the moment you do so, you die!"

"I will not," gasped the trembling and prostrate man.

"Swear it," said Bob.

"I do," gasped Bill.

"Remember—remember!" said Bob, endeavouring to make his voice even more unnatural than did the tow in his mouth. "Rise!"

Dancing Bill staggered to his feet. His face was ashy pale, and he trembled so violently that it was with the greatest difficulty he could stand.

"Look upon me," said Bob. "I have but to touch you, and you wither like this oak; and descend to eternal torments. So beware, you seek not to harm her, who has been a good wife to you."

"I—I will not. I swear I will not," gasped Bill.

"Remember your oath, 'tis death to break it; for I am ever by your side. Beware — beware!"

And drawing his cloak over his breast, and hiding his hands beneath its folds, Bob closed his mouth and glided away in the dark shadow of the tree.

CHAPTER LXXXI.

GRIPE'S DEPARTURE FROM THE HALL — THE STEWARD AND THE OFFICER ON THEIR WAY TO THE LOCK UP.

FOR a few moments, the little eyes of the weazened-faced steward glared upon the door-way through which Dick the Poacher had disappeared.

Then they turned with an inquiring glance upon the smiling face of Squire Henley.

The squire dropped his eyes, and walked to the further end of the hall, and the constable, whose fingers were twined about the collar of the little steward's coat, forced Gripe towards the opened door.

It was then that the steward's countenance changed.

It became pale as marble.

The smile vanished, and a look of blank despair took its place.

His limbs trembled, and his chest heaved with passion and disappointment.

Never had Gripe been so moved before.

A moment since, and he could have crushed the squire.

Now he was powerless.

They had changed places once more.

The steward was again the servant, and Henley the master.

And that master was armed with the evidence of his defalcations, and could consign him to prison.

Bitterly did he curse the poacher, for depriving him of the packet he had so strangely obtained.

Bitterly did he curse his own folly, in not waiting to produce it in a court of justice.

And as these thoughts coursed hurriedly through his mind, he ground his teeth with rage.

"Now, sir," said the constable, who felt in anything but a good humour, at being called out of bed to take the charge. "I can't stop here all night; so come on."

And Gripe felt the pressure on his collar tighten, and himself being thrust anything but gently forward, along the hall.

"Stay a moment," said Gripe, endeavouring to conjure up his usual cool tones of voice, and little smirking smile, "I will not detain you long."

"I can't stop," said the man.

"Only a moment," said Gripe.

"Well look alive, then," growled the officer. "If you have anything to say, say it; and be sharp."

"Squire," said Gripe, turning to Henley, "will you suffer me to be dragged from this house like a felon?"

"You are one," said Henley, coolly.

"And you," said Gripe.

Henley turned pettishly away.

"Squire," said Gripe, loudly. "You triumph now, but your time will yet come. Aided by Dick the Poacher, you have deprived me of that, which would consign you to an ignominious doom. But, though it shields you for a time from the vengeance of the law, it is for a time only; and that time a short one. I go now to a prison, but I warn you, Squire Henley, robber of the widow and orphan, not to appear in a court of justice against me, or, by hell, I will hurl you from the witness-box into the felon's dock. Be warned, squire, for though I have lost the proofs of one crime, I hold the evidence of another."

Henley started and turned pale.

"Beware, Squire Henley! Beware!" said Gripe. "The steward will yet be master of the lord of Henley manor."

Henley answered not.

His eye fell beneath the eagle glance of the little steward.

A strange feeling of fear took possession of his heart.

He almost regretted that he had gone so far.

But it was now too late to retract.

He could feel that the eyes of the domestics were upon him.

He must go on with the work he had commenced.

Without raising his eyes, he waved his hand to the officer.

"Come," said the constable.

"I am ready," said Gripe, and he moved to the door.

But on the threshold he stopped.

"Squire," he said, "I go not to suffer the penalty of a crime which you have imputed to me, but to unfold to the world the deeds of one who stepped from poverty to affluence by villany, who rose to his present position by fraud and robbery, and whose wealth is stained by—"

"Officer, do your duty," exclaimed Henley, in a voice choked by passion.

"Aye, well may you tremble at my words," exclaimed Gripe, as the officer forced him over the threshold. "Look upon the pale-faced villain! See the guilt written upon his brow; Henley, beware—beware!"

Then drawing his little figure up to his full height, Gripe walked firmly along by the side of the officer.

He did not consider himself utterly ruined yet.

The agitation of the squire had led him to hope.

Henley's fears might lead him to believe that Gripe still knew more than he did.

His words might awe the squire into silence, and compel him to keep away from the court of justice.

If so, Gripe would escape.

Gripe's motto was never despair.

And he resolved to cling to it now.

For some time he walked on in silence.

But as they neared the county lock-up, the steward said in a bland tone of voice,—

"Well, Mr. Grabham, I should think the squire ought to have known better than to have called you out of bed in the middle of the night to have made a fool of himself."

The officer gave vent to a sort of grunt.

"He wouldn't have done it if you had not made a knave of yourself, I suppose," he growled.

Gripe shrugged his shoulders.

"Strange things happen in this world," said Gripe. "Sane men go mad and mad men become sane. So I suppose Squire Henley will recover from his madness in a short time."

"I don't understand you," remarked the constable.

"Don't you now," said Gripe.

"No, indeed."

"Well, then, Squire Henley is mad." said Gripe.

"Is he!"

"Yes."

"He didn't seem like it," said the officer. "On the contrary he seemed to know what he was about, when he refused to let you rob him any longer."

"My dear sir,—"

"No I ain't," said the officer, "so come on. You walk so slow I am getting cold."

"Never be in a hurry." said Gripe, "hasty deeds are often repented; always bear in mind, Mr. Grabham the words of the bard,—'Wisely and slow; they stumble that run fast.'"

"I wonder then that you did not remember them," said Grabham, "and not been quite so fast with the squire's money."

Gripe winced.

He felt that Grabham had him there.

But he wished to make the officer believe that his guilt existed only in the diseased mind of Henley, so he said in the same calm tone,—

"Mr. Grabham, I pity you."

"Pity me!"

"Yes."

"What for?"

"Your ignorance."

"My ignorance," repeated the officer, while an indignant flush rose to his face, and he pressed his knuckles into the neck of the little steward, till Gripe was ready to howl with the pain.

The flush of wounded pride in the face of Grabham gave place to a broad grin, as he inflicted this chastisement upon the man who could presume to assert that he was ignorant.

"Yes, sir, your ignorance!" exclaimed Gripe, snorting under the pressure. "Your ignorance of human nature. Any one could have seen that the squire was either drunk or mad."

"Could they."

"To be sure they could."

"I couldn't."

"That's because—oh!"

This last exclamation was called forth by the hard knuckles of the officer, who, forseeing the remark of Gripe would be anything but complimentary to himself, worked his hand a little lower down the neck of the steward, and forced his knuckles not over tenderly into the flesh.

"What's the matter?" asked Grabham, chuckling to himself.

"I was afraid my neck might hurt your knuckles," said Gripe, feeling as if it would have afforded him infinite pleasure to kick the shins of the officer.

"Oh, dear no," replied Grabham, "they are not so soft as yours. Honest toil hardens the hand and softens the heart. Hurt them, bless you, no. Just feel how hard they are."

And Grabham pressed them so tightly against the side of Gripe's neck, that the little man almost became black in the face.

He felt a secret pleasure in torturing the little man.

He knew the character of the little steward, and, though a constable, he was still a man with a heart in his breast that could feel for the sufferings of the oppressed, and many a time had he pitied those whom the unfeeling Gripe had driven forth homeless into the cold world.

Mr. Grabham was certainly much annoyed at being called out of his bed at so unseasonable an hour to take the charge, but he decidedly felt a pleasure in having Gripe in his clutches, and he resolved that not a few who had suffered at the steward's hands, should know on the following morning that Gripe was in prison.

"Perhaps you will just be kind enough to take your fingers from my neck," said Gripe.

"Can't."

"Why not?"

"You might attempt to escape," replied the officer.

"Escape!"

"Yes."

"I have not the least intention of doing so," said Gripe.

"Ain't you!"

"No."

"Well, I certainly have not the least intention of giving you a chance," said the constable.

"You need have no fear of me," said Gripe.

The officer burst out into a loud fit of laughter.

"No fear of you!" he exclaimed.

"You need not indeed," said Gripe.

"Well, I reckon you are about right there, Mr. Gripe," said Graham. "There's not enough of you to fear."

"What do you mean!" exclaimed Gripe, his hitherto calm temper becoming ruffled.

"Simply what I say," replied the constable.

"Then be careful what you say, sir!" exclaimed the steward—Oh!oh!"

Grabham's knuckles again pressed very unpleasantly into Gripe's neck.

"Just walk along quietly, sir, if you please," said the officer. "Honest people must not be roused from their beds by such unseemly noise as you are making."

"I'll report you, sir; I'll—oh!—oh! you'll choke me," gasped Gripe.

"Then walk quietly, and be silent, or I shall do my duty in spite of everything," said Grabham.

"It's no part of your duty to choke a man," exclaimed Gripe.

"I have no wish to do so," said the constable, coolly.

"Yes, you have."

"No, I have not."

"You are trying to choke me," exclaimed Gripe.

"God forbid," said Grabham, "that I should do such injustice to a fellow creature. That is no part of my calling. That office is left for the hangman, Mr. Gripe, and heaven forbid that I should be the means of robbing the poor man of one of his victims, by choking you myself."

"Insolent scoundrel!" exclaimed the steward. "You shall repent of this. You shall soon find out whether—oh! oh!"

Again the officer's knuckles were pressed into his neck, and Gripe, in utter despair, became silent.

In a few minutes the lock-up was reached; the door opened by the officer, and Gripe thrust forward somewhat roughly into the dark and strangely-built place.

CHAPTER LXXXII.

TIME'S CHANGES—THE APPEAL OF DANCING BILL TO MARGARET.

THREE months have passed away; the buds of spring have expanded into the blossoms of summer; the seed has become a plant, impregnating the air with a delightful fragrance, and the earth teems with luxuriant vegetation, watered by the gentle showers of spring, nurtured by the warm sun of summer.

Three months!

How short a time, yet how great the changes in this wide world, in so short a space.

Every grain of sand in Time's hour-glass bears with it, as it passes on, a record of hope or fear, love or misery; and so they will each, as they pass on their way to eternity, till chaos comes again, and all things cease.

During the three months which have passed since our last chapter, the Boy Actor and his friends had been travelling the country and working the fairs with more or less success, and are now building their booth at Coventry.

Margaret is still with them. Her health and spirits are somewhat improved, and she is happy in the belief that Dancing Bill is by this time in America, as she has never seen or heard of him since the night when the arm of Buskin Bob saved her from his vengeance.

Contrary to the expectations of Mr. Gripe, Squire Henley *did* prosecute him, for appropriating money entrusted to him, to his own purpose, and he was committed to prison for twelvemonths.

This was a fearful blow to Gripe.

As soon as the sentence was pronounced, he endeavoured to make a statement about the squire, but was hurried away to the cell by the officer.

Dick the Poacher had remained at home with poor Minnie, and had turned his attention to his farm, which now bid fair to become profitable.

It was while Charlie, Buskin Bob, little Harry, and the Brothers Tumblini, who had again joined them, were building the booth on the evening before the commencement of the fair at Coventry, that Margaret, at the request of the clown, strolled some little distance from the fair field with a jug in her hand, to procure some beer for their supper.

She had arrived at the house to which she had been directed to proceed, when a hand was placed upon her shoulder.

With a start she turned hurriedly.

Her face became deadly pale.

Her limbs trembled violently.

With a choking sensation in her throat, she gasped,—

"Bill, you here!"

"I am, Margaret," replied the harlequin.

For he, indeed, it was whose hand had been laid upon her shoulder.

But very different was he in appearance to when she last saw him.

His dress was that of a well-to-do man.

The long beard and whiskers had been shaven off, and the moustaches trimmed neatly.

For some moments Margaret stood gazing upon him.

Her bosom rose and fell with powerful emotion.

Dancing Bill, too, seemed to be suffering from his feelings.

His face, which had become pale and thin from suffering, looked even more pale.

His eyes were sunken.

His gait faltering.

There was a nervous twitching about the mouth.

A restless glance in his eye.

And every moment he looked around him as though he feared the officers of justice were at his side.

Truly, indeed, a guilty conscience knows no rest.

A soul stained with crime fears the echo of its own voice.

"Margaret," he said, after a long pause, "will you not speak to me?"

"I—I thought you were miles away," she stammered.

"And you hoped so."

"I did."

"Can you then forget your husband?" he asked, in a husky voice.

"Would that I could," she replied, and as she spoke a tear trembled on her eyelid, and rolled slowly down her pale face.

Bill watched it, and a sigh escaped his breast.

"Why do you linger in this country?" asked Margaret.

"Because I cannot leave it," he replied.

"Why?"

"I fear to go."

"Rather should you fear to stay!" she exclaimed.

"I know it, Margaret," he whispered, "yet I cannot go alone."

Margaret made no reply.

"Wife!" he exclaimed after a pause, and in a husky whisper,

The columbine started and shuddered.

"Ah!" he muttered, "that word is hateful to you. Is it not so?"

Margaret averted her head, and replied not.

"I know that it is," he continued.

"Could you think it otherwise?" she asked.

"A wife should be a wife in weal or woe," said Bill.

"To you I have ever been a true and faithful one," she said, with emotion.

"But are so no longer," he said bitterly. "For better for worse you took me, and swore to stand by my side. But now, when I most need your advice, your company, you turn from me with loathing and disgust, desert me in the hours of my wretchedness."

"'Tis your own fault, Bill, that you are wretched," said Margaret. "I always strove to make you happy but received blows for my work. You can blame none but yourself for your sufferings. Your own base, evil passions, alone have made you what you are."

Bill sighed.

He felt the truth of this.

"Margaret," he said after a pause. "I have wronged you much. I would become a better man."

"Do so," she replied "and none could rejoice more at the change than I, your poor, broken-hearted wife."

"Margaret, am wretched; life is a burden to me. I feel at times that I am going mad!" he exclaimed. "You could save me."

"Me!" she exclaimed.

"Yes, Margaret, you," he replied.

"How?"

"By forgetting and forgiving the past," he replied, endeavouring to grasp her hand.

But the woman drew back with a shudder.

She could not take the hand of her husband. There was blood upon it.

It was stained with the life stream of her friend.

"Forget—oh, never, never!" she exclaimed; "would to heaven that I could. No, no; sleeping and waking, by day and by night, that fearful crime preys upon my soul, renders my life a misery, eats away health and youth, and buries my hours in agony."

"What can your suffering be compared to mine?" he asked sadly.

"You are guilty," she replied. "I am innocent."

"True, Margaret," said Bill, "but if you, who are innocent, can suffer, what must I feel who am guilty?"

"Alas, alas!" she murmured, dropping her head upon her breast.

"Alas, indeed!" exclaimed Bill, with a shudder.

"Oh, Margaret; much as you may feel the villany of which I have been guilty, you can form no conception of my agony. I cannot rest; sleeping and waking, the face of that woman haunts my mind. I see her as I walk along the streets. I see her at my bedside, in my dreams. I hear her cries for vengeance on her murderer in every puff of wind. I cannot sleep. I cannot sit. I must keep on—on, ever flying from the spectre at my side. Margaret, this state of mind will soon kill me. I cannot be alone and live. Solitude is fearful! Oh, Margaret! wife, save me from madness, save me from myself!"

And he grasped the wrist of his wife in his trembling hand.

"Touch me not," she almost shrieked.

"Margaret," he gasped, "as you hope for salvation yourself, save me."

"How can I save you?"

"Leave me not, keep by my side!" he exclaimed, "for I dread to be alone."

"Impossible," she replied.

"No, no; say not so."

"It cannot be."

"It must—it must."

Margaret shook her head.

"Fly to America!" she exclaimed, "as you promised to do. The change of scene may afford you some relief."

"Alone; no. I will go anywhere with you by my side, but I cannot go alone."

"Oh, Margaret, leave me not, and I will study your every want; obey your every wish. Drive me not from you. The fearful visions which haunt my imagination will flee from you, for you are innocent. Margaret, wife! as you hope for mercy hereafter, deny it not to me in this world!"

"Seek it there," said Margaret.

And she pointed upwards to the clear blue sky.

Bill shook his head.

A deep sigh broke from his breast.

"'Tis vain," he said.

"Not so."

"I can expect no mercy there," he said, in a tone of bitterness.

"It is from heaven alone you can hope to find it," said Margaret solemnly.

"That is closed to my prayers for ever," said Bill.

"No," said Margaret; "for it is written whosoever repenteth shall be saved."

"But I am lost—lost!" he exclaimed, in a tone of agony. "No, Margaret; there I dare not look for mercy! Life is to me a burden. Yet I fear to die—fear to leave this world of misery for that there!"

And with a shudder he pointed downwards.

"Let your thoughts wander to heaven," said Margaret.

"'Tis useless."

"Think it not," said Margaret.

"Think—'tis useless to think," he exclaimed. "Margaret, I know—"

"What?"

"That I am doomed."

"To what?"

"Eternal torments!" he gasped.

"Speak not thus," said Margaret. "It is beyond our power to fathom the will of heaven. It is not given to us to know whether the hand of mercy be extended or refused."

"To me it is."

"To you!"

"Aye, to me."

"You know not what you say," answered Margaret.

"Would that I did not," exclaimed Bill—"would that I dared hope."

"Hope and trust," said Margaret, in a solemn tone. "The sinner that repenteth at the eleventh hour shall be saved!"

"Margaret," gasped the trembling man "had you seen what I have seen, you would not speak thus."

"What have you seen?"

"That which curdled my blood in horror, and drove me nearly to madness," exclaimed the guilty man, trembling violently. "I have seen him who goaded me on to crime, to murder!"

"Who?" gasped Margaret.

Dancing Bill cast an anxious glance around him.

Then he bent his head down till his lips almost touched the cheek of his wife and hissed in her ear,—

"The devil, Margaret, the devil!"

Margaret started.

She believed now, that her guilty husband's reason had tottered from its throne.

His sufferings, she thought, had driven him mad.

She raised her eyes with a look of pity to his pale face.

She extended her hand and laid it upon his breast.

"Bill," she said, "there—there is no devil which prompted you to sin; there is the devil which haunts your imagination, and peoples it with visions of your crimes. 'Tis the voice of conscience, speaking in tones of thunder, and upbraiding you for your sins."

"No, no," said Bill, with a shake of the head. "I have seen him, spoken to him!"

The superstitious nature of the guilty man led him to believe that Buskin Bob, whom he had seen at the haunted oak, was indeed what that worthy wished him to think he was..

Not for one moment did Bill think it was a being of this world.

Margaret gazed with an expression of pity and horror upon the guilty man, then turned to go.

But Bill sprang forward, and caught her frantically by the wrist.

"Margaret, Margaret!" he exclaimed, "for heaven's sake do not leave me."

"I must," she said, calmly but resolutely

"Pity me; oh, pity me," pleaded the harlequin.

"I do, from my heart," she said.

"Then stay with me," he pleaded.

"Impossible."

"Oh, no, no!" he exclaimed, clinging more tightly to her arm.

"Bill," exclaimed Margaret, "end this scene, so painful to us both. Go your way, and let me go mine."

"I cannot, dare not leave you," he exclaimed.

"You must."

"I—I will not."

"Go in peace," she said, "and heaven forgive you the misery you have inflicted upon me."

"Margaret."

"I will hear no more!" she exclaimed, endeavouring to wrest her arm from his grasp.

"In mercy,—"

"Go."

"Come with me?"

"I cannot."

"Yes—yes."

"I will not."

"In mercy."

"Let go your hold."

"Do not—do not leave me," he pleaded.

"I must—I will!" she exclaimed, tearing herself away.

"Margaret!" he exclaimed, bounding after her and grasping her shawl.

"Away—away!" she shrieked, "or I will denounce you."

The hand of the guilty man relaxed its hold, and Margaret bounded forward towards the fair-field.

"She is gone—gone," gasped Bill, clasping his forehead in his hands, "and I am alone. No, not alone; for there, there is my victim. I see her glassy eyes fixed upon me. I hear her cries for mercy ringing in my ears. Will she never leave me, will that pale face and bleeding bosom never vanish from my sight. Never, till I have paid the penalty of my crime on the gallows."

CHAPTER LXXXIII.

MARGARET RETURNS TO HER FRIENDS—THE PROCESSION AT COVENTRY.

FINDING herself released from the grasp of her guilty husband, Margaret sped along towards the spot where the booth was being erected.

Her heart beat violently.

Her limbs trembled.

But fear of pursuit by Dancing Bill, lent her strength, and she hurried on.

She feared that Bill would follow her.

But not once did she look behind.

A sigh of relief escaped her breast, as she came in sight of the half erected booth.

But then her strength gave way.

She slackened her speed, and gasped for breath.

In a few moments more she had reached the booth.

"Hi! here we are," exclaimed Charlie, wiping the perspiration from his brow with the back of his hand, and advancing towards her, "first let's have a pull at that, Margaret, for I'm precious thirsty."

And stretching out his hand, he grasped the mug which Margaret still carried, and raised it to his lips,

Then finding that it was empty, the clown lowered it from his mouth, and looked first into the inside of the jug, and then into the pale face of Margaret, with a look of questioning surprise.

"Why, I'm blowed if there's any in it," he said at length.

"Strike me comical, if you ain't been brewing that beer!" exclaimed Buskin Bob, coming out to the side of Charlie.

"I began to think you was never a coming back with it."

"No more she ain't," said Charlie.

"How do you make that out, when she is here?" asked Bob.

"But she ain't brought the beer," said Charlie.

"How's that?" asked Charlie.

"Don't know."

Bob peeped into the jug, then turned to Margaret for an explanation.

But as his eyes rested upon her pale face, he started back.

"Why, what's the matter, Margaret?" he exclaimed hurriedly.

But the columbine replied not.

Bob bounded to her side.

"You ain't well," he said. Perhaps it is only the heat, go in and sit down."

"Yes, yes," said Margaret, moving towards the broad steps which led up into the caravan.

Bob shook his head mysteriously, and again looked into the jug.

"I suppose she felt queer, and turned back said Charlie."

"I reckon that's it," said Bob. "Send Harry, for it. Poor thing, she ain't got right yet."

"No," said Charlie, "and it strikes me, she never will."

"Why?" asked Bob.

"I think she frets about that damned husband of her's," replied the clown.

"Do you?" said Bob, putting on a look of surprise.

"I do."

"What makes you think that?" asked Bob.

"I don't know," said Charlie; "but sometimes I notice she looks dull and miserable, and thoughtful. I believe she often worries about him, and more fool she, for he ain't worth a thought."

"Not half a one," said Bob, and, he added to himself, "you'd think a good deal less of him, my friend, did you know as much of him as I do."

But Bob thought it better to avoid as much as possible entering into conversation about Dancing Bill, so he turned and beckoned to Harry, who was standing some short distance from him.

The boy bounded to his side.

"Go and fetch some beer," he said, "for strike me comical, if I ain't melting all away."

The boy took the jug and the money, and was out of sight in a minute.

This had the effect of preventing any more being said on the subject of Dancing Bill, and Charlie and Bob re-commenced the work of building the booth for to-morrow's fair.

In a short time the booth was completed, and the pantomimists entered the caravan to partake of their evening meal.

Margaret had returned to her couch to prevent any inquiry as to the cause of her returning without the beer.

Buskin Bob was the only one who suspected the real cause of the emotion exhibited by Margaret, but he kept silent, and the meal passed over without any remarks, other than of an ordinary character.

On the following day the fair opened, and our friends once more solicited the favour of the public.

There was no change in the character of the entertainment from what we have hitherto seen, save and except increased confidence on the part of Harry and Mary in meeting the faces of the audience.

Buskin Bob and Charlie Evans tried their utmost to draw in the people, but spite of all their endeavours, they had to perform to half-empty houses.

The fair did not pay.

It was the worst they had yet attended, and on the third day, not all the glowing accounts of the wonders to be seen within, could fill more than three rows of benches in each house, and when the curtain fell upon the last house, Charlie felt happy that the Coventry fair was over.

The amount taken during the three days, was hardly sufficient to pay the expenses, and the good hearted clown's face wore a look of sadness for the first time since he had purchased the caravan.

"Well, Harry," he remarked, to the Boy Actor, "Coventry has been failure, I am sorry to say. But it has been no fault of mine. I have done all in my power to draw the people in. I have bawled myself hoarse, but all to no avail."

"Never mind, father," said Harry. If the people would not favour us with a visit it is no fault of yours. We can hardly expect all sunshine and no showers. Perhaps the next fair may make up for the failure of this."

"I hope it will, my boy," replied Charlie, "for we can ill-afford to meet with two such bad runs. I did expect that Coventry would have proved a success."

"And no doubt it would," said Bob, "if it wasn't for the procession."

"What procession?" asked Harry.

"Why, the Lady Godiva procession, to be sure. The folks are husbanding their money for that."

"To be sure they are," said Charlie, "I had forgotten all about it."

"I hadn't," said Bob, "and strike me comical if I don't think we can turn a failure now into a success."

"How?" asked Charlie, eagerly.

"Get engagements in the procession," replied Bob. "There's no fair for ten days, and we can reach it from here in two. So what do you say to going to see if all the posts are filled up?"

"Good," said Charlie "we will do so in the morning."

"I'm with you, strike me comical if I ain't," said Bob.

"And I too," said Harry.

Charlie smiled at the promptness, with which the boy showed his eagerness to work for the general welfare of all.

But he shrugged his shoulders as he remarked.

"I fear you would not be required."

"Why not?" asked Harry.

"Ah, why not?" said Bob.

"What could he do?"

"He would do for a page," said Buskin Bob.

"A page?"

"Yes."

Charlie shook his head.

"He'd do first rate," said Bob.

"He can't ride."

"What of that?"

"He'd be thrown off."

"He can walk, I suppose?"

"Well?"

"And he could lay his hand on a horse's bridle, I should say."

"Ah, I see, a walking page," said Charlie.

"Exactly."

"Certainly, he could do that."

"And so could Mary."

"Yes."

"Then we may as well seek engagements for all four," said Bob.

"So we may."

"I shall be so glad if we succeed," said Harry.

"I don't think there is much doubt but what we shall," remarked Bob. "Those who are getting up the affair will be more willing to employ professionals than any one else."

"And besides, we can find our own dresses if required," remarked Charlie.

"That's another step in our favour," said Bob.

No. 21.

"Well, then, to-morrow you and I will seek out the people who have the management of the affair," said Charlie, "and see what can be done."

On the following morning, Charlie Evans and his friend Buskin Bob, applied for engagements in the procession, and as there were several still vacant they were accepted, together with Harry and Mary as pages.

Charlie and Bob who had learnt to ride while engaged in a travelling circus, were to assume the characters of armed knights, and Harry and Mary were to undertake the characters of pages to them.

This was better than the friends had expected, for the young folks would thus remain with them during the march through the town.

The pantomimists hastened back to the caravan, to make the young folks acquainted with their success.

The terms they had made were very satisfactory to themselves, and although, when added to the proceeds of their last three days labour, they would not make up the takings of a good fair, still it would prevent them making use of any of the small sum Charlie had put by for a rainy day, as he himself expressed it.

The day of the procession broke bright and glorious, and the pantomimists rose by times to prepare for their labours.

As they wended their way to the rendezvous from whence the procession was to start, they found the street rapidly filling with persons of each sex, anxious to get a good view of the procession.

"Strike me comical if we shan't play to a larger audience to-day, Harry, my boy, than ever we have done before," said Bob, casting his eyes along the High Street, whose pavements were fast becoming blocked up by the eager sightseers.

The boy's eyes kindled as he followed the looks of his companion, and observed the mass of heads stretching away far up the High Street of the town.

In a short time they arrived at their destination, and attired themselves in the costume selected for them.

The time arrived for the procession to start.

Harry and Mary, attired as pages, laid their hands upon the bridles of the horses, which Charlie and Bob, attired as knights, armed cap-a-pie, bestrode more gracefully than many would have given them credit for. The gates were opened, and the procession started forth amid the ringing of bells and the thundering cheers of an English mob.

Along the High Street the procession wended its way slowly.

So dense was the crowd, that it seemed almost impossible that ever it could pass through it.

Harry cast an anxious glance along the route.

The huge mass in front for a moment appalled him.

He thought of Mary.

"What if the crowd should close in upon and crush her."

His hand trembled upon the bridle of the steed which Buskin Bob rode.

Bob saw the face of the youth pale, and he stooped over his horse's neck.

"Harry," he said, "what is the matter?"

"I fear we shall be crushed to death," replied the youth.

"Not a bit of it," said Bob. "The crowd a-head will open as we go on as it does now. Cheer up, a knight's page should not have pale cheeks and trembling hands!"

The boy smiled, and becoming re-assured by the words of his friend, he strode on more firmly.

The end of the route was reached at last, and the labours of the pantomimists were over.

It was with a smile of joy that the Boy Actor grasped the hand of Mary.

He had suffered much anxiety on her account, but now that they had forced through the crowd the glow returned to his cheek.

———

CHAPTER LXXXIV.

A YOUTHFUL ADMIRER—AND A YOUTHFUL DEFENDER.

In the procession rode a youth, the son of one of the directors of the *fete*.

His position was close behind that of Charlie Evans and his daughter.

He was an effeminate-looking youth, with a supercilious sort of smile always on his features.

But there was a look in the small twinkling eyes which betokened a sensual passion.

The only son of a wealthy man, spoilt in childhood, of a wayward nature; he would have his own way.

And the father, ever willing to grant him money and indulgence, the youth formed companionship with those who would rather excite the depraved passions of his nature, than endeavour to curb them.

Though young in years, he was old in sin.

He had expressed a wish to form one in the procession, and the indulgent father, much against his will, had granted the request.

His sensual gaze had fastened on the face of Mary from the moment that she appeared, attired in the costume of the page.

Her bright eyes and lovely features caused a pang to shoot through the heart of the young libertine.

He resolved not to lose sight of her, and as the young girl took up her position, William Frampton forced his way behind her.

Throughout the whole route, he saw nothing but the graceful form of the clown's daughter.

He had eyes for none but her.

And when the procession had wended its way to its destination, he hurriedly dismounted his horse, removed his dress, and waited the appearance of Mary.

He resolved to find out her destination.

With this intention, he watched and waited till she left the place with her father and his friends.

Little did Charlie Evans know that the footsteps of his child were being dogged by a youthful libertine.

Frampton followed them to the caravan, and a sigh escaped him as the little door closed upon her slender form.

But he did not leave the spot.

He stood gazing at the door for some time.

"I must discover her name," he muttered.

"I must see her again. Her beauty has charmed me. She is poor, no doubt. I am rich, and gold will purchase anything. She is young, but what of that? I am young, and have the means to pander to her every wish. I must find some means to force myself into her company. But how—how?"

The door of the caravan opened.

Charlie ran hurriedly down the steps.

The watcher withdrew from the spot.

He must not excite suspicion.

Especially the suspicion of the man who had left the caravan.

For he was the father of the girl whom his unholy passions prompted him to watch.

He had heard her call him such.

So he hurriedly darted away from the spot.

When Charlie had got out of sight, Frampton returned to the front of the caravan.

"How can I obtain an interview with her?" he muttered. "I can see no other way than staying and watching for her leaving the booth alone."

Scarce had these thoughts ran through his mind, than the little door once more opened, and the graceful form of Mary ran down the steps, and hurried along towards the town.

She had left the booth to procure something for supper.

The heart of the youth bounded in his breast.

Quickly he strode after her.

Out of the fair field into the road went Mary, followed at a few yards' distance by the youth.

Once or twice she looked behind her, but no suspicion entered her mind that the youth, who kept the same pace between them, had any design to molest her.

Humming a ditty, she kept on her way, till she had arrived at a deserted part of the road.

The footsteps behind her quickened, and in a few moments Frampton was by her side.

He looked boldly, almost insolently, into her face.

Mary drew back, then stepped into the road, and hurried on.

But the youth again made his way to her side, and said,—

"I saw you in the procession to-day."

"Did you," said Mary, and she quickened her pace, evidently hoping to get rid of one who wished to force his company upon her.

"Yes," he replied, still keeping pace with her. "And I was charmed with your beauty."

Mary made no reply.

And finding that the youth still kept up with her, she stood still, thinking that perhaps he would continue on his way.

But the youth stopped also.

"Yes," he said again. "I was charmed with your beauty, for who could be otherwise."

"Which road do you travel, sir?" she asked, indignantly.

"The same as yourself, Mary, for such I heard you called," he replied.

"Be kind enough then to go on, sir," said Mary, "for my road lies different to yours."

"Now don't be offended," said the youth, with a supercilious smile. "Surely you do not object to being told you are beautiful."

"I object to being annoyed by a stranger," she replied haughtily.

"I hope to be better acquainted with you ere long," he said.

"Then I have no wish to become acquainted with you, so please to go your way, and leave me to pursue mine, free from any further molestation."

"You are too severe," drawled the youth, "I wish to be your friend."

"Indeed!"

"Yes, indeed I do," he continued. "It is not every poor girl who would refuse the friendship of the son of a wealthy man, whose fortune he will inherit at his death. Now don't be obstinate, your pretty face has charmed me; and I declare I have fallen in love with you at first sight."

And as he spoke, the youth endeavoured to take the hand of the young dancer.

But Mary indignantly drew back, and failing to secure her hand, he grasped her shawl, which fell from her shoulders as she bounded into the road.

For a moment she stood gazing upon the youth, as he held her garment in his hand.

Then with a flushed cheek, she stretched forth her hand to take it from him.

"You shall not have it," he said, "till you purchase it with a kiss."

"Give me my shawl," she said, the tears starting to her eyes.

"It is yours on the condition I have named," he replied, offering the garment to her.

Mary stretched out her hand to take it, and as she did so Frampton threw his arm around her neck, and endeavoured to imprint a kiss upon her lips.

Mary struggled and screamed; but the youth, fired with her resistance, essayed the more to accomplish his desires, and as he forced her head back, and was about to imprint a kiss upon her lips, he received a blow upon his forehead, which sent him staggering back some few paces, and ere he could perfectly recover his balance, another blow was dealt him between the eyes, and he fell into the road, as the arm of Harry Marston, the Boy Actor, encircled the waist of the almost fainting girl.

CHAPTER LXXXV.

DANCING BILL'S JOURNEY TO SEEK GRIPE—HIS SUFFERINGS—A SURPRISE.

PERHAPS of all the fallacies in the world, there is none more deceitful than a man believing that he can drown sorrow or remorse in the bowl filled with intoxicating liquors.

There are some who, at the approach of misfortune or calamity in any shape, instantly fly to drink, in the vain belief that they will find relief in its fumes.

The brain, worried by affliction; the mind, lacerated by misery, is but rendered worse by the depressing effects of drink.

It is like dropping oil upon a burning wick.

For a moment it blazes up with increased lustre; but the next instant the brightness fades, and it becomes even more gloomy and dimmed.

Still, it would be hard to persuade many that they but enhance their sufferings by believing in this sophism.

It cannot be rooted out, and, spite of all the

arguments brought to bear against it, they cling to the belief till, their constitution ruined, they find but too surely they have been feeding the disease; adding fuel to the fire which consumed them, only to learn the fatal truth when it is too late to stay its ravages, and save the structure from utter ruin.

In the vain hope to drown the cries of conscience, Dancing Bill, the harlequin, sought relief from its whisperings in the arch demon brandy.

To obtain the intoxicating liquor he had sold everything he possessed, and driven himself to starvation, in which state we saw him when he met Gripe, the little steward, on his way to London.

The twenty pounds he had received from that worthy had set him up again, and he returned to Barnstable, where he took all that he could lay his hands on in the hidden cavern, and resolved to leave England and try his fortunes in America.

But he feared to go to a strange land alone, and still hoping that his wife would at last be prevailed upon to accompany him, he hung about the country, spending the money which would have procured him a passage, and left something for his wants on his arrival, till it dwindled away and nothing was left to pay his passage with.

Still he craved for drink—drink to drown the voice of conscience.

The musket and the hunting-knife were sold for this purpose, and now he was alone in the world without a friend—without the means of procuring shelter.

The depressing effects of the liquor drove him almost to madness, and, as he had said to Margaret, he could hear the cries of his victim in the breeze—see her pale face and blood-stained form in every step.

Conscience never slumbers.

Its whisperings will make themselves heard; but would the imagination play so fearfully upon the constitution were it not excited by that which is so fallaciously believed to still its upbraidings.

Dancing Bill inflicted more misery upon himself daily.

As the fumes of the liquor wore off, his spirits sank, his nerves became more and more weakened, till at length he started at his own footfall, and turned pale even at his own shadow.

The fright he had received at the hands of Buskin Bob, too, had tended greatly to unnerve him; and, his brain weakened by suffering and intemperance, he could not bring himself to search for an explanation of the strange object he had encountered at the haunted oak.

He trembled at the very recollection of that night.

He believed that it was Satan himself who had accosted him.

Weakened in body and in mind, without shelter, without food, without the means of procuring drink, he resolved to visit Barnstable again, and seek out Gripe and endeavour to prevail upon the little steward to minister to his wants.

With this determination Dancing Bill started on his journey.

Walking by day and sleeping under haystacks or in barns by night, he arrived at length, foot-sore, weary, and literally starving at Barnstable.

It was about mid-day when he arrived at the spot where he had met the steward on the night that he gave up the papers.

He dragged his wearied and attenuated form along towards the old manor house, and questioned every person he met for information as to where Gripe was to be found.

It was not till the shades of evening began to close around him that he learnt from a wayfarer, whom he accosted, that the person he sought was in prison.

This was a serious blow to Dancing Bill.

His hopes of succour were gone.

He seated himself by the wayside and gave himself up to despair.

Whilst hope of relief existed he still dragged on; but now his last chance was gone; his brain tottered, his limbs refused their office, the pangs of hunger gnawing at his vitals became unbearable, and he laid his head back against the fence which parted the green fields from the high road and closed his eyes, believing that his last hour had come, and that Death had set his seal upon his guilty brow.

Yet with all his sufferings he feared to die.

How could he meet his Maker?

How could he answer the dread question,—

"Hast thou obeyed my commandments?"

He was wearied of life. Yet he prayed for it now—prayed that the edge of the scythe might be averted, and that he might live—live on, though every moment was fraught with terror—every footstep jarred upon his soul lest it should be that of those who came to bear him to justice and the reward of his sins. Yet he could bear all rather than death, for,—

"The fear of something after death,
    The undiscovered country from whose bourn
    No traveller returns, puzzles the will
    And makes him rather bear those ills he has
    Than fly to others that he knows not of."

Truly indeed has the poet said,—

"Conscience makes cowards of us all,"

and the shivering and guilty wretch, emaciated with want, with the hand of every honest man against him, with the sword of justice hanging over his head, the gallows looming in the distance, an outcast from society, a burden and a misery to himself, feared to seek relief from his sufferings in the cold and silent grave.

After a time he rose with some difficulty to his feet, and glanced around him.

His eyes encountered a bright light, shining from a window, some distance along the road.

"I will struggle to reach it," he murmured, "and ask for bread. Oh, heaven, what a whip have I made to scourge myself. I must beg for food, or I shall die, and then—then—oh, the thought is fearful. I cannot—must not perish. Food—I must have food; they will not refuse me; I will struggle to reach that house, and beg of them to save me from death."

He grasped at the palings, and drew himself along the road.

But so weak had he become, that he was compelled to rest every few minutes.

Still, the fear that death would overtake him, urged him onwards.

Grasping at the rails, he dragged himself, rather than walked, towards the house, from which the light came.

The moon rose, and lighted up his path, but he shuddered as his eyes ever and anon rested upon his shadow.

Still on—on.

The light loomed larger, and nearer, but he feared he would be unable to reach it, so faint was he.

Thus an hour passed; and he stood at the door of the farmhouse.

He struck upon the panels with his knuckles then a sickness came over him, and he leant against the doorpost for support.

In an instant his summons was answered.

Bill raised his head, he tottered back, staggered, and fell to the earth, as he gasped forth,—

"Dick the Poacher!"

CHAPTER LXXXVI.

DICK THE POACHER ENDEAVOURS TO REVIVE THE HARLEQUIN—THE SENSES RESTORED—THE RECOGNITION.

AT the mention of his name, Dick the Poacher, for he indeed it was, who had answered the summons of Dancing Bill, started back, as the tones of the wretched man fell upon his ears.

The voice was familiar to him; but he could not call to mind, when and where he had heard them before.

But as Dancing Bill staggered and fell to the earth, the poacher sprang forward.

"Minnie, Minnie!" he called out to his wife, "bring a light, here is some poor wretch who needs assistance."

His poor idiot wife, who was sitting in the kitchen, from whose window Bill had seen the glimmer of the lamp, sprang to her feet, and grasping the light, hurried to the side of her husband.

"See, Minnie!" exclaimed Dick, pointing to the prostrate body of the harlequin before the door. "Some poor fellow is here ill or in a fit; hold the light, Minnie, while I endeavour to lift him up."

The poor idiot held the lamp in such a position as to throw its rays upon the heap of humanity which lay across the doorway.

Dick bent over the prostrate form, and raised its head on to his knee.

He felt that the hand and face of the man was cold, and a shudder ran through the frame of the good-hearted fellow, as the idea occurred to him, that the wretch he held in his arms, had paid the last debt of nature.

"Hold the lamp lower, Minnie!" exclaimed Dick, peering into the features of Bill, and endeavouring to trace the lineaments now so pale, stiff, and rigid.

Minnie stooped and threw the rays of the light full upon the face of the man.

"I have seen these features before," muttered Dick. "but where—where?"

And he laid his finger upon his brow, as if to assist his memory.

"Poor man, poor man," muttered the imbecile. "Cold—pale. The birds do not sing, Dick; the grass is withered; see it is dry, not green, Dick—not green."

And she pointed down at the herbage at her feet.

"It is the rays of the lamp streaming upon the blades, that changes their colour, Minnie," said the poacher, "that is all. I will carry the poor fellow into the kitchen, he must not lay here to die, be he whom he may."

And the strong man raised the weak and attenuated form of the guilty wretch in his arms.

"Go on, Minnie," he said. "I will follow you."

The idiot stepped back into the house, and Dick followed her with his inanimate burden.

But the moment he had crossed the threshold, Minnie shuddered.

This was not lost upon Dick.

"Why do you shudder, Minnie?" he asked.

"Bad man—bad man," she replied hurriedly.

And as she spoke, she shrank further away from the inanimate form.

"Good or bad, Minnie," said her husband, "we must not forget the duty of a Christian. Look! his pale thin face speaks of want and suffering. He is but the skeleton of a man, worn down to a shadow by illness or starvation. Minnie shall we refuse to give a helping hand to the suffering or the oppressed?"

The tones of his voice, and the words he had uttered, caused the poor wife to start to his side.

"No, no!" she exclaimed hurriedly. "We must be kind, we must be good; or the birds will not sing around the old house, and the grass will wither at our footsteps."

"I knew you did not wish me to leave the poor fellow where he fell. No, Minnie, we have little to give, but that little we will give freely."

"Yes, yes!" she exclaimed, setting the lamp down upon the table, and again returning to the side of her husband, she took the thin hand of the guilty man in her own.

But as she pressed the cold fingers she again shuddered.

"Why is this?" thought Dick. "Suffering has shattered her reason, but heaven seems to have implanted in her soul an instinct denied to those who have the full use of their faculties. Why, then, does she shudder when she gazes upon this miserable wretch?"

Dick laid the insensible form down upon a couch in the kitchen, and leant thoughtfully over it.

But Minnie drew back to the table and stood watching her husband.

"I have seen these features before," muttered the poacher thoughtfully, "but where, I cannot for the life of me think. There are strange resemblances in this world, yet I cannot be mistaken, for did he not recognise me at the door?"

And taking the lamp from the table, he held it so as to throw its rays full upon the thin, pale face of the harlequin.

He gazed long and intently upon those sunken eyes, and thin visage; then he placed his hand on the breast of the prostrate man, to feel if any pulsation yet remained.

The heart beat faintly, and a look of pleasure lit up the bronzed countenance of the poacher.

"He lives, Minnie!" he exclaimed, turning to his wife, "and that is all. The heart still beats, but so faint is its pulsation, that I almost fear we shall be unable to revive him. But we will do our utmost to call back the fleeting breath. Give me the brandy, Minnie."

The idiot walked across the room and opened the door of a high cupboard, and took from one of its shelves a small black bottle, which she placed in the hands of her husband, and then returned to the table as though she feared contact with the form upon the couch.

Dick drew the cork, and placed the neck of the bottle to the lips of Dancing Bill.

But the teeth of the prostrate wretch were clenched so tightly, that the liquor ran over the sides of his mouth down on to his neck.

"Poor fellow—poor fellow!" muttered Dick, condolingly.

Then pouring some of the brandy into the palm of his hand, he bathed the temples of the harlequin.

Grasping the thin hands in his own, he chafed them in the hopes of causing the blood to flow more freely through the veins, and again he applied the neck of the bottle to the blue lips of the sufferer.

Then he drew back a few paces, and eagerly watched the effect of his work.

Gradually the poacher perceived the muscles of the face to relax, the lips parted slightly, and the bosom heaved.

Then a long, deep-drawn sigh emanated from the prostrate form.

"Good," said Dick, with a look of pleasure beaming in his dark eye, as he turned towards his wife, who, pale and trembling, watched his every movement. "There is life, Minnie, so there is hope. Poor fellow—poor fellow, what must he have suffered to have been brought down so low."

Minnie answered with a sigh.

Again the poacher placed the neck of the bottle to the lips of Dancing Bill.

A groan came from his throat; a shudder ran through his frame, and his eyes opened.

For a moment the poor suffering wretch remained quiet, then with a wild, unnatural stare he gazed around the room.

"You are better now," said Dick, placing his arm under the neck of Dancing Bill and raising his head.

The harlequin still gazed in the face of the poacher with a wild look.

"Here, take a draught of this, and you will soon be all right," said Dick, placing the bottle again to the lips of the half insensible man.

The eyes of the harlequin brightened as the brandy poured down his throat.

"There, it will do you good," said Dick, taking the bottle from his lips, and allowing the head of Bill to once more fall back upon the pillow.

As Dick returned to the table and placed the bottle thereon, the glance of the harlequin followed him.

Recollection was fast returning.

He tried to raise his head from the couch.

With a great effort he did so.

The light of the lamp fell full upon his features, which were fast assuming their natural expression.

Dick gazed thoughtfully and anxiously upon him.

Then the poacher started with a suppressed cry.

Now he recollected where and when he had seen those features before.

A look of disgust overspread his features, but in a moment it gave place to an expression of pity.

In health and strength he could despise the wretch before him, but in suffering and want, pity took the place of disgust.

Though a poacher, he was a man, and he resolved to extend a helping hand to one who so ill-deserved sympathy.

CHAPTER LXXXVII.

THE YOUNG PLAYERS — THE DAWN OF LOVE — JEALOUSY—SAD FOREBODINGS.

WITH clenched hand and flashing eye, the Boy Actor stood gazing down upon the prostrate assailant of little Mary.

With a cry of joy the young girl had flung her arm around the neck of her youthful protector, and her bosom rose and fell with the emotions which the conduct of the unprincipled young libertine had engendered in her breast.

Surprised and abashed, the youth lie upon the ground at the feet of the Boy Actor, with the blood pouring from his nose, and his head aching from the force of the blow dealt him by the protector of the young girl.

Like most persons of unprincipled nature, he was a coward.

He trembled before the indignant glance of the youth, whose age and size would bear no comparison with his own.

A good cause is ever half the battle, and this was felt by the young libertine, as he lay, half-fearing to rise to his feet, lest he should receive further chastisement at the hands of the youth who had arrived so opportunely for Mary upon the spot.

After the first feeling of gratification was over, Mary burst into tears.

The severe expression on the face of the Boy Actor changed in a moment to one of pity and condolence, and he pressed the form of the young girl to his breast, as he muttered,—

"Don't cry, Mary, he shan't touch you again. I'll fight for you while I can stand, though he is bigger than me."

Mary raised her tearful eyes to his face, with such a look of love and tenderness, that the heart of the Boy Actor bounded with an indescribable feeling in his breast.

His arm tightened around her waist, and unconscious of what he did, he strained her to his breast, and their lips met in a long, lingering kiss.

It was the dawn of love in the youthful hearts of them both; the affections of childhood had given place to a passion, if not more fervent, at least more ardent.

But as though some unseen monitor rebuked them, they started from each other's embrace, and their cheeks became flushed with their blushes.

"Come away, Harry," she said, as the young libertine staggered to his feet. "He will strike you."

"He dare not," said Harry, proudly drawing himself up. "I do not fear him. I feel as if I had a man's strength in my arms, and could thrash twenty such blackguards as him.

But contrary to the expectations and fears of Mary, the youthful libertine made no attempt to molest them further; but on the contrary, grinding his teeth and casting a malignant glare upon them, he sneaked away like a beaten cur down the road.

The eyes of the young friends watched his retreating figure for some moments, then turned their gaze upon each other.

But in an instant their eyes dropped, and they looked upon the ground.

The rich blood mounted to their faces once more, and each appeared to be very much confused.

Why was this?

They scarcely knew themselves.

Harry tried to speak with that freedom he had ever been in the habit of using, but his tongue seemed tied.

The pretty little playmate and fellow-worker in their Struggles for Bread, had in his eyes changed from the child to the woman, and he felt that restraint which holds in awe the free advances of childhood.

From that moment their feelings were changed towards each other. Not that they loved each other the less, but that love had taken a different shape.

Young indeed they were. Still, the first bud of affection had opened in their hearts, and the flower of young love was fast expanding to maturity.

Childhood's gambols had passed away.

That long, lingering embrace had drawn forth the hitherto hidden passions from the well-springs of the heart, and implanted in their breasts a feeling so different to that which they had hitherto experienced, that they approached each other now with a restraint that they had never before felt.

"If you have no objection, Mary," said the Boy Actor, after a pause, and raising his eyes half frightened to the pretty blushing face of the fair girl, "I will accompany you on your errand."

"Objection!" she said. "Ah, I shall be only too happy if you will come."

"And I only too happy to be with you," he thought, as he started on beside her.

Then there was another pause.

Harry wished to break the silence, yet could find nothing to say.

No subject could he start to break the monotony of their walk.

"How is this," he thought, "I never felt so lost for something to say before. Nor has Mary ever seemed so dull; she does not laugh so merrily, run so wildly away from me, nor tease me as she always has done. What can be the cause of it. It must be that rascal's annoyance that has damped the spirits of us both."

This was the only conclusion he could arrive at.

At length he remarked,—

"Why did that fellow interfere with you, Mary?"

"I don't know," she replied.

"Did he want to steal your shawl?" asked the youth.

"I do not think so."

"How did he come by it?"

"As I ran away from him he caught hold of it to stop me, and it came unpinned in his hand," said Mary.

"Yet he would not give it you back."

"Not till—till—"

"What?"

Again the tell-tale blood rose to her cheeks, and she cast her eyes to the ground as she murmured,—

"Till I kissed him."

"But you did not, did you," said Harry, hurriedly.

"Oh, no!"

"But why did he want to kiss you?" asked the boy, a new feeling for the first time entering his breast, and clouding his brow.

It was the first pang of jealousy.

That attendant upon love, from which it would seem the affection of the heart is seldom or ever free.

"I cannot say," replied Mary, in answer to Harry's question.

"Have you ever seen him before?" asked the youth.

"Never."

"Strange."

"Very."

"Where did he first speak to you?" asked Harry.

"Where you saw him."

"Did he meet you?"

"No," replied Mary. "He followed me from the fair field."

"Followed you."

"Yes; I tried to avoid him but could not. At last he spoke to me."

"Yes."

"And I stepped into the road, in the hopes that he would pass on."

"And he did not."

"No. He spoke to me again," said Mary.

"What did he say?"

"That—that—"

And the blushes again suffused her cheeks.

"What?"

"He had seen me before."

"Yes."

"At the procession."

"Well."

"That I was pretty," said Mary.

Harry clenched his hand and grated his teeth.

There was pain to him in anyone admiring the beauty of his companion.

"And that he loved me," continued Mary.

"He said so!" exclaimed Harry.

"He did."

"I'm glad I knocked him down!" exclaimed the boy.

"Why?"

"For loving you."

Mary burst out into one of her ringing laughs, but suddenly checked herself as she saw the look of pain which crossed the face of the Boy Actor.

"I told him to go about his business, but he would not, and when I endeavoured to turn back he stretched out his hand to stay me. It was then I left my shawl in his hand, and when I asked him for it, he refused to let me have it unless I kissed him. Then you came up."

"And if I had not come up, Mary?" queried the youth.

"I should have returned to the booth without it," she replied.

"You would not have complied then with his wish to regain it," said the boy.

"No," she said hastily.

A gleam of joy glanced from the eyes of the boy.

"I'm so glad of that," he exclaimed.

"Why."

"Because—because—"

"What?"

"I don't know," stammered the boy, in a confused tone, "only I feel I could not bear to know you had kissed him."

"You couldn't," she said, with an arch look.

"No," exclaimed the boy. "I—I don't know why, but I think I should feel very unhappy if you kissed anybody, Mary."

"Then I would not make you unhappy, Harry," she said tenderly. "For I am sure I would not gratify the whim of any rude stranger, and I hope I shall never meet him again."

"It wil be well for him if you do not," said Harry. "For I feel that I should serve him worse than I did to-day, if he dared to offend you again."

"We shall never meet him, I daresay," remarked Mary.

"I hope not," thought Harry, "for my sake."

Yet an indescribable feeling took possession of his heart, as he gave utterance to the words, that it was not the last time they would meet.

A something whispered to him that the youth he had struck down would be a thorn in his side, and a feeling of hate towards him sprang up in his breast.

It was the first person for whom he ever entertained animosity.

He felt no such feeling, even, towards Dancing Bill, as he did towards the youth he had met for the first time in his life that day.

Mary, however seemed to have forgotten the circumstance, for the smile returned to her cheeks, as she kept on her way.

Not so Harry.

He could not forget.

That instinct for which it is not in the power of man to account told him that he had made an enemy of one whom till now he had never seen—who would strive to blight his happiness, and that of the girl who he now felt was dearer to him than his own existence.

The foreboding pressed with increased weight every minute upon his mind, and he became sad and gloomy, and spite of all his endeavours to shake off the feeling in his heart, it grew in strength, till it rendered him miserable.

CHAPTER LXXXVIII.

SHADOWS OF EVIL—A MISTAKEN IDEA—THE LIBERTINE AND HIS THOUGHTS.

At one period or another, a dark cloud is sure to obscure for a time, the bright sunshine of man's existence.

Were it not that happiness was every now and then crossed by sorrow, the human heart could not appreciate the value of peace and joy.

To go through life smoothly would render us callous to the sufferings of our less fortunate fellow-creatures.

Therefore it is by a wise dispensation of Providence, that all mankind are made to feel the stings of poverty, misfortune, or sorrow.

A dark cloud will enshroud at some time or another; enshroud the happiness of all.

Even on the sun's bright disc, a black spot can be detected.

Love, perhaps the noblest of all the passions, is the most liable to a dark shadow.

The Boy Actor loved; though he knew not the passion which had taken possession of his heart.

The beautiful and gentle Mary, the poor clown's daughter had won the noblest affections of his soul.

Her gentle nature had implanted in the bosom of the Boy Actor, a ray of happiness he had never before experienced.

But there were dark clouds looming in the distance, and the happiness engendered in his soul, was yet to be overcast.

"Coming events cast their shadows before," and the Boy Actor's heart was filled with dark forebodings.

That instinctive dread of evil which at times rushes upon our hearts, and for which we strive in vain to account, had taken possession of his soul.

In vain he strove to shake it off.

There, like a nightmare upon his heart, it sat, and not all the sophistry of his youthful mind could hurl the incubus from its throne.

It was therefore with mingled feelings of pleasure and dread that Harry Marston bade the pretty Mary good night, and sought his couch.

For some time he strove in vain to court the drowsy God,—

"To steep his senses in forgetfulness,"

he could not woo him to his pillow. Somnus would not weigh his eyelids down till the first grey streak of early dawn lit up the eastern sky.

But even whilst the body rested, the mind was still at work.

The portals of the brain were opened, and shadows flitted before them.

Shadows of the libertine and Mary.

And he awoke, when the bright sun was high in the heavens, unrefreshed in body and in mind.

Still the dark cloud hung like a funeral pall upon his soul, and weighed his spirits down.

In vain he strove to shake it off and seek its silver lining.

Superstition reveals a weak and ignorant mind. But is there one who is not more or less prone to it. We believe that all mankind are superstitious in a greater or less degree. Many pretend to laugh it to scorn, but they themselves are not wholly free from its influence.

At times there is a strange and indefinable weight about the heart which leads our thoughts to the belief that something is wrong, that something is about to happen to us, or those near and dear to us, and spite of all the arguments we can bring to bear upon it, we cannot shake it off.

It is seldom, indeed, that this strange, oppressive feeling is not the forerunner of some evil, or sickness.

MARY EVANS.

And in the case of the young players it was no exception.

The youthful libertine, whom his hand had struck to the earth, possessed a spirit as unforgiving as his nature was degraded.

The blow he had received awakened all his evil passions, the principle of which was revenge.

His cowardly and ungenerous nature led him to ponder upon the chastisement inflicted upon him by the protector of the pantomimist's daughter, and he vowed never to rest till he had had a deep and bitter revenge for the blow.

His subtle and crafty spirit could not return and give blow for blow.

No.

He would strike again, but in the dark and behind his back.

No. 22.

The embrace which had been denied to him, yet granted to his assailant, rankled in his heart.

It fanned his youthful blood, and poisoned all the nobler qualities of his soul.

Shame and confusion now gave place to feelings of hate and revenge.

His vanity too was wounded.

He had been spurned by the daughter of a strolling player.

He, the son of one of the most wealthy and influential gentlemen of Coventry.

He, the heir to vast estates; the scion of a proud and ancient lineage.

Spurned by one so far beneath him in the scale of rank and station.

The thought was more than his proud soul could bear.

And to be struck down by the hand of one who had no standing in society, was gall to his heart.

Not once did it occur to him that the young players had shown themselves more noble than he had done.

It never occurred to him that virtue and justice are nobler qualities than wealth and lineage.

Like many pampered scions of wealthy houses, he believed that gold could buy truth and honour, virtue and happiness, peace and content.

To him gold was the balm to heal every wound and minister to every wish.

But, like many others of the same class, he had found to his cost, that virtuous poverty is not always to be assailed with impunity, and the hand of a poor and honourble man, sometimes descends with fearful force upon the head of a rich, unprincipled, and insulting villain.

But if gold cannot always buy honour it can purchase revenge.

And to this the mean spirited and ignoble seldom hesitate to stoop.

The young libertine resolved to be revenged, not alone on Harry for the blow, but on the girl for the contempt with which she had presumed to treat him.

His dignity was wounded.

He had been repulsed by a strolling player.

He who had stooped so low as to condescend to notice one so far beneath him.

Beneath him—Heaven save the mark.

Were the gold the standard by which to measure mankind, honour and virtue would fall low indeed.

"Curse her!" he muttered between his clenched teeth, as he strode along, holding his silk handkerchief to his bleeding face, "the miserable, poverty-struck thing. But I will be revenged for this; I have condescended to stoop to think of her, because she was pretty. I lowered myself to honour her by my notice—her, a strolling player, a dancer at a penny show, and she, forsooth, must ape her superiors by acting a virtuous indignation, as if that were a commodity which ever was to be found in the composition of those who followed such a calling. Does she think I am such a fool as not to know, that to those of her sex who follow her profession, virtue is but a name."

How many have made a similar remark, with regard to those who follow the stage.

The youthful libertine who has dared to assail a poor and defenceless girl, because she struggled for bread before the footlights, is not the only one who has made such an assertion, and pointed to the actress as a thing to be shunned and abhorred.

Such insinuations have come from those who know better.

From men whose hatred to the enjoyments of their fellows, or from their own fanatical views, are led to utter the unblushing and shameful lie, and strive to bring into contempt those who often read a better moral, and teach a nobler lesson from the stage, than is read from the pulpit by those who, in their frenzied zeal, profane the gospel and desecrate the drama.

In every class of the community, in every grade of life, in every calling, there are good and bad members; but it is a disgraceful shame that the actress and the ballet girl should be made the mark by many at which to hurl the venomed lie of unchastity and level the finger of scorn.

Behind the curtain virtue stands forward as proudly, as in the homes of honourable justice-loving families, and is to often contaminated by the presence of those who presume to revile it.

Why should this class of the gentler sex be thus unblushingly and ignobly vilified.

And more often by those who profess peace and good will to all.

Also it is hard to tell the motives which prompt the wicked falsehood.

Fanaticism may do much towards it, for the fanatic stoops often to lie to serve a theory to which he is wedded, and in the sacred name of religion excuses his acts; as if religion counselled such unholy work. No, it teaches us to shield the erring, not belie the fair fame of the virtuous and the true.

It is that hatred to all that do not hold the same opinion as themselves, to all who seek relaxation and amusement and instruction in other places than those devoted to the wild ravings of a sanctified hypocrite; it is the mean and base revenge of a fanatical scoffer at other teachings than his own; it is prompted by a debased mind and ungenerous spirit, and deserves the contempt of all honourable right-thinking men.

He that makes the assertion, that on the stage virtue is but a name, gives utterance to a scurrilous and wicked lie, and should be rewarded by the scorn of every one to whom truth and justice are words to be honoured and respected.

No pity should be extended to him, but,—

"A whip placed in the hands of every honest man,
To lash the rascal naked through the world."

Grinding his teeth with rage, the youthful libertine hurried on his way towards his own home.

And the dark thoughts in his breast grew darker and darker.

He was resolved that little Mary should yet see him again.

And then there should be no chance of escape for her.

He would humble her proud spirit.

He would teach her that poverty was no match for wealth.

That virtue, however much prized, was still to be bought.

He would be revenged upon the Boy Actor.

He could find the means to accomplish his desires with him in several ways.

And he would find them.

That blow had struck deep in his heart.

But he would strike one which should fall more heavily upon his foe, than did the one he had received fall upon himself.

He would strike not at his body but at his reputation.

He was a strolling player.

A vagabond.

And the libertine's father was a justice of the peace.

A man who felt little or no pity for the poor.

For in his eyes poverty was a crime.

To consummate his vengeance would be an easy task.

And the libertine chuckled to himself as he entered the proud dwelling of his father.

Poverty will harden the hands; but oftener wealth hardens the heart.

CHAPTER LXXXIX.

THE MURDERER AND THE POACHER—AN IDIOT'S FEARS—A NIGHT'S VIGIL.

TIME flies!

On iron pinions borne, it cleaves its passage through boundless space to its destination—eternity.

Swift, indeed, its flight, yet it leaves in its wake changes, which, even the records of history cannot encompass, or its pages in one month would form a book more huge than the wondrous pyramids that rear their lofty heads above the dessert wild.

Changes as countless as the sands of Egypt, as numerous as the bubbles that break on the sea shore amid the raging of a storm.

"Who can compute them?

None but God.

Were man to set down every change in his own existence, what a monument of records might be piled upon his grave.

It would tower high above the surrounding pedestals of marble, and contain a far more faithful epitaph than is to be found upon the sculptured granite which records the virtues so often extolled by interested or sorrowing friends.

Still, if it is not in the power of man to reveal the changes of time in the aggregate, he at least can record a few of its particles.

Every drop of water, every grain of sand, every moment as it rolls by bears its record, and swells the history of the world.

They may pass unheeded, yet nevertheless they could "a tale unfold," these small disregarded grains in the vast bulk of the universe.

However, it is but with a few out of the millions who people this world with whom we have to do.

It is only the changes in the lives of the Boy Actor and those personages who have hitherto played their part in this drama of real life, that we have to record and follow step by step their adventures and vicissitudes in their Struggles for Bread.

We left Dancing Bill, the harlequin, in the home of our old friend Dick the Poacher, and his imbecile wife.

The utter prostration of body and the anxiety of mind from which he had been suffer-

ing, made sad inroads upon his once robust constitution, and ere he had been an inmate of the old farm-house an hour, reason tottered from her throne, and he was in a raging brain fever.

His wild incoherent mutterings, and his frantic struggles with some imaginary being, rendered it necessary for Dick to sit beside the couch on which the poor wretch lie, to save him from inflicting injury upon himself.

Minnie looked vacantly upon the raving man, she knew not what to make of it, still she shuddered as the poor wretch started up and glared wildly around, or muttered several broken words in a thick tone.

"Don't be frightened, Minnie," said Dick, as he flung his strong arm around the waist of the struggling wretch, and laid him back upon his pillow, "but go to bed."

But Minnie hesitated to obey the wish.

A something seemed to keep her lingering by the bedside of the raving man.

"Poor fellow," said the kind-hearted poacher, "his sufferings have driven him mad."

"Mad, mad!" iterated Minnie, as though talking to herself.

"Yes, dear," replied Dick.

"Is that madness?" she asked.

"Yes."

Minnie gazed incredulously into the face of her husband for some moments, then she exclaimed, suddenly,—

"Then I am not mad! ah, no—ah, no."

"You Minnie?" said Dick.

"Yes, people say I am mad," she replied, "but they lie, Dick, darling. Ha, ha!"

Dick heaved a heavy sigh, and turned his gaze from the face of his wife to that of the prostrate man.

"No, no," continued Minnie, "I am not mad; no one fears me, for I do not grind my teeth, and fight like him. I should die if I was mad; but I am not mad—I am not mad!"

"No, Minnie," said Dick, "but go to bed and leave me to look to this poor man; you are tired and need rest. Come, Minnie, go to bed."

For a few moments she lingered sadly by his side.

"I would rather stay with you," she said, "there's danger. The birds do not sing, Dick, and when the grass withers, and the birds are still, there's danger, there's danger!"

"But the birds do not sing at night, dear one," said Dick, sadly.

"But the air is clammy, like death, like death," she muttered.

"Poor thing," thought Dick, "perhaps she imagines he will die. 'Tis not unlikely, and better that she be not here when his soul flies to its maker."

And bending over the prostrate and now quiet Bill, he istened very intently to his breathing.

The breath, though quick and short, was regular.

"He sleeps," said Dick, again turning to his wife. "It will do him good, and perhaps in the morning he will be well again. Now go to bed, Minnie."

The wife took up the lamp with a sigh, and holding it so as to throw its rays full upon the face of the now sleeping Bill, she laid her hand upon her husband's shoulder, and looked fixedly into his eyes.

"Dick," she said, in an impressive tone of

voice, and the vacant stare seemed for a moment to have left her face, the birds never sing whilst he is near; the grass withers at his footsteps; bad man, bad man."

"We haave all our faults, Minnie dear," said her husband.

"But the grass does not wither at the steps of all," she said.

"No," replied Dick, "nor would it at his, Minnie."

The woman shook her head.

"It would, Dick, it would," she said, casting a furtive glance at the pale features of the harlequin, and then bending down her head till her face touched that of her husband. "Blood kills the green grass, and it withers."

"Blood, Minnie?" said Dick, looking up in her face in surprise.

"Aye, Dick, blood!" she exclaimed, grasping his wrist and nodding her head towards the harlequin. "Can you not see it upon his hands, upon his forehead? Dick, there is blood there, there is blood there!"

Dick the Poacher rose to his feet, and taking the lamp from the hand of the idiot, he held it over the face of the insensible man, whilst he gazed intently upon the brow and hands so pale and thin.

"Blood, Minnie?" he said, after a pause, "there is no blood here, it must have been the blue veins upon his hands and forehead, brought out so prominently by the wasting of flesh, caused from hunger, that you fancied were blood."

And he placed the lamp upon the table, and seated himself again with a deep sigh.

"Ah, well," sighed the poor imbecile, the vacant look again returning to her features.

"I suppose I am mad, Dick; people say I am mad."

"No, no, Minnie, only mistaken, darling."

She shook her head.

"The birds will not sing to-morrow, and the grass will wither for there is blood here, blood."

Dick started from his seat and clasped his wife in his arms.

"Minnie!" he exclaimed, "the sight of this poor starving wretch affrights you. I am sorry that I took him in, but I could not bear to feel that a fellow creature lay dying at my door, and I would not give him shelter. I have met him before and know him to be a bad disposed man; but, Minnie, we are learnt to be charitable to the erring. Cuold I see him die upon the step, and close my door in his face? I have known what suffering is and can feel for the sufferings of another. Minnie, heaven knows I would not pain your gentle heart intentionally, but, how must I have pained my maker, had I have refused to extend a helping hand to one of his ceatures bowed down with want and disease."

The eyes of the woman dropped before the look of her husband.

Her hand trembled in his, and she was silent.

"Go to bed, Minnie, and pray for him," said the poacher, as he pointed to the sleeping man.

"I will pray that the birds may sing and the grass may remain fresh and green," said Minnie, "for them there is happiness and all is well."

"Do so, Minnie," said her husband. "Go, and God bless you."

The imbecile threw her arms around his neck, and imprinted a kiss upon the bronzed cheek of her husband.

Then, with a sigh, she left the apartment and proceeded to her chamber.

The eyes of the poacher followed her till she was lost to view.

Then he seated himself again by the side of the couch on which Bill lay.

"Poor girl," he muttered, "fate has been cruel to her; affliction has fallen heavily upon her soul, and through her love for me. Heaven has deprived her of reason, and its will be done; but I sometimes think and feel that it has engrafted in her soul an instinct denied to rational beings. How often has she warned me of danger when I saw it not, thought it not, and therefore, her words to-night, must sink deep into my soul. What can she mean by blood? There's no blood here. Does that instinct with which she is gifted lead her to read the character of this man in the lineaments of his face. It may be so. 'Tis said the blind can hear more acutely than those who have their sight; may not the idiot, therefore, from a similar cause, be enabled to read the character of those with whom they come in contact, with greater accuracy than can they to whom a bountiful providence has vouchsafed the faculties of reason. I believe it is so. She has detected the cruel nature of this wretch, and her gentle soul shudders with horror at contact with one who can degrade his manhood by offering insult and violence to a weak and defenceless woman."

For some time, Dick the Poacher sat watching the guilty man, smoothing his pillow, or bathing his heated brow with cold water.

The harlequin slept till near daylight, when Dick, tired with his vigils, had allowed his eyes to close for a few moments.

Suddenly a movement of the raving man caused him to start.

Dancing Bill had sat up in the bed, and his eyes were fixed with a wild unnatural stare upon vacancy.

His arms were extended as though he were endeavouring to keep off some imaginary object.

His hair seemed to literally stand on end, and a look of abject terror was upon his face.

Dick shuddered as he gazed upon him.

"Keep back, keep back!" gasped the harlequin, moving his hand as though in the act of pushing back something from him. "Spare me, spare me! I have not harmed her. I swear I have not. I have kept my oath. Do not bear me away to eternal torments. Let me live, only for a day, an hour. Have mercy. I am yours, but not now—not now; only one hour; oh, spare me—spare me!"

Dick absolutely trembled as he gazed upon the foaming lips and strained eyeballs of the guilty man.

"Lay down," he said, gently, throwing his arms gently around him, and forcing him softly back upon his pillow. "Compose yourself, you will be better soon."

With a shriek that rang through the apartment, Dancing Bill struggled to throw off the arms of the poacher, then exhausted and powerless he sank back panting upon the pilolw of the couch.

Dick bent over him for a few minutes till he felt satisfied that he had again fallen into slumber.

Then with a sigh he turned and sat down again.

"What can he imagine he has seen," soliloquised Dick, with a shake of the head. "Conscience perhaps is pricking him for some of his wickedness, and now, upon this bed of sickness, he feels all the pangs of misery he has inflicted upon others. 'Be sure your sins will find you out,' is a passage not to be passed lightly over. The man who will not bridle his evil passions is sure at some time or other to be punished for allowing them full scope. His sins, doubtless, lay heavily upon his soul, and now, in the moments of his sore affliction lie with fearful weight upon his heart, and conjure up to his diseased brain phantoms of imaginary justice, at which he shrinks appalled."

And the poacher, taking the jug of cold water in his hand, sprinkled it upon the brow of the guilty man, and strove to allay the burning of his fevered brain.

Day broke, and the guilty man slept soundly.

For the first time since that fatal night of the storm, when his coward hand struck the hellish steel deep into the heart of her, who had never by deed or word injured him, Dancing Bill's slumber was free from the visions of that pale face and bloodstained form.

The guilty man had for a time found relief from the whisperings of his conscience in madness.

When slumbering nature had again awoke to life to joy : and the hardy sons of toil had risen from their refreshing couch, and commenced the labours of another day.

Dick the Poacher, leaving the sleeping man in the care of his idiot wife, stole forth into the fresh morning air, to seek medical advice for him who had craved his aid.

As Dick threw open the door of the old farmhouse, a feathered songster rose from the grass at his feet, and took its flight heavenward, carrolling a song of praise and thanksgiving for another.

Dick stood for a moment on the threshold, then turning to Minnie, exclaimed,—

"Hark! the birds sing and the grass is green and fresh, matured by the dews of night."

The idiot listened.

The notes of the bird smote upon her ears.

A look of childish pleasure overspread her vacant features.

A smile beamed for a moment in her expressionless eyes.

She clasped her hands together, and with a sigh of relief, exclaimed,—

"Heaven be praised!"

Dick smiled and stepped over the threshold.

For some few moments, Minnie stood straining her ears to catch the notes of the lark, as it winged its way higher and higher towards the clouds.

Then she turned and looked upon the pale and attenuated form of Bill the harlequin.

As her eyes rested upon his white face, she shuddered and drew back.

"There is blood upon his brow," she said. "I see it there—blood, fresh and red. Ah, I knew it; the birds song is hushed, and there is misery around the old farm."

Stepping to the window she gazed up towards the light blue clouds, and listened again for the notes of the lark.

But all was still.

Not a single note smote her ears, and as she gazed the little warbler descended once more to the earth.

His downward flight was uncheered by song, the welkin rang not with his joyous notes.

Silently the poor imbecile turned from the window.

Sadly she seated herself upon the chair which her husband had occupied through the night, and anxiously awaited the returning footfall of Dick the Poacher.

———

CHAPTER XC.

DICK MAKES A FRIEND—A KIND RESOLVE.

WE have said time flies.

So it does.

With even and unerring course it passes on towards eternity.

Never does it deviate in its stride, but keeps on the "even tenor of its way."

Yet to the wretch doomed to expiate his guilt upon the scaffold how quick must its flight appear.

How swiftly must the moments roll by as, through his barred windows, he gazes upon the first grey streak of dawn—the last shades of evening.

The echoes of the prison-bell seem scarcely to have died away, ere another hour is tolled forth and the guilty man shudders at the flight of time.

But in an adjoining cell may be incarcerated one to whom it may appear time stood still.

To him time drags its weary course along till minutes appear hours, and hours seem days.

Imprisoned for a term of years, his soul pants eagerly and impatiently for the time to arrive, when his prison-door shall be opened and he shall once more inhale the breath of freedom.

But to him it seems the time will never come, when he is bidden to go forth to the world and sin no more.

All of us, at some period of our existence, have chidden the rapid flight, or the laggard strides of time.

Youth chides its hardiness; manhood marks the velocity of its speed.

But there are times when youth impatiently watches its strides, and age chides its slowness.

Time never seems to fly so slowly as when awaiting the return of an absent one.

To poor Minnie the moments rolled tediously away, as she impatiently awaited the return of Dick.

Scarce had he been absent a quarter of an hour, when she rose from her seat beside the couch of the sick man, and walking to the door, looked forth in the hopes of seeing the returning figure of her husband; although she well knew that the distance he had to go to seek medical aid, could not be accomplished in double the time.

Back to her seat, with a look of disappointment on her face, only to leave it again in a few minutes on the same fruitless errand.

Backwards and forwards, from the bed to the door, every few minutes, strode the poor idiot, only to return disappointed and dispirited to the side of the sick man.

At length she perceived the stalwart form of her husband, accompanied by the village doctor, coming towards the house.

Impatiently she awaited their approach.

She could not feel comfortable alone in the presence of the sick man.

They seemed to walk very slowly, yet the poacher and the medical man were striding over the ground at no mean pace.

Minnie met them at the threshold.

"Well, Minnie," said Dick, "has he woke up?"

The woman shook her head.

"I am glad of that," said Dick, "he might have frightened you in his ravings."

Then, taking his wife by the arm, he led her back into the kitchen followed by the doctor.

The doctor was a rather diminutive person, with a bald head and somewhat pompous style, but withal a kind-hearted little man.

He was near sixty years of age, and had set up in business in the very house he now occupied thirty years before.

He had striven hard to make a fortune, but the fickle goddess would not be wooed by him, and he was now, after thirty years practice, as poor as the curate of the little church, which could be seen from the old farmhouse.

It was not so much perhaps that he could not find customers, as his customers could not find money to pay him liberally for his visits and his medicines.

Fate had certainly dealt hard with him, but it had neither soured his temper or hardened his heart.

In rain or sunshine, night or day, the little gentleman was ever ready to answer a call, and he hurried as quickly to the bedside of the sick labourer, as to that of the influential farmer.

He was somewhat out of breath with the quick pace at which he had accompanied Dick, but he stayed not to rest.

Placing his hat upon the table, and wiping the perspiration from his bald head with a blue cotton handkercheif, he hurried to the couch, and bent over the form of the prostrate harlequin.

Thrusting his handkerchief into his coat pocket, he felt the pulse, raised the eyelids, and parted the lips of the sick man.

"Humph!" he exclaimed, turning to Dick and Minnie, "sad case—very."

"What is the matter with him?" asked Dick.

"Been delirious."

"Yes."

The doctor shook his head.

"Brain fever!" he exclaimed, "that's what is the matter with him."

"I thought so," said Dick.

"And you thought right, sir," said the doctor.

"Brought on by want, I expect," said Dick.

"Want of what?"

"Food."

"More than that. Mind ill at ease. The mind, sir—the mind—excessive worry, or something of that sort."

"He looks bad indeed," remarked Dick, "starved, in fact."

"So he undoubtedly is," said the doctor, "but that is not the only cause of his present ailments."

"What do you think is the cause?" asked Dick.

"That is not in my power to say." replied the little man. "I can read any disease in the body but not in the soul, that is not in the power of man."

"True," said Dick. "Then you do not think that hunger has brought him to this?"

"Hunger will bring a man as low as this, but the symptoms would be different," said the doctor. "We all have our trials and vicissitudes, and each bears them according to his strength. No doubt, the frame, weakened by the want of food and necessaries, hurried on the malady, although it is not its absolute cause. A man may suffer from palpitation of the heart and live for years, but a sudden shock at any time may deprive him of life."

Again examining the prostrate man the doctor put on his hat and prepared to depart.

"I will send you the medicine," he said, "directly I get home, and with a little care I trust he will soon be restored. "Is he any relation of yours?"

"No," replied Dick. "I found him last night weak and ill, at my door, and as a man and a Christian I took him in."

"Then he is a stranger to you?" said the doctor.

"Not quite, for we have met before," replied the poacher, "though it was only for a few moments."

The little doctor opened his eyes very wide and gazed into the face of the poacher with an almost rude stare.

"Dick," he exclaimed at length, "your heart is in the right place and I honour you for it. It is not every man in the country would act as you have done, burden yourself with a stranger, and one, too, suffering from a disease which, at any moment, may take a more dangerous turn, and, like the adder nourished in the bosom, turn and sting you?"

"I have but done as my heart prompted me to do, extend a helping hand to one powerless to help himself," said Dick.

A look of admiration beamed from the eyes of the doctor.

"His recovery may be of long duration and the expense of medical attendance heavy," said said the little man.

"No matter, sir," answered Dick. "I will not do things by halves. I have stretched forth my hand to aid him, and he shall not fall now if I can hold him up."

"And what reward do you expect for your kindness?" asked the little man.

"Reward, sir!" exclaimed Dick, hastily, as his face flushed crimson, "I expect no other reward than the knowledge that I have done my duty to a fellow creature, and my God!"

"Nobly spoken!" exclaimed the doctor, extending his hand to Dick. "I have heard men call you rogue, vagabond, poacher, and seen them shun you as they would a pestilence, but I feel proud and happy—honoured, I will say, to grasp the hand, and call that man friend who can give utterance to such sentiments, and so kindly succour a suffering fellow creature."

And the little man shook Dick's hand, with much fervour.

"There is a green spot in every heart," said Dick, "however callous. I know that men shun me, look upon me unkindly, but they know me not."

"No," said the other, "or they would honour instead of despise you. Let them think what they may, say what they like, but I feel it no disgrace to stand uncovered in the presence of Dick the Poacher!"

And the doctor took his hat from his head as he gave utterance to the words.

A flush of pride crossed the face of Dick.

There was at least one who could respect him.

His lips quivered with emotion as he said,—

"Men judge me from what they have heard, not what they know. Some day those who affect to despise me now, may look upon me with a kindlier glance. I have my faults, as other men, and where is the one who has not? 'Tis human to err, and were the failings of mankind stamped upon their foreheads, who would not draw his down low over his brow?"

"True, Dick, true," answered the doctor, and hence, should we be more charitable towards our fellows and,—

'The faults of others kindly o'erlook;
Such deeds to the heart would give credit;
Were all our bad acts writ in a book
Where's he, would not blush when he read
    it.'"

"You are right, sir," said Dick, "the heart of man is disposed to evil, and the judge is often the greatest sinner."

"But no man shall ever judge you in my presence," said the doctor, "at least, not unjustly. This good act counterbalances any bad ones you may have committed; but you shall not be alone in your work of kindness. I insist upon sharing it; my visits shall be gratuitous, and so shall my medicines. I am poor, it is true, but not so poor but that I can assist in a good deed. Now don't say a word, I will have my own way, and together we will work for the restoration to health of this man. We will cast our bread upon the waters, and who knows, Dick, but we may find it after many days."

And shaking the poacher again by the hand, the little doctor put on his hat and hurriedly left the farmhouse.

Dick stood gazing after his retreating figure for some time, then turning to Minnie he said,—

"A good action brings its own reward. Yesterday I was the despised of all men, to-day, one has grasped in friendship the hand of Dick the poacher."

CHAPTER XCI.

THE RECOVERY OF THE HARLEQUIN—THE DESK AND THE PACKET—BASE INGRATITUDE.

DAYS passed, and Dick and his wife watched beside the couch of the sick man.

Mr. Barnett, the little doctor, was unremitting in his labours, and strove to tax science to the utmost, to bring back to health and strength the guilty harlequin.

The friendship of Dick and the doctor increased daily, and the worthy son of Æsculapius, instead of smoking his pipe of an evening in the snug parlour of the village inn, often sat in the kitchen of the old farm house with Dick and his wife, and passed a pleasant hour over a jug of ale.

In a fortnight the attentions of the doctor and Dick were rewarded, and Bill awoke once more to consciousness.

To the consciousness of his guilt.

It was towards evening, and while Dick sat watching at his bedside, that the wretched man opened his eyes and gazed around him.

"Where am I?"

"With friends," replied Dick, starting up with a look of joy upon his face.

His noble nature could not resist a feeling of happiness at the recovery of one whom he well knew to be a worthless scoundrel.

"With friends?" iterated Bill, and then with a sigh closed his eyes again.

"Minnie, Minnie!" called Dick.

"Yes," replied his wife, coming in from the porch where she had been sitting at her favourite occupation, listening to the birds.

"Come here, darling," he said, "look, look!" and he pointed to the form on the bed.

Minnie followed his finger with her gaze, and then turned an inquiring look upon his face.

"He has recovered, is well again. Our work has not been in vain," said her husband.

Minnie cast a vacant glance upon the bed, then turned aside with a sigh,

"Why do you sigh, Minnie?" asked her husband.

"Because the birds do not sing, and the grass is yellow," she replied.

"But they will sing to-morrow, dear one," he replied hurriedly, perceiving that she was in one of her melancholy moods. "The shades of night are falling, and they have gone to roost, till the rising sun shall wake them again to life and joy."

"Ah, me," she sighed, clasping her hands and dropping her eyes to the ground.

"Are you not glad Minnie, that this poor man is well again?" asked Dick after a pause.

"Are you?" she asked without raising her eye.

"In truth I am."

"So am I," she said, "when you are happy I am glad. But the birds are silent, and the grass withers."

"Come—come, Minnie," said Dick, throwing his arms around her waist and drawing her to his breast. "You are sad to night, look up and smile, for you know I love to see you smile, Minnie, it cheers my heart."

The poor woman smiled a sickly smile, then her features relapsed into the same expressionless form they had worn before.

Like a faint sunbeam struggling through a murky cloud, it died almost ere it was born.

Dick felt a choking sensation in his throat as he looked upon that expressionless face.

"Oh, God!" he murmured to himself, "what would I not give to recall her fleeting senses, my poor loved Minnie."

And he pressed her to his heart and imprinted a kiss of love and tenderness upon her lips.

The eyes of Dancing Bill again opened, and were fixed upon him.

"Minnie, my own dear wife!" he exclaimed. "Oh, what would I not give to see a smile live for a minute on your cheeks; what would I not sacrifice to see you again what you once were. Oh, heaven, I think I should go mad with joy were reason to return!"

And he pressed her passionately to his heart.

"You love me, Dick, always love me," she said.

"Love you, God knows that I do!" he exclaimed. "I loved you with all the fervour of my soul when—when the smile on your cheek faded not and the eye was bright, but how much more do I love you now—now that cruel fate has robbed you of reason. Love you, aye, Minnie, for are you not my wife. Have I not sworn to love and cherish, and that love will live whilst life lasts, my poor, poor wife."

A deep groan startled the poacher, and turning hurriedly, he perceived that Dancing Bill had covered his face with his hands.

Releasing his hold of Minnie, the poacher sprang to the side of the bed.

"What can I do for you?" he said. "Ask anything you will, and if in our power to grant it it shall not be asked in vain."

But the only reply he received was a deep sob.

Dick stood gazing for some moments upon the sick man then turned away with a sigh.

"He weeps," he whispered to Minnie. "Come away, and leave him to his grief."

And the poacher strode to to the door followed by his wife.

Sitting down in the porch with Minnie beside him, Dick became lost in thought.

At length he raised his head.

"Minnie," he said, in a low tone, "our work I think has been more happy in its influence than I had hoped for."

Minnie only raised her head, she made no reply.

"We have restored him to reason, and a sense of the duty he owes to me, to whom he has not been over kind."

Minnie still remained silent.

"Perhaps this illness may lead him to think better of one whom he professed to love, yet treated harshly, his wife."

"Wife," repeated Minnie.

"Yes, dear, for he has a wife."

"Where?"

"I know not."

"A wife, and not here," said Minnie.

And the expressionless features were lighted up for a moment, as she gave utterance to the words.

At this moment, casting his eyes across the stream, Dick perceived the form of the worthy doctor wending its way towards the house.

Leaping to his feet, Dick hurried forth to meet him.

He was anxious to make him acquainted with the state of his patient.

"Good evening, Dick," said Barnett, "how's your patient?"

"His senses have returned," said Dick.

"Happy to hear it, very happy," said the little man, stopping short and drawing forth his blue cotton handkerchief commenced wiping his bald head.

"Yes," said Dick. "I am happy to say that reason has again returned."

"I felt sure we should be able to restore that," said Barnett.

"And that was what I feared could not be restored," said Dick.

"Then I did not, it was his health that troubled me the most."

"Would to heaven," said Dick, "you could restore reason to my poor wife."

The doctor shook his head.

Dick sighed as he observed him.

"That, then, is irretrievably lost," he mut. in a tone of agony.

"I fear it is," said the doctor.

"I would give all the wealth in the world did I but possess it," said Dick, "to see her once again what she was; but that is impossible."

Barnett laid his hand upon Dick's arm, and stopping short in his walk, looked up into his face.

"There is nothing impossible to God," he said, pointing upwards.

"Is there hope?" exclaimed Dick eagerly clutching at the arm of his companion.

"Whilst there is life, there is hope," said the doctor.

"Oh, that I could feel there was hope," said Dick. "Could I think you had the skill to restore her—"

"Dick, I have not the skill, would to heaven that I had. Time may do much to restore her shattered senses, but the work must be left to him who can make the blind to see and the lame to walk."

Dick sighed heavily and silently they walked to the house.

As Barnett passed the poor imbecile in the porch, a look of pity stole across his face.

But he spoke not to her.

He strode into the kitchen and up to the bedside of Dancing Bill.

"Well, well," he said, taking his wrist between his fingers, "this is cheering, very, to see you so far on the road to recovery, you'll soon get on now, and we shall not be long before we see you as happy and strong as ever."

"Happy," murmured Bill, with a shudder.

"Happy, yes, why you are happy now, ain't you, at finding you have improved so much," said Barnett.

A deep sigh was the only response.

The doctor looked pityingly down upon him.

"Ah," he muttered, "just what I expected; some secret grief has brought about this illness. But he must be kept quiet, Dick, or he may have a relapse."

The poacher nodded.

The doctor prepared to take his leave.

"Will you stay?" asked Dick.

"Not to-night," replied the doctor, moving towards the door.

When he had gained the porch he took the hand of Minnie in his own and pressed it somewhat tightly.

A strange tremor ran through her frame, the lustreless eyes brightened.

The expressionless face became animated, and a smile played around the mouth of the little doctor.

"Whilst there is life there is hope, Dick," he

said, laying his hand upon the poacher's arm.

"Speak," said Dick, quickly, who had observed the sudden change in his wife's look the moment that Barnett took her hand in his own.

"Good night; I am in a hurry," said the little man, as he quickly darted off through the porch.

Dick turned to his wife, with the words of the doctor on his lips.

"What can he mean?" he earnestly muttered. "Heavens, can he detect one ray of hope—can he believe that her reason may yet be restored, yet fear to tell me so lest my heart should burst with joy. I must know more; there is an import in his words, 'whilst there is life there is hope;' can there be hope for her, for me?"

Heaven grant it may be so. I will hope, hope on; may the dark hours be fading away, and the light of reason again dawn in her soul. 'Tis all I ask, to render me happy, all—all."

And he placed his arm around the waist of his wife, and looked long and anxiously into her eyes, as though he would read there the consummation of his hopes.

From that day Dick watched the movements of the doctor closely every time he visited the farm, and this was nearly every day, but not one word could he gain from him which led him to believe that Barnett considered there was any prospect of her recovering her reason.

Still, Dick observed that every time the doctor came he shook his wife by the hand.

Still, he could discover nothing in this but an ordinary salutation.

Yet it was not lost upon the poacher, that the eyes of Minnie always brightened beneath the pressure, and her features became animated.

Meantime, Dancing Bill rapidly recovered his strength, and was able to rise from his bed and sit in the porch during the bright sunshine.

But there was a look of sadness on his brow; a nervous twitching of the lips when any one approached him.

This Dick accounted for by the weakness of his nerves, which the good-hearted poacher believed must have been sadly shaken by his illness.

The moment Dancing Bill began to utter his thanks for the kindness shown him, Dick always changed the subject, and as Bill never once mentioned his wife, Dick took care not to bring up her name.

He wished Dancing Bill to imagine that he had forgotten all about her, and his own disgraceful acts.

The kind heart of the poacher rebelled against giving utterance to a word which might tend to wound the man to whom he had extended the hand of hospitality.

So another month passed, and Dancing Bill was recovered in body.

Not in mind.

That was diseased past all cure.

He still feared to be alone, and dreaded the time when he must leave the old farm house and start forth again, friendless upon the world.

Still he could not remain much longer.

He felt he must go.

He well knew that whilst there was a probability of his strength giving way, or a relapse, that Dick would not suffer him to depart.

But, he likewise felt that to appear anxious to prolong his stay might give rise to suspicions, which, perhaps, would ultimately reveal him to them in his true character.

At length he felt that it was time to take his departure, as there could now be no further reason for him wishing to prolong his stay.

He lay, tossing uneasily upon his bed, thinking what he should do, and whither he should go.

He dreaded to apply for an engagement in any part of the country, yet now he knew that to leave it was impossible without money, and he had not a coin in the world.

As he lay thinking and trembling at every sound, his eye wandered around the apartment, and the light of the lamp, which Dick left every night burning upon the kitchen table, revealed to his gaze a small writing desk which Minnie had left upon a side-board.

She had brought it down at the request of Dick a few hours before, and had forgotten to take it to her chamber ere she retired to rest.

In a moment the base nature of the harlequin rose uppermost in his heart.

He rose from his bed and silently crossed towards it.

Pausing for a moment to listen, he placed his hand upon the lid.

It yielded, and he gazed in upon its contents.

It was filled with papers.

Thrusting his hand down beneath them, he assured himself that it contained no money, and he was about to close the lid when his eye rested upon a packet, the cover of which appeared familiar to him.

He grasped it in his hand and bore it to the lamp.

He checked the cry of surprise which rose to his lips, as he perceived it to be the one he had sold to Gripe.

"I am penniless," he muttered, "and must leave this place. This may procure me money, nay, it will save me from starvation. I will go now, for I hold the means to procure food; and ere they rise from their beds I can place miles between us."

Hurriedly attiring himself, he silently left the house without one thought of how basely he was repaying all the kindness he had received at the hands of the man he was robbing. The adder turned and stung the hand that warmed it into life.

CHAPTER XCII.

THE DECLINE OF THE YEAR—THE PANTOMIMISTS SEEK ANOTHER FIELD FOR THEIR LABOURS—THE ACTOR TURNS AUTHOR.

THE golden corn had been garnered; the hot sun of summer was fast losing its intensity; the leaves of the trees were becoming tinted and dry, and falling to the ground at every passing breeze.

Autumn had come.

It ushered in a glorious harvest; but it shut out the travelling pantomimists from further Struggles for Bread in the line they had adopted, that of visiting the fairs, and extolling the wonders to be seen to the country lads and lasses in the caravan.

The season was over; the last fair had been held, and there was no more work with the booth till the next spring.

So the old shaggy horse was sold.

Poor old fellow, his labours had been heavy at times, but he had found a kind friend and indulgent master in Buskin Bob, and it was not without a pang of regret that the pantaloon saw him taken away by his new owner.

Bob patted his neck, smoothed his shaggy mane, and hoped he might be struck comical, if he didn't feel grief at their parting.

But there was no hope for it. To keep him idle throughout the winter could be ill afforded by the pantomimists.

The season, if not an extraordinary good one, had at least not been altogether unsuccessful, but still, Charlie felt that it would be unwise to saddle themselves with the expense of the quadruped, and perhaps be unable to start again next season for want of funds.

The caravan was put up for the winter on a piece of waste ground, and the friends took a small house in the neighbourhood of Tiverton, in Devonshire, some few miles from the scene of our opening chapter.

There was now six months before them ere they could solicit the patronage of pleasure seekers to their caravan.

Six months. The money they had would perhaps have kept them from want during that time, but Charlie Evans was too careful a man to live to-day and trust to providence for the morrow, even had he not considered that the money he held was Harry's, and not his own.

Again, he had no wish to start for the fairs on

the ensuing year, without funds, so he resolved to seek engagements for himself and friends, and if unsuccessful, risk a portion of it in opening a theatre for the winter season.

To this all were agreed, and Charlie, and Buskin Bob, applied for engagements in their usual line of business.

But in this they were unsuccessful. So procuring a list of the closed houses, they resolved at length to enter upon the management of the Crown Saloon, and endeavour by the production of a good pantomime, to draw good houses, and good profits.

Their arrangements having been made, the friends once more commenced their Struggles for Bread.

The depressive feeling which we have seen take possession of the Boy Actor had worn entirely out, and he was again as cheerful as ever.

But in the presence of Mary—now on longer little Mary, for she had grown wonderfully, and bade fair to become a tall and stately figure—he felt a strange reserve.

Too young almost to know the reason of the emotions, he could not bear to be separated from her for an hour, yet still felt confused and nervous when by her side.

He had almost forgotten the adventure near the fair-field, an adventure which had been to him a turning point in his existence.

Margaret, too, had greatly improved; though she could not but think, and often too, of her husband; but she concluded that, finding all his attempts to persuade her to again join him, futile, he had left the country.

Buskin Bob, however, at times became thoughtful and silent.

His usual happy nature seemed overclouded.

And strange as it may appear, he was invariably sad when Margaret was near.

Charlie believed this change to be caused by his tender nature becoming afflicted by pity for the poor columbine, and her blighted existence, but Bob knew better than that.

The cause was different.

It arose from a feeling which even he himself acknowledged to be a bad one.

Pity is akin to love, and from pity the nature of Buskin Bob had roved to love.

Yes, Buskin Bob loved Margaret.

But he knew that love was unholy; knew that the woman on whom his affections had lighted, was the wife of another.

And that other a murderer.

He shuddered even at his own feelings.

Yet he could not eradicate them from his heart.

Do what he would, argue with himself as he would, Bob could but acknowledge that he was in love.

And that the woman he loved was another man's wife.

We have said Bob was a noble-hearted fellow; and indeed we have had several proofs of the truth of this assertion.

He was a man who would not willingly injure a worm, yet he would have leapt with joy, had he heard that Margaret was free.

For then he could offer her a hand and heart, and by a life of study and kindness strive to make her happy.

True, he had the power to make her free, by handing over to justice, the villain whom she called husband.

But at this course, Bob shuddered.

He could not bear the idea of having the life of a fellow creature upon his hands; though that life had been justly forfeited to the outraged laws.

Again, could he ever hope to unite his destiny with that of the woman whose husband he could be the means of consigning to an ignominious doom.

No, even though his death severed the fatal bond, and rid her for ever of a wretch at whose name she shuddered with horror.

So Bob nourished the secret in his own breast; and day by day it fed upon his vitals, saddened his nature, and threw a veil of melancholy over his happy soul

Margaret could not become his wife.

Buskin Bob had not fallen so low in the scale of humanity to ask her to become his mistress.

He felt the wish to make her his wife was dishonourable, but the desire to make her his mistress contemptible, and an insult to one who had already been fearfully injured by him, who had sworn to love and cherish her, and throw around her tender form the shield of his manhood and protection.

Thus things stood when the Crown Saloon fell into their hands.

Like most places of its class, the little theatre contained few properties, and those were in a dilapidated and worn out state, so that it required the attention of all to get things in working order.

Still, three months was a long time to wait for any reward of their labours, and it yet wanted that time to the first night of the pantomime.

Therefore, Charlie resolved to open at the beginning of November; but as he well knew it would be madness to expect good houses for two months before Christmas, he set his wits to work to find out how he could make the house pay till the Boxing day, for the pantomime was to be played in the morning, as well as the evening, Charlie having found the benefit of this arrangement the year before.

Of course it would be ridiculous to go to any great expense at present, so the friends resolved to play small pieces, that would only require a few extra beside themselves to sustain the characters.

With this they set themselves to work to concoct pieces to suit their requirements, from various dramas, cutting out characters, in some places, doubling them in others, and adapting the pieces so as to suit the limited company.

This, of course, was a great injustice to the author, who would scarcely have recognised the fruits of his labours, and, perhaps had, the pantomimists have given that fact one thought, it might have prevented their wholesale slaughter. The wrong they were doing did not enter their minds, the practice in many of the provincial theatres being so common that it is thought nothing of.

It is scarcely justice, however, to those who, at the labour of their brains, and the sacrifice of many hours of incessant thought, produce the dramas from which the players make their bread to be thus treated; but the author in very few cases is little studied by the managers. They will grasp with avidity at a piece that is a sure success, but of one which they may entertain the slightest doubt they will throw aside, and often, despite the request of its writer for an answer to their decision or respecting it, a return of the manuscript, they will not take the trouble to hunt it up from among the rolls of paper in the room; and give the author the trouble to make innumerable applications for its restoration, and at the same time deprive him of seeking a market for it elsewhere.

Certainly theatrical managers have something else to do besides studying those who place manuscript in their hands, many of which are utterly worthless; but still, a drama, no matter how long, takes but a short time to read, and a manager can generally form an opinion as to its merits, ere he has waded through one act, therefore their prevarications and off-puttings are unjust, for if a piece be successful the manager receives the greatest share of the profits, and surely that class who—

"Put money in his purse,"

should be studied and honourably treated by him, even though the work submitted to him be worthless.

This is not the case with all, but it is with many, and it is an injustice and a shame that those who profit from the workings of others, brains should deal thus unkindly with their contributors, for it is a fact that manuscripts are sometimes detained for months, nay, years; in spite of the repeated applications of their writers.

But, as we said before, this is not the case with all, and we doubt whether Charlie Evans would not have honestly acknowledged in a few days whether any manuscript placed in his hands was worthy of production or not.

But Charlie was not in a position to procure new pieces; the house would never have borne the expense; so he resorted to the old dodge of cutting and contriving to suit place and company.

Harry watched this work intently for some time; then, without saying a word to the others, he resolved to try and write a piece with characters for each of them.

Hunting about the theatre, he soon made himself acquainted with all its properties, and knowing the necessity of keeping down expenses, in vain he sat about concocting a drama, for which, if Charlie should consider it worthy a place on the boards, the properties in the house could be brought into play.

Night after night, for several hours after the friends had retired to rest, Harry sat at his work, and in the course of a little over a week, he produced a little piece in two acts, entitled "The Faithless Tar."

On the morning after the completion of his labours, and whilst the pantomimists were at breakfast, the youthful author drew forth the labour of his brains, and placed it in the hands of Charlie, without saying a word.

The clown turned it over two or three times in his hands, then opening it, and looking at the title, laid it down on the table beside him, remarking, with a shake of the head,

"Harry, we have little money to spare, my boy, in the purchase of manuscripts, had it been offered to me, I should have told the author so,

in order that he might seek a market elsewhere, and obtain a recompense for his labours at the earliest moment. When was it given to you?"

"Oh," replied Harry, "I have not had it long. You will read it, won't you."

"I don't see the use of doing so, as I cannot afford to purchase it," said Charlie.

"The author don't want anything for it," said Harry, with a smile. "He only wants to know if it is fit to play."

"It ain't fit to play if it ain't worth paying for," said Buskin Bob. "Strike me comical if it is."

"No," said Charlie, "for the labourer is worthy of his hire, and he knows it, so if the writer of this requires no recompence depend upon it it is worthless."

A flush suffused the cheeks of the Boy Actor as he remarked,—

"You cannot say till you have read it."

"I only judge from what you say," replied the clown.

"Still I am anxious that you should look at it," said Harry.

"I will do so," replied Charlie, "if you wish it."

"I do indeed."

"What makes you so anxious?" asked Charlie.

"Oh, I only want to know your opinion," replied the youth.

"Strike me comical if I don't think there is a part in it he fancies for himself," said Bob, "eh, Margaret?"

The columbine smiled.

"Yes," she said, "I suspect as much."

"Well, I'll look it over, it won't take long," said Charlie, "and then it can be returned."

So saying, he took up the roll, and commenced reading down the whole of the little page, having only glanced at the title of the play before.

"Whew!" he whistled, raising his eyes from the paper to the face of the boy, who sat anxiously watching him, while a smile broke over his good humoured features, "the cat's out of the bag."

"What's up?" asked Bob.

"No wonder he was anxious to have it read," said Charlie.

"Why?" asked Bob.

"Listen," said Charlie, commencing to read from the paper— "The Faithless Tar; a nautical drama, in two acts, by Harry Marston!"

"Harry Marston!" exclaimed Margaret.

"By Harry!" exclaimed Mary, a gratified blush suffusing her cheeks, as she turned her lustrous eyes full upon the youth's face in a questioning glance.

"Strike me comical, never!" gasped Buskin Bob.

"A fact," said Charlie, "now I can see it is his handwriting."

"Oh, read it, father, do read it!" exclaimed Mary. Then, as she detected the eyes of the youth fixed full upon her, she blushed till the colour mounted to her temples, and turned her head confusedly away.

"Read it, Charlie," said Margaret.

"In course you'll read it, and read it out loud, too, for all to hear," said Bob. "Strike me comical, now, only to think of his writing a drama on the sly."

"Pour out another cup of coffee, Mary," said the clown, "and then I'll begin."

This was done.

"Now, silence," said Charlie, "and we shall see what the first production of Harry is worth."

Each prepared to listen, and the clown read the piece through to his attentive listeners.

When he had concluded, he laid the manuscript down, and extending his hand to Harry, said,—

"Well done, my boy, it does you credit, and we will open the 'Crown' with it, and I only hope it may be appreciated by others as it is by me."

"So do I," said Bob, "strike me comical, there!"

CHAPTER XCIII.

FIRST NIGHT OF THE NEW PIECE—BUSKIN BOB'S ADVICE—DARK THOUGHTS AND SAD FOREBODINGS.

SELDOM or ever was author kept so little time in suspense.

In less than an hour he knew the fate of the offspring of his brain.

True, it met with a favourable reception.

But had it been worthless, it had taken no longer to read.

What a pity it is, then, that writers should be kept so long in ignorance of their fate.

But Harry was fortunate, far more so than many, for he submitted his production to friends not to strangers.

He might have fared otherwise, perhaps, had he taken it elsewhere.

It would doubtless have been detained for some time, and after being assured that the greatest attention should be paid to it, and at each fresh application for an answer, being told that it would require some slight alteration either in dialogue or situation, have it returned to him, after the lapse of several months, unperused, and, sometimes, unopened.

It is a good thing to have a friend at court, is an old saying, surely it would prove a blessing to many to have a friend behind the scenes, for favouritism goes a long way. He is pretty well sure to benefit by the friendship, though it is doubtful if the public are not the losers by this favouritism, as works of merit are often refused to place a trashy piece, produced by a friend, on the boards.

It must not be thought that managers are so unmindful of their own interests as to discard works of sterling merit; it is not thus. The fact is, they do not often take the trouble to look at the productions of unknown authors, hence they often lose a novelty, and a chance of emolument.

But many still persist in this course, and not a few have experienced dull houses from no other reason.

In the provinces, pieces are changed every week, but we doubt if this would be so, did the managers follow the example of many of the London theatres, and not be so penny wise and pound foolish.

However, be all this as it may, Harry had the gratification of knowing that the drama was appreciated, and he now only longed for the opening night to come, to see whether the public would look as favourably upon it as did his friends.

The few days that intervened between the time of his placing his manuscript in the hands of Charlie and the opening night, seemed to pass away very sluggishly.

It was but his own impatient spirit, for the time came round equally as quickly as if he had been anxious to stay its flight.

The piece was rehearsed, and all were letter perfect, and a smile of pleasure was on the face of the youth, when, a few moments before the rise of the curtain, the characters assembled on the stage.

Buskin Bob, who was made up for the unfaithful tar, looked every inch a sailor, whilst Charlie Evans, to whom was assigned the part of the deceived wife, made up for the character to perfection.

Margaret, of course, had her part, and so did Harry and Mary.

The bell rang, the heart of the young author beat violently, and the curtain rose to a wellfilled house.

The piece proceeded, each doing their utmost to make it go well, and their labours were repeatedly rewarded by well-earned applause.

It was evident to all that the little drama was a triumph; but it was the last scene that told better than all, which could scarcely be heard for the shouts of laughter, which were called forth when the injured wife finds the faithless husband, and after knocking him down with their child, thrown from her arms at his head, proceeds to administer corporeal punishment upon her half intoxicated spouse with a rope's end, and from which the faithless tar is only rescued by his messmates, who then rush on to the stage.

The curtain fell, and the piece was over.

Having stood for some few moments on the stage—a gleam of pleasure in his eye, a feeling of gratification in his heart.

He was about to turn away, when Buskin Bob laid his hand upon his shoulder.

"Well, Harry," he said, "are you well satisfied."

"Indeed I am," replied the youth, a glow of pride on his cheeks.

"The piece was successful."

"Beyond my expectations."

"But not your hopes?" said Bob.

"No."

"Success is a great thing, Harry," answered Bob.

"Yes."

"A pleasant thing?"

"Very."

"But it is sometimes a bad thing," said the pantaloon.

"Bad?"

"Yes."

"Why?"

"Shall I tell you?"

"Do."

"Because it ministers to pride."

"Well."

"And kills the better part of human nature," said Bob.

"How."

"By making men conceited."

"Conceited."

"Yes."

"Of what?"

"Their abilities."

The youth smiled.

"Success often leads us to think better of ourselves than others."

"It would not me," said Harry.

"Perhaps not."

"Why should it?"

"I can't say, but it does many," said Bob. "Men who by their natural talents, or some stroke of luck, meet with success, often turn round upon their old and tried friends with scorn."

Harry looked pained.

Did Bob think he would.

He felt wounded at the words of the pantaloon.

He looked fixedly in Bob's face.

It wore the same look as ever.

"Bob," he said, "I am not one of those of whom you speak. Success to me would be happiness, because I might share it with those I love."

Bob grasped his hand.

"I know it, Harry," he said. "I feel it. Strike me comical if I ever thought otherwise. I have only said what I have done that I might say more."

"Go on."

"You are young."

"Yes."

"The young heart, like the young tree, is easily twisted into any shape. A pressure brought to bear upon the green sapling, and it is often twisted out of shape: the tall, straight, and beautiful stem becomes crooked, and spite of all, it never recovers from its deformity. The pressure of success often acts upon the soul of youth as force upon the sapling bends it to deformity, crushes down its nobler qualities, and gives place to vanity and arrogance."

A blush overspread the face of Harry.

"Harry."

"Bob."

"I speak not to wound your feelings," said the pantaloon.

"You do not."

"I fear I have."

"No."

"Yet you blush."

"Do I?"

"Yes."

"I did not know it."

"Perhaps not," said Bob, "but the face often pourtrays the feelings of the heart."

"You have not hurt me," said the youth.

"I am glad of it, for I had no intention of doing so."

"I am sure you had not."

"No, Harry, I only said what I did, that I might warn you in time," said Bob.

"Of what?"

"Allowing yourself to be carried away by your success to-night," said Bob.

"I shall not."

"Do not, my boy. I am many years older than you, and have seen a few ups and downs in life, strike me comical if I haven't, and I have learnt that success and applause have often done more to destroy the true nature of man, than ever it has done to kindle it. I am happy for the success of anyone, but I cannot help feeling a pang of sorrow, when I find that it makes man forgetful of what he once was, and leads him to look upon those who were his former friends, with a patronising air, a glance of pity, or a word of contempt."

"Me it never will!" exclaimed Harry, as a tear rose unbidden to his eye. "No, Bob, success will never make me forget that I was a poor orphan boy, without a friend in the wide wide world, but Charlie and you and Mary. I know that I am ambitious, but ambition only leads me to help those who have so kindly helped me. I would be more than I am, better than I am, but come weal or come woe, never will Harry Marston, the poor orphan boy, forget those who so kindly protected and sheltered him, and shared with him the little they could get in their arduous Struggles for Bread!"

"Nobly spoken!" exclaimed Bob, shaking him by the hand. "You are made of the real stuff, and your heart is in the right place. There keep it, my boy, in spite of the designs of knaves, and the flatteries of fools. Let success crown a man's labour and he is surrounded by both. Heed them not, for they have but their own base purposes to serve; and their friendship is only professed not practised. The true friend is he who stands beside you in adversity and sorrow, not him who only basks in the sunshine of your prosperity, and flies at the approach of the first dark cloud. So be warned, Harry, my boy, be warned in time, and depend upon it, you will never regret following the advice of the poor strolling player, Buskin Bob; you won't, strike me comical if you will—there!"

And giving the hand he still held in his own another hearty shake, the pantaloon darted away to his dressing-room, to prepare for the next piece and talk with his old friend and fellow-worker Charlie Evans, over the success of the first production of the youthful author.

Harry watched him till he disappeared behind the wings, then heaving a sigh, he muttered,—

"Heaven has indeed been kind to me since my poor mother's death. If her angel spirit is permitted to look down from heaven, how happy must she feel to know that I have such kind friends. How gratifying to her must be the knowledge that the poor orphan she left alone in the world is surrounded by those whose only aim is to guide his footsteps in the paths of honour, justice, and truth. How shall I ever be able to repay them for all their kindness to me. I know not yet, I will strive my utmost to make them happy. To Charlie I will be a true and obedient son, to Bob a true and stanch friend, to Mary, what to her," he added thoughtfully, "a kind a loving brother. I will seek her, lest she, too, think my success has made me cold. No, no, it shall only warm my heart towards them and spur me on to cheer their path and ease their Struggles for Bread!"

And with a glowing cheek the happy youth sprang to the wings and looked around for Mary.

But his eye detected her not.

"She is in her room," he muttered to himself.

But he did not, as he used, fly to her.

A few short months since, and he hesitated not to enter her dressing-room.

He saw no harm in so doing.

Felt none.

But now, he dreaded to approach within its precincts.

Something seemed to hold him back.

What?

He knew not.

Could not divine the cause.

A change had come upon them both.

And that change was love.

Felt for the first time when he so nobly stood forward to protect the pantomimist's daughter, from the indignities of a ruffian.

So he awaited her appearance at the wings.

Minutes flew by and she came not.

He paced up and down, anxious and uneasy.

A feeling of sadness again stole over him.

Yet he could not tell why.

There was nothing unusual in Mary remaining in her room.

For the poor girl was often hard at work every moment she could get.

At any other time he would have felt no surprise at this circumstance.

He would have come to the conclusion that she was stitching way at some doublet or pant that required mending ere it could be put on.

But now no such thought ever entered his head.

"Why was she not ready to congratulate him on the success of the piece.

Why had she shut herself in her room.

He could not rest easy.

With uneasy strides he paced the sides sadly and thoughtfully.

Suddenly he started, like a nervous girl, as the hand of Charlie Evans descended on his shoulder.

"Hi! here we are!" exclaimed the clown. "Hallo, what in the name of fortune is the matter with you?"

"Nothing," exclaimed the youth, in a confused tone.

"Well, then nothing makes you look precious miserable," said Charlie. "I expected to find you in high glee."

The youth sighed.

"Sighing, too, when you should be laughing," said Charlie. "Why, if I had been the author of that drama, I verily believe I should laugh for a week for joy at its success. Well, you meet good fortune in a strange way, and no mistake."

And the clown thrust his hands deep into his pockets, and stood gazing at his young protégée with a half anxious, half comical look for some minutes.

"What, in the name of peace, is the matter with you," said Charlie, at length. "Why are you wandering up and down the place like a hyena in his cage, with your hands clasped behind you, and your eyes fixed upon the floor. I have it, thinking of a plot for another drama.

"No, indeed" replied the Boy Actor, "my thoughts were far from that."

"Then I should like to know what they were about," said Charlie, "for they cannot be pleasant ones I am sure."

Harry's face was suffused in blushes in a moment.

He felt the hot blood rising to his cheeks, and he turned his head away.

Charlie eyed him intently.

"Nothing you're ashamed of," he said, at length.

"Ashamed!" exclaimed the boy, turning hurriedly round, and fixing his eyes upon his interrogator.

"No, Harry," said the kind hearted clown, "I did not expect they were, though I made use of the word. But come, what ails you—you look queer, you are not well my boy. I hope you are not ill."

And the clown laid his hand kindly upon the arm of the youth and gazed steadfastly into his face.

"No, father," replied Harry, "I am not ill, yet I feel sad.

"At what?"

"I cannot tell."

"Not tell."

"No."

"That's strange."

"But true."

"Come, cheer up," said Charlie. "Are you not satisfied at the success of the piece?"

"Oh, yes."

"And yet you are sad," said the clown, in a puzzled tone."

"I am."

"What's the reason?"

"I cannot give it."

"Cannot!"

"Indeed, no."

"Has anything occurred to make you unhappy?" asked Charlie, anxiously.

"Not that I know of."

"Charlie shook his head.

"Strange," he muttered to himself.

Then turning to Harry, he said,—

"Cheer up, cheer up. It must be the heat and noise, combined with your anxiety to know how the piece would go, that's all."

Harry tried to call a smile to his face.

But it died ere it was born.

At this moment Buskin Bob approached.

"Hi!" said Charlie.

"Here I am," said Bob, darting to his side.

"Just look at him," said Charlie.

And he pointed to the Boy Actor.

"I can see him without a microscope," said Bob, "strike me comical if I can't.

"What do you think of him?"

"Why the same as I always did," was the reply.

"Then I don't."

"Don't!"

"No."

"How's that?"

"Take a good look."

Buskin Bob did as he was requested.

"Well," said the pantaloon. "I've got his likeness to perfection."

"And what do you think of it?" asked Charlie.

"Same as ever."

"And no alteration?"

"None."

"Then I do."

"Where?"

"Why there."

And the clown pointed to the face of the Boy Actor.

Bob's eyes followed the clown's finger.

"Humph," said Bob, looks rather grumpy, "strike me comical if he don't."

"That's it."

"What's up?"

"Don't know."

"Well, he does, I suppose," said Bob, carelessly.

"Says he don't," replied Charlie.

"What, don't know what's the matter with him?"

"So he says."

"Then if he says so, strike me comical if he don't mean it," said Bob.

"Well, he does say so."

"Then rest assured he speaks the truth," said Bob, emphatically.

"It's a rum go to look miserable, feel miserable, and not know the cause, ain't it?" said Charlie.

"Well, rather," said Bob, with a grin, "but strike me comical if I don't think I can tell."

"What?" asked Charlie.

"Why, he is in love."

Harry gave a sudden start.

"In love," said Charlie, "ha! ha!"

"Yes, in love," said Bob, "that always makes people miserable, you know."

"Why, in the name of fortune, who can he be in love with?" laughed Charlie.

"Why, with you, to be sure," replied Bob.

"With me?"

"Yes, your make up was so capital, you looked a woman to perfection, and I almost fell in love with you myself."

"Ha, ha!" laughed Charlie. "But there, I will soon find one to bring back gladness to your heart, my boy. I'll fetch Mary to you, and see what she can do."

And the good-hearted clown darted away in the direction of his daughter's dressing-room.

Again the tell-tale blood mounted to the forehead of the youth.

He strained his eyes eagerly after the form of Charlie Evans.

Bob could not but observe this, and he fell into a train of thought.

Could it be possible the words he had spoken were truly uttered.

Was the youth before him really in love.

Had that strange feeling really taken possession of his heart.

Had his affections become centred on the clown's daughter.

Such he had believed would one day be the case.

But not so young.

Bob shook his head.

He was puzzled.

But he made no remark.

He only stood watching the changing colour, as it rose and fell upon the cheeks of the Boy Actor.

Charlie soon re-appeared.

The eyes of the youth were raised anxiously to his face.

The clown shook his head with a grin.

"She'll soon put you to rights," he said.

"Did you tell her he had got the blues?" asked Bob.

"No," replied his friend. "I couldn't."

"How so?"

"But I will," said Charlie, "when she comes by. She ain't in her room."

"Not there!" gasped Harry.

"No," said Charlie, looking suddenly up into the face of the boy, at the strange manner in which he had given utterance to the words.

Harry's face had become pale as marble.

Charlie and Bob sprang forward.

"Not there," gasped Harry, again. "Not there. Oh, heavens!"

CHAPTER XCIV.

THE LIBERTINE AT WORK—THE MEETING AT THE FAIR—THE PURSUIT—THE CONFERENCE IN THE LANE—THE VILLAIN AND HIS EMPLOYER.

ARRIVING at his home, William Frampton, the youthful libertine, hurriedly sought his own room.

He flung his hat upon the table, and his body into a chair, and for a few moments remained buried in thought.

Then he rose and paced across the room.

He started as he saw the reflection of his face in a mirror on the wall

And he ground his teeth with rage and shame at the sight his features presented.

His eyes were swollen, and fast becoming black, and altogether he presented a picture, by no means flattering.

Then he thought how should he account to his father for his appearance.

Should he tell him the truth.

No.

For then he would not only stamp himself as a villain, but also as a coward.

He resolved to hatch up some tale to satisfy his parent, and bide his time to be revenged on his assailant and Mary.

Bathing his face, and destroying all the traces which he possibly could of the punishment he had received, he strode to the room in which his father sat, and, to surprised inquiries, answered, that he had fallen heavily to the earth, and struck his face against a projection by the wayside.

The tale passed current, and after a few words of advice and condolence, no more was said of the matter.

And in a few days the circumstance was forgotten by the father.

Not so the son.

He neither forgot nor forgave.

Time only added fuel to the fire of revenge that smouldered in his heart.

Plan after plan did he conjure up, by which to minister to his desires.

But no sooner were they matured, than they were discarded, and his evil mind sought others less dangerous, and more certain of success.

Thus months wore on.

But still, during this time he was far from being idle.

Day after day, he followed the progress of the caravan, and stood at some distance, gazing with bitter hatred upon the youthful players, as they laboured upon the parade.

Excusing his absence from home, he travelled the country, still keeping the same course as the pantomimists, and day by day his all absorbing passion strengthened.

At length the last fair was over.

Still he was no nearer the consummation of his wishes.

His revenge had not yet been gratified.

But still he resolved to track them like an evil spirit through the world.

MINNIE THE IDIOT.

The smiling face of the lovely girl fired his passions.

The noble countenance of the Boy Actor rankled in his heart.

Whilst watching them, day by day, his eye had often encountered the form of a man, always standing about the same distance from the caravan as himself.

The constant appearance of this individual at each town the booth was raised, excited the curiosity of the dishonourable youth.

There is a freemasonry in crime; and one culprit can generally detect another.

Frampton from the first believed that this individual was actuated by no very honourable feelings towards those in the caravan.

And of this he soon became assured.

Cautiously making his way up to the spot where his fellow watcher had taken his stand on the last day of the last fair, he stood beside and appeared to be deeply engaged in watching the performances going on outside the booth.

But Frampton paid little heed to them; beneath his lashes his eyes strayed to the face of the man beside.

It was pale and haggard, and there was a restless and nervous twitching of the mouth, and constant movement of the eyes, as though he feared to encounter the glance of some unpleasant object.

But a flush overspread the face of the man, as Harry bounded on to the parade; and he locked his teeth together, and hissed between them,—

"Curse him; but for him, I had not been what I am!"

Then, perceiving the eye of Frampton fixed upon him, he turned deathly pale and moved away from the spot.

Without appearing to have noticed the act or words of the man, the youth continued to appear engaged in watching the performance, but in reality, by a side glance, he was following the movements of the man.

He saw that he was not alone in his hatred of the Boy Actor.

He felt that the time drew nigh to be revenged on those who he had sworn to injure.

The words of the man led him to believe that in him he might find a willing tool to minister to his desires.

And his heart bounded at the thought that perhaps the hour of vengeance was at hand.

When the outside performance was over, the man moved away, and left the fair field.

Frampton followed him.

Once or twice the man cast an hurried glance behind him, and quickened his pace.

Still the youth followed, keeping the same distance between them.

In this way they walked on for about the space of half a mile, when the man turned hurriedly down a narrow lane.

Quickening his pace the youth soon stood at the entrance to the lane.

He looked down it.

A cry of disappointment escaped him.

He stamped his foot in rage.

The man was nowhere to be seen.

For a moment Frampton stood irresolute; whether to proceed or go back.

He felt that he had lost sight of one who would have been serviceable to him.

Of one who, like himself, would stop at nothing to be revenged on those he hated.

But the opportunity was lost.

For a moment he wavered.

Then darted down the lane as speedily as he could.

There was a turn in the lane about a hundred yards down it.

This he quickly gained.

He looked anxiously forward.

The man was some distance on before him, and going along at a swift pace.

Frampton resolved to come up with him if possible, so started into a run.

The man turned his head, and seeing himself pursued, urged himself forward at renewed speed.

Frampton now thoroughly despaired of overtaking him, and was about to give up the chase, when the man slipped and fell heavily to the ground.

Again the youth bounded forward.

And the man as speedily rose to his feet.

But it was evident that he had been severely shaken by the fall, for though he strove to fly from his pursuer, he was unable to do so other than in a slow and staggering gait.

A cry of joy broke from Frampton's lips, and in a few moments he was within a few paces of the man.

But he was brought to a sudden standstill, by the man turning furiously round upon him.

The look of pleasure on the youth's face, now gave place to one of fear.

He cast his eyes hurriedly around.

They were alone.

What if the man meant mischief to him.

He almost repented that he had followed him.

He resolved to fly.

But again his decision was changed, as the man exclaimed,—

"What do you follow me for? Keep off, or it may be the worse for you. I will never be taken alive—never!"

In a moment the youth perceived that the man he had followed, was a wretch flying from justice.

He saw that he had him in his power.

And he resolved to work upon his fears, if he could not upon his inclinations.

"I intend you no harm," he said, hurriedly.

"Then why do you follow me?" asked the man.

"Because I seek a friend," answered the youth.

"A friend!" said the man.

"Yes."

"I know you not."

"But I know you."

"Ah!" gasped the man; and his face became even more pale than it was.

"I know you to be one, who, for a handsome reward, would stand my friend."

"What do you require?" said the other, who, at the mention of a reward, unclenched his hands, and approached the youth.

"First let me tell you," said the youth, "that I stood beside you at the fair."

"I know you did."

"And I overheard the remark you made," said Frampton.

"What remark?"

"A remark called forth by the appearance of the boy on the parade."

"Well."

"The words you then uttered proved to me

that you bore him no good will," said Frampton.

"What of that?"

"Much."

"I don't understand you."

"You soon will."

"Shall I?"

"Yes."

"Go on then," said the man.

"I believe that boy has injured you," said Frampton.

"Perhaps he has."

"I am sure he has."

"Why."

"From your words."

"Oh."

"And from another reason."

"What's that?"

"He has injured me."

"You!"

"Yes."

"How?"

Frampton coloured to the temples.

He could not muster courage to stamp himself as a coward.

And this he must surely do, did he speak the truth.

"No matter how," he said, after a pause, "enough that I hate him."

"So do I, and all in that cursed booth," said the man.

"And I would be revenged upon him and the girl."

"The girl!"

"Yes."

"What girl?"

"The manager's daughter."

"Ah!"

"I would. From your words I believed you to be actuated by the same desires as myself, hence the reason I followed you."

The man now seemed to recover from the fear which had first taken possession of him, for he approached still nearer the youth.

"Why should you believe so?" he inquired.

"Not only from the words which escaped your lips, but from the knowledge of the manner in which you have followed the caravan from town to town."

"Ah!" exclaimed the other, in surprise, "then you—"

"Have done the same."

"For what reason?"

"Revenge."

The man eyed the youth closely.

He was anxious to see if he could detect in his features anything that belied his words.

But he could not.

He mused thoughtfully for a few moments.

At length he said,—

"You say revenge prompts you to seek me, because you think I entertain the same feelings towards those you name."

"Just so."

"What circumstances have brought about these desires on both sides, it would be as well for neither to inquire into; it is sufficient that we hear the ill-will."

"It is," said Frampton, only too anxious to conceal the cause as regarded himself.

"Then what do you require of me," asked the man.

"Your assistance."

"And for that if I consent," asked the man.

"I will reward you handsomely," replied the other.

"You."

"Yes, me."

The man looked hard at him.

"Do you doubt me?" said the youth, indignantly.

"Not your will."

"What then?"

"Your ability."

"How so?"

"You are very young."

"But I am rich."

"And I am poor," said the other, "very poor."

"That is all the better," said Frampton.

"Why so?"

"Because it will be to the interest of both to deal fairly by the other."

"What do you require," asked the man, fixing his eyes steadily on the face of his companion.

Frampton looked eagerly around to make sure that no one was within hearing.

Not a soul was to be seen, and he said,—

"I love that girl."

"Love her!"

"Yes."

"She is but a child."

"I am but a boy."

"In years, yes—In crime," he added to himself, "a man."

"That boy stands in my path."

"Does he?"

"He does. He has insulted me, and the girl, too. I would humble their proud spirits, and teach her to know that, when one of my station sinks so low as to condescend to look favourably upon a poor strolling player, my overtures are not to be treated lightly with indignity and scorn."

"What would you then," said the other, evidently somewhat puzzled.

"Tear her from those who would protect her," replied the youth, "and make her that by force, she refuses by persuasion."

The man started back a few paces.

He eyed the youth from head to foot, as if he doubted the evidences of his senses.

But the demoniac look upon the face of Frampton, convinced him that the youth meant every word he had given utterance to.

"You would tear her from her father," he said.

"And her lover."

"Lover!"

"Yes."

"Who is that?"

"The boy you cursed a short time since," said Frampton. "I will learn her how to despise the offer of one so far above her, and embitter the heart of him, who dared to stand forward in her defence."

"I hate that boy," said the man, "and would do anything to make him wretched."

"I am glad of that," said Frampton, "for then you have a greater incentive to enter my service, as by serving me you minister to your own revenge."

And taking his purse from his pocket, he counted into the hands of the man five guineas.

"There," he said, "that is an earnest of what I will do for you, if you consent to serve me."

The man's eyes sparkled as he held the gold in his extended hand

"I will serve you," he said, in a determined tone.

"And you shall find me no bad paymaster," replied the other.

"Name your work!" exclaimed his companion.

"The seizure of that girl. Place her in my power, and I will double that sum."

"I will do it," said the other, "if only to be revenged upon him who struck me down like a dog on the parade."

CHAPTER XCV.

THE PLOTTERS AT WORK.—THE ABDUCTION OF MARY—THE RECOGNITION.

ON the opening night of the Crown Saloon under the management of Charlie Evans, about an hour before the time of opening the doors, two persons entered the parlour of a publichouse a few doors from the theatre.

One was a youth of genteel exterior, the other, a man attired in somewhat poorer habiliments.

There was a peculiarity about the features of the latter.

His eyes were sunken, and a restless expression hovered in them; his cheeks were pale, and his whole appearance denoted one who had seen much suffering.

A pair of black bushy whiskers and moustache, which he wore, served only to make his cheeks more sallow, and give to him the appearance of a man in the last stage of consumption.

The parlour was empty at the time they entered, and after calling for refreshments, they sat down close together, with their backs to the door and window.

"Your disguise is perfect," said the younger of the two men, addressing his companion.

"Yes, I flatter myself the make-up is good," replied the man.

"No one would recognise you now, I am sure," said the younger personage.

"Nor do I wish them too," said the other.

And as he spoke he cast an anxious look towards the door.

"You seem nervous," remarked his companion.

"Do I," said the other, sharply.

"Yes. And I have often noticed that you start at the slightest sound."

The other made no answer.

"If you have any fear of meeting with any one you have no wish to see, I am sure they would never know you, so greatly are you altered."

"Since when?" asked the other, thoughtfully.

"Since our meeting in the lane," resumed the youth.

"Aye," sighed the other, "I have altered much within a few months; but there, no one will know me now, and that is sufficient for our present purpose."

"Quite," said the other.

"Then to business."

"You are sure you are on the right track," said the young man, after a pause, "and that the girl will really be at the theatre to-night."

"Quite sure," was the answer.

"But how do you propose to get her in our power?" asked the young man.

"That must depend upon circumstances," said the other. "The reason I have brought you here is that I may learn when she is on and when she is off."

"But how can you learn here?" asked the other.

"Some of the supers are pretty well sure to drop in here before they go to the theatre."

"Well?"

"We can stand a glass to them, and worm out of them all we desire to know," said the man.

"Good," replied the other. "I am impatient to see what this night will bring forth."

And the youth rose from his seat, and gazed out of the window into the street.

The other sat with his eyes fixed on the fire, which burned in the large grate.

Thus they continued for about a quarter of an hour, when the door opened, and two young men entered the apartment.

The eyes of the man twinkled, and he nodded meaningly to the youth, who turned from the window at the entrance of the new comers.

The strangers called for their favourite beverage, and drew their chairs near to the fire.

Meantime, the man with the black whiskers kept his face studiously turned from them, and appeared to be busily engaged with his own thoughts.

But in truth he was listening eagerly to every word uttered by the last arrivals.

It was not long ere he discovered from their conversation that they were engaged at the Saloon, and still keeping his face averted, he remarked,—

"The Crown opens to-night under a fresh management."

"Yes," replied one of the men, "and good luck to it, say I."

"You are fond of theatricals perhaps," remarked the man with the whiskers.

"Well, as to being fond of them, I can't say that I am or I ain't. If I could get a living in any other line I would throw up the profession to-morrow."

"Oh, I see, you are connected with the theatre."

"Yes."

The man with the black whiskers filled his glass to the brim, and handed it to the man who had spoken.

"Will you drink with me," he said.

"I don't mind if I do," replied the other, taking the glass. "Your health."

And raising the vessel to his lips, he drained it off.

"I have often thought I should like to see the back of a stage," said the black-whiskered man, "it must be a strange sight to one who has never been behind the curtain."

"Ah, you may well say that," replied the man. "'It's not all gold that glitters,' and that you soon find out at the wings. It looks very pretty from the front, but the charm is gone when you look from behind. The beautiful landscape becomes a daub then; the jewels are but tinsels; the stage but a workshop."

"Indeed."

"Yes, indeed; you have never been behind then."

"No."

"Then you would be surprised," said the man.

"Do you think this place will answer," said the man with the black whiskers, after a pause.

"It's hard to tell," said the other. "But I think it stands a good chance, for you see the expenses ain't much."

"Ain't they."

"No. The people that's got it all play themselves."

"All of them?"

"Yes, even a girl and boy."

"Why, what can they do?" asked the man, innocently.

"Well, I can't say yet, for I have only seen them at rehearsal."

"Are they young?"

"Yes, rather. Certainly they can make up to look older."

"Do they play to-night?"

"Yes. The boy has written a piece to suit himself and the girl, and they both play in it to-night."

"I should like to see it, but I can't spare the time."

"It's first piece," said the man, "and a short one. It won't play above an hour and a half."

"Do they go all through it?" asked the man with the whiskers, filling the glass and handing it to the other.

"Yes, right up to the last act, except the girl, she ain't on then, and she is the only one in the whole company that is off."

"And all the others are on the stage then."

"Every one for the tableaux but her, I almost wonder he didn't bring her on then, for the company is very small, and every one is a help."

"Well, so it is."

"I must be off now," said the man. "I must be dressed in a quarter of an hour. Why don't you go in and have a look at us."

"I should like much to do so," said his interrogator, "but the fact is I am not at liberty till eight o'clock."

"Well, the last scene will be on then, if you like to come up behind, you can."

"But how do you get there?"

"Go down the gateway at the side of the house, and you will see a little door before you. Push it open, and walk up."

"But will they allow strangers to do so?"

"Not as a rule they don't, but if you like to come and have a look you can do so, for if any one says anything to you, say you want to see Joe Smith, that's me; but there, no one will say anything to you, for the reason that there is no one to do it but the girl, and she ain't at all likely."

"Well, I am much obliged to you, but I don't think it's likely I shall have a chance," said the man, turning his features farther into the shade, as the other rose.

"If you do, you can come up without any fear, so I'll say good day if I don't see you again, for I have hardly got time to dress. Come on, Tom."

And the next instant, the two men hurried from the room.

The youth watched their forms till they had passed by the window, then walked across the room, and sat down beside the man with the whiskers.

"Well," he said.

"Better than I expected," remarked the other,

"the girl will be left alone by herself during the last scene."

"But she will be surrounded by those who will protect her."

"I tell you that will be the time for us."

"How so?"

"We must make our way on to the side, and seize her, whilst the others are all engaged on the stage."

"Are you mad?"

"No."

"You must be."

"Why so?"

"So daring an act would be sure to bring down upon us exposure and defeat," said the youth.

"It is our only chance, for then she will be alone."

"But within call of others."

"True."

"Then it will be madness."

"Not so."

The youth shook his head.

"Not if we watch for a favourable opportunity."

"I cannot see any."

"I can."

"Explain.

"You heard that man say that the whole company were on the stage except her in the last scene."

"I did."

"While all are thus engaged we have but to pounce upon her."

"And if she cry out?"

"We are safe."

"Safe!"

"Yes."

"How?"

"Those on the stage cannot leave it till the piece is over and the curtain falls."

"Are you sure?"

"Quite."

"Yet I fear."

"What?"

"Assistance."

"There is none at hand."

"I would we could find some other means to put our wishes into execution," said the youth.

"I can see none other."

"Can we not seize her on her way home."

"When?"

"After the house is closed."

"No, for then she would be protected by her father and others."

"On the way to the theatre then."

"When?"

"To-morrow."

The other shook his head.

"She would still have them with her who would defend her to the last, and besides, daylight does not favour such a plan."

"True."

"Then if you really wish to get her in your power—"

"Wish to get her," interrupted the youth. "I shall know no rest till I do."

"Then there is no time more favourable than to-night."

"To-night be it then," said the youth.

"We will remain here a short time longer, and when the piece is in full swing, we will go and reconnoitre the passage to the stage door."

"Yes, we had much better make ourselves

thoroughly acquainted with the place before we proceed to business," said the youth.

"True."

Some time longer the two individuals sat together, each apparently deeply engaged with his own thoughts.

At length the elder of the two, raising his head, said,—

"If this work is done to-night, you are prepared to fulfil your promise, I suppose."

"I am," replied the other.

And taking a purse from his pocket he held it up before the eyes of the man with the whiskers.

"That's all right. Business like ours can't be done on credit."

"Why not?"

"Rogues should never trust each other; they have no pull."

"Rogues," said the youth, an indignant flush overspreading his face.

"Aye, rogues," replied his companion.

"You are not very complimentary."

"'Tis best to speak plain. You have no reason to be offended at the title, as you strive your best to earn it."

"Still, I don't like the word," said the youth, biting his lips in vexation.

"Well, I shall not use it again," said the man. "So come, and let us look about us."

So saying, he rose and walked to the door, followed by his companion.

Casting his eyes up and down the street, the man with the black whiskers led the way towards the theatre.

There were a few boys hanging around the entrances, but otherwise the place was quiet and deserted.

"This is the way to the stage door," said the elder of the two, pointing to a gateway.

The youth approached, and looked down a narrow dark passage, at the end of which was a door, through the chinks of which streamed the rays of a light.

"That is the stage door then?"

"It is. The passage is dark, and nothing can be seen from the street, so it will be easy to bear her down it to here."

"And then," said the youth, "how will it be best to proceed?"

"You saw the place I pointed out to you where they let vehicles for hire."

"I did."

"Can you drive?"

"Well."

"That is good, since you will have no need to bring another into the secret. It is now half past seven: the last scene is at eight. Go and engage a vehicle and bring it to this gate."

"And you will do the rest?"

"Yes."

"And you will bring her to it?"

"I will; and then you must drive off as fast as possible."

"I will go at once."

And the youth turned to seek a vehicle to suit his purpose.

"Stay," said the other.

"What is it?"

"The money."

"What money?"

"The price of this night's work."

"But it is not yet done."

"True; but I must have the money first," said the other.

"This is not fair."

"It is."

"It is not."

"But it is. When I have torn that girl from her friends, when I have served your purpose, you may play me false."

"Do you suspect me?"

"I do."

"What!" exclaimed the youth, firing up.

"Silence," said the man. "I have no wish to make others as wise as ourselves. You have no need to be so fiery, because I tell you the truth. I do suspect you, for your deeds are dishonourable."

"Then what guarantee have I that you will not sell me when you have been paid?"

"This. I hate the father of that girl with an undying hatred. I would do any deed, however black, to be revenged upon him. What greater vengeance could I have than to tear away his child, and place her in the arms of a libertine who seeks to destroy her honour. Boy, your vengeance is not called forth by sufferings so acute as mine. I tell you, I will do this work, but I will be paid first."

The youth drew forth his purse, and counted ten guineas into the hand of the other.

"That is right," said the other. "Now away, and meet me here as the clock strikes eight."

"You will not deceive me?"

"I will not, so help me heaven!"

And as he spoke he darted into the narrow passage.

The youth sped on his way, and quickly engaged a fly, the box of which he mounted, and drove to the spot where he had left his companion.

Meantime, the man passed through the stage door, and stood at the bottom of the steps listening intently.

Thus he stood for some time, when he heard the voice of Charlie Evans.

He ground his teeth in rage as the tones fell upon his ears.

The clown was giving the necessary directions for the last tableau, and in another minute the listener knew, from the clapping of hands in front, that the last scene was on.

Taking off his overcoat, he crept noiselessly up the steps.

At that moment, the figure of Mary passed within a foot of him. A smile of triumph lit up his face, and he flung his coat over her head, lifted her in his arms, and bore her rapidly down the steps, along the passage, to the fly, at the door of which stood the youth. Without a word he thrust her into the vehicle, but as he did so, Mary succeeded in releasing herself from the covering, and, stretching out her hand, tore off the black whiskers; then her lips parted, and she shrieked out, "Dancing Bill, the Harlequin!"

CHAPTER XCVII.

THE FLIGHT—THE STRUGGLE IN THE CARRIAGE—THE END OF THE JOURNEY—AN UNLOOKED-FOR MEETING.

WITH a smothered curse Dancing Bill thrust Mary back upon the seat of the vehicle, and leaping in, placed his hand over her mouth to prevent her giving any alarm.

"Mount the box, and drive off as fast as possible," he exclaimed, to Frampton, who stood, pale and trembling, with the handle of the door in his hand.

"Do not let her scream," said the youth.

"No fear of that," replied Bill, pressing his hand with brutal violence upon her mouth. "Quick, or we shall have them discover her loss ere we get away!"

The youth cast one more glance upon the young girl, who was struggling in vain to wrest herself from the arms of the harlequin, then closed the door, mounted the box, and taking the reins urged the horse to its utmost speed.

Away went the vehicle over the hard road, jolting and swaying in its course, and the heart of Mary sank within her.

Finding her struggles vain, she relaxed her efforts, and sat sobbing and motionless on the seat.

Finding this, Bill relaxed the pressure of his hand upon her mouth.

No sooner had he done so, than Mary, by a violent effort, succeeded in freeing it altogether, and gave utterance to a loud cry.

"Curse you!" exclaimed the ruffian, springing upon her, "another cry like that, and it shall be your last."

And once more he essayed to stop her mouth with his hand.

"Oh, no, no!" she pleaded, grasping at his wrist.

"Will you swear to be quiet, then?" said Dancing Bill, savagely.

"Yes, yes!"

"Mind you do, or it will be the worse for you," said the ruffian.

The girl sank back with a sigh.

"Why am I served thus?" she said, after a time, during which she had been conjuring up how to escape.

"You'll know all, in good time," said Bill.

"Oh, in mercy's name tell me what is the meaning of this outrage," she pleaded.

"Shut your mouth," said Bill, "or I'll shut it for you."

And he raised his hand threateningly as he spoke.

The young girl shrank farther back, tremblingly.

"Oh, let me go back to my father!" she sobbed.

"Damn your father!" exclaimed the ruffian brutally.

"It will break his heart!" she murmured.

"I hope it may!" exclaimed Bill, brutally.

"Oh, why, why; he never harmed you," said Mary.

"It's a lie!" exclaimed Bill, furiously.

"Oh, no; he would not harm you, he would not harm a worm. He is too kind, too good. Oh, let me out of this carriage! let me go back to him, in mercy, let me go back!"

"I tell you no!" exclaimed the harlequin, "so let that suffice you."

"Where are you taking me?"

"To your future home."

"My future home?"

"Yes."

"What do you mean?" gasped Mary, in tones of surprise and terror.

"Just this," said Bill "that youth you saw at the door has taken a violent fancy to you; but that you already know."

"Ah," gasped Mary, "I thought I had heard his voice before, but I could not see his face. Is it him who Harry struck down for insulting me at Coventry?"

"That's where he comes from," said Bill, "and very likely it is the same; but that's nothing to me. All I know is he has taken a fancy to you, and has engaged me to assist him in carrying you off."

"Oh, Bill, Bill!" said the poor girl, again bursting into tears. "How can you lend yourself to this wicked act?"

"How can I!" exclaimed Bill. "Because I would be revenged upon Charlie."

"Upon my father!" she exclaimed.

"Yes."

"For what?"

"For what?" iterated the harlequin, grinding his teeth together, and hissing out the words, "for what."

"Yes, for what?"

"For the blow he struck me," exclaimed Bill, "for the taunts he has heaped upon me, for the wrongs he has done me."

"He wrong you?"

"He—yes, he."

"Oh, no, no."

"But, I say, yes!" exclaimed Bill.

"Indeed, indeed, you mistake. He would not wrong you. Oh, no! He is too kind, too good, too noble. See what he has done for Margaret."

"Curse him, yes. What has he done? torn her from me, kept her from her husband, biassed her mind against me; robbed me of my wife, curse him!"

"He rob you of your wife!" said Mary. "Oh, no, he only pitied her, held forth a helping hand to assist her when ill and starving; gave her freely from the little we had, and in return for this you belie him, and insult and injure me."

"Silence!"

"I will speak. I could bear anything but hear him spoken ill of."

"I speak the truth."

"No, Bill, no. You do not speak the truth. You lie!"

"I lie!" exclaimed the ruffian, fiercely.

"I repeat it—you lie!" exclaimed Mary.

"Curse you!" roared Bill, foaming with rage, and all his coward nature rising uppermost, "take that to close your mouth."

And he struck the poor girl a sharp blow on her cheek with the palm of his hand.

"Coward and villain!" exclaimed Mary, springing up hastily.

But the ruffian rose also, and grasped her in his arms.

"Let go!" she shrieked.

Bill strove to force his hand over her mouth, but so violently did she struggle, that he could not succeed, and Mary gave vent to scream after scream.

Goaded to fury by her cries, and fearful that they would bring some passer-by to her assistance, Bill forced her down upon the seat, and held her there with his knee.

"By hell!" he exclaimed, "if you utter another word, I will cut your throat from ear to ear."

"Murderer!" gasped Mary.

"Ah!" exclaimed Bill, and he staggered back at the word.

Thus released, Mary sprang up, and dashing her hand through the window of the door, she shrieked aloud,—

"Help—help!"

In an instant Bill was upon her.

With brutal violence he forced her down upon the seat.

And pushing her head violently back, he strove to bury her face, and drown her cries in the coat which she had thrown off her, as they placed her in the carriage.

Having done this, he anxiously looked from the broken window to see if her cries had given rise to pursuit.

But he could perceive no one following the vehicle, and that the place where they now were was deserted.

With a sigh of relief, he drew back into the carriage.

"So you thought to summon assistance did you?" said Bill.

"I shall be suffocated!" exclaimed Mary, from beneath the coat.

"Will you cry out again," he said, "if I release you?"

"No," gasped the poor girl.

Bill drew the coat from off her head.

"You hurt me," she said. "Your hand stops my breath."

Bill hesitated for a moment; and then, thinking it would not be to his future interest, perhaps, if the girl suffered any injury at his hands, and believing there was now little chance of her obtaining assistance, he let go his hold.

"It will be better for you," he said, "to remain quiet."

With a deep sigh, Mary leaned her head back against the padding of the carriage, and covering her eyes with her hand again burst into tears.

Dancing Bill watched her intently.

For some minutes the poor girl gave free vent to her grief.

Her overcharged bosom rose and fell with the powerful emotions that reigned in her breast.

She thought of her father, and his grief at her absence, of Harry and Buskin Bob, and she became powerless.

Still the carriage rolled on at a swift pace, and she perceived that its course was along a road between the fields.

She wondered where she was being conveyed to, but every time she looked up to ask Bill the question, she fancied she could see, in the dark, the forbidding countenance of the harlequin gazing upon her, and she was silent.

The pace at which she was being hurried along, led her to believe that she was some considerable distance from the place of her abduction.

This was a new source of grief.

For she feared to hope that Charlie would be able to trace her.

She gave way to despair.

And sobbing and clasping her hands in agony, she sat quiet and dejected.

The carriage still continued to roll on with unabated speed.

Fences, hedges, and trees whirled past, looking to her like shadowy spectres in the dim light.

The clatter of the horse's hoofs, and the rumble of the wheels on the hard road, alone broke the silence.

Thus another quarter of an hour passed.

A quarter of an hour of anxious thought and miserable suspense.

Then she perceived a few lights in the distance, towards which they were rapidly hurrying.

Their faint glimmers seemed to endow her with fresh hopes.

She resolved to appear resigned to her fate, in order to prevent Bill from folding her head in the cloak, or placing his hand over her mouth again.

But she also determined to call aloud for aid when the lights were reached.

Seated in the back of the carriage, she could plainly distinguish them, whilst her companion, being seated with his back to them, could not possibly have detected their vicinity.

The vehicle still rolled on, and Bill was the first to break the silence.

"You find it a little more sensible to be quiet, don't you?" he asked.

Mary replied only with a sigh.

"You see now what you gain by it," he continued. "If you had only howled again, I would have kept your head in this coat the whole way."

Then he relapsed into silence for a time.

"You ain't got much farther to go," he said, at length, "before you are put out of your misery."

"You will suffer for this outrage," said Mary, "some time or another. My father and his friends will leave no stone unturned to trace me, and then—"

"I shall be out of it altogether, interrupted Bill, "my share in this transaction will end in a few minutes."

"Your share?"

"Yes. I am only engaged to see you safe to your destination, and then, my work is finished."

"And what then?" asked Mary.

"Oh, you must ask the young gentleman who has taken such a violent fancy to you," said the harlequin.

"Gentleman," she sneered.

"Yes, such he calls himself, and I suppose he is one."

"He is a ruffian, like—"

But Mary paused quickly.

The fear of the coat was before her eyes, and this she dreaded, now that they were so near the lights she had been watching.

"Like me, ah," said Bill.

"No, no!" she gasped. "I meant—"

"It. No doubt you did," said the harlequin, "well, it matters little what you think, only be careful what you say, or I will have your mouth stopped again, in no time."

"Oh, no, no!" pleaded Mary.

"Be careful, then."

"I will."

"You had better," said Bill, sneeringly, and again he relapsed into silence.

Nearer and brighter became the lights, and Mary perceived they were fast approaching a town.

Her heart beat high.

She could almost hear its throbbings.

She drew her handkerchief from her pocket, and wrapped it round her hand, taking care that her knuckles were well covered.

She shifted silently along the seat.

Then she gazed eagerly through the glass, and waited.

The first light was passed.

It beamed from the window of a small house, and cast its faint glimmer in at the window of the carriage as it rolled past.

In the sudden glance, she perceived that Bill was reclining on the opposite side, with his arms folded across his breast.

It was but a momentary glance that she obtained of his features; but a shudder ran through her frame as the small ray lighted up his pale and haggard face, now devoid of whiskers.

Another light was passed, and then another, yet still Mary sat quietly peering from the window out into the darkness.

Then suddenly she leapt to her feet, and dashing the hand, around which she had wound her handkerchief through the window of the carriage, she screamed out with all the strength of her lungs—

"Help, help! Murder! help!"

The crash of the falling glass, and the sound

of her voice, as it broke on the stillness and echoed around, caused the youth who was driving, to pull suddenly up, and the fly was brought to a stand-still.

In a moment, Dancing Bill had sprung upon her, and bore her back from the window.

"Damn you!" he roared, "but I'll not give you another chance."

"Help—hel—mur—" she shrieked, as she felt his hand upon her mouth, and struggled for breath.

Frampton had leapt from the box, and now flung open the carriage door.

"For God's sake," he exclaimed, "keep her quiet now, or she will bring the whole town upon us."

"Damn her!" exclaimed Bill, "she promised not to make a noise, and this is how she keeps her word; but I'll take good care she don't fool me again, for I'll stop her tongue if I force her teeth down her throat in doing it."

"Don't hurt her," said Frampton, "but mind she does not give any further alarm, or we shall be stopped and suffer for it."

"I'll take care she don't," said Bill. "How far have we to go?"

"Not a quarter of a mile into the town," was the answer.

"Then mount the box, and drive on quickly," said Bill, "and I'll hold her tight till you stop."

Frampton shut the door, and mounted to the box; but just as he was about to seat himself, he felt the reins turn violently from his grasp, and he received a violent blow in the face, which knocked him completely over into the road, and ere he could utter a single cry, the fly was urged forward at terrific speed.

Dancing Bill, who now had all his energies taxed to their utmost to keep Mary quiet, so fiercely did she struggle, did not observe the form of the youth as it fell, but he heard the sound of his body as it struck against the earth, and holding the girl firmly with one hand, he lowered the window with the other, and thrusting his head out he said,—

"What's the matter?"

"Nothing," was the answer he received, and he drew in his head.

In about five minutes the fly drew up opposite a roadside inn, and the driver leaping to the ground, opened the door, and stood behind it.

"Is this the place?" said Bill.

"Yes; make haste and bring her out."

Bill sprang out into the road, and drew Mary after him from the vehicle.

But the moment that her feet touched the ground, Dancing Bill felt his throat grasped as in a vice.

"Villain!" roared a voice in his ears.

It was not the voice of Frampton, but one that he had heard before.

"Ah!" gasped Bill, as a cold perspiration broke out upon his brow.

"Rascal!" exclaimed the man, throwing the harlequin round, so that the light from the window of the inn might fall full upon his own face. "You little expected to meet me. Me, whose kindness and hospitality you repaid, by basely robbing the man who succoured you. Serpent, I nourished you, and you turned and stung me, but your sting shall recoil upon yourself. So, beware of the vengeance of Dick the Poacher!"

CHAPTER XCVIII.

THE SEARCH FOR THE MISSING ONE—ANXIETY OF THE PLAYERS, AND GRIEF OF THE BOY ACTOR.

For a few moments Charlie Evans and Buskin Bob stood gazing in mute surprise upon the pale face and trembling form of the Boy Actor.

They knew not what to make of his emotion.

At length Charlie, seizing him by the arm exclaimed,—

"What is the meaning of this? why did you reiterate the word, 'gone,' so strangely?"

"I know not," said Harry; "but I fear—"

"Fear what?" asked Charlie, hastily.

"That Mary has gone."

"Gone where?" asked Charlie.

"Gone!" exclaimed Bob.

"Yes, gone!"

"But where, where?" asked Charlie, his good-natured face suddenly becoming as pale as that of his protégé.

"I know not!" exclaimed Harry; "but, father, a strange feeling has taken possession of my heart, a foreboding of some evil to Mary; you say she is not in her room; she is not here, where then can she be?"

"Somewhere about the house," said Charlie.

"But where?"

"You make me uneasy, Harry!" exclaimed the clown.

"I will search for her."

"And so will I," said Bob, running hastily across the stage to the opposite wings.

Charlie again sought the dressing-room of his daughter.

Anxiously he cast his eyes around it.

A sigh of relief escaped him as his eyes lighted upon her walking attire, hanging against the walls.

"She is about the place," he muttered. "What a fool I am, but that boy has made me quite nervous."

And conjuring up a smile to his face, he left the room and returned to the spot where Harry stood.

The youth looked up anxiously and inquiringly.

"Well," said Harry.

"She is about the house somewhere," replied the clown.

Harry shook his head.

"Her clothes are in her room," remarked Charlie.

"Thank God!" exclaimed Harry, fervently.

"I declare you put me quite in a fright, said the clown, with your pale face and strange manner.

"Strike me comical, if I can find her," said Bob, coming up.

"Ask Margaret if she is in her room," said Charlie.

"I have."

"And she is not there," said Harry.

"Not there?" said the clown, anxiously.

"No, strike me comical if she is," replied Bob.

"Where can she have flown to," mused Charlie.

"Has she gone out?" asked Bob.

"She can't have done," replied the clown.

"Why not?"

"Because she has not undressed," replied her father.

"Well, it's a rum go, strike me comical if it ain't," said Bob.

Harry shook his head sadly.

"I will change," he said, "and seek her."

"She is sure to be back directly," said Charlie, "the puss is up to some of her games, hiding away somewhere."

"That's it," said Bob, "and she'll soon make her appearance when she is tired."

Harry walked moodily away to the dressing-room, and commenced hurriedly to divest himself of the garments in which he had played his part, and don his ordinary attire.

Still the same feeling was upon him.

The weight at his heart seemed to bow him down.

He could not change quick enough.

His impatience was so great.

Whilst he was thus engaged, his friends were making a vigorous search for the missing girl.

Both Charlie and Bob did not believe for a moment that she had left the house.

Yet they were puzzled to account for her disappearance.

Certainly circumstances were against the idea that she had left the theatre.

It was not likely she would do so in the garments she wore for the character she had sustained.

Every room was searched.

But in vain.

Every person in the company was questioned as to whether they had seen her.

But all shook their heads.

Charlie and Bob now became almost as anxious as Harry.

Property-chests were opened and looked into, but of course no Mary was to be found ensconced therein.

And when Harry once more made his appearance beside his friends on the stage, he perceived nought but blank looks in the faces of all.

"Have you found her?" was his first question.

"No," said Charlie.

"No," echoed Bob.

Then for a moment the players stood gazing upon each other with thougtful glances.

"Have you looked everywhere?" asked the boy.

"Everywhere I can think of," said Charlie.

"Strike me comical," said Bob, "if a corner a mouse could hide in has escaped us."

"Then she has gone," said Harry, in a sad tone.

"But where—how," said Charlie.

"What object could she have in leaving the house?" asked Margaret.

"If she has," said Bob, "strike me comical if she ain't gone mad."

"I cannot think she has left it of her own free will," said Harry.

"How then," said Charlie.

"I fear she has been carried away," replied the boy.

"Carried away!" said Bob.

"By whom?" said Margaret.

"I don't know," replied Harry, "but I think she has."

"For what purpose?" asked Margaret.

The boy shook his head.

And again the players lapsed into silence. Suddenly Bob started.

"Charlie," he said, and his voice trembled.

"What?"

"Are the traps all fast?" asked the pantaloon, anxiously.

"The traps!" said Charlie, with a start. "Good heavens! she surely cannot have fallen through."

"Oh, see, see!" gasped Harry, rushing to the centre trap, and stamping upon it, whilst Charlie and Bob tried those at the sides.

All were fast.

"I could have sworn that I looked to them," said Charlie.

"They are all fast," said Bob, "but I'll go under the stage and see if she's there."

"And I will come with you," said Harry, quickly.

"Bring a light then," said Bob, "or strike me comical if we shan't stand a good chance of breaking our shins, in the dark."

A light was quickly procured, and Bob descended the steps on which Dancing Bill had stood a short time before, and opening a door at the bottom of them, entered the large space under the stage.

But only a heterogeneous mass of old scenery, timber, and rubbish, met their gaze.

"Just hold the light up, Harry, my boy," said Bob.

The boy did as requested, and Bob examined the bolts of the traps, to make sure that they were shot full home in their sockets.

"Well, thank God, she ain't fell through the traps," said Bob, making his way over the rubbish. "Now we have looked everywhere we can think of, and strike me comical if I ain't perfectly licked."

"She is not in the place," said Harry.

"No," said Bob, "and where she can have got to, attired as she is, puzzles me, strike me comical if it don't, there!"

"Oh, Bob, we must seek her!" exclaimed the boy.

"We must, if she don't come back before the house is over," replied the pantaloon.

"At once, Bob, at once!" said the boy.

"We can't."

"We must!"

"Impossible."

"Oh, no."

"Oh, yes," said Bob. "The overture is finished, and the people in front, are clamouring for us to begin."

"Let them wait," said the boy, impatiently.

"And ruin the place on the first night?"

"Better that than lose her!" exclaimed Harry.

"Tush, tush!" exclaimed Bob. "She ain't far off, depend upon it. She is wild, and giddy, and will be back soon."

"Heaven grant she may," sighed the Boy Actor.

"You take it too much to heart," said Bob. "She is a silly girl to leave the house as she has done, but she is young, and thoughtless; when she gets older she will know better. Come on, my boy."

And Bob passed up the steps on to the stage, followed by Harry.

"She is not there," said Charlie.

"No," replied Bob.

Charlie looked anxious and pale.

"Where can she have got to?" he murmured.

"I expect she has thrown a cloak over her dress, and foolishly strayed out for something," said Bob.

"That must be it," remarked Margaret.

"I wish she would return," said Charlie, "for I feel anxious and uneasy."

"She'll be back soon, depend upon it," said Bob, "so make yourself comfortable on that score. Hark how impatient the people are. We must leave her for the present and begin, or they will stamp the house in."

"We must," said Charlie. "Confound the girl, I'll rate her soundly for this freak. Clear the stage. Ring up Bob."

In an instant the stage was clear, and Buskin Bob rung up the curtain.

It was a fortunate circumstance that neither Mary or Harry were cast in the second piece, or it could not possibly have proceeded."

To such a state of mind had the youth worked himself, that he would have been unable to utter a single word.

The piece commenced.

But the eyes of the players wandered anxiously from the stage to the side where the steps were, in the hope of seeing the form of pretty Mary at the wings.

But no Mary came.

Charlie became more and more dispirited, and walked through his part without the least spirit.

Bob was no less anxious, but he had not a father's anxiety.

The good fellow saw how things were going, and he resolved to do his best to save the piece.

And nobly he did it.

Never did he play with more spirit; never did he laugh so loudly and so merrily.

But little did those in front, as they showered down their applause upon him, know that though the face wore a smile, the heart of the player was aching.

Harry could rest no longer, so he left the house, and made his way into the street.

Anxiously he cast his eyes about in all directions.

Not a shop but he peered into; not a figure but he rushed eagerly forward to see if it was that of Mary.

Every moment he became more and more dejected.

Sadly he returned to the stage, and as he mounted the steps to the wings, his eyes were filled with tears.

Impatiently and sadly he awaited the fall of the curtain. The green baize rolled slowly down at last, but still no Mary was there to glad his eyes with her sweet smile and silvery voice.

CHAPTER XCIX.

MARY PLEADS FOR DANCING BILL — DICK THE POACHER AND THE RESCUED MAIDEN.

IF ever a guilty wretch stood paralysed in the presence of the man he had injured, Dancing Bill was the one.

So sudden and so unexpected had been the meeting between himself and Dick the Poacher, that every faculty became numbed.

He had not the power to shake off the grasp upon his throat.

No, he could not raise a hand to protect himself.

His eyes started almost from their sockets, beneath the pressure of Dick's fingers, and a thick foam gathered round his mouth.

His knees knocked together, and he trembled in every limb.

He tried to gasp out an appeal for mercy, but his tongue refused to give utterance to the words.

And he stood glaring in abject fear upon the man, whose kindness he had repaid with such base ingratitude.

The indignation of Dick the Poacher was so great, that it threatened the total destruction of the base-minded harlequin.

Is is doubtful whether the guilty man had not paid for his ingratitude dearly, had it not have been for Mary.

The moment she found herself on the ground, and freed from the hold of Dancing Bill, her first impulse was to fly.

Whither she knew not.

For the place in which she found herself was strange to her.

Still the moment she felt her feet touch the earth, and her limbs free, she bounded forward.

But the next instant she paused in her flight.

A cry of joy broke from her lips.

She clasped her hands in thankfulness.

The tones of the voice that saluted her ears were familiar to her.

She had heard them before.

And they were tones she had never forgotten.

She recognised them instantly.

And a look of joy overspread her pretty face, as she turned and by the light of the inn lamps, distinctly saw the features of Dick the Poacher.

What a change come over her young heart in an instant.

A change great indeed; from grief and fear to joy and hope.

She knew that she was now safe, and she sprang forward to the side of Dick.

She cast a hurried glance around her in search of Frampton.

But he was nowhere to be seen.

The light of the lamps streaming full upon the features of the two men, as they stood confronting each other, revealed to her, the face of Dancing Bill, distorted and fast becoming blackened.

A cry of horror broke from her lips, and she sprang to the side of Dick.

The wretched harlequin, writhing with pain, turned a beseeching glance upon her.

In an instant all her hatred for the man had vanished.

Pity took possession of her breast, and she laid her small white hand, upon the muscular arm of the poacher.

Dick cast his eyes down upon the upturned face, so pale and pleading.

"Spare him," she said.

"Spare him," repeated Dick, "can you forgive him."

"I can."

"For bearing you away from those who love you," said Dick.

"We should be merciful," said Mary.

"We should be just," said Dick.

"And forgive our enemies," said Mary, shuddering with horror, as her eyes again encountered the glance so appealingly cast towards her, by the man who had so basely assisted to tear her from her friends.

"He deserves no pity," said Dick. "He will but turn and sting the moment the heel is taken from his head."

"Let him go," said Mary. "He is too base and contemptible to merit even the indignation of a right thinking man."

"He is indeed a contemptible villain," said Dick. "A dog, who bites the hand that feeds him; a reptile, who stings the breast that warms him into life! I have a long reckoning to settle with him! I have stood his friend, and he has repaid that friendship with the basest ingratitude."

"Yet have mercy; vengeance is not for us," said Mary, who could not but feel a pang of pity for the wretch whose glance pleaded to her for intercession.

"Enough," said Dick, for your sake I free him. But beware, Dancing Bill, we must yet settle accounts. Contemptible viper, you have to thank her, whose ruin you sought, for the mercy I extend to you."

And he thrust Dancing Bill violently from him.

The base-hearted scoundrel staggered under the force of the push, and it was with difficulty he saved himself from falling to the ground.

But the instant the grasp on his throat had relaxed, he cast a wild and hurried look around him.

His energies returned in an instant.

His first thoughts were to fly.

The road was clear.

The fracas had caused no alarm to those in the inn.

Only the poacher and Mary, who clung to his arm, were near.

One hurried glance he fixed upon Dick.

Then, with the speed of a deer, rendered doubly swift by the fear of the consequences of his evil deeds, he bounded down the road.

With an exclamation of rage, Dick sprang after him.

But scarcely had he taken half-a-dozen steps, when he recollected that Mary was without a protector.

He drew up, and returned to her side.

"He has escaped me," he said, bitterly.

"Let him go, he is unworthy of your indignation," said Mary.

"True. But he has robbed me of that which is of inestimable value to me, and to—"

Dick paused ere he finished the sentence.

"Whom?" asked Mary.

"No matter," replied Dick.

Mary saw that he was unwilling to say more, so forbore to question him further.

For a few minutes Dick paused in thought.

Then turning hurriedly to the girl by his side, he said,—

"It was a fortunate circumstance that brought me to this part of the country."

"It was, indeed," replied Mary.

"I heard your screams and the fall of broken glass," said Dick, "and wishing to learn its cause, I stepped from the shadow of the hedge, into the road, as the driver of this vehicle opened the door, and then I heard the voice of Dancing Bill, and feeling assured that some villany was a-foot, I prepared to thwart it."

"Where is the youth who drove me here?" asked Mary.

"Lying senseless in the road, some distance from here, I doubt not," said Dick.

"Senseless?"

"Yes."

Mary opened her eyes questioningly.

"Whilst he was talking to Bill at the door of the carriage, I mounted the box, and as he attempted to do the same, I struck him down, and drove on to here."

"Then it was his fall we heard," said Mary.

"It was."

"Is he dead, do you think?" asked Mary, with a shudder.

"I hope not," replied Dick, "for I would not have the blood even of a wretch like him, upon my hands."

"I trust he is not."

"There is little fear of that," said Dick; "the blow may have stunned him, perhaps."

"I hope that nothing more fearful has happened," said Mary.

"You may quiet your fears," said her companion. "Dick may be a poacher, but not a murderer."

"Oh, no."

"But come, you must return to your friends. How is it that I find you thus, attired only in your stage dress?"

Mary informed him of all that had transpired

"I must convey you back to the theatre. Your friends will suffer much anxiety at your absence."

"They will indeed," said Mary.

"But their hearts will be gladdened when they know that you are safe," said Dick.

"And doubly so, when they know that my saviour is yourself," said Mary, looking up into the bronzed face of the poacher.

"Dick the Poacher need do some good acts to atone for his bad ones," said Dick.

"Bad," she said, "oh, no."

"Yes," replied Dick; "but there, let that pass, I must now convey you back to those who, doubtless, are in agony at your absence."

"If you will point me out the road to take," said Mary, "I will trespass upon your kindness no longer."

"My kindness?"

"Yes."

"My duty, rather," said Dick. "No, no! you return not alone. I will see you safe back to your father."

"It may put you to much inconvenience," said Mary.

"It would put me to more to feel that, perhaps, you had fallen again into the power of that ruthless man."

"He would scarce dare to harm me now," said Mary.

Dick shook his head.

"You know him not," he said.

"Alas! I know him too well," replied Mary.

"His base nature would prompt him to be revenged on you," said Dick.

"For what?"

"For what he has received at my hands," replied Dick.

"He would not be so base."

"The coward is ever revengeful," said Dick, "he would hurl all the fury of his villany upon you for the squeezing I gave him. Bill is not the one to face a man before his face, though he hesitates not to strike behind his back; but with a woman it is different. In her presence he shows his courage, heaven save the mark. There it is that all his valour, all his bravery, is revealed in its true character. He will fly from the glance of a man, but he will strike at the face of a woman."

"The wretch!"

"Aye."

"Poor Margaret," sighed Mary, "how I pity her."

"So do I," said Dick, "fate has tied her to a villain; but were I her, I would snap the bonds that bound me, and crush the reptile that could sting the one he swore to love and cherish."

Mary looked with pride into the face of her companion.

"Come," said Dick; "the air is cold, and you are but thinly attired. Get into the vehicle, and I will convey you back to the theatre."

"Oh, how can I thank you," said Mary.

"I need no thanks. I should be less than man did I refuse to do my duty," said Dick.

And he led her to the door of the fly, and assisted her into it.

"Your journey back will be more pleasant than the one hither," he remarked, as he closed the door. "Make yourself as comfortable as you can, and I'll soon restore you to your friends."

Mounting the box, Dick seized the whip, and in another moment the vehicle was on its way to the theatre.

———

CHAPTER C.

FLIGHT OF THE HARLEQUIN—THE POACHER'S MIS-HAP—THE PISTOL SHOT—THE PURSUIT—THE MAIMED LIBERTINE.

WITH a feeling of gratitude, and a sigh of relief, Mary sank back upon the cushioned seat of the carriage.

She could not but think now of the anguish of mind her absence would cause to her friends.

In imagination she pictured her father and Buskin Bob searching everywhere for her, and the grief of Harry, when he saw that search was fruitless.

How impatiently she watched the trees and the hedges as they seemed to fly past the window of the carriage.

The speed of the vehicle would not keep pace with her thoughts.

And yet it rolled over the hard road at a great speed.

Meantime, Dick kept a good look out ahead.

He expected that the force of his blow upon the forehead of the youth, and the fall therefrom had left him stunned in the roadway.

The poacher kept his eyes fixed upon the ground in advance, determined to leap from the box and draw the youth, did he still lie there, to the side of the road, lest he should be run over by any vehicle that might pas.

It was very dark, and Dick strained his eyes to the utmost, in search of Frampton.

He pretty well knew the spot where he fell, so he did not slacken the pace of the horse till he had neared it.

Then he drew the reins, and continued at a walking pace, casting his eyes right and left in search of the object.

Presently he perceived a black mass in the centre of the road.

He drew up hurriedly, and believing it to be the youth who had sought to make Mary his own, he leaped to the ground quickly.

It was well for him that he did so.

The moment that Dick brought the horse to a standstill, the figure in the road leapt to its feet, and the loud report of a pistol, staggered the poacher as he rushed towards it.

By the quick flash, Dick perceived the features of Dancing Bill, and as he sprang forward he felt a heavy blow upon his shoulder, and he was hurled to the ground.

At the same moment, the horse, startled by the report of the pistol, bounded forward, and tore along the road at a maddening speed.

For a moment, and a moment only, Dick the Poacher remained upon the earth.

In that short space he had realised all that had happened.

He sprang to his feet, and bounded after the carriage, heedless of anything but the safety of Mary.

As he did so, a loud and defiant laugh broke upon his ears.

And the voice of Dancing Bill saluted him from the opposite side of the road.

"Ha, ha!" he laughed. "Dick the Poacher! who triumphs now?"

Muttering a smothered vow to be less merciful the next time they met, Dick sped on.

Anxiety for the safety of Mary lent him speed; but still the horse, frightened and furious, bore the carriage every moment farther and farther from him.

As he dashed wildly on, a loud shriek of pain fell upon his ears.

But his whole thoughts, being centred in the occupant of the carriage, he heeded it not, but kept on his way.

He saw that to overtake it was impossible, but he hoped that something might stay the progress of the affrighted beast.

On then he ran, panting for breath; and on, still on, went the carriage with its frightened occupant.

Meantime, Dancing Bill who, when he had perceived the approach of the carriage, as it was being driven along by Dick, had taken a pistol from his pocket, which he always kept loaded, and laid himself down in the road, with the intention of destroying the man he had so basely treated for all his kindness.

Fnding that the shot had not taken effect, he dashed hurriedly to the opposite side of the road, to which Dick had fallen, hurled down by the vehicle, as the horse started in its fright, with the intention of leaping the hedge, and seeking safety in flight.

But when he perceived that Dick paid no heed to him, but bounded after the carriage, he stood gazing at his form, as it flew along the road, with an expression of fiendish delight in his features.

"Curse him," he muttered, savagely, at the

same time placing his hand to his neck, which felt sore and swollen from the pressure of Dick's fingers. "He has escaped and I have one foe the more. I had hoped to have rid myself of any further fear on his account. Still, if he has escaped there is little chance of the girl doing so. Either she will be thrown out and killed, or jump out, and break her neck. I don't care which, so long as she is done for, for then I shall have had my revenge on Charlie Evans for the blow he struck me; and Dick, too, the fool, to think that anything he could do for me, could render me forgetful of his taunts and violence. No, I hate him more now than ever. He is a thorn in my side, and I will strive my utmost to destroy him."

So saying, he walked leisurely along in the direction which the carriage had taken.

"Where the devil can Frampton have got to," he muttered. "I must find him. I must not lose sight of him. He is a weak fool, and I shall be able to play upon his well-filled purse. I have known hunger and want, but he must keep me from it for the future. I have him on the hip. The fear of exposure will make him consent to any demands of mine, and I promise him they shall not be moderate ones. Ah, what was that."

And Bill paused suddenly, and looked anxiously around.

In a moment his whole bearing was changed.

His abject fears once more took possession of his breat.

His heart beat violently.

A cold perspiration broke upon his brow.

He trembled.

"Again!" he gasped, as a groan saluted his ears.

"That sound! It terrifies me! It is the same as those uttered by her on that fearful night, when the elements warred with each other, and the earth shook with their fury."

And he looked nervously and fearfully around him.

The lights in the town were now extinguished, and all was darkness before and behind him.

He felt his hair stand literally on end, now that he felt he was alone, in that dark and silent road.

Again a low moan floated by on the breeze.

"Will she ever haunt me," he muttered. "Shall I never be freed from her presence. Never! I see her pale face in yonder darkness. Oh, that look! horror! horror!"

And Dancing Bill closed his eyes, as though he would shut out some horrible vision.

But in vain.

He saw it still.

Saw that pleading look for mercy.

That pale face and blood-stained form.

He shuddered violently, and almost feared to move forward.

Then, as if goaded on by some fearful impulse, he bounded along the road.

He had gone about a dozen yards, when a groan, so long and so heartrending in its intensity, caused him to stop suddenly, and utter an exclamation of fear and horror.

"Oh, help! for mercy sake, help!" came now clearly to his ears.

For a moment Bill stood irresolute, whether o go forward or turn back.

He had resolved to pursue the latter course, when the voice again broke the stillness.

"Here! here!" it said. "Oh heaven! do lift me up, my limbs are broken."

In a moment the whole truth flashed upon Dancing Bill.

He sprang into the road, in the direction from whence the sound proceeded.

He recognised the tones.

They were those of William Frampton, the youthful libertine.

Casting his gaze downwards, Dancing Bill perceived the youth lying in the roadway.

He bent over him and laid his hand upon his arm.

"Frampton," he said.

"Oh, you are here, thank God," gasped the libertine.

"What is the matter?" asked Bill, as he placed his arm beneath the head of the prostrate youth.

"My legs are broken."

"What?"

"My legs are broken," iterated the libertine.

"Broken?"

"Yes."

"How?"

"By the wheels of the carriage," replied the youth.

"What carriage?"

"The one I drove."

"Did you fall from the box?" asked Bill.

"No I was struck down."

"By whom?"

"I know not."

"I do."

"You!"

"Yes."

"Who?"

"A man to whom I bear no good will," said Bill.

"Curse him."

"And the wheels passed over your legs," said Bill.

"Not then."

"When?"

"A few minutes since."

"What, as it went back."

"Yes; I had recovered from the blow, and a heavy one it was, and was standing by the hedge there, when I heard a vehicle approach from the town. As it came nearer I saw it was the same from which I had been hurled, and that there was no one on the box. I rushed forward to seize the bridle, but the horse reared, and threw me, and then dashed on, and the wheels passed over my legs."

"They may not be broken." said Bill.

"Alas! I fear they are."

"Try to stand."

"I cannot."

"Try."

"It is in vain."

Bill lifted Frampton to his feet.

Then leaving go his hold of him, the youth fell with a cry of pain.

"They are broken," said Bill.

"Yes, I am punished for my guilty work," said Frampton.

And so thought Bill, but he spoke not a word.

"Where is the girl?" asked Frampton.

"Gone."

"Where?"

"To the devil, I hope," said Bill, savagely.

"Has she escaped you?"

"She has."

"How?"

"The man who knocked you from the box drove on till he arrived at the inn at the entrance to the town."

"Well."

"There he pulled up."

"Yes, yes."

"And before I discovered that it was not you who opened the door, I was seized, and the girl rescued."

"And did you not resist?" asked Frampton.

"Of course I did."

"Well."

"It was not well. What chance had I of rescuing her," from five or six said Dancing Bill.

"Then he was not alone," murmured Frampton.

"No."

"The girl, what of her?" asked the youth, faintly.

"Why you see, as soon as the door was opened, I was seized by three of the fellows and the girl taken away from me."

"Yes."

"Then she was put into the fly again," and one of them drove off with her," said Bill.

"And you could not prevent them," said Frampton, bitterly.

"No, but directly they were gone, I hurled those who held me to the ground, and made my escape," said Bill.

"But there was no one on the box when I endeavoured to stop the horse," said Frampton, with some difficulty, from the pain he was suffering.

"Don't you know how that was," said Bill.

"No."

"Then I do."

"How?"

"I made all speed I could and overtook the fly."

"Well."

"I seized the driver and dragged him from the box."

"Yes, yes."

"And was about to mount and look for you when—"

"What?" interrupted the other, impatiently.

"The horse took fright."

"Well, well."

"I was hurled off the wheel, and the animal dashed on carrying the girl behind him," said Bill.

A bully is ever a coward, and a coward is ever a boaster and a liar, and Dancing Bill was no exception to the general rule.

He thought it best to put as brave a face on his actions as he could.

So he glossed over his want of courage with acts of heroism which he never performed.

"Well, she has escaped us for a time," said Bill, after a pause, but it can't be helped. Better luck next time."

"Lift me up and bear me to some place," murmured Frampton, "where I can have a doctor, or I shall die."

Bill raised him up again, and supported him by his arm.

"Oh, groaned the youth, as his feet once more touched the earth."

"Are you in much pain?" asked Bill

"Fearful."

"This is an unlucky piece of business," said the harlequin.

"If it had not been for her cursed squealing it would never have happened," said Franton.

"Certainly not."

"You are to blame."

"No."

"Yes."

"Why so?"

"You should have prevented her call for help," said Frampton.

"I nearly forced her teeth down her throat in doing so," said Bill. "I only wish I had quite done it, then they might have stuck in her windpipe, and prevented her hollowing."

"Well, its no use now to quarrel about it," said Frampton. "What's done can't be undone. Lift me to the side of the bridge and go to the town for some vehicle to convey me there."

"To the town?"

"Yes."

"The one where you were going," said Bill.

Yes, I have friends there," said Frampton.

Bill carried the maimed youth to the side of the hedge and sat him down beneath it.

"Fly," said Frampton, "I am faint."

"And so am I," said Bill, with the work I have done to night.

"But you have the use of your limbs, for heaven's sake make all the speed you can, for it may be too late."

"I shall not be able to procure anything to convey you from here to-night," said Dancing Bill.

"Why not?"

"Because it is so late."

"What of that?"

"Every inn and house in the town is closed."

"Still, you can rouse some one up," said Frampton.

"But will anyone come?"

"Yes."

"Who?"

"Anybody you may ask," said the youth, "if you tell them an accident has occurred."

"But will they believe me."

"Why should they doubt you?" asked the youth.

"I am a stranger in this part of the country."

"Then the hospitality extended will be greater," said Frampton.

"Well, I'll go and see."

"Do so, and in heaven's name be speedy."

"All right."

"Would that it were," groaned the youth, as he lay his head back against the hedge. "But, alas, I fear it will never be all right with me again. Oh, what a fool I was not to await some other opportunity to get her into my power. To be foiled thus is madness, and at the very moment, too, when I believed I had humbled her proud spirit, and broke her heart. Curse her, I will yet become her master, and she my slave. I have vowed to make her mine, and, in spite of all, I will yet do so. Foiled as I have been, yet disappointment but adds to my resolves. If I love her, I also hate her, and that hate shall goad me on, till I have consummated the desires of my heart. For a time she will escape me; for a time she is free from all molestation, but only for the time which is necessary to restore these shattered limbs, then will I crush her heart and happiness, even as the wheels of that carriage have crushed me!"

CHAPTER CI.

THE PANTOMIMISTS ON THE SCENT—THE MEETING IN THE ROAD.

FINDING that Mary did not return to the Crown when the piece was over, and the curtain fell, Charlie and Bob hurried to their dressing-rooms.

"Not returned," said Charlie.

"No," said Bob.

"I have been so unhappy," said the clown, "that I had no heart to play."

"Nor I, strike me comical if I had," said the pantaloon.

"And yet you saved the piece," said his friend.

"Did I?"

"Yes."

"How?"

"By the spirit you threw into your part," said his friend.

"Then it was like watered gin," said Bob, "very weak indeed."

"No," said Charlie, "your spirits were damped

No. 26.

as much as mine by the absence of Mary, but you saw that it was necessary to make a struggle for the good of the house, and nobly you did it, Bob, though I know your heart ached, whilst you expressed so much mirth."

"Ah!" sighed Buskin Bob, drawing off his tights, "the life of a player is a strange existence — strike me comical if it ain't. He laughs often when he could cry, and cries when he could laugh; he quaffs imaginary draughts of wine, from jewelled goblets, partakes of sumptuous fare from sparkling plates, and yet, at the same time, hunger may be gnawing at his vitals, and he knows not where to lay his head."

"True," said Charlie. "But, Bob, I must seek this girl. I cannot rest. My heart misgives me. I fear I know not what."

"So do I, strike me comical if I don't," said the pantaloon, "and all I can say is, that Buskin Bob don't lay down on his bed till she is found."

Charlie grasped his friend's hand.

"I won't be long," said Bob, "before I'm ready to start."

And the good-hearted pantaloon hurriedly changed his clothes, flinging those he took off in a heap on the ground, not waiting, as was his wont, to fold them neatly, and place them on the bench.

In a few minutes, the friends had attired themselves, and were ready to depart.

Hurrying on to the stage, they met Margaret and Harry.

The eyes of both were moist with tears.

"Go home, Harry," said the clown, "we shall find her, I dare say."

"In course we shall," said Bob. "Strike me comical if you won't fret yourself to a shadow, and only be fit to play the ghost all the rest of your life, if you take on like this."

"Where are you going, father?" asked the youth.

"To search for Mary."

"I will come."

"No. You remain at home."

"No, no," said the boy.

"Well, as you like," said Charlie. "Margaret, will you remain here or go home?"

"I will remain here, if you are likely to return," said Margaret, who had not yet changed her playing costume.

"We shall no doubt do so," said Bob.

"Then I will await you."

"All right," said Bob.

And the three hurried down the steps, and out into the street.

When they had got there they paused.

"Which road will you take," said Bob.

"I am undecided."

"I have looked this way," said Harry, pointing to the right.

"Then we will go this," said Charlie, turning in the opposite direction.

And he strode on.

Bob remained behind looking down into the gutter by the kerb.

Something there had caught his eye, and he stooped to examine it.

It was a rosette of white ribbon.

He picked it up and looked anxiously at it for a few moments.

"Strike me comical," he muttered, "if that isn't the very rosette I saw Mary make up for her slippers. Now how did that come there?"

"Bob," called Charlie, who having missed his friend, had turned back a few paces.

Bob looked up, and beckoned to Charlie.

In a moment both the clown and Harry were by his side.

"Ain't that Mary's," said Bob, placing the rosette in the hands of his friend.

"To be sure it is," said Charlie, "it is the one she made a few nights since."

"Strike me comical if I didn't think so," said Bob.

"Where did you get it?" asked the clown.

"Found it."

"Where?"

"There."

And Bob pointed to the kerb.

Harry run to the spot indicated, and looked around.

"Father," he said, hurriedly.

"Well."

"Look here."

"What is it?"

"The mark of wheels."

"Well I reckon there's nothing particularly strange in the mark of wheels in a public road, said Bob.

"No; but some vehicle has drawn up to the gateway," said Harry, pointing as he spoke to the passage leading to the stage door.

"So there has, boy," said Charlie, "for see where the horse has pawed the ground."

Bob examined the spot.

Then he shook his head ominously.

"Some one has either got in or out of this vehicle here," said Bob, "for look at the things about."

"It is Mary who has got in said Harry.

"Mary."

"Yes."

"What object in the world could she have in going away," said Charlie.

"Charlie" said Bob after a pause, "it was not here I picked up the rosette. It has been torn from her slipper, and strike me comical if I don't begin to think that, she has been carried off by some one."

"Good heavens!" exclaimed Charlie.

"My own thoughts, and fears!" exclaimed Harry.

"But who—who?" gasped Charlie, now as white as when making up for clown, he smeared his face with the French chalk.

"Time may show," said Bob, "but now heaven only knows."

Charlie darted out into the road, and examined the indentations in the earth caused by the horse's feet.

"The vehicle has gone this road," he said, "by heavens I will follow its track, though it be for a thousand miles."

"And strike me comical if Buskin Bob, ain't with you on that journey," said the pantaloon, "let it be a rough or a smooth one."

"And I too," said Harry.

"Stop" said Bob, "we shall soon loose the traces in the dark. We had better take a property lantern with us."

"Good thought," said Charlie. "Harry get the dark lantern from the property room."

The boy bounded back into the theatre, and in

the course of a few minutes, returned with th article in question.

"Draw the slide for the present," said the clown, "we have no wish to excite curiosity, and here we can see all we wish to."

So saying, Charlie strode on, followed by Harry and the pantaloon.

It was a painful journey which the players had to perform.

Painful alike to the mind and the body.

For the stooping position in which they continued their course, in order to follow the marks of the wheels, caused them no little pain in their backs and loins.

They kept on their way for some time, the light from the lantern, which was now turned on, streaming upon the hard earth; when Buskin Bob, placing his hand behind him, stretched himself up.

"Strike me comical," he said, "if I ain't doubled myself up into a ball many a time when doing the hanky-panky business, but it never give me the backache like this."

"I should not mind the backache," said Charlie, with a sigh, "were it not accompanied by the heartache as well."

Harry sighed.

His back and and his heart ached also, and he felt more miserable than ever he did in his life.

His dismal fears had been realised.

The moment of his success had been dimmed by the loss of her, he now felt he so fondly and purely loved.

What if they were destined to never meet again.

The thought was terrible.

It conjured up to him a life of misery and despair.

Her presence he felt was necessary to his existence.

Her absence would cause a blank in his heart, which nothing could fill up.

Every moment his thoughts became more sad.

Every step, his anxiety the more intense.

Still on they went.

Not a word was spoken for some time.

Each was busy with his own thoughts.

Harry yearned for the presence of her who had taught him to love; whose beauty and gentleness had engrafted in his heart a feeling of affection, which he experienced for none other being in the wide world.

Charlie yearned for his daughter; the offspring of his early love; the companion of many a bitter hour; the guardian angel of his home and life.

Buskin Bob was sad because of the loss they all experienced, unhappy because his friends were in grief, sorrowful because a dark cloud had overwhelmed their happiness.

Still on, along the dark and dreary road.

The mark of the wheels could be traced sometimes distinctly, at others scarcely had they left an indentation.

Here and there they were lost for a few yards, but soon discovered again, and on, with bent bodies, and strained eyeballs, went the poor players in their search for Mary.

In this manner they continued on their journey for the space of an hour and a half, when they were suddenly startled by a peculiar sound at the way side, some short distance before them.

Simultaneously they paused to listen.

Again the sound was heard.

"What's that?" asked Charlie.

"Strike me comical if I can tell," said Bob, shading his eyes with his hand, and peering into the darkness of the distance.

"It sounded like a cry of pain," said Harry.

"I thought it was a groan," said Charlie.

"Oh, heavens, can it be Mary!" exclaimed the youth, in a tone of poignant grief.

"From whence came it?" said the clown.

"From there," said Bob, pointing to the hedge which skirted the road.

"I will go and see what it was," said Harry, and he moved forward as he spoke.

"Stay," said Bob, clutching him by the arm, "give me the lantern, I will go."

And he took the lantern from Harry's hand.

At that moment the same sound smote their ears.

"Some one is in pain," said Charlie, "see who it is, Bob, and if we can aid them."

Bob held the lantern so as to throw its powerful rays before him upon the ground, and stepped forward to the spot from whence the sound proceeded.

Suddenly he paused.

Right before him, seated upon the ground, with his head supported by the hedge, was a youth, with a face pale as marble, and a look of most intense pain upon his features.

Bob sprang to his side in an instant.

The soul of the good-hearted fellow was touched at the suffering evidently endured by the youth, and stooping down, he laid his hand upon his arm and said kindly—

"What is the matter? why do you lie here?"

"Oh, I am dying, I fear. Oh, this pain is unbearable. I—I shall faint. Oh, will he never return with the means of conveying me to the town. Oh, oh!"

"Here, let me raise you to your feet," said Bob, grasping the youth by the arm.

"No, no!" shrieked Frampton. "I cannot stand, my legs are broken."

"Ah!" exclaimed Harry, who recognised the features of the youth in an instant, "where is Mary? where is she?"

CHAPTER CI.

BILL'S RESOLVE—THE HARLEQUIN FIRES THE CROWN SALOON—ENTRAPPED

DANCING BILL the harlequin, had only proceeded a few steps on his journey towards the town, when the sound of voices fell upon his ears.

He paused and listened.

The sound came from the direction where the maimed youth lie.

It was evident that there was some person coming along the road, and the idea struck Bill, that they would fall across Frampton, and as he had no wish to be seen in the town by any one, he resolved to leave the youth to his fate unless he should receive succour from those who were advancing.

It was true that Frampton had been taken to the side of the road, and laid beneath the thick hedge, but the harlequin had no doubt that he would be found, even in the darkness.

The part he had played that night he felt certain would soon be known, now that Dick had escaped, and he deemed it more than likely that a search would be made for him in order to bring him to justice for carrying off Mary.

Now, Bill might have faced all this chance of punishment had that been all he had to fear.

But he knew that he was also guilty of robbery and murder.

Should he fall into the clutches of justice for the lesser crime, might he not suffer for the greater?

At least, he was pretty well certain that Dick the Poacher would have no mercy.

He could not expect him to do so.

The part he had played at the house of the poacher was so base, that he could not expect the least pity even from the most forgiving.

If he once fell into the clutches of the law, he feared that circumstances would turn up to fix upon him the fearful crime he had committed on the night of the storm.

And even if there was no suspicion of his being the guilty man by others, his never-slumbering conscience seemed to whisper, "I shall betray myself."

So Bill resolved to fly from that part of the country as quickly as possible.

He was now provided with money; for, like most guilty people, he was suspicious and distrustful, and had made sure of his reward before he had performed his agreement

So, all things considered, he resolved to make himself scarce.

Buttoning up his coat, to protect himself from the cold night air, and bitterly cursing the circumstance which had deprived him of his warm wrapper, he was about to leap the hedge which skirted the road, and make his way along the other side of it, till he had passed the approaching party, when an expression, uttered by one of the coming pedestrians, caused him to pause, and strain every nerve to catch their conversation.

He felt his limbs slightly tremble as he listened.

He clenched his teeth together to stay the malediction which he felt rising to his white lips.

All the bitterness of his wicked nature was once more aroused.

"So, so," he hissed, "he is on the road. I could swear to his voice in a moment. Ha, ha! Mr. Buskin Bob; the flight of the bird has been discovered, and the hunters are out and on the scent."

He peered around nervously and with anxious gaze.

"Curse him!" he continued, "he has scented the right track, but the hare has doubled on the hounds, and the scent is lost. I hope she may have her neck broke before they find her. Ah! there is Charlie, too, and the boy. I should know their tones a mile off. Curse them!"

Then he listened intently again for some moments.

For a short time all was still, save the rustling of the leaves, dried and withered, on the road side, as the passing breeze caught their parched edges in its invisible grasp, and drove them, leaping and spinning in grotesque fashion, along the hard road.

Dancing Bill scrambled over the hedge and stood in the field.

The road wound round slightly near where the harlequin stood, and the darkness rendered it necessary that he should use some little caution, to prevent being heard or seen by the players.

Stepping slowly and cautiously along by the side of the hedge, he strained his eyes to see through its interstices into the high road.

Presently he imagined he could see the forms of the pantomimists.

Lighter and more silent, if possible, became his steps

He must not be seen by them.

They would suspect he was there for no good purpose, perhaps hit upon the truth at once, and accuse him of bearing off the clown's daughter.

Keeping close to the hedge, he stealthily moved onwards.

His teeth were clenched, and he hissed through them,—

"Oh, that it would be safe to send a bullet at him now. It should tell him that I have neither forgotten nor forgiven the blow on the parade; but no, no, I must wait for my revenge; but it shall come—it shall come, as sure as fate."

At this moment, the groans of the maimed youth, as he lay writhing beneath the hedge at the roadside, fell dismally on his ears.

"They will hear him," he soliloquised, "and he will be discovered, by those he has played so strange a trick. That's unfortunate for him. But perhaps not. For if the girl is killed, which I hope she will be, and the fool holds his tongue, who's to know that he had any hand in her being carried from the theatre. Ah, but there's Dick," he added, after a pause. "He'll know him again, and it will be all up with him. Well, it don't matter to me much, as long as I get out of it. Yes it does though, for I had made up my mind, that he should pay me well for my silence. Damn these people, they are always starting up to thwart me."

And with a growl, the villain was about to pass on his way.

However, the groans of the maimed libertine continued, and a sudden flash of light upon the hedge behind which Dancing Bill was, caused that worthy to start violently, and then stand still as a statue.

The light was none other than that, thrown from the dark lantern, carried by the Boy Actor, upon the prostrate form of the suffering Frampton.

But the suddeness with which it lit up the dark hedge, caused the guilty harlequin to tremble violently.

The sudden start caused his heart to throb, till its rapid beatings became almost audible, and his hair seemed to stand on end.

Truly the nerves of the guilty man had been severely shaken.

Crime finds its reward often by making the feelings and thoughts of the guilty a hell of torture.

It was several moments before Dancing Bill recovered from the shock, and ere he had done so, the pantomimists were bending over the crippled youth.

Bill's first impulse, then, was to fly from the position in which he stood, but the conversation which ensued chained him to the spot.

He soon discovered that the players' sympathy were aroused for the crippled libertine; and that they were resolved to bear him to the town, and seek some assistauce for his hurt.

But Bill heard more than this.

He heard that which caused his heart to bound within his breast.

From the conversation of the pantomimists, he learned that Margaret, his wife, had been left at the Crown Saloon alone.

Alone there!

How long and how anxiously had he watched for a chance of again seeing her alone.

He could not rest whilst she was away from him.

He would give anything, everything, to be enabled to again prevail upon her to live with him.

But Margaret studiously avoided being alone, so that she gave him no chance to plead his cause again to her.

Long and anxiously he had watched and waited.

But all in vain.

Now she was alone in that theatre, and her friends hurrying further from her.

There was a chance, at least, of seeing and speaking to her.

Perhaps with none near she would again consent to share his home.

Certainly his cruelty had driven her from him.

But would she have denied his prayer had she not been biassed by others.

He believed not.

He felt assured that, were it not for the pantomimists, Margaret would forgive and return to him.

He felt her absence acutely.

He dreaded to be left alone.

He resolved to seek her, now that there was not likely to be any one to interrupt them.

And he waited only till the players moved from the spot with the suffering Frampton; then he darted on for some distance further, leaped the hedge into the road, and started off as quick as he could towards the town in which the Crown Saloon was situated.

The night seemed to become blacker every minute, and one by one the stars went out.

The air, too, blew more cold and chilly than it had done, and Dancing Bill hurried forward, expecting every moment to be deluged with rain.

But the threatened storm came not.

Still, Bill slackened not his pace.

On he went as fast as possible.

Urged along by the hope of seeing his wife, and inducing her to forsake the protection of those he hated.

When he entered the town, he felt a chill fall upon his heart.

So silent was it, that it struck him as though all within were dead.

So long as trees and fields alone were passed Bill cared litttle for the silence, but, now that he was surrounded by buildings, the quiet seemed to oppress and appal him.

This may seem strange, especially to one who had always been accustomed to travelling by night or early morn.

But it is easily accounted for.

The guilty heart could find no rest; the voice of conscience ever upbraided him, and day by day weakened his nervous system, till the rustle of a leaf, the shadow of a tree, anything and everything, rendered him fearful, wretched, and miserable.

Stealthily he approached the saloon.

The place was now bathed in darkness, and the quiet of the grave reigned around.

Bill pushed open the gate of the passage, which led to the stage door.

But here he paused.

He listened.

All was still, still as the grave.

He felt assured that Margaret was on the stage, and he longed to meet her; to plead to her, yet he feared to enter that building.

Hesitatingly he stood, grasping the top of the gate with his hand.

"Perhaps, after, all my pleadings and persuasions will be in vain," he muttered, "and I shall have to leave the place without her. I dare not tear her from here, lest the vengeance of him I met at the haunted oak, fall instantly upon me. I must not use violence to her; but would that I could think of some means to bear her from these enemies of mine, for enemies they are to me, when they coerce my wife. But what—what means can I devise—why, none; none!"

And he struck his clenched hand upon his breast fiercely.

That movement, slight as it was, altered the whole tenor of his thoughts in a moment.

Truly it is said, from little things great causes spring.

The blow which Dancing Bill inflicted on his own heart, rebounded with fearful violence upon the head of Charlie Evans and his friend.

It had struck a cord which vibrated with terrible force.

In an instant the scene on the parade was before his mind's eye.

His lips quivered as he felt all the passions that day's work had loosened in his heart.

His eye flashed fire, as, in imagination, he beheld the indignant clown, striding over his prostrate form with upraised hand.

The demon of revenge once more started from its half-slumbering position, once more seated itself on its throne in the black heart of Bill the harlequin.

With starting eyes, clenched teeth, and dilated nostrils, Bill looked around him.

Out into the dark street his eyes wandered, only to return and rest with a fearful gleam upon the walls of the Crown Saloon.

"Never would Charlie Evans been manager of this place," he muttered, "had I succeeded in my hopes with the Royal Star. Had I triumphed that night, the stain of blood had not rested on my soul, the cries of the victim had not have drowned the raging storm, and Margaret might ere now have bowed to my will. But this man is a thorn in my side, a serpent in my path. I hate him, as man never hated man before. But for him I had not been a guilty wretch, flying from justice, but for him, curse him! ah, why should I hesitate, the stage door is open, and the path is clear. It is but a match applied to the lumber beneath the stage. But Margaret is there, she will perish. Let her, for then I shall feel that the only evidence of my guilt, is destroyed, and be at rest. But ha, ha, rest with the pale face of my murdered victim ever before me. Rest! no, no, there is no rest for me. Let me think. Margaret must not die, not by my hands, at least at present. No, no, she must live, and my revenge must die. Never, I have sworn never to rest, till I have encompassed the ruin of this man and his friends. What better time than this. None. I have failed once but now success is certain. But Margaret, Margaret; I have it. I will fire the old scenes and lumber beneath the stage, then, as she finds the house on fire, I will rush to her rescue. Ha, ha, the devil prompted that idea, for I will serve a double purpose, feed my revenge and minister to my hopes. Ha, ha! It shall be, a glorious night yet. The flare of the burning pile shall light me to Margaret's forgiveness. I will become her saviour to be her master once more."

Could he have seen his own features at that moment, he would have stood appalled.

Never had he looked so fearfully demoniacal.

But then never had he felt so bitter as then.

He looked quickly up the street.

All was still.

Not a sound smote his ears.

Not a figure met his gaze.

With compressed lips he turned from the gate and stealthily moved along the narrow passage.

But he paused suddenly.

The echoes of his own footfalls startled him.

Yet his steps was not heavy nor quick.

On the contrary, it was soft and slow, but its sound fell jarringly upon his ears.

Once more he moved forward.

Once more the echo of his footfalls reverberated through the narrow stone passage which led to the stage door.

But he hurried on, now, for his ear, ever alive to the slightest sound, had become accustomed to the noise.

He gained the stage door, and stood upon the step at the threshold, and forcing it with his hand, it opened with a creaking sound.

The little square passage was now before him, and on the right of which were the flight of wooden steps leading to the wings, whilst straight before him was the door which led into the large space beneath the stage.

In the little passage or hall, a small lamp was burning, and Bill could also see that the stage was not wholly in darkness, for a weak, sickly ray of light penetrated the wings, and threw their shaddows on to the wall of the building and the top of the wooden steps.

" Now, Charlie Evans, " I will pay you the debt I have so long owed you. Whilst you seek for your lost daughter, and minister to the sufferings of him who sought her ruin, the man you have made your enemy till death, is toiling to embitter your existence, and sow the seeds of misery and despair, around your Struggles for Bread. But first let me see where Margaret is."

And placing his hands upon the wall at the side of the steps, he crept up them till his head was above the level of the top step, and he could see on to the stage between the wings.

In an instant, he withdrew his head and commenced to descend the steps.

There was a gratified smile upon his features now.

Yes, Dancing Bill smiled.

There was a gleam in his eye which bespoke satisfaction.

And Dancing Bill, the guilty harlequin, was satisfied.

And why ?

He had seen his wife.

He had seen her whom he had so basely treated.

He had seen her whom he had promised to love.

Her whom he had promised to protect.

His eyes had rested upon the woman whom his brutal nature had driven almost to the brink of madness.

The coward and the bully had obtained a glance of one he had so cruelly wronged.

His heart beat with hope and gladness, instead of shame and sorrow.

Margaret, who had changed her dress, and now only awaited the return of her friends, was seated beside a small property-table, in the centre of the stage, which was only lighted by the dim rays of a small lamp.

By the light of this, Margaret was learning, or rather trying to learn, her part, for her anxiety respecting the absence of Mary would not allow her mind to dwell fixedly upon the words before her.

The light played upon her now pale countenance, as her head was bent over the folio of written paper, giving to her features a still more deathly pallor than she in truth possessed.

Dancing Bill had seen this, but not one regret arose to his heart for being the author of all her sufferings.

No, not one thought of regret ; not one qualm of conscience.

That she was necessary to his happiness and comfort, he could not deny, but that she deserved either sympathy or respect, he did not consider for one moment.

She was there, and that was enough for him to know then.

She was where he could easily reach her, and bear her to the open air, and for this act he doubted not to merit her gratitude.

Her romantic nature, as Dancing Bill styled it, would prompt her to forget the past, and reconcile her to his company, for the future.

And so, without further ado, Dancing Bill opened the door which led under the stage, and glared in upon the heap of old properties, and scenery, which lay piled in heaps, here and there, in the semi-darkness.

The door to this place opened outwards, hence Dancing Bill had to pull it towards him, to gain a view of the space beneath the stage.

But the stage door, or outer entrance to the court, opened in the contrary manner, and the least push from the outside, would instantly open it.

Bill saw in an instant that it was necessary, to prevent being seen about the hellish work he contemplated, to secure this door.

So, placing a piece of timber, of which there were many in the little hall, against the door and the wall, he felt thoroughly secure from any sudden discovery.

This done, he pulled open the door again, which led under the stage, and thrusting his hand into the large space, drew forth a piece of old scenery, the torn and dilapidated canvass of which was to serve as the torch to fire the pile.

Then he listened, to make sure that his movements had not been overheard by his wife.

Not hearing any sound indicative of her having left the position she occupied when he looked upon the stage, Bill placed his foot behind the door, so as to hold it open, and held the piece of painted canvass over the lamp.

"Now," he thought, as the flame of the lamp was drawn upwards towards the canvass, "this light carried to the heap of rubbish beneath the centre trap, will soon raise a flame, that will light Charlie Evans to the wreck my vengeance has made. Margaret, you have scorned my pleadings, but you will scorn them no more. Dancing Bill, your triumph is at hand; and by the consummation of your vengeance, hurl those you hate upon the cold and pitiless world once more to Struggle for Bread."

Again that demoniac look overspread his features.

He withdrew the now flaming piece of canvas from over the lamp.

With one glance at the steps, he darted through the door, under the stage, and into the very centre of the heterogenous mass of scenes, oil-pots, fat-pots, shavings and saw-dust.

He cast an hurried glance around.

Not a soul was to be seen.

With one chuckle of delight his eye took in the piles of inflammeable matter heaped up in every direction.

His hand trembled, and for a moment he hesitated.

But it was only a moment.

Then he hurled the fatal torch into the centre of a heap of old scenery.

Scarce had the flaming canvas touched, than it was on fire, and lighting up the dark place beneath the stage.

With a half suppressed cry of joy and triumph, Dancing Bill darted to the door, but ere he reached it it was closed to with a loud bang.

Bill sprang forward to thrust it open.

His efforts were in vain.

A shriek of horror broke from his lips.

Again he tried to open it.

It was useless, the door was fastened.

CHAPTER CII.

AGONY OF DANCING BILL—FEARFUL POSITION OF THE COLUMBINE—DESTRUCTION OF THE SALOON —A DARING ATTEMPT TO SAVE MARGARET—THE FATAL BEAM—HORROR AND DISMAY—THE DISAPPEARANCE.

CONSTERNATION and horror now reigned where triumph had held sway.

In the mement of success Dancing Bill had learnt the truth of that proverb, "there's many a slip 'twixt the cup and the lip."

In the very moment that he believed his long sought vengeance was about to be consummated, and that he would succeed in bearing away Margaret, and gloat in triumph at the work his hands had made, he discovered that he was himself a prisoner in the fiery pile.

Reason appeared to be tottering from her throne.

He could but stand in speechless amazement.

He could only glare with bloodshot eyes upon the now fast-closed door.

Cold drops of perspiration broke upon his face.

His pulse stood still.

The blood seemed to have become stagnated in his veins.

A shudder ran through his veins.

His limbs trembled.

He strove to catch at the door.

But his strength seemed to have flown—his energies were paralysed.

The flames had taken a firm and terrible hold.

The thin, dry wood which composed the frames of the scenes lighted instantly, and fizzed and crackled, and spit and flared, and spit and glowed around him.

Every moment they spread farther and farther around.

Like fiery serpents they leapt and danced, and sported with renewed vigour, and with another shriek of agony, Dancing Bill flung himself upon the heap he had fired, and endeavoured to trample it out.

But, as if in mockery of his struggles, the flames only leaped the more furiously, and drove him back with their forked and fiery tongues.

Further and further spread the fiery element.

Higher and higher arose the forked tongues of flame towards the stage above.

And thicker and closer every moment became the huge clouds of dense smoke, which rose from the smouldering rubbish at his feet.

To extinguish the fire his hand had raised was now impossible.

Destruction was before him.

Death stared him in the face.

Death in the most horrible form.

Frantically he tore the half-consumed pieces from the heap, and trampled upon them, in the vain hope to crush out the fire.

His hands were burned in his endeavours, and the soles of his boots were so hot that he almost shrieked with the pain they caused his feet.

Fire had the mastery, and a terrible master it was to him.

Despairingly he looked around.

Fire—fire—nothing but fire—everywhere.

Again he sprang to the door.

Again he strove to force it open.

He threw his body against it, but in hollow mockery the echo of the blow reverberated through the place.

Horror! horror! It was fast, and he was powerless to move it.

He thrust his fingers between the door and the post against which it shut; but torn flesh and bleeding skin alone was his reward.

Where was it fastened?

How was it secured?

By whom had it been closed?

Such questions rushed rapidly through his mind.

But no answer came to them save the crackling of the burning wood, the hiss of the smoking canvas.

Despair—abject despair now took possession of his soul.

Again he flung himself upon the door, and shrieked aloud.

But the flames hissed his cries to scorn, and the thick black smoke choked him.

Blow after blow, with frantic rapidity, he rained upon the door, and shriek after shriek for help rose from his parched throat.

Truly his position was a fearful one now.

He felt that his hour had indeed come.

And more still.

He would be the murderer of his wife.

In a loud and agonising tone he shrieked her name.

He called upon her for help.

He supplicated aid of her to whose appeals for mercy he had so often refused to listen.

But those cries were unheard.

And if heard they were unheeded.

"Oh, God," he yelled in agony, "spare me —spare me! Heaven have mercy!"

The words he uttered, jarred back upon his ears with fearful force and meaning.

Those words had been uttered by one before.

They had mingled with the pitiless storm.

They had rose over the smooth green grass which had been dyed with blood.

Blood shed by his hand.

And now they were shrieked forth by a murderer.

Uttered by one who would not listen to them.

How could he hope for mercy?

He who never granted it.

He felt that he had no right to expect the boon he craved.

Yet, in utter despair, he prayed for it again and again.

He prayed.

Dancing Bill, the wife-beater, thief, and murderer, prayed.

What a mockery.

What an insult.

And yet, in his despair, he hoped that prayer would be answered.

But the moments passed on with relentless stride.

The flames spread wider and wider, rose higher and higher, and the smoke became denser and denser.

The heat, too, was fearful.

It scorched his hands and face, and blistered his body.

His garments were like a case of heated metal upon his limbs and back, and only required a gust of air to burst them into flames.

The smoke blinded him, and the heat parched his lips and tongue.

Still nearer and nearer the fire approached to where he stood by the door.

In his frenzy he held his hands before him, as though to thrust them back, but as they reached him, and their forked tongues twined themselves around his arms, and licked even his very face, he gave utterance to a shriek of heartrending despair, and fell insensible to the ground.

And over his prostrate body, leaped and twined the devouring element; dancing in mad glee, like furious demons let loose from hell, and spluttering, spitting, and hissing in devilish triumph, over their bloodthirsty and inhuman victim.

And now they rose upwards, licking the stage on which, that night, the poor players had Sruggled for Bread.

When Dancing Bill had entered the space beneath the stage, to carry out the diabolical work his hellish mind had suggested, he did not observe that the piece of timber which he had placed against the outer door, had become shifted from its position.

But so it had.

By some means it had slipped, and the instant that Dancing Bill let go his hold of the door which led to the space under the stage, it dropped right down, and fixed itself so firmly against the pannels, that the greater the pressure brought against it, the firmer was it fastened.

Thus it was that the harlequin found himself secured in the furnace that his own hand had kindled.

Whilst the guilty man was struggling below the stage, we will see what happened to his poor ill-used wife above.

In anxious suspense she had seated herself at the table, and waited the return of the pantomimists or news of Mary.

Hours passed, and still no one came back to the theatre.

The time seemed to pass on in sluggish strides, and weary and dispirited, Margaret opened the part for which she had been cast the following evening, and endeavoured to study the lines.

But her mind could not be brought to bear upon it, and though her eyes rested upon the leaves of manuscript, her thoughts were wandering away to poor Mary and her friends.

She was thus engaged, when a thin stream of light smoke rose from behind the flooring of the stage at her feet, and a strong smell of something burning saluted her nerves.

For a moment Margaret sat gazing irresolutely upon the vapour as it rose through the cracks in the floor, and formed itself into fantastic shapes around her feet.

But it was for a moment only that she sat thus.

Her mind instantly embraced the real state of affairs, and she sprang to her feet.

A loud cry broke from her lips as she did so.

For, the instant she rose, a huge cloud of vapour arose from the spot on which she had been seated.

And as she cast her eyes down in dismay, she perceived a bright light through the chinks of the floor.

Her features assumed a livid hue now.

Her frame trembled, and she clutched at the table to save herself from falling.

Her bosom rose and fell with the various and conflicting emotions which shook her breast.

"Oh, God!" she gasped forth, "the house is on fire!"

And then her strength deserted her quite.

She staggered forward.

She clutched at the table as her brain became dizzy.

Then she fell, with a fearful cry for help upon her lips.

A cry which was answered by one as loud and heartrending.

It was uttered by Dancing Bill, her guilty husband.

But Margaret heard it not as it echoed around the stage.

She had fainted.

The horror she had experienced had been more than she could bear, and reason for a time had tottered from its throne.

And as she lie, the smoke rolled up through the clinks of the stage, denser and denser, blacker and blacker, till it enveloped everything in almost utter darkness.

And beneath the boards on which she lay, the fire burned brighter and brighter, fiercer and fiercer.

The boards beneath her became scorched, and their heat, causing pain to her limbs, awoke her from the trance into which she had fallen.

Reason had returned.

The horrors of her situation were again thrust upon her with redoubled violence.

With a cry she sprang to her feet.

With a glance of agony, she looked around her.

Above was enveloped in a thick pall of black smoke.

Below, the bright flames thrust their forked fiery tongues through the cracks.

She knew that the huge lumber room below was one mass of fire.

She knew, too, that in another moment the boards beneath her feet would be burned through and fall in, and that the flames would then seize upon the wings, scenes, and flies, and the whole house be one huge roaring furnace.

"Oh, God!" she muttered, "Bob and Harry must have fired the place in their search for Mary."

As she spoke, she sprang towards the steps which led to the stage door.

She hoped to be enabled to leave the house ere the flames rose through the flooring at her feet.

But vain was that hope.

As she gained the steps, a huge body of black smoke rolled up them, and forced her back.

A cry of horror and despair broke from her lips, and again she essayed to pass down the stairs.

But again was she driven back by the poisonous and suffocating vapour.

In an agony of despair she leant against the side wall.

Her eyes filled with tears.

Her heart rose and fell with emotion.

Her legs almost refused their office, and she felt weak and powerless as an infant.

"What—what can I do to be saved," she exclaimed. "Oh, heaven, spare me from this fearful doom!"

Once more she approached the steps.

"I must pass out this way, or remain to die," she said. "Oh, what a death. Fire! fire!" she screamed. "Help—help!"

She bounded forward down two or three steps, in spite of the volumes of smoke, which rose against her, to bar her only passage to safety.

But here she was brought to a fearful pause.

Through the black smoke shot the lurid flames, as they burned through the doors the harlequin had been powerless to open.

Their long tongues leaped towards her, and with shriek after shriek, she sprang back, up the steps, to the side of the wings.

On, with a roar and a hiss; on, with forked tongues, and smoking crests, came the devouring, death-seeking element. On, up the steps to the stage, driving the shrieking and bewildered woman in horror before them.

All hope of escape by the steps was effectually cut off.

What was to be done?

What hope was there left her now?

None.

There was no other means of exit from the theatre, but by the front doors of the house.

They were securely fastened, and Charlie Evans had the keys in his possession.

All hope was gone.

On rushed the flames, up the steps, curling their heads round to the wings, which had been drawn back to give full effect to the last set scene of the nautical drama.

Leaping, and darting, the fiery element made its way towards them; licking the boards, as it stretched its long forks towards the frames of light wood-work, over which the bedaubed canvass was fastened.

On, still on, nearer and nearer!

The flames have seized them at last, and leap and twine themselves around the wings, stretching their forked tongues upwards to the network of wooden grooves, in which the scenes are run on and off, and driving the affrighted woman back on to the stage before them, only to stand appalled with horror, as the flames burst through the traps in the floor at her feet.

Cry after cry, shriek after shriek, she uttered.

But the roaring of the flames, and the cracking and snapping of the dry timbers, as the destructive element seizes on its prey, and enfolds it in its fiery embrace, drowns her voice, and back, still back, she retreats, in horror and dismay.

Is there no hope, must she perish in the flames.

Will the slumbering townspeople never awake, and come to her rescue.

Will not the glare of the flames, the cracking of the burning timbers, arouse them to the truth of what is going on in that theatre.

It will, it does.

Above the roar of the devouring elements, ring loud the voices of men, as windows are thrown up, and cries of horror break from the throats of half aroused sleepers.

And now for some distance around the Saloon the cry of many voices rise in the night air, and that cry is,—

"Fire!"

That terrible word, screamed from a dozen throats, is echoed back by a hundred, and over the sleeping town "Fire! Fire!" floats in agonised tones.

The fire has been discovered at last; and hundreds are hurrying to the spot from every quarter.

Margaret heard the cry, and her heart bounded with hope.

But the flames burst through the boards of the stage, and myriads of sparks encircled her form.

And as the flooring falls, charred and powdered, into the space below, she sees a huge sheet of fire, into which, it seemed, she must sooner or later fall.

Like one in a dream, she stood fascinated, glaring into the fearful, glowing furnace, but the smoke rose up in thick volumes, and she staggered along the smouldering boards, towards the footlights.

Her only chance to prolong her life, is to leap over the small orchestra into the pit.

This she prepared to do.

But too late, a sheet of flame forces a passage into the orchestra, and all retreat is cut off.

"Oh, heaven, have mercy!" she gasped, turning her gaze upwards.

What a fearful sight met her eyes now.

The flames have curled up the wings, and seized upon the borders, which are now one sheet of fire, and the fearful element is twining around and over the flies; and now, wings, grooves, borders and flies, are one sheet of flame, tearing, roaring, hissing to the roof, and seeking some outlet there, into the air beyond.

Oh God! What a fearful position was Margaret's now; flames below, above, and on either side of her; all round was she hemmed in by sheets of fire, and thick, black, suffocating smoke.

In despair she clasped her hands together, and sank down upon her knees.

Insensibility was fast stealing over her; death, in its most horrible form, encircled her on all sides.

Crack, bang, crash, and the flooring of the stage falls through, piece by piece, into the glowing pit, and up rise showers of sparks into the air.

Smash, rattle, and the windows of the building are forced out by the heat, and the flames, rushing through the openings into the outer air, light up the surrounding buildings with a lurid glare.

The murmur of a thousand voices are mingled with the flames, and fall in bitter mockery upon the columbine's ears.

Louder and louder, they roar and hiss; the flames have broken through the roof, and are leaping in mad fury high up over the fated building.

Another loud cry from the assembled multitude outside; a cry that gains strength every moment, till it swells into a roar.

The engine has arrived, and a hundred willing hands are stretched forth to work it.

Down upon the stage fall the half-consumed and blackened timbers, which formed the flies, and grooves, crushing in the charred flooring, as though it were tinder, and giving the flames below a greater scope.

Plank after plank disappeared, into the burning vortex, and Margaret once more sprang to her feet, in an agony of despair.

Scarce had she done so, than she felt the boards on which she stood sinking beneath her weight, and she bounded a few steps further towards the centre of the stage, just as they fell through, and were lost in a volume of sparks, which rose up and settled on the hands, face, and dress of the frantic woman.

All hope is gone now, for she feels her new position as dangerous as her former one; the boards are cracking on which she stands.

Scarcely had she stepped off them, than they snapped and fell through like their predecessors.

In vain she sought a hold for her feet; step where she would, her weight crushed in the charred timber.

There was but one chance now, but one spot where she could hope to prolong her life a few moments.

That was on a beam which had supported the flooring, the under side, and sides of which glared with fire.

With one glance to heaven, she stepped upon it. A strange, hissing noise, caused her to look up, and through one of the windows she perceived a stream of water was being forced.

But it planted no hope in her breast now, the fearful element had too strong a hold.

But she watched it as it fell, and as it deadened the flames around the window, she saw a man forcing his way through the blackened orifice.

With one shriek for help, she extended her hands towards him.

He stood upon the blackened sill, amid the smoke and water; then down he leaped into the flames beneath.

A cry of horror broke from her lips, and she closed her eyes. Her brain swam; she tottered along the rafters, and would have fallen into the pit beneath, but a strong arm encircled her waist.

The man had reached her side, and a dozen faces, half-blinded by the smoke, peered through the window.

The man lifted Margaret in his arms, and moved along the rafter, around which the flames curled, and those at the window watched him with breathless anxiety, till observing that the flames had nearly burned through the tottering support, they called upon him to hurry across it.

Grasping Margaret firmly in his arms, he darted forward, but their united weight was too much for the charred joist to stand, and with a loud crash it parted in the centre.

An immense cloud of sparks and smoke arose around them, and when they had subsided, those at the window strained their eyes in vain to detect the form of Dick the Poacher, and the woman he had perilled his life to save.

CHAPTER CIII.

THE STEWARD RELEASED FROM PRISON.

MR. GRIPE, the late steward of Squire Henley, sat on the rude stone seat which ran along one side of the small cell in which he had been confined for twelve months.

Twelve months had the little steward been an inmate of that cold, cheerless apartment.

Twelve weary months had he been working out the sentence meted out to him by the court.

And twelve months of misery was it to him.

His weazened face had become even more thin and wan. His little form had wasted away, till he was but a shadow of his former self.

But, fearful as was the punishment to him, it had not eradicated the feelings of his nature.

Revenge on the squire was now all he cared for.

Revenge, deep and bitter, for the trick he had played him.

It was this which buoyed him up during the long, lonely hours of his imprisonment.

But the twelve months were now ended.

The term of his sentence expired on that day.

He sat gazing upon the door of his cell.

That door through which he was to pass to liberty—liberty!

Oh, how the word warmed his soul, and caused his heart to beat.

With what emotions his breast heaved as he muttered the word.

None but those who have been denied their freedom can know the blessing of liberty; none but those situated like Gripe could realize all the pleasures of freedom.

How anxiously he listened to the foot-fall of the warder as he passed the passage beyond the door of his cell.

There was music in the sound now, though it had smote upon his ears, and struck deep into his soul as a death knell before.

But now—now it would stop before that iron-bound door, and unbar the passage to sweet liberty.

No wonder, then, that his eyes were strained upon the door, his ears to catch every sound.

As the first grey streak of dawn penetrated through the small, barred casement of his cell, Gripe had arose from his couch, and waited the summons of the warder, to appear before the governor and receive his discharge.

How wearily did the moments seem to roll on their course.

How tardily the sun rose, and threw the long, bright, slanting rays through the bars of his prison window.

With what breathless anxiety he listened for the chime of the prison-bell, as it told the hours as they passed on to eternity.

Six hours had he sat thus, waiting and watching the long-looked for liberty.

The prison clock struck the hour of twelve, and as its sound floated through the passages of the prison, and reached the ears of Gripe, he felt that never before had music so sweet and comforting saluted his senses.

The echoes of the last stroke died away, and silence—deep, painful silence—reigned once more throughout that sombre building.

But not for long.

A loud footfall on the stone floor of the passage without his cell saluted the strained ears of the little steward.

He rose from his seat and moved close up to the door.

The footsteps beyond drew nearer and nearer, and paused at last before the door of his cell.

Gripe's lips quivered, and a smile played around his weazened features.

The rattle of a key in the lock grated upon his ears.

With a long, deep sigh of relief the steward staggered backwards to the stone seat, and sank down upon it.

The key was turned in the lock, and the door of the cell opened.

Gripe clasped his hands together, as though in thankfulness, as he looked upon the tall form of the warder on the threshold.

The face of that functionary, usually so stern and rigid, is relaxed and smiling.

Never before had he appeared so good-tempered.

The steward's opinion was changed in a moment, and he rose from the seat on to which he had sunk, and approached him.

"Good morning, Mr. Gripe," said the man.

"Good morning," replied Gripe, looking surprised at the salutation.

"You will have no objection to follow me to the governor's room, I suppose," said the warder.

The little weazened face of Gripe beamed with smiles.

"Oh, no, no," he replied, "I shall only be too happy."

"No doubt," said the warder, "this way, if you please."

And the turnkey, turned and left the cell.

It was the first time he had done so for twelve months, without locking it.

Gripe bounded over the threshold into the passage.

His little eyes swept round the dismal place, now not half so dismal to him as it had always appeared.

The dark stone walls, hitherto so cold and cheerless, seemed to shine in the rays of the sun as they forced their way through the high barred windows.

The long line of iron doors on either side, struck no chill to his heart now, and he bounded forward with a light and buoyant step.

The little form, was bent up to its full height, the little smile once more played on the little face, and the little grey eye gleamed with joy and triumph.

On, through the long passage, impatient at the slow pace of the turnkey, walked Gripe towards the private room of the governor of the gaol.

In a few moments the steward was ushered into the presence of that functionary.

Seated before an office-table, covered with papers, Captain Lirrington awaited his presence.

As Gripe entered, the governor raised his eyes from a paper he held in his hand, and fixed an eagle-like glance on the little steward.

If he expected the eye of Gripe to flinch before his gaze he was mistaken.

All the cool bold manners of the steward had returned with the dawn of liberty.

He returned the gaze as cool and fixedly as the governor's.

"Your term of imprisonment has expired," said the captain. "You are now free to go forth from these walls and mix with the world outside, and I sincerely trust that the lesson you have learned may never be forgotten, and that the punishment you have received may deter you from further crime."

Gripe listened patiently till he had ceased speaking, then brushing his hair back from his forehead, and advancing a step nearer to the governor, he said—

"To younger and more criminal men your words of advice would do honour, but to me, sir, who has been imprisoned in this place for twelve months upon the evidence of a villain, whose machinations I endeavoured to thwart, they have but little weight. I have been confined here by one, who, but for his wealth, had taken my place, but for a longer term.

"You refer to Squire Henley," said the governor.

"I do."

"Having the honour of his personal acquaintance, it would be vain for you to endeavour to gloss over your own guilt by assailing the honour of an upright gentleman," said the governor.

"I will show, sir," said Gripe, "whether Squire Henley be the man you believe him to be, or whether I, who so long transacted his affairs, have been punished justly or not."

"I am not your judge," said the governor. "I am only an officer of the law, consigned to a duty, which, I trust, I shall ever perform to the satisfaction of all; therefore, I can hold no conversation upon the matter. Here is your discharge, and I give it to you with pleasure, for, believe me, I had rather open these prison doors to give freedom to a fellow creature, than usher one into confinement!"

So saying, he rose and left the apartment.

Gripe followed him with his eyes till he had passed through the doorway, then turned to the warder, who still stood beside him.

"Now," he said, "is there any more ceremonials to go through ere I am permitted to leave this accursed place?"

"Yes."

"What?"

"One."

"And what is that?"

"Change your clothes, that's all," said the man, with a grin.

"Ah, I had forgotten," said Gripe, looking down at the prison dress which he wore.

"You would have soon been brought to your recollection," said the man.

"Should I?"

"Yes. You wouldn't have gone far before you would have discovered that you were rather an object of interest."

"No, I suppose not."

"This way, then," said the man, walking out of the apartment.

Gripe followed.

The turnkey now led him into another apartment, where he lifted a bundle from a shelf, and placed it in the hands of the steward.

"Here are the clothes you wore," he said, "when I first made your acquaintance. You can put them on, and, no doubt, you will feel a little more comfortable in them, than you do in those you now wear, at all events, they will not look so conspicuous, or attract so much attention outside the prison."

Gripe hastily untied the bundle, and allowed the garments he wore on the night of his being led away in custody from the hall, to fall on to the floor at his feet.

The little smile became brighter, and the eye dilated, as he gazed upon them.

Then he hurriedly threw off the prison clothes, and attired himself in his own garments.

Now, indeed, he felt himself once more.

His little figure was drawn up to its full height, his eye kindled, and he was once more Gripe the steward.

Down the long passage to the outer door of the prison he strode alongside of the turnkey, his form erect, his glance more patronising than ought else, and when the door was thrown open, he stepped over its threshold as coolly and calmly as though he were governor of the goal, instead of a prisoner just set at liberty.

The door closed behind him with a loud clang.

He stood before it, inhaling the breath of freedom, but that gave not so much joy to his heart as did the thought that he was now at liberty to work out his revenge on Squire Henley.

CHAPTER CIV.

GRIPE AND THE OFFICER—THE STEWARD'S INDIGNATION AND RESOLVE.

GRIPE stood for some moments gazing around him ere he attempted to leave the spot.

He seemed in no hurry to get away from the vicinity, from the place in which he had been so long immured.

Anyone would think that he would only be too anxious to turn his back upon the dark frowning walls.

Shame alone would have induced many to leave the spot as quickly as possible.

But not so Gripe.

Another feeling, more deep than shame, had hold of his soul.

That feeling was revenge.

Revenge on the man who had consigned him to a felon's doom.

It was that which absorbed his whole thoughts now.

The bright sunlight, from which he had been so long barred, the pure breath of freedom, which he had not inhaled for so long a time, was unheeded. Darkness had set upon his soul—the darkness of revenge.

The moment his foot had stepped over the threshold of the goal this feeling had taken a deeper and firmer root in his heart, and when at length, he had turned away from the frowning walls, he took the road to the old manor house.

Yes, towards the old manor house strode Gripe the steward.

Too well he knew that as he passed along he would be recognised by many—many who had heard with pleasure of his misfortunes, and who would feel a pang of regret that he was again cast loose upon society. But he only smiled, his cold, heartless smile, and kept on his way.

How many a poor wretch, less guilty than he, would have shunned the vicinity of his crimes.

But not so Gripe.

What cared he for the jeers of those he had so deeply injured; what cared he for the scowling glances, and the pointings of the scornful fingers of honest men.

Not an atom.

He had suffered for his crime, paid the penalty of the law, rendered atonement to justice, and was free.

For what?

To begin the world again, and struggle to redeem the character he had lost; to mount the ladder of reputation, step by step, till once more he stood at the top, an ornament to society.

Yes, Gripe was free to do all this.

But would he—did he intend to try to do all this.

No!

Gripe had but one course marked out for him by himself—one resolve, and that was the destruction of Squire Henley.

But how was he to proceed.

He was alone in the world now, without money, without a home, without friends.

Surely this was sufficient to make any one despair.

But it did not Gripe.

He had bent under the pressure of circumstances, but the weight once removed, he sprung up again, firm and resolved as ever.

The want of money was all that he considered stood in his way.

This he felt he must have, to enable him to wait to mature his plans.

But where was he to get it?

He never possessed many friends, and those he had he knew would now shun him. So to attempt to borrow funds he felt would not only be unavailing, but that he would lay himself open to refusal after having sought the favour.

There was but one with whom the steward felt that he had no slightest chance of success.

That was Takeall, the broker and auctioneer.

There was a probability of obtaining assistance from him.

Not that Takeall felt any particular respect for Gripe, not that his heart was in the right place, and could be softened by the sufferings of his friend, but because Gripe knew a great deal that would not redound to the credit of the broker, did he open his mouth and give utterance to all he could say.

It was fear alone that would induce the broker to assist the steward, and Gripe ultimately made up his mind to make that the instrument by which to minister to his present requirements.

When he had come to this descision, Gripe quickened his pace, and hurried on along the road to Barnstable.

Hitherto he had met none whom he knew, but as he trudged along, his head erect as ever, his gaze suddenly encountered the tall form of Mr. Grabham, the constable.

In an instant, an indignant flush overspread his face, and his little grey eyes twinkled with malignant light.

He had not forgotten the treatment he had received from that worthy officer, on the night he was borne to the lock-up, nor had he forgiven it either.

Gripe was not the man to easily forget or forgive.

But he still walked on at the same pace, still kept his head erect, and stared boldly at the officer, as he neared him.

In a few minutes Grabham stood directly before him.

Gripe was about to pass him with a contemptuous curl of the lip, but the officer, stepping fairly in his path, said—

"So you are out, Mr. Gripe, I see."

"And so you will find ere long," replied Gripe, irritably.

"Don't lose your temper, Mr. Gripe," you used to be the coolest and calmest dispositioned man in Devonshire, but there, twelve months in gaol is enough to sour the temper of an angel."

"Stand aside," exclaimed Gripe. "I have nothing to say to you now."

"Oh, haven't you."

"No, but I shall have much some other time," said the steward, malignantly.

"Indeed."

"Yes, indeed."

"Upon what subject, may I ask, Mr. Gripe."

"You will see all in good time," replied Gripe.

"I should like to know now," said the officer, his eye twinkling with a mischievous light, and giving a shrewd guess as to what the steward meant.

"No doubt you would, but you'll know quite time enough for yourself, and too soon to be pleasant," said Gripe, endeavouring to pass the officer.

"Ah, I see," said Grabham. "Close confinement has played upon your brain. But there, you will soon be all right now—that is if you mind what you are about."

"I shall do as I please," retorted Gripe.

"You mustn't do that," said the other.

"Mustn't I."

"No."

"What's to hinder me," asked the steward, impatiently.

"The law, Mr. Gripe—the law," said Grabham.

"Damn the law," said Gripe, furiously, once more endeavouring to pass the officer.

"Be careful, sir, be careful," said Grabham, taking a secret pleasure in annoying the little man. "The law is very powerful, and should be respected, you, at least, have come to know that, for you have felt its force."

"And the force of your knuckles, too, thought Gripe, but kept it to himself.

"And you shall feel its power, too, sir," he added, aloud.

"Me?"

"Yes, you."

"Indeed."

"You shall, or my name's not Gripe," exclaimed the steward. "You shall learn to treat your prisoners as men, sir, not beasts."

"I do not understand you," said Grabham.

"Don't you?"

"No."

"You soon will."

"I am glad to hear it," replied the officer.

"You shall soon find out, though you are one of the law's myrmidons, you have not the power to choke a man," said Gripe.

"I am not the hangman," said the officer, coolly, "or I would not stand here now talking to you, for I do not believe I could converse with one it would be my painful duty to strangle some day."

Gripe fairly foamed at this, and stamping his little foot upon the ground, he exclaimed,—

"You rascal—you—you—"

"Ha, ha!" laughed Grabham. "Mr. Gripe your ordinary coolness has deserted you."

"Coolness be ——."

"Don't swear, sir, don't swear; it is a bad habit; and often leads to worse. Good day to you, Mr. Gripe, and don't let me get you in my clutches again."

"Go to the devil," raved the little man.

And the steward pushed the officer aside and darted past him.

"Gripe, Gripe," called Grabham, after him,

"you can hardly believe the excitement there was when you were put in limbo, it was almost a general rejoicing throughout the county."

"I'll make you smart for your insolence," yelled the little man, "I'll—I'll—"

"Choke yourself with passion, and rob the hangman of his fee," said the officer, with a chuckle, "if you give vent to your feelings in that way."

Gripe turned furiously, his fists clenched, and his teeth set firm with rage.

"If you insult me I'll crush you," he roared.

"Ha, ha, ha!" laughed the officer, looking down upon the little man. "Why, Mr. Gripe, you are mad, and have no right to be at liberty."

Gripe looked up in the face of the officer, scarcely knowing what to think or how to act.

The coolness of the man somewhat disconcerted him, and with a smothered curse he turned away indignantly.

Grabham watched him in silence for two or three seconds, then raising his voice, he said,—

"Ah, Mr. Gripe, there's not been a single execution levied upon the goods of any poor devil in Barnstable during the last year, and Takeall will have to dispose of his business, unless you obtain a situation as steward in the county."

Then, with a chuckle, he turned away and left the steward, to pursue his course.

Foaming with rage and indignation, Gripe strode on for some distance, ere he cast a glance behind him, to assure himself that he was free of the presence of the officer.

The last words of Grabham, however, strengthened his resolve to pay a visit to the broker.

That worthy, he believed, would be glad to see him, who ever else would be sorry; for to Takeall he had been a valuable friend.

A great deal of business he had placed in the broker's hands, and his absence from the town must have sadly interfered with the profits of the auctioneer.

To Takeall's office, then, should be his destination.

The broker was a crafty man, one to whom honour and feeling were but words; self interest was centered in his soul, and if Gripe could only show him that he might be a gainer by still standing his friend, the steward doubted not that he would yet be able to carry out his plans, and strike a terrible blow at those who had excited his anger and revenge.

He soon forgot his interview with the officer, and strode along the road with a quick, yet steady step.

The smile had returned to his face, the gleam to his eye.

Already he felt himself able to cope with the squire, and hurl his defiance in his face.

"Once more the hound is on the scent," he muttered to himself, "and he will not rest till he has run down the game. Squire Henley, you might have made me your friend, but you chose to make me your foe. For a time you have lived secure, now tremble, for the leash is slipped and the chase once more begun!"

CHAPTER CV.

THE BROKER'S OFFICE—TAKEALL AND THE STEWARD—THE THREAT.

Mr. Takeall, the sworn-broker and auctioneer, sat on a high stool, before a high desk, in the little front room of his house, and which room was the office in which he always transacted business.

A long quill pen was stuck behind his ear, and his right hand rested upon the soiled cover of a large account-book, which he had closed with a loud clap a few moments before.

His eyes rested upon the green blind, which half-covered the window of the apartment, and there was an expression of ill-temper about the lineaments of his face.

The shades of evening were drawing in, and the office was bathed in a semi-darkness.

It was rather over his usual hour of retiring to the comfortable upstairs apartment, and his whole appearance denoted that he was anything but pleased at being confined in the office, when the time had arrived for him to place his slippered feet on the ornamental fender, which graced the hearthstone of his private sitting-room.

Suddenly his glance shifted from the green blind to the door, which slowly opened, and gave admittance to a tall, thin young man, habited in a suit of rusty black, who nervously entered the room.

"Well, sir," exclaimed the broker, the moment the head and shoulders of the new comer presented themselves, "am I to wait here all night, because you will crawl when you ought to run?"

"I am sorry I kept you waiting in the office, sir," replied the young man, closing the door after him, "but the poor woman promised to pay if I waited till she could raise the money."

"And you did wait?"

"I did, sir."

"Then you are a fool, Jacob, a great fool, for your pains," said Takeall.

"I thought it best, as you refused to make any further applications for the rent," said the young man, drawing a canvas bag from his pocket, and counting out thirty shillings upon the desk.

"Thought it best; it was the worst thing you could do. If you had come away when you found she was not prepared to pay, I could have levied on her goods and chattels in the morning," exclaimed Takeall.

"But, sir, though she could not meet the demand at the moment, she did so a short time after."

"Yes, but if you had not waited she would not have troubled herself to procure the money immediately."

"That's why I did wait."

"Humph!" "you will never be fit for this line of business; your friends have made quite a mistake in sending you to it; you are no good at all."

"I endeavour, sir, to do my best," said the young man, mildly.

"And always do your worst," exclaimed Takeall, dropping the money into his pocket.

"Thirty shillings, one quarter's rent of the cottage. And the place is decently furnished, too. If you had come away without the money I could have put an execution in, and though she has been able to obtain it now, she might have had some difficulty in doing so, when people knew the brokers were in the place, you see now what you have done by waiting, prevented me leaving her goods. How do you think I can keep this office if you are so short sighted. You must not wait, it is the worst thing to do. What is a small percentage on the rents collected, nothing compared to what is to be made by a distress. There, shut up the office and go home, and remember that if ever you want to make a broker, you must seize, sir, seize."

"But, sir, replied the young man," it is hard, very hard, to lose a home."

"What's that to us. Business is business, and if we refuse to do our duty we shall soon have to shut up the office altogether."

The young man sighed and turned to the window, the shutters of which he began to close.

"Humph," muttered Takeall, as he left the room, "times are bad enough without that fool making them worse. Why, I haven't made a single seizure since Gripe was lugged off to gaol. He was the man, the business hasn't been worth half what it was. None of these ridiculous feelings entered his heart. He always did his duty; he knew what duty was. What a fool to allow himself to be found out. Ah, if he were only back again in his old berth I should thrive again."

Takeall flung himself into his easy chair, and commenced mixing a bowl of punch, the ingredients for which had been placed upon the table ready for him as soon as he left the office.

This done, he took a long clay pipe from a sideboard, and having filled it, and lit it, commenced puffing out huge volumes of smoke.

"His time is up, or nearly so," he soliloquised, as he watched the blue vapour curling fantastically up from the bowl. "What will he do, I wonder. The squire won't have anything more to do with him, and what's more, he will have no business with those who do. It's a pity he allowed himself to be found out; a great pity for himself, and a great loss to me. But, there, it's no use to regret, but I only wish the present steward was like him. He ain't half sharp enough, not half."

There was a gentle tap at the room door.

"Come in," growled the broker, laying down his pipe, and peering at the door as if he would look through its panels.

The door opened, and Jacob, the clerk, stood upon the threshold.

"Ain't you gone yet?" growled Takeall.

"No, sir. As I was going out a person requested to see you," replied the clerk.

"To-night?"

"Yes, sir."

"What does he want?"

"I don't know."

"It's past office hours," said Takeall. "I can't see him now."

"So I told him; but he said he must see you."

"Who is it?"

"I don't know."

"Some one in arrears, I suppose, to come

pestering at this time. Tell him to call to-morrow."

"He is very importunate, and said you would be glad to see him," said the clerk.

"Go and ask him his name," said Takeall.

The young man turned to obey the order, when Gripe, who had followed him up the stairs, pushed him aside, and entering the room, said,—

"There is no necessity. He will answer for himself."

Mr. Takeall, who had raised the pipe from the table to convey it to his lips, let it fall, and it lay shivered to atoms at his feet, whilst his eyes opened to their utmost width, and he stammered out,—

"The devil!"

"Not exactly," replied Gripe, quickly, and making a motion towards the clerk, who still stood on the threshold, with the door in his hand, undecided whether to leave the spot or not.

"You can go, Jacob," said Takeall, waving his hand.

"Good night," said the clerk, drawing the door close, and leaving the worthy pair to-gether.

Then Gripe advanced to the surprised and confounded Takeall, and held out his hand.

But the broker did not take it.

He stood hesitating.

Gripe's countenance changed.

The smile on his face vanished, and a look of anger took its place.

"What," he said, "do you refuse to take my hand."

Takeall tried to stammer out a few words, but did not succeed.

His mind had become bewildered by the re-collection that he had heard that the squire had threatened to have nothing whatever to do with any person who should feel disposed to hold communion with the guilty steward after he had served his term of imprisonment. Takeall was a worldly man; self interest was his god. At present he only saw that his interest lay in con-forming to the wishes of the squire.

"What!" exclaimed Gripe, "do you give me the cold shoulder. You, who I have made what you are; you, who I can hold up to the scorn of every honest man."

And the little steward raised his voice to its utmost pitch.

The coldness of Takeall was the unkindest cut.

"Hush!" gasped the broker.

"You scout me after all I have done for you," continued Gripe.

"No, no!" exclaimed Takeall, hurriedly, ex-tending his hand. "I—I was only surprised at seeing you."

"And annoyed," retorted Gripe, sarcasti-cally. "It's the way of the world; the devil who is unfortunate enough to get found out, is scouted even by those who, even a thousand times worse than himself, is fortunate enough to escape!"

"I don't scout you," said the broker.

"Then why this coldness," asked the steward.

"I only waited to be sure that my clerk had left the house, before I recognised you," said Takeall. "You can trust no one, and that fool might have betrayed your presence here."

"And if he did, what then?" asked Gripe.

"The news might travel to the hall."

"Well?"

"And then I should receive no more of the squire's patronage," said Takeall, "and I can ill afford to lose that, as business stands now."

"And so, to keep that, you would turn upon an old friend," said Gripe; "turn upon one who can crush the squire at any moment!"

"You have tried that, and failed," said Takeall.

"I have," replied the steward. "But if I have failed, it has only been for a time; experience has made me wise, and I must act in a different manner to bring about my desires; desires did I say? resolves, rather. He has escaped me, but only for a time. Takeall, you know me to be a man of my word; a man, who, when I once take a case in hand, go through with it. You know, too, that I am not one to grasp at a shadow and lose the substance!"

"I do."

"Then listen. The squire is in my power, and I only require the means to bring him to my feet! the means to wring from him gold to purchase my silence. What money I had has been handed to him to repay him for that which I took, and I am now penniless, with the prison taunt upon me, the brand of felon on my brow. I want a friend, I want money, and for these have I sought you."

Takeall shook his head.

"Business has been so bad," he said, "so very bad lately."

"Curse the business," said Gripe furiously. "Shall business stand before friendship."

Takeall was silent.

"I want money for my present necessities," said Gripe, "and, Mr. Takeall, you must provide it."

"Indeed I cannot," replied the broker, quickly.

"But I say you shall," exclaimed Gripe, bring-ing a chair down with great violence upon the floor, and flinging himself into it.

Takeall looked at the little steward from head to foot for some moments.

"When you have taken my likeness," said Gripe, cooly, "perhaps you will sit down, and come to business, since business and not friend-ship is to be the order of the day."

And the little man folded his arms across his breast, leant back in his chair, and waited for Takeall to seat himself.

Fearing to arouse further indignation in the breast of Gripe, and well knowing that the steward could "a tale unfold," not very creditable even to a sworn broker, Takeall sat himself down and awaited uneasily for Gripe to speak.

"Glad to see your obstinacy is not beyond reason," said the steward, slowly unfolding his arms, and placing his elbows on the table, whilst he looked steadfastly at his companion. So Mr. Takall, the man who has been the means of placing you in the position you occupy, may go to the devil, for all you care, before you will consent to assist him, who as often assisted you."

"It's not that," stammered the broker, "its—its—"

"Your greedy disposition," interrupted Gripe, cooly.

"No, no."

"Yes, yes, I am down in the world now. I am no longer able to give you employment, to put money in your purse. In fact, I am useless to you, and may starve and rot in the ditch for all you care. But mark me, Mr. Takeall, I won't be kept down, and it's not to your interest to keep me down either, for I can pull you down with me, and I will, too, if you refuse my request.

"What do you want?" said Takeall, anxiously glancing at the cool, calm, and imperturable countenance of the steward.

"Money."

No. 28.

"I assure you that I have but very little," said Takeall.

"And I assure you," said Gripe, "that you are a liar."

"What, sir," exclaimed Takeall, leaping to his feet. "What, sir. A liar! I will allow no man to call me a liar."

"Sit down," said Gripe, "and be cool, or I may yet call you a robber in the bargain."

"Me, a robber! me, me!" exclaimed the broker.

"Yes, and a mean spirited contemptible robber, to boot," said Gripe. "You see, twelve months' imprisonment has not quite subdued me; has not quite crushed every particle of spirit out of me, for I can upraid you, the powerful broker of Barnstable, the man whose look strikes terror to the soul of poor but honest men, whose presence is abhorred and whose actions are accursed."

"I must do my duty," said Takeall nervously.

"Duty, is duty, but is it duty when it is exceeded; when, for a few paltry shillings, a home is broken up worth more pounds; when a man perjures himself to put the proceeds in his own pocket, eh, Mr. Takeall, eh!"

Takeall hung his head, and beat his foot nervously upon the hearthrug.

"I have been in prison," continued Gripe, "I have stood in a felon's dock. My name has become a bye-word in the town, men point at me with scorn, call me robber, and turn from me with disgust. I have been held up to infamy and shame, but, Mr. Takeall, I consider myself an honest man when compared to you. I have condescended to ask you for means to supply my wants, and you have refused them. Now I demand them, and deny me if you dare."

"Mr. Gripe."

"Mr. Takeall."

"You forget yourself."

"I have but just remembered," said Gripe. "I have hitherto believed you a man, but now I find you a mean spirited villain, a thing who would cringe and fawn around the legs of him who could aid you in your dirty business, one who would kick his friend the moment he is unable to help you further. But if I could help you in your filthy calling, I can also hold up to the eyes of the world its mysteries, and bring down upon you the indignation of every honest man. By my aid you have risen to the position you occupy, and by my aid, too, you shall descend from it, unless you condescend to look with more favourable eyes, and extend a more generous hand towards me; you are the only one to whom I can apply for assistance, and you cannot, dare not, refuse it. Though a branded felon, I have my foot upon your neck, and if you struggle to free yourself from its pressure it will prove fatal to yourself."

CHAPTER CVI.

THE DANGERS OF MARY — A CHRISTIAN AND HIS WORKS — THE ANNOUNCEMEMT AND ITS EFFECT.

ON went the fly over the hard, dark road, bearing Mary along in terror and dismay.

Clatter, clatter, went the iron-bound feet of the affrighted animal, striking fire from the stones, and jolt, jolt, went the vehicle, swaying from side to side of the deserted highway.

Mary clung in terror to the seat, and sank down upon her knees, on the bottom of the carriage.

She had heard the pistol-shot and she could not think otherwise than that Dick the Poacher had been wounded, and now lay upon the road-way far behind.

In her terror she knew not how to act. At one time she thought of opening the door of the vehicle, and leaping out into the road.

But as she rose to put this resolve into execution, a sway of the vehicle flung her on to the back seat, with fearful violence.

It was well for her, that it did so.

It called to her mind the danger she sought, and she sat trembling with terror.

Had she have taken the leap, there is little doubt, but that it would have been a fatal one to her.

The furious rate at which the animal sped along, would have placed her life, as well as her limbs, in jeopardy.

On went the horse in its mad career, and Mary clasping the window frame of the door, shrieked aloud for help.

But the clatter of the horse's hoofs, and the rumble of the wheels alone answered her cries for succour.

Trees and hedges flew by with the rapidity of lightning, and as her affrighted gaze rested on the roadway, the very ground seemed to rush from her.

Truly her position was a fearful one.

Bitterly did she feel the loss of her protector.

She murmured a prayer to heaven for succour, but still on, on, went the vehicle.

So fearfully did it sway from side to side, that she expected every moment to be dashed from it to the ground.

But spite of the mad speed, and blind fury of the animal, it still kept the centre of the road-way.

By degrees Mary became more calm, and endeavoured to think of some means of attracting notice to her position, or staying the career of the affrighted animal.

But none presented themselves.

"Surely," she thought, "the beast cannot long hold on at this fearful pace. It must soon tire, and then I may be enabled to descend from the vehicle, with less chance of danger."

This idea quickly rooted itself in her mind, and she determined to wait patiently.

But spite of her determination, her patience was soon exhausted.

To her, minutes appeared hours, and it seemed that the animal rather quickened, than slackened his pace.

Then she thought of the agony of mind, her father and his friends were enduring, and wondering whether Dick was really wounded or killed.

These thoughts but added to the anguish she already endured, and she clasped her hands together, and bowed her head upon her bosom.

Tears came to her relief at last, and she wept. Her overcharged heart could bear no more.

Still on with a rattle, a rumble and a swing; on with quickened speed, towards the town.

On, with that poor frighted young girl, whom a villain's hand had torn from her friends.

Like a vision too bright to last, a cottage appears at the roadside for a moment, and then is lost.

Another, and another are whirled past the window of the vehicle.

Mary knows now that she is in the outskirts of the town.

She clutched fiercely at the door, and thrust her head through the window.

And out upon the still night air, her voice rang loud and clear,—

"Help—help!"

But the tones float away on the breeze, and the clatter of the hoofs, and the rumble of the wheels, alone break the stillness.

Now several cottages are passed by rapidly, and the town is but a short distance.

She shrieked louder and louder.

Still the horse hurried on.

The tones of her voice seem to incite the animal to increased speed.

He swerves from the centre of the roadway, and the vehicle is dragged on to the path, by the roadside.

The pathway being much higher than the road, the carriage is almost overturned, and shrieking louder and louder, Mary clung to the window.

Still there is no response to her cries for aid.

House, after house, are passed in quick succession.

The trees, fields and hedges, are fast fading from her sight, and long rows of cottages are on either side.

"Help—help!"

The horse rears madly at the sound of her voice, and plunges across the road.

There is a violent shock, and the carriage is dashed against a tall fence, which skirts the grounds of a gentleman's estate.

It rights itself however, and hurries on, only to strike violently again, at another spot.

So fearful was the second concussion, that the window which had remained uninjured, is shattered into fragments.

With a loud cry, Mary falls back on the seat.

Again the carriage is hurried into the centre of the road, and once more it is forced on to the pathway.

The horse finding the rise an obstacle to his flight, plunged and reared, and dashing on still more fiercely, the wheel is locked in the post of a gateway.

Another plunge, and with a loud crash, the wheel is torn from the axle, and the body of the coach falls violently to the ground.

With a desperate clutch, Mary opened the door, with the intention of leaping out.

But the animal again plunged forward, dragging after him in his mad flight the dismembered carriage.

Bump—bump! crash, crash, and over on to its side falls the fly.

Loud and heartrending was the cry that arose from within, but still it kept on its mad course, bearing the now bruised and bleeding girl, along the high road of the town.

Crash, crash, and the body of the vehicle is splintered into a dozen pieces, and the panels are scattered about the road.

Another plunge, and Mary is flung forward.

A wild shriek, a fearful blow, a numbness of the limbs, a dizziness of the brain, and the poor girl lies bleeding and insensible by the roadside; whilst the animal rears, and plunges far away, with the shafts splintered, and the wheels lying on their boxes, over the road of the now slumbering town.

And there lay poor Mary upon the hard ground, her light theatrical costume stained with blood, and torn to shreds, lay amid the *débris* of the fly, which had borne her so far away from the Saloon, only to bring her so near back to it, and then leave her insensible upon the dark roadway.

But her cries, and the noise of the crushed vehicle, had aroused the inmates of the house before which she lie, and in a few moments after she had been hurled to the ground, a light appeared in several of its windows.

A few moments more, and two men appeared, making their way down the long gravel walk of the garden, towards the gate.

The foremost evidently a servant, bore a large horn lantern in his hand, whilst the one who followed close behind him, attired in a long dressing gown, would seem from the deference with which the former treated him, to be the master of the house.

Arriving at the gate, the man with the lantern hastily threw it open, and holding the light high above his head, passed into the road, followed closely by his companion.

"Hold the light this way, Joe," said he, with the dressing gown, looking in the direction where the poor girl lay.

"Yes, sir," replied the man, holding the lantern so as to throw its dim rays in the direction indicated.

"It's what I thought," said the first speaker, fixing his eyes upon one of the panels of the shattered fly, "a carriage broke down, or broke up, or something. Hullo! hold the light here, Joe, hold it here. Good, heavens, what is this. As I live a girl insensible, and habited in—why it must be some one from the theatre, yonder. Hold the light up, Joe, that's it, just so."

And bending down over the prostrate form of Mary, the gentleman gazed eagerly, and compassionately, upon the pale face, down which a thin streak of blood slowly trickled.

"Poor thing—poor thing!" he exclaimed, "she is senseless and bleeding, perhaps dead. Hold the light a little higher, Joe, and I'll carry her into the house."

The man adjusted the lantern as desired, and anxiously gazed down upon the still pale form of the poor girl, whilst his master, lifting her tenderly in his arms, gently bore her towards the gate.

"It's a rum affair this, sir," said the man, looking with a puzzled air first at the girl and then at his master.

"A sad affair, very," was the reply; "but hold the light, so that I can see I do not knock her against the trees—poor thing, poor thing!"

And the men hurried along the gravel walk to the house, with his inanimate burden.

When arrived at the hall door, he was met by two children, one a boy the other a girl, and two or three servants, all hastily attired.

Each pressed round with eager and anxious inquiries.

"Stand back all of you," said the gentleman.

"What is it, papa?" asked the boy.

"Heaven only knows," replied the man. "A poor girl nearly dead. Here, Joe, saddle the grey mare, and ride for the doctor. Bring him back with you. Stand back there. Light me up to the spare bed-room."

"Papa, papa!" exclaimed the youth, who had been intently gazing upon the features of

Mary since the moment she was carried into the house. "Don't you know who it is?"

"No, my boy."

"I do."

"You do—eh?"

"Yes, papa, I know who it is," replied the youth. "It is the girl who played Desdemona at our party.

"What!"

"Look, papa. You must remember her pretty face—I'm sure you must."

The gentleman paused, and looked fixedly into the pale face of the insensible girl.

"Why," he exclaimed in tones of amazement, "it can't be—yes—no—well, I really do believe it is."

"I am sure it is, papa," said the youth. "I knew her again directly."

"How could she come to be in this state," muttered the old gentleman. "Well, it is a strange coincidence, very. I wish the doctor would make haste."

And the kind-hearted man hurried up the stairs with his inanimate burthen, to a room on the second floor of the mansion, where, with a deep sigh, he laid her down upon a richly curtained bed.

He threw himself in a chair by the bedside, and sat anxiously gazing upon the poor girl. In a short time Mary showed some signs of re-recovery, and the anxiety of those around her became almost painful in its intensity.

The gentleman moved the others back from the bedside, lest when she opened her eyes and rested them upon strangers, a too sudden shock should be given to her already weakened system, and muttered something about the man being a very long time gone.

With a deep drawn sigh Mary at length opened her eyes, only to close them again.

At the moment she did so, Joe tapped at the door of the room, exclaiming,—

"Doctor will be here in a minute, sir."

In about half an hour the doctor entered the room, and apologised for his delay by saying he could not get along on account of the Crown Saloon being on fire.

As the words left his lips, Mary started up in the bed, "Fire!" she exclaimed. "Oh, my poor father!" then sank back again insensible.

CHAPTER CVII.

THE IDIOT AND THE GALVANIC BATTERY—A GOOD MAN'S WORK—A SOUL LIGHTED WITH JOY.

IT was on the same day of the evening of which Dancing Bill and the youthful libertine Frampton had put their design into execution of bearing off Mary, that Mr. Barnett, the little village doctor, sat in the little room called the surgery.

He was seated before a small table, on which were several well-worn books, and a small galvanic battery, which that day had arrived from London.

There was a smile on his good-humoured countenance, and a merry twinkle in his eye, as he alternately turned from the battery to a small book which lay open before him.

"Ah, ha," he chuckled to himself, as he laid his finger on one particular line in the book. "Science will turn the world upside down one

of these fine days. What wonderful things does it not bring to light—what numberless theories does it not overthrow."

Then taking the blue cotton handkerchief from his pocket, he commenced rubbing away at his bald pate till it shone like the surface of a mirror.

"Were I a young man now," he continued, talking half aloud, "I might hope, by studying the mysteries of science, to raise myself to a prouder eminence than that of a village physician; but the sere and yellow leaf dances before my eyes, and I cannot hope to attain any position at this time of life. Still, I may yet do one act for which a life is worthy—still leave behind me the record of one deed which shall confer a blessing upon those who now suffer. Poor Minnie, it must have been a dreadful shock that deprived her of her faculties. Still, I fondly hope that a shock of a different nature may yet restore them."

And once more the old gentleman fixed his eyes upon the book, and slowly moved his fore-finger along the leaves.

For some time he remained buried in its perusal, then starting up, he closed the book to with a loud bang.

"Oh, Dick, Dick," he muttered, "heaven grant that I may have a surprise for you on your return."

Then looking up, at an eight day clock which stood in a corner of the room, he said,—

"She will soon be here now. She promised to come and I will get the battery in order," and the old gentleman commenced adjusting the machine before him.

Then he sat down and waited.

Presently there came a low knock at the door.

"Come in," answered the doctor, hurriedly, and at the same time starting from his seat.

The door opened slowly, and Minnie the idiot stood upon the threshold.

Her face was even more than usually sad in expression.

Her eyes were downcast, and there was a nervous twitching about her lips.

"Come in, Minnie,—come in," said the little man in his usual bustling manner, and at the same time placing a chair before the battery.

Minnie slowly walked into the apartment and silently sat down in the chair placed for her.

"Well, how do you find yourself to-day, Minnie?" said the doctor, seating himself before her and taking her hand in his own.

A sudden beam of light shone in the dull eye of the poor woman, then the orb became as dull as before.

Mr. Barnett, whose gaze was fixed close upon her eyes, slowly shook his head.

"You are not so well to-day, Minnie," he said.

"The grass withers, and the voice of the birds are hushed," she replied sadly.

"But the year is at its full," said the doctor. "The green face of nature becomes changed then, and the song of the birds is not so melodious as in the spring and summer."

"Ah, me," she sighed.

"Come, cheer up, Minnie, Dick will soon return to glad your heart," said Barnett.

"Dick?"

And the dull eye brightened.

But it was only for a moment.

It was dull and heavy again, and the pale face became even more pale.

"Yes," said Barnett, "he'll soon be back at the old farm. He is a noble fellow, Minnie."

"Would I could hear the birds sing," she muttered.

"And so you will, Minnie."

"No, no."

"Why not?"

She slowly shook her head.

"They will sing no more, nor ever again will the grass be green."

"But why, why?"

"Dick is in danger."

"Of what?"

But she replied only with a shake of the head.

"Come, you are dull, cheer up. Look here, Minnie, here is a pretty thing I have had sent me all the way from London."

And the doctor rose from his seat and pointed to the battery.

Minnie turned her dull glance towards it.

"Does it sing?" she asked.

"Sing, Minnie."

"It's not a bird."

"A bird, Minnie, oh, no, it is a little machine. If you only lay your hand upon it, it will work directly."

"What work?"

"Look here. Place your hand there, so," said Barnett.

But Minnie hesitated.

"Don't be frightened, Minnie, I have had it sent expressly to show you. Now do just catch hold of it there, so—so—"

Minnie stretched forth her hand hesitatingly.

Barnett, watched her with breathless surprise, as she did so.

But ere her fingers came in contact with the battery she drew back.

"No, no," she said.

"Why, not?"

Minnie fixed her eyes doubtingly upon him.

"You do it," she said.

Idiot as she was, she had yet cunning sufficient to know, that if there was danger to be apprehended, Barnett would not touch the battery.

He saw the drift of her mind in an instant.

He stretched forth his hand, and touched the apparatus.

"There, you see, Minnie, it cannot harm you," he said.

Still the woman hesitated.

Barnett became fearful lest her fears should upset his hopes, and a shade of disappointment crossed his benign face.

"Minnie," he said, after a pause. "Do place your hand there, it will make the birds sing again."

"And the grass grow," she asked hurriedly.

"Yes, luxuriant and green," he replied.

"Ah, then Dick will return to the old farm and poor Minnie," she sighed.

"He will indeed."

She stretched forth her hand and touched the battery.

Barnett could hardly repress the cry of joy which rose to his lips.

But he did suppress it, and leaned eagerly forward, straining his eyeballs into the pupils of Minnie.

Brighter and brighter became the gleam in her dull orbs.

The inanimate expression of her face slowly gave place to an intelligent beam, her pale cheeks became tinged with a ruddy glow, and then back she sank upon her chair.

"Minnie," gasped Barnett.

She raised her head quickly.

The eye was still bright.

The features no longer bore the expression of idiotcy.

Science had indeed benefitted the idiot.

For a moment she remained silent.

Then she bounded from her chair, and flung herself on her knees at the feet of the doctor.

She clasped her hands convulsively together, then raised her now bright eyes suffused with tears to his.

"Minnie," he gasped, "speak—speak!"

"Oh! God my heart is too full for utterance," she gasped.

The old man clasped his hands, and turning his eyes to heaven, exclaimed—

"Great God, I thank thee. She is saved—saved!"

Then unclasping his hands, the old man threw himself forward, and flinging them around the neck of the kneeling woman, bent his head down upon her shoulder, and wept.

They were tears of joy and thankfulness.

Barnett, had brought science to his aid, and the idiot was once more sane.

The overcharged heart, overcharged with joy, soon found relief and he lifted Minnie to her feet. He pointed to the battery and uttered the one word—

"Minnie!"

Poor woman, she saw it all in a moment, and flinging herself into his arms, she sobbed upon his breast.

"Oh! Dick, Dick," she gasped between her choking sobs; "where, where are you. Oh! I must fly to him. Oh! joy. How can I bless you."

"Minnie!" said Barnett, solemnly pointing upwards, "think not of me. "There, there your thanks are due. Science is great and powerful, but He is greater and more powerful. To Him must you turn with thankfulness. I have my reward in being able to render happy the man whose generous and noble heart I so much respect, Dick the Poacher."

Down, down sank Minnie at his feet, and poured out her thanks to Him who sways the destinies of the world.

CHAPTER CVIII.

THE PANTOMIMISTS ON THEIR HOMEWARD JOURNEY —THE RESCUE FROM THE FLAMES

BUSKIN BOB and Charlie Evans raised the maimed youth in their arms, and bore him towards the inn, before which Dick had surprised Dancing Bill.

The exlamation of Harry had scarcely been noticed by either of the pantomimsts, and Harry himself determined to make no further remark, till the young libertine should have been cared for by his friends.

Tenderly the poor players bore him along the highway, casting looks of commiseration on to the pale face of the young man, now distorted by pain.

Harry led the way with the lantern, and in a short time they arrived before the inn.

The house was now clothed in darkness.

Not a glimmer of light was to be seen at any of the windows.

The inhabitants had all retired to rest.

After knocking for some time at the door, they gained admittance to the inn, and the youth was placed in bed, and medical attendance summoned for him.

Harry was anxious to question him respecting the loss of Mary, but the worthy doctor enjoined silence, stating that he must be kept quiet, as the least excitement might be fatal.

Harry was compelled to give way, and with a disappointed look he turned to follow his friends from the inn.

The peculiarity of his manner attracted the notice of Buskin Bob, who inquired its cause.

"I am certain that he could tell where Mary is to be found," replied the boy.

"He tell?"

"Yes."

"What can induce you to think so?" asked Bob.

Harry then informed his friends of the adventure in the road, and how he had rescued Mary from the insults of Frampton.

This set Charlie Evans thinking.

Still he could not bring himself to believe that the youth he had assisted to carry to the inn, was likely to have had any hand in the loss of his daughter.

He was so young.

His own generous nature prompted him to look upon others in a kindly light.

So, after a few moments, he remarked—

"There is something strange in Mary's absence, certainly; but depend upon it, Harry, that youth knows no more about her than we do."

"I fear—" commenced Harry.

"Strike me comical if you have done anything else this last six hours," said Bob, "try and hope, and perhaps things will turn out brighter."

"I have hoped," said Harry.

"Hope on then," said Charlie.

"Hope ever," chimed in Buskin Bob, "though, strike me comical if I haven't often tried it in vain."

"And so we shall now, I fear," said Harry.

"I hope not," said Bob. "What do you think of doing now, Charlie?"

Charlie shook his head.

"I hardly know what to do," he replied.

"I don't think it is of much use going further on this way in search of her," said Bob.

"I wish that fellow would have opened his mouth," said Harry, "and told us all he knew."

"Nonsense," said Bob.

Harry sighed but said no more.

There was a something which told him that his surmises were not incorrect.

"We will return to the Saloon," said Charlie, "and see if she has been seen or heard of, perhaps she may be there now."

"I hope she is," said Bob. It is a strange affair, but I hope it will end all right, strike me comical if I don't."

And in silence the three players retraced their steps along the road towards the Saloon.

Each busied with his own thoughts, they strode on, looking down upon the ground for some time, when Charlie, happening to raise his eyes, perceived a bright sheet of light in the clouds.

For a few moments he kept his gaze fixed upon it in silence.

Brighter and brighter it grew each moment, till at length, with an exclamation of horror he gasped out—

"Bob—Bob, there's a fire!"

"Where?" exclaimed Harry.

"Where?" exclaimed Bob.

"There, just over there!" said Charlie, pointing with his finger over the top of some high trees which skirted the road.

"Strike me comical," drawled out Buskin Bob. "Good heavens! it can't be—"

He did not finish the sentence, but clutched nervously at Charlie's arm.

The clown turned his gaze hurriedly upon the pantaloon's face.

Their eyes met.

A deathly pallor overspread the features of both.

"God forbid!" gasped Charlie, "but it is close there."

"Oh, heavens!" gasped Harry, "you do not think it is the Saloon?"

"No, no," answered Charlie and Bob simultaneously.

But the tremulous tones in which the words were uttered told but too plainly their fears.

"Oh! let's run, let's run," exclaimed the boy, quickening his pace.

Both Charlie and Bob required no incentive, and they started off at the top of their speed.

In a short time they came to a turn in the road.

The town now lay directly before them.

An exclamation escaped the lips of each.

For a moment they seemed paralyzed.

Before them the long rows of houses were lighted up by the glare of the flames, and huge volumes of smoke rose high into the clouds, and hung like a funeral pall over the theatre.

A hum of many voices rose on the night-air, and was borne plainly to their ears.

The poor pantomimists stood and looked, as though spell-bound, for a moment.

Then, with a deep sob, Charlie Evans buried his face in his hands as if to shut out the sight before him.

Bob caught him by the arm.

"Charlie, Charlie!" he gasped.

"Ruined—ruined!" exclaimed the clown.

"Don't give way now," said the good-hearted pantaloon. "The hand of misfortune indeed lies heavily upon us. There is no disguising the fearful truth now. The Saloon is on fire, and our Struggles for Bread have been in vain, but don't despair, Charlie, don't give way thus, it's hard—damned hard, but strike me comical, I wouldn't give way so, Charlie, I—I wouldn't."

And the poor pantaloon, fairly overcome with his feelings, burst into tears.

Yes, the hot-scalding tears rolled down his worn features, his over-charged heart could bear no more, and thus it sought relief.

Those tears disgraced not the poor player, no, they ennobled the soul that could feel so acutely for the misfortunes of his friend.

But violent grief seldom lasts long, and Buskin Bob recovered himself quickly.

"Come," he said, "our place is there."

And he pointed towards the burning edifice.

"This night's work has done me up quite," said the clown. "The loss of Mary, and now the ruin of this boy's hopes, ah, I cannot bear it."

"Do not think of me," exclaimed Harry "do not think of me, for myself I care not, but for you, you. Mary and Bob."

"And Margaret," gasped Charlie, "oh! God we left her there."

"Margaret!" exclaimed Buskin Bob, and he clutched the shoulder of Charlie nervously.

"Heaven grant she has escaped," said Charlie hurrying forward again.

"If not, I will tear her from the flames, exclaimed Bob. "Quick, quick, Charlie; ah! how my heart beats; quick—quick."

And Buskin Bob darted forward at a fearfully swift pace, followed by Harry and the clown.

The ground scarcely touched their feet now.

Anxiety and despair seemed to lend wings to their speed.

Nearer and nearer they drew towards the Saloon.

Higher and higher rose the flames into the air.

Louder and louder sounded the shouts and cries of the mob which surrounded the scene of destruction.

Without slackening their speed for a moment, they reached the outside of the crowd, which momentarily gathered in strength and density.

But amid a volley of oaths and execrations, the pantomimists forced their way through the crowd, right up to the walls of the theatre.

But here they were seized by the constables, and forced back.

Buskin Bob, whose anxiety overcame his reason, broke from the officers, and again endeavoured to make his way towards a low window, through which streams of water were being poured from the hose.

The officer seized him again.

"Stand back!" he exclaimed.

"I will not!" exclaimed Bob.

"I must do my duty, if you are fool enough not to see the danger you run."

"Take your hands off!" exclaimed Bob, "there is one there I must save!"

"Stand back."

And again the officers endeavoured to force back the pantomimists.

Goaded to fury by the resistance offered to his desires, Buskin Bob raised his hand to strike at the man, who but performed his duty, and would doubtless have suffered from his impetuosity, had not a voice called out.

"Let them be, the house belongs to them, they are the new proprietors."

This had the effect of inducing the officers to offer no more resistance to the pantomimists, and Buskin Bob sprang towards the window, opening at the moment, that several voices called forth,—

"Quick—quick! the beam is breaking!"

Close behind Bob rushed the Boy Actor and Charlie Evans, all unmindful of the danger to which they presented themselves.

They gained the opening, they forced their heads above those assembled, and a cry of horror broke from their lips as they perceived Dick the Poacher and Margaret sink into the flames.

But ere that cry had died away, Buskin Bob sprang upon the window sill.

A dozen hands were stretched forth to stay him, but he thrust them from him, exclaiming,—

"I will save her, or perish in the attempt!"

And with one fearful spring he leapt through the opening, amid the cloud of sparks from the broken beam.

"And I," exclaimed Charlie Evans, "will save that man or die!"

And ere he could be prevented, he had followed Buskin Bob into that fiery place.

The boldness of the acts held those around the window spellbound for a few seconds; but as they perceived the pantomimists bearing through the fiery embers the forms of Margaret and Dick the Poacher, a loud shout arose from their throats.

Frantically they cheered the brave men; they stretched forth their arms towards them, and urged them to struggle on.

But the cries were unheard or unheeded by Charlie and Bob, as with panting breath and burning clothes they struggled to reach th opening through which they had entered.

It was a fearful struggle, the weight of the inanimate bodies in their arms, the heat of the flames, and the overpowering smoke told fearfully upon them; but still on they struggled.

They reached the opening, a dozen hands grasped them, and together with their rescued burdens they were drawn through and lowere to the ground.

Then their brave natures gave way, and they fell insensible beside those they had saved.

CHAPTER CVIII.

CONCLUSION.

ABOUT a fortnight after the events recorded in the last chapter, some men, whilst clearing away the ruins of the Crown Saloon, discovered under a heap of rubbish, the remains of Dancing Bill, the harlequin.

The guilty man's body had suffered little from the flames, the mass of rubbish which had fallen upon him protected his form from the fire, but he had suffered a fearful death from suffocation. Concealed between his shirt and his heart was the packet he had stolen from the house of Dick the Poacher, and for which Henley and Gripe had so deeply plotted.

This packet was placed in the hand of Mr. Hardy the magistrate for the county, and the gentleman who had discovered Mary bleeding on the road-side after she had been thrown from the fly.

Mr. Hardy, who as soon as he had discovered that the proprietors of the Crown Saloon were the same he had met with, exerted himself to the utmost to assist and relieve them, and Charlie, Bob, Harry, Margaret, and Dick, were inmates of his house.

The players and the poacher were in a fair way of recovery, and were assembled in one of the rooms when Mr. Hardy arrived with the packet, and explained, how it had fallen into his hands.

Dick no sooner saw it, than he recognised it in a moment, and then it was that Margaret became acquainted with the fact that her husband was no more.

To say that she grieved for him would be

false, for he had saved himself from the gallows by his own wicked deeds.

At the request of Dick, the packet was now opened. It was the last will and testament of one James Playford, dated one day before the hour of his death, and in which he gave and bequeathed to his son Richard Playford and his daughter Emma Marston all his goods, chattels, and estates in the manor of Barnstable, Devonshire.

When it was read, Dick said,—

"That will was made by my father, and bears date one day before his death. Shortly ere he died, Squire Henley, then a substantial farmer, used his utmost endeavours, to prevail upon my father, to disinherit me and my sister, who had married a man beneath her station, and to make a will in his favour. Squire Henley produced a will, purported to bear the signature of my father, in which he is made the heir to all his property; and which property he has enjoyed for many years. The packet you hold in your hand, was in my sister's possession, and though I had some suspicion of its nature, I never really knew till now, that he had not disinherited us. But I can now see the cause of her never producing it and obtaining her rights. Squire Henley, and his unworthy steward, Gripe, had contrived to weave around me a web, out of which I should find it difficult to escape; they having laid a snare for me to fall into. Several stacks were fired on the estate, and suspicion pointed to me; it was known that I bore them an ill-will, and it was so contrived, that had they charged me with the crime, I could not, though innocent of the charge, have rebutted it. It was the dread of my having to suffer for this crime, that must have induced my sister to bear with poverty so long, to save me from a felon's doom. She is now dead, and this boy, her son, is co-heir with me to these estates. Sir, you have already extended to us the hand of friendship. To you I leave the work of justice, fully assured that you will befriend us still."

Great indeed was the joy of the pantomimists, at the discovery that the Boy Actor was in a fair way of being enabled to live without struggling for bread as a strolling player.

Days wore on, and the discovery of the will, found its way to the ears of Henley.

The squire saw that his evil course was run, and as he could see that not only would he be ousted from the property he had so long kept from the rightful heir, but that he would be sure to suffer for forgery, and perhaps murder, for if they exhumed the body of James Playford, they would find traces of poison, administered by his hands; he resolved to defeat justice, by death, and placing the muzzle of a pistol in his mouth, he blew out his brains.

Gripe and Takeall, who had at last sworn eternal friendship, and resolved upon making the squire's purse their own, thus found themselves defeated, and a quarrel ensuing between them, Gripe made public several guilty acts of the broker, who in return, turned upon the steward, and as it often happens, that when thieves and rogues fall out, honest men get their due, the poor people who had been so shamefully robbed, and suffered so much at their hands, demanded justice, and got it.

Gripe and Takeall stood side by side in a felon's dock, were chained wrist to wrist, in a convict ship, and worked side by side in a convict settlement.

Mary soon recovered from the injuries she had received, and the bloom of health once more sat upon her cheeks.

But who can describe the meeting of Dick and Minnie, who pourtray the feelings which reigned in their hearts, feelings of unutterable joy and happiness, and thankfulness for the boon received at the hands of Doctor Barnett, the aid of science and the will of God.

It was a boon greater than the wealth of the world, and appreciated at its true value.

Dick and Minnie never indeed happy now, and the light sunshine of love and peace reigned where dark clouds had so long held sway.

Mr. Hardy had been true to his word. His legal experience had obtained for Dick and Harry their inheritance, and the uncle and nephew took up their abode at Henley Manor.

But Charlie Evans was not allowed to depart from them, and the worthy clown and his pretty daughter, found a home in the old hall.

Buskin Bob, after the lapse of six months from the date of the fire, sought the hand and heart of Margaret.

The columbine could not refuse him and consented to become his wife.

Bob wished he might be struck comical if he didn't love her all the better for being the widow of a man who had deserved death at the hands of the hangman.

And so they were married. Margaret had bound herself to the man who would shield and protect her. No more the ruffian's hand would be raised against her in anger, but shielded by the love of one whose heart was prompted only by impulses of justice, love, and truth, she would find that happiness in the after part of her life which was denied her in her youth.

The Boy Actor and his friends retired for ever from the profession, but still their love for the stage and its votaries never died. They could not in their prosperity forget the hours of adversity, and were ever ready to extend a helping hand to the poor player.

In due time Harry led Mary to the altar, and never did they have cause to regret the union.

Happiness alone reigned throughout Henley Manor, and the players, ever studying the parts of justice, honour, and truth, shed around them blessings on every hand, and many a prayer was uttered for their welfare by those who partook of the benevolence of the Boy Actor, or sought his aid in their Struggles for Bread.

THE END.

www.ingramcontent.com/pod-product-compliance
Lightning Source LLC
Chambersburg PA
CBHW08083825O626
47161CB00009B/3117